Acclaim for the authors of *Where the Heart Is*

KATE WELSH

"Kate Welsh writes an extremely poignant
and emotional story...."
—*Romantic Times* on *A Family for Christmas*

"Kate Welsh handles a very difficult subject
with a delicate, loving hand."
—*Romantic Times* on *For the Sake of Her Child*

IRENE BRAND

"Rich with interesting characters,
heart-warming emotions..."
—*Romantic Times* on *Tender Love*

"A tender story..."
—*Romantic Times* on *Autumn's Awakening*

MARTA PERRY

"A splendid romance beautifully
demonstrating the multiplicity of love."
—*Romantic Times* on *A Father's Promise*

"Beautifully written with a perfect balance
of story elements and true romance."
—*Romantic Times* on *Since You've Been Gone*

WHERE THE HEART IS

KATE WELSH

IRENE BRAND

MARTA PERRY

Love Inspired®

Published by Steeple Hill Books™

STEEPLE HILL BOOKS

Steeple
Hill®

ISBN 0-373-78524-0

WHERE THE HEART IS

Copyright © 2003 by Steeple Hill Books, Fribourg, Switzerland

The publisher acknowledges the copyright holders
of the individual works as follows:

FOR THE SAKE OF HER CHILD
Copyright © 1998 by Kate Welsh

CHILD OF HER HEART
Copyright © 1998 by Irene Brand

DESPERATELY SEEKING DAD
Copyright © 2000 by Martha Johnson

Visit us at www.steeplehill.com

Printed in U.S.A.

CONTENTS

Books by Kate Welsh

Love Inspired

For the Sake of Her Child #39
Never Lie to an Angel #69
A Family for Christmas #83
Small-Town Dreams #100
Their Forever Love #120
*The Girl Next Door #156
*Silver Lining #173
*Mountain Laurel #187
*Her Perfect Match #196
*Home to Safe Harbor #213
*A Love Beyond #218

*Laurel Glen

Silhouette Special Edition

Substitute Daddy #1542

KATE WELSH

is a two-time winner of Romance Writers of America's coveted Golden Heart award and was a finalist for RWA's RITA® Award in 1999. Kate lives in Havertown, Pennsylvania, with her husband of over thirty years. When not at work in her home office creating stories and the characters that populate them, Kate fills her time in other creative outlets. There are few crafts she hasn't tried at least once or a sewing project that hasn't been a delicious temptation. Those ideas she can't resist grace her home or those of friends and family.

As a child she often lost herself in creating make-believe worlds and happily-ever-after tales. Kate turned back to creating happy endings when her husband challenged her to write down the stories in her head. With Jesus so much a part of her life, Kate found it natural to incorporate Him in her writing. Her goal is to entertain her readers with wholesome stories of the love between two people the Lord has brought together and to teach His truth while she entertains.

FOR THE SAKE OF HER CHILD

Kate Welsh

For those who believed: John, Heather, Kristen, Daddy, Mother, Debbie and my wonderful critique partners—Ardath, Bobbie and Martha. Your support has helped make a dream come true.

Prologue

"Why aren't the lights on?" Amanda Powers stared at her house from the drive, her stomach unaccountably jumpy. She rushed from the car to her front door. The unlocked front door did nothing to calm her disquiet.

"Keira?" she called, snapping on the hall light. Only silence greeted her. "Keira?" Silence. "Jesse?" she shouted, now irrationally calling for a baby too young to answer.

Dropping her coat and briefcase to the floor, Amanda rushed from room to room along the hall, turning on lights as she went. Empty. The rooms were empty. Could Jesse have taken ill? Had Keira taken him to the doctor—worse yet to the hospital? She dashed to the message board tacked to the refrigerator but there wasn't a note explaining the absence of Keira, her sitter, and Jesse.

She went back to her son's nursery but rather than finding evidence that Jesse was ill, Amanda was stunned to see that the diapers she'd left stacked on the shelf above the dressing table were gone. The closet was empty too, and all the drawers of the little chest she'd refinished just before his birth.

Like an automaton, she moved to the empty crib. And there she found the note. An innocent-looking eight-and-a-half-by-eleven sheet of paper told Amanda what her mind had refused to believe. What every parent fears and thankfully only a few ever face.

"I need a son. There was no other way. Keira."

Amanda walked to the kitchen and lifted the receiver on the wall phone. Surely, the world had stopped spinning.

"New Orleans dispatch," the voice at the end of the line drawled.

Amanda recognized Harry, her late husband Jess's partner. He'd been on dispatch duty since a shoot-out had left him paralyzed and Jess Powers dead. "It's Amanda," she whispered, her voice weak and shaking. "Keira—the sitter—she's taken my baby."

Chapter One

Garth Jorgensen checked his watch again. Five minutes past eight. One minute since he'd last checked, he thought, dragging a hand through his hair. "Where could she be?" he muttered and stood to pace the porch as he had been doing for over an hour. It wasn't long before he threw himself back into the swing that sat in the shadows of the wraparound porch. After a short time, he hiked up his sleeve and checked his annoyingly accurate watch. Even the happy, night sounds tortured him. How could the earth spin and all its creatures go right on chirping when his world had fallen apart?

A small car that had seen better days rattled into the drive just then, and Garth's heartbeat thundered in trepidation. The moment of truth with Amanda Powers had arrived. He wished he had an excuse to flee but he had no choice. This was what had to be done—what he had to do or never have a moment's peace again.

Garth stood as she approached her front door, his courage flagging. From his shadowy corner of the porch he watched her, unable to speak now that the confrontation had arrived. He wondered again what she was like.

Was her personality sunny?

Did she always look on the brighter side the way Jason did?

Did she still search, still hope?

He didn't doubt it. The copies of the newspaper articles the private detective had given him were heart wrenching and left no doubt as to the magnitude of the loss she'd suffered.

Because of him.

She bent and slid her key into the gleaming brass lock. The only feature Garth could make out was a fall of honey blond hair that swung forward over her shoulder, hiding her face.

Garth cleared his throat and stepped into the light. "Excuse me." To his dismay the words seemed to thunder across the space that separated them.

Amanda Powers gasped and backed away, holding her keys like a weapon. "What do you want?"

Garth winced at the tremor in her soft voice and the fear in her violet eyes. Stupid! How could he have been so stupid as to sneak up behind a woman at night?

"Sorry to startle you. I wasn't thinking. My name's Jorgensen. Garth Jorgensen." His words seemed to catch in his throat. "I—I'm, from Philadelphia. Pennsylvania." He paused, the rest of his well-rehearsed opening lines having fled his brain. This was going to be even tougher than he'd imagined!

"Are you Amanda Powers?" he asked, trying a new approach. Garth patted the pockets of his bomber jacket. Finding what he sought, he stepped more fully into the light and reached out to pass the woman a copy of a seven-year-old newspaper article. It outlined the first six months of her desperate search. A search that had failed. "Are you *that* Amanda Powers?"

She didn't even glance at it. Her eyes stayed riveted on his face. She paled visibly in the harsh light of the carriage lamps that bracketed the polished wooden door. She took a hasty step backward and almost fell over a potted plant. The woman looked as if she might faint.

Amanda Powers dragged her gaze away from him and frowned as she tilted the page he'd given her to the light. Her hands began to shake.

"Jesse! Is this about Jesse? Do you know something about him? Please, tell me anything, anything at all that could help me find my son."

Garth's heart twisted to think of all the hours of anguish she must have suffered and all the joy he'd had over the past seven years. He swallowed. He couldn't put off the moment for another minute. "I think I've been raising your Jesse as my son. His name is Jason. That is," he added haltingly, "*I* have called him Jason."

Amanda felt her world spin and tilt. Could it be this incredibly simple? After all this time, when she'd exhausted nearly all her resources, could a man just show up on her porch to end her search? It could be another hoax, she warned herself. Don't get your hopes up! Why would he admit to kidnapping?

"That could be rather a dangerous claim, Mr. Jorgensen. Kidnapping is a federal offense. A death penalty offense."

"Yeah, I'm well aware of that. But believe it or not, I only recently learned that Jason isn't my son."

Amanda's spirits plummeted. "Then you must be wrong. My son was six months old when Keira Jagger disappeared with him. He wasn't switched in a nursery."

"Look, Mrs. Powers, this is a long, rough story. Could we go inside or maybe sit on the swing? It's been a bad few weeks for me and I'm just about played out."

Amanda stared at the man who claimed to have her son. It was uncanny how much he looked like her late husband, Jess. His eyes were the same brilliant blue and nearly the same shade of chestnut hair swept across his wide forehead. His cheekbones were high and his cheeks slightly hollow. His chin had the same little cleft that Jess had muttered about every morning while shaving.

Amanda wondered if this man's resemblance to her dead husband was the reason she felt a twinge of sadness for him—the man who claimed to have had her son all these years. There were lines of strain around his eyes and mouth, his brow furrowed as if he had one winding of a headache. She waved him inside on instinct.

"Thanks, Mrs. Powers."

Amanda ushered him into the first room off the center hall.

It was the only room in the house not crowded with packed boxes, except the one where Jesse had slept his first six months. That room had remained unchanged. She still hadn't gathered the courage to finally pack up the nursery. It felt too much like an admission that she'd never see her baby again.

She sat in the chair opposite the sofa and watched the tall good-looking man rake his fingers through his longish hair, then settle himself on the edge of the sofa.

"I guess I should start at the beginning," Garth Jorgensen said after a tense moment. "As much of the beginning as I've been able to piece together. A couple of months after your son disappeared, my wife, Karen, showed up after being gone for over a year. She had a child with her. She said he was my son. Please understand that I didn't doubt it for a second because he looked like pictures of me when I was his age. He still does."

"You and your wife were separated?"

Garth nodded. "Karen was…difficult. Things between us had been strained for some time. One day, she walked out of my life. I waited six months to hear from her, then I instituted divorce proceedings. Our marriage and anything I'd felt for her had been long dead."

He clasped and unclasped his hands. "But then she showed up with Jason. My mother had a baby picture of me on the piano for years. Jason was the image of me at that age. I had to take Karen back for his sake." He hesitated as if the next part were difficult to admit. "The truth is that I realized that Karen was…unstable. The problem was unmistakable within minutes of her arrival. I was afraid to trust her with the baby. I got her to agree to therapy but she kept getting worse. She killed herself by driving into a bridge abutment at nearly a hundred miles an hour before Jason was a year old."

"She killed herself?"

"She tried to take Jason with her that day but my mother stopped her."

They stared at each other for a long moment. "Then the

person who may have taken Jesse is dead,'' Amanda said at last. Curiously, she felt none of the victory she'd always imagined words such as those would bring. She felt only a hollow sadness. It was as Pastor Kendrick had always maintained. Vengeance was not man's province but the Lord's. ''Provided that the boy you call Jason is my son,'' Amanda added, afraid to pin too much hope on the word of a stranger.

''There really isn't much doubt. I hired a detective to find you when I first realized the truth.''

''Why did you suddenly find out that Jason wasn't your son after all this time? Why are you so sure Jason is my Jesse?''

''I had cause to go though Karen's things recently. I found a picture of you and your baby that was taken as you were leaving the hospital.'' He drew an envelope out of his inside pocket. ''On the back is written 'Amanda and Jesse come home.' It wasn't Karen's handwriting. I had it checked out. My investigator found you through it.''

Garth held out the envelope. Amanda reached out hesitantly. Her emotions warred.

Look at it.

No don't. He could be wrong. He could even be lying.

Why would he do that?

He could be another reporter. Don't do this to yourself. Don't believe him! You'll only be disappointed again.

Amanda closed her eyes and sent a desperate prayer winging toward heaven. It was certainly not her first prayer for Jesse's return but hopefully it would be her last. She gripped the envelope and ripped it open. And then she knew. Her prayers had finally been answered. Her search was over. Her baby found.

Tears of relief and gratitude filled her eyes. ''Thank you. Thank you for coming forward. Take me to my son. Is he in New Orleans?''

''It's not that easy, Mrs. Powers.''

Amanda forgot feelings of gratitude amidst her need to hold Jesse again. ''Not that easy? Mr. Jorgensen you're in possession of a kidnapped child. I'm willing to give you the benefit of the doubt when you say you had nothing to do with his kidnapping but you had better not try to keep me from him.''

"There are...complications. You have to understand, Jason knows nothing about you. He thinks I'm out of town on business. He has no idea about any of this.''

"If you were this sure, why on earth didn't you prepare him?"

He dropped his gaze to the floor but not before she saw the utter devastation in his compelling eyes. Her scalp prickled as a cold sweat sent a shiver down her spine. The dinner she'd eaten at her desk turned to stone in her stomach. "What is it? Why didn't you talk to Jesse about this before you came here?"

"*Jason.* Get used to calling him Jason. He doesn't know who Jesse is.''

"And whose fault is that?"

"Karen's," he said, honesty shining in his eyes, then he put his head in his hands. "Man, I wish I knew how she got so close to you, so close to Jason. I wish I knew how a kid could look so much like me and not be mine.''

Amanda felt his pain and finally understood the confusion she'd seen in his eyes earlier. When he looked up at her, his blue eyes swam with tears he quickly blinked away. Amanda stood and pulled Jess's police photo out of a nearby box. "This was my husband, Mr. Jorgensen.''

Garth Jorgensen stared at the photo then looked up at her again. "He could be my brother. He could almost be *me.*" Jorgensen frowned, narrowing his eyes in deep thought. "The article about the kidnapping didn't mention when he died.''

"My husband never lived to see his son. He was killed six months before Jesse was born." She mentioned the date in an automatic afterthought.

He muttered under his breath and handed the picture back. "Did the press mention that you were pregnant when your husband was killed?" Amanda nodded. "That's it then. Karen and I were in New Orleans that weekend, Mrs. Powers. I remember the date because the trip was a last-ditch effort to save a marriage that had nothing left to save. We'd had what I thought was a rational discussion Saturday afternoon and decided to separate. She was relaxing, reading the local paper when I went out on an errand. But she was gone when I came back. A note said she hated goodbyes.''

"But what does that have to do with her stealing my son?''

"I can only assume but she probably saw the article and the picture of your husband in the paper.''

Amanda could scarcely believe anyone could be that evil. "You think she saw got the idea to steal my son before he was even *born?* Could she have been that...that...?'' Any word other than *evil* failed her.

His eyes were bleak. "*Sick.* She was that sick.''

"Excuse me.'' Amanda stood and left, needing the refuge of Jesse's room. She walked to the crib and fluffed the little pillow—now yellowed with age. Trying to ignore its dusty smell, she hugged the teddy bear who'd guarded the empty crib for so many lonely years. Then she turned away. A sudden vision of the note as it had once lay atop that pillow flooded her mind.

I need a son. There was no other way.

Amanda walked to the other side of the room and sat in the rocker Jess had bought when she'd told him about the baby. She rocked, haunted by the thought that because of Jess's murder, she'd lost her son as well. Old anger swelled in her heart. Her husband had been so careless with his life in his search for acclaim—his search for earthly success. Now it seemed his death had even led to his son's kidnapping. She closed her eyes and prayed for peace and the ability to forgive Jess one final time.

Amanda looked up at the sound of footsteps. Peace eluded her but strength filled her in its absence. "You asked how she got so close, Mr. Jorgensen. I'll explain after you tell me why Jesse still doesn't know that you aren't his father.''

Garth nodded and looked around the little room. It contained so much less materially speaking than the nursery he'd furnished for Jason but he was sure every bit as much care had gone into its planning. How did he tell this woman that she'd found her child but could still lose him?

He looked around the room again and realized that Jason's room at home now held bunk beds and that teddy bears had given way to outer space. This room probably hadn't changed since Karen had taken the baby. Questions bombarded him. In Amanda's mind, hadn't her child grown at all in his absence? It made him wonder if that would be a normal reaction? He stared down at the empty crib. How strong had the ensuing years left Amanda Powers? Could she take hearing the rest of the truth?

Her wry voice called him from his troubled thoughts. "I'm not delusional, Mr. Jorgensen. My friends call it my shrine to Jesse but it's not. I just couldn't put his things away. It felt like a lack of trust in God. I've always tried to have faith that He'd bring my son back to me. And now that He has, I'd like that explanation you promised. Why am I supposed to be so all-fired patient before I see him?"

Garth turned back to her after sucking in a fortifying breath. Sitting in the tall rocker, she looked small and fragile and quite lovely. Her soft Southern accent wafted through the air as if her words had been spoken by an angel. He'd bet she'd never had trouble settling Jason for the night the way Karen had. A lullaby on the lips of Amanda Powers would surely soothe the most fretful child. But there was strength in her that belied her vulnerable appearance and she wanted the answer he dreaded giving.

"Jason's...ill."

"Ill? How ill?" she asked in a hushed whisper. It was as if she feared even stirring the air.

"He's in Children's Hospital in Philadelphia. This time it's just a secondary infection."

"This time?"

"There's no easy was to say this, Mrs. Powers. Jason has leukemia."

Amanda looked out the window of Garth Jorgensen's twin engine plane. He'd strapped her into the copilot's seat hours earlier. They'd stopped so he could top off his tanks at small local airports on the way to Philadelphia. Flying had never been one of Amanda's favorite modes of travel, but in Garth's small plane, it was more like a roller-coaster ride than air travel. It was a perfect metaphor for her life in the last few hours.

Amanda had always hated roller coasters.

She turned her head and listened as Garth spoke to the tower. He'd been cleared for landing. Amanda gripped the armrests even harder. She'd learned that there was only one thing worse than flying around in a toy plane and that was landing in one. She closed her eyes to pray as the ground came rushing up to meet them but the peace and assurance the Lord had always given her seemed to have deserted her.

An eternity later Amanda felt Garth's hand on hers. "You can let go now. We've stopped." Amanda focused on Garth, pleased for some inexplicable reason to see that an amused grin had lightened his care-worn features.

Amanda smiled, too. "It's not like riding in a 747, is it?"

His grin widened. "It's not like flying one, either."

"You pilot them, too?"

"Used to. I quit the airlines when Jason came along. That's when I started Liberty Express. That hangar," he said, pointing to a large building, "is our headquarters."

Amanda stared at the huge, freshly painted, cinder block structure. It had a Liberty Bell logo hanging over the large main doors. What sort of man had raised her son? His clothing didn't allude to wealth, but if he owned all this he had to be wealthy. Would he use that wealth to try to keep Jesse? "You own an airline?"

Garth didn't seem to hear the suspicion she knew was rife in her tone. "I'd dreamed about it for years. It's small but we're doing well. I had just added a cargo transport division to the commuter flights about the time Jason took sick."

"It sounds as if you changed your entire life because of him?"

Garth nodded. "He gave me a reason to chase the dream. I wanted something to pass on to him. I may go back to flying the big boys now."

Amanda had heard the pride in his voice when he'd pointed out the building that housed his company. Now he seemed not to care about it at all. "What about Liberty Express?"

"Whether Jason recovers and is able to grow up and live a normal life or not, I no longer have a child to pass Liberty on to. What's the use? Come on," he nearly growled. "Let's get to the hospital. We have a nine o'clock meeting with Jason's doctors."

"You've been flying all night. You haven't slept."

"Believe me, Mrs. Powers, I've missed more nights' sleep in the past year than I can count. And before Jason took sick, too. An airline pilot works long stretches at a time."

As he punched the correct floor on the elevator, Garth's stomach knotted. He was a mess, he thought ruefully. Not only hadn't he slept the night before, he hadn't slept in nearly forty-eight hours. He felt as if he'd eaten a handful of Mexican jumping beans. Glancing at Amanda, he realized that he wasn't the only one strung out.

"You're as nervous as a cat in a room full of rocking chairs. I promise, I've told you the truth about Jason's prognosis. And his doctors here at Children's Hospital are some of the best in the country."

"Then why couldn't I see Jesse first?" she asked as he directed her down a sterile-looking corridor.

Garth frowned. "Jason! His name is Jason. You can't slip."

"Why not? He has to be told who I am."

Garth sighed. She had longer to wait to claim her son. A lot longer. For him it was a reprieve—for her a sentence. He ushered her into the conference room. Someone else would have to explain why Jason couldn't be told her true relationship to him right away. He just couldn't do it!

Three doctors stood as they entered. Garth introduced Bill Wood, his lifelong friend and Jason's pediatrician; Matthew

Hernandez, the oncologist, and Shelly White, Jason's psychiatrist. Doctor White took over the reins of the meeting immediately. "You must be Amanda," she said, holding out her hand.

Garth watched Amanda hesitantly take her seat, then listened to a recap of the last ten months of agony Jason had gone through. The first course of chemo. The first big disappointment when the blessed remission ended. Then the second course Jason had finished two months earlier. His heart ached when he saw Amanda's radiant face as she looked at the father-and-son picture taken of the two of them a couple of months before Dr. Hernandez had diagnosed the disease. He'd been such a beautiful child. But the ravages of the second full course of chemo showed in the next photo Shelly handed over.

The shock and pain on Amanda's face had him fighting tears once again. Garth felt that way every time Jason vomited as a result of the medicine they all hoped would save him. He felt again the panic and sorrow as he heard Jason crying and found him putting the hair he'd scraped off his pillow into a box. "I'm going to glue it to my baseball cap," he'd shouted, wiping furiously at his tear-stained face. "It's still my hair even if it's not on my head!" he'd told Garth in an uncharacteristic spurt of anger.

Garth had cried himself to sleep that night. Sometimes he felt so hopeless. What kind of God would let a child suffer like this?

"What are his chances?" he heard Amanda ask.

"We're not certain," Bill Wood replied after a quick glance at Garth. "Jason has been on the donor list for a bone marrow transplant for months but we're having trouble. So far none of the potential donors have been a good enough match."

"What about me?" Amanda asked.

Dr. Matt Hernandez shook his head "Doubtful. It's a question of what is called HLA Tissue Typing and it's much more specific than just blood type or parentage. You see, Jason got his genes from both you and your husband. In cases where there has been a lot of intermarriage, as in some ethnic groups or people from small villages, it would be more probable. In large American cities like New Orleans that doesn't usually happen.''

"But Jess and I were from a small town. Nearly everybody was related in some way or another. Could that increase the chances?"

"It helps but it's still just a chance. And you have to be aware of the degree of discomfort—"

"This is my child we're talking about! I'd cut off my right arm to help him."

"That's what Garth said, too," Bill murmured. For the first time, Garth wondered if having his best friend—his champion—at this meeting was a good idea.

Amanda looked toward him for the first time since the meeting began. "Is that when you found out Mr. Jorgensen wasn't his father—when they tested him to be a donor?"

"Actually, we knew their blood types were all wrong from the beginning. We just didn't discuss that with Mr. Jorgensen at the time," Shelly replied.

"Why not? I might have found Jason sooner."

Bill Wood stood and stalked to the window then turned abruptly. "Because, Mrs. Powers, he was suffering enough already. Garth was devastated by Jason's illness and none of us thought it was necessary to tell him his dead wife had been cheating on him. That was the only logical reason we could surmise at the time."

Amanda blushed. She hadn't meant to be insensitive but it had all been so much of a shock. "Oh, Mr. Jorgensen, I'm so sorry."

"There's nothing you need to apologize for. No one's blaming you for any of this mess. You and Jason are the victims here," Garth said, shooting an angry glare at Dr. Wood.

"And you're not a victim?"

"Leave it, Bill!"

She studied Garth out of the corner of her eye. He'd been silent until then since entering the room. She looked down at the picture of him and her son. The illness that had decimated Jesse had done its work on Garth, too. She'd bet he had aged a year for every month since the photo was taken.

"How did you find out?" she asked, turning to Garth.

"While discussing Jason's condition with one of the specialists here, I learned that with my blood type I couldn't be Jason's father."

Amanda looked away from the pain in Garth's eyes. "What would be the procedure when you find a donor?" she asked the oncologist, hoping to dispel the tense, thick silence.

"Now that Jason is in remission again, if we find a donor we'll use radiation and chemotherapy to oblate all of the stem cells in Jason's body. We use transfusions to artificially elevate the red cells and hemoglobin. Then we do the transfer of bone marrow from the donor. The healthy bone marrow has what you could think of as a built-in homing mechanism that tells it where it belongs within Jason's body. Eventually it will grow into mature, cancer-free blood cells."

"What are the chances that it will work?"

"It's quite successful in cases like Jason's but it isn't risk free. The danger comes in the time just before and after the procedure. He'll be in isolation because he's open to any and all diseases. And because his body's natural disease-fighting mechanism has been completely destroyed, he won't have the ability to fight anything off."

"Is there anything else? Why is he hospitalized now?"

Bill Wood took the question. "Jason cut himself on some broken glass. Just a minor cut, really, but because his resistance is low, the wound became infected and didn't respond to oral antibiotics. I admitted him to watch him and administer intravenous antibiotics. It's a precaution."

Amanda nodded, calmer now, reassured that Garth had been truthful about Jason's condition. "When do you want to test me and when do I see my son?"

Shelly White cleared her throat. "As I explained, you can't

simply tell him who you are. Emotional upset could affect his chances. He's in remission but stress could endanger it."

"Then what do you propose I do?" Amanda asked, a hollow, sick feeling settling in her stomach.

"I think it would be best for you to be typed first. If you can be a donor then we can introduce you to him as such. If not, as a hospital volunteer."

Amanda propped her elbow on the table, leaned her forehead on the palm of her hand, letting her eyes drift closed. *I understand, Lord, I really do, but I want my Jesse back. Now! Tell me what to do.* The answer came to her and she knew it was the right one. She looked up at Dr. White. "I want to meet him now, as a volunteer. I can spend more time with him that way and if I can be the donor it will only bring us closer together."

"That's as good a plan as any. Garth, do you have any objections?"

Garth stood and shrugged. "Why ask me? I don't have a right to object." He grimaced. "In fact, I don't think I have any rights at all any more where Jase is concerned."

Dr. Wood scowled. "If not because of your love for him, then you have rights because a lot of the money for Jason's treatment has come out of your pocket and from the foundation your employees set up to help you with all the bills."

Garth gave the doctor a hard look. Always uncomfortable with the word *love* he stood. "I'm going up to visit Jason then I've got a flight."

Amanda watched Garth leave. He'd sounded so bitter. So sad. She hated that her good fortune had to hurt someone. His pain touched her deeply. Perhaps too deeply.

Minutes later, Amanda approached the room at the end of a third-floor hall with equal parts dread and anticipation. As she pushed her volunteer cart forward, the sounds and smells assaulted and soothed her by turns. Tears and laughter mixed, creating the bittersweet music of life and death—joy and pain. The smell of flowers and antiseptics warred, not quite defeating each other but blending into a smell that she knew would remain in her memory for all time.

Turning the last corner, she spotted Garth. He stood next to the doorway. His long straight back was pressed against a brightly painted mural of dinosaurs and vegetation. At his sides, his tightly clenched fists vibrated—in anger or pain Amanda couldn't tell. He stared straight ahead as if unaware of the sights and sounds around him, his expression blank.

Amanda drew up to him and stopped. She gasped at the pure anguish on his face. The sound drew Garth's attention at last.

"Is he awake?" Amanda asked.

"Awake?" Garth's attention seemed distant as the horizon they'd flown toward all night.

"Jes— I mean Jason. Is he napping or can I see him?"

Garth chuckled as if delighted despite his own pain. "He's poring over a book on New Orleans I picked up on my way to your place yesterday." His sudden grin faded quickly with a grimace of inner pain.

Amanda felt a pull so strong she had to force herself not to flee its danger. A moth to a flame, she reached out and gripped his arm, struck by the thought that, even as he traveled to arrange giving up the child he loved, Garth had remained a typical parent until the end. He hadn't come home without a present. "If he liked your gift, then what's wrong? Is he worse? What?"

"He…" Garth swallowed and wiped at a tear that leaked onto his hollow cheek. "He looks at me with such trust and I have to stand there and lie. I've always told him I'd be there for him no matter what and now it's a lie."

"You can be there for him as long as he needs you. As long as you need him. I want what's best for my son. If you're what he needs, then he should have you in his life."

Garth turned his head and looked at her with near desperation in his eyes. "I can't just walk away. I have to see this through with him. You see that, don't you?"

"Mr. Jorgensen, I just told you I did." Amanda put her head

down and squeezed her temples, fighting off the ache slicing through her head. "This is all so unfair," she said in a broken whisper.

"Nobody ever said life was fair. I've got that load of freight to deliver and one to pick up in Scranton. When you go in, try not to act shocked because of how bad he looks. He's sensitive about it. His hair hasn't grown back in yet. And remember his name's *Jason.*

"I'm...ah...sorry you have to face this alone but I just can't be there when you meet him. I just can't lie to him again today."

Amanda smiled. "I'm not alone, Garth. Jesus is always with me. He's kept me going for seven years. He won't desert me now."

"You sound like my mother," Garth said, but instead of admiration for the faith she apparently shared with Garth's mother, there was bitterness tinged with ridicule in his tone. "Where was your God the day Karen took your baby from you? And why did He let you find him when he's so sick a scraped knee put him in here?"

Garth turned and left as if he knew his question had no answer. None he wanted to hear, anyway. Amanda stared after him as her favorite scripture—the one that had kept her going for seven long years—floated into her thoughts. *All things work together for good to those who love God, to those called according to his purpose.* That would have been her answer but Garth clearly wasn't in any mood to listen. Seeing again the rigid set of his shoulders as he disappeared down the hall, Amanda wondered if he ever would be.

Chapter Two

Amanda stepped quickly out of the cab onto the sidewalk in front of Children's Hospital, then rushed toward the entrance, anxious to meet Jesse. No, Jason! She had to remember that or she was going to endanger his health. And he did look so weak. He'd been asleep the day before and Amanda, after watching him sleep for a couple of hours, had left at a nurse's urging.

Amanda had resented the intrusion but understood when she'd seen herself in a mirror. It hadn't been a pretty sight. The dingy mirror in her motel room that morning showed the improvement sleep, a shower and fresh makeup could make. Amanda smiled. What was it her grandmother used to say about women and makeup? "Even an old barn looks better with a fresh coat of paint." It certainly held true for her today.

After picking up her volunteer cart, Amanda rushed to Jason's room. A high-pitched giggle and the sound of a deep voice froze her in her tracks.

"Well, thanks for the high praise, son. I'll have to come up with as nice a compliment to give you now."

"How about my head has a healthy shine today?" a laughing child asked.

"Oh, I don't know. I swear I see a little peach fuzz dulling that chrome dome," a voice she recognized as Garth's responded.

Garth's unkind comment hit Amanda like a physical slap,

but what shocked her more was the child's giggle that followed in response. Then a thick silence descended.

"It'll grow back, won't it, Daddy?" All the glee had left the boy's tone. "And I really will be healthy again?"

"Hey! Of course you will. You'll be totally healthy—and hairy," he quipped in a lighthearted voice, "in no time. I promised you, didn't I? Have I ever broken a promise?" There was a long pause. "Well, there you have it. A Garth Jorgensen promise is as good as gold. Why, I'll bet you we find a donor any day. That'll really cinch it."

Amanda braced her back against the door and pushed inward. She couldn't wait longer. "Hello there. My name's Amanda Powers. I'm the new volunteer on this wing," she announced, hoping she sounded more cheerful and matter-of-fact than she felt. She backed her book and toy laden cart into the room then turned, hoping she was once again mentally braced and ready for the sight of her dangerously ill son.

She wasn't ready. Not by a long shot! Her plump, healthy baby was now unrecognizable in this thin, tired boy in the hospital bed. How could Garth manage to joke about Jason's appearance?

"Hi. I'm Jason Jorgensen. This is Garth Jorgensen. He's my dad. We don't look much alike right now but we used to. After I saw *The King and I,* I decided I was the king in a former life."

"You believe in reincarnation?" Amanda asked, fascinated by so adult a statement from so young a child but worried about what he'd been taught.

"Nah. I was just joking," he waved away the notion with an arm attached to an IV tube that connected to the bag hanging over his head. Amanda stared in fascinated horror at Jason's hand where the needle penetrated. "I like what my dad told me better."

Amanda glanced at Garth who remained silent, his face a noncommittal mask. "What did he teach you?"

"That 'cause I'm a kid, if I die I go right to heaven and

being there puts this life to shame. He says there's a room in a palace just waiting for me. And Dad says that if I get too tired of fighting, the angels will take me there. But if I want to get better, then he'll help me keep fighting.''

"I—I see. We'll all help you fight, Jason," she said, surprised that Garth would handle the subject the way he had. How had he found the strength inside himself to tell the child he held dear that he was free to leave life behind if he needed to? Especially since he seemed to rail against God because of the illness that might take Jason.

"I won't give up though," Jason promised staring at Garth. "Dad says I'm a fighter. Right, Dad?"

Garth nodded, still silent. Amanda watched a poignant exchange between father and son. Garth stood and looked at his watch. "I've got to be going, kiddo. I'll bring you that treat if you promise not to give the nurse a hard time about today's blood tests."

"Ah, don't worry about me. I bet these are the best marks yet. I studied hard for 'em this time!"

Garth chuckled as Amanda wondered at the strange combination her son seemed to be. She'd just had a rational, very adult conversation about death with him and yet he had the wonderful faith in God that few other than children seemed able to hold on to. Seconds later he'd gladly accepted bribery from Garth for his good behavior then wisecracked like a boy three times his age. He seemed and—considering his bald head and thin face—looked like a little old man with the body and voice of a child.

Garth leaned down and kissed the boy, tugged on the teenager's cap, and allowed the old man in Jason to draw strength from their embrace.

"Nice meeting you, Mrs. Powers," Garth said. "Have a nice visit but don't let him chew your ear off."

Amanda watched Garth leave then turned to Jason. They were father and son, as much as she hated to admit it. She, the one with all the legal rights, was on the outside looking in. It might not be right or fair but that was how it was.

"Sure hope these tests are good," Jason muttered, shaking his head. Again, he'd aged.

"You seem to want it for more than just that it means you're getting better. Why?"

"My dad needs me and I'm getting awful tired of fighting. I'm his reason for living. He told me that once. It was before I got sick. It wouldn't be fair not to fight till I can't anymore. It isn't just me, you see?"

"Yes," Amanda said, choking on tears she dared not show. "Yes, I see. You love your father very much."

Jason nodded. "My dad's a real live hero."

"Hero?" Amanda frowned. They'd called Jess, his real father, a hero, too. Wanting it—the accolades, the admiration—had killed him. Why thoughts of Garth traveling the same dangerous path bothered her, Amanda couldn't say. She only knew that inexplicably it did.

"...but Dad stayed in the Air Force Reserve," her son was saying. "He was in Desert Storm and he saved a whole lot of people. I was there when he got his medal and a general talked about how my dad risked his life to save soldiers he didn't even know. Dad quit though when I got sick. Grandmom lives with us and my aunt Christina only lives two miles away from our house. They take care of me when he's working and when he used to go away. I sure miss my aunt Chris. I prayed she'd come see me today."

A tap on the door drew Amanda's attention. "Aunt Chris! Guess what! Jesus answered my prayer. I wanted you to come today and here you are. Just like you said. He really answers some prayers quick."

"Just don't forget the other part," the tall blonde in the doorway said.

"I know. He's telling me to wait when I pray about my leukemia. Come meet my new friend."

As the door pushed fully open, the young woman walked in

with a balloon and a gift. Her classic features and bright blue eyes marked her as Garth's sister at once, even though she had light hair instead of Garth's rich chestnut.

"So, what's this I hear about my klutzy favorite nephew and a broken bottle? Honestly, I go on a business trip and you wind up in here. What are we going to do with you?"

Jason shrugged. A gesture so like one she'd seen Garth make that it made Amanda's heart ache. "Give me my present?" he asked hopefully.

Garth's sister handed over the gift and turned to Amanda with a smile. "Hello. I guess you're new around here."

"This is Mrs. Powers. Her first name's Amanda," Jason said as he tore into the package. "She's the new volunteer. I was just telling her about what a big hero Dad is."

Christina's smile faded. "Mrs. Powers. I...I'm pleased to meet you."

"It's good to meet you, too," Amanda said, realizing Christina knew who she was and that the meeting was not a pleasure for the other woman at all. She cast about for something to say that would ease the awkward situation. "Jason was just telling me that your brother is in the Air Force Reserve."

"*Was.* He resigned his commission about a year ago."

"When I got sick," Jason said, his tone suddenly sullen. "I wrecked everything by getting sick. He'd be a major by now if it wasn't for me!"

"Jason Jorgensen! What a thing to say. Your father loves you. He didn't give a fig about his rank and you know it. He quit to spend more time with you."

Jason sank back on his pillow after a careless shrug that was anything but careless. He clearly felt he'd become a burden on Garth. "'Cause I might not be here for long."

Christina whispered, "Get his shrink," as she passed Amanda to sit on the bed next to Jason. "Is it time for a pity party?" she asked gently as she settled next to her nephew.

Amanda didn't wait for his answer. She pushed her cart into the hall and went to the nurses' station to call Dr. Shelly White.

What had happened to the happy little boy Garth had left in her care? She knew it was foolish but she felt as if she had somehow failed her son already.

Garth entered the hospital just after dark. His stomach hurt from lack of food but hunger would have to wait. Most nights he stayed far past regular visiting hours, helping get Jason settled for sleep. Often he even stayed until his son dropped off.

His son? Not for long. No, that wasn't true. Legally he didn't have a single right to call Jason son but in his heart that boy would be his son into eternity. Garth stabbed the button, calling the elevator. How could Karen have done this?

"You gettin' on the elevator or what, mister?" an impatient voice snapped from behind.

Garth looked up startled to see an open elevator before him. He stepped in, apologizing to the elderly man whose path he'd inadvertently blocked. Minutes later, he stepped into Jason's room, surprised to find Amanda embroiled in a Monopoly game with the only eight-year-old business tycoon he'd ever met. He smiled when he saw the healthy stacks of colorful money tucked under Jason's side of the board. Jason appeared to be over the setback Chris had called his office about and Amanda looked about ready for the poorhouse. It didn't take a genius to figure out who owned all those little red hotels lined up around the board.

"You could lend me the hundred and fifty," Amanda was saying as he let the door drift closed. "I'll be past Go by my next turn."

Jason wiggled his eyebrows. "Or you could sell me..." He paused and tapped his chin. "Let's see...how about your Electric Company."

"*My last utility?* You little rat! You've been after those since I bought the first one."

Jason snickered. "And now I've got all but one! Come on, Mrs. Powers, pay the rent." Snidely Whiplash had nothing on his son, Garth decided wryly.

"But I can't pay the rent," Amanda sighed dramatically, picking up on the joke.

"But you must pay the rent," Jason ordered in an unnaturally deep voice.

"I'll pay the rent!" Garth shouted, then strode forward and plopped down a paper bag in the middle of the game board.

The game forgotten, Jason scooped up the bag and tore it open. "Wow! Are these all for me?"

Garth raised an eyebrow. "You have a guest, kiddo."

"Oh! Sorry, Mrs. Powers. Would you like one? They're my Grandmom's cookies. She's the best baker in the whole world." Garth's heart contracted painfully when he saw the nearly worshipful look in his son's eyes when he looked at her.

"I guess I'd better not pass up the world's number one cook's cookies," Amanda replied, her boundless love easily readable in her eyes.

Garth wondered what it would be like to have Amanda Powers look at him like that. He pushed the thought away. He was no good at relationships. And even if he were, getting more involved in Amanda's life was out of the question. It could only lead to more heartache than he could stand.

His son obviously had other ideas. "No, she's a lousy cook. She's just a great *baker*. Mrs. Powers hasn't eaten, Dad," Jason hinted. "And I know you haven't."

"Then she shouldn't have another cookie. It'll spoil her appetite."

Jason pressed on. "Dad does anything to avoid Grandmom's cooking. He comes straight here and eats on his way home. He uses me as an excuse. Why don't you take Mrs. Powers to dinner? She ate breakfast and lunch here and she's got to be starving. She'll think Philly has awful food."

"I'm sure Mrs. Powers knows hospital food doesn't represent the best Philadelphia has to offer. I'm also sure she doesn't need me to prove it to her." Garth didn't glance at Amanda but that was probably a mistake because it left him looking into his son's disappointed eyes. The kid had had a rough day with all the tests and whatever had upset him while Chris had been there. Garth decided it wouldn't hurt him to take Amanda out for one meal and it would undoubtedly put a smile back on Jason's face.

From now on he'd just avoid running into Amanda—set up some kind of schedule with her. "But then again, I wouldn't want a pretty lady to be forced to eat the food here—and I use the term loosely—for a third time in one day," Garth agreed. "It might just do her in."

"Great," Jason said. "I guess you ought to get going."

"Going? I just got here," Garth protested. "Don't you want to finish your game with Aman...ah...Mrs. Powers? I was supposed to finish reading that mystery to you tonight."

"I'm kind of tired, Dad. I don't think I'll be awake much longer." His yawn was expansive. And fake!

The kid belongs on a stage, Garth thought, biting his lip to keep from laughing. "Perhaps Mrs. Powers has other plans."

"Amanda. Her name's Amanda, Dad. Her friends called her Mandy when she was my age."

Garth looked at Amanda. Color had flooded her cheeks. Her violet eyes were wide with embarrassment, giving her a look of utter vulnerability. She looked like a Mandy at that moment—young and achingly sweet. "I guess we'd better go eat, Mandy," Garth said as he took her hand and led her, unresisting and obviously quite dazed, to the door.

Amanda stopped short and turned. "We'll call this game a draw since you're too tired to keep playing. See you tomorrow."

"Hey! I had you beat. I want a rematch!"

Amanda laughed and the sound vibrated right through Garth. "Any time," she promised, then turned back toward him with a bright smile.

Amanda glanced at Garth as the car passed beneath a streetlight. He gripped the wheel tightly and a muscle throbbed in his jaw. The man radiated tension. Was it simply her presence or had some doctor told him something about Jason that they hadn't told her? Was this second remission over?

"Is Jason all right?" she asked.

Garth smiled. It was the helpless sort that came in spite of pain and fear. Love was the only emotion Amanda could think of that could produce such an expression. "He seemed fine to me," Garth answered. "In rare form. He finally found a new pigeon to play Monopoly with *and* he got his way. We're having dinner together, aren't we?"

"I meant his health. Today's tests."

Garth shook his head. "We'll hear tomorrow on those. What about yours? Did you get any feel for whether you're a match or not?"

"There was a problem in the lab, so my tests were put off until tomorrow." They lapsed into an uncomfortable silence. "If…ah…you'd rather not go to dinner with me, I'll understand."

Garth blinked as if surprised that she'd draw such a conclusion from the silence that had stretched between them. "Huh? Not go—? Oh, no." He sighed and pulled into the parking lot of an Italian restaurant. "I'm sorry if you misunderstood. It's been a lousy day. Maybe it's *you* who should rethink dinner with *me.*"

"It's my being Jason's mother that has you this upset though, isn't it?"

Garth turned toward her. "It's the future and the past that have me tied in knots, not the present. None of this mess is your fault. Jason's your son. I meant what I said yesterday during the medical briefing. You're the victim in this. Jason, too. He's missed a lot of years with you because of what happened and now, even if he lives, he'll still lose the life he's known."

Garth got out of the car then and circled it to open her door, then directed her toward the restaurant. Amanda glanced up at his handsome profile and admitted the truth to herself. She was attracted to him, against all logic and sane judgment—against her promises to herself. This dinner together was definitely a bad idea.

But thoughts of past mistakes fled when she noticed Garth's troubled expression. It reminded her of something Jason had said earlier. *"I'm his reason for living."* Garth had said essentially the same thing the night he'd flown her to Philadelphia. He was ready to give up on the business he'd worked so hard to make succeed. Despite tough economic times and the odds against a small carrier succeeding in the northeast, Garth had made his dream come true. His dreams had apparently ended the day he'd confirmed her existence.

"Finding me doesn't have to mean you'll be out of his life," she told him as they took their seats. "Jason would resent me if you just disappear. We need to find a way to—"

"Share him? Come on, Amanda. He has a long recovery ahead. He's not just a piece of baggage we can ship all over the country. You live in New Orleans. You have a job. Friends. A home. I live here. It's not as if I could drop over once or twice a week even though I'm a pilot."

"All my job in New Orleans meant to me after Jesse—I mean Jason—was born was a means of support. Even after he was taken, the job just paid for my search. My friends have drifted away because they were uncomfortable with my continuing to look for my son. Jason is my main concern. It can't be a good idea to take him away from all that's familiar to him."

"Are you saying you'd think of moving here?"

Before Amanda could answer, a waitress stepped up to their booth. Since Amanda had done no more than glance at the menu, she ordered spaghetti. Garth dittoed her order then looked at her, silently demanding an answer.

"I have no family," Amanda said softly. "I recently sold my house for money to continue the search for Jason." She looked down at the tablecloth. "I had yet to sign a lease on the new apartment I planned to move into and the company I work for has offices here. I might be able to get a transfer. It would be better for Jason to stay close to his doctors and your family...and...and you.''

Garth stared at Amanda, clearly taken aback.

''You *don't* want him out of your life do you?'' she asked.

Garth bristled, ''Of course not, but—'' His gaze drifted over her shoulder then back to her face. ''I don't know if it's a good idea for us to have too much contact. Jason's been trying to... well...''

Amanda didn't bother to fight the smile that tugged at her lips. ''How could I help but notice. He wants you to date, doesn't he?'' she asked with a slight smile.

Garth chuckled helplessly. ''You can't imagine. Ever since he noticed other kids had a mother and not a grandmom to take care of them. His first-grade teacher and I got on a first-name basis. Not because I took her out but because of the truly bizarre ways Jase had of getting me up to his school. The kid's fixated on getting me married. Frankly, it's not something I ever intend to do again. Women want more than I can give—feelings I can't give or believe in.''

''Do you mean love?''

''That's a pretty, dressed-up name people have given lust and possessiveness.''

Amanda grimaced. Her marriage hadn't been very happy, either. But Garth seemed to reject the very basis of marriage. She, on the other hand, still believed there was a man meant for her out there somewhere. But next time she would marry for companionship...friendship...not passion and attraction. Next time the man would be someone as committed to her faith as she was, not someone who might just give lip service to her Lord in order to lure her into marriage. She knew she never again wanted to tie her life to someone who didn't share her values. ''I understand,'' she said. And she did understand why he felt what he did even though she didn't agree with his definition of love. Karen had really done a number on this man.

''No, no I don't think you do. Your marriage was a happy one. I'll bet Jess Powers was your childhood sweetheart.''

"I was young when we met but that wasn't a guarantee of happiness," she hedged.

"No, but I married in haste and you know what that leads to. Karen was a flight attendant, beautiful and sophisticated. I wanted to believe what we had together was enough. We were married in a quick ceremony in Las Vegas between flights. I managed to break my mother's heart and ruin my life with one stupid decision that was based on lust."

"Your mother didn't approve of Karen." Their lives had run along such close parallel lines it was uncanny, though they had come away from their similar experiences with such different views on love. Amanda hoped Garth didn't also feel the same kind of attraction for her that she felt for him.

"Karen had an obsessive personality. Mom saw through her in minutes. Karen had decided to marry me so no lie was too big, even to pretending to be a different kind of person than she really was. She told so many lies that I couldn't wade through them after a while."

Amanda felt a chill. Yes, their lives had run very parallel. Right down to being fooled by the same woman. "She lied with truthful eyes," Amanda said. "I should know. I trusted her with my baby. I called the police minutes after I found them gone but I still couldn't really believe Keira had stolen him. I was holding her note and I still couldn't believe. She was my friend. She was my labor coach. She held me when I cried because Jess would never see him."

"That's something we've both avoided talking about with each other since that night at your house," Garth said, looking pensive. "I know this may seem strange but I need to know what happened. How she got away so clean. A baby is a real happening on an airline. They usually scream so loud I can sometimes hear them all the way in the cockpit. The air pressure bothers their ears."

Amanda could see that Garth needed to hear what she'd gone through but she couldn't understand why. Perhaps he needed to know what had happened in Jason's life when he wasn't with either of them.

"It was a day just like any other," she began. "I came home from work expecting to see the lights on in the house. But it was dark inside. And it gave me an odd feeling. Then the front door wasn't locked. There was no answer when I called out. They weren't in any of the day rooms. There was no message on the refrigerator explaining that she'd taken Jesse to the store or anywhere else. I started to really panic then. I thought that perhaps he'd gotten terribly sick and Keira had rushed him to the doctor's or a hospital. I ran into Jesse's room looking for evidence that she'd dressed him in a hurry. Or that he was sick. But most of his clothes were gone. Then I found the note and I called Jess's old captain. He notified the FBI immediately but it was already too late."

"What did the note say?"

"That she needed a son. That there was no other way. She turned my life into a nightmare because she needed my son. So she just took him." Amanda swallowed hard. Even after all this time, after having miraculously found Jesse again, the pain, the unbearable panic and self-reproach of those first days still overwhelmed her.

"Karen told me she'd had the baby in New York City," Garth said.

Amanda shrugged, shaking off emotion, speaking calmly. "All the authorities were ever able to learn was that Keira had boarded a plane to Maine that morning at about the time I got to work. She rented a car that was abandoned in Michigan. There was never a trace of them after that. They had simply vanished."

"She must have gone to New York at some point because that was where she found out about the child who was born and died within a few weeks. She must have gotten a copy of his birth certificate. My detective says that's easy to do. When she showed up in Philly, she said Jason was six months old. I think he may have been older than she said. He walked early, talked early. But I guess I was a typical new father. My kid was brilliant.''

"His birthday is August twenty-sixth," she said with a sad smile.

Garth sighed. "We've always celebrated it on November second.''

"Why do you think she told you she'd given birth in New York? Suppose you had decided to check out her story. She might have been found out."

"Because she had been in New York. There was always some element of truth in her lies. The envelope with Jason's birth certificate in it was addressed to the name she claimed to have assumed when giving birth. It matched the mother's name on his birth certificate and the father was listed as unknown.'' Garth looked up from fiddling with his salad. In his eyes she saw something she couldn't define.

"Garth, what's wrong?"

"Even after all the lies, I believed her story of taking an assumed name and leaving my name off the birth certificate to punish me for wanting a divorce.'' Garth looked back down and stirred his salad. "My biggest disappointment when the marriage fell apart was that I'd probably never have a child. And she knew it! Could I have been desperate enough for a son that I turned a blind eye to the truth when she presented me with one? I'll tell you something, Amanda. It haunts me to think I might have.''

"What did you do when you found out you weren't Jason's father?"

"I was hurt, furious. I still had Karen's things in the attic because I'd had my mother pack it all up and store it there for Jason some day. Then I found out she'd lied to me about being Jason's father. I started going through it all, throwing it out. It was a good thing Jason was in the hospital because I acted like a maniac. Then I found the picture of you and the baby.''

Garth rubbed his eyes. "When I read the back, this sick feeling hit me like a ton of bricks. I just stared at it and sank down onto a box. The baby looked so much like Jason. I hired a detective. He didn't tell me right away but he started looking for the death certificate on Jason—the real Jason. When he learned that the boy had died within a month of his birth, we knew Karen hadn't given birth to Jason at all. We started searching for you.''

Amanda found herself once more choking back emotion. But this time it was Garth's pain she felt. ''So, how can you say you turned a blind eye? You did the right thing as soon as you knew.''

Garth gave her a sad smile, one absent of joy. ''Now if the FBI just believes in me half as much as you and my mother seem to. It's my word against a dead woman's that I wasn't involved, you realize. I was in New Orleans with her when your husband was killed. That could look pretty bad. Even if they believe me, they could ground me until they're sure. I can't afford that right now.''

Amanda grabbed at a chance to add a little levity to the discussion. She really thought Garth needed it right then. ''Ground you? How about taking away TV for a week?'' she teased with a chuckle in her voice.

Garth rolled his eyes and grinned. Amanda breathed a grateful sigh that she'd been able to lighten his mood. He shook his finger at her, teasing her back. ''It is not polite to ridicule a man's professional buzzwords.'' Then he sobered. ''I'm a pilot, Amanda. I have to stay in the air. I can't afford not to fly.''

Unconsciously, Amanda reached out and covered his hand. She was immediately sorry she had. It was all there. Everything Jess had made her feel and more. The need to comfort. The need to be near. That wonderful, undeniable electric jolt at the slightest contact. But for Garth there seemed no such reaction. He only looked worried. Her compassion warred with her fear of repeating past mistakes. Compassion won, as usual. This situation could be serious for Garth. ''Did you see an attorney?''

''He said he'd go to court and get the judge to allow me to

fly because it's my livelihood if the FBI does ground me but it could take days or a week just to get the hearing scheduled.''

"Garth, none of that's going to happen. I'll talk to the FBI agent who's handling the case and make sure he believes you. I don't think you need to worry about it, but while we're talking about your business may I ask you a question?''

When Garth gave her a noncommittal shrug, Amanda decided to take it as a yes. "Is Liberty Express in financial trouble?'' she asked.

Garth dragged his free hand through his hair, then shrugged again. "I've got medical insurance but it doesn't cover everything. The foundation my employees and family have set up for Jason has helped but...'' Garth grimaced. "My house carries a second mortgage now. The business, too.''

Amanda felt a little guilty for her initial thoughts on seeing Liberty Express's offices the morning of her arrival. Not only had he not planned to use his wealth to keep her son, he'd already spent it all to save Jason's life.

Her heart softened even more toward him. She hated to see him weighed down with so many problems. But then if there was one thing she'd learned since Jesse's abduction, it was that life was rarely fair. Garth had learned that lesson, too. She could tell by the way he'd spoken the night before. She hated to see him learn it again and again.

There was a pause while Amanda gathered her courage. They had other things to discuss. There were things *she* had to know and understand. And one request to make of him. "About Liberty Express, please don't do anything about selling it. Now is an emotional time for all of us. Promise me that you won't make any decisions until Jason's well. You might later regret anything you do.''

Garth didn't think she understood. "I promise to think about it. But you have to understand that when I started Liberty it was for the future but now I don't have a son to pass it on to. Without that there's no reason to keep hanging on to a dying dream. I may as well go back to measuring success in dollars alone.''

Amanda opened her mouth to comment but stopped. ''I'm glad you'll think over your decision. Now.'' She took a deep breath. ''About Jason. I'd like to talk to you about him. A-about the leukemia. I have questions.''

Garth clenched his teeth. He couldn't take much more tonight. He'd made a big mistake asking her to relate what she knew of Jason's kidnapping and its aftermath. He'd thought hearing about her past pain would somehow lessen the agony he was going through at present but it hadn't. Instead, he felt not only his pain but hers as well and he felt responsible for both.

He was sure the questions she needed answered were questions she had every right to ask. But he hated to think about the past year, let alone talk about it. Memories of the terror he'd faced when learning of Jason's illness and of all the suffering Jason been through since flooded his memory. And all he had to hang on to was the hope that he'd made the right choices. And that was no comfort at all. One remission had ended, hadn't it?

He was so afraid he'd made a wrong decision about the chemo and that he'd put Jason through all that for nothing. It was that fear that ruled when he practically snarled his own set of questions. ''What exactly would you like me to tell you? That the first round of chemo failed? That it decimated Jason? That I'm responsible for putting him through all that pain for nothing? That I approved it a second time because I couldn't face losing him?'' Garth knew his tone was sharp and cutting but he was helpless to change it. He was bleeding, too.

He watched Amanda take a careful, deep breath before she responded to his spate of questions. ''Actually, it isn't really his medical treatment I have questions about but the way you talk to him and some of the things I've heard you say to him.''

The blood pounded in Garth's head. ''Are you questioning the way I've raised Jason thus far?''

Amanda sat straighter in her seat and now her eyes blazed. "I'm not questioning a thing! I was trying to compliment you! I think it's admirable that you'd tell him about heaven when I've heard you question God out of his hearing."

"Of course I question. I've held him while he vomited for hours on end and got so weak he couldn't roll over himself to keep from choking. I've watched him go from being the best ball player on his team to not being able to lift a bat. One day I found him gluing his hair to the edges of his hat so none of the other kids would know his hair had fallen out."

"And that's why you joke with him about it?"

Garth nodded. "Because, sometimes, if you don't laugh, you cry. Laughter keeps things in perspective for him. It helps him see how unimportant his appearance is if the chemo will save his life. Fear is a big enemy for Jason. To help him cope, I told him some of the fables from the Bible that my mother and father told me."

Amanda reached out and grasped his hand with hers and Garth glanced away as his heart skipped a beat. He would not acknowledge any attraction he felt toward Jason's mother. It was emotional suicide.

"They're not fables, Garth. They're promises and guidelines," she whispered, that soft Southern lilt in her voice soothing his jangled nerves and awakening feelings he feared to acknowledge.

He took a deep, steadying breath, retreating to familiar ground. He went a round with his mother at least once a week. "I challenged you to explain God and His selective blessings to me already. When you have an answer, we'll talk about it. In the meantime, if you want to help Jason you can help him keep the balance he's achieved. It's a delicate one."

"I understand and I'll try to help him fight, too." Amanda looked past her own pain to the same feelings reflected in Garth's eyes. His pain was worse, though. It had to be. He didn't believe God's hand was on the situation. She wouldn't push further now. It had been a long day for both of them. "Tell me about before. Tell me about Jason growing up."

Garth's smile was sad but quickly became wistful and often joyous as he talked about the boy they both called son. Their shared mood was pensive and serene until he climbed in the car beside her and she gave him her motel's address.

"What on earth possessed you to take a room there? I thought you were at the Ronald McDonald House near Children's."

Amanda stiffened at his tone. "As they say, there was no room at the inn and this is the only place I can afford for an extended period. It isn't that bad."

"Amanda, please—it's awful, and you know it!"

Amanda blushed. "It is a bit seedy. I'll concede that point, but I can afford it."

"You're checking out tonight," he ordered.

"And where, pray tell, do you think I'll sleep? I told you, it's all I can afford. Once the sale of the house is complete I'll move to something more suitable."

"I won't have Jason's mother staying in a place like that. You can stay at my house," Garth countered.

"I can't stay at your house. It wouldn't be right."

"For goodness sake, woman, you're in Philadelphia, not some judgmental small town. Who do you think would care? And don't give me that tired old business about it not being a good witness to your beliefs. Besides that—I live with my mother!"

Amanda giggled at his indignation and, though she still had some concerns, she gave in. It would only be for a short time. "All right, all right. Since your mother will be there, I'll stay till I can get a transfer to the Philadelphia branch worked out or the sale of the house goes through. Does that suit you?"

Garth pursed his lips and nodded but he had a strange look in his eyes. Almost as if he regretted his invitation.

"I could probably afford something a bit better if you'd rather I look around tonight," she countered, not wanting to be more of a burden on him than she already was. Just her presence in Philadelphia, near Jason, must be almost more than he could bear. Now the woman who was going to take his son away would be staying in his house. He couldn't want that.

"I wouldn't have invited you if I didn't want you here." Garth said. He muttered something that she could have sworn sounded a lot like, "That's the problem," but she couldn't be sure because it was lost in the noise of the engine starting. Praying that she'd heard wrong, she dismissed the idea. The same temptation couldn't possibly be visited upon her twice in one lifetime.

Could it?

Chapter Three

Garth grabbed Amanda's suitcase out of the trunk and led the way up the front walk from the sweeping drive. He tried to look at his house with the eyes of someone used to the French Quarter, Southern plantations and shotgun houses with homey wraparound porches. His two-hundred-year-old, three-story, stone colonial in the suburbs of Philadelphia spoke of Americana, dignity and grace. Her house was surrounded by colorful flowering bushes and perennials, his by a stone wall, sedate shrubbery and ancient trees.

Did she think it looked pretentious and cold? Or did she see what he had the first time he'd seen it—a home. To Garth, the house was a sign of everything he'd had as a child—and then lost. He'd found what he'd lost here with Jason and his mother, Frieda. For six years these four stone walls had meant home and security. Now he'd lose it once again. Oh, he'd still have the house but the home he'd built within its sturdy exterior would be gone.

The outdoor lights came on and lit up the grounds and the house itself. Amanda gasped. "Oh, Garth, this is lovely. I feel as if I just stepped into Colonial America."

"It's almost that old," he told her, smiling. He knew he shouldn't let himself care what Amanda thought but her approval mattered. And that meant she was trouble. He wanted Amanda in his life and he had no business thinking or feeling that way. He had to be crazy. Why had he invited her here? He'd promised himself that he'd stay away from her! How could he avoid someone who was living under his own roof?

The front door opened, drawing Garth's attention off his troubled thoughts. His mother stepped out. She was a small, gray-haired, gentle-looking woman but Garth, at six-two, still tried not to cross swords with her. He cringed inwardly. He'd thought of his mother only as a chaperon to ease Amanda's worries. What his mother was going to be was trouble with a capital *T*.

Amanda was the woman who would take away the grandson his mother had helped raise from infancy. There'd be resentment and anger at first. Frieda was a mother hen of the first water. But that would only be at first. Because Amanda was also what his mother would call a good Christian woman. And Frieda Jorgensen had been trying to find a woman like Amanda for him for years. Most women would shun Amanda indefinitely but his mother was not most women. She would more likely see blending of their lives as the will of the Lord—the Lord she vehemently espoused to him at every opportunity. A Lord he no longer served.

"Garth, what are you doing home so early? Nothing's wrong with Jason, I hope," she said when they reached her.

"Jason's fine. More than fine," he answered, thinking of the self-satisfied grin Jason had worn when they'd left for dinner. Garth took a fortifying breath and tried to get ready for the fallout his foolish offer to Amanda of a place to stay was going to cause. He stepped to the side, ushering Amanda forward. "Mom, this is Amanda Powers."

"Oh." That one syllable was so packed full of fear and worry that Amanda stepped back. Her foot slid into the edge of the flower garden and she lost her balance. It was instinct that made him wrap his arms around her waist so she wouldn't fall. But it wasn't instinct that made his heartbeat accelerate. Garth's gaze flew from the top of Amanda's head to his eagle-eyed mother. She propped a hand on her hip and raised an eyebrow, her forehead wrinkling with contemplation. Garth groaned silently, afraid she'd seen his reaction to Amanda's nearness. He hoped against hope that there would be no time for her and Amanda to get into a discussion of personal belief systems.

His mother smiled. "Welcome, Amanda. Call me Frieda."

Garth closed his eyes and sighed. He'd seen it coming, hadn't he? Unfortunately he'd seen it too late. His mother knew how Amanda's nearness had affected him. And now his goose would be cooked once they got to know one another. Why hadn't he just offered to pay for better accommodations for her elsewhere?

"I'm so pleased to meet you," his mother continued. "Jason's told me all about you."

"Jason told you about me?"

"Oh, indeed. He called me for just that reason. You two got on like a house afire, I hear. I'm glad someone's treated you well. Just for the record, I wondered what had gotten into my son when he came home without you last night," his mother continued. "I suppose you stayed at the Ronald McDonald House."

Amanda laughed. "Actually, there was no room there. I stayed at a motel but Garth didn't think it was safe. I wasn't entirely comfortable there but it did have a wonderful little church just down the street. I went to services there last night."

"Wednesday night services? How nice!" his mother replied with a wide, Cheshire cat smile. "You just come right on in."

Garth groaned. Well, that hadn't taken long!

Amanda turned and looked at him. She was so confused it was almost funny. Almost. But not quite. It had taken all of ten seconds to throw a second, and more accomplished matchmaker in the mix. Worse, by ten the next morning, she'd be in league with Jason. "Watch her," he whispered in Amanda's ear. "We usually wind up doing exactly what she wants. She might look like a pushover but she steers us all with an iron hand."

"Garth Colbey Jorgensen, what tales are you telling this young lady?"

"No tales. Just warning her about you, Mom."

"What could you warn Amanda about where I'm concerned? I'm just a nice old lady. Come in, dear. I'll see about your room."

An hour later Garth was in the study adjacent to his room. He was ready for bed but he had a few things to work on and he was getting nothing done. The events of the evening and Amanda were on his mind.

He sighed heavily as he remembered his mother's last question as they'd entered the house. What was he warning Amanda about? Nice old lady? His mother was already at work! That's what he was worried about! The gleam that had come into her eyes had still been there when he'd parted company with her and Amanda.

Ten minutes later Garth realized he was pacing and that his mother could hear the floor creaking. He dropped quickly into his desk chair, trying to focus on the report he had to finish. Liberty Express was always a welcome distraction.

Garth was deep into facts and figures when, from just down the hall, the silvery notes of a song rose above the muted sound of the running shower. Amanda's voice was as sweet as the lyrics she sang.

She'd promised to call the FBI agent who was in charge of Jason's case and add her endorsement to his character. Why couldn't she have been vindictive instead of so understanding? He'd at least have a chance of guarding his heart if she were.

Amanda slipped beneath the covers and let her head sink into the feather pillow. She closed her eyes and inhaled the smell of sheets dried outdoors in the sun. They smelled of fresh air and the housewifely pleasure of crisp, clean beds. She'd never take that wonderful aroma for granted again. To think foolish pride had almost kept her from such a simple pleasure! "Thank you for this special night, Lord," she whispered. "And for the simple pleasures of life."

Her eyes sprang open at the sound of footsteps in the hall. They ended with a crash and a split second later a very male hiss followed. Garth! Her peace fled as thoughts of him flooded her mind.

Wasn't this just like life? Garth had experienced the joy of raising her son for the past six years and to envy and even resent him for that would have been only human. Yet, after meeting him she had a hard time not liking him. Amanda shook her head ruefully. Be honest, she told herself, you more than like him. Even though they were poles apart on fundamental issues, she was more strongly drawn to him than she had been even to Jess Powers. Why did she have to be attracted to the one man in the universe she shouldn't be? He didn't know the Lord. In fact, he was downright hostile about Him. And he'd sounded alarmingly like a man who measured his worth on his success—just the way Jess had. There was also his adamant belief that *love* was a word used to dress up domination, need or lust. Yet even with all those strikes against him, he was so very attractive—everything she'd promised to avoid and then some.

She'd tried to tell herself that the feeing that arced between them was because of their mutual love for Jason. But that was a lie. She'd felt something stir in her heart when she'd fallen against him and into his arms on the front walk earlier. And what she'd felt had nothing to do with mutual feelings for Jason.

And then there was Garth's mother. The older woman had clearly decided to throw Amanda and Garth together. And her reasons were easy to understand. Mrs. Jorgensen didn't want to lose Jason and what better way to keep him right where he was? It made perfect sense.

What was she to do? First, Jason had innocently pushed her and Garth together for dinner. Then Mrs. Jorgensen, not so innocently, stepped into the act with hints about how wonderful a husband Garth would make the right woman and what a wonderful father he was. And Garth had seemed embarrassed at the hospital when Jason had all but strong-armed him into asking her to dinner. He clearly didn't want to be near her—which she should understand and even be grateful for. Instead, she was insulted. Which she shouldn't be. But was.

It was all too much!

Amanda rolled over and deliberately thought of what tomorrow would bring. Another visit with her son. Her tests. Needles! No, that was worse.

She went back to prayer but the last thought that drifted through her head was that she'd be less afraid of the tests if Garth were with her during them.

Garth checked his watch as he waited for the traffic to clear. He glanced up at the hospital. The sun glinted off the windows and the light-colored facade. He didn't dread it today. He felt good. Better than he had in months. The results were in and Amanda was as close a match as they were likely to find. He couldn't wait to tell her and see her reaction. Hear her reaction.

He shook his head. Amanda was the most curious mix of childlike exuberance and femininity he'd ever encountered. She giggled when she was happy but stoically hid her fears and sorrows. She relied on her Lord for strength with a child's faith but was tough as old shoe leather when she had to be.

Garth stepped into the street and rushed forward. He couldn't wait to see her. It wasn't wise but he could fight just so many battles at one time. Five minutes, two corridors and one elevator ride later, Garth pushed open the door to Jason's room. He was surprised to find Jason looking disheartened. "Hey, buddy. Why the long face? That cut giving you fits?"

"Na. I hardly feel it. She didn't come see me, Dad."

"Who?"

"Mrs. Powers. I think I may have made her mad. I mean, everyone isn't as good as you about losing games to a kid."

Garth sat on the edge of the bed. "She wasn't the least bit upset. In fact, she likes you so much that today she had a test done to see if she could be a donor for that transplant Dr. Matt has been talking so much about."

"She did? Wow." Jason's eyes lit up but just as quickly the

flame of happiness dimmed and his face screwed up in a look of total consternation. "But she hates needles."

"So?"

"I mean she *really* hates them, Dad. Yesterday she got all white and her hands started shaking and it was *me* getting stuck. The nurse made her sit down and put her head between her knees. I sure hope she didn't get too scared."

Garth eyed Jason, trying to decide if Amanda was really as terrified as Jason said or if his son was attempting to set another matchmaking trap. Garth frowned as a thought filtered through the suspicion.

"She didn't come to see you at *all* today?" he asked Jason who shook his head, looking sad and worried.

And now Garth was worried about her, too. Wild horses wouldn't keep Amanda away from her son. It bothered Garth how much he wanted to assure himself that she was all right. "Would it make you feel better if I went and made sure she's okay?"

Jason perked up in a flash. "Would you? I really want to make sure she's okay. It would be my fault if she wasn't. Thanks, Dad."

Feeling like a man on his way to an execution—his own— Garth left Jason and went looking for Amanda. He stopped first at the nurses' station near Jason's room. "Excuse me, Cindy," he said to the perky blonde behind the desk.

Cindy Kelly looked up from the chart in her hand. "Mr. Jorgensen, what can I do for you?"

"I wondered if you'd heard anything about that new volunteer who's spent so much time with Jason. Amanda Powers. She had tests today to see if she could be a donor for Jason. Ah...he missed seeing her."

"Amanda Powers? She's resting down the hall. Room 302. She went into shock during the tests. She's fine but—"

"Shock? From tests? What did they do to her?"

Nurse Kelly's smile was indulgent. "She's fine. She fainted. That's all. Really. But I'll go—"

Garth spun away and bolted toward 302. He entered the room as quietly as he could, not wanting to wake her if she was asleep. She was, her blond hair spread like gold across the pillow. He longed to feel the silkiness of those strands slip through his fingers. He raked his hand through his own hair instead. In sleep, her face was peaceful as if she had put her fears and troubles aside for a while. She was beautiful.

Garth reached out to touch her but pulled his hand back just short of contact. He wanted too much from this woman. He cared too much about her, too. But Amanda Powers was not for him. A tap on the door drew Garth's attention.

He opened it to find the young nurse, Cindy Kelly. He followed her into the hall. "I wasn't sure I was supposed to tell you she was in there. Her being Jason's mother and all." Garth felt the blood drain out of his head. Cindy Kelly reached out to him. "Mr. Jorgensen, are you all right?"

Garth gritted his teeth and grabbed the door frame in a death grip. She took a wary step backward and Garth followed her into the hall. "Jason can't find out," he warned. "We were told not to tell him."

Looking perplexed, the nurse nodded. "I'll make sure that no one tells him. We'll even instruct the cleaning people since it's all over the hospital grapevine."

Garth stood stunned as the nurse hurried back toward her station. Amanda had told their secret! Feeling angry and betrayed, he shoved the door to Room 302 open again and stalked to the bed. He looked at the woman in the bed with new eyes and wondered why he'd been such a fool to believe her willingness to wait. Would he never learn?

"Amanda," he barked.

Amanda's eyes flew open as she shot up in the bed. She could just make out the scowling face of the man who'd haunted her dreams. But he'd haunted them with a smile not a frown. "Garth?" She looked around at the darkened room. "Oh, goodness! How long did I sleep?"

"I'm not sure. I came looking for you because Jason missed

your visit today. He was worried when I told him about your test.''

Her son had *missed* her and he'd *worried* about her. Elation spread through her but just as quickly it vanished. Amanda felt a keen disappointment take over her spirit when Garth's annoyance penetrated the after-fog of sleep. Jason, not Garth, had cared. In fact, she seemed to have angered him.

Pushing dangerous notions and foolish wishes for Garth's goodwill aside, Amanda stared at his tight expression. Was Garth jealous that Jason had worried about her? Or just angry that she'd carelessly allowed Jason to become upset?

''I'm sorry he's worried,'' she said as she swung her legs out of the bed and stood. ''I'll go see him and get out of the way so you can have your visit.''

''Are you sure you can hold your tongue with *him* at least?'' Garth snapped.

''Hold my tongue about what? What on earth are you growling about?''

''They all know that you're Jason's mother, Amanda. Just how many people have you told?'' he accused.

Amanda sat back down, her knees collapsing under her. She stared at Garth in shock but then righteous anger flooded her. ''How dare you accuse me of spreading my relationship to Jason around? I don't know how anyone found out but it wasn't from my lips. I've searched too long for my child to endanger him now!''

''Then how did they all find out?''

''How should I know? All I know is that I haven't told anyone.'' Even in the low light it was obvious from his mutinous expression that Garth doubted her. Amanda's outrage grew as she shoved her feet into her shoes. ''You don't believe me. You really don't believe me! You know, Garth, trust has to go both ways. When you told me you didn't have anything to do with the kidnapping, I believed *you* and you were a stranger! You should know enough about me by now to know how much I love Jason, yet there you stand accusing me of doing something to hurt him. You have a heck of nerve and a warped view of people.'' Amanda didn't wait for a reply but stormed out the door.

Garth followed her slowly to Jason's room and entered quietly. Amanda had already taken a position at the foot of the bed and had just finished setting up the Monopoly game board on the dinner tray table. He gritted his teeth. She was supposed to have a quick visit and leave. He sauntered in and sat on the bed next to Jason. This was his time. He didn't have much of it left with Jason and he wanted every precious second. It was selfish but he was too mad to care.

Jason looked up and smiled. "Hi, Dad. Want to play with us?"

Amanda swallowed nervously when she saw Garth's expression but stiffened her spine and with it her resolve. He might look mad enough to chew her up and spit her out but she wouldn't be intimidated. How dare he accuse her? This might be his time to visit but so what! He'd had all the years she should have had with her son already. And she could still lose Jason before she'd ever really gotten him back. Let him learn to share!

Garth's eyes bore into hers in a silent signal. *You're trespassing.*

She glared right back. *Tough.*

"Sure, I'll play," Garth answered, then added almost defiantly, "You're the hat, right, *son?*"

Jason tipped his cap and laughed before handing Garth a marker. "And you're the car. Right?" Her son smiled at her. "It's as close to a plane as he can get. Dad likes speed. What's your choice? I've got a cute dog here or Grandmom always picks the thimble. Hey, how about the iron? You're a woman. There's a wheelbarrow and a horse, too, but they're guy things. Right, Dad?" Jason teased, elbowing Garth in the ribs.

Amanda felt her muscles relax. She couldn't be in the same room with her son and stay angry. "You little chauvinist! I'll have you know I hate ironing. I'll take the horse. I used to ride a lot. My grandfather had a little farm and a big old gelding named General. I used to ride whenever I had a chance.''

Jason frowned as he counted out Garth's fifteen hundred dollars start money from the bank. "What kind of horse is a gelding?''

Garth chuckled and gestured to Amanda indicating that the question was all hers. She cleared her throat, determined not to let the nature of the question ruffle her. This was her first chance to be a parent to her son in seven years. "Well, you see stallions are hard to handle. So, at a certain point, they're altered and then they're called geldings. You see?'' She clapped her hands together. "Let's get on with the game. Shall we?'' she suggested, feeling as if Garth had set her up.

Garth went on the attack. Monopoly ceased to be a game to him. He played ruthlessly. It quickly became evident that this was personal. Under the jovial face he'd put on for Jason, he was still furious with her. Amanda felt sorry for his real competitors as she paid her rent for landing at his Park Place hotel.

"You owe me ten more dollars, Mrs. Powers,'' Garth demanded as he counted the currency she'd just handed him. "Can't you count or are you a cheat, too?''

"Dad? It's just a game. That's what you always tell me.''

Garth looked for a split second as if he might snap at Jason. Even though his expression changed in the blink of an eye, she quickly handed over her last ten dollars and stood up. She couldn't in good conscience let Garth's anger at her boil over onto Jason. "Listen, guys, that did it for me tonight. I think I'll grab a cab and run on home. May the best man win. I'll get by to see you tomorrow, Jason. And Mr. Jorgensen, from now on, I'll make sure I'm gone before you arrive. I'm sorry I encroached on your private time with your son tonight.''

Garth watched in stunned silence as Amanda disappeared.

"Did you have a bad day or what?'' Jason asked, glaring at him and tearing his cap off.

Garth grimaced. "I think *or what.* I suppose you want me to go apologize.'' Jason nodded.

He did have things to discuss with Amanda and he didn't want his mother to be party to that discussion. Garth stood, not happy to find himself leaving so early. He deeply resented losing a second night with Jason. "I'll be back and maybe bring Mrs. Powers with me."

Jason crossed his arms in a stubborn pose. "Only if you're calling her Amanda again."

Garth hurried down the hall in time to see Amanda's blond hair flow behind her around a corner. He heard the stairwell door slam shut as he rounded the corner. Garth ran after her down the steps, calling several times but Amanda just kept racing ahead. Garth made it to the exit door just after she did. He reached past her head and slapped the door shut just as she started to pull it open.

Amanda froze. She wasn't frightened. At least not physically. Garth wouldn't hurt a fly but she knew he would protect Jason no matter what the threat. She shivered. He thought she'd tried to hurt Jason by revealing her relationship to him. She refused to turn around, somehow knowing she'd lose something vital if she did.

They stood there for a long minute with Amanda feeling Garth's closeness to her core but determined to ignore it. Garth took her by the shoulders, finally, and turned her to face him, breaking the stalemate.

Their eyes locked, hers combative, his filled with regret. "I'm sorry," he whispered. His caressing gaze robbed her of her anger. "I should've known you'd never do anything to hurt Jason."

Amanda found she couldn't look away. "You have a lot on your mind."

"I'm tired. I'm worried about—" Garth's fingertips trailed across her cheek and Amanda felt a spark pass between them. "No. No, there's no excuse," he whispered as he bent his head. "Just like there's no excuse for this." His lips found Amanda's in a gentle salutation. "No excuse at all." He kissed her again, his kiss expressing his longing yet no less gentle. The spark blazed into something so powerful it left Amanda weak and shaken. Garth broke the kiss but his arms engulfed her and pressed her close. "This is wrong. I know it but I just don't care." His lips covered hers again.

And Amanda realized what it was she'd been afraid she would lose if she turned around and looked at Garth.

Her heart.

Chapter Four

The stairwell door suddenly smacked into Amanda's back and threw her even more tightly against Garth's solid frame, the dangerous moment thankfully shattered. As one, they moved to the side like automatons, both shocked and a little horrified, though for their own diverse reasons.

A small ferret of a man in a white lab coat squeezed through the door. It was obvious that he had a good idea what he'd interrupted. "Sorry," he said with a knowing grin as he stared at Amanda.

Amanda remembered him from the lab when her tests were done. She remembered the way he'd stared at her and that he was a terrible gossip. She ducked her head, feeling a flush rush up her neck to heat her face. She had no doubt that he would add this latest story to the other, making her and Garth tomorrow's top subject on the hospital grapevine. He might even be the person who'd told everyone about her true relationship to Jason.

Garth stepped between them and blocked her view of the interloper. "Sorry," the man said again as he scurried up the stairs. This time he sounded as if he meant it.

Once the man was gone, Garth turned and reached for her again. Amanda sucked a strangled breath, afraid of the things he'd made her feel but wanting to feel them all the same. She'd never felt anything with her husband that even resembled what she felt minutes ago in Garth's arms. And that reckless need for Jess had nearly destroyed her, she reminded herself. She couldn't risk this. She had to fight it because feelings like these couldn't be trusted—couldn't be good.

She had to remember the pain she'd felt losing Jess to his obsession with worldly adoration and his death in its pursuit. She had vowed never to risk so dangerous an involvement again. And to break that rule for a man like Garth—a man who so openly disdained her faith and sought after worldly success—would make her ten times a fool. And Amanda would be no one's fool again. She'd found it wasn't a role she liked playing.

As he stepped closer, Amanda planted her hand in the middle of his chest. "You're right," she said. "This is wrong."

Garth stared down at her. Regret and something that shouted loneliness flashed in his eyes before they went hard and cold. He snatched his hands off her as if burned and stepped away. "Sorry," he said.

Amanda wasn't sure what he'd apologized for. The kiss, the interruption or her refusal to accept another. She wasn't sure she wanted to know, so she didn't ask. "It was just a kiss," she said and turned toward the door silently confessing the lie.

"Just?" he asked, clearly dubious.

She turned back to confront him only because she knew it needed to be done. "It can't be more." Amanda almost hoped he'd disagree.

Garth's eyes narrowed, assessing her. Amanda met his gaze with determination. His jaw tensed. "Whatever you say."

Amanda turned to leave again but Garth stayed her with a hand on her shoulder. She backed away, determined to keep him at a distance. "What?"

Garth's hand dropped and curled at his side before relaxing. "Jason wants us to come back," he admitted. "I'm in the doghouse with him for growling at you."

"Is he upset?"

"No. More like determined." Garth shrugged, his grin a bit sheepish and very reluctant as he buried his hands in his pockets. It was an expression she was quickly coming to associate with his reaction to Jason's precociousness. "I'm to return with you and be addressing you as Amanda if I know what's good for me. He can be a tough little guy when he digs in his heels."

"And it's equally tough on you to tell him no just now."

"Yeah," Garth admitted. "But he's right this time, even though he doesn't know why I acted the way I did. I really am sorry about the way I treated you upstairs. I know you care about Jason as much as I do. I shouldn't have doubted you but I have a hard time trusting since Karen. Come back, please."

Amanda didn't want hard feelings between them any more than she wanted the ones she'd felt when he'd kissed her. She nodded and followed him up the stairs to Jason's room. He was sitting with his legs and arms crossed, waiting like a Middle Eastern potentate when they entered.

Garth tried to be firm. "I asked *Amanda* to come back but don't think I did it because you told me to. It's you who obeys me, remember?" Jason lost a bit of the superior look in his eyes and nodded. "There was something I had to talk to both of you about," Garth continued as he took hold of Jason's hand. He smiled. "Your last tests were the best they've ever been, son, and—"

"I feel great, too. Does that mean I can come home again?"

Garth shook his head. "'Fraid not. You have to stay here because Amanda's test results are in, too. We've got a near perfect match, kid."

Jason's gaze flew from Garth to her. A grin split his face but his eyes were nearly worshipful. Amanda felt tears well up when he reached out and took her hand with his free one. Amanda glanced at Garth who studied their clasped hands then her face with sober eyes. It hadn't escaped Amanda's notice, either, that Jason was an undeniable link between them.

"So, now they bring in the heavy guns Doctor Matt told me about?" Jason asked. The trepidation in his tone drew the attention of both adults. Jason's smile had faded and there was apprehension in his eyes.

"I'm afraid so," Garth warned with a grimace.

Amanda had thought Jason and Garth would both be elated. "What heavy guns?" she asked.

"They'll start the chemo again plus do full body irradiation so that, when they do the transplant, your stem cells will replace his. Remember? We talked about this. Then when his body makes blood, it'll be cancer free."

"Will you be here more often like you were before?" Jason asked Garth.

"I'll be here as much as I can be. Grandmom will be here with you, too, and maybe Amanda could come more often. You wouldn't mind, would you, Amanda?"

"I'd be glad to visit more often. Jason's my favorite patient."

"It'll be worse than before, won't it?" Jason asked.

Garth held out his arms and Jason let go of her hand so he could nestle into Garth's embrace. "Dr. Hernandez doesn't think it necessarily will be. They're going to try a new drug to keep you from getting too sick. Hey, cheer up. This is good news."

Garth glanced at Amanda. It was obvious that she hadn't really understood all the transplant would entail. He knew she'd been told but now he remembered that no one had explained just how sick it would make Jason. He could see she was upset and unable to do what she wanted—to hug Jason the way he could in his role as Jason's father. It was unfair to her that he was free to offer comfort to her son but for the life of him he couldn't think of a way to include her.

They stayed with Jason until after ten when he finally fell asleep. Then they tiptoed out of the room. "What happens now?" Amanda asked as they headed for the elevator.

"They'll begin the chemo and radiation tomorrow. Jason will be in isolation pretty soon because he'll be prey to any bacteria or viruses that come along. He'll get weaker because the infusion therapy will wipe out his blood cells. He'll hold down less food and eventually go on IV feeding entirely. It'll be rough going but it'll be worth it when it works." Garth stared at Amanda and answered the question in her eyes. "It has to work."

Amanda spent the next morning with Jason, then she went to the Philadelphia branch of her company to see if she could secure a transfer. Her timing couldn't have been better. The same job she did in New Orleans would be available in the Philadelphia office. Highly recommended by her boss back in Louisiana, Amanda soon found herself welcome at the Pennsylvania office. That left her with a four-month leave of absence to spend with Jason.

She couldn't wait to share her news with Garth. The ease with which she was able to transfer to Philadelphia had to have been heaven-sent. But Amanda's elation burst like a pin-stuck balloon when she stood in Jason's doorway and found Garth holding Jason's head as he vomited. He looked so small and even paler than he had before. Helpless. Exhausted.

Amanda fought tears as she listened while Garth spoke in soothing tones to their son. At that moment, Amanda realized that Jason was *their* son. Garth was as much his father as she was his mother and always would be. She would never have her baby all to herself again.

Just then Garth noticed her in the doorway. Their eyes met and he stiffened as if he'd seen into her heart to the resentment and jealousy she felt. But Garth's eyes betrayed him, as well. In the split second before he masked his thoughts in the face of her bitterness, she read so much worry and pain that she backed out of the room, ashamed.

She ran. She ran from the past. She ran from the future. But most of all, she ran from the present because she didn't know what else to do. There were too many things happening. Too many feelings bombarding her heart.

Amanda sought refuge in the hospital chapel. Drawn there by the need for the kind of comfort that only He could give, she begged for guidance and the strength to deal with all that life had suddenly thrown at her. She did what she'd learned at her mother's knee. She sat in the quiet, and listened. Not to herself but for a still quieter voice. She waited for Him to speak to her.

Amanda couldn't hide from the truth, sitting before her Lord. Her upset wasn't caused by Jason's illness. The leukemia caused fear and worry but not this churning turmoil. No. That was all tied up in Garth.

It was a very human emotion to feel resentment toward the man who'd had all the good years of Jason's life. It was what most people would call a normal reaction. But she knew feelings of resentment were wrong. Those emotions flashed through her anyway even as she fought them. They were feelings and emotions she didn't even want to feel, because of the kind of person Garth had turned out to be.

Garth was a good man. A decent and caring man who'd probably been hurt just as badly by Karen Jorgensen as Amanda herself had. He'd been good for Jason. She couldn't have asked for a better father for him, except for his lack of faith in God. And he even seemed to hide that from the boy.

But none of that was the overwhelming problem that had set her into flight from Jason and Garth. The problem was that she was drawn to Garth for her sake and not Jason's. And that frightened her.

The only solution seemed to be that she had to keep Garth out of her life as much as possible. He just made her *feel* too much and she'd made that mistake once already with Jess. And if that weren't enough, she had no way of knowing if Garth was drawn to her for herself or her claim to Jason. Amanda wondered if even Garth knew.

"Amanda," Garth said from the chapel doorway, "are you all right?"

Amanda felt the now familiar stirring deep in her soul at the sound of his voice. She stood and turned to face the first man she could love since her son's father. The flashing memory of a flag-draped coffin, a sea of blue uniforms, the smell of thousands of carnations and the sound of a twenty-one gun salute chased away any thoughts of falling in love again. It was just too dangerous with a man like Garth. Too familiar. Around him she really did feel too much.

"I'm fine," she lied. "It was a shock seeing him like that. He was fine this morning."

"I feel as if I lied to him. The antinausea drug isn't working with the new program. It's going to be bad."

Amanda hugged herself, her empty arms aching. All the resentment flooded her again. "I can't stand this. I want to hold him! I'm his mother but to him I'm just a kindly stranger, not someone to turn to for comfort."

"You're much more, Amanda. You're giving him a chance at life and he knows it. He's grateful."

"I don't want his gratitude!" Amanda was torn by conflicting emotions. "I'm his mother, I want his love!"

Garth understood the feelings behind Amanda's uncharacteristic outburst, though he wrestled with the concept and meaning of love daily. He wished he could tell her that Jason wanted her for a mother as badly as she wanted to be able to be his mother. But it wouldn't be fair. Because Jason wanted her to be more than his mother. He wanted them to be a family. Besides the fact that they'd really just met, Garth never intended to have another wife.

Karen had cured him of marriage for good. He was not foolish enough to believe he'd caused Karen's problems but he knew he hadn't handled them right, either. Her stealing of Jason and her subsequent suicide were ample proof of his failure. There were no happily-ever-afters for some people. And he was one of those people.

"It'll take time. For your sake, I wish we could walk in there right now and tell him the whole story. But we can't. Just be there when he needs you, Amanda, and pretty soon his gratitude will turn to something more. Then he'll turn to you."

Garth watched the internal struggle going on inside Amanda as it reflected on her face. She'd been robbed of so much and he knew from the look on her face when he'd glanced up to see her standing in Jason's doorway that she blamed him.

She wasn't alone. He blamed himself. He hadn't recognized Karen's illness until it was too late. He'd been so wrapped up in his career and what he wanted from marriage that he'd fooled himself into believing that Karen was just spoiled and demanding. He hadn't even considered that she might be mentally ill. By the time he recognized her actions as an illness it was too late. He'd already called it quits in New Orleans. And when he'd cut her loose, she'd apparently turned around and come up with an insanely brilliant scheme to steal her way back into his good graces. She'd stolen Jason from Amanda. The damage was done. And he'd become a father.

For a while, anyway.

Garth ran through the parking garage and into the hospital, not caring if anyone stared at him. Jason was in trouble. Damn! He'd been doing so well. After that initial bad bout, the anti-nausea drug had taken hold. Then two hours ago, Garth's mother had called but he'd been deep in negotiations on a new contract. The secretary of the man he'd been meeting with hadn't understood the nature of the call. He'd been angry but had masked that anger because he needed the business her boss's company would provide. When he'd left, he'd broken every speed limit on the expressway.

Would that elevator never come? he thought as he jabbed the button repeatedly. Garth ran through the conversation he'd had with his mother for the hundredth time since jamming his key in the ignition and peeling out of his parking spot.

Jason had become hysterical over something he'd seen on television. Frieda Jorgensen had promised to do whatever was necessary to calm him but she wanted Garth and Amanda to hurry right over. Garth had hoped he'd be able to calm Jason down before Amanda saw him since she'd only be able to enter his room as a new friend. Unfortunately by now, Amanda had probably gotten there before him and had been forced to stand by and watch her own son being comforted by another. And there was always the possibility that Jason would lash out at her because he thought she was a hospital employee.

The past year hadn't been without incidents like this. Even the mildest mannered kid acted out once in a while when practically every adult he saw came into his life to inflict one kind of pain or another. Even volunteers who only played games with him to help occupy his time had been targets at those times. He could only hope Amanda's reception hadn't been too bad.

What had Garth so worried this time was that his mother's tone had sounded different from those other times. As if something had shaken Jason badly. Garth checked his watch. Where was that elevator? And what had set Jason off?

Garth heard the frantic click of high heels on terrazzo. He turned and saw Amanda racing toward the elevators from across the lobby. She looked as frantic as he felt but he hid his worry. Too many times since meeting Amanda, she had needed to shore up his faltering strength. Now, from somewhere deep inside he had to do the same for her.

At that moment the elevator finally came. Garth stepped inside and held the doors open for Amanda. He quickly stepped backward as Amanda rushed inside. "Garth," she gasped as the doors slid shut behind them. She stayed facing him and sagged, clearly exhausted, against the closed elevator doors. "How is he? What happened? I decided to take a cab but it got caught in a huge traffic jam on the Schuylkill. I'm so sorry it took me so long."

Garth shrugged trying to look nonchalant and not give away his roiling emotions. "Don't worry about it. I just got here myself. I was in a meeting and didn't get the message. As for Jason, I'm sure it isn't anything to be too frantic about. He's gotten upset before over tests and whatnot. Sometimes he just can't take any more poking and prodding. Mother did say though that this time it was a television show that upset him."

"What could he have seen on television?"

Garth leaned his back against the wall and jammed his hands

into his pockets to keep from pulling her into his arms and comforting her. "Maybe he saw something negative about bone marrow transplants. I don't know." All Garth really knew at this point was that his mom had sounded frantic and nothing shook his mother.

Matt Hernandez met them outside Jason's room. His words were quick and concise, his manner grave. "I don't care what you have to say or do. Calm him any way you can. It's imperative that you reassure him."

Reluctant yet impatient, Garth pushed open the door to Jason's room without any response to Hernandez. Jason lay in the bed looking smaller and more forlorn than Garth had ever seen him. His big violet eyes, the only trait he seemed to have gotten from his mother, were red rimmed and swollen. Worse there was a panic in them he'd never seen before. Even the day he'd heard that leukemia could be fatal. "Hey, kiddo, what's the trouble?"

Jason looked up as a tear rolled out of the corner of his eye and into his ear. "You lied to me," he said in a barely audible whisper.

Garth frowned and leaned closer. "Son, I've never lied to you."

"Yes, you did. I'm not your son."

Garth felt a knife thrust through his heart as his blood drained into his toes. For a moment he couldn't breathe. "Jason, where did you hear something like that?"

"The man on 'The Nick Terry Show.' He said I don't belong to you. He said I'd have to go live with Mrs. Powers. He said she was my mother and that my…moth…your…your wife… stole me when I was a baby. Why, Daddy? Why did you lie to me?"

Looking into the devastated eyes of his son, Garth knew the full depth of the heartbreak he'd already been feeling for weeks. "I didn't lie, Jason. You look just like me and I didn't know what she'd done. She'd been gone awhile and when I saw you,

I accepted what she said. You were my son from the moment I saw you."

Jason's bottom lip quivered. "I'm so much trouble and all and I'm not yours anyway. I guess you don't want me anymore."

Garth stared at Jason, staggered. "Jason, that's not true! I'll always want you and think of you as my son but you see... Amanda...is—"

Garth's mother stomped on his foot. Hard. "For goodness sake, Garth. Stop pussyfooting around. Can't you see that Jason's upset and worried about how all this will affect him? You can't keep your plans a secret any longer, thanks to some wretched person who blabbed the whole story to that tacky, morning talk show.

"Jason, lamb." Frieda took a deep breath. "What your father has been trying to keep as a surprise is that he and Amanda have decided that the best solution for all of us is to be a family. They're getting married. Garth will still be your father and you'll have Amanda for a mother."

Garth stared at his mother. Was she out of her mind? The silence in the room seemed answer enough. One glance at Amanda told him she was as appalled as he was by the whopper his mother had told. Did she really think a savvy kid like Jason was going to swallow a tall tale like that?

"Really?" Jason asked, hope a living thing in his voice. Garth stared down at Jason—a different Jason, a changed Jason, a happy, beaming Jason. "You still want to be my father and Mrs. Powers is really my mother? She's going to live with us? For real?"

Garth turned toward Amanda again. He bristled. She was as white as Jason's sheets. Okay. His mother had dropped a real bomb here. He wanted to give her a piece of his mind, too, but did Amanda have to look so...so horrified? He might not be a movie star but he wasn't some monster. And his house might not be the governor's mansion but it was a pretty terrific house, second mortgage and all. He didn't share her faith, but he wasn't a bad person. Did she have to look as if marriage to him would be a fate worse than death?

What was he thinking? Of course it was! For him, too. He didn't want a wife. Especially not one who looked so horrified at the prospect of having him for a husband. He glanced back at Jason, who had begun to look worried again, and leapt from the frying pan into the fire. Jason was all that mattered. He'd walk through fire to save him.

Garth took two long steps, which put him next to Amanda. She still stood barely inside the room. He smiled and, putting an arm around her, pulled her to the bed to stand with him beside Jason. "Since your grandmother let the cat out of the bag, son, I guess it's time we shared our plans with you. Right, sweetheart?" Garth said and squeezed Amanda's shoulder.

"Absolutely," Amanda answered. Her mind in a whirl, she forced a smile in Jason's direction then looked at Garth. He looked…stunned when she wrapped her arm around his waist. Good! Two could play at this game. Whatever the game was.

"And you're really my real mom?" Jason asked. "And you looked for me for years and years until you found me?"

Amanda nodded. "I looked for years and years but actually, it was your father who found me," Amanda corrected. She was annoyed at Garth but she had to give Garth his due. "He found out that his wife had kidnapped you. So he looked for me. He made me so happy. It was like a dream come true when he told me where you were."

Jason pushed himself up in the bed. It was the most strength and determination he'd displayed in days. "He was your Prince Charming," Jason said dreamily. "He rescued you and you fell in love. Right?"

Amanda felt like Alice just after she'd blundered down the rabbit hole. How could the child who'd rationally discussed heaven and death with her and who beat her twice a day at Monopoly believe in fairy tales? "That's not—" Amanda broke off when Garth squeezed her arm.

"That's about the size of it," Garth put in.

"Do I call you Mom?" Jason asked.

"You can call me whatever you feel comfortable with."

"Mom, I think." Jason stared off into space for a few minutes. "What do you want to call me?" he wondered. "Is Jason my real name, Mom?"

Amanda had never heard so wonderful a sound as "Mom" on her son's lips. She had waited so long. *Mom.* Her heart swelled with mingled pain and joy. "I named you Jesse but I don't expect you to use that name unless it's what you want. You're Jason now. That's even how I think of you."

Jason looked ponderous. "It's my real father's name, isn't it?"

"You were named for your father. He died before you were born."

"He died because he was a hero like Dad!" Jason frowned. "I remember what you told me about your husband. When he tried to save a lady in a holdup, he got shot."

Amanda nodded as she vowed to remember what Jason had innocently reminded her of. Garth and Jess certainly were two of a kind. And, because of that, she had to find a way to undo the damage Frieda and Garth had done with this engagement story. True, they could make it a long engagement, using Jason's health as an excuse and never marry, but the pretense would put them in contact with each other too much.

"Mom," Jason said as if from a distance. "Isn't that a good idea?"

Amanda had no idea what he'd said but she decided a non-committal answer was better than letting him know how distracted and upset she was. "I suppose," she said.

She was surprised when Garth glared at her. "Son, I'm not sure. You're going into isolation any day. That's short notice and your doctors might not let you come anyway. I think we'd better wait until you're at home and on the road to recovery."

"But that could be months! I want you to get married now. Why does everything have to get ruined because I'm sick? If I were dead, you two could be happy and have other kids. You wouldn't have to waste all your time here with me.''

"Jason! Don't talk that way! It isn't true," Garth said. "The time we spend with you is precious. Besides that, it was you who brought Amanda and me together. You're an important part of our lives. Nothing would be the same without you.''

Jason brightened. "Then you'll get married in the hospital chapel and get them to let me go. I want us to be a family right away!"

Amanda held her breath. Garth would think of something. She'd seen how fast he was when dealing with Jason's machinations. Her heart stopped when he nodded in defeat. "I'll see what I can do.''

"Well now," Frieda said with a smile worthy only of a cat with canary indigestion. "If there's going to be a wedding, you and Amanda better not waste a minute. I'll stay with Jason this evening and you two can go see Reverend Pittman. I'll call him and smooth the way. I'm sure he'll be delighted to perform the ceremony here. And I'm sure you've got a great deal to discuss between you.''

"But I'd like a word with you, Mother," Garth said, his teeth gritted in a semblance of a smile.

Frieda waved aside Garth's reasonable request. "You don't need me to plan your wedding. Run along, children. I'll see you both at home after visiting hours.''

Amanda followed Garth out of the room after kissing Jason on the forehead. "Why did you agree?" Garth snarled as soon as the door closed on Jason and Frieda.

"Me!" Amanda squeaked. "It was you who acted as if we'd planned it all along. I was so shocked that I answered a question I didn't even hear. It was your mother who trapped us. How could she do this?"

"You saw how upset he was. He calmed down right away when she said we'd be a family. What else could she have said?"

Since Amanda didn't have a better answer, she asked another burning question. "What are we going to do?"

Garth's jaw hardened with determination. "We're going to get married."

Chapter Five

Amanda gaped at Garth. "Are you out of your mind? I refuse to even consider marrying you!"

Garth's eyes suddenly blazed. "You wanted Jason to know you're his mother and now that's happened. What are you going to do with that privilege? Walk in there and burst his bubble?"

Amanda's temper flared, too. "Your mother shouldn't have created the *bubble* in the first place!"

"Look, Amanda." Garth inhaled deeply and let his breath ease out. "This is about more than just my mother's…story. The bubble I'm talking about is his security and I've been that security for as long as Jason remembers."

"I'm not debating that, but I would have been there for him if I could have. If I'd been allowed to."

"And I'm not debating that. And for the record it was Karen's fault that you weren't a mother to Jason all those years. Not mine," Garth continued. "I can't tell you how sorry I am that all this happened. I even feel partly responsible. She may have hoped to hold on to me through the baby. But guilt aside, I also know Jason can't lose me right now. The connection forged between us in the past seven years can't be wiped out by your arrival on the scene and your rights to him. I thought for a while it could, but hearing his take on this made me realize that I was wrong. I hadn't thought he'd feel deserted or that he'd been too much trouble. I wish it didn't have to be this way but that's the way it is."

"You don't want to marry me any more than I want to marry you. That's what you're saying."

Garth nodded. "That's what I'm saying. But I'm willing to put aside my feelings for Jason's best interests."

"I hardly even know you!" Amanda railed. "And this is about more than feelings."

Garth shrugged. "It doesn't have to be a real marriage and we can end it when Jason's health is secure."

Amanda turned away and walked into the nearby solarium. She stared out over the city and wondered if anyone else in that sea of humanity faced so monumental a decision that day. No, she corrected herself, there really wasn't a decision and that was the problem. She'd been forced into a corner by a gossip and a desperate grandmother.

But more was at stake here than Jason's health and peace of mind. She had to wonder if Garth saw this marriage as a way to increase his legal chances to stay a part of Jason's life. And what of her vow never again to become unequally yoked to an unbelieving partner in marriage. This marriage, that he seemed all too willing to toss aside when it no longer suited his purposes, for her would be a lifetime commitment no matter what an earthly court decreed. She could never stand before a minister of the Lord and vow her life to Garth with an option-out clause in the marriage contract tucked in the back of her mind.

It was all too much. Here she was still trying to cope with finding Jason and discovering him ill—now it looked as if she was trapped into a sham of a marriage with a man she feared she could easily love. No matter what, Amanda knew she was bound to be hurt. Because if she agreed, it would be her duty to try to make their marriage work. And if she took that course, how could she possibly guard her heart in case he did toss her aside as soon as Jason was well? Amanda wondered if she even had a right to try protecting herself when that would mean giving less than her all to her marriage.

Her only choice seemed to be to agree and pray that Garth would see how rewarding marriage could be. She'd be a good wife to him and hope he would begin to feel for her some of what she had begun to feel for him. She'd also use any opportunities presented to her to show him the kind of peace and joy putting the Lord back in his life could bring.

Amanda turned from the sight of the towering city to face Garth. She leaned against the windowsill and crossed her arms. "I need to pray about this, Garth. It's a big step."

Garth's eyes went as hard as diamonds. "I don't see what you need to *pray* about. Jason's life or your temporary inconvenience. It won't be all that long. I want out of this marriage as much as you do."

Amanda fought the urge to flinch. Why did he react so badly to any mention of her faith and how could he look on a vow made to God as inconsequential? "Exactly how long do you intend for us to stay married?" she asked tightly.

"Until Jason is stronger and has adjusted to our new roles in his life. Then we can separate amicably."

"Amicably?" she repeated, but the question in her voice told of her doubts. "And what about Jason at that point? Where does he fit into the *amicable* divorce?"

"All I ask is that you let me see him. As I said, you were right about that. I can't just drop out of his life. After the way he talked just now, I'm afraid he'd think I don't care about him. I want him to always be able to trust in my feelings for him even though I'm not his real father."

Amanda's anger drained. Garth once again seemed to be thinking of her son first. But the loss of her anger left a void and a question that had been nagging at the back of her mind. Why did Garth, who obviously loved Jason with every fiber of his being, never say the words? To Jason or anyone else for that matter. She shook her head clearing away the deep questions that kept gnawing away at her. It was the practical she had to deal with just then. "Garth, you are his father but I still want an agreement worked out up front. I'd be eroding my right to sole custody with a marriage to you. I can't risk losing him again. I don't even have any guarantee that it wasn't you who leaked our story to that show. Maybe you and your mother thought keeping a legal foot in the door was worth the gamble with Jason's health.''

Garth's jaw hardened even more. His eyes glittered and she could almost see steam come out his ears. Amanda was ashamed. For a second she'd considered the possibility of a conspiracy between Garth and Frieda Jorgensen but had dismissed it the next. These people loved her son, so why had she said that? Just because the word seemed to be missing from his vocabulary?

''Garth, I—''

''What happened to all that trust you talked about yesterday?'' he asked through gritted teeth.

Amanda wished his anger didn't make her feel so awful. It meant she cared and that almost guaranteed she'd be hurt badly eventually. ''I'm sorry. I guess it went out the window with my sense. I shouldn't have said that. I shouldn't even have thought it. I'm afraid, Garth. Can you understand that?''

Garth stared at her with a hard uncompromising look in his eyes. ''Don't worry, you'll get your agreement. And while we're on the subject, I have a demand of my own. I want a prenuptial agreement stating that you have no claim on Liberty Express or the house.''

Amanda was once again surprised at the way Garth's cold anger affected her. She felt like crying. ''Fine.'' She forced the word past nearly trembling lips and turned away. ''Just give me a few minutes in the chapel and I'll have my answer.''

Dear God, is it already too late? Do I already care too much? Amanda asked silently as she walked toward the chapel. She entered, her mind in a whirl, fears overwhelming her. *Why did I even hesitate? What choice do I have?* She looked around, peace an impossible commodity, the voice of her Lord silent in the face of thundering anxieties. Amanda turned and left. Garth had been right. What was there to pray about? She had no choice.

Amanda stared at the woman in the mirror. The ivory lace, tea-length dress was something out of her fantasies. How had she wound up dressed like this in the middle of her worst nightmare? Ah yes, Amanda thought, that first run-in with my would-be mother-in-law's iron will....

"Amanda you can't wear that to your wedding!" Frieda exclaimed in horror as they left the hospital.

Amanda sighed, gazing down at her blue-flowered dress. "Why can't I wear this? It's perfectly presentable."

"Tomorrow you'll be a bride and you can't wear a dress you wear all the time no matter how nice it is. Garth's seen you in that more than once."

"I didn't have time to plan my trip north. I just threw some things in a bag."

"It isn't that he's seen you in it," Frieda explained, slowly as if Amanda were missing some or most of her marbles. "This should be a special occasion. A celebration!"

"Then why do I feel as if I'm a lamb being led to slaughter?" Amanda hated the sullen tone in her voice.

"How long are you going to keep this up?" Frieda snapped.

"Keep what up?"

The older woman took Amanda's arm and pointed her toward the curb and the taxi stand. "How long are you going to keep up the pretense that you aren't attracted to my son? Amanda, I've seen the way you look at Garth. He's quite a catch, if I do say so myself."

"Garth is a very nice man," Amanda hedged as she climbed into the taxi. "But so was my husband."

"Nice, but he's not what you need?"

Amanda nodded.

"And your late husband was a believer. Is that it?"

Amanda bit her lip. She just couldn't lie to this woman who'd helped raise her son. "It isn't my place to judge Garth or Jess. Let's just say Jess wasn't a committed Christian. I thought it wouldn't matter. After we moved to the city, Jess changed. He cared about other things besides our marriage and the family we'd planned."

"And those things hurt you?"

"No. Those things were more important than me. And as for being attracted to Garth, I was as attracted to Jess. *Attraction* is another word for *temptation* as far as I'm concerned. My old pastor used to say that temptation doesn't happen with things that are good for us."

Frieda sighed and closed her eyes. "Oh, Amanda, I can't believe I got you into this. I knew in my heart it wasn't fair to you but I love my son. I confess I've seen you as a sort of godsend for Garth. I hoped that through your example he'd see how wrong he is for not trusting in the Lord. He just can't keep on carrying the burden he has in these years alone. He needs to rely on the Lord. He needs His strength. His comfort."

Amanda shrugged. "Don't count too much on me to help bring him to the Lord. I doubt he'll be looking at me as any great example. I'm going to try, but you have to realize that Garth sees both of us as fools who believe in fairy tales. Besides, according to Garth this marriage is only a temporary arrangement."

Frieda balled her fist in her lap, deep disappointment evident on her face. "I could shake that boy for turning his back on everything he once believed in."

"Once believed?"

"As a boy, he loved the Lord so much. I thought..." Frieda trailed off, her eyes filling.

Amanda reached out and grasped Frieda's hand. "What is it? What did you think? What happened?"

"It isn't all my own story to tell. Actually, my part of it was settled a long time ago. But what turned Garth against the Lord is another story in a way. It's how my problems affected him so it's his story now. I think you should ask him. I don't want him thinking I've been interfering more than I already have."

"Would you answer one question for me?"

"If I can, dear."

"I've noticed that Garth never says the word *love*. Even to Jason. It could be that I'm imagining it but—"

"You aren't imagining a thing. No, he doesn't acknowledge love any more than he does the Lord. And before you ask, it is because of the same thing. Ask him if the opportunity presents itself. Right now I have a question for you. Does Garth understand that you'll consider yours a marriage for life?"

"No. And I have to ask you not to tell him anything about this conversation. If he stays with me, it has to be of his own free will, just as if he turns to the Lord, it has to come from his heart. Not his lips. I need you to understand that I could very easily love Garth more than I ever did Jess. I know that already. But if Garth can marry and plan to end that marriage so easily, then I can't trust him with my heart."

Frieda pursed her lips and set her shoulders. "I understand completely but you still have to look the part for Jason. Suppose we stop on the way home. I know a lovely little dress shop in Haverford. They're sure to be able—"

Tempted, Amanda interrupted before she could weaken. "No, I—I can't."

"Why?"

"It wouldn't be wise."

Frieda batted her hand at the air in front of her. "Oh, fiddle with being wise. Neither you nor Garth seem to think this marriage is going to last, but I believe this was meant to be. If it does turn into something wonderful and lasting, would you want to look back on tomorrow and remember yourself in your blue-flowered dress?"

"It isn't exactly a rag," Amanda hedged, refusing to let herself hope that there could be a happily-ever-after for her and Garth.

"It just won't do!" Frieda reiterated, losing her patience. "Jason will think it's strange for you to wear a dress he's already seen. It will upset him. He's already asked if your dress has pearls and a train."

"I don't think—"

"That's right! You've got it. Don't think. Driver..."

And that's why I'm wearing this beautiful dress, Amanda thought as she stood in a room across the hall from the chapel of Children's Hospital in Philadelphia. She fingered her dress, the most beautiful, expensive, over-thirty wedding dress the Lysette Shop could furnish.

She'd meant to hate everything the proprietor showed her and had done herself proud until the sneaky woman had brought out and installed Amanda in the dress she now wore. Frieda had seen something Amanda couldn't hide and had declared the dress sold and her wedding gift to Amanda. The price tag had horrified Amanda but Frieda had waved away any protests. Matching pearl combs and a pair of lacy pumps were soon added to the growing pile on the counter.

Amanda grumbled, "I feel like a Thanksgiving turkey. All trussed up, dressed up and ready for sacrifice."

"Well, you look absolutely beautiful," Frieda said from behind her as she fussed with the combs in Amanda's hair. Frieda had insisted that Amanda apply what she called "full party makeup" as well. So she looked in the mirror and saw eyes that looked even larger than usual. Amanda hoped Jason wouldn't be able to see past the eyeliner, blush and lipstick to the fearful woman beneath.

"Thanks to you. I don't think anyone back home would recognize me. I doubt Garth and Jason will, either."

Christina Jorgensen, Garth's sister and Amanda's maid of honor, laughed. "Garth is in for a surprise. That's for sure."

Amanda fiddled with the engagement ring Garth had given her and insisted she wear. It was for appearance's sake only, he'd assured her. "I'm not sure I can do this," she admitted.

Christina took hold of Amanda's cold hand and squeezed gently. "Of course, you can. I'll be right there by your side. It's a maid of honor's job to help out the bride."

"And if you get tongue-tied, I'll just shout out the I do's for you," Frieda teased.

Amanda smiled but she wasn't at all sure if the older Jorgensen woman had made a promise or a threat. She looked up into Frieda's smiling face and detected nothing but support. But still, she wondered. "This really isn't what Garth wanted, either," Amanda said.

Frieda raised an eyebrow. "Is that what you think? Let me tell you, nothing and no one has ever made my son do something he didn't want to do."

"You can say that again," Christina agreed.

Amanda allowed a small hope to spark in her soul.

"And on that subject, Garth asked me to give you these. This is your wedding gift," his mother said.

Amanda stared at the flat jeweler's box Frieda had placed in her hands.

"Open it," Christina demanded.

What looked like an antique seed pearl choker and matching earrings lay on a bed of age-yellowed satin. "Oh, my goodness!" Amanda's eyes flew to Frieda's then Christina's.

"Grandmother's wedding jewelry," Garth's sister said.

The spark of hope flared in Amanda's heart. Why would he give her these if he meant to end the marriage? "But, why would he do this? I can't accept these under false pretenses."

"Oh, yes you can!" Frieda exclaimed. "Those will be Jason's one day to give his wife. It's a tradition. One I'd thought Garth had forgotten. It's a good sign. Now, let's get those on you."

"Who knows how long this marriage'll last?" her smug maid of honor added cryptically as she handed Amanda a small cascade of gardenias and baby's breath while her new mother-in-law finished with the clasp. "These are from him, too. He said he remembered you grew them."

Amanda felt her eyes fill. "Why did he have to make such sweet gestures?" She bent her head to smell the heady sweetness of her flowers.

Frieda chuckled. "Oh, you've got lots of surprises ahead of you being married to my son. He is, after all, *my* son."

There was a knock on the door. "Everything's ready," a voice called from the hall.

"Here we go," Frieda said cheerfully. "Curtain's going up."

Amanda swallowed. It was curtains for her. That was for sure! *Oh, help me Lord!*

Chapter Six

For Amanda, the short walk across the hall to the chapel was sheer torture. There weren't just a few butterflies ricocheting around in her stomach. This was more like a whole flock of sparrows.

Her steps faltered on the threshold as a nurse began to play the wedding march on an acoustic guitar. Amanda looked around at the curious staff who'd squeezed into the tiny chapel next to several of Garth's employees and a handful of his family and friends. It struck Amanda that she'd never felt so alone in her life, not even standing at her husband's graveside amid scores of consoling strangers who hadn't a clue about her real feelings.

She sought out Jason with desperate eyes and found him sitting on a high stool at the foot of the plain altar between Dr. Bill Wood, Garth's best man, and Christina. Jason looked frail and tired but his eyes shone with delight and excitement. She glanced at the pillow in his lap. He had his own special part in the ceremony. Since he was too weak to walk up the aisle, Garth had dubbed him the official ring *keeper*. Amanda looked at her son's face again. It was his look of hope that gave her the courage to step fully inside the chapel.

But fear and isolation surrounded her. Jason was the only one in the room who was there for her and even *his* affections were divided. Jason glanced back at the cross over the altar and Amanda remembered that she was never alone. Then a deeper realization dawned. Her Lord would have to protect her from hurt because deep in her heart, Amanda knew her fear sprang from a foolish, dangerous wish that Garth wanted this marriage because of her as much as because of Jason.

Garth startled her when he stepped to her side even though the plan had been to meet her at the altar. Amanda looked up and saw sympathy and understanding in his compelling gaze. He took her trembling hand and tucked it around his arm, covering her hand with his. Any remnant of loneliness fled.

"It's going to be okay," he whispered.

Amanda smiled up at him tentatively and Garth felt his heart catch. She was a lovely, brave and incredibly noble woman. What man wouldn't want her for his wife? He thought she deserved so much more than a man like him who'd failed so miserably at his first marriage. He hated failure. In fact, thanks to his father's constant haranguing, he feared it. That was why his total failure with Karen had hurt so much.

He wondered suddenly how all this had come about. Could his mother be right about lives being directed by God? Could He really have used Amanda's tragic loss of her son and his own near loss of that same child for good? How else had he wound up marrying someone who deserved so much better than him? Garth couldn't smother the sudden wish that his mother was right about a lot of things, especially that someday he and Amanda would look back on this forced wedding as a miracle.

Jason beamed at them when they drew even with him. The next minutes seemed to speed by so fast that Garth found himself doing as he was told without thought. The minister began the traditional words of the ceremony. His sister, Chris, acting as Amanda's maid of honor, took her bouquet as Jason handed the rings over. Amanda repeated the same empty promises he had but with such a ring of truth to them that he found himself wishing she really did mean them.

Then it was over. In the eyes of everyone there, he had just taken a wife. Garth looked from Amanda to his mother and sister, then glanced up at the ceiling toward the heavens. Had he taken a wife before Him as well?

Garth once again obeyed a voice on the periphery of his thoughts and leaned down to drop a simple peck on Amanda's cheek. But she turned her head just then and their lips met. Met and clung for two, then three lingering seconds before he somehow marshaled the willpower to step away.

They stared at each other.

"Where are you taking Mom for your honeymoon?" Jason asked into the ensuing silence. Garth looked away from Amanda and forced a laugh. He turned and scooped Jason into his arms then settled him in a wheelchair. "Somewhere you're not, kiddo," Garth told Jason as he tugged on the peak of his ever-present Phillies cap. Garth's quip drew a laugh from everyone but Amanda.

"I'll push Jason back, Garth," Chris said. "You should escort your new wife upstairs. Wait a few minutes though, Jason has a surprise planned in his room," she added in a whisper.

Amanda grabbed his sleeve and Garth turned back to face her as his sister pushed Jason toward the door. He was surprised to see near panic in Amanda's eyes. "We can't leave the city. He needs us. I can't go. Not now. I just can't. You have to think of an excuse. I'd feel as if I'm deserting him."

"Are you implying I wouldn't?" Garth growled. All traces of the strange, altered state of reality into which he'd fallen during the ceremony fled. How could he have forgotten the way she'd fought this marriage or the low opinion she had of him?

Amanda put her hand to her head, then looked back up at him. "No. Of course not." Garth noticed tears well up in Amanda's violet eyes, seeming to drown their vibrant color in sorrow. "I just can't go away," she continued needlessly. "Just going home at night hurts."

Garth's anger melted, though her revulsion over having to marry him still stung. "Amanda, I was only trying to break the ice and pass off Jason's question without a real answer. I have no intention of taking you anywhere but home. It was a joke."

"Oh. I...I guess I overreacted. I'm sorry, Garth. I should have realized that."

"It's okay. I'm sorry, too. It was probably a bad joke." Garth took Amanda's arm and directed her toward the door.

Amanda smiled up at him, violets seeming to sparkle in her still moist eyes. "If Jason weren't sick, it would have been funny. Really," she assured him. "I should have recognized that kind of male humor. It's something Jess would have said. Cops are notoriously irreverent."

Garth stiffened at the reference to her former husband. Before he recognized his own jealousy he said, "Pilots aren't that different from cops. We both wear uniforms and some of us never come home from work again, either. Who knows, maybe I'll go down in flames one of these fine days and you'll be rid of me."

Amanda felt the blood drain from her face and she quickly looked away. How could he think she'd wish him harm? Had she somehow given him the impression that she did? True, she didn't trust him. She was afraid to, because she knew he couldn't wait for the day Jason was healthy so he could divorce her. Her lack of trust was only because it would be so easy to love the man. Certainly not because she hated him!

Just then Amanda noticed Bill Wood's head peek out the door to Jason's room as she and Garth approached and she lost her opportunity to contradict his assumption. In a voice that sounded like a caricature of a wedding palace master of ceremonies, Bill said, "And now, ladies and gentlemen, for the first time ever, may I present Mr. and Mrs. Garth Jorgensen."

They walked in and found Frieda, Christina, Bill Wood, Dr. Matt Hernandez and his sister who'd played in the chapel. There was a cake on Jason's bed table.

"My goodness. Who arranged all this?" Amanda gasped.

"I did!" Jason beamed. "Me and Doc Wood. But you guys got to cut the cake and give it out, then toss your bouquet real fast, Mom. That way my nurses can go and we won't have so many people in here." Conspiratorially, in a stage whisper Jason said, "We don't want to get Doctor Matt or Doc Wood in trouble with their bosses."

Amanda laughed and she and Garth made short work of the cake. She hated to toss her flowers away but knew it was foolish to feel sentimental about them even if they had come from the most wonderful man she'd ever met. Jason's nurses left after one of them caught her bouquet.

Amanda felt a tap on her shoulder as Maria Hernandez, Matt's sister, began to play a slow tune. "I think this is our dance, Mrs. Jorgensen," Garth said.

Turning into his arms, Amanda tried to ignore the song's promises. They would not grow old together. There was nothing in their future but the ending that had begun the day they'd met. Amanda blinked away the hot tears that burned at the back of her throat. *I think I've made a big mistake, Jesus. I'm sorry I didn't take the time to listen to your advice.*

Amanda gave up trying to get back to sleep. It was nearly dawn anyway. Thankfully the sun would soon chase away the night. Her wedding night. She shook her head ruefully. Hers had certainly been an unconventional one.

She glanced around her room and remembered her surprise when Garth had gathered her in his arms at the front door. But fairy tales were for children. He'd deposited her in the front hall, turned and walked back out of the house. She'd heard him return hours later, sometime after two.

Amanda watched as the sun rose, its light filtering through the bare but majestic trees that surrounded Garth's house. Garth's house. Jason's house. Even Frieda called it home. But it wasn't Amanda's home and it never would be. She'd given up any right to it without even a thought.

Now that all was said and done, she realized that she should probably have found a lawyer to represent her interests. She'd signed both the prenuptial agreement Garth had wanted and the custody agreement she'd demanded, reading only the latter.

When Jason was well enough and they divorced, Garth would have Jason with him every other weekend, one month of the summer and on alternating holidays excluding Christmas. That had been the one item she'd had an objection to. She wanted Jason's Christmases for the next seven years. She'd already missed six of them, she'd told Garth, and he'd acquiesced immediately, grateful that she'd planned to allow him as much time as she did. Amanda had dismissed his thanks. The arrangements were for Jason, not Garth, she'd told him, trying to remain detached.

As for the financial agreement that included the house, Amanda hadn't even thought to read it. Garth owned nothing she wanted.

"Amanda?"

She pivoted toward the door. "Come in," she called. Garth pushed the door open but stood in the hall wearing a robe with a towel hooked around his neck. "If you want a ride into the city, I'll be ready to leave in about an hour."

"But, Garth, that's an awful lot of trouble. I can take the train," she told him needing a bit of distance after the soul-searching minutes she'd just spent. "Taking me to the hospital's too far out of your way."

"It's no trouble. All I'll do is get off the expressway, drop you off and get back on at the next exit." He glanced at the window. "It looks like rain. You'd have to take a cab from the train. Come on. Shake a leg."

"You shake me up enough already," she muttered.

"Did you say something?" Garth asked then chuckled.

Amanda scowled, wondering what he'd heard. "And just what do you find so funny?" she asked as he turned and sauntered down the hall.

Two hours later, Amanda managed to keep herself from bolting from the car before Garth pulled to a complete standstill. She did open the door as soon as the car rolled to a stop but Garth reached out before she got her seat belt off. He brushed her hair off her shoulder. She froze at the feel of his fingers brushing her neck.

"Amanda," he whispered. "You've scarcely said a word all the way in. Don't I even get a thank-you for driving you?"

Appalled by her lack of manners, Amanda turned her head to apologize and thank him. But Garth wanted more than words. His lips settled over hers.

Amanda forgot fears and worries. She forgot the rest of the world.

Beep! Beep! Beep! "Hey, Mack, kiss the old lady at home will ya? I got a fare to pick up!"

Amanda jerked back. Garth glared out the back window at the taxi behind him, then looked back at the passenger seat. Amanda had slipped away in the blink on an eye. He smiled as he watched her disappear through the large glass doors into the hospital lobby. The cabby beeped again and Garth waved off his complaints as he faced front and pulled away from the curb.

The kiss confirmed Garth's suspicions. Yesterday when they'd gone to Jason's room for the wedding reception, Amanda had stayed as far from him as possible while going through all the motions expected of her. He'd been a bit insulted but he couldn't resist having her near when Maria had played that song. The dance had been a spur-of-the-moment decision but it had been an eye-opener.

Amanda wasn't as against this marriage as she'd seemed. When he'd demanded the dance, she'd melted as if as powerless to resist him as he was to resist her. But there was more than physical desire at work on his side. This wasn't just the lust Karen had once inspired.

He'd never missed Karen the way he did Amanda and that was after knowing her such a short while. He'd see something and think, I wish Amanda had seen that. Or he'd hear a news story and wonder what Amanda would think of it. Jason would say something delightful and he'd wish she were there to share the moment. Now that his pride wasn't so sore, he wondered if he wasn't falling in love with her.

Love.

Until Amanda had come into his life he been unable to even think the word. Now more and more it and its meaning floated through his head at the oddest times.

But even if he did love her it didn't matter. He couldn't let it. He didn't have the right to hold Amanda in a marriage with a man she didn't love and who she'd been trapped into marrying.

That was the question that had sent him out of the house on his wedding night. He knew it had been wrong to dump Amanda in the foyer without so much as a goodbye. But after that dance and then having given in to the romantic gesture of carrying her over the threshold, he'd had no choice. One word and he'd have been begging her to let him make their marriage real. And that wouldn't have been fair.

Garth wound his way through traffic and arrived at the hangar without the slightest idea what the answer to his dilemma was or what to do next. Sometimes he wished he had a father to turn to but then he never had. Love hadn't mattered when he'd needed it most.

In the back corner of his mind a voice whispered that he always had and still did have a Father. A Father who would not fail him as his mortal father had. He stubbornly silenced the voice.

"So, Matt Hernandez thinks they'll do the transplant at the end of next week?" Garth asked Amanda as they made their way toward the parking garage. They'd been married a week and had fallen into a routine. Unfortunately, the routine kept them apart for all but an hour a day. She'd hoped for more time to show him how good marriage could be.

"He thinks from the way the tests look that Jason will be ready sooner than he thought."

"That's a break." Garth's voice broke and he stopped walking. He took a fortifying breath. "I can't stand this. He looks worse now than he ever has." Garth grimaced and raked a hand through his hair. "I'm sorry. I keep falling apart on you."

Amanda noticed a small sitting area to their left. She took

his arm and motioned toward the seats. "You're entitled to lean on someone, Garth," she told him as she sat next to him. "It's been a long year for you. I don't know how you do it alone."

"Well, it's been a tough seven for you and you haven't fallen apart," he replied.

"Garth, first off, that was not falling apart." She gave him what she hoped was a reassuring smile. "But as far as how I survive, I've told you. Jesus takes care of the worry and gives me peace. I still have to handle everything that comes along but He's there for me to lean on. If you'd ask Him for help, He'd be there to hold you up, too. Believe me."

"Maybe I don't want *His* help," he snapped. "What kind of a God lets anyone, let alone a child, go through the torture Jason has? What kind of God deserts a kid who believes in him?"

Amanda knew an opportunity when she saw it. She'd bided her time and now it was here. "Deserted? Garth, take off the blinders. Look at Jason. Does he look deserted to you? Ask him what his faith gives him. It isn't a lack of pain. It's the strength to endure it without becoming angry and bitter. I wish I could understand you. Your mother says you were a believer once. What happened to you?"

"Did my mother tell you about my God-fearing, lying, cheating father?"

The hatred and bitterness in his tone shocked Amanda to her soul. He always sounded angry whenever the subject of God or prayer came up but now he sounded as if he were a different man. Amanda could do no more than shake her head.

"I didn't think so. If I had any faith, he killed it." Garth's eyes seemed to blaze brighter with every word he spoke. "The way he almost killed my mother."

"I don't understand."

"Did she tell you about him?"

"Only that he was demanding and that he asked too much of you and your sister sometimes."

"Sometimes? Try twenty-four hours a day. None of us ever

measured up or were perfect enough for him. He was a very godly man,'' Garth said sarcastically. ''An elder in the church. He—'' Garth broke off and started to turn away but Amanda reached out to stop him.

''I'd like to understand,'' she said.

''He took a lover. One of the women who worked in the church office. He was the church treasurer and she worked with him. When Mom found out and confronted him, he didn't deny it or say he was sorry. He told her he'd been waiting until I graduated from high school to tell her. He had it all figured out. She was supposed to leave him. Then in a couple years, he'd marry the woman who'd comforted him when Mom deserted him.''

Amanda's heart felt as if a fist were squeezing it. Something told her Garth's father's plans didn't go that way at all. ''What happened then?''

''He didn't know I'd heard. I went to the pastor. Told him what was going on under his nose. He asked Dad to give the woman up.''

''That's as it should have been, but what did that do to your relationship with him?''

''I never saw him again. He left the night the pastor called him in and confronted him. He never came back home. He moved in with *her*.''

''And your mother?''

''I take care of my mother. I did then and I do now. I've given her more than he ever did or could. I made a success of myself in spite of his opinion of me.''

Once again, Amanda noticed his emphasis on success measured only in terms of money and security. ''I meant that she doesn't seem to be bitter at all.''

''She *loved* him too much. She didn't realize it but she was under his thumb—brainwashed into believing everything he said. It was as if he had dominated her for so long that she couldn't think for herself. He tried to do the same thing to my sister and me. I think she might have gone along with him if I hadn't short-circuited his plans. She even visited him before he died. He asked forgiveness. Can you imagine that? Mom lost her home and most of her friends and came close to a breakdown because of him and he wanted her forgiveness. A day late and a dollar short, as far as I'm concerned."

"He didn't ask to see you?"

"I didn't go! I wasn't listening to his lies. Nothing he could have said or done would have earned him my forgiveness."

"Garth, it's never a day late or a dollar short to ask forgiveness. Surely you understand that. There's nothing any of us can do to earn forgiveness. It's a gift. To give and to receive. Look at the good thief. He asked forgiveness and Jesus promised him paradise. There wasn't anything the thief could do to earn it, hanging there on the cross the way he was, except ask. His repentance was enough."

"So you're saying my father was forgiven all the wrongs he did. He destroyed all our lives and God just forgives him." Garth snapped his fingers. "Just like that!"

"Yes. Garth, you have to get over this idea that it was God who turned His back on you. It was your father. Not your Father in heaven but a man—a flawed man to be sure but we're all flawed. We're all sinners."

Garth's gaze had lost none of its anger. "I guess you'd have gone. You'd have forgiven him."

Amanda shrugged. "I'd like to think I would but I don't know. He wasn't my father. It wasn't my mother he betrayed. I'm sure he disillusioned you on more levels than I can imagine. I can't judge what you did but I will tell you that you need to forgive him—for *you* not him. You need to undo the damage he's done to you so you can put it all behind you. Hatred takes too much energy and is just too destructive to hang on to."

Garth raised a sardonic eyebrow. "I'll never forgive that man, Amanda. Never. Besides, it *is* behind me. I'm a grown man who doesn't need childish crutches to get by. I do it on my own."

"And it wears you down." Amanda smiled sadly and

squeezed his hand where it lay on his thigh. She was tempted to bring up his aversion to love or at least talking about it but perhaps she'd pushed far enough already. "Just think about it, okay?"

Garth stared at their hands for a long minute then looked up into her eyes. Amanda had never seen his eyes look so stormy but it wasn't anger that churned in their blue depths. She had no idea what it was—but anger it wasn't. And it made her nervous.

"Didn't you say something about going home?" She stood before he could voice the emotion she saw in his turbulent blue gaze.

Garth blinked. "I hoped maybe we could stop for dinner. I didn't get time to grab lunch and breakfast was forgettable."

"Sounds good," Amanda said. It meant the possibility of good food, which with Frieda around was in short supply, and more time in Garth's company. That was a combination that she just couldn't bear to turn down no matter how tired she was. "I didn't have dinner, either, and lunch was...*very* forgettable."

Garth groaned on her behalf. "Don't tell me my mother brought lunch in again when she visited Jason today."

"I didn't have the heart to turn her down and I thought this time it would be okay." Amanda wrinkled her nose. "I just don't understand how anyone could ruin egg salad."

"It's the cloves. She insists they add something. I think she was born without taste or smell or something." Garth chuckled. "Sweetheart, you're going to have to risk hurting her feelings. It isn't going to get any better. You're the only person I've ever known who's eaten what she cooks for this long and lived to tell the sad story."

"I...I...ahem..." Shocked by the endearment, Amanda paused to recover. "I'd hate to make her feel bad."

"She ought to be used to it by now." Garth smiled in the darkness that engulfed them as they entered the parking garage. *Sweetheart* had just slipped out but it had really rattled her. He'd found he enjoyed rattling the unshakable Amanda. Then a troublesome thought struck. *Why did I call her sweetheart?*

Chapter Seven

"No! No, wait!" Jason sat up straighter in bed. "Don't turn it off yet. Look! Isn't that where Dad flew those guys?" he asked.

Amanda looked up and watched with cold dread as the weatherman explained that sudden fierce thunderstorms had developed over western Pennsylvania and West Virginia. She remembered how anxious Garth had been about the day's itinerary. This was the first flight Liberty Express would make ferrying the executive of a large agriculture products company based outside Philadelphia. It was the company Garth had been meeting with the day Jason had found out the truth about who she was. It was hard for Amanda not to resent the CEO of the company for leaving orders not to be disturbed. It was because of him that it had taken Garth two hours to reach the hospital.

"What's wind shear, Mom?" Jason asked, dragging Amanda back to the present.

"Wind shear? Oh, I missed that. What did they say?"

"That the airports were still open but that pilots had reported wind shear and they have light craft warnings in effect."

"I think it's some sort of weird wind that makes flying difficult," Amanda answered as nonchalantly as possible. All the while her mind flooded with memories of large airliners whose crashes had been blamed on wind shear. "I don't know much about that sort of thing." Her stomach muscles felt like quick-setting concrete. What if Garth tried to fly in that? Wasn't his plane considered a light craft? And he was already an hour late.

"Hey, Mom, don't worry. Dad knows what he's doing."

Amanda stared at Jason, trying to decide if she'd frightened him. "I—I'm not the least bit worried."

Jason nodded gravely. "Sure," he said sounding unconvinced. He pushed away his barely touched dinner tray. "I can't eat this stuff. Did they hire Grandmom as a cook?"

Amanda forced a chuckle, though his continued lack of appetite wasn't good. "That's not nice."

"Neither is Grandmom's cooking," Jason quipped with an exaggerated grimace. "Let's finish the game we started."

Two hours later, Jason looked up from his board game. "I'm worried now, too, Mom. Dad always calls when he's going to be late. Maybe you could call his office. They might have heard something."

"What a good idea! Now, why didn't I think of that?" Amanda pounced on the phone and punched out the number.

It rang twice. "Liberty Express, Marge speaking." Garth's secretary sounded as anxious as Amanda was.

"It's Amanda, Marge. Jason and I wondered if you've heard from Garth."

"Not since they landed in New Castle. That was around noon. They still had quite a jaunt ahead of them. The boss'll be beat when he gets in. I'll have him call as soon as he lands. Are you planning to stay with Jason until then?"

"Yes. Yes, I am. I'm sorry if I bothered you. Jason was worried. Is anything wrong?"

"Now don't get upset but Garth's plane is...is..."

"Is? Is what?"

"The tower at Pittsburgh lost contact with Garth. But he'd said he was going to try to put down somewhere outside the storm's path. It was pretty fierce out there and communication was patchy." Marge took a deep breath. "Please don't worry. He's a wonderful pilot. Remind Jason that Garth's an ace. That man was practically born with wings. He's probably sitting out

the worst of it in some drafty hangar. He wouldn't want you
two to worry.''

Amanda hung up knowing she couldn't tell Jason the full
truth even though Marge had been wrong. Amanda wasn't just
worried. She was frantic. She remembered with stunning clarity
Garth's final words to her in the chapel after the wedding. *Pilots
aren't that different from cops...some of us never come home
from work again, either. Who knows, maybe I'll go down in
flames one of these days, and you'll be rid of me.*

She'd never bothered to deny that she might want to be rid
of him.

''Miss Marge hasn't heard from him either, huh?''

''Not in a while,'' Amanda said casually, ''but last she heard
he planned to wait out the storms on the ground.''

Jason shook his head. ''Uh-uh. Dad told me last night that
he had to get the men where they were going or he'd have to
pay the plumber.'' Jason stopped, screwing up his face. ''No,
that wasn't it.''

Amanda felt her heart sink as Jason's meaning became clear.
''You mean the piper? He'd have to pay the piper?'' she asked.

Jason nodded then added quickly, ''But like I said, Dad's
the best pilot in the world. If anyone could get them there safe,
it's Dad.''

Amanda smiled. She knew Jason was worried and trying to
protect her. She'd seen him do it countless times with Garth
and, like Garth, she hid the fear lurking in her heart as best she
could. *What if no one could have flown through those storms
safely?*

Garth jogged across the street from the parking garage. He
grimaced when the sun burned through the fog with a sudden
burst of light and heat. Marge said Amanda had sounded worried because no one had heard from him. And that had been
last night.

Amanda must be frantic by now. Garth smiled as it occurred
to him for one selfish second that if Amanda was worried, it
might mean she cared for him as more than just the man who'd

raised her son. But he banished the joy. He hated the thought that Amanda had suffered a second's distress on his account. He had no right to be glad if she'd begun to care because there was no future for them.

The remark he'd made after the wedding about the dangers of his job had echoed in his mind all night as he cooled his heels at Mayport Field. The tiny airfield in the mountains of West Virginia was just a fly speck on the map and consisted of an army surplus Quonset hut and three sheds. The storms had been right on his tail and Henry Mayport lost telephone communication and power before Garth could tie down his plane. Phone service had still been out that morning when he'd taken off.

He'd paced all night thinking about that snide remark. He should have explained that his profession was less dangerous than many. There were even statistics he could have cited that said more men were killed in cars going to nice, safe office jobs than were killed working as pilots.

Garth found Amanda in the solarium near Jason's room. She was curled up in a big chair, hugging her legs, her head on her up-drawn knees, her thick hair hiding her face. Garth knelt next to her and pushed back her tousled hair. Her eyes were shadowed after what the nurse on duty said had been a sleepless night. Garth smiled gently. "Amanda... Mandy," he whispered. "Wake up, sweetheart."

Amanda's head shot up. "Garth! You're okay! Oh, thank you, Lord."

Garth couldn't believe his good fortune when Amanda launched herself against his chest and hugged him for all she was worth. But before he'd even had time to enjoy the feel of her in his arms, she pulled away, jumped up and glared at him. "Why didn't you call? Do you have any idea how worried I...J-Jason was."

He stood and leaned against the back of the chair. He just couldn't suppress a grin he felt grow on his face. He'd heard the admission she'd unsuccessfully covered. And she wasn't getting away with it. He raised an eyebrow and crossed his arms. "Jason was? Or you were? Which is it?" he taunted playfully.

"Both! How could you do it? How could you put your life in danger for business? For money? You could have been killed! And for what? A company. Success! If your crash had been worse, you'd all be dead!"

Garth frowned. "Crash? What crash?"

"Now what crash do you think I'm talking about?"

Garth spread his hands helplessly. "I don't know what you're talking about."

"Play dumb, then!" Amanda shouted and planted her hands on her hips. "But I know you crash-landed before you could get to the Pittsburgh airport. They told Marge and Marge told me."

"No!"

Tears filled Amanda's eyes and she furiously scrubbed them away. "Don't lie!"

"I do not lie!"

"They told her they lost contact with you, so you may as well tell me the truth."

"Amanda, listen to me," Garth demanded, losing his patience a bit more each time she accused him of lying. "They lost contact with me because I turned back and flew out of their range. I was trying to get away from the storms. Another storm pattern cropped up in my path so I headed into West Virginia instead of back to Ohio. I set down at a little field in the mountains."

Amanda was clearly confused. "But…but you told Jason you had to get those men where they were going. You *had* to keep flying!"

Garth was shocked to utter silence by the certainty in her tone. There was more going on here than worry, his careless remarks or her reaction to them.

"You wouldn't give up!" she continued. "It wouldn't matter to you one bit that Jason was here worrying." Amanda paused for a breath to continue her diatribe. "*Jason* who isn't supposed to get upset. *Jason* who is the only reason you got into this stupid marriage."

Garth felt sudden defeat weigh him down. Why had he ever let hope glimmer into his heart that perhaps he could make her happy? That, perhaps, he could make their marriage work. He'd made her miserable from the day he'd met her. Since before he'd met her considering that he'd had Jason while she'd longed for her son. Why did she have to make him care!

Cold anger replaced hurt and defeat and Garth was thankful for his irrational feelings. "You could have explained my absence last night by saying I'd stayed over in another city. You could have saved Jason all the worry you say he suffered. Now if you'll excuse me, I'd like to go reassure him. And I'd appreciate time alone with him. I missed my visit last night."

Amanda watched Garth stalk out of the solarium, then sat down in defeat. She hadn't meant to anger him but perhaps that was better than his figuring out why she hadn't been able to lie to Jason. Why she hadn't been able to hide her own worry or think clearly enough to formulate a simple lie.

She loved him.

And she'd thought she'd lost him.

And now that Amanda had faced that truth, she had to face another. He hadn't even tried to call. He hadn't even thought of her. There really was every possibility that, to him, she was just a means to keep Jason. One thing was a certainty. She had fallen in love with a man just like her late husband. Jess wouldn't have called, either.

After two hours, Amanda wandered down the hall to Jason's room. Tired and emotionally spent, she arrived just as Dr. Matt Hernandez did. He put his arm around her shoulders, misinterpreting her despondency. "Hey. Cheer up. I know Jason looks bad but it's not any worse than usual. And I come bearing good news for a change. Jason's ready. We can do the transplant tomorrow. See Cindy before she goes home and she'll give you your instructions."

"Do I stay in the hospital tonight?"

Hernandez shook his head. "That's not necessary. Have Garth bring you in by six. You'll be prepped and ready by seven." The oncologist put his hand on her shoulder. "Come on! Cheer up! This is it! It's all downhill from here."

Amanda forced a smile. "Right. Downhill. Let's tell Jason." She pushed open the door.

"Come on. Open that tunnel wide," Garth told Jason as he tried to coax him to eat with an absurd-looking spoon. The handle was shaped like a train with a spoon on the end. The electronic sound of a train echoed through the room. Absurd though it was, Jason giggled, opened his mouth and ate some Jell-O.

"You don't eat for me like that," she accused mildly.

Jason gave her a wan smile. "I'm a train tunnel. At lunch I get to be an airplane hangar."

Matt picked up the box containing the airplane spoon, dumped it out and activated the engine noise. "These are great, Garth," he said. "Especially now. Jason needs to build up his strength if he's going to be hitting home runs again soon. And since tomorrow is his transplant, I'd say the other teams better get ready for some competition."

"Tomorrow?" Garth asked.

"Tomorrow?" Jason asked at the same time.

"Tomorrow. Garth, you need to have Amanda here by six. The lab's been scheduled and I've got the best man to work on Amanda. It's easy stuff for Jason here. Just like another transfusion for you, fella."

"And then I'll be better?" Jason asked, his eyes suddenly bright.

"Then we test every day and watch that cell count start climbing." He unrolled a plastic sheet that had the outline of what looked like a three-foot high thermometer printed on it. "We'll hang this chart on the wall for you to color in. You'll be able to chart your own progress. You can fill in every healthy new blood cell you grow. Right now your thermometer's nearly empty. First few days, the rest go. Then after a while they'll start building again. When it's all full, we'll start talking about when you get to go home!''

"Home." Jason sighed. He sounded like poor Dorothy pining for Kansas.

Amanda glanced at Garth for the first time. He hadn't said a word and sat looking pensive. The anger had disappeared from his expressive eyes. "How long do you think it will be before we see some results?" he asked, speaking at last.

Hernandez glanced at all three of them. "Okay, this is how we count. Today's day minus one. Tomorrow's day zero. The next is day plus one. At day plus fourteen we should see a small change in the cell count. That cell count will get higher every day. Right, pal?" He tugged on the brim of Jason's red Phillies cap.

"Right!''

Garth heard it again. There was a loose board under the wall-to-wall carpet in Amanda's room that squeaked whenever someone stepped on it. Considering the rhythm of the squeaks he'd guess she was pacing.

Guilt assailed him. They hadn't had a chance to talk alone. Not about their disagreement or even tomorrow's procedure. His sister had come in then his mother arrived just as Christina was leaving. He'd had to get back to Liberty Express for a meeting with his accountant and his mother had promised to take Amanda home.

Squeak. Sque-e-e-ak!

The noise set Garth's teeth on edge. This had to stop and it looked like it might be up to him to put a stop to Amanda's pacing. He'd realized, as he watched Amanda's mixed reaction to the transplant being scheduled, that he'd been foolish to react to her anger with a show of his own. There had to be a reason for her to fly off the handle, and instead of probing gently, he'd acted like the proverbial bull in a china shop. He hadn't even explained that he'd tried to call.

Squeak. Sque-e-e-ak!

Garth threw back the covers and pulled on a pair of jeans. Neither one of them was going to get any sleep tonight if they didn't talk. He tapped on the connecting door. "Amanda?"

Squeak.

Silence. Garth smiled. "Come on, Amanda, I know you're awake. I've heard you pacing."

Sque-e-e-ak! "Oops," Amanda muttered.

Garth chuckled. "I'm coming in so I hope you're decent. If you're not, better cover up." He pushed open the door in time to see her toss a robe over a long T-shirt and sit on the side of the bed. She looked up and Garth was horrified to see how pale she was. "Good heavens, Amanda, are you ill?"

"No."

She wouldn't even look at him. "You aren't still upset about this morning, are you? Look, I'm sorry I snapped back at you. I should have remembered that you'd had a bad night. I should have told you that I couldn't call because the storm knocked out communications before I got to the hangar." Amanda remained silent.

Garth sighed. He hated seeing her like this. "Amanda," he said as he walked to the bed then sat next to her. Being closer didn't help. Garth could feel the tension coming off her in waves but he could only see the top of her head. "What is it? And don't say nothing."

He tried to think and nothing came to mind. She'd hugged him for all she was worth that morning then her mood had done a one-eighty and she'd nearly taken his head off. He put his crooked knuckle under her chin and encouraged her to look at him. Her violet eyes were almost glazed. "Amanda, you're acting—"

"Crazy?" she asked.

Incredulous, Garth stared at her for a full five seconds. "Amanda, you are not crazy!"

Fire flared in the violet depths of her eyes. "What do you think of someone who'd rather go through twenty hours of labor without anything for pain rather than have anyone come near her with a needle? Don't placate me! Go ahead. Tell me that's not crazy.''

"That's not crazy! *Karen* was unbalanced. *You* have a phobia.''

"Phobia, schmobia! This is my son's life and I'm sitting in here shaking in my slippers, wishing tomorrow just wouldn't come. I feel so stupid and so incredibly selfish.''

A fat tear rolled from one of her eyes and tracked across her cheek. Garth couldn't help himself. He leaned forward and captured it with a soft kiss. He sat back quickly. That felt too close, too real, for their temporary marriage.

"You are *not* selfish,'' he told her. "Not once have you flinched from doing what was best for Jason. Well, you weren't too crazy about marrying me, but it's not your fault you resented me because I'd been raising Jason.''

Amanda shook her head. "Oh, don't think that. I don't resent you. You've been a wonderful father to him. Anyone can see that.''

"Well, I'm sure not your ideal husband.''

"But that's not because you're not attractive or nice.''

Garth barely resisted the urge to groan. Nice! Why did she always have to think of him as nice. There was nothing wrong with nice, of course. His mother had raised him to be—well—nice. He held out his arms and she came to him, leaning and snuggling against him. Garth smiled against her hair and stroked her back. She sighed and relaxed. No, there was nothing wrong with nice at all.

They sat that way with Garth murmuring comforting words and caressing her back and hair until Amanda raised her face to his. "I'll be fine alone. You must be tired, Garth.''

"No more tired than you. I managed to catch a few hours of shut-eye. From what I've heard, you were up pacing all last night, too. Come on, get under the covers and scoot over to make room for me.''

"But—''

"Amanda, I'm not going to get a wink of sleep unless I'm

sure you're okay and sleeping soundly. I'm not here to make demands. I came in here to find out what was wrong and how to help. Now move over a bit.'' Garth settled next to her, heavy jeans and all.

She sat staring at him, wide-eyed and shocked. "But—" she said again.

Garth slid down in bed then reached up and put one fingertip to her lips. "Sh-sh. Just trust me." He wove his arm behind her, cupped her head with the palm of his hand and pulled her down so that her head rested on his shoulder. With his other arm he stretched to turn off the light, plunging the room into darkness.

"Did I ever tell you about the Saturday Jason woke up early when he was almost six?" Garth asked in a hushed tone. "They'd learned about not littering in kindergarten the day before. He apparently looked out and saw the Saturday paper on our lawn. He snuck out so he wouldn't wake us and *cleaned* up the lawn. Once he picked up our newspaper, he wondered if everyone else had papers littering their lawns, too.

"Mom and I woke up about an hour later to find twenty newspapers in trash bags in the kitchen. It took another hour to get the paperboy on the phone, get the house numbers he'd delivered, then to go and ask everyone if their papers were missing."

Amanda smiled in the darkness. "Were they angry?"

"No, not really. They thought it was funny. So did we."

Garth chuckled. "Then there was what Mother calls the popcorn incident. He was about four and a half. We were lucky he wasn't hurt. You see, he'd read a book about popcorn. He was reading by then which was pretty scary since we didn't teach him. Well, anyway, in the book, the bear parents went out and left the children alone and they decided to make popcorn."

"What did he do?"

"Fortunately, Jason didn't fill the house with popcorn even though he used enough to. Unfortunately, my mother has nothing on him when it comes to kitchen disasters. The book didn't give a recipe. He put about four inches of oil into the bottom of an old pressure cooker we use to pop popcorn. Then he dumped the whole bag of popping corn in and turned the mess on.

"I'd been flying all night and had probably been asleep three hours when he climbed up on the bed and woke me. Jason never likes to upset people so he starts explaining things gently. 'I opened all the windows and doors but I can't get the smoke out of the house.' I catapulted out of bed like I'd been shot from a cannon."

Amanda chuckled so Garth launched into another and yet another story. He spoke in soft, quiet tones as he ran his fingers softly through her hair. He talked about funny incidents, heart-warming moments and his hopes and dreams for Jason's future. After nearly an hour, Amanda's breathing changed, slowed, deepened. She slept at last and, exhausted, Garth let his own eyes drift closed. He gave himself up to the joy of feeling Amanda in his arms as soft tendrils of sleep wrapped around him in the darkness. He didn't even realize where his last thoughts went.

Could you find a way for it to always be like this, Lord? Please.

Chapter Eight

Amanda climbed her way out of the mists of sleep toward the far-off sound of a buzzer. At first she thought it was a fire alarm but the smell that greeted her wasn't smoke. It was sandalwood and spice. Garth's unique aftershave.

She forced her grainy eyes open and noticed the dent in the pillow next to her. Heat rushed to her cheeks as she hit the snooze bar on her alarm clock. She didn't want to get up. She wanted to pull the covers over her head rather than face Garth. She'd acted like such a fool last night! Crying and shaking over today's procedure.

Amanda shook her head ruefully. Some witness to the peace of the Lord she was. It was a good thing He didn't rely on mortal men to fill His kingdom. If He did, at the end of time it would be a pretty empty place.

But then Amanda remembered that it was by the deed and actions of men that Garth had judged God. What kind of confidence had she shown in His power?

Amanda bowed her head. *Lord, please watch over me this day. Pour out Your peace on me and show Garth how mighty a God You are by healing our son. And, Lord, if You could work on his heart about the sanctity of marriage I'd appreciate it. I love him and I don't want to lose him even though he confuses me. He's such a good person. This plan he has to just walk away from me and his vows doesn't fit. I know he's Yours, Lord. Please show him the way back to You.*

A noise drew Amanda's attention. She looked up as Garth peaked his head in the door. He smiled. "Feeling better this morning?"

Panic once again flooded Amanda, washing away all thought but one. The transplant! Needles! Long needles! Great big, fat needles! Amanda shuddered.

"Calm down," Garth said, his smile gone, compassion in his gaze. "You're going to be fine."

Amanda tightened her grip on the blankets and with it her control over her runaway emotions. "What I'm probably going to do is make an idiot of myself again. What I'm *not* going to do is let it stop me," she promised.

Garth walked to the bed and sat next to her, his hand resting on her knee. "I never thought for one moment that wild horses could stop you from doing anything you could to help your son—or anyone else for that matter."

Amanda smiled, warmed by his regard. "Thank you," she said and continued trying to sound confident. "And don't worry about me. I'll be just fine today."

Evidently Garth saw right through her bravado. "If you need me I'll stay with you. Just let me know."

"Jason's going to need you more than I do, Garth. He's not as confident as he pretends." Amanda lay her hand over his. "I'll get through this with the Lord's help. I always have in the past."

"You shouldn't have to rely on some distant entity that you can't see."

"But I can feel His presence and His peace when I don't let my own fear overwhelm me."

"Like last night?"

"No. Last night I forgot to stop and listen to His voice inside me. I'm afraid I've been doing that a lot lately. But He took care of me anyway. He sent you to me. You helped me get through the night."

"You frustrate me. Do you know that?"

"How?"

"Because I want to believe you when you say things like that." Amanda felt his hand ball into a tight, quaking fist under her palm. "But I just can't."

Amanda smiled and gently squeezed that hard, frustrated fist under her hand. "You're a hard nut to crack. I'll give you that. But you'll crack. He has His hand on your life, Garth. Mine too. He's intertwined them for some purpose. We just don't know what it is yet."

Garth rubbed his free hand over his face. "Enough of the metaphysical at 5:00 a.m., okay?"

She moved her hand to his arm, giving him another gentle squeeze. "I can't explain it, but I know something good will come of all this."

"I'm sorry, Amanda, but I can't imagine anything good coming out of this mess. But I do have an idea that I believe would help get you through today." His eyes suddenly went serious and his smile faded. "Every time you feel yourself start to panic during the procedure, think about Jason. Not the Jason you've come to know." He pulled a picture out of his pocket and handed it to her. "This is Jason. It was taken just before he got sick."

In the picture her son had a full head of gleaming hair and a bright, sunny smile. He was hanging upside down from a rung on the ladder to his now deserted tree house.

"The kid's part monkey. Maybe we'll find out he's part cat, too. That would give him at least one life left, right?"

Amanda nodded and just stared at the picture. Something good had to come of all the suffering this boy had faced in the past year. It had to!

"Are you sure she's all right?" Garth asked the pretty young nurse at the desk. He'd known Maria Hernandez for five years. She'd worked her way through nursing school as his part-time secretary. It was through her that he'd found Jason's oncologist. Matt was her brother.

Maria hissed something under her breath, then looked up from the chart. "What did I tell you five minutes ago?"

"That she was fine," Garth admitted.

She nodded. "That's what I said, but I also promised to tell you if anything changed. She was fine then and she still is. Have you got any reason to believe I'd lie to you?"

Garth shrugged. "You might not want to upset me."

Maria Hernandez sighed. "You ought to know me better than that. I don't give a hang if you're upset. Now leave me alone with my charts. You know I hate paperwork, Garth Jorgensen."

Garth knew. He also knew he was acting like a complete fool but he couldn't seem to help himself. All he could see in his mind's eye was Amanda's pale face, her eyes full of fear and the brave smile she'd plastered on her face as he'd left her. "She's afraid. Is this going to hurt?"

"Ah! A way to prove that I'll tell you the truth. Sorry to say it's going to hurt plenty."

"Nurse Hernandez," Jason's oncologist growled from behind Garth. "We do not frighten already worried family members."

"We do when they act loco, *mi hermano!*"

Matt Hernandez chuckled and turned from his sister to Garth. "I was down there a little while ago. Amanda said to tell you she's fine. That sometimes facing a fear is the only way to get over it."

Garth sighed and raked his fingers through his hair. "But is she fine or trying to ease my mind? She's like that."

"*She's fine.* I thought you were going to stay with Jason."

"He's with my mother. He wanted me to find out about Amanda."

Hernandez laughed. "I just left Jason. He tossed you out! Come on. Let's get you something to eat."

Garth felt his face heat. "No, I'll go back and tell Jason Amanda's doing okay." Riding the elevator back up the three floors to Jason's isolation room, he couldn't help wishing that he'd asked to be allowed to stay with Amanda.

"Hey, kiddo," Garth said when he pushed the door open to find his mother and Jason collaborating on a game of solitaire.

Jason was so weak it broke his heart. "We're almost there," he told his son. "Your mom's getting through this like a real trouper. They'll be up within the hour. Doctor Matt was in, I hear?"

"He said the same thing about Mom." Jason eyed Garth with suspicion. "Are you going to play now or keep hopping up and down?"

Garth chuckled then rubbed his hands together. "I was only trying to distract you. But since you've thwarted my scheme, I'll just have to beat you fair and square."

Jason grinned. "In your dreams. I'm Monopoly champ of the hospital."

"You hear this smart-mouthed kid, Mom? I think it's time to take him down a peg or two."

"Oh, at least two," Frieda Jorgensen agreed. "I think I'll go get a cup of coffee and a cruller."

Garth didn't protest. He knew wearing a surgical mask and gown bothered his elderly mother but while Jason had no ability to fight infection they had to be extra careful. Jason was too listless to play more than one trip around the board so Garth got out the crossword puzzle book and pretended to be in dire need of his help. Jason fell asleep in the middle of the first puzzle.

He never even woke when the transfusion bag of precious bone marrow arrived. He slept while the transfusion was hooked into a line that had been fed through a vein in his arm to a place near his heart. It was through that line that he was fed, infused with medication, transfused and now given the marrow Amanda donated. It couldn't start working fast enough for Garth.

Amanda arrived half an hour later looking wan yet cheerful. Still, Garth couldn't help but worry about her. She stood by Jason's side but soon retreated to a chair. As the minutes rolled by she put her head back and drifted off to sleep. It was only then that her face began to mirror increasing levels of pain. Garth finally couldn't take it anymore and gave in to the uncontrollable urge to cosset her. He walked over and crouched down in front of her.

"Amanda," he whispered and took her hand in his. "Come on. Let's get you home."

Her eyes popped open quickly but were glazed with pain. "No, I haven't even talked to him yet today. I should be here. I'm fine. Really."

In a pig's eye, Garth thought, remembering Matt's warning that she would be in considerable pain. "Then let's go grab lunch. Jason hasn't moved a muscle. He'll sleep that long for sure."

Amanda looked like a deer caught in a bright pair of headlights. He stood and offered her his hand. She tried gamely to stand but sank back down, shaking from the pain. Garth shook his head and squatted down to his previous position.

"How come you're so stubborn? You hurt, Mandy. Didn't your doctor tell you he'd give you something for pain?"

"I don't like pain medication. Besides, he's next door by now. I'll be fine. It just took me by surprise."

"Next door? You mean at the adult hospital?"

She nodded and Garth stood. "I'll be right back."

Amanda watched Garth stalk out. Was he angry or concerned? She never knew what he was thinking where she was concerned, yet she could practically read his mind when his thoughts were on Jason. It was darn frustrating. She got her answer minutes later when he returned with a wheelchair. The look in his eyes was gentle, his brow creased with worry.

"Come on, Mandy. It's past time someone looked after you. Chris is on her way in. She'll stay with Jason."

"You—you're going to look after me?"

He carefully scooped her up. "You have a problem with that?" he asked and smirked as if to say *Do you have a choice?*

Amanda sighed and dropped her head on his shoulder. "No. No problem at all."

Garth lowered her into the chair and she felt suddenly bereft without the shelter of his arms surrounding her. She'd been alone so long. A tear trickled down her cheek. Amanda quickly wiped it away but another replaced it on the other cheek. Garth smoothed that one away. "Poor Mandy. You've had a heck of a time lately." He kissed the top of her head and started the wheelchair forward. "But I'm here now to take care of you."

Amanda closed her eyes and prayed he always would be.

Hours later Garth paced across the room then returned and stood next to Amanda's bed to watch her pale face once again as she slept. She lay so frighteningly still. He smoothed a stray lock of hair off her forehead, then traced her delicate features with his eyes then his fingertips.

"I love you," he whispered. "I didn't want to. I can't tell you that I do but that doesn't mean I don't. It just means that I'm no good for you. Funny, isn't it? I've crash-landed a 727 in a swamp and I wasn't anywhere near as terrified as I am of ruining your life more than I already have. I just can't take the thought of failing you the way my father failed me."

"Garth," he heard his sister call softly from the doorway. "Is Amanda all right?"

"She's sleeping," Garth answered not taking his eyes off his wife.

"Then what's wrong? You look troubled."

Not willing to reveal his inner torment he voiced a lesser worry. "It's just that she's sleeping so soundly. They gave her a shot and it must have helped because she fell asleep."

Chris shrugged. "So, she's asleep. The shot will probably take time to wear off."

"That's what the nurse said but it's been hours."

"Come across the hall and I'll tell you about Jason."

Garth nodded but didn't move. "Why wouldn't she tell me she was in pain? Why did I have to guess?"

"Come on. I think we need to talk." Chris took his arm and marched him across the hall to the solarium. The news about Jason was that he was still sleeping peacefully but Chris had Garth's welfare on her mind. "Why do you think Amanda didn't tell you how bad she felt?"

"I don't have a clue," Garth answered, confused.

Chris blew her bangs off her forehead with a furious puff of air. "You're right. You don't have a clue. About anything! She probably didn't tell you because she assumed you were more interested in Jason."

"I'm interested in her, too," Garth grumbled.

"Sit," Chris ordered and took his hand after settling across from him. "Don't you think it's time you told her just how much you care?"

"No. I can't do that. I promised her this arrangement was temporary. It's the only way. I want her to be happy."

"Amanda's been alone a lot of years. Do you really think she wants to stay that way?"

Garth grimaced. "Well, as much as I'd like to be the one to change all that, I'm not the man for the job." Garth slumped down in the sofa. "I'm just not good at making women happy."

"What?" Chris asked, incredulous.

"I failed Karen miserably, Chris. You know that! I swore I'd never be like our father and then when the going got tough I asked her for a separation. And because of that, she stole Jason from Amanda. I was so wrapped up in my own needs that I didn't notice that she was sick. I'm afraid that stealing Jason was her way of trying to hold on to me."

"Are all men this stupid or does it just run in our family?" Chris let go of his hand and slapped the arm of her chair. "Karen was a deeply troubled person! She had no conscience, no sense of right and wrong. She was like a spoiled child until the day she died. She stole that boy to get you back. Because she had to have every toy she wanted. She might only want to break it but no one else could have it. That's all you were to her. A toy. A pet. Then she realized she couldn't have you and she decided to break you instead. When she couldn't do that, she decided to destroy Jason to get at you but Mom stopped her from taking him with her that day."

She reached out and gripped Garth's hand, frowning at him, willing him to hear her. "You didn't fail at your marriage. You tried everything in your power to help her—but she didn't want help. She didn't want to change. Don't let her succeed in ruining the rest of your life. This is your chance for true happiness. You can't let it slip through your fingers. You love Amanda.''

Chris held up her hand like a traffic cop to stop his denial. ''Don't. I saw your face in the mirror when I came in to her room. I'm great at lipreading.''

Restless and uncomfortable, Garth stood and wandered to the window and sat on the wide sill. ''But Amanda's probably counting the days until she can divorce me and have Jason mostly to herself.''

''Amanda's a true Christian, brother mine, so I'm sure she doesn't take her marriage vows that lightly.''

''But divorcing eventually was part of our arrangement. As for her calling herself a Christian, is that supposed to mean something to me? Our father was always talking about serving God and it didn't stop him from divorcing our mother. Besides which, her religion is more of a deterrent than a recommendation. And it goes both ways before you say I'm prejudiced.''

Chris pinched the bridge of her nose and sighed. ''It isn't a religion. It's belief in Jesus Christ.''

''It's hogwash,'' Garth muttered.

''I'm not going to get into this debate with you again. It's a waste of breath.'' Chris's blue eyes flashed as she stood. ''Sometimes I can't believe Mom raised such an idiot,'' she added in a far more loving tone. She touched his shoulder and strode out of the room.

Amanda rolled over and a dull ache in her pelvis brought her awake. In the dimly lit room, she could just make out the dial of her watch. ''Dinnertime,'' she mumbled and sat up. A shadow at the corner of her vision made her gasp.

Garth sat forward and smiled. Amanda felt her traitorous heart skip. ''Welcome back to the land of the living.''

Amanda's head felt muzzy, her eyes dry, her mouth like cotton. ''What happened?''

"They gave you something for pain that should have put you out for three, maybe four hours. You've been asleep for twelve. It's 6:00 a.m."

"It's morning? Then why are you here?"

He raised an eyebrow. "I wanted to be."

"Oh."

Two hours later, Amanda sat curled up with a blanket on the wide windowsill of the solarium down the hall from Jason's isolation room. Normally, during the afternoon hours it was full of children. The sounds of their delicate laughter echoed in her mind and tortured her. Jason hadn't laughed today. He just lay still, his eyes listless and dull. He was so sick. She hadn't been prepared for just how sick he would be.

She hadn't understood.

Wiping the tears that tracked down her cheeks, she turned toward the sound of footsteps in the hall. Garth, his face creased with worry, stood just outside the door. "He—" His voice cracked and he tried again. "He fell asleep."

Amanda's lip quivered and another tear fell. "I beat him at Monopoly. Oh, Garth. What if it doesn't work? I never asked. What happens then?"

Garth walked toward her and she went to him. "It has to work. This can't all be in vain. It can't." He gathered her in his arms. "Are you feeling any better today?"

Amanda nodded, her head bobbing against Garth's chest. He's right, she thought. This has to work. It just has to! *Oh please, Father, make Jason get better. Give him back to us.* Amanda glanced up at Garth's strained face. *And please, let Garth see Your power and compassion through Jason. Use all this pain for good.*

Garth stared out into the night remembering the last two weeks. He'd felt as if he'd been living in a nightmare. So had Amanda. So had Jason. Jason's discomfort, due to the side effects of the transplant, had been extreme. Garth had sat with Jason in his lap one night for hours before sleep finally slipped under the pain. Since that day, the only nourishment he'd been able to get was through IV feedings. His weight had gone down to forty pounds. Transfusions of packed red cells and hemoglobin had been practically all that kept him alive.

But today he'd taken an uphill turn. It was a small step on the long road to recovery, but Garth would never forget the moment when he'd fully understood what Matt was saying....

Matt Hernandez sat in a chair at the base of Jason's bed, studying that day's test results. Garth and Amanda stood next to Jason on either side of the bed. It was a moment fraught with tension and hope. Hernandez looked up. A wide smile graced his features. "We've got a white cell count!"

Garth looked up from Jason's puzzled face into Amanda's eyes. They were once again flooded with tears. But this time they were tears of joy.

"Is that good? Does that mean I can go home soon?" Jason asked.

"Slow down there, pal. This is just the start. You've got to give it time," the doctor explained.

"How much time?"

Garth laughed. "What's this, kiddo? A new version of, 'Are we almost there?' You know we told you that you could be here for three more months."

"The rest of your time here will go by so fast you won't believe it," Amanda promised. "Every day you'll feel better, stronger. We'll play games with you and I'll bring you books and arts and crafts projects to do."

"But I want to come home and be a family."

Garth sat down next to the bed. "We're a family right here. A house doesn't make it happen."

The scene blurred in Garth's mind and his eyes focused on the present. He saw Amanda's reflection in the window behind him where she sat on the sofa in the home Jason longed for. She was doing something with her hands, her graceful fingers moving over the material she held. "What's that?" he asked.

"Jason asked for his own pajamas. Everything he has is way too big in the waist. So I'm putting drawstrings in the waistband with the elastic. That way he can grow into them again without realizing how much weight he's lost."

"Maybe we could get him a pair of sweats with a drawstring to wear when he comes home."

"It sounds like such a long way away," Amanda lamented.

Garth chuckled. "You're as bad as Jason."

"I've always been impatient for things to happen. I guess he gets it from me."

Garth walked over and sat on the end of the sofa. "What was his father like? What does Jason get from him?"

Amanda frowned, deep in thought. "I don't know. I've never seen Jason healthy except as an infant and I don't think I ever saw Jess sick. Or sit *still* for that matter. He was always on the go. He was a bit of an oddity in a town on the edge of the bayou. Hardly anybody over the age of twelve moved if they didn't have to."

"That's how I noticed Jason was sick. He was never still, either, until then."

Amanda smiled wistfully. "I don't think he slept six hours a day when he was an infant. I bet no mother in New Orleans was more exhausted than I was."

"How did you and your husband wind up in New Orleans?"

"Dreams. Young love. I wanted to go to a school in the city and Jess wanted to be a big-city police officer. When my parents died, Jess offered to put me through college. He'd already been accepted to the New Orleans Police Academy. We got married and moved to the city. After I graduated, I worked for a while then got pregnant. A couple months after that Jess was killed."

"That must have been hard on you," Garth said. "Being alone like that."

"Having the baby alone was nearly unbearable. At least I thought it was. Then he was kidnapped and I thought I was going to die. But now I know that nothing can ever be worse than watching him suffer.''

Garth agreed but he knew that losing Amanda would run a close second. His sister's advice echoed in his head. Could theirs be a real marriage? After pondering that monumental question for several moments he thought of the more important one. The one on which the entire answer hinged, since Amanda's happiness was fast becoming one of Garth's main concerns. Was he capable of being what Amanda needed?

''I heard Jason say that you'd told him his father died a hero?'' Garth asked, deciding that since she'd been happy with Jess Powers, he would be her measuring stick for a man. He might as well get some idea of what kind of man had made her happy. No telling where he'd fall when compared to a husband slain in the line of duty.

Amanda looked up from her needlework, a stunned look on her face. ''What?''

''If it's still too painful for you to talk about him, I understand. Forget I mentioned it.'' He wasn't sure he really wanted to hear about Amanda's first husband.

''Painful?'' She smiled. ''Jess died over seven years ago, Garth. It isn't painful to talk about him. But it is pointless. Yes, Jess was a hero. Whatever that means. He died being a hero. To me that means he died and never saw his son born—never got a chance to be a father. I never cared about the accolades Jess received. They didn't make him a good husband. They didn't bring him back.''

''Was he a good husband?'' The answer could hurt, but he had to know.

Amanda raised an eyebrow as if it were something she'd never thought of. ''A good husband? Jess never did anything by half measure so I guess that's what he tried to be. I was the envy of a lot of police wives because Jess didn't drink and he'd never have looked at another woman. He never brought the tensions of his work home, either. Jess saw the world in black and white—good or evil. Jason reminds me a lot of him in those ways.''

Garth had to wonder if there was any hope for him at all. He was far from the paragon she'd described. ''It sounds as if he was perfect,'' Garth commented.

''No one is perfect, least of all Jess. We had good times and bad. Just like every married couple.''

Garth saw a glimmer of hope. ''You had differences of opinion about some issues?''

Amanda nodded. ''And he was killed before we were able to resolve them. I told you *I* didn't care about the accolades but at the end they were all he *did* care about. He'd work a second shift and be so wrapped up in his police life that he'd forget all about me and never call. So there I'd sit, worrying all night that something had happened to him and he'd just have forgotten to call. As the years went on, he took more and more extra duty. He became obsessed. We grew very distant.''

One mystery solved, Garth thought. That was why she'd so easily believed he hadn't called the night he'd sat out that storm in the hills of West Virginia. She'd been furious with him and he couldn't help wondering if he'd gotten caught in some old unresolved anger she held toward Powers. ''You sound angry with him. He didn't choose to die, Amanda.''

''But he didn't choose to live, either. He could have waited for backup that night. He didn't. His partner was crippled and he was killed because Jess insisted they move in before their backup arrived. Jess lived on the edge and he liked it that way. An adrenaline high, he called it. He died for nothing but I'm not angry at him. I forgave his foolishness long ago.''

''You sure took off on me that night you thought I hadn't called to let you know I was grounded at Mayport. Are you denying it had anything to do with Powers?''

''I said I forgave him. I didn't say I'd forgotten. You never forget. It felt like the same thing all over again, is all.''

''You seem like an unlikely pair,'' Garth commented, hoping to understand what had attracted her to Powers now that he knew something about him. Hoping knowledge of her past would give him some key to how to win her for his future. If indeed he did decide to try winning her. He was still not convinced he could be what she needed.

Amanda nodded. "He was always a little wild but basically he was a good man. Then my parents died in a boating accident. Jess was there, urging me to go away with him. Telling me he wanted me." She hesitated. "He was an experienced twenty-two to my very naive eighteen."

"Are you saying he pressured you to marry him?" Garth asked.

"I—I…in a way I suppose you could say that. And I'm sure he isn't the first or last man to go after what he wanted any way he could get results. He was going away from everything familiar and he wanted me to go with him. I really do believe he loved me. I just wish I didn't feel he manipulated me to get what he wanted." The pain and disappointment she swore she no longer felt was there for anyone to see or hear.

"We were young. I was suddenly alone. I loved Jess and he was leaving. He used every weapon in his arsenal to make sure I went with him. He even professed faith in Jesus, and I believed him even though my pastor didn't."

"And that's the real issue for you, isn't it?"

"If the Lord had been foremost in his heart, getting medals and his name in the papers wouldn't have been important enough to risk his life for," Amanda said.

Garth stared into space, declining to make a comment. Jess Powers had hurt Amanda, that was for sure. He'd thought he needed to be more like Powers when the opposite was the case. Now he could see it. His similarity to Powers stood in his way, not his failure to measure up to the man.

And there was nothing he could do about it. Amanda was lost to him.

Because while his career was no longer the center of his existence, her Lord would never be either.

Chapter Nine

"Okay, troops," Garth said as he picked up the box of games and toys Jason had accumulated over his long hospital stay. "Do we have everything?"

Chris hefted the two plants she'd been assigned to carry. "Check," she called with a wide smile and headed for the door.

His mother held up her load—a suitcase in one hand and a fistful of strings that were attached to a dozen colorful balloons in the other.

"Check," she said and followed her daughter out of the room.

"Looks like everything to me," Amanda said and tucked a huge stuffed dog under one arm and an oversize Easter bunny under the other and marched out the door after his mother and Chris.

"Hey," Jason protested. "Didn't you guys forget some-body?"

Garth frowned. He looked around the bed and in the closet. "Now, let's see. Games and toys. Suitcase. Balloons. Plants. Stuffed animals. No. I don't think we forgot anything."

"You forgot some*body*. Me!" Jason squealed and hopped to his knees on the bed, his bright, ready smile proof that through his illness and the long months of isolation, Jason had retained his wonderful sense of humor.

Garth widened his eyes. "Well I think you're right, kiddo! You were supposed to come home with us today, weren't you?

Do you think you could hang around another day? We've all got our hands full here.''

"No way. I'm going home. We're havin' a party.''

Garth laughed and held the door open so Maria Hernandez could push a wheelchair into the room. "Is this rotten father of yours pulling your leg?'' Maria asked.

Jason plopped his cap on his head, his lower lip pouted out. "Yeah.''

Maria planted her hands on her narrow hips. "Don't worry,'' she told Jason in a stage whisper. Then to Garth in a formal tone that was totally un-Marialike she said, "I'm afraid he'll have to leave today, Mr. Jorgensen. We need this room for someone who's really sick.''

"And I'm all better.'' Jason's eyes glowed with increasing strength and vitality. He slid off the bed and jumped into the wheelchair. "I'm outta here,'' he called over his shoulder as Maria pushed him toward the door and his future.

"Yeah,'' Garth whispered past the lump in his throat as he looked around the now empty room that had been all their home away from home for too long. "We're all outta here.''

After lunch Garth swung Jason up onto his shoulders and carried him to his room. He'd talked Jason into resting on top of the covers. It was a compromise they'd reached when Jason was two and a half. The rest usually translated itself into a two hour nap. Garth had learned quickly that *nap* was a word to be avoided at all costs.

Once inside the room, he plopped Jason on the royal blue comforter that covered the top bunk. "Let's lose the shoes, shall we?''

Jason looked ready to argue on principle but nodded with a grimace. "Good idea. They're too small anyway. Could I have a pair of those really rad high-tops? You know the ones that have heels that light up when you walk?''

"Yeah, sure. Maybe we'll go to the shoe store tomorrow.'' Garth was so happy that Jason's feet had grown, a sign as far as he was concerned that his son was getting better, that he'd have agreed to gold-plated combat boots.

Jason stabbed his fist into the air. "Yesss!"

"But for now, you settle down," Garth ordered. "You know the drill. You don't have to sleep. You just have to rest."

In the hall, Garth nearly bumped into Amanda who'd been watching from the doorway. He saw the longing in her eyes and made a mental note to step aside that night so she could put her son to bed for the first time.

Amanda made an effort to look stern but her smile blossomed as warm as ever. "You should be ashamed of tricking him that way. He won't be awake for five minutes and you know it."

Garth chuckled. "How do you think I survived all those years when he needed naps? If he didn't sleep when he was an infant, he sure didn't when he was two or three or four, either. I see parenting as sort of survival of the smartest and that kid would give a rocket scientist a run for his money. By the time he was three, I considered taking up ballet to help me keep on my toes."

"From the sounds of it, he's outsmarted you on many an occasion."

Garth dropped his arm around Amanda's shoulders and led her toward the stairs to the first floor. He could hear his mother and sister talking in the kitchen beyond. He felt guilty but he wished they weren't there. He'd held back for so long. Been careful to keep his distance except for small gestures for so long. He didn't know how much longer he could wait. "Hey, I'm not the only one he's gotten the best of. Ever hear the one about Smokie, the neighbor's cat and the day Jason decided he needed a bath?"

Amanda laughed and, as always, it did something to Garth. It flipped a switch. One position of that switch was labeled Father—the second was labeled Healthy, Needy Husband. Garth stopped in his tracks, halting Amanda's progress down the hall. He took a deep breath.

He'd spent the months of their marriage trying to keep his

hands off her, trying to respect their agreement for a platonic relationship. He'd spent a lot of time trying to get to know Amanda. Trying to learn what she wanted from life.

He had decided to put an all-out effort into building the kind of relationship between them that would make a woman like Amanda happy. He was fairly confident he could succeed. Hadn't he succeeded at everything in his life with the exception of marriage to Karen? And marriage to Amanda would be nothing like those nightmare days. It would be worth all the effort because he could no longer conceive of life without her.

He had buried his true feelings behind a facade of friendship. But his resolve had worn thin over time and now he was afraid it was gone. He wanted Amanda. He wanted her for his wife. His real wife.

He looked down into her sparkling, violet eyes as she looked up at him. Then they turned warm and inviting and a ragged sigh escaped her lips. Garth lifted a hand to her hair. She wore it pulled away from her face in a braided arrangement that made her look about seventeen and made him feel like an adolescent again.

"You're so beautiful," he whispered against the delicate shell of her ear. He tugged her closer and tilted her face to his. Garth hadn't kissed her in so long. He'd been so very careful but he knew if he didn't kiss her right then, he'd lose his mind.

He'd already lost his heart.

Garth watched her eyes soften as he lowered his head toward hers. He'd been afraid she might pull away but he'd steeled himself for disappointment for no reason. Instead, she melted against him and reached up to sift her fingers through his hair. Her touch felt so right. "Amanda, I—" He shook his head unable to say more. He decided to let his kiss do his talking for him.

Amanda's lips under his made Garth think of tomorrows. Possibilities. A future with her in it. He had come to need Amanda in his life more than he needed air to breathe.

Then the voices of his mother and sister drifted up the stairs and shocked him back to reality. He would not seduce Amanda into making theirs a real marriage. She would have to settle for a man who could not share her faith. If Amanda decided to change their agreement it would be because she decided to— not because they'd consummated their marriage and she felt trapped.

He pulled back and put her away from him. "I'm sorry," he said, furious with his own weakness. "This isn't part of the bargain."

Amanda's violet eyes suddenly blazed. He'd never seen her so angry. "Then keep your hands to yourself!" she said through gritted teeth, her Southern accent suddenly thick enough to cut with a knife. "And let me tell you one more thing, Mister Jorgensen! If you apologize to me one more time for kissin' me, I'll clobber you. When I want an apology, I'll ask for it. Excuse me. Our guests are doin' the lunch dishes."

Amanda waited in Jason's room for Garth to help him finish his bath. She was anxious to tuck him into his own bed for the first time. It was another precious first Garth had given her and she loved him for suggesting it. It was tough staying angry at someone who was so considerate.

The problem was that Garth was too considerate at times. Like earlier that day in the hall. How on earth was she supposed to make this marriage last a lifetime when he continued to apologize for every kiss? Each apology served as a reminder that, to Garth, theirs was a temporary union. She couldn't help but feel rejected and the pain of those rejections increased with each passing day.

She sighed and looked around Jason's room. It spoke of budding masculinity, intelligence and creativity. Jason seemed to have participated in nearly every sport organized for boys. On one wall hung a collage of sports equipment, only some pieces of which she recognized.

He had a set of drums in one corner and a computer station in another. Jason was into the computer age in a big way. He was also a consummate Trekkie. The latter interest seemed to have inspired the scheme for decorating the entire room. It looked like a child's bedroom right off the *Enterprise.*

She chuckled, remembering the days he and Garth spent killing time in the hospital. Over the past three months, they'd built models of every starship ever conceived from the first *Enterprise* to *Voyager.* Her heart swelled at the memory of Garth's and Jason's heads bent close together in serious conference over a mock-up of the far wall of Jason's room.

She walked over and set one of those carefully constructed models into a swaying motion. Last week she'd helped Garth suspend the starships on fishing line from the ceiling in front of a wall mural of the Milky Way galaxy, which took up the whole wall.

It was a room that had been decorated with loving hands. The furniture had a space-age quality, the bunks built of bright red metal tubing. The white Formica bureau and desk, with their bright royal blue drawers and red knobs, looked indestructible. Garth had even found a deep blue carpet scattered with stars that he had matched in the ceiling. The stars on the ceiling glowed in the dark.

Amanda picked up Jason's discarded sweat suit and went to the closet to hang it up. She laughed when she slid the pocket door open. The closet walls always tickled her. They were the same deep matte blue as the bedroom ceiling but a grid work of white tape had been applied over it.

"You still think it's funny but you wouldn't laugh if it had been you," Garth growled in her ear, amusement showing through his gruff tone. "I almost went cross-eyed doing that."

Amanda turned. "What would a 'Star Trek' room be without its own holo suite?" she asked.

Garth rolled his eyes. "You're as bad as Jason. Now I know where it comes from."

"So, how come you went to so much trouble for a closet?"

"I figured he'd keep it neat if he wanted to show it off and I had extra paint."

"Mom, isn't that the coolest closet?" Jason said as he came

into his room all fresh from his bath. "Dad didn't want to do it but I won so he was stuck."

Amanda lost a short battle with a grin when she glanced at Garth who winced. "Extra paint, huh? What did you win?" she asked her son but kept her eyes on Garth.

"*Interloper*. It's a video game. Want me to show you how to play it?" Jason asked.

"Get the gleam out of your eyes, son. There's plenty of time for video games tomorrow. Right now you need to get some sleep. Now come here and give me a big hug and kiss. Then I'll see you in the morning. Mom's going to read to you tonight."

Jason dove into Garth's arms and was wrapped in a bear hug as Garth scooped him up. "You're not working tomorrow, are you?" he asked Garth.

"Not tomorrow but the next day, son. That temporary pilot left last week. I've got to get back to working my regular schedule. Money doesn't grow on trees, you know."

"But I thought we could take Mom to see Philadelphia. She's never seen the historical sights or the Franklin Institute. We should take her to the art museum and the zoo, too!" Jason squealed and bobbed up and down in Garth's arms. "And maybe Adventure Park. It'll be open on the weekends soon."

"We'll see. Don't forget you have schoolwork to catch up on and I'll still have office work to handle besides my flight hours. We'll fit in what we can. Okay?"

"Sure," Jason answered, only a little disappointment showing in his tone. "Will my tutor start coming again soon, too? She's cool. Not as cool as Mom but she's cool, you know?" Jason directed his attention toward Amanda. "Um, Mom, about breakfast. Do you think you could cook mine? I never had my own mom cook breakfast for me and that pizza you made for dinner was really awesome."

"And while you're at it, could you make mine, too?" Garth asked. There was the same little-boy hopefulness in his face as had been in Jason's. They looked so much alike that sometimes she forgot they weren't really father and son.

Amanda reached up and ruffled Jason's hair. "Grandmom and I already worked out the division of the housework. She has her jobs and I have mine."

"You're going to be the cook I hope?" Jason asked.

"Well, you see, sweetie, I hate doing dishes. Always have, so I was reluctant to take over the kitchen," she confessed with a twinkle in her eye.

Jason looked horrified. "But we'd help you. Wouldn't we, Dad?"

"Sure," Garth answered.

Amanda clapped her hands and smiled. "Wonderful! I'd *hoped* you'd both say that. Since I'm now chief cook, we'll all be the bottle washers."

Garth chuckled. "I think we've been set up, kiddo."

Jason sighed dramatically, then said dreamily, "Oh, I don't care. Won't it be great not to get waked up by a smoke detector?" He levered upward in Garth's arms and whispered in his father's ear, then dove into the top bunk.

Garth laughed. "Me too, son," he said cryptically, kissed Jason, then left.

Amanda wondered about Garth's answer and Jason's secret question all the while she read Jason a story, heard his prayers and tucked him in.

"You too, what?" she asked Garth when she found him at the desk in his office.

Garth looked up from his papers with a roguish grin curving his lips. He rolled his leather armchair away from the desk and snagged her around the waist, pulling her close. He gave her a quick, smacking kiss. A kiss that he didn't apologize for. "I like you a lot better than his tutor. So does Jason. She was his last matchmaking effort before he met you." She squirmed away, profoundly confused by his vacillation from cold to affectionate.

"Should I be jealous?" she teased.

But Garth's eyes turned suddenly serious as they captured Amanda's. "No. I swore I'd never get married again. Until I met you, no one even tempted me."

"But you were forced into this marriage," Amanda countered.

Garth raised an eyebrow, still holding her gaze. "Was I?" he asked, then went back to reading the report on the desk. Amanda stared at his bent head wondering what was going on. It would take a lifetime to figure this man out. Shaking her head she turned and left.

Garth braked to a stop as the traffic came to a standstill once again. Amanda didn't care about the traffic jam. She was fascinated by the hustle and bustle of the city. The downtown area was a well-blended mixture of old and new. This was their first outing as a family that wasn't shopping or a movie. Amanda could scarcely contain her excitement.

"Do you and Jason go to the Franklin Institute often?" she asked Garth who was busy looking for a break in the traffic.

"Several times a year."

"What if Jason's bored?"

Garth reached out and put his hand over hers where it rested on her knee. "He's going to have a good time showing you all his favorite exhibits. They rotate special exhibits but others were here when my parents brought me. They have a lot of exhibits on technology. And Jason's crazy about technology," he added as the lane on their right cleared and he steered into it.

"Look, Mom. There's the art museum."

"I want to grab the first parking place I can so keep your eyes peeled for a spot you two."

"There, Dad. On that side street!"

"Way to go, kiddo," Garth said as he made a sharp right.

Garth watched Amanda as she played virtual reality volleyball with Jason. The silhouette of her figure was reflected on a tall wide screen. To him, she was perfection. Evidently several other men thought so, too. They all watched her with awe in their gazes. She wasn't very good at the game but she was something to watch all the same. The only trouble was he didn't want them looking. Amanda missed the "ball" one last time and let out an outraged cry as the screen went blank.

"Next group," the operator of the exhibit called out. Amanda bent to pick up her purse and tripped into Garth's arms as she came upright. He smiled and held her longer than was necessary, neatly getting his message across to all the men who'd been watching her. She was his.

"Can we eat now?" Jason asked.

"Again?" Garth asked, teasing his son for the wonderfully voracious appetite that had come with his healing. Jason's color was healthy and he was beginning to outgrow his jeans. He even had a fuzz of dark hair on his head. Garth caught himself grinning. Life was good. In fact, today it was downright wonderful.

Amanda suggested a quick stop at one of the snack bars. Garth took the opportunity to indulge Amanda with her favorite new food—Philly soft pretzels with gobs of mustard. She gobbled hers even faster than Jason, then they went off to find the train. All three of them climbed all over the big engine. They investigated it thoroughly, teased each other and playacted a train robbery until Jason grew bored. Garth jumped down, then reached up to swing Jason to the ground. But it was hard to see his son so full of energy and not give him a big hug. He usually resisted the impulse for Jason's sake but this time it was too great a temptation.

Amanda stood in the engine compartment and watched Garth hug Jason. She felt left out for a second, then fought off the stupid jealousy that still cropped up at odd moments. Jason couldn't have a better father and it wasn't Garth's fault that this was the first outing of this kind she'd ever had with her son.

Determined to join them, Amanda looked about in search of a way to the ground. As she took her first step out onto a piece of ironwork, her foot slipped. She gasped as her own weight pulled her hand loose and she lost her grip on the bar she'd held. Amanda knew a split second of terror as the hardwood floor rose up to meet her. But in the next heartbeat, she found herself cradled in strong arms and against a hard chest. Garth's chest.

Instinctively, Amanda wrapped her arms around his neck and found her gaze snared by his blue eyes. She thought the angels were surely proud of the color God had painted there. "Wedges of sunlight," she murmured as she stared, mesmerized by the golden flecks she'd never noticed before.

Garth, too, stared then gave his head a quick shake. "Are you okay?"

"Okay?" she asked, confused and still a bit disoriented by the fall but mostly by his nearness. "Oh! Yes. I'm fine." Did her voice sound as breathless to Garth as it did to her?

"You didn't hit your head on the engine when you slipped, did you?"

"No. Why?" she asked and cursed her still vague tone.

"You said something about wedges of sunlight. I thought you hit your head and were seeing stars or something."

"Your eyes have wedges of yellow in them. I never noticed."

"Oh. I guess I never did, either," he said, still not taking his eyes off her.

Then a little voice said, "You can put Mom down now, Dad. Everybody's staring. She'll be careful from now on, won't you, Mom?"

Garth dropped her almost like the proverbial hot potato. One second she was cocooned in his embrace waiting for a kiss and the next she couldn't help but feel abandoned as she found her feet on the hard wooden floor. He backed away, his jaw rigid and his eyes blank of expression where seconds earlier they'd been open and achingly vulnerable. Or was that her overactive imagination? Or her hopeful heart?

"Jason wants to see the air travel exhibits next," Garth said taking two more steps backward.

Amanda refused to show him how empty his sudden desertion made her feel. "Oh, good! Since you're a pilot you can explain to me what keeps those things in the air. I've never understood."

Garth smiled, if a little stiffly and Amanda relaxed. At least he hadn't apologized for the near kiss. That was a bit of progress anyway.

"Come on, then. If these exhibits don't explain it to you, you'll never understand it."

"I'll never understand it," Amanda said, throwing up her hands. Garth looked on with amusement as Jason once again manipulated the wing.

"But Mom don't you see—"

"I see the smoke going over the wing," she interrupted. "It's lovely but it doesn't explain a thing. Where's the air come from?"

"Daaadd!" Jason whined, "she still doesn't get it. You try again."

Garth held up his hands and not in mock surrender. "Nope. I know when I'm licked. Might as well accept it, son. In aviation circles, she's what we call a hard case. I think it's time for the planetarium."

"Oh, yes. That sounds like a good idea," Amanda said.

"That's what you said about *this* exhibit," Jason chided.

Garth grinned at her, then scooped Jason up on to his shoulder. "Come on, kiddo. I think we've all had enough of the aviation world for one day."

Jason wilted dramatically against Garth. "More than enough."

"I'm not all that bad!" Amanda protested as she walked purposefully over to the hot-air balloon exhibit and pushed the button that started the burner. "I understand how this works. Heat the air and the air inside gets lighter—the balloon goes up. It cools off and it comes down. Simple. Airplanes weigh too much. They should drop like rocks. They're in a class with bumblebees as far as I'm concerned. They definitely should not be able to fly."

Garth sighed and shook his head. "A hard case, son. So, on to the planetarium? Jason can rest during the show."

"But I don't have to nap, right?" Jason asked his inevitable question.

Of course, Jason did nap and Garth was glad he'd sat their son between them. In a darkened movie theater with the stars above and a pair of amorous teens in front, having Amanda right next to him would have been more temptation than he could have resisted. He'd have kissed her within five minutes of the darkening of the lights. And he'd already almost kissed her long and hard in the middle of the institute earlier. That just wouldn't do. Because Amanda was worth the wait.

After the show, they visited the future exhibits and the one honoring historical accomplishments like the telegraph. Jason played for a while trying to master Morse code before they moved on to the scheduled paper exhibit.

"Where shall we eat?" Amanda asked when the demonstration drew to a close.

"I've got a picnic basket in the car," Garth said. "Suppose we go over into the park, eat, then come back in?"

Jason looked dubious. "A picnic basket that Mom doesn't know about? Dad, you didn't let Grandmom—"

Garth chuckled. "Do I look like a fool? *I* packed it."

Jason grimaced. "Dad, you cook as bad as Grandmom."

"But I know I can't cook! Oh, ye of little faith! Wait until you see the feast I bought when I went out to gas up the car this morning."

"Good, because I'm starved. Jason is, too!" Amanda said.

Garth loped ahead of Amanda and Jason. He went to the car, picked up the insulated basket, blanket and bag of toys he'd brought, then he went to meet them in the park across the street from the institute. Since it was a weekday and school was in session, the park was nearly empty. He spread the blanket out in the sun while Amanda listened to Jason's discourse on flying once again. He chuckled at Jason's exasperation when she still didn't get it.

"Chow time," he called out, changing the subject.

"What did you buy?" Amanda asked.

"Sit," he ordered and pulled her down next to him. The gourmet deli not far from their house specialized in box lunches. He took out the plastic boxes and handed them around. "Ham and cheese on white with crusts trimmed, potato salad and a sweet pickle for Jason."

"Way to go, Dad! My favorite. What do I get to drink?"

"A Ben's Berry-Berry Cooler." He felt in the basket. "And it's still cold. A turkey on a sourdough roll with diet mayo and lettuce with a tossed salad for a certain Mrs. Jorgensen."

Amanda chuckled at Jason who was tearing into his lunch. "Thank you. My favorite. And what do I get to drink?"

Garth grinned and pulled out a thermos. "Iced tea for the adults. Jason and I have almost the same lunch except I eat my crusts."

Amanda grinned up at him. "Good boy." She yanked on the dark curl that always fell over his forehead. "Crusts make your hair curl. My nana said so."

Garth traced her abundant waves. "What did you have to eat for these?"

"Hmm. Let's see. Carrots for my good eyes. Crust for curls. I remember. Potato skins!"

"Potato skins? Mom, your nana was as nuts as Grandmom."

"Jason, that wasn't kind," Garth admonished. "Your grandmother is older and she has a few..." Words failed him.

"Eccentricities?" Amanda supplied, fighting a grin.

"What's that mean?"

Now Garth was fighting a grin. "It means that when you're seventy, you can say what you want and pip-squeaks like you aren't allowed to poke fun."

Jason looked at his plate. "I'm sorry."

"It's okay, pal. I know there are a lot of rules but your mom and I are here to teach them to you. No one's mad. I just want you to treat people with respect.''

Jason nodded.

"Are you going to eat that salad or just play with it?" Garth asked his son after a few minutes of silence.

Both he and Amanda went off into gales of laughter over the way Jason hugged his plate to him and quickly took a big mouthful of salad. But later, when he put his head down and drifted off for one of his rests that were definitely not naps, they watched in contented silence until a backfire from a truck woke their son and he was once again raring to go.

Chapter Ten

"Come in," Amanda called and glanced up as her secretary, Julie, appeared in the doorway. In her hands was a crystal vase of white roses with sprigs of baby's breath and airy ferns intermixed in the bouquet.

"Flowers," the young woman sang out, a bright smile gleaming in her face.

Amanda felt her heart pick up its beat as it always did when Garth made one of these gestures. "My goodness! Again!"

"Your husband certainly didn't spare any expense this time."

Amanda stood and rounded the desk to take the vase. She took a deep breath. "The whole room smells like a rose garden."

"That's because your Garth sent you the whole rose garden. Two dozen! I counted. What's the excuse this time?"

Amanda set the bouquet on the credenza behind her desk and plucked the card from its center. "Thanks for waiting up for me. The dinner, even three hours late, was the best. G."

"He was late last night. I waited up and kept his dinner warm," Amanda explained.

"Woooeee, that man's crazy about you," Julie declared.

"He's just grateful," Amanda said suddenly downhearted. Lately she and Garth were like ships passing in the night, or the morning depending on his flight schedule. She didn't see enough of Jason, either, for that matter.

Though she had a good position at a large insurance company, it wasn't as fulfilling as she knew staying at home would be. She wanted to be Jason's mother and Garth's wife, not the head of the actuarial department. But if Garth went ahead with the divorce, she'd need to support herself and Jason.

"Why so glum all of a sudden?" the young woman asked. "I wish that man of mine would send me flowers once in a while."

Amanda shrugged. No one but Garth's family knew about their arrangement. Sometimes she longed for a listening post. And Julie might just be the perfect person. Wise beyond her years and a devout Christian, her secretary might just have been sent by the Lord as a friend.

"I miss him," Amanda admitted. "We see so little of each other with me working. Garth has an erratic schedule. Sometimes he flies at night. If I'm here during the day, when are we supposed to build a marriage?"

Julie stared. "Build a marriage? Woman, you've got yourself a great marriage." Amanda didn't respond but just stared at the flowers. "Don't you?"

"I don't know what I've got, Julie." Amanda bit her lip trying to keep the tears at bay. "I'm so confused."

"Back in a sec," Julie said, then turned and walked out of the office, returning minutes later with two cups of coffee in her hands. She kicked the door shut on her way past. "Let's take a break and have a little girl talk, shall we? You look like you could use it. Sit and talk, girl!" she ordered.

Amanda obediently sat back down at her desk as Julie took the chair in front it. "Garth didn't want to marry me," Amanda began. "At least I don't think he did. And I didn't want to marry him but I had no choice. At least I don't think I did. So you see, I'm not sure what I have."

Now Julie looked as confused as Amanda felt. "Start from the beginning, okay?"

Amanda did, pouring out the whole story starting with meeting Jess at fifteen up to the present. She was surprised that so many years condensed into so few words. Then Amanda realized how little living she'd done in the years her son had been missing.

"Why are you here?" Julie asked.

"Here? In Philadelphia?"

"In this office," Julie replied. "Amanda, your life isn't here. You need to be with your family, as you said, building a marriage. Don't get me wrong. I'm not one of these people who think a woman can't have a career and a successful marriage. That's the calling the Lord has given some women. Good as you are at your job, this isn't your calling. I've seen you with decorating magazines, poring over the pages for ideas. Have you put even one of those ideas into effect?"

"No. Garth made it very clear that the house was his. He even wanted a prenuptial agreement."

"Yeah, but that was in case of divorce. You aren't going to get divorced. That man's crazy about you." She tapped her chin. "But something's holding him back. What you've got to do is show him how good having you around is. And the only way to do that is to *be* around. Go home and make it your home, Amanda. Put your stamp on it."

"It sounds like it could be a good plan."

"You've got everything to gain by trying it. I'm sure going to miss you around here, girl."

Amanda laughed. "You've hardly had time to get used to having me here. You're saying I should quit?"

"Can Garth support you? Is your policy your family's medical insurance or can you go on his plan?"

"I guess so. I could have put Garth on my plan when we got married but I forgot all about it with Jason so sick. Jason!" Amanda smacked herself on the forehead. She couldn't believe she'd forgotten something so important! "I've always carried Jason on my insurance because I wasn't sure what kind of condition he'd be in when I got him back. My insurance should have picked up Jason's bills all along. I imagine they still can. Garth's pretty tight financially right now because of all the medical bills. He said he had to take out a second mortgage on the house and on Liberty Express, too. It would help him so much to get that money back. It'll probably be a real tangle but I think they have to pay.''

"You better get that all squared away before you even consider quitting. You don't need your salary, do you? I don't want to advise you to quit work if you can't afford it.''

"No. It just goes in the bank. I wanted to contribute but Garth doesn't want me to spend it except for my expenses. I imagine that's because he knows he won't be supporting me or Jason after the divorce.''

"But there isn't going to be a divorce,'' Julie corrected. "Keep telling yourself that. Continue on as if you never heard the word. Make plans just as if you never agreed to it. Go home tonight and show that man what he'd be missing if he let you get away.''

"You really think being at home might help?''

"Pray about it and in the meantime talk to personnel about this insurance thing.'' She pointed to the flowers and smiled widely. "A little gratitude got you them. No telling what getting his business and house out of hock might get you.''

"It's a big step. This job means financial security for Jason.''

"Like I said, pray about it, Amanda. Then give notice if the Lord confirms it in your heart. I just know He wants Garth as your husband.''

Garth picked up the envelope and stared at it. He had a ton like it in the drawer. The return address read Children's Hospital of the University of Pennsylvania. "Another bill,'' he said, with a sigh. Suddenly, though he'd just gotten up, Garth felt exhausted. He even toyed with the idea of adding it unopened to the others in the drawer. Why did he want to know how much more money he owed?

Selling Liberty had already begun to look like the best solution. His only acceptable solution. Declaring medical bankruptcy was not an option. He would provide for his family. He had to!

Headhunters representing three different major carriers had called in the last month looking to fill empty slots. He had promised jobs waiting with two of them and had already flown as a fill-in pilot for one of them—his old airline—last week. And the money from the sale would just about pay off every last one of the bills that had been piling up. He looked again at the offending envelope. It would have until today, that was.

Selling sounded so easy except that he didn't want to sell. Amanda had asked him to wait. And he had. But he couldn't stall much longer. Potential buyers didn't wait forever.

Garth turned the envelope over in his hand. Something told him to tear it open so he did. And he just stared. It was a check. Not a bill. A check. Credit for payments made in error it said. A hundred thousand dollars. About five thousand more than the second mortgages on the house and Liberty Express.

What in the world was going on in the hospital accounting office? If he wasn't an honest man, he'd run right out and pay off the mountain of debt burying him. Instead, shaking his head over the monumental errors made by today's whiz-bang computers, Garth picked up the phone and dialed the hospital.

Ten minutes later he hung up and sat, staring at the check. His check. Not one printed in error. Amanda had seen to it that she was now to be considered the primary person responsible for Jason's bills. Garth could feel his pulse beating in his temple. Did she think him incapable of supporting her and her son? Had he ever given her any indication that he needed her money?

His father's strident tones rang in his ears, conjured up from deep-seated memories. *A pilot? Where do you think you'll learn to be a pilot? What kind of an occupation is that? You'll never support a family with that kind of pie-in-the-sky dreaming. Get your head out of the clouds, boy.* But Garth hadn't been able to and he'd hated himself for having foolish dreams. Then pleasing his unpleasable father had no longer mattered. So he'd gone to his congressman and before he'd known it his dreams were happening. He was an officer in the United States Air

Force and headed for top gun school. And he could support a family very well, thank you.

Garth didn't want to think about Amanda's motives. He just wanted to let her know what he thought of her lack of faith in him. He picked up the phone and dialed her at work.

"Actuarial department—"

"Amanda Jorgensen," he snapped and grimaced, realizing that he'd taken out his anger on Julie, Amanda's friendly, young secretary.

"Hi," Amanda said, her voice annoyingly cheerful.

"It's Garth. I'd like to talk to you if you have a minute."

"What's wrong? You sound upset."

Garth could barely speak he was so angry but he managed. "Did you change Jason's records to make you responsible financially for his medical care?"

"Well, technically—"

"Yes or no!" Garth demanded between clenched teeth.

"Yes," Amanda said, sounding confused and annoyingly innocent. "It was the only way to straighten out the mess. Red tape at—"

"Have I ever given you any indication that I am unable or unwilling to provide for you and Jason?"

"That wasn't the issue. Jason is my son and therefore—"

"He's my son, too. You've said so often enough. He took sick while in my care. I am perfectly capable of paying for his medical expenses."

"I never said you weren't. But—"

"But nothing! I'll leave the hospital's refund on your dresser. I don't pretend to know where you got all that money but you can just put it back in whatever account it came from." Not caring to hear empty platitudes about his financial reversals or the extraordinary number of expenses he'd incurred because of Jason, Garth hung up.

Amanda sat staring at the phone in stunned silence. What on

earth had just happened? Why did nothing she did where Garth was concerned go right!

"Did the phone self-destruct after I connected you?"

"Was he rude to you?" Amanda asked, shocked that Garth would take his anger out on someone innocent of any wrongdoing. Wait a minute. What was she thinking? She was innocent, too!

Julie waved a careless hand in the air as she sat across from Amanda. "Don't worry. He just growled your name. So, what did you do to put the thorn in the lion's paw?"

"A cardinal sin. I claimed against my health insurance for all of Jason's expenses and got a bundle of money returned to Garth. Clearly, I should be taken out and stoned!"

"Now calm down and let me get this straight, girl. You went ahead and got his house and business out of hock and he's *angry?*"

Amanda nodded. She didn't know what to feel. Hurt? Anger? Her anger had already ebbed away. Right now she was numb. But hurt was nibbling away at it. Get angry again, she told herself. It hurts less.

"The way I see it, your man has a real problem where money's concerned. And you could react two ways. I don't think handing him his head would be very constructive, however satisfactory."

"Right about now it sounds like a pretty good idea to me."

"Or you could call his mother and ask her why she thinks Garth reacted to good news so badly. Could be that the answer might just drain all that anger away. Then you could let Garth know that even though you understand why he acted the way he did, he hurt you. Make him grovel around for forgiveness. It's better than a good scream any day."

Amanda laughed. "Julie, you are a godsend."

"Yeah. Yeah. That's what they all say. Then they give notice and go on their merry way, leaving poor Julie to train another boss."

"I think I'll call and talk to my mother-in-law. She may know what this is all about."

* * *

Amanda walked up the front path a bit earlier than usual that night. She couldn't put off the coming confrontation any longer. Frieda met her at the door.

"I sent Jason over to a friend's to play. I didn't want him upset. Garth's barely been civil all day. Try to remember that he acts like this when he's hurt."

"Julie's lion with a thorn in his paw." Amanda smiled. "I'm in good company anyway. I'm not the first Christian to confront a lion. Where is he, anyway?"

Frieda grimaced then chuckled. "In his den."

Amanda snickered. "We shouldn't be laughing. This is serious."

"Of course it is. Don't you spare his feelings. I heard the volume he used when he called you this morning. He deserves to eat some crow." The older woman chuckled again. "Do lions eat fowl?"

Garth looked up as Amanda walked into his study. She hadn't bothered to knock. "We need to talk, Garth," she said as she plunked herself down in the chair across from him.

"The check's on your dresser. I don't want to discuss it further."

"You prideful fool! That money represents all you've paid so far that is *now* paid by my insurance. I've carried health coverage on Jason since he was born. Why shouldn't I claim against it? Jason is your son by virtue of your love for him and his for you, but I gave birth to him. I can't see the harm in using the insurance I paid for for years! My policy predates yours, so I had to be the one on record as being chiefly responsible. Your policy picked up the rest. Much of what you paid had to be returned."

Garth had a sinking feeling in the pit of his stomach. He'd made a complete fool of himself. "Insurance?"

"In-*surance!*" Light suddenly dawned in Amanda's eyes. "Good heavens! You thought I sent them a check? Where would I get that kind of money?"

"Life insurance on your husband. Wise investments. I don't

know. Why didn't you tell me about this?'' Garth asked, raking a hand through his hair.

"Because no one told me it had been settled. I didn't want to get your hopes up once I found out how much money was still outstanding on Jason's account, so I decided to wait and tell you when I was sure both coverages would pay for everything. These things usually take time but because I'm an employee, personnel promised to speed up the process. I guess they forgot to tell me it had all been worked out."

Garth took a deep breath. "Amanda, I'm so sorry. I acted like an idiot." He spread his hands in a gesture of helplessness. "I don't know what else to say."

Amanda fixed him with a long, level stare. "You can start by telling me where all that anger came from. I think you owe me that much."

Her request shocked him. Especially since he didn't know why he'd gotten so angry. It was all tied up with Jason. Money. And Amanda's opinion of him. He'd thought that he'd failed her at the most basic of levels. That she didn't trust him to provide for her and Jason. That she saw him as a foolish dreamer...just the way his father had. But that was ridiculous! His father was dead and buried. He had no effect on Garth's life at all. Did he?

Not one to lie to himself once he stared the truth in the face, Garth admitted that it had been his father's berating voice he'd heard in his thoughts just before making the call to Amanda. Now he really felt like an idiot. How could he admit that to Amanda? The woman he wanted to share his life with. The woman he'd been trying to woo for months into remaining his wife. Well, if he didn't want all that work to go to waste he'd better think of something to explain his outburst—or admit to the truth.

Garth sighed. Painful as it was, the truth was his only option. He would not lie to Amanda. "Did you ever have a dream? One that was so far above the realm of possibility that it seemed almost unattainable?"

"Going to Tulane," Amanda said. "But I worked hard at the local community college. Then I got a grant because my parents were killed and Jess offered to pay the rest."

"Did you have the dream before your parents died?"

"They told me to work my hardest, pray for it and trust in the Lord."

"That's pretty much what Mom told me. My father, on the other hand, called me a fool chasing a pie-in-the-sky dream— among other things. I was going to be a failure as a man and be unable to support my family."

"And it seemed to you that I was saying the same thing?"

"Stupid, huh?"

Amanda shook her head. "Not stupid. Garth, I understand that supporting your family is important to you. But do me a favor. Ask yourself if succeeding to the level you have would have been as important to you if your father had been like your mother. If he'd supported your dream. I'll just bet you never had to do anything to earn her love and respect."

"No, Mom's always been there for both Chris and me. She never criticized us unless it was constructive. I guess maybe I'd be a little more relaxed about succeeding if he'd been like her. But he wasn't, Mandy. He tore us down at every opportunity. If I made a hit in a Little League game, it would have been a home run if I'd just hit the ball a little harder."

Garth could feel the old anger and resentment begin to burn inside him. His hands seemed to ball into fists of their own accord. "I remember getting an A on a really tough calculus test. He found it necessary to mention that it was a shame I missed the *easy* extra credit question. Not only did no one else get that extra credit question right, but my father couldn't do second-level algebra to save his life. He had no idea if that question was easy or not."

"But you've proven him wrong," Amanda said and scooted to the edge of her chair so she could reach across the desk. She took his hand and uncurled it so it lay flat on the desktop. "You are what you said you'd be. How long are you going to let his memory do this to you, Garth? You need to forgive him and put the past behind you.''

"I told you before, I'll never forgive him. Not for what he did to Mom or the way he treated Chris and me.''

"Do you think your mother still goes through all these push-and-pull emotions where your father's concerned? She seems rather serene to me. She's put that part of her life behind her. She's able to live in the present and for the future. I don't think you can make that claim, can you? You're still the kid whose father didn't appreciate his test grade.''

Garth stared at his hand, now flat on the desk and covered by hers. Emotions with no names warred in his heart and mind. "Until you pointed it out to me, I thought I'd gone beyond being that kid. But forgive him? I don't think I can. He hurt us all so badly.''

"Do you have any idea how much energy it takes to hate someone the way you do your father? Your hatred makes you drive yourself harder than necessary. I know my situation with Jess wasn't the same but I had to come to a place where I forgave him.''

"I've never understood how Mom was able to make her peace with my father.''

"Why not ask her?''

Garth nodded, still staring at her soft hand. He was so ashamed of the way he'd acted. Maybe he would talk to his mother about that last meeting with his father. Amanda deserved so much better than a man like him. He'd just have to try harder. He had to make sure he never flew off the handle like that again. He had to make Amanda happy—had to be the man she needed him to be because there was no longer any chance that he could just let her go.

He looked up not knowing what to expect and found her smiling at him. "Now I have my own apology to deliver,'' she said. "I'm sorry I didn't tell you what I'd set in motion at work.''

"Your apology is unnecessary, Amanda. I overreacted.''

"Yes, you did but your overreaction doesn't negate my mistake. A marriage is a partnership. Partnerships don't function well if both parties act independently." She took a deep breath and rushed on. "So, before we have another misunderstanding, I remembered about the health insurance on Jason when I was talking to Julie about quitting my position."

"Quitting?" Garth couldn't believe what he'd heard. "Your job? You want to quit? I thought you wanted to work."

Amanda shrugged. "So did I. But I don't. I want to stay home and be a wife and mother. I've missed so much of Jason's life already that every day I spend away from him drives me crazy. Plus, your mother isn't getting any younger. She deserves a chance to kick back and give up some of the responsibilities of running a house and caring for Jason. So, if you have no objection I'd like to give my notice. We can still carry the double health insurance for up to three years by paying the premiums, just to be on the safe side where Jason's health is concerned."

Garth was almost afraid to breathe. Had he heard right? Amanda believed in him? She'd begun to see their marriage as a marriage, not some bargain struck under duress? She was willing to trade her job—her financial security—to stay at home and take care of him and Jason?

He might be reading too much into her gesture, though. She had said she missed Jason. And it would be just like Amanda to worry as much as he did that his elderly mother carried too much of a burden. He'd better not get his hopes up too much. Better to be practical. Safer, he decided.

But then an optimistic thought occurred to Garth and he hung on to it like a lifeline. When she'd mentioned continuing her health benefits, Amanda had said *we can still carry* which committed her to their marriage for at least three years. He had three years to show her how happy they could be together.

Chapter Eleven

Amanda gave her notice the next morning and, as Julie had predicted, was invited to return at any time. She prayed that returning to work was not part of her future. Insurance had never been her plan for the future anyway.

The next two weeks seemed endless, especially since Garth's schedule was more crammed than usual. He'd explained that he'd taken on more work, hoping to keep himself in the black so he wouldn't have to sell Liberty. Though he didn't need the work, he felt he should honor the commitments. But consequently, Amanda felt more isolated from him than she ever had.

Then finally her first Monday at home dawned. Garth rushed off to work with the promise to be home for dinner and Jason's tutor arrived at nine. After seeing Jason settled with the woman in the den, Amanda returned to the kitchen for a cup of coffee with Frieda.

Glancing around the utilitarian kitchen, Amanda's thoughts turned to color and style. How she wished she could redecorate Garth's home! There was nothing really wrong with this room except that it was dated and a little dingy. The rest of the interior of the house, with the exception of Jason's room, needed help, too. The formal areas especially needed a major overhaul. Japanese minimalist, chrome and glass had their place but, in Amanda's humble opinion, it was not in a two-hundred-year-old colonial.

Not knowing exactly who had chosen the odd pairing nor how much of the current decoration Frieda had chosen, Amanda was reluctant to approach the subject. The last thing she wanted was to offend Garth or his mother. Amanda realized how little she really knew about Garth. She didn't even know how long he'd owned the house. She almost let the whole subject lie but once again Julie's words of wisdom flowed through her thoughts. *Go home and make it your home, Amanda. Put your stamp on it.*

"Frieda, how long has Garth owned this house?" Amanda asked before she could once again lose courage.

Frieda tapped her chin. "Well, let me see. I didn't move here until after Jason came to us. I think he bought it right after his marriage. Though I don't remember them doing much to fix it up for some time. Even so, the effort was rather piecemeal," she snorted in disdain. "Truth be told. Not all of the problems in that partnership were due to Karen's mental illness. Neither one of them slowed down their schedules long enough to work at a marriage."

"Then Garth and Karen didn't decorate it together?"

"No. As I remember it, Garth planned the outside work." Shaking her head she added, "And Karen handled the inside." Her tone provided Amanda all the encouragement she needed. Frieda didn't approve of her late daughter-in-law's taste, either. Amanda gave the kitchen another close look. It didn't fit with the rest of the house.

"Oh, not this room, dear. That one wasn't much for the kitchen. This is the way it was when Garth bought the place. I've thought about trying to do something around here for years but, to be honest, I just didn't know where to start. It seems like such a monumental task and I'm not as young as I used to be. Would you consider it?"

Amanda breathed a sigh of relief. "That's what I was trying to get around to asking. I really think this house cries out for something a little more suited to the period. So, you wouldn't mind it if I tried a few new things?"

"I wouldn't mind it if you called the Salvation Army and

emptied the whole place.'' Frieda giggled like a schoolgirl, then wiggled her eyebrows. "In fact, that might not be such a bad idea.''

Later that day over dinner Frieda brought up the subject with Garth. "Amanda mentioned the decor around here today.''

Garth looked around. "What decor?'' he asked, sounding genuinely confused.

Frieda chuckled. "Exactly her point. Tell Garth what you'd like to do, dear.''

Leave it to Frieda to just blurt out a sensitive subject. Amanda took a deep breath. "Well, actually I didn't have any definite plans. Just sort of a general idea of suiting the decorating a little more closely with the architecture and period of the house.'' Remembering how proprietary he was about the house she added, "You wouldn't feel I was intruding, would you?''

"Intruding?'' Garth asked, frowning. "Amanda, this is your home.''

"But—'' About to bring up his past attitude and the prenuptial agreement, Amanda stopped. Now, in front of Frieda and, of course, Jason, was not the time. "But it would mean more than paper, paint and carpets. The furniture's all wrong for what I had in mind.''

"Good. I hate most of it anyway.'' He thought for a minute. "All of it actually, except for the stuff upstairs in my study.''

"That furniture was from your apartment, wasn't it?'' his mother asked, casting a determined look in Amanda's direction.

Garth nodded, so Amanda jumped in with a few suggestions to brighten up his private domain without changing its basic style. "You're probably more qualified to decide what it should look like than I am,'' Garth responded. "I'd kind of like to see what you can do with this old barn. I suppose you'll want to hire a decorator.''

Amanda's stomach dropped. Was he saying he didn't think she could do it on her own? "I hadn't planned on it. Do you want me to? It's your decision, after all." *It's your house* she almost added.

"Karen did, but to tell you the truth, if this place is an example of what a decorator would do, I'd rather you go it alone."

Now her heart pounded. Not only did he not mind her changing his home but he trusted her to do it right. "It might get messy for a while."

"Not a problem." Garth grinned. "If I could live with that thing in the family room that's supposed to be my easy chair for all these years, I can live with anything. I'll give you my credit card. Get whatever you want."

"Don't you want to have some input into what I do?"

Garth stared at her for a moment, then shrugged. Sometimes she thought they must look like wary children, both afraid to say what they wanted, both afraid it was too much to ask. "Is that what you'd like? You wouldn't mind me looking over your shoulder?"

"I thought we could make some of the decisions together," she ventured, praying he'd want to work with her—as a real married couple would.

Garth smiled. A little dimple in his cheek appeared and his eyes sparkled. He suddenly looked ten years younger than when she'd first met him. "Just let me know where and when."

Amanda smiled, too, unable to look away from his beloved face. She felt a bond forming between them that hadn't been there before. *Please. Please, let this mean something!*

"Mom? Dad?" Jason's worried voice cut through the connection with Garth and they both turned toward their son. "I like my room. Don't you?"

"Oh, goodness. I wasn't thinking of changing a thing in there," Amanda declared. "Except maybe we could do something about the stash of books under that bed. Some rolling drawers maybe."

Jason sighed dramatically then his eyes lit. "I thought of something my room could use."

"Not if it has anything to do with white tape!" Garth exclaimed and poked Jason in the belly.

Jason giggled. "I thought maybe a dog bed next to mine."

"Why would you want a dog bed?" Amanda asked. "You don't have a dog." Light dawned when Garth snickered. "Oh, you'd like to change that as well?" She looked toward Garth, gauging his reaction. But Garth had turned his head toward his mother. Amanda followed his gaze.

"Well, don't everyone look at me!" Frieda exclaimed.

"If I remember," Garth said tapping his forehead, "you've been the stumbling block in the past."

"Now that Amanda's here, I have no objection. As long as I'm not the one who has to take care of it. Which is why I objected. I had to feed that mongrel of Garth and Christina's for years after they left. You two had the fun when you visited and all I ever got was nearly knocked down every time I gave him his bowl." She huffed and stood to clear the table then stopped, a thoughtful look crossing her face. "Well," she added with a fond smile, "at least *he* enjoyed my cooking."

"He sure did, Mom. He ate enough of it under the table," Garth said in a muttered aside as the door to the kitchen closed behind Frieda.

Jason hooted and Amanda gave them both a reproving look as she stood to collect some more dishes. "You are both incorrigible." Just inside the kitchen she stopped to reflect. Garth hadn't been offended by her interest in the house. In fact, he'd seemed pleased. She looked around the kitchen. She couldn't wait to get to work!

Over dessert, plans for a trip to the SPCA began to form. Amanda couldn't have been more pleased. They were beginning to look and feel like a real family.

"You're sure that's the one you want, son?" Garth asked, eyeing the puny puppy in Jason's arms. Jason, and frankly he, had always preferred bigger dogs, not ankle biters. This one would clearly never grow to be anything but ankle high.

"He's so friendly." Jason sighed as the little dog licked his face once again.

Garth had to give the mutt several points for personality if not looks or stature. A nondescript gray, his wiry fur stuck out at weird angles. This was one ugly dog.

"The shepherd pup looks real friendly," Garth said encouraging Jason not to discount one of the more obvious choices.

"But don't you see...almost anybody would want him. But this puppy...well..."

"Has problems," Garth supplied, being as kind as he could. Garth took the dog from Jason and held the squirming little body next to his chest. And his heart melted when the pup looked up at him, his tongue darting out to give Garth a big puppy kiss. His left ear drooped while the right perked up at attention, his big, brown, puppy eyes full of canine admiration. "Hold still and stop with the kisses, buster. That's not going to get you anywhere with me," Garth lied, trying to maintain some decorum and his image as a tough guy for his son.

"Buster! What a great name, Dad!" Jason reached up and ruffled the dog's unruly fur. Garth's melted heart puddled somewhere in his chest. He even got to name him. Oh, how he'd wanted a dog when he'd been Jason's age. His chance had only come after his father had exited their lives. But Garth had left for the air force a little over a year later.

"And Mom did ask us to get one that's not too big," Jason added unnecessarily.

Garth was going nowhere without Buster. "And she did say not to get one with a pedigree because they're sometimes harder to train. He's sure not in that category. We'll take this one," Garth told the approaching attendant who looked instantly confused.

"That one? But we don't have any records on that one. We just found him in a box on the doorstep. Can't say I'm surprised. The note said he'd been a big disappointment. Runt of the litter. We're not even sure what he is." He chuckled. "Except a pretty ugly dog."

Offended on behalf of the newest member of the Jorgensen clan, Garth glared. "He's the one. It's him or none. Right, Jase?"

Jason's head bobbed as he jumped up and down. "Right on, Dad!"

Garth filled out what felt like more papers than he had the last time he'd bought a car, then after purchasing a dog carrier, he and Jason started their trip home. They stopped on the way though, to buy everything an abandoned doggy needed to make him feel like a part of the family.

"Garth, what is it?"

"A puppy," Garth told Amanda, once again offended on Buster's behalf. Were he and Jason the only people who saw Buster's potential?

"Well, he is small. I—I did say to go for one on the small side. And he sure doesn't have a pedigree. Nope. No AKC papers attached to old...what did you say Jason's going to call him?"

"Jason decided on Buster."

"But Dad named him. Said something like, 'You're not going to get to me with all those kisses, buster.' And I said, 'Buster! Let's call him Buster.' And so his name's Buster. What a great doggy name! Did you see all the stuff Dad bought him? Squeaky toys and a bed for my room and that new stuff so he won't get fleas, and leather chewies so he won't want Grandmom's slippers. He's gonna be the best little dog anybody ever had. I'm going to take him outside and show him the dog igloo we got. It's kind of big for him but it's the smallest one they sold."

Amanda turned to Garth after watching Jason and his small gray shadow run out the back door. "Runt of the litter? Garth, they don't usually use that term unless they are expecting a certain size within a litter."

"That was what the note said that was left with him. Can you imagine abandoning him like that on the front steps. Out in the woods the way the SPCA is? He could have been hurt by a predator before anyone found him.''

Amanda stepped up to him and put her hand in the middle of his chest. ''You're just an old softy, aren't you? You heard that story and just had to take him in.'' She tiptoed and planted a smacking kiss on his cheek. ''You're a nice man, Garth Jorgensen.'' She moved forward to give him another friendly kiss and Garth turned his head. Their lips met. And the small token offered became so much more.

To both of them.

Amanda dabbed the last touch of paint on the wall and climbed down from her high perch on the ten-foot ladder. She stepped back to admire her masterpiece. The border of ivy vine she'd stenciled on the soffit over the kitchen cabinets looked exactly the way she'd hoped it would.

This afternoon, when the kitchen set she'd bought arrived, the room would be complete. It still amazed her that rock maple had been hidden under the chipped paint on the cabinets. What some people did to wood! Now stripped of their color and hand rubbed to a smooth patina, the cabinets looked more like antique furniture. And it had cost next to nothing.

Amanda had saved a bundle by using sponged-on paint and joint compound to give a textured colonial look to the walls and by refinishing the existing cabinets. She'd also haunted area thrift shops, estate auctions and house sales looking for a trestle table and benches. She'd finally found them at a bargain price. An older woman had sold her the set at a fraction of what Amanda knew it was worth because it was going to a family and not to some ''snooty'' antique dealer. Amanda loved the sound of that. Family.

Smoothing her hand over the polished granite countertop that had arrived and been installed that morning, Amanda smiled. Now here she'd splurged but it had been well worth it, as had the hand-hewn panel that matched the cabinets and disguised the modern look of the dishwasher and refrigerator. The other big-ticket item had been the professional stove that, because of its utilitarian design, lent itself to the antique flavor she'd given the room.

Garth had spent the week away on a long charter, ferrying a state senator around on a campaign tour of Pennsylvania. Amanda couldn't wait for his return. When he'd left, the kitchen had been a disaster with doorless cabinets, an exposed subfloor and several holes in the plaster. It had been the perfect place to begin training Buster but hardly looked promising as a redecorating job. And now all she had to do was clean up her paints and sweep the new slate gray tile floor.

"The men are here with the table and benches," Frieda called from the front of the house just as Amanda put the broom in the closet.

Three hours later, she placed an old jar with a bouquet of daises on the table. She looked around in tired anticipation as Jason called out. "Mom! Come quick. I think there's something wrong with Buster's paws. They're all swollen and even bigger than they were last night."

"I'm in the kitchen," she called, not as concerned as Jason. Amanda chuckled. Since Wednesday, three days after Garth took off and five days after the puppy had come home with the hearts of her men firmly in his grasp, Amanda had suspected that she hadn't gotten one of the things on her doggy wish list. Buster was not going to be a little dog. His paws, so small that everyone had believed he'd never reach knee high, had… flowered. Sneakered feet thudded and puppy nails clicked as the pair came bounding into the room.

Hunkering down, Amanda picked up the squirming little dog. "Now, let's see." She poked and prodded each little puppy paw. The puppy was all paws. "Jason, I think his paws are just fine. He's just growing but his paws are growing a lot faster than the rest of him. What this means is that Buster isn't going to be a little dog when he grows up the way everyone thought. He may have been taken away from his mother a bit too young and so he seemed as if he were destined to be a little dog, but he was just a very young puppy."

"How big?" Jason asked, clearly not disappointed by this new development, just curious.

She put her hand off the floor. "Big-big." It was an underestimation, she was sure.

"Wow!" He stood. "Hear that boy? You're not a runt after all. Let's go tell Grandmom."

"I'm sure she'll be thrilled," Amanda said as the two raced off to find more adventure together. The *beep-beep* of a horn drew her to the back door then as Garth hopped out of his car.

He looked up and smiled. That dimple she'd never really taken note of until recently peeked out. He tilted his head and said, "Should I come around front or is the kitchen safe to navigate these days?"

Amanda folded her arms and tried to look annoyed at his teasing. "And I said you were nice? I stand corrected. I'll have you know that the kitchen is completely safe," she said as he reached the house. "And finished," she added when Garth stopped in his tracks just inside the door.

"Amanda! This is incredible." Garth dropped his bag and walked to the cabinets. He caressed the rock maple then the granite counter. Then he turned to her.

Amanda wished she could read his mind. Did he understand that this had been a labor of love for her? She voiced her big worry. "Then you like it? It isn't too...I don't know... rustic?"

Garth shook his head. "I feel as if I just stepped into the pages of a magazine. The 'after' photograph. You were wasted in insurance, Amanda. You should have been a decorator."

A smile bloomed on her face. "Actually, that's what I started out wanting to be. Insurance was just a job I qualified for because my major was in business. I minored in art and courses I hoped would get me into decorating later. But...well it was too tough to get into it. Real bottom-level starting salaries." And Amanda had felt honor bound to find a good paying job. Jess had spent so much on her education that she'd grabbed at

the first job she could find. It was supposed to have been temporary.

"How did you do all this in a week? You must have worked
around the clock."

Amanda didn't dare address the subject of her hours. "It took
longer than a week if you think about it. The place was already
torn apart when you left. Everything had been ordered. You
helped me pick out the stove. The carpenter you called had the
cabinet doors to finish so they'd match the refrigerator and dishwasher panels he was making for us. The floor was almost
ready for the tile masons. All that prep work is the part that
takes the time. It usually looks its worst just before it all comes
together. That's where we were when you left."

Garth reached out and snagged her into his arms and hugged
her tightly. Amanda's heart skipped several beats then picked
up its usual, if quicker, rhythm. "Thank you," he whispered
into her hair. "I never realized having a wife could be this
wonderful."

Garth tiptoed into the kitchen and shut the door behind him.
It was two in the morning. He didn't want to wake anyone else
just because sleep was further away now than when he'd gone
to bed at midnight. He opened the fridge and pulled out the
carton of milk. As he shut the door, he couldn't resist running
his hand over the wooden panel. Even in the dark the scope of
Amanda's efforts overwhelmed him.

He turned and grabbed a glass out of the cabinet and once
again his fingers caressed smooth wood as if he had no control
whatever over his actions. Which was even more true now that
he'd learned how much of the work Amanda had done herself.
With loving hands. That's what showed the most. That she'd
cared about the room. He closed his eyes. Hopefully that was
a sign that she cared about the man standing in the room at the
moment.

He took a swallow of the cool milk. Marriage. He had so

much to learn. It was a partnership, Amanda had said. Tomorrow they were going to pick out some furniture. She'd insisted. And he was glad. In fact, like a kid, that was why he couldn't sleep. He wanted tomorrow to come—to be here now!—so he could be with her.

Amanda.

It seemed that nearly every waking moment this past week— *Oh, be truthful with yourself at least, Jorgensen, nearly every moment for months*—was filled with thoughts of her.

He hated the nights the most all. It was the one time she wasn't his. The one time of the day when he couldn't pretend that the gulf between them didn't exist. He wanted her. It was that simple and that complicated. It didn't matter if she was all made up and dressed in fashion magazine splendor or if her cheek was streaked with paint and her clothes were full of it. He loved her and wanted to show her how much since the words seemed forever stuck in his throat.

"Garth? Son, is that you rattling around out here?"

Garth chuckled. "It better be or you have a milk-drinking burglar in your kitchen."

Frieda chuckled, too, and flipped on the under counter lighting. "Not my kitchen any longer." Frieda looked around. "It's Amanda's. She made it hers. She's a wonderful wife to you, son. Don't be a fool and lose her."

"I'm trying not to, Mom." Garth sighed and ran his fingers through his hair. "But you should know that sometimes marriages don't work out. I'm working as hard as I can but—"

"Work? Is that what you think Amanda deserves?"

"Marriages take work."

Frieda reached out and grabbed his free hand. She squeezed so tight it was almost painful. "Marriages take love. Any work involved is a labor of that love. Don't you ever think anything can substitute for the love part. I know. I tried."

Garth was not encouraged as he leaned his hip against the counter and crossed his feet. "But you lost the man you—"

He shook his head refusing to call the blind loyalty his mother had shown toward his father love. "Why try?"

"I lost because all the *trying* in the world couldn't substitute for the fact that he didn't love me. He never had."

Garth saw red. "So you forgave him by blaming yourself?"

"No, son," Frieda said, shaking her head now. "I forgave him because he asked me to. He was wrong, wrong, wrong in what he did. By going to that woman, he committed sin. He asked me to marry him when he knew he didn't love me. That was wrong, too. But I did something wrong, as well. I said yes, knowing full well that he didn't love me the way I loved him."

Frieda shook her head again and took a sip of Garth's milk. "I was going to work at that marriage and make him love me. It doesn't work. We proved that."

Had he ever understood what his family had been about? "Why did he ask? Why did you say yes?" Suddenly, Garth needed to know. Needed to see that there was no correlation between his and Amanda's forced wedding—between what he felt for Amanda and what his parents had or hadn't shared.

"He wanted his grandfather's business, but he knew it wouldn't be handed over to him until he had a wife. I was always there in the background, adoring him. Ever since we met in high school, I loved him. And then, suddenly he saw me. He thought I would be the perfect wife. In his defense, I think he tried to love me but... Well, anyway, I forgave him. I had to." When he would have protested, Frieda put her hand up halting his objection. "I had no choice. Don't you understand that, yet? It was for myself. I needed to let go of the hate. And really, when you think about it, Almighty God forgives anyone for anything they've done as long as they ask it in the name of His Son. How could I refuse? His Son let himself be nailed to a cross and took all our sins on His shoulders and He forgives us even though we were the cause. It would be pretty small of me not to do the same. Wouldn't it?"

Garth, now haunted by more than his need for Amanda, got

very little sleep that night. Exhausted, his eyes drifted shut at last. Words and names swirled in his mind, disturbing even that respite.

Forgiveness.

Jesus.

Father.

Love.

Amanda.

Chapter Twelve

"Dad? Could I talk to you?" Jason asked.

Garth looked up from the lawn mower that refused to start. He'd been puttering around with the thing for an hour and still hadn't a clue what was wrong with it. Jason was a welcome interruption. He sat on the cement floor of the garage and gestured for Jason to join him. "What's on your mind, kiddo?"

Jason settled on the cement floor facing Garth and leaned back on his elbows, his feet crossed at the ankles. A mirror of Garth's own position. "What's my name?" Jason asked.

"Jason," Garth answered automatically, momentarily confused. Then he understood. "Well, legally it's Jesse Powers."

"But I don't want to be Jesse Powers. I don't want to hurt Mom's feelings, either, but I think I'm Jason Jorgensen. And so do all my friends at school. My teachers, too."

"Oh, I see," Garth said. He did see but he let Jason explain.

"I'm weird enough to all of them already. When I go back to school, I'm going to have to explain it *and* my leukemia again. And now Mom is Mrs. Jorgensen, too. Right? When you guys sign my stuff, we'll have different names. It's like I'm not part of the family. Who am I, Dad?"

Garth sat up, crossed his legs Indian style and scooped Jason into his lap. "You're our son. Legally you aren't my son. You're my stepson but you know that doesn't matter, don't you? I couldn't be any more your father if I'd been there when you were born."

"But I don't want you to be my stepfather. I know my real father was a hero but I want to be Jason Jorgensen again. Teddy Connors was a foster son first. He used to be Teddy Upsall. Then the Connorses adopted him and now he's Teddy Connors. Can't you adopt me? I want you for my father. My real father's dead and can't be my father anyway."

Jason seemed to get more and more worked up as they talked. Garth knew that if the boy was worrying about this too much it could undermine his recovery. But then, talking about this to Amanda wasn't going to be easy, either. He'd have to approach her in just the right way after quite a bit of thought. And unfortunately, back to school time was approaching. "I'll tell you what? I'll see what I can do. You put this out of your head, okay. Mom and I will work something out. I'll talk to her about it and we'll let you know when it's all fixed. Okay?"

Jason jumped up and gave Garth a tight hug around his neck. "Thanks, Dad! It's great how I can always talk to you. So, what's wrong with the mower?"

Amanda waved goodbye to Garth at the back door and watched him drive off. She stood there until the car disappeared from sight and, some minutes later, realized she was still staring after him like a moonstruck idiot. *Get a grip, Amanda. The man barely knows you're alive,* she told herself. He hardly spoke a word to her anymore. She refused to dwell on the lacks in her marriage as long as she still had one.

She grabbed her tape measure, her notebook and pencil and headed for Garth's upstairs study. Frieda had explained that his office was on the second floor because Karen hadn't wanted her "creation" downstairs marred by Garth's old comfortable furnishings. There was a small room on the first floor she hoped to fix up as a surprise for Garth and furnish with his own familiar things. She walked in and looked around with a critical eye.

There was nothing wrong with the burgundy leather furniture. In fact, it was perfect for a man's study. The bookshelves were well made and had lovely detail work. The tables were another thing altogether. They had to go.

The styling of the desk was perfect but she wasn't sure if it needed refinishing. It was so covered with papers that Amanda couldn't really see the top. As she moved some flight plans he'd been working on to the side, she came across a letter from the lawyer who'd handled the prenuptial agreements for them.

"A hearing in the case of the adoption of Jesse Powers is set for 10:00 a.m. on August 19 before Master Fletcher." The sentence glared up from the page at her. *Adoption.* The word telegraphed itself painfully into Amanda's brain. Garth had started proceedings to adopt Jason.

Wouldn't that negate their previous agreement? That agreement he'd stated that he had no rights to Jason but that she was granting visitation rights. If he adopted Jason, that would give him the legal right to vie for custody in the event of a divorce. An event Garth had promised would happen.

All Amanda's old fears resurfaced. *Had* he married her to strengthen his claim to Jason as she'd originally thought? Had he just been trying to lull her into a false sense of security by not mentioning this adoption to her? She battled back the tears that flooded her eyes until she reached her room.

The constant uncertainty about her relationship with Garth had finally taken its toll. An overwhelming sense of fear and doom settled over her soul. Burying her face in her pillow, Amanda gave free rein to her tears.

When they were spent, anger began to replace the pain. She rolled to her feet and stalked to the phone. Garth, however, was already in the air. As she dropped the phone in the cradle, Amanda realized she had just almost done the exact thing to Garth that he had done to her over the medical expense refund.

Seconds later, Amanda found herself deep in prayer about her marriage and her unrequited love for her husband. Why was she married to a man who couldn't love her?

Because you didn't ask Him, a voice in her soul whispered. *You just went ahead and married Garth. You didn't give Him a chance to solve the problem. Now you live in fear and suffer the pain of being unsure of your husband.*

Amanda stayed in her room all day, feigning a splitting headache. Between bouts of tears, she prayed, asking forgiveness for not asking the Lord's direction about marrying Garth and for the wisdom to approach him in the right way about what she'd seen. She had to learn his true motives, yet not cause a rift between them if those motives were pure ones. She found no answer as to what she would do if they weren't. About Jason or her broken heart.

Garth tossed his jacket on the chair in his study and looked around. He noticed the notebook lying on the desk that Amanda used to record all the information on her decorating. Next to it was a tape measure. He picked up the book and found the page she'd labeled for his study still empty. She hadn't written anything on the page. Her headache must have come upon her just after he'd left for the office.

Worried, he went to her room and tapped lightly on the door so he wouldn't wake her if she was deeply asleep. When no answer came, Garth decided to just peek in to see if she was all right. But Amanda wasn't sleeping. She was sitting in a chair on the far side of the room. Even in the gloomy light he could see that she look terrible.

"Amanda?" he called. "Didn't you hear me knock?"

She looked up and nodded.

Alarmed by her puffy, red-rimmed eyes, he walked in and toward her. "What's wrong? You look as if you lost your last friend?"

"Leave me alone. Please. I'm fine. I just need time to sort out a few things."

Garth frowned. Sort out? What could she possibly need to sort out? He started to back out of the room but the sadness in her tone stopped him. If there was something he'd done to put that look of utter desolation on her face, he had to know. How could he make sure she was happy if he didn't know what made her *un*happy? "Maybe talking to someone would help. You know, put a fresh perspective on whatever it is you're wrestling with.''

"Actually, your perspective is all I guess I need. When I went to check your desk to see if the top needed refinishing, I saw a letter from your lawyer scheduling a hearing about your adoption of Jason. What adoption? We never discussed it. And why do you want to adopt him?''

Garth sighed. This is what he got for not being up front about all this. The problem was that he hadn't been able to decide how to approach her. He'd made up his mind to say something soon. Definitely in the next few days before he had to go out of town. "I was going to talk to you about this soon. It isn't something I'd even thought about but I should have. *We* should have.''

"We already made provisions for you to have visitation rights...ah...later...ah...after we—''

"But we're married now,'' Garth stressed, sick of thinking about that agreement. "And Jason's upset *now*.''

"Jason's upset? About what? He never told me he was worried about anything.''

"Confused is more like it,'' Garth explained, calmer now that he was able to focus on his son. He sat down on the bed opposite her chair so he could see her expression better. "He doesn't know what to call himself when he goes back to school.''

Now confusion clouded Amanda's eyes. "Call himself? We decided months ago he was Jason to all of us.''

"But legally he's Jesse Powers. He wants to be Jason Jorgensen the way he always has been. He's afraid the other kids will single him out even more if he comes back with a new name. If you'd looked further, you'd have seen a form to change his first name as well.''

Amanda didn't seem too angry when she asked, "Why didn't anyone discuss this with me? And if you're going to change his name for him why must you adopt him?''

"The form would only change his first name. He asked me

to adopt him, Amanda, and that would change his last name. I just didn't know how to ask you. But time was important since Jason was so upset about school and the confusion his new name would cause. He also said that since he was the only one in the house whose name was Powers that he didn't feel like part of the family. I figured that at least if the paperwork got started the school would object less to his keeping his name the same since legally it would be that way soon anyway.

"I hope you'll forgive me for not talking to you about this sooner. I really did intend to. I just kept putting it off. I got the ball rolling, figuring I'd come up with a way to bring this up without upsetting you. I'm sorry you were hurt, especially since that's what I was trying to avoid. If you object, I'll try to explain to Jason that you want him to keep his father's last name."

Amanda's lower lip quivered and she launched herself into his arms. "I don't care. You're his father. I forgot all about his name. It's okay. It's really okay." Garth held on to her tightly when she started to cry in earnest. Eventually, she quieted and he realized she was asleep. Careful not to wake her he tucked her in and sat down in the chair. What had he done or said that made her cry if she was truly okay about the adoption? One thing was certain, Amanda was insecure in her position in his life and it had made her unhappy. Maybe it was time he began to show her how he felt about her.

"Is it comfortable?"

Garth gave the recliner he'd just tested a wistful look. "But you said you wanted to stick to authentic furnishings."

Amanda blew her bangs off her forehead. And this man teased her for not understanding how airplanes fly! "Garth, the kitchen-family room addition is completely separate from the historical section of the house. It has French doors to a deck for heaven's sake. They did not have decks during the Revolutionary War."

"Or refrigerators or dishwashers," Garth added, catching on, she hoped.

"Exactly. We'll just decorate that part of the house and, of course, the bathrooms with a colonial flavor. That's what I did in the kitchen."

Garth seemed to consider this. "So, I can have the recliner but not that entertainment center I liked?" He grinned and she knew he planned to tease her about something. She'd seen that look on his handsome face too often not to recognize it. "Amanda, this may come as a shock to you," he continued setting her up she was sure, "but, there weren't any electronics around then, either."

"Very funny. Do you understand why we can't buy that entertainment center?"

He shook his head. "Not really. It was oak. They used oak for furniture back then."

"Arrgghh! The entertainment center you liked was too modern looking. Think of the hours someone would have needed to spend planing and sanding all those rounded edges." She took his hand and dragged him over to the sofa they'd already decided on. She flipped through the swatches of available fabrics. "See this fabric? We cover that chair in this fabric and it gives it the right flavor just the way it does for this traditional sofa."

"But what do we do about the TV, stereo and VCR?"

Amanda smiled, seeing her own opportunity to tease him. "Well, we could upholster them." At his look of horror she laughed. "But I have a better idea. I found something. It's an antique armoire. I thought if you like it, we could have Mr. O'Brien put shelving in it."

"That way we hide all the electronics."

"By George, I think he's got it!" Amanda exclaimed.

Garth chuckled and leaned down to kiss her in full view of the other store patrons. It was a lingering kiss—an arms-wrapped-around-her kiss—and it had a powerful effect on Amanda's emotions and senses.

"Let's go look at the bedroom furniture next," he said after lifting his lips from hers. The tone in his voice betrayed the effect the kiss had on him as well.

Dazed, Amanda let him take her hand and lead her to the salesman. Garth confused her more and more each day. What did he want from her? If he wanted what she thought he did when he kissed her like that, then why did he hold himself back? She had sent him every kind of signal she could think of to let him know that his attentions were welcomed but he'd always frowned and backed off. Way off.

At least until yesterday, she realized. He'd been away for a week. Did absence really make the heart grow fonder? she wondered. Amanda didn't think so. Their lack of contact while their work schedules kept them apart had done just the opposite. Was this sudden change she saw only gratitude for her work on the kitchen? Yesterday he had kissed her and had remained sweetly affectionate all afternoon and evening. But they'd still gone to separate rooms at day's end.

She looked up at him as he chatted with the salesman. He glanced at her, his eyes still warm as he smiled and gave her hand, the one he hadn't let go of, a squeeze. He sure hadn't backed away this time. *Please, Lord, don't let this be just gratitude.*

Two more weeks went by. Two weeks of warm, firm hugs. Two weeks of spicy, spontaneous kisses and hand holding. Two weeks of growing affection and attraction. The violets arrived just as Amanda put the final touches on the newly finished master suite. Frieda brought them to her and gave her a sly smile as she left.

The note read: "Violets to match your eyes. Have dinner with me. Just me. Pick you up in the family room at seven. A real date. G."

Amanda looked around the room and smiled. One mystery solved. At least she hoped so. Garth had gone along with any suggestion she'd made while they worked together to plan the house. Except one. The violets also matched the bedroom wallpaper Garth had stubbornly insisted upon. Amanda sniffed the nosegay in her hand. Not much aroma but so very sweet, nonetheless.

"You look beautiful," Garth said as he stood when Amanda came into the family room.

"Wow, Mom! Be careful not to spill anything on that dress. It's real fancy!" Jason added from his place on the floor. "And you know how messy spaghetti is."

Amanda glanced down at her royal blue dress. She'd bought it weeks ago but had never worn it, embarrassed by its soft, flowing, romantic style in the face of her platonic relationship with her husband. She tilted her head and considered Garth for a long moment. "Thank you. Both," she added with a smile for the two men in her life.

Garth swallowed with difficulty as he walked toward Amanda.

She looked up at him, her violet eyes sparkling and said, "You look very handsome, yourself."

And Garth breathed a mental sigh of relief. It was the first time she'd seen him in a suit and tie since the wedding. He wasn't really a suit-and-tie kind of guy. He'd worn uniforms for so many years that he was always unsure what tie went with what. He was also more nervous tonight than he had been the night of his first date, so it was good knowing he hadn't made a fashion faux pas with a navy suit, navy-and-white striped shirt and a paisley tie.

"I still don't see why I can't come," Jason grumbled. "I'm always good in restaurants. You both always say so. And I'd try to be neat and I wouldn't even ask for dessert."

"Not tonight, Jase," Garth said, never taking his eyes off Amanda. "Tonight's just for grown-ups." He leaned down and kissed her without thinking.

"Oh, yuck. Are you two going to start getting mushy like Todd's parents? I told him I didn't have to put up with this!"

Amanda giggled in the back of her throat and Garth lifted his head to glance at his son. He couldn't help but grin at the horrified expression on Jason's face. He treasured this kid more than life itself, but Jason was murder on a romantic moment.

"And that attitude, young man, is precisely why tonight is for grown-ups only. Now, give us a kiss good-night and we'll see you in the morning."

After they got in the car and Garth started down the drive Amanda glanced back at the figure waving furiously from the living room window. "He was really disappointed not to be coming with us. Do you suppose we—"

"No. We shouldn't." Garth didn't slow the car a bit. "All parents leave their children with sitters. Mom isn't even that. She's part of the family. He didn't care a bit about our plans until he found out that we were going to the Casa Roma. The kid's not part Italian is he?"

"Nope, just French," Amanda said, then laughed. "All Cajun French except for maybe an Indian maiden way back."

Garth shook his head and pulled to a stop at a red light. "Weird. I look enough like Jess Powers to be his double but we don't even have nationality in common."

She looked at him, suddenly serious. "You have nothing at all in common with Jess except your looks," she said quietly.

Garth's heart suddenly thundered in his chest. He stared at Amanda, her face illuminated by a nearby streetlight. He really thought he saw love in her eyes. He wanted to trust that love existed all of a sudden. That love didn't hurt. "That's the nicest thing you've ever said to me. I know he hurt you, Mandy. I want to make you happy. I want that more than my next breath. I—"

The blare of a horn made them both jump.

"The light's green," Amanda said, having glanced forward when he looked behind to see why the guy behind had leaned on his horn.

Muttering about lousy timing, Garth drove through the intersection and on to the exclusive Casa Roma. Reservations being what they were at the posh new Main Line restaurant, they were seated immediately at a table screened off by lattice and greenery. Garth had stopped by earlier in the week and had asked for this specific table. He'd left nothing to chance about this entire night. He put his hand in his pocket, anxiously feeling for the small, velvet jeweler's case. She had to say yes. If she didn't, he was afraid he'd disgrace himself and cry like a baby, which was another reason he'd wanted so private a setting.

"Garth, this is lovely. I'd heard about this place but never imagined it could be this perfect," Amanda said. "Thank you for bringing me here."

"No. Thank you."

Amanda's smile faltered. "Thank…me?"

Garth didn't know what he'd said wrong but she'd looked stricken for a few seconds before stiffening her spine and trying to achieve the same smile once again. This one was a poor imitation.

He took her hand and kissed her knuckles. Her hands weren't as soft as they'd once been, a testament to all her work. Work? "Mandy, not thank you for all you've done at the house. Although we all appreciate what you've done. To be honest, the inside of the place always made me feel like a fish out of water, but that's not what tonight's about. I meant thank you for coming into my life and making what I thought was a full life so much better.

"I know, I'm lousy at this," he groaned. "It still sounds like…gratitude, doesn't it?"

She nodded, but a little smile played at the corners of her mouth.

"It's not. I…" The words *I love you* seemed forever buried so deep within himself that he couldn't find them for anyone, even Jason. He reached for them but came up with, "I don't want to lose you."

"I'm not going anywhere," she assured him.

But Garth was far from assured. And he wanted—no needed—her assurance that she would always be there, so this time he reached for the diamond wedding band he'd had made. It would replace the one that had been his grandmother's—the one given as part of that unholy bargain they'd made to keep Jason's health on an even footing. The one that meant a possible end to the first real happiness he'd ever known.

"Promise me," he said and handed her the box. "Marry me. Be my wife. Forever. For real, Mandy. Not just Jason's mother but my wife. Lie in my arms at night and smile at me in the mornings. Be there to make coming home after work special. Look at me when Jason's friends leave after a weekend and smile because we're tired and we're still together."

Amanda bit her lip against a rush of tears. This was so much more than she'd thought possible the first time marriage between them came up. And so much less than she'd hoped for because now that she loved him so deeply, she'd hoped for his love in return. But if not love, what was it in his eyes? It didn't matter, she told herself stoically. This was enough. It had to be.

"Garth, I already did promise. You would have needed to tell me to go because I will never leave you."

His eyes narrowed. "Chris said that but we haven't slept—"

"That's not the point. I made you a promise before God in that chapel. I always intended to keep it. No matter what. Even if you asked for the divorce, I would have been your wife in my heart on the day I died."

"So, you'll stay because of your vows," he said, his jaw tight.

Amanda looked down at the box he'd pressed into her hand. She'd mentioned God and now she could feel his anger building a wall between them. Needing a distraction, she opened the box. She didn't even try to stifle her gasp of delight. Nestled on a bed of white satin was a diamond wedding band, each small setting a copy of the one on her engagement ring. She looked up and saw pain in his eyes instead of anger.

Putting the ring on to the first knuckle, Amanda whispered, "In the beginning that was true. But that isn't the reason anymore." She extended her left hand and he took her hand but lowered his eyes, hiding his feelings. Amanda pressed on anyway. It did no good for her to hold back words that had never hurt her the way they had Garth. Maybe if he heard them enough he'd believe them. "I'll stay because of you. Because of the man you are. Because of the husband I know you can be. I'll stay because I don't know if I could leave you now even if you asked me to. I need to be with you, Garth. You're already my husband—in my heart as well as on paper. I love you."

Garth didn't say anything. She told herself it didn't matter. He just pushed the ring gently the rest of the way onto her finger to nestle it next to the other two he'd already given her. He looked up then, longing and frustration roiling in his eyes. It was as if he wanted to say he loved her, too, but couldn't get the words out. She knew instinctively that when he finally said, "I need to hold you," it was far less than he wanted to say but true nonetheless. He stood without letting go of her hand. "Dance with me."

Amanda smiled as a quartet began to play somewhere in the room. "My, you did have tonight planned. Music on cue. Imagine that."

Garth chuckled and pulled her to her feet, gesturing behind her. "They'd just picked up their instruments. My timing doesn't seem to be bad tonight after all."

When they reached the dance floor, Garth tugged her close and Amanda went willingly, closing her eyes and resting her cheek on his shoulder. It felt so good to be in his strong arms, knowing he was hers. Knowing that there wouldn't be a divorce. If she didn't have his love yet, she had hope that someday she would. There was all the time in the world.

They danced several numbers in a row when Garth whispered. "I need to hold you."

She looked up into his molten gaze. "You already are."

He shook his head. "Not like this. I need more, Mandy. I need you. Tonight. Every night."

"Me too," she said, her throat tight with emotion. "But Jason's still up. We'd have to explain why we're home so early."

Garth grimaced then sighed. "Maybe we'd better eat something. Dance a little more. Something—anything to kill time.

He'll be up for at least two more hours." He kissed the knuckle where his rings rested. "I know it sounds selfish but I want this to be just about us."

And it was. Just about them. For the rest of the night and into the early morning hours. It was about them and a union the Lord had blessed months earlier.

Amanda's prayers were answered.

She was Garth's wife.

Amanda woke to the sound of Jason's running feet and her name bouncing off the wall of the hall.

"Mom!" Door open. Door slam. "Mom!" Feet pounding to the top of the stairs. "Grandmom! I can't find Mom!"

"So much for discreetly taking my mother aside and explaining the change in...our uh..."

She giggled at his hesitancy. "How about we just say our relationship?"

Garth cleared his throat. "Good word," he said.

Amanda rolled over. "You're blushing!"

"Amanda, I do not—"

"Dad, I can't find Mom!" Jason called as he threw open the door and burst into the room with a full head of steam. His eyes widened. "Dad, how come your face is so red? Oh, Mom, there you are." He ran and dove between them on the bed. "You promised me pancakes for breakfast. It's past ten! Grandmom said not to keep looking for you but, Mom! She's threatening to make them herself. You've got to get up!"

"Threatening? Don't you mean offering," Amanda reproved.

Jason shook his head fiercely.

"Burned on one side—raw on the other," Garth muttered. "In defense of our son, Mandy, he means threatened."

"Okay, go tell Grandmom I'm on my way down."

"Hold on right there, son. We need a new rule here."

Jason wrinkled his nose. "Another rule?"

"Yes. Another rule. An important one. Now that this room's been redone, your mother is going to share it with me. You are never to barge in here like that again."

"Why?" Jason asked. "I always have."

Garth searched for the right words. Did this parenting thing never get any easier? "I wasn't always married, son. You're old enough to understand that your mother needs her privacy. Like Grandmom."

"Why?"

Amanda chuckled.

"Let me put it to you this way," Garth said with a glance at Amanda. "Would you like Debbie Culver walking in on you when you're in the bathtub?"

Jason blushed. "No! Oh! I get it! Okay, I'll knock."

"*And* wait for permission to come in. Got it?"

"Wait for permission," Jason said and nodded. "Got it."

"Good," Garth replied, then gave Jason a light, playful smack on his backside. "Now beat it so we can get dressed." Jason bounded off the bed and sailed out the door. "And get dressed yourself," Garth called after the retreating figure who'd forgotten to close the door behind him.

An hour later Jason ran out the back door with Buster tripping over his own paws as he followed. They watched from the window over the sink as Jason attempted to teach the puppy the rudiments of fetching. Amanda sighed wistfully and nestled her head on Garth's shoulder, her arms wrapped around his waist. He smiled and dropped his cheek on to her soft hair, hugging her back.

"He looks better and better each day," she said. "It's great having him here with me but I can't wait till he can go to school like a regular kid."

"But for now he is here. Almost all the time. And this isn't going to work."

"What's not going to work?" she asked, her voice suddenly wobbly and tinged with fear.

Garth cringed. *Open mouth—insert foot, Jorgensen.* He tipped her chin up and kissed her forehead. "I meant what I said about us last night and nothing's going to change that. What I meant was that just now us being here with Jase and

Mom isn't good. We need time alone, Mandy. Just you and me. We need that honeymoon we never had and now's the perfect time."

"Go away? But what about Jason?"

He tipped her chin up farther so he could see her beautiful eyes. "Jason'll be fine. You said it yourself. He gets better and better each day. He's cured. I can feel it." He smiled at the thought.

"But—"

"My mother's here. Chris can stay here while we're gone to help out in the evenings. It isn't as if that isn't a familiar routine for him and it doesn't have to be for long. Just a few days."

"But the house and—"

"The house will be here when we get back and you can decorate to your little heart's content."

"What about Liberty Express?"

"It's been two years since I took a real vacation. The other pilots will be thrilled to take my hours. I've done it for them enough times."

"But you always say it isn't good business to have a plane sit idle. That's why you hired that temporary extra guy when Jason was so sick."

"It won't be idle. We'll be using it."

Amanda swallowed with obvious difficulty. "Using it?" she squeaked.

Garth chuckled. "If I didn't know better, Mrs. Jorgensen, I'd say you didn't trust my flying."

"Oh, no. It's just that the plane you brought me here in was so small. And bumpy. And noisy."

"And safe and convenient. No schedule to keep but our own. No annoying airport security to get past. No lines. No flights delayed for a dozen stupid reasons."

Amanda raised her eyebrows. "My, you do hate to fly commercial, don't you?" she teased.

"I wanted it to be just us but if my plane really scares you we'll fly commercial."

"No," she laughed. "Alone's just too tempting to resist. Besides, I trust you. Jason assures me you're the best pilot in the whole wide world. Where would we go?"

"I was thinking sort of a short tour. Maybe start out with Niagara Falls for a couple of days. Then a friend of mine has a resort in the Catskills. Riding, swimming, tennis. That sort of thing. It's on Hunter Mountain. Real pretty country. Come on, Mandy. It wouldn't even be for a full week. We have to be back for the hearing on the nineteenth. How about it?"

"It sounds wonderful. When would we leave?"

"It'll take a couple of days to arrange everything at work and make reservations. I'd need to file a flight plan, too. Then we'll be all set."

Amanda threw her arms around Garth's neck and pulled his head down for a kiss. He closed his eyes willing the rest of the world away.

"Oh, excuse me," his mother said as she quickly backed out of the room.

Garth groaned and opened his eyes. Amanda winked and chuckled. "Maybe you could make those arrangements in one day?"

Chapter Thirteen

Amanda glanced at her suitcase where it rested by the door. She was all packed and ready for their honeymoon trip. And so excited she felt like a kid on her way to Disney World instead of a thirty-something woman on her way to Niagara Falls.

They'd leave after lunch but first there was church.

Normally Amanda looked forward to those couple of hours on Sunday morning. They rejuvenated her and washed away the hassles of the week. But today she felt as if she were leaving a part of herself behind. Garth.

After checking her hair in the mirror one last time, Amanda turned to follow Frieda and Jason to the car. But as she passed the stairs she stopped. Once again her thoughts turned to Garth. How did he while away the time when the rest of them were at church? What was he doing and what was he thinking right now? From experience, she knew he wasn't getting ready to go with them.

As usual he'd made himself scarce after breakfast, avoiding the inevitable questions from Jason and invitations from her and his mother. Fighting the melancholy feeling that had come over her, Amanda forced herself to move forward. She needed this even if Garth refused to realize that he did, too.

Garth pushed aside the drop cloth that hung over the window in the empty front bedroom. He watched, his fist clenched, as

Amanda backed down the driveway. The car hesitated for a long moment then slowly drove away.

He threw the cloth back into place. Why couldn't she have given up church to be with him for just this week? This was supposed to be the day they started their honeymoon. Why couldn't she have wanted to be with him more than her God?

He guessed that was what he'd always wanted. Someone who put him before everything and everyone else. Someone who would count on him for everything. But she couldn't count on him for everything the way she counted on God. He remembered that bleak look in her eyes when he excused himself from the breakfast table—a tacit refusal to accompany her to church. Garth wanted more than anything to make Amanda happy and more often than not he made her miserable.

He couldn't protect her or Jason the way God could, either. Jason had gotten sick while under Garth's protection. Sure, God hadn't protected him then, either, but Amanda had said God would use all that pain and anguish for good. She'd said that He had a plan. And He obviously had since it really was Jason's illness that had brought Amanda to them.

Was she right? Could it all be that simple? He sighed, remembering a time when he'd believed it was.

Now with the future looming on the horizon, he had to wonder about a lot of things. Like what made him think he'd be able to do any better in the future than he had in the past? Garth raked his unsteady hand through his hair. The answer scared the life out of him. He just didn't see how he could go it alone anymore.

If only Amanda were there to tell him that he'd do fine. Anger flared in his heart once again. He needed her! Why couldn't she have stayed home?

What stopped you from going with her? Pride? Because you said you didn't need her fairy tales and crutches? You wanted to go it alone. Why start whining about how hard it is now?

"Because it doesn't have to be this way!" Garth shouted at the voice that had been whispering to him from a distant corner of his mind for years. His voice echoed in the empty room—in the deserted house. And this time he listened.

It didn't have to be this way. It didn't!

He could go back to the one source of strength that had never failed him. Things might not have been easy when he was young but he'd always had his faith to bolster him even in the roughest of times. Even when he'd learned his father's plans to get rid of his wife and take a new one.

Garth slid down the wall to the floor, momentarily shocked. But then he thought back to the night he'd chucked it all and turned his back on his faith and his Lord. It *hadn't* happened when he'd stood in the hall outside his father's study. Somehow through the years he'd convinced himself and everyone else that it had been.

But it hadn't.

No, it had been after the meeting with the pastor when he'd told him what he'd learned. He hadn't gone to the man because he wanted to protect his church from scandal and disgrace. He'd gone there with a spirit of revenge in his heart against his father. His father had betrayed them all and had to pay with the one and only thing that had ever mattered to him. He had to lose his church.

After he'd told his tale, Garth had felt ashamed. He'd rushed to judgment, and committed his own sin of seeking vengeance. Then anger had taken hold of his young heart. He had all the guilt and his father expressed nothing but anger at him for his betrayal. And then Garth's anger had exploded. He'd turned his back on God the same way his father had turned his back on his family.

And that was why he was still angry. His father had sought forgiveness and been granted it. Garth had never admitted that he'd been wrong. In deed and in motivation. He should have let his parents deal with their own marital problems. But he hadn't and for all that he'd never sought forgiveness and so he still felt guilty—and angry. In fact, Garth realized with yet another pang of guilt, in going to the pastor and shutting his father out, he had been guilty of the same sort of pride and perfectionism his father had always shown toward him.

Garth dropped his head back against the wall and closed his eyes.

Amanda's drive to the small stone church that sat nestled in a wooded area took only a few minutes but today she felt as if she'd driven miles. She felt so far away from Garth. Probably because they'd scarcely been out of each other's sight since he had taken her to Casa Roma the other night. If only he'd come with them today, she thought, as she slid into the pew after chatting with several of the other parishioners.

Lost in thought and prayer, Amanda automatically opened her mouth to sing along with the choir when the music started. But the joyful noise she'd intended to sing unto the Lord turned into a gasp when a beautiful, clear, tenor voice next to her sang the opening words of ''Amazing Grace.''

Though Amanda had never heard Garth sing, she knew instantly that it was his voice raised in praise. She pivoted and stared up at him. He stood in the aisle, singing from memory. Tears of joy clogged Amanda's throat and blurred his beautiful smile, but her ears still worked just fine and it was plain that Garth meant each word. How or why he was there, she didn't know.

But she rejoiced.

He leaned down and kissed her cheek and settled his arm around her when the pastor took his place at the podium and dismissed the children to their classes. Curiosity and overwhelming joy all but obliterated the message for her, though Garth seemed intent on the lesson. Finally the congregation rose as one to sing the final song of the service.

''How? What happened?'' she asked as soon as the pastor disappeared up the aisle to greet his parishioners as they filed out.

Garth shrugged. ''I felt left out. I missed you after you drove away and I was angry that I was alone. I started to worry about you and Jase. I felt weak and afraid of the future. Afraid I'd fail you both. I needed to hear you telling me I was doing okay by you and Jason. I needed you and I was furious that you weren't there.''

"But you knew you were welcome, didn't you?" Amanda said, worried that she'd somehow failed him when he'd needed her.

"I knew. I was just plain stubborn. Then this morning I suddenly realized that it was me who'd stayed home. It was me who'd cut himself off from all this. The joy. The comfort. The forgiveness. A part of you. This part of you. And Him."

Amanda reached up to lay her palm on his cheek. "Oh, Garth, I'm so glad you finally understand."

Garth took her hand in his. "It may take a while to work it all out. I'm carrying a lot of baggage because of my father that I've never dealt with. But at least I can admit it now. I see it for what it is and I see that he was just a man. Imperfect. Flawed. Not an angel or a god. And his mistakes were his, not God's. Not mine."

"And now we can share everything," Amanda whispered.

"Even eternity," Frieda said and held out her arms to her son, tears rolling down her wrinkled cheeks. "Welcome home, son. Welcome home."

Five days later Amanda thought back to the scene in the church as she watched the trees fly by beneath them. She and Garth were returning from their honeymoon. Their wonderful honeymoon that had started last Sunday in church. Closing her eyes she shut out the view of the trees remembering how the pastor had returned to where she and Garth stood and presented him with a Bible. He'd been saving it, he'd said. The man had known Garth's father, had been with him at his death. Edward Jorgensen had sent his son a message to be delivered when he was ready to hear it. The pastor decided then was a good time.

Amanda still reserved judgment on that one.

She knew it had shaken Garth's fledgling faith but only for a couple of seconds. Garth had done the right thing in going to their pastor, his father had said. There were no hard feelings.

That was it. He hadn't asked for forgiveness for all the pain he'd caused. He hadn't said he was proud of Garth or his accomplishments.

But Garth had nodded after a few heartbeats and held her against his side, obviously feeling her reaction. "It's okay. It doesn't matter that he didn't ask my forgiveness. It just matters that I'm forgiven," he'd whispered and she'd heard the amazement in his voice.

Amanda's first thought had been that she wanted to hurt Garth's father posthumously until she saw that it really didn't matter to Garth. But it made her more aware than ever that sometimes being a Christian was a tough road to follow and that no one succeeded all the time. Especially not her.

And speaking of roads, she thought now, there were none below them. Only millions of acres of trees. "We're really in the wilderness, aren't we?"

"Yeah, this section of the Catskills is pretty sparsely populated. In the winter, skiers flock up here but at this time of the year, before the color really blooms, it's pretty much just the locals."

"I meant that I haven't seen a road in an awfully long time."

Garth chuckled. "The roads are there. They're hidden by the trees. I could look for an interstate if it would improve the scenery for you."

"But if you had to land..."

"This King Air is Liberty's newest plane, Mandy. I had it gone over nose to tail by the best mechanic around before we took off. Relax."

"I am. Really," she lied. She knew that quake in her voice gave her away so she changed the subject a bit. "I still feel guilty that you took a plane this big out of service just because the Piper scared me when you flew us to Philadelphia. You should have just used that one."

"I wasn't having you trembling in your seat the whole trip, sweetheart. It wouldn't have been fair. This is supposed to be fun.'' Garth reached over and gave her hand a quick squeeze before returning it to the yoke. Where she wanted it anyway!

"Still, those twenty-five seats sitting empty back there make me feel guilty.''

Garth flashed her a crooked grin. "It would have been worth it if the bigger plane had given you a bit more confidence in my flying.''

"It isn't your flying ability that worries me. It's Newton and Murphy's laws that keep me on edge.'' Amanda forced a smile. She was only half joking but he didn't need to know that!

Garth raised an eyebrow. "Newton and Murphy?''

"Sure.'' Amanda shot him a wry smirk. "What goes up must come down? If anything can go wrong it will go wrong?''

"Mandy, nothing's going to go wrong,'' he promised. Then, after reaching to flip a switch on the control panel, he twisted to face her, leaning negligently on the arm of his seat. "So, what was your favorite part of Niagara Falls?''

Amanda's eyes strayed to the now guideless yoke. Garth reached out and took her chin. "Look at me. It's on autopilot. This is called changing the subject. Now, what was your favorite part?''

"How do you pick a favorite part of a dream come true?'' she answered, unable to look away from his compelling gaze. "I guess Monday afternoon and the picnic in the state forest.'' For Amanda, having Garth whisper that he wanted her to have his baby almost made her most fervent dream come true. The only thing that could have made that moment more perfect would have been hearing the words "I love you'' whispered as well. Someday, she told herself once again.

Someday.

He leaned forward and closed the gap between them, joining his lips to hers in a fleeting kiss. "Mine was the nights,'' he whispered from inches away. "Scenery and hiking and picnics could never compare to holding you in my arms.''

Amanda didn't bother to correct his misconception. "I'll

never forget the nights, either. Do you think one of those nights will give you your wish?''

"Wish?''

Amanda nodded. ''The wish you made on the picnic.''

She watched as the memory of his picnic wish surfaced. He grinned. ''If not we'll just keep trying.''

''Mmm-hmm,'' Amanda agreed, leaning back in her seat and closing her eyes. ''That sounds like a plan, thought I doubt it will be necessary. I have a feeling Jason's going to have a brother or sister in the spring,'' she said, opening her eyes, not wanting to miss his reaction.

Joy then tenderness stole over Garth's features. ''Really?''

Amanda nodded.

''How can you know so soon?''

''I'm so tired I can hardly keep my eyes open and I've only been awake for what? Five or six hours? This is just the way I was within days of conceiving Jason.''

''Wow,'' he said, his tone more reflective than excited. ''Think Jason will be pleased?''

''I hope so,'' she said, unable to keep the wistfulness out of her voice.

''Miss him?'' Garth asked.

Amanda turned her head and opened her eyes again. He looked rather jaunty in his flight jacket, Liberty Express baseball cap tipped back on his head and wearing those official-looking headphones. ''Not as much as I'd have missed these last days with you. Thanks for insisting. We really did need this.''

''Why don't you try to get some sleep?'' Garth looked at Amanda, smiled and then winked. ''You might be sleeping for two now.''

After settling back and closing her eyes again, Amanda muttered, ''You just want me unconscious so I'll stop twitching at every noise.'' Garth's chuckle was the last thing she heard before she drifted into sleep.

Amanda's nap ended with a crash the likes of which she'd never heard. She catapulted upright, her heart pounding. The plane dipped sharply then bounced back up—hard. Amanda felt as if her stomach were still in free fall. Her next confused perception was that night had fallen around them suddenly but there was too much ambient light for that. The plane was vibrating like a car being driven along railroad tracks. She could see Garth's hands gripping the yoke in what looked like a life-and-death struggle.

She looked at his face. The look of strain carved there was answer enough to her unasked question. It was a life-and-death struggle. Then Garth's gaze met hers.

"Don't fall apart on me, Mandy. I need your help." Once again the plane shook, buffeted by surging winds. "I can't take my hands off the yoke."

"What happened to that autopilot thing?"

"Not working—like a lot of the other systems. I need you to put your hand on one of the knobs on the control panel. Okay. Now, move it over two to your left."

The plane dropped altitude suddenly, leaving Amanda's stomach what felt like a hundred feet above them. Once again, Garth fought for and gained control of the rocking craft as thunder and lightning crashed around them.

"Did I do that? I swear I didn't touch anything."

"It was the wind. It's okay," he said as the plane evened out again. He glanced back at her hand. "That knob only sets the radio frequency. Turn it to 121.5. That'll put us on the emergency band. Good. Now move your hand down one and to your right. Turn that one to 7700. Right. That puts the transponder on an emergency setting. They'll be able to zero in on us on their radar screen when I raise a tower. Say a prayer there's one not too far away. This bird's in sad shape."

"That's so they can find us, right? Are we lost? Don't you know where we are?"

"With my instruments out I can't pinpoint our location exactly but I've got a good idea." He sounded so confident that she almost missed the slight inflection in his tone.

"Where are we?" she asked, dreading what she guessed might be a vague answer.

Garth grimaced. "Somewhere over the Poconos."

Amanda sighed. "What happened?"

"A thunderstorm came from nowhere. Nobody was reporting it. Lightning hit the starboard engine. Now sit back and get your head against the headrest. And Mandy, I meant what I said about praying. I don't want to lie to you. We're in real trouble here and I'm going to have to concentrate on flying."

Then in a controlled voice Garth spoke into the headset he wore. "Mayday. Mayday. This is LIB 7985. Anyone within range come in, please."

He sat a bit straighter. "Canadensis tower. This is LIB 7985. I'm experiencing what looks like a total electric failure after a lightning strike," he answered what must be a voice coming through his earphones.

"A Beech King Air.... It hit the starboard engine.... I've been losing oil pressure and fuel ever since.... It's still up and running rough. I can't be sure for how long.... One passenger. My wife. Have you picked up my transponder reading...? Roger. Changing course to those coordinates."

Amanda released the death grip she had on the arm of her seat to touch his arm. "What?"

"The electrical system's acting up. So's the engine that was hit."

"I heard. It sounds like a big problem."

"The electric is the real trouble. Not too much works right without it. Like the autopilot. But we got lucky. There's an airfield only about fifteen minutes to the southwest. We'll be landing there." Garth immediately made the course correction he needed to put them back on course. The plane banked. Not smoothly, but he did seem to get it to do what was necessary.

Amanda could feel perspiration bead on her scalp. Her fingers were already numb from the tight grip she kept on the arms of her seat. She marveled at how calm and competent he was. "Are we going to crash?" she asked, her voice nowhere near as steady as Garth's.

"Not if I can help it. I've got too much to live for and so do you. We just found each other and Jason needs us. And there's that baby you seem so sure we'll be having in the spring." He looked away and she could see the muscles of his jaw tighten as if he were fighting for control.

He glanced back at her, his eyes misty. "Amanda, I'm going to need more help. Do you remember asking me what that crank in the back of the plane is for?"

"You said it was the manual crank for the landing gear."

"Yeah. I need you to go back and turn it as far as you can. As hard as you can. Can you do that?"

"You also said you'd never used it."

Garth's grin was as easygoing as she knew he could make it. "Well, there's a first time for everything, sweetheart."

Amanda twisted in her seat and stared backward down what she'd thought of as a short aisle earlier. Then the plane pitched to the side and lost altitude. She sat frozen. How was she going to get there? What if she wasn't strong enough to crank down the landing gear?

"I can't leave the controls, Mandy, and that gear won't come down automatically with the electric system off-line. Come on. You can do it. Undo your safety belt. Get down on the floor. I want you to crawl back. I don't want you falling and hurting yourself. This is about as steady as I can hold her."

Garth didn't add that injured or unconscious she'd be little help to them and he didn't relish landing with no chance that the gear was down. As it was, with no indicator lights to show that the gear had locked, they could only hope and pray that it did. "Remember, turn it as far and as hard as you can."

Three minutes went by in agonizing slowness for Garth as he took instructions from the tower and Amanda crawled to do her best with the crank. The control tower had called out emergency equipment but that didn't give him much confidence. This wasn't Philly International's tower he was linked up with.

It was a small backwater airport. He was lucky they had radar. He'd flown in and out of there several times. Their tower was two stories tall and the emergency team consisted of gas station attendants, a café waitress and a cook who'd been a medic in the marines.

Once again, a sudden wind shear tossed them around like a feather in a wind tunnel. A crash and a screech at the back of the plane nearly had him abandoning the controls. "Amanda!"

"I'm okay. A little bruised but I'll live," she called. "I think I got the gear down. The latch on the door to the rest room came loose and hit my head."

Garth didn't miss the irony in her voice when she said that she'd live. She *had* to live through this. Even if he didn't. "Then belt yourself in back there," he called.

"But I want to be with you," she shouted back.

"It's safer back there, sweetheart."

About a minute later, there was a shuffling next to him as Amanda wiggled back up into her seat from the floor. "But I want to be with you," she repeated. "Garth, if the landing gear is down, why didn't those three red lights turn green the way you showed me when we landed in New York?"

"Because the electrical system's out." Amanda held his gaze and somehow with just her eyes, she forced him to tell her the rest. "We can't know if it locked, Mandy."

"Until it does or doesn't collapse?" He nodded. "I'm scared, Garth. If we don't make it, what's going to happen to Jason?"

The starboard engine choked just then causing the plane to falter even more. Garth fought for control then feathered the engine. The plane dropped a bit more altitude but that was okay. He'd be taking her down soon anyway. For good or bad. This ride was almost over. He glanced at Amanda. Pale, frightened and thinking of Jason. She'd been cheated of so much.

Please, dear God, don't let her be cheated of seeing Jason grow. Don't cheat her of having our baby. Give me the strength and wisdom to do this right. Lock that landing gear.

''Nothing bad's going to happen to Jason because nothing's going to happen to us. God didn't bring us together just to take us away from Jason. I've been in tougher spots than this and lived to tell the tale.''

But never with the woman you love—the mother of your son—sitting next to you, he thought. He looked at her long and hard, memorizing each feature in case memories had to last an eternity.

The woman he loved.

And are you ever going to get up the guts to tell her how you feel? It's only a little word. And it'd mean so much to her. Are you going to cheat her of hearing you say it? One or both of you could die and you'll never have said it. She'd never know, he chastised himself silently.

''Amanda, there's something I have to tell you before I take us in for a landing. It's not the best setting or circumstance. I can't even hold your hand let alone hold you in my arms the way I want to but I think it had better be now, sweetheart. I—I love you. I love you with all my heart. I'm sorry I never told you how I felt before, but the word wouldn't come. It was thrown back in my face so often as a kid that I swore never to say it again. Then even when I wanted to, I couldn't. I didn't mean to hurt you.''

Amanda's smile was gentle as she blinked back tears. ''I was hurt, but it doesn't matter because I love you. All that matters is that you do.''

Garth's attention was snatched away just then. The tower had a visual sighting on them and started giving runway and special emergency instructions. The blue lights of the runway came into sight for him as well. Garth braced the yoke with his knees and took a second to give Amanda's cold hand a squeeze. ''Okay, sweetheart, here we go. Put your head down on your knees and lock your hands behind your head. Pray real hard, Mandy, I want a hug and kiss when this is all over.''

Garth lined them up and started the rocky descent. *Hold us up, Lord. And set us down easy,* he prayed.

After all the fear and worry, Amanda nearly laughed at how perfect the landing went. When she felt the plane roll to a stop, she would have laughed. She really would have, but she was too busy shedding tears of joy in Garth's loving arms.

Epilogue

Garth ran through the hospital lobby and dove for the call button at the middle of the bank of elevators. He bumped into an older man who had approached from the other direction. "Sorry," Garth said, then turned to the controls and repeatedly stabbed it. "Come on. Come on."

"In sort of a hurry, son?"

"Yeah. My baby's having my wife! Three weeks early!" Garth exclaimed and stabbed the call button again. "Why isn't this elevator coming?"

"Don't say?" The old man chuckled, raising one of his thick gray eyebrows. "Sort of nervous, too. This your first?"

Garth shook his head. "Fourth. Well, third really. I wasn't around for the first. Sometimes I'm almost glad I wasn't. My wife's afraid of needles. Has them natural. It's awful. She needs me." He stabbed at the button again then again when it refused to stay lit.

"Ah, son. The elevator's here. You'll want to be getting on, won't you?"

Garth turned toward the old man's voice and rushed into the elevator, stabbing the number five on the control panel. "Bye and thanks," he shouted over his shoulder seconds later when the elevator doors slid open and he charged out. Jason was there to greet him.

"Mom's fine. So's the baby. But you better get in there," he said directing Garth toward Amanda's labor room at a fast clip. "Doc Hernandez was by a few minutes ago and said it won't be much longer."

"If you're here, who's with Ian and Patrick?" Garth asked.

"Grandmom, Aunt Chris and the terrors are in the waiting room. We've got everything under control. You go take care of Mom," his son ordered. "And give her my love."

Garth nodded and entered the room where their child would be born—three weeks early. Amanda looked toward him and smiled. It was one of her brave, I'm-in-pain-but-okay smiles. It didn't calm his pounding heart a bit. "I'm getting too old for this, lady," he quipped as he took her hand and smiled. No IV. She'd once again managed to convince the staff that an IV wasn't necessary. He lifted her hand and an eyebrow.

Amanda chuckled. "They really respond well to hysterics around here."

Garth leaned forward and kissed her forehead just as her hand tightened on his. "Jason sends his love. How far apart are the pains?"

"Right...on top...of one...another," she said through gritted teeth.

Garth looked around at the empty room and felt the blood drain from his head. "Then where are your doctor and all the nurses?"

"Ah, the sound of a panicking father. Sweet music to my ears," Maria Hernandez, now Doctor Maria Hernandez, said. Garth glanced at the doorway as she rushed in, an entourage of begowned women hurrying in behind her. "I was just dressing for the occasion," she continued. "Glad you could make it. Sorry about the unscheduled arrival."

"Are you sure this isn't too early?"

"Babies arrive this early all the time. No sweat. So, Mom. Ready to push this one out into the world?"

Garth was exhausted. Which was ridiculous. It was Amanda who always had to do all the work. He grinned knowing he looked like an idiot. She'd outdone herself this time. Little Jessica was perfect. She didn't look a bit like Ian or Patrick, who both looked like their mother. She was the picture of Jason. Same thick dark hair. Same stubborn little chin. It had been almost like watching Jason being born. Except at the end when he'd seen that he finally had a daughter. Jessica.

Garth hoped Jess Powers was in heaven looking down. He hoped he understood why they had named their daughter after him. He hoped Jess understood why his son no longer carried his name and that he was proud of the tall, healthy boy he'd fathered.

Six years had passed with no recurrence of Jason's leukemia. He was considered cured by the medical community. Though God had somehow let Garth know that years ago, it was nice to have science confirm it.

He walked toward the waiting room but stopped when he heard Ian's five-year-old voice. ''Tell us again how God used you to make us all a family.''

''It was just like a fairy tale,'' Jason said, never tiring of telling the tale, ''only it was real, like the miracles and stories in the Bible. A bad thing happened to Dad when he was young and he just didn't think he could love anybody ever again. And then he met this woman. She was sort of like one of those witches is in a fairy tale—a real bad lady—so it was good that Dad didn't love her. Anyway, she stole me from our mom when I was a baby. When the bad lady took me to Dad, he thought I was his son. He loved me right away but I'm not sure he knew it yet. Then the bad lady died.''

''How she died?'' two-and-a-half-year-old Patrick demanded.

''Ah...'' Jason hesitated for a second. ''She sort of fell into her own cauldron from what I hear. Well, anyway. Dad was still sad 'cause of the thing that had happened years before. He didn't find anybody else to love besides me until God finally stepped in. He let me get real sick and so Dad was real worried. And it was no fun for me, either, let me tell you.''

''But it was worf it,'' Patrick said, obviously well versed with this, Jason's favorite story.

"It sure was worth it. Me getting sick let Dad find out who I really was. So, then he went on a search for Mom."

"Just like the prince in Cinderella," Ian added.

"Right. But instead of a shoe, Dad found a picture of Mom and me in the stuff the bad lady left behind. That led him to Mom. When he found her he put her in his plane and brought her to me. Then I could finally start to get better. While I got better, they fell in love and lived happily ever after."

Garth stepped into the doorway of the waiting room, love overflowing his heart as he looked at his family and remembered the days when he and Jason had been alone. God truly had been good to him, Garth thought as he wiped away a tear. He'd sent Amanda to Garth. And though she had only married him for the sake of her child, Amanda had come to love him and had restored Garth's ability to believe in love. And best of all He had expanded their family so they both had more people to shower their love upon.

"Boys." Garth smiled. "The Lord sent you a sister."

*   *   *   *   *

Dear Reader,

I hope you've enjoyed *For the Sake of Her Child.* It was a true labor or love. Nothing can compare to the joy of doing what you love while serving the Lord. I hope I've done that by showing how He took two evil deeds, the murder of Amanda's husband and the kidnapping of her son, and made them work for good.

No matter how bad things are in our lives, as was certainly true for Amanda, Garth and little Jason during his illness, the Lord is in charge and can make all things work out.

Sometimes we pray and feel that He hasn't heard, but we need to remember the lesson Jason learned so young. Sometimes the answer is yes, but often it's wait. It may take years for Him to answer, but He *will* answer, just as it took years for Amanda to be reunited with Jason.

Remember also, sometimes His answer is no. We may lose a loved one, as Amanda did with her first husband, but He still may have good things in store for us. We just have to keep on believing and praying.

It took me a lot of years pounding away on first a typewriter and later a keyboard to get a manuscript accepted for publication. My nails wore grooves in my keyboard. But the Lord's answer was wait. And you know what? I believe that first sale probably felt a little sweeter for me than for some others who sold their first book.

So, whatever it is you're praying for, trust in the Lord. If achieving your heart's desire will be good for you, it'll happen. If it doesn't, then maybe He knows something you don't!

God bless,

Kate Welsh

Books by Irene Brand

Love Inspired

Child of Her Heart #19
Heiress #37
To Love and Honor #49
A Groom To Come Home To #70
Tender Love #95
The Test of Love #114
Autumn's Awakening #129
Summer's Promise #148
Love at Last #190
Song of Her Heart #200

IRENE BRAND

Writing has been a lifelong interest of this author, who says that she started her first novel when she was eleven years old and hasn't finished it yet. However, since 1984 she's published twenty-four contemporary and historical novels and three nonfiction titles with publishers such as Zondervan, Thomas Nelson, Barbour and Kregel. She started writing professionally in 1977 after she completed her master's degree in history at Marshall University. Irene taught in secondary public schools for twenty-three years, but retired in 1989 to devote herself to writing.

Consistent involvement in the activities of her local church has been a source of inspiration for Irene's work. Traveling with her husband, Rod, to forty-nine states of the United States, Hawaii being the lone exception, and to thirty-two foreign countries has also inspired her writing. Irene is grateful to the many readers who have written to say that her inspiring stories and compelling portrayals of characters with strong faith have made a positive impression on their lives. You can write to her at P.O. Box 2770, Southside, WV 25187 or visit her Web site at www.irenebrand.com.

CHILD OF HER HEART
Irene Brand

Chapter One

If you get burned, you'll have to suffer alone with the blister!

The thought flashed unbidden into Sonya Dixon's mind as she paced the floor of her third-story apartment. With her marriage crumbling around her, why would she remember a remark her father had made over two years ago? She had paid scant attention to what he had said then, and she hadn't thought of the words since, for she had loved Bryon so much it hadn't occurred to her that the future could hold any problems.

Sonya paused at the double windows, pulled the heavy draperies and watched as darkness settled over Omaha. She opened one of the windows and shivered at the hint of frost in the air. In the distance she heard a school band playing at a football game. Seemed like only yesterday she had changed the clocks to daylight saving time, looking forward to a long summer of fun, but the wonderful season had ended in a nightmare of misery and frustration.

You might as well stop dawdling and deal with that letter, Sonya's conscience prodded, but she stared out the window until the streetlights came on and the scent of exhaust fumes stung her nostrils. The room behind her was unlit, but when she turned, the white envelope lying on the floor made a little island in the darkness.

She picked up the letter, flipped on a light, kicked off her shoes and flopped down on the couch.

"It's only a joke, so why should I let it upset me?" she

muttered. She crushed the letter in her hand, refusing to read it again. When the telephone rang, Sonya threw the wadded paper across the room and, with a smile, lifted the receiver.

"Okay, Bryon, it was a good joke, but I didn't appreciate it much," she said immediately.

"Sonya?" The voice on the line wasn't Bryon's. "Oh, Mother." Sonya's smile faded and disappointment drenched her spirit.

"What was that all about?" Marilyn Sizemore asked. "What joke has Bryon played on you?"

"Only a little argument between us, Mother. I'll tell you about it sometime. What's new with you?"

"What's new with us?" she gasped. "You write and tell us we're going to become grandparents again, and then ask, 'What's new?' What could be greater news than that? Are you feeling all right?"

"Sure, I'm great. I've been to a doctor, and he's says I'm right on schedule. So don't worry about me."

"How's Bryon? Is he excited?"

"He's a little slow to catch on to the idea," Sonya said dryly. "How are Dad and the rest of the family?"

"Everything is fine here." Her mother rambled on about news of the family in Ohio, and Sonya made the proper responses when her mother paused.

"Say, Mother, I'm expecting a call from Bryon, so maybe we shouldn't talk any longer."

"Is he away?"

"Yes, on a business trip."

"But you always go with him. Are you sure you're all right, or are you keeping something from me?"

With a laugh, Sonya tried to assure her mother. "You're borrowing trouble. I told you, I'm fine."

"I want to be there for the birth. You say the baby is due in March?"

"Yes, around the first of the month. Goodbye, Mother. Thanks for calling."

Sonya terminated the conversation with relief. Bryon was sure to telephone in a few minutes, and she wanted the line open.

While she waited for the phone to ring again, Sonya surveyed her surroundings. Plush brown sectional furniture rested on a beige carpet. The draperies picked up both the brown and beige tones of the other furnishings. A superscreen television stood in one corner of the room with two reclining chairs arranged around it. Bryon's golf and bowling trophies dominated the mantelpiece. Most of the wall hangings had been gifts from Bryon's parents, as were the two antique oriental vases on the end tables. Mrs. Dixon had found the vases in China when they had stopped there on their round-the-world tour last year.

"Be careful of these, Sonya," her mother-in-law cautioned. "If Tom knew what I paid for them, he would cancel my credit cards."

With trembling hands Sonya lifted a framed portrait standing beside one of the vases. *Their wedding picture!* All of her friends had been envious because she had been the one Bryon had chosen—he was considered the catch of the university campus.

It was not only the splendor of his tall, well-muscled body that made Bryon attractive, but he was handsome, as well. His eyes and hair were brown, his teeth straight and startlingly white, and he possessed a personal magnetism that had captivated Sonya at their first meeting.

Sonya's blond beauty marked a vivid contrast to Bryon, although she, too, was rather tall with a slender body. In the picture her large blue eyes gleamed soft and gentle and happy. Long blond hair hung loosely over her shoulders. Sonya fingered the short curls covering her head now and wished she had never complied with Bryon's wishes that she cut her hair.

When the phone hadn't rung by ten o'clock, Sonya prepared a vegetable salad and turkey sandwich and took them to the living room. She placed the food on a snack tray and went back for a cup of hot tea. She avoided the dining area, although she should have been accustomed to eating alone, after the past six weeks.

Sonya turned on the television to watch the news while she ate. She had no interest in what was happening outside her own walls, but she needed to hear the sound of a human voice.

While she watched the numerous commercials leading up to the newscast, Sonya couldn't forget the crushed letter lying beside the couch.

"Good evening," the anchorwoman's voice entered the room. Sonya listened as the anchorwoman reported the world's events, yet Sonya's thoughts kept returning to the crisis in her own life.

The doorbell rang, and Sonya eagerly flipped off the television. Had Bryon forgotten his key? She ran to the door and jerked it open, kicking the letter to one side as she did so.

"Bryon, what do you think—" Sonya began, but the words died in her mouth. "Oh, hello, Leta, I thought Bryon had forgotten his key again."

Sonya didn't want to be rude to her neighbor, who owned the apartment building and lived across the hall, but could she possibly listen to Leta's problems tonight?

"Are you busy, Sonya?" Leta Barton's dark eyes wore a woebegone expression, and Sonya couldn't turn her away.

"No, come on in. I'm waiting on a call from Bryon."

"I thought he was due home yesterday."

"I thought so, too, but apparently I was mistaken in the date. Do you want a sandwich or some tea? I'm having a late dinner tonight."

"I'm too mad to eat, but I'll take some tea."

Sonya brought a cup and the pot of tea and placed them on the table in front of Leta. "Help yourself." Sonya sat down opposite her friend, who had curled her petite frame into a roomy chair. Leta looked lovely as usual, Sonya noticed, with her coffee-brown skin and dark hair complemented by the rust and gold hues of her stylish autumn dress.

"That woman has been bothering me again," Leta said.

In the two years they had lived beside Leta, her neighbor had gone through a second divorce, and Sonya had been obliged to hear a blow-by-blow description of each shattering episode.

"She follows me around. Everywhere I go, she's there. If she wants my ex, she's welcome to him, but I want her to leave me alone."

Sonya had often given Leta advice on how to deal with her marital affairs, but tonight any suggestions she might offer seemed almost laughable.

"I'm sorry you're having these problems, Leta, but I don't know what you can do about it."

"I'm going to protect myself—that's what. I'll go to the police and get a court order of protection, and if she comes near me again, she'll have a court official to deal with. She stole my man, and now she's trying to drive me crazy." Her black eyes sparkled, and she poured another cup of tea.

Sonya knew Leta wasn't serious. She had listened to her vent her frustrations before.

"Surely she must have some reason for her behavior."

"She's jealous because the judge awarded me a huge settlement so I can live in this luxury apartment. She thought when she got my husband, she would get all of his money, but my lawyer took care of that. With these apartments, I'm set for life." Leta laughed delightedly.

"Then if you're fixed for life," Sonya advised, "you shouldn't bother about her. If you just ignore her, maybe she'll leave you alone."

Leta took a swig of tea and stood up. "Oh, I'd never make trouble for her. My ex-husband will bring her enough grief, believe me. But it does help me to let off steam talking that way. Thanks for listening." As she started toward the door, Leta saw the crumpled letter. She stooped to pick it up and handed it to Sonya.

"You'd better put that in the wastepaper basket. You know how touchy Bryon is about a messy apartment."

The letter felt like a hot potato, and Sonya had the urge to throw it from her again. She locked the door behind Leta, and with the paper still in her hand, she paced the floor for several minutes. The smell of tea and salad dressing was strong in the room, so she stuck the paper in her pocket, took the dishes to the kitchen and placed them in the dishwasher.

Maybe I was mistaken. Perhaps it didn't say what I thought it did. She took the sheet from her pocket and straightened it.

Dear Sonya,
I want out! Since you're so delighted with the little cherub, you can have it all to yourself. I won't be coming back. Pack my clothes, and I'll notify you where to send them. It was fun while it lasted.

Bryon

Again she thought of her dad's remark about the blister. Had he realized even then that Bryon would be an unstable husband? Her parents had objected to her marriage, but she had thought it was because she had left college at the end of her sophmore year to marry Bryon, who was going to take her to Nebraska to live.

When they had voiced their concern to Bryon, he'd said, "I'll send her to college. The Omaha branch of the University of Nebraska is only a few miles from where I'll be working. No problem—she'll get her education."

Bryon had soon forgotten that promise, and because he had been determined to have her with him all of the time, she hadn't argued about it. She couldn't complain about his attention to her during their two years of marriage. He'd rented this luxurious apartment, where he often entertained business associates and their wives. He needed a hostess for those affairs, and Sonya couldn't do that and go to college. At times Sonya had marveled at the ease with which she'd given up her dreams of graduation and becoming a social worker simply because Bryon had asked her to do so. Actually, Sonya had been extremely flattered that Bryon had loved her so much he hadn't wanted her out of his sight, but in light of Bryon's behavior the past few weeks, she had occasionally wondered if Bryon really loved her that intensely, or had he been selfishly thinking of himself, always wanting her at his beck and call. Whenever these thoughts occurred, Sonya had felt guilty and unfaithful. Of course Bryon loved her! He was an ideal husband.

In his position as vice president of a brokerage firm, Bryon traveled frequently, and he wanted Sonya to travel with him. How could she have been so fortunate—a country girl from Ohio having an opportunity to travel to so many large cities and resort areas? They had lived a perfect honeymoon existence until that afternoon in early August when she had come home from the doctor.

She was sure of her pregnancy even before she had consulted the obstetrician, but she hadn't told Bryon about it. She suspected he might be displeased, but she hadn't anticipated the depth of his wrath.

He'd been dressing for a dinner party when she'd scurried into the apartment. In her excitement, she had forgotten about the engagement.

"I thought you weren't going to make it. You have only thirty minutes to dress. Where have you been?" He was buttoning his white shirt and poring over his tie selection on the closet door.

Sonya laid aside her purse. "I'll shower quickly and dress." It was a relief to put off telling him.

Before she entered the bathroom, Bryon repeated, "Where have you been?"

"To the doctor."

His hands stopped in the midst of fashioning his tie, and he turned quickly.

"Are you sick?"

Sonya was gladdened by the concern in his voice. Bryon had never talked much about his childhood, but once he had mentioned that when he was in elementary school, his mother had been sick, and he'd been sent away to live with his grandmother for two years. "That was the saddest time of my life," he had said. Perhaps he was afraid if she became ill, he would be abandoned again, but surely that wasn't a normal reaction for an adult.

"Are you sick?" he repeated.

Sonya couldn't control the smile that spread across her face. "No...I'm pregnant."

Abject silence followed her statement. The anger spreading across Bryon's face took away any desire to talk that Sonya might have had, and Bryon looked as if he had been struck speechless. When he found his voice, Sonya cringed with fear.

"Pregnant," he shouted, and Sonya feared Leta would hear him. "Why have you done this? I told you to take care of that sort of thing before we married. Why did you allow this to happen? You know I don't like kids."

And why didn't he? He ignored the children of their friends so much that she was often embarrassed by him.

"I've used the same type of birth control since we were married, but any doctor will tell you that no method is completely safe," Sonya said, hastening to defend herself.

"Well, you march yourself right back to that doctor in the morning and have him do something about it."

"What do you mean?" Sonya asked, and she sat down on the water bed to still her trembling legs, but the sway of the mattress made her dizzy.

"I've told you I don't want kids. Get rid of it."

"You don't mean an abortion?" Sonya cried.

"Certainly. That's no problem anymore."

Sonya's shock turned to anger. "Forget that, Bryon Dixon," she said. "You're as much responsible for this child as I am. You'll have to learn to like it." She went to Bryon and put her arms around him, speaking more tenderly. "You might not like kids now, but your own child will be different. It might be fun to have a baby."

He jerked away from her. "Babies stink. They cry. They vomit on you. This apartment would be crowded with toys, a crib and dozens of other things. How can I entertain my friends with a baby here?''

''The Shraders have children, and they give delightful parties.''

He looked at her appraisingly. ''But think how you'll look. Your beauty will be ruined forever. I want a wife to keep me company, not one who sits home breeding.''

Surely he didn't consider her a possession, like the trophies he so proudly displayed on the living room mantel. Sonya's pulse raced, and her head throbbed. Bryon couldn't be saying these things!

He gave his tie a final jerk and bolted out the door without waiting for her.

He hadn't come home until early morning. It was the first night they had spent apart since their marriage, but certainly not the last one as she soon found out.

Trying to rid her mind of the incident, Sonya laid aside the letter and picked up the evening newspaper. But she could barely skim the headlines because her mind continued to think about Bryon. His behavior during the past weeks had changed completely from their first two years of marriage. He had never before spent long evenings away from home or gone on business trips without her. Now, if he entertained his friends, he did so somewhere else rather than at the apartment. He never mentioned her pregnancy. How could the mere mention of a child cause a man to change so much?

Sonya had ignored his changed attitude. When he was home, she prepared his meals. She looked after his personal needs as she always had. She hadn't nagged at his long absences. When they talked, she acted as if their relations were normal, even after he started sleeping in the guest bedroom.

Sonya privately nursed her hurt, fully believing that when the baby arrived, Bryon would be happy about it. And even with his letter, she still couldn't believe that he would actually leave her. They had shared such a beautiful love. How could he change so quickly?

If it had been true love, he wouldn't have changed, her conscience needled.

Sonya didn't go to bed until after midnight as she tensely awaited a telephone call and listened for the sound of his key in the apartment door. Then she felt his arms around her, and they shared the bliss that she'd missed so much. She gave a glad cry, which awakened her, and she sobbed when she realized that he hadn't come home—she had been dreaming.

As she struggled out of bed the next morning, she shuddered when she looked in the mirror.

"No wonder he left me," she moaned.

The combined effect of morning sickness and Bryon's rejection had caused her to lose weight. As yet, she didn't outwardly show her pregnancy, but she was only a shadow of the beauty queen that Bryon had pursued. She hadn't slept well for weeks, and the black circles under her eyes made her appear old and haggard. Even her hair looked listless and drab.

While she sat on the side of the bed waiting for her nausea to lessen, she felt a slight movement in her womb, the first outward sign she'd had that a new life grew within her. She pressed her hand to her stomach. It had been so fleeting, just a fluttery feeling, really. For a moment she thought she'd only imagined it. But no, it had been real. A real baby lived and grew inside her now. The idea was almost overwhelming.

I can't do much about the weight loss, Sonya thought as she examined her image in the bathroom mirror, but I can at least do something with my hair. I'll call the beauty salon for an appointment.

By the time Sonya returned from the beauty shop, the mail had been delivered, and she looked eagerly through the collection of bills and junk mail hoping for a letter from Bryon saying it was all a mistake. Nothing!

Sonya put the bills in the desk where Bryon would find them and trashed the other items.

Knowing she couldn't go through another night of suspense,

Sonya finally dialed the brokerage firm and asked for Riley Shrader. Riley and his wife, Lola, were close friends.

"Hi, Riley," she said. "This is Sonya."

"I didn't know you were back, Sonya. How did you like San Francisco?"

"Oh, I didn't go with Bryon this time. That's the reason I telephoned. Do you know when he's returning? I looked for him day before yesterday, but I must have been wrong. Has he been delayed?"

A long silence ensued, and Sonya said, "Riley, are you still there?"

"Yes," Riley answered, and his voice sounded strained. "I was checking to see if I could find Bryon's schedule. I don't seem to have it."

"Then I won't bother you anymore. Let me know if you learn anything."

Why had Riley thought she'd gone with Bryon? Had he told his friend that? She had wondered why Lola hadn't telephoned during the past week. Had Bryon shared his dissatisfaction with the Shraders?

Sonya settled down to another evening of waiting and wondering. Surely Bryon would telephone tonight, if for no other reason than to learn her reaction to his letter.

When the bell rang at eight o'clock, Sonya moved weakly toward the door. This had to be Bryon, but she took the precaution of checking through the peephole. Riley and Lola Shrader stood in the hallway.

"Have you heard from Bryon?" she whispered as she opened the door. "Is there something wrong?"

She swayed on her feet, and Riley led her to the couch.

"Steady, Sonya," he said. "I'm sure Bryon is all right. We stopped by to check on you."

"I appreciate it," Sonya said hoarsely. Her mouth felt dry and hot.

"You don't look so well," Lola said. "Are you sick?"

"I'm pregnant," Sonya admitted. Because of Bryon's attitude, Sonya had told no one except her parents about the baby. "I'm having the usual morning sickness, and I'm not sleeping well. I'm tired all the time. The doctor says this is normal, and that I'll feel better soon."

Riley and Lola were the parents of three children, and Sonya expected them to be happy about her condition, but instead, tears came to Lola's eyes, and Riley refused to meet Sonya's gaze.

"What do you know that I don't?" Sonya asked with bated breath.

"I suppose you have to hear it," Riley said. "Bryon asked for a transfer to the San Francisco branch, and he starts work in that office tomorrow. He's been there this week looking for lodging. None of us at the office had any idea that you weren't with him, until you telephoned today."

Sweat drenched Sonya's hands, and she clutched the arms of her chair. She stared at Riley. Was this really happening, or was she dreaming again?

"When did he ask for the transfer?"

"About a month ago. Didn't you know he was doing this?"

She shook her head, and Lola cried, "But what's happened? I didn't think there was any happier couple in Omaha than you two. What went wrong?"

Sonya rose wearily from her chair, picked up Bryon's letter and handed it to Riley. Lola moved close to him and read the message over his shoulder.

"Bryon mentioned before we were married that he didn't want any children, and I didn't care one way or another. He blames me for becoming pregnant, although I haven't done anything different than we've always done. He demanded that I get an abortion, and when I refused, he hasn't had anything else to do with me. We've been living under the same roof, but that's all."

"The brute!" Lola said.

"I've been patient, thinking that he would change his mind

when he got used to the idea, but I never suspected that he would go this far. All day long, I've been asking myself if I've deluded myself into thinking he loved me, but in spite of my doubts, I can't give him up."

"Is there anything we can do?" Riley asked.

"I don't know what to do myself," Sonya admitted. "I suppose I'm still in shock. I keep thinking it's a bad dream."

"I wish it were, but he's gone," Riley said. "He cleaned out his office and took everything from his desk with him."

"Did he go alone? Has anyone else from Omaha been transferred?"

Riley stared at the toe of his shoe, but he finally said, "No one else has gone."

He stood and laid a sympathetic hand on Sonya's shoulder.

"If he doesn't telephone me, I'll get in touch with him some way," Sonya said. "Perhaps you can give me the address and telephone number of the San Francisco branch." Sonya put her arm around Lola. "I do appreciate having you come by."

"Would you like me to spend the night with you?" Lola offered as she hugged Sonya tightly.

"No, I'll be fine." Sonya forced a smile, but the moment the door closed behind the Shraders, she picked up one of the oriental vases that Bryon's mother had given them. She hurled it across the room, and when it hit the opposite wall with a crash, fragments shattered all over the carpet.

"Maybe there's a little Leta in all of us," she muttered.

Grabbing a pair of scissors, she headed for the guest bedroom. "I'll pack his clothes for him," she said, and she jerked shirts and trousers off the hangers, threw them in a heap on the floor and tramped over them. Lifting his ties from the rack, one by one, she cut them in two and tossed the pieces on top of the clothing.

When the last tie was mutilated, Sonya hurled the scissors from her and, sobbing, she collapsed on the bed where he had slept. The scent of his cologne enveloped her, and in her fancy,

Bryon lay beside her, holding her in his arms, moving his lips over hers. *How can I live without him? How dare he walk off and leave me?*

For two days Sonya cried. She didn't leave the apartment, no one phoned, and the doorbell was silent. She didn't shower; she didn't eat. She didn't care much what happened to her. Each day when the mail fell through the slot, she searched it quickly—nothing but bills and junk mail, no word from Bryon.

When she awakened on the fifth day after she had received Bryon's letter, Sonya stirred with a new determination.

"Even if I don't care what happens to me, I have a life growing within me. I have a responsibility to it, so I'm going to start fighting. I have to survive." But in spite of her brave words, Sonya was scared. What if Bryon didn't come back, and she had to rear the child by herself? For a moment she hated Bryon intensely for worrying her so much, but she swiped the tears from her eyes. Of course, she didn't hate her husband; she loved him.

Chapter Two

The doorbell rang before Sonya finished her breakfast. Eager to speak to someone, she hurried to the door. Through the peephole, she saw Leta.

"Come in, neighbor. Join me for a cup of coffee."

"Bryon already gone to work? I don't want to interfere with his schedule."

Was there any reason for further secrecy? she asked herself.

"He isn't here," Sonya said, heading back to the kitchen. She poured a cup of coffee for Leta and asked, "Do you want some toast, too?"

"No, just the coffee. You look terrible. What's the matter with you?"

"Bryon has left me."

Leta strangled on a sip of coffee and stared at her. Did it take something this drastic to shock Leta into silence? Sonya wondered.

"When did that happen?" Leta finally asked.

"He went on a business trip to San Francisco ten days ago, and I've learned it's a permanent move." She briefly apprised Leta of the events of the past few days.

"You mean he didn't tell you he was leaving! The dog! Another woman, I suppose?"

That thought hadn't occurred to Sonya. Surely not! Bryon often laughed about the girls at the office who flirted with him, but he'd never indicated he took any of them seriously.

"No, there's no other woman. He left because I'm pregnant, and he didn't like that."

"My word, Sonya, you do have trouble! At least when my two men walked off, I didn't have a passel of kids to trouble me. Men often start straying when their wives are pregnant. How far along are you?"

"A bit more than three months."

"Of course, even if it is another woman, he'll probably beg to come back after the baby's born and you regain your good looks."

"I don't know what to do, Leta. Bryon took care of all our business affairs, and if he's gone, I won't even have an income." Sonya hadn't thought of this before, but now it filled her with panic. What would she do for money?

"You need to see a lawyer. Bryon needn't think he can walk off and take no responsibility for you and that child. Don't you have any idea about your finances? He always paid his rent with a check, so you have a checking account."

"His uncle died and left him several thousand dollars a few months back. That's in a savings account. Of course, Bryon makes a big salary, but we spend lots of money, too." Sonya thought about their affluent tastes. Bryon wouldn't have anything but the best clothes and furniture. He loved his fancy, foreign car and eating out at the best restaurants in the city.

"I have an electrician coming to do some work, and I have to go," Leta said, "but I'd advise you to check into your affairs quickly. If he's the kind of skunk who won't assume his responsibility as a father, it's hard to tell what he'll do."

"I still think this is just temporary," Sonya insisted. "He really isn't the kind of person to act this way."

"You poor thing! You still love him, don't you?"

"Of course I love him. When you've been in love with someone for three years, you don't forget it overnight."

"More the pity for you! If a man mistreats me, I can fall out of love mighty quick. I tell you, see a lawyer. When a man starts to stray, he keeps it up. You'll be better off without him."

"I don't feel that way, Leta, although I may be stupid to still care for him," she added sadly.

When Leta left, Sonya showered, styled her hair and dressed in brown knit slacks with matching cotton blouse. After applying her makeup carefully, she peered in the mirror.

"I really don't look too bad now." No one would suspect by looking at her that she was pregnant, so surely Bryon hadn't left because of her appearance.

The long day loomed before her. What could she do? She needed milk and bread, so perhaps she should go to the grocery store. She checked her purse—less than ten dollars—that probably wouldn't be enough, but she wouldn't need many groceries if Bryon wasn't coming home.

Their checking account was joint, so she could write a check, even though she didn't often do that. Since Bryon had been an accountant before he became a stock broker, it had seemed simpler to let him take care of paying bills.

She couldn't find the checkbook, nor could she find the file in which Bryon stored the statements of their savings account. Sonya's hands shook, but she still refused to believe the obvious. She searched the desk for an hour, but she couldn't find any of their financial records. In her purse she found one check that she carried for emergencies. She could buy groceries with that, she supposed, but what if there wasn't any money in the checking account? They overspent occasionally, causing Bryon to borrow from his father.

Frantic with worry, Sonya left the apartment hurriedly and walked three blocks to the branch bank where Bryon conducted their business. She handed her ID card to the teller.

"I'm Mrs. Bryon Dixon. I'd like to know the balance in our checking and savings accounts, please."

"Just a moment," the young woman said. She punched some information into the computer on her desk, and Sonya waited impatiently drumming her fingers on the marble ledge in front of her. The music wafting throughout the bank, intended to be soothing to the customers, rattled on her nerves like a nail drawn across a windowpane.

"There's a balance of $929.38 in your checking account, but the savings account is closed. One withdrawal closed it two weeks ago."

"Thank you very much," Sonya said through lips so stiff she could hardly move them. She stumbled out of the building and paused. *Which way do I turn to go home?* She wandered around a few minutes and finally stopped an elderly man.

"I'm looking for the Sandhill Apartments. Could you direct me to them, please?"

"Turn north, ma'am. You can see the roof of the building from here."

Strange she could remember the name of the apartment, but not the location. *Was she losing her mind?* she wondered as she trudged home.

When the elevator reached the third floor, Sonya ran down the hall to Leta's apartment. The electrician was still there, but, noting Sonya's agitation, Leta dismissed him quickly. When the door closed behind the man, Leta asked, "What has happened?"

"Bryon has taken all of the savings, and there's less than a thousand dollars in checking. I don't even have a checkbook. What am I going to do?"

"The first thing is to take the money out of that checking account before he snatches it."

"I have one check in my purse."

"That's all you need. Go to the bank and close that account. This afternoon I'm taking you to see my lawyer."

Sonya didn't think she could walk to the bank again, and when she went for the car in the garage beneath the apartment house, she noticed Bryon's empty parking place. She had supposed his car was at the airport, but no doubt he had driven to California since he didn't expect to return. When traveling by plane, they usually took their old car to leave at the airport, but she hadn't questioned his decision to drive the new car and leave the old one for her. Come to think about it, she hadn't questioned anything that Bryon did. She loved him and trusted him completely, why should she have doubted him?

Sonya filled out the check for $929.38, drove to the bank's drive-in and received the total amount in cash. Returning to the apartment, she spent the rest of the morning looking through Bryon's desk. The gas and electric bills, car payment, and credit card statements totaled more than the cash she had.

Leta rang the bell at one o'clock. "Ready?" she said.

"Why is it necessary to see a lawyer? For one thing, I don't have any money to pay attorney fees."

"Lawyers are used to waiting for their money until the divorce settlement is made."

"Divorce! I don't want a divorce."

"Even if this is just a separation, you'll have to make some arrangements for him to support you."

"I'll get a job."

"That's assuming you can find a good job right away! Besides, Bryon should pay child support." She pointed to the desk where Sonya had stacked the bills. "Someone will have to pay those, and you know you can't. If you get a job tomorrow, it will be weeks before you would receive a check."

"When is our rent due?" Sonya gasped, realizing that she hadn't considered that obligation.

"You're paid through the rest of this month, but don't worry about that."

Sonya reluctantly followed Leta out of the apartment building. As Leta drove along busy Dodge Street, she said, "The lawyer's name is Daniel Massie. He represented me in my last divorce. Before I went to him, I'd heard he was always on the woman's side, and I believe it. He surely held my ex's feet to the fire."

Leta parked in an underground garage. "Massie's office is on the fourth floor of this building. I telephoned and made an appointment, so I'll introduce you and then wait in the reception room. You'll be more at ease if you talk to him alone."

"I don't know what to say, and I'm scared."

"No need to be. He's a gracious man."

Sonya's stomach heaved, and she nearly retched during the elevator ride to the fourth floor. She pressed sweaty hands to her abdomen and leaned against the wall, thankful that no one else except Leta had witnessed her discomfort.

Daniel Massie greeted Leta warmly when they entered his office, and after the introduction, he turned to Sonya with a smile and shook hands with her.

"I'll be in the waiting room," Leta said.

Massie motioned Sonya to a chair beside his desk. Daniel Massie was a man at whom people, especially women, took a second glance. Even as he leaned back, at ease in his leather chair, he exhibited a hint of latent authority. He was not handsome in the usual sense, yet his face was made up of winsome features—brilliant gray eyes, small wrinkles at the corners of his eyes and a warm smile. Yes, it was a face meriting a second glance, but although he had the kindest eyes she'd ever seen, Sonya couldn't meet his gaze.

What kind of person must he think she was when her husband had deserted her?

"What can I do for you, Mrs. Dixon?"

"I don't know," she murmured. What a dumb remark! And she made it worse by stammering, "I didn't want to come, but Leta thought I should."

What had happened to her self-confidence? she wondered.

"How old are you?" the lawyer said.

"Twenty-three. I've been married two years."

"Not quite as old as my mother was when my father went off and left her with two children to raise. That was twenty-five years ago when I was five years old, but I still remember the problems she had."

Sonya twisted her purse straps. The telephone rang, and Massie engaged in a short conversation with another client relating to an automobile accident. Water gurgled in the aquarium in the corner, and Sonya riveted her eyes upon the black and gold fish zipping gracefully through the bubbling water. The leather furnishings of the room weren't new, but they had quality, and Sonya deduced that Daniel Massie had a thriving law practice much beyond what she could afford.

When he replaced the receiver, he said, "Mrs. Barton briefly outlined the nature of your problem, but perhaps it would be better if I hear it from you."

In halting sentences, Sonya unburdened the trauma of the past two months, leaving out nothing. It was easier to talk to a stranger than her friends. "The worst thing about it is that we had been very happy up until that point. I just can't believe that my life could change so drastically."

"On what criteria do you judge the happiness of your marriage?"

Was he suggesting that they hadn't been happy? The nerve of the man!

Almost belligerently, Sonya said, "We lived in a large apartment in the best part of town, lavishly furnished, and we vacationed at luxurious places. Bryon bought me expensive jewelry, and he insisted that I buy nothing but designer clothing. Of course we were happy."

"But it takes more than material things to make a happy marriage. You've mentioned nothing about tenderness, mutual respect and devotion."

"We had those, too," Sonya said with downcast eyes. But had they? Daniel Massie had given her something to think about.

"Do you want me to contact your husband?"

"Oh, no, I don't want to make him any angrier. And I can't have you working for me when I can't pay you. Perhaps you can just advise me."

The lawyer pondered a moment. "Do you have family to help you financially?"

"My parents live in Ohio and would probably help me if I asked, but I won't ask them. They were opposed to my marriage, and I remember my grandmother's old adage, 'If you make the bed, lie in it.' It's my problem, and I don't expect to burden them with it.''

"Then it might be a good idea for you to talk with a marriage counselor. You'll need help from someone.''

"I'll handle it myself. I still think Bryon will come back.''

"Even so, I suggest that you send those current bills to your husband. If he's been caring for the finances, he'll have to continue to do so. Also, if you won't let me contact him, you'll have to. Find out exactly what he intends to do. And I must warn you, Mrs. Dixon, from his actions, I think he means to make this a permanent break. If he sues for divorce, you'll need an attorney.''

"I don't believe in divorce.''

"You may not have a choice, and if he files, you must have help.'' Daniel Massie smiled slightly. "You won't let me help you. You won't call upon your parents or a marriage counselor. But you must face reality. Mrs. Dixon, I've been through this with many other women. You can't handle it alone. You'll need help to get through this,'' he added gently.

Sonya stood to leave and found that her legs scarcely sustained her body. She held on to his desk for support. The lawyer quickly left his chair, came to her side and took her arm.

"Perhaps you should sit down for a few minutes,'' he said, with concern in his voice. "I'll call Mrs. Barton to assist you.''

Sonya shook her head. "I'm all right now. How much do I owe you, Mr. Massie?''

"Nothing at all today, since I haven't done anything for you.''

"I won't accept charity.''

"It isn't charity—I never charge for a consultation of this type. If you need further help, then we can consider a fee. But there is one thing you can do for me.''

She looked at him questioningly, suddenly suspicious of his motives. What kind of woman did he consider her?

"I'd like to have you talk to a friend of mine, a professional counselor as well as a minister.'' He picked up a notepad, wrote a name and handed it to her. ''His name is Adam Benson, and he and his wife, Marie, will come to you anytime day or night when you have a special need. I've written down his home and office phone numbers.''

''I don't need to talk to a minister or a counselor. I can handle this alone.''

''I'm sure you believe you can. But there comes a time in each life when human resources, and our own self-determination fail us. When those times occur, people who don't have a higher power to sustain them will be overwhelmed by the pressure. I don't want that to happen to you, Mrs. Dixon. Please take this card.''

This man is really concerned about me, Sonya thought, and she took the card from his hand.

''Thank you,'' she murmured and walked weakly from the office.

Leta took Sonya's arm and helped her to the elevator, and Sonya was thankful to have a friend to lean on.

''What did you think of Daniel?'' Leta asked, as she drove out of the parking garage.

''He was all right, I suppose.''

''He makes a good appearance before a judge. I think he's very handsome.''

''Maybe so. I was so embarrassed to be telling my problems to a stranger that I hardly looked at the man, but I was surprised that he seemed to be really interested in my welfare. After all, he must see dozens of people with such problems in a week's time. How could he be interested in each one?''

''I don't know, but he is. He makes all of his clients believe that solving their problems is his first priority. I've heard of a few cases when he's represented abused women in getting their divorces and has charged no fee at all, simply because they couldn't have gotten a divorce otherwise.''

Sonya thought about that. It was rare to find a person who helped others so selflessly. Daniel Massie was an unusual man.

* * *

The letter she'd been looking for had arrived when Sonya entered the apartment. She tore open the flap of the envelope with trembling hands:

Dear Sonya,
By this time you will have recovered from the shock of my earlier letter. As you may have gathered, I want a divorce. I hope you'll be reasonable and not cause trouble about this, for I have no notion of returning to Omaha. You can send my clothes to the address below.

Bryon

Sonya dropped the letter on the floor and stamped on it. She picked up the second oriental vase and hurled it across the room. The shattered pieces joined the fragments of the other vase she hadn't cleaned up from the carpet. If she was only a possession to Bryon, perhaps if she destroyed everything else, he would turn to her.

She went to the desk, picked up all the bills that had accumulated in Bryon's absence and stuffed them into a stamped envelope. Angrily she scratched out a note. "If you want your clothes, you can come after them." Before she lost her nerve, she sealed the envelope, ran downstairs, and dropped it in the mailbox in front of the apartment house.

The next morning Sonya went to the unemployment agency and applied for work. Even as she filled out the blanks, she realized that she was a poor candidate for a job. She had no experience at anything. Being the wife of a successful stock broker wasn't much of a recommendation for employment, and she'd taken only basic subjects her two years in college, so she had no training in any field.

What was it her father had said? "Please don't get married before you finish college, Sonya. The day will come when you'll wish you had that degree." But Sonya had ignored her father's advice and listened to Bryon instead. "But I don't want to wait, Sonya. If I leave you here and go off to work somewhere else, you might find another man you want to marry. I want you with me always. Don't I mean more to you than a college diploma?''

Sonya shook her head to rid her mind of such perplexing thoughts and continued to fill out the job application.

The clerk who interviewed her was sympathetic and kind. She suggested that Sonya should enroll in some kind of job training at a vocational school. After scrutinizing Sonya closely, apparently taking in her expensive clothing, she said, ''If you need financial help, there are federal grants available.''

But that wouldn't take care of her living expenses in the meantime.

''I'll give that some thought,'' Sonya told the woman. ''Thank you.''

Acting upon Leta's advice, Sonya spent the next week going from one business establishment to another filling out work applications. Each personnel officer was kind, but the answer was always, ''We'll telephone you if there's an opening.'' Meanwhile, Sonya's small hoard of money dwindled rapidly.

Several times she looked at the telephone number that Daniel Massie had given her. Did she need counseling? She found it difficult to discuss her problems with anyone, even her mother, who had telephoned again, wondering why they hadn't heard from her, but Sonya hadn't mentioned Bryon's absence.

Finally, when she had given up hearing from him, Bryon telephoned. The joy she felt when she heard his voice made her body tremble like a breeze-wafted aspen leaf.

''Oh, Bryon, I'm so glad you called.''

''I doubt you will be when you hear what I have to say. First of all, tomorrow, I'm sending a friend of mine to pick up my belongings. Be sure you send everything.''

''Bryon, please, don't you intend to come back?''

''I think I made that plain to you before. I intend to divorce you.''

''But you can't do that! Bryon, I still love you. I need you. Why are you treating me this way?''

She began to sob and he hung up on her. It was hours before

Sonya stopped crying. She would have been better off if he hadn't called, as she'd developed a numbness about his absence, and now her heartache started again.

His clothes still lay where she had thrown them two weeks ago, and she picked them up lovingly, chagrined at the mess they were in. She worked for hours pressing the garments to make them as neat as he liked his clothing. There wasn't anything she could do about the mutilated ties, and she questioned whether she should send them. If she didn't, he would probably demand to know where they were, so she stacked them with his other things. Sonya had hoped that this menial service for Bryon would serve as a catharsis to rid her mind of the unkind thoughts she'd been having about her husband. Instead she actually felt unclean to love so wholeheartedly a man who no longer loved her, and perhaps never had.

She telephoned Leta early the next morning. "Bryon is sending someone after his clothing today. Do you have any large cartons that I can use for packing?"

"I'll have the janitor bring some to your apartment, and I'll help you pack. You shouldn't have to do that by yourself."

When Leta saw Sonya's stricken face, she was unusually quiet, and she didn't make any caustic comments about the tears Sonya shed as they tied the boxes. Leta put comforting arms around Sonya's shoulders and said, "Cry all you want to. I know you won't believe me now, but you'll get over this. You'll be happy again."

"You're a good friend, Leta, and I've found I don't have many. Bryon has been my life for three years. The friends we had were *his* friends. The Shraders are the only ones who have shown me a bit of kindness since Bryon left. I feel like a pariah. Bryon is the one at fault—why does everyone shun me?"

"I don't know," Leta answered, patting Sonya's trembling shoulders. "Mostly it's because they don't know what to say to you. They don't intend to be unkind."

"And I'll have to lose you, too, Leta, since I can't go on

living in your apartment and not pay rent. The rent will be due next week, and as you know, I can't pay it."

"Hush that kind of talk. I'll carry you until you get on your feet."

"But I can't afford this apartment on what I'll be able to make. And I hate to ask you, but could you buy the furniture? I don't know that I have the right to sell it, but if you could buy it, that would give me some money to rent a smaller place. You could rent this as a furnished apartment, couldn't you?"

"I often have calls for furnished apartments, and I'll buy the furniture if you're determined to move, but don't decide now. I have plenty of money, and I have no intention of setting you out on the street." She kissed Sonya's cheek and released her. "This is a tough break, little lady, but you'll come through it all right. Let me know when they come for Bryon's clothing, and I'll have the janitor carry the boxes down to the lobby. You shouldn't lift them."

All day Sonya waited, but it was after five o'clock before the doorbell rang, and she was surprised to see Gail Lantz, one of the women from Bryon's office. Gail had attended most of the parties they'd had in the apartment. She was a divorcee, but she usually came in the company of a single man from the office. Sonya and Gail met occasionally for lunch.

"Hello, Gail," Sonya said. "Come in. I'm glad to see you." What a relief to know that all of their old friends hadn't deserted her!

"I don't have time to visit. I came for Bryon's things."

Gail was a petite brunette with a helpless look in her eyes, who prompted protective instincts from others. Until today, Sonya had never detected any arrogance in her personality.

"Oh, I didn't know who he was sending." She stepped back into the apartment. "They're boxed and in the bedroom. The janitor will carry them downstairs."

"Two of the men from the office are with me. They'll carry the boxes."

The men, both of whom had often visited their apartment, pushed a luggage carrier down the hall. Mute, Sonya motioned them to enter. They spoke, and after that, refused to meet her gaze.

Sonya followed them into the bedroom. They stacked the boxes on the carrier while Gail riffled the dresser drawers. She added Bryon's jewelry box and several books to the stack. When she picked up Sonya's jewelry box, Sonya said, "That happens to be mine. Or do you have orders to take my things, too?"

Gail fingered several of the gold chains and lifted the diamond necklace, Bryon's last-year's Christmas gift. She dropped it back into the box and closed the lid. "You'd better put those in a safer place. You won't be getting any more."

From the nightstand drawer, she took an album filled with pictures of Bryon's childhood and youth activities. She brushed by Sonya and went back into the living room, where she collected the trophies and plaques that Bryon had won at bowling and golf tournaments.

"Where are his golf clubs and bowling ball? He wants those, also."

Sonya pointed to the closet beside the hallway. She had lost the power to speak. Gail handed Bryon's sports equipment to the waiting men, and as Sonya listened to the carrier squeaking down the hall removing all evidence of Bryon from the apartment, she couldn't have been any more disconsolate if they had been wheeling Bryon out in a casket.

Before Gail left, she took a letter from her purse. "Bryon also wanted me to give you this." Her brown eyes flared maliciously.

Sonya couldn't lift her arm to take the E-mail letter, so Gail laid it on the table, exited into the hall and slammed the door.

Gail! Was she the other woman Leta had warned her about?

Sonya locked the door, as she didn't want anyone to come in. She had about reached the end of her endurance, and if she came completely unwound, she didn't want anyone to witness it.

She forced herself to pick up the message Gail had placed on the table.

Sonya,
I've paid the bills you sent, and I think it's only fair to tell you that I'll pay no more. I've arranged for the telephone to be disconnected, and the electric and gas will be shut off the last of the month. If you had been reasonable when I asked for a divorce, I wouldn't have gone to this extent. As far as I'm concerned, you can fend for yourself.
Your "loving" husband, Bryon.

The last of the month. So she had three more days to live in this apartment. Even if Leta permitted her to stay rent free, she couldn't live here without utilities.

The telephone rang several times before Sonya finally answered it.

"Mrs. Dixon, this is Doctor Hammer's office. When we submitted the statement for your last office call, the insurance company rejected our request stating you were no longer on that policy. I'm sure it's a mistake, but I thought you should check it out."

"Thank you for calling. I'll look into it."

"And don't forget your next appointment in two weeks."

Sonya replaced the phone. Of course, there wasn't any mistake—Bryon had removed her from the policy. What could she do? She had no job, no money, no insurance for the birth of her baby, no friends, no nothing.

Laughing wildly, Sonya charged around the room kicking the furniture. She looked out the window. What did she have to live for? Three floors down. One quick jump would end it all. It would be practically painless and easy. She unlatched the window and climbed out onto the ledge. The traffic roared below her. She looked down fearlessly. On the count of ten, she would jump.

"One."

I've always feared heights. Shouldn't I be afraid now?

"Two."

The clouds are pretty today. They remind me of the sky in Ohio when I was a child. I used to pick out all kinds of figures in the clouds—animals, continents, states. Can I do that now? Why, yes, that one looks like an angel. Is it my guardian angel? "I looked over Jordan, and what did I see? Angels coming to carry me home," she sang dreamily.

"Three."

The first time Bryon had seen her, he'd said, "Gee, you're beautiful. Where have you been all my life?" She had been so proud that Bryon had chosen *her*. Was that why she had always done what he'd wanted her to? Come to think of it, she had never refused to do anything he'd asked until he had demanded she have an abortion. Maybe Bryon wasn't as perfect as she'd thought. Was she only a possession to him? Was he kind only when he had his own way? But she refused to believe it, for to concede that Bryon's character contained many flaws would reflect on her own judgment.

"Four."

The trees above her were beginning to display colored foliage. She had always liked fall; too bad she would miss all of the beauty.

"Five."

Would Bryon feel sorry when he heard the news? Would he realize he had caused her death? Maybe she should have left him a note.

"Six."

I should have written my parents, but there's no time. If I don't do this now, I might lose my nerve.

"Seven."

The pavement looked inviting. I must remember to fall on my head. Sonya envisioned that her landing would have the sensation of settling into a water bed.

"Eight."

When I awaken, where will I be? That was a sobering thought, but Sonya counted on.

"Nine."

She released her hold on the brick wall and leaned forward, but she staggered back when the ringing telephone shattered the stillness.

What am I doing on this window ledge? she thought frantically. When the telephone continued to ring, she scampered back inside the living room.

Grasping the receiver as if it were a lifeline, she said breathlessly, "Hello."

A resonant voice answered her. "This is Adam Benson. Daniel Massie gave me your name. When would it be convenient for my wife and me to call on you?"

"Could you come right now?" Sonya gasped. "I'm desperate. I'm afraid of what I'll do if I'm alone anymore. I need help. Please come right away."

Chapter Three

By the time Adam Benson rang her doorbell, Sonya shook like a woman with the palsy. Her throat was dry, and when she opened the door she seized the man's arm.

"I'm Adam Benson, and this is my wife, Marie." His brown eyes gleamed with compassion, and he murmured, "My dear, trust us."

Marie Benson put an arm around Sonya and led her to the couch.

Adam said to his wife, "Make some tea, and see if you can find something for her to eat."

"I'm not hungry," Sonya murmured between stiff lips. Marie disappeared in the direction of the kitchen, and Sonya heard her opening cabinet doors as if she were at home.

"I almost did a terrible thing," Sonya confided to Adam. "When the telephone rang, I was standing on the window ledge ready to jump to my death. How did you know I needed help at that exact moment?"

"You've been on my mind since Daniel suggested you needed some counseling. This evening when I was praying, I felt an overwhelming urge to telephone you. Daniel has also been praying for you."

"I can't believe I'd do such a thing. It was almost as if I were in a trance. I knew what was going on, but I seemed to be standing outside my body watching the whole thing."

"It's quite common for a person who's been driven to the depths of despair to have suicidal tendencies."

Marie returned with a pot of tea and some sandwiches, and the aroma of the tea nauseated Sonya. She clutched her stomach.

"I can't eat anything," she insisted.

"But you must eat, Sonya, and especially drink the tea. Adam and I will eat with you. We didn't take time for dinner."

"I've not eaten much for several weeks. My stomach feels as if it's been tied in knots. I hate to eat alone."

Marie sat beside Sonya and patted her hand. "Try to relax. You don't have to bear your burden alone anymore. We're here to help you."

The Bensons were middle-aged. Adam was a short, slender man, who wore brown-rimmed glasses. His wife tended to plumpness, and she had dark hair sprinkled with gray. Her gray eyes glistened with warmth and friendliness; her voice was soft and cheerful.

Nibbling on sandwiches, the Bensons talked to each other, discussing ordinary happenings around Omaha—the ball games and the fall and winter concerts planned by the fine arts department at the university. Sonya occasionally added a comment to their upbeat words. They didn't refer to her problem, and to her surprise, in a short while she realized that she had eaten a whole sandwich and her tea was gone. She poured another cup of tea and settled back on the sofa feeling better than she had for a month.

When the food was gone, Adam said, "Sonya, we're here to help you, not interfere in your affairs. If you want to tell us about your situation, we're ready to listen."

"What did Mr. Massie tell you?"

"Only that you had some problems, and that you might contact me."

"My husband has left me," and, having had the courage to admit that, Sonya launched into the experiences of the past months. She talked for more than an hour, often breaking into sobs and occasionally walking around the room twisting her hands. Marie finally pulled her gently to the sofa and sat holding Sonya's hands tightly as she talked. When she faltered, Adam asked a brief question to encourage her to continue.

"What worries me," Sonya said as she finished, "is what did I do wrong? Why did this happen to *me?* I've tried to be a good wife. I've been faithful to my husband. Why did this happen to me?"

"I know this is small comfort to you," Adam said, "but there are thousands of young women in this country who have suffered a similar fate. And I don't think you have done anything wrong. Your husband is obviously a selfish man without any consideration for others."

"That isn't true!" Sonya hurried to defend him. "He's always been considerate of me until this incident. It's out of character for him to behave like this."

"Then let's just say that your husband has a problem. A man who walks out on his responsibilities should seek help himself."

"I doubt he would see it that way," Sonya said, realizing that her two statements about Bryon were inconsistent. "But I have been wondering if there is something in Bryon's past that I don't know about, some incident that would cause him to resent my bearing a child. I can hardly believe it, for his family seems well adjusted and live a normal life-style, and they are prosperous. I feel sure that he wouldn't see any need for change in himself."

"Then if he won't seek counseling, either jointly or alone, all we can do is work with your situation. You must believe that you're going to surmount all these difficulties and come out of this a stronger woman than you've been before."

"I don't see how I can make it." Sonya shook her head. "I've looked for a job with no luck. I must move out of this apartment soon, and my money is dwindling rapidly."

"Please believe me—you're going to make it all right. Tomorrow, we'll discuss plans for your future. Our immediate problem is to bring you safely through the night.''

"I'll stay with her," Marie said.

"Oh, I couldn't let you do that. I'll be all right."

"It's quite likely you will have other despairing moments as you struggle to deny what has happened. If you won't allow Marie to stay, then I'll give you two telephone numbers. There are counselors at these phones around-the-clock ready to listen, and whenever you feel that life is more than you can handle, telephone them. They'll listen or give advice, whichever you need most.''

"But my telephone service will be discontinued tomorrow!"

"Sometimes it takes a few days for the telephone company to follow through on those orders. We'll trust that will be the case in this instance.''

Before they left, Marie handed Sonya a small book, entitled, *No Easy Way Out*.

"Please read this book," Adam said. "It's the story of a young woman in this town who went through a difficult marriage. She thought she was taking the easy way out, but the woman who wrote the pamphlet believes healing comes through facing one's problems." He took Sonya's hand. "How is your relationship with God, Sonya? I feel I must ask that.''

"My parents started taking me to church when I was a tiny girl, and Bryon and I go to church occasionally. I do believe in God.''

"How long since you've read your Bible?"

Sonya dropped her head. "Not since I've been married."

"Then I would suggest that you read it. God can help you, but you need to reach out to Him.''

Desperation surged over Sonya again when the door closed behind the Bensons. She looked out the window and then checked to be sure the latch was securely closed. She pushed several chairs in front of the window to deter her if she tried to climb out again. The street lamps radiated brightness, and blurred streaks of automobile headlights pierced the darkness.

Sonya shuddered when she thought of where she might be now if the Bensons and Daniel Massie hadn't been concerned.

She looked at the two numbers Benson had given her. Would there be someone to listen if she telephoned? She dialed one of them, and a pleasant voice answered, "We Care. May I help you?"

Sonya laughed nervously. "I only wanted to know you were there in case I do need you. Adam Benson told me to call when I have a problem."

"Someone will be here all of the time," the woman assured her. "When you feel a problem coming on, telephone. We'll listen."

Sonya ran the sweeper, dusted the furniture and did a load of laundry. Still not sleepy, she picked up the pamphlet Marie had given her. She started reading the story of Alice Simmons.

She tried to remember where she had heard that name, but couldn't quite recall. Then she remembered, she'd heard the woman's name on the news some months ago. Alice Simmons was related to someone well known in the city—Sonya didn't remember who.

She did remember that Alice's death by her own hand had attracted a great deal of attention in the local news. Alice had married a hardened criminal without any knowledge of his illegal activities. She had suffered abuse of all kinds, and had finally left the man to live with her grandmother. Her husband had continued to harass her, and unable to get rid of him, she had finally committed suicide. Sonya could see her own situation in that of Alice, and again she longed for the release that death would bring.

But the pamphlet continued, "There's no easy way out. Trust God with your problems. Deal with them head-on, rather than ignore them."

These words spoke to Sonya's immediate need, for she had been feeling guilty that she had actually planned to take her life. She couldn't imagine why she would be tempted to do such a thing, but in light of Alice's experience, her action must be a normal response to what she had been through.

During Adam's counseling, he had told her to remember, "When your burden seems the worst, a way out will be provided." She repeated the words over and over, and she went to bed, clutching the paper Adam had given her. She dreaded to turn out the light, but she went to sleep right away. Suddenly she awakened overwhelmed with heaviness and despair.

God can't help me. Adam Benson can't help me. Nobody can help me. I'll do what Alice Simmons did. Surely I can be as brave as she was.

Sonya slid out of bed and headed for the window, but she became conscious of the slip of paper in her hand. Her shaking fingers reached for the telephone, and she dialed the number for We Care, fearing no one would answer.

"We Care. May I help you?"

"Yes, please. I'm considering taking my own life."

The woman's voice at the other end of the line spoke soothingly, "Tell me what's bothering you, ma'am."

At the end of a half hour, Sonya terminated the conversation feeling relaxed, although the woman hadn't said much. She had simply let Sonya talk, but that had been comforting. Remembering the woman's last words from the Bible, "Weeping may endure for a night, but joy cometh in the morning," Sonya went to sleep again.

Once more during the night, she awakened, shaking violently. She dialed the number. A man answered and, speaking calmly, he discussed the good things in life, ending with, "Why don't you try remembering all the pleasant times you've enjoyed through the years. Usually they outweigh the bad days."

After considerable effort, Sonya blocked out the past two years and thought of her childhood on the farm. She envisioned fields of growing corn, ripening wheat and the scent of new-mown hay. She eventually went to sleep, to be awakened by the ringing telephone. The sun shone brightly through her windows.

She reached for the phone receiver. "Good morning, Sonya. This is Marie Benson. How do you feel?"

"Tired, but safe, thanks to you and your friends."

"Adam and I want to talk with you again. When will it be convenient for you?"

"As soon as I shower and have breakfast. Do you know, I actually feel hungry this morning?"

"Great! That's a good sign. You've started on the road to recovery."

The warm shower took away some of Sonya's weariness, but when she started to dry her hair, the dryer wouldn't work. She tried the light switch—no power. So Bryon hadn't been fooling—he'd had the power company disconnect the electricity. No doubt the telephone would go next. Fortunately the water was provided as part of their rent, so she wouldn't be completely without utilities until she could find some other place to live.

Without electricity, she had to be satisfied with a glass of milk and untoasted bread for breakfast, but though she had felt hungry, she threw most of the bread in the garbage. Her obstetrician had given specific instructions about her diet, and she knew she must be more careful, but not this morning. She made an effort to greet the Bensons with cheerfulness, but after she reviewed her tense night, Adam said, "You probably still aren't out of the woods as far as despair is concerned, but you know how to handle it now. Let's deal with your immediate problems. As I see it you have several options, and if we had more time, we could make long-range plans, but it's obvious you'll have to make a change in living arrangements right away."

"What options do you suggest?" A sense of frustration threatened to overpower her again. If it were only herself, she could live anywhere, but she had to have a place for her baby.

"You can go to your parents and stay until after the birth of your child. Surely they would take you in."

"I know they would, and they'll be furious when they find out I haven't come to them, but when I disregarded their wishes by marrying before I finished college, I don't think they should be burdened with my mistake. My dad said if I was burned, I'd have to suffer with the blister by myself.''

"I doubt he meant that," Adam said with a smile. "I have three children, and I know how your parents will feel. Besides, it will be a burden to them whether or not you go home."

"It may come to that, but not until I've exhausted every other possibility."

"You can go on welfare. The agency will provide you with food and shelter, as well as a health card to take care of your medical expenses."

Sonya shook her head. "Why should the taxpayers be burdened with my mistake?"

"Then your only other option is to take legal action immediately, to force your husband to support you until after the child is born. You might feel it isn't a problem your parents or the public should share, but you can certainly realize that he has an obligation."

"But I want him to come back to me. If I force his hand that way, he'll be angrier than ever."

Adam smiled. "Since you don't like any of my suggestions, what do *you* want to do, Sonya?"

"I want my husband to come home. I want him to love our child as much as I intend to."

"I don't mean to be cruel, but the likelihood of that happening is slim. And if he should return, I doubt it will be in the immediate future. He'll run the gamut of willfulness before he'll return to you."

"Then if that won't happen, I'll find a job to support my baby and make a home for us," Sonya replied firmly. "I want to be independent."

"If that's your desire, we'll do what we can to help you. It's going to be difficult for you to get much of a job until after your child is delivered, but perhaps we can find something to tide you over until then." Lines of perplexity creased his face as he considered her problem.

It amazed Sonya that this couple—these strangers—were so genuinely concerned about her welfare. She had never seen them until yesterday, but now they were making her future their greatest priority. Was it the depth of their spiritual faith that fostered this concern? If so, it was certainly a level of spirituality she would hope to attain.

"What about the opening at our school, Adam? She wouldn't need any special training for that," Marie said.

A smile lit Adam's brown eyes. "A good idea, dear." Turning to Sonya, he said, "We operate a day school in our church building—nursery through the sixth grade. Just yesterday, one of the aides in the nursery class resigned. You would fit in nicely, but the salary is low. I'm not sure it will support you and allow you to accumulate enough for your medical bills."

With hope dawning in her heart, Sonya said, "I'd like to try it. I'll be frugal."

Adam looked around the lavishly furnished apartment and said, "Sonya, it's a trait you'll have to *learn*, since you haven't been living that way."

"I didn't live this way before I was married. My parents reared a family of four on an Ohio farm, and we didn't have many luxuries. I'll admit it will be hard, though, because I've learned to like this way of life."

"There's an apartment complex near the church, subsidized by the government to provide housing for low-income people. They base your rent on what you can afford to pay. We'll take you there to see if they have any vacant apartments."

"You could walk across the street to work, so there wouldn't be any travel expense," Marie added.

"I'll not put you to all that trouble. I have a car and can drive there. I don't know how much longer I can afford to operate the vehicle, but at least it's paid for."

The Bensons overrode her objections and took her in their car to the Washburn Complex in a newly developed area on the west side of Omaha. They pointed out their church, the Community Lighthouse, a shingled building of modern architectural design. The four-story apartment complex faced the church.

The manager of the apartments said they did have some space available in single apartments and two-bedroom units.

"It will have to be the single apartment," Sonya told her. "I can't afford anything else."

But she was hardly prepared for the small area she was shown. The living, dining, and kitchen space was about the size of her bedroom in the apartment she'd shared with Bryon. A small bathroom contained a shower, but no tub. The apartment was unfurnished, except for a refrigerator and stove.

"If you can't provide your own furniture, we can supply it for you," the manager said. "We have a sofa that can be made into a bed at night, a small table for the kitchen and a few other items available. We can fit up the room nicely."

"I'll appreciate having you do that," Sonya said, knowing that none of her massive furniture would fit into the tiny space. Some of the enthusiasm that had been generated by the Bensons' help faded, and she wondered why Bryon would sentence her to living in such a humble place.

Sonya made arrangements to move in the next day, the last day the rent was paid at the Sandhill Apartments. There was no need for delay. Leta had already agreed to buy their furniture, and without a telephone or electricity, the place wouldn't be livable. She couldn't take advantage of Leta's friendship and live at her expense.

Before the Bensons left her at the Sandhill Apartments, Adam said, "We'll check on you tomorrow night, and you can plan to start working on Monday morning. Will you need any help moving?"

"No, I can load everything in my car and make more than one trip if necessary. I can't express my appreciation."

Sonya's throat was dry, but her eyes watered. Bitterness filled her heart, and she wanted to rail at somebody. But not the Bensons—they had done the best they could.

"Don't try—just pass along some kindness to others who need it," Marie said with a smile.

As she walked upstairs, Sonya marveled that it had been easier to take help from strangers than from her own parents. Perhaps it was because they had not stood in judgment of her and had seemed so willing to help. Could their obvious submission to following God's will account for their generous spirits?

Leta protested Sonya's sudden move. "I think it's a mistake, but do what you think you must. If I was in your place, Mr. Bryon Dixon would have been forced to pay for your lodging and expenses in this apartment for a reasonable amount of time. You see how I'm living, don't you?"

"But you were glad to get rid of your husbands! I want to keep mine, although I admit I might be foolish to feel that way."

"You won't keep him by kowtowing to him. He'll show you more respect if you speak up for your own rights."

In spite of Sonya's protests, Leta helped her pack and went with her on the first trip to the apartment. When she saw the small room, Leta exploded, "This is quite a comedown. It isn't right for you to live in such a place! You can't possibly be comfortable here."

"I can't help it, Leta. It will take half of the salary I make at the school to even pay the rent on this apartment, and how I can eat and save any money for doctor's bills, I don't know. I'll just have to make do." But in spite of her brave words, thoughts of the future terrified her.

The closet was too small to hold even Sonya's winter clothing, and they left her summer garments in boxes and stacked them in the corner. Sonya had made an effort to hold back her tears, but both she and Leta were crying before they finished unloading the car.

"Look on the bright side. At least I won't have to buy any clothing—I have enough to last me for years."

"Oh, yeah," Leta retorted. "Have you given any thought to

how your body is going to expand? You won't be able to wear any of these clothes much longer. Please, Sonya, go to Daniel Massie and have him contact Bryon. It isn't right for him to go scot-free while you're so hard up.''

But Sonya shook her head and bit her lips to keep them from trembling. "All I have to bring now are my kitchen supplies and a few knickknacks. Let's go."

Sonya thought she had cried until there couldn't possibly be any more tears left, but before she left the apartment for the last time, sobbing constantly, she looked at each item, caressing them lovingly. She and Bryon had such fun picking out their furniture. She stood a long time in their bedroom, thinking of their more personal moments. Had she failed him? What was wrong with her? If she could only get past the feeling that she was at fault, she might be able to accept it. How could she have prevented his leaving?

When she locked the door, she dropped the keys through Leta's mail slot. She absolutely couldn't talk to anyone else today.

Sonya placed a few vases and pictures in the new apartment. Even with these possessions around her, the room seemed alien. She ate a light supper, and then started her hardest task. She had to notify her parents. What if they tried to telephone and learned the number was no longer in service? She had caused them enough trouble, and she couldn't let them have that worry.

Since there wasn't any desk, she sat at the small dining table to write.

Dear Mother and Dad,
Bryon left me about a month ago. He's living in California and has no intention of coming back to me. I moved today to the address on the envelope. I do not have a telephone here. I'm starting to work Monday as an aide at a nursery school in a nearby church. Please do not worry about me. I'll be all right.

Sonya.

Adam and Marie Benson came by to check on her, but they had to call at a funeral home, so Sonya had a long evening before her. She watched the small black and white television she and Bryon had used in the kitchen, but the problems of other people soon palled.

It was still too early to retire, but she decided to see if she could unfold the couch into a bed. Considering her other luck lately, Sonya was surprised that it opened so easily. The bed was comfortable enough, but she knew it would be aggravating to fold and unfold it every day.

When she finally turned off the light, well after midnight, Sonya wished for the comfort of the We Care persons, but without a telephone, she couldn't contact them. No, she was on her own now—either to succeed or fail. *But I'm not on my own,* and the thought brought her upright in bed. She pushed the light switch and rushed over to the luggage piled in the corner. When she was packing, she had unearthed her Bible. Adam Benson had said the answers were there, if only she could find them. When she found the white Bible her parents had given them for a wedding present, Sonya turned it over in her hand as if it was some foreign object.

"God," she whispered, "I feel awful, neglecting you all these years and then turning to you when I'm in trouble. But truly, God, I have no place else to turn. Was it necessary for me to be brought this low so that I'd realize how I was straying from my childhood faith? If so, help me now. Direct me to some words that will give me peace of mind and help me through this night and the difficult days ahead."

Sonya had no doubt that God heard her prayer, and she opened the Bible to the book of Psalms. After she turned several pages, Sonya read words she didn't even remember were in the Bible. "God is our refuge and strength, a very present help in trouble." And in Psalm 94, she read of David's struggle when violent men would have overcome him, and she committed to memory the words, "Unless the Lord had been my help, my soul had almost dwelt in silence. When I said, my foot slippeth, thy mercy, O Lord, held me up.''

Sonya kept repeating those words in her mind when she returned to bed, and when worries about the future threatened to intrude into her thoughts, she gritted her teeth and whispered, ''When I said, my foot slippeth, thy mercy, O Lord, held me up.''

Chapter Four

When she awakened again, her bedside alarm showed twelve o'clock. At first, Sonya thought it must be midnight, until she realized the sun was shining in her windows. It was the first good night of sleep she'd had since her estrangement with Bryon. She left the bed and looked across the street to see that people were leaving the church, and she was sorry she had missed going.

Her stomach rebelled at the odor of fried bacon permeating the apartment, and she rushed to the bathroom. With the adequate ventilating system and soundproof walls at Sandhill Apartments, they had hardly realized they had neighbors. But the walls here must be paper thin, she thought. Children ran in the room above her, a television played in the room beside her apartment, and the wails of a crying baby filtered in from across the hall.

Weak with nausea she crept back into bed and slept for another hour. After all that sleep, she should feel rested, but she didn't. Moving slowly to the kitchen area, she toasted a slice of bread and made a pot of strong coffee. Boxes of kitchen utensils and groceries crowded the cabinet top, and she had many other things to unpack, too. She had to generate energy somehow. She must get the apartment in order before tomorrow when she started to work.

While she sipped on the coffee and nibbled the toast, Sonya wondered how she would like a full-time job. She had worked for her parents on the farm, but she'd never had a salaried position. Such inexperience would have made any job difficult, but when she felt so lousy, she doubted she could give a satisfactory day's employment to anyone.

Sonya forced herself to finish a glass of cold milk, as her doctor had instructed. During the afternoon while she unpacked boxes, her stomach crawled with hunger, but when she tried to eat, the very scent of the food caused her to gag. The work was finished by four o'clock, and she faced a long evening.

She drew on a jacket over her sweats and went down to her car. Several children played football in the parking lot. She slid into the car, ignoring the glances of three men lounging on benches. She had intended on going to see Leta or the Shraders, but she remembered that the gas gauge had shown empty yesterday. Should she use her small hoard of money to buy gas for pleasure riding?

She got out of the car when she noticed the men staring at her, and that one of them, a short man with a handsome face, had headed in her direction. "Need any help?"

"No, thank you. I've decided to walk."

"Anytime you need any help, let me know. People are neighborly here."

She rushed out of the parking lot, trying to avoid the man's attention. Walking would be better for her, anyway, but she needed companionship.

The area around the Washburn Complex had sprouted many housing developments. The larger houses were surrounded by a brick fence, and it was obvious that spectators would not be welcomed. Sonya walked west along a street of moderate houses until she came to a corn field. A brisk breeze rattled the dry blades, and the heavy, drooping ears on the stalks awaiting the picker reminded her of the farm at home.

Sonya retraced her steps, tears in her eyes. When she passed the Community Lighthouse, cars poured into the parking lot. Families entered the first floor carrying covered trays and picnic baskets. Momentarily, Sonya was tempted to follow them, but glancing at her dirty sweats, she moved on. She hadn't even showered today—she couldn't inflict her presence on them. No doubt Adam and Marie Benson would welcome her, but she didn't want to spoil their evening when they'd been so kind to her. She wasn't fit company for anyone tonight.

When she entered the lobby of the apartment house, Sonya went to the telephone booth. She hesitated about spending the quarter, but she had to talk to someone. Not the Shraders, for they usually ate out on Sunday nights. Surely not her parents! Leta? Maybe, but in the end, she dialed the number of Bryon's parents. She had always called his parents "Mother and Father Dixon," but would that be appropriate now?

When Mrs. Dixon answered the phone, Sonya said, without any salutation, "Hello. This is Sonya. We haven't talked for several weeks. How are you?"

"Well enough, I suppose. Tom is snoozing now. He's been golfing all afternoon. Has Bryon come back from San Francisco yet?"

Mrs. Dixon's voice sounded normal, and Sonya concluded she didn't know about her son's perfidy.

"Didn't he tell you? He isn't coming back. He's left me."

Mrs. Dixon's gasp couldn't have been feigned. "I can't believe that. What has happened?"

"I really feel that Bryon should be the one to tell you, because he's the one who initiated the separation. I'm very bitter about it, so it's best if I don't say anything until you've heard his version of the situation."

"When did this happen?"

"I had a note from him a few weeks ago saying that he didn't expect to return...and he had someone come for all his possessions. In a later letter he indicated that he would no longer be responsible for my support, so I had to move. I'm living at the Washburn Complex. I have a one-room efficiency here."

"Why that's a welfare establishment!"

Sonya laughed shortly. "It's certainly not luxury living, but it's all I can afford now."

"I'm going to contact Bryon and get to the bottom of this, and I'll be in touch with you again. Is your telephone number the same?"

"I don't have a telephone. I'm calling from the lobby. I'm sorry to trouble you with this, but if Bryon hadn't told you, I thought you deserved to know."

Sonya could hear Mrs. Dixon crying softly, and she hung up the receiver gently. She had never been overly fond of her in-laws, but she did feel sorry for them. They would feel keenly the fact that their only son's marriage had failed.

Adam Benson was on hand to greet Sonya the next morning when she timorously entered the ground floor of the church building. She arrived at eight o'clock, thinking she would be early, but numerous cars had pulled up at the door and unloaded children while she had crossed the parking lot.

"I'm sorry I'm late," she said to Adam. "What time should I come to work?"

"You aren't late because we hadn't discussed your hours. About all you can do today is meet our other staff and observe. Tomorrow, you should come at seven o'clock and plan to work until two. We try to accommodate parents who go to work early. A few children are here after two o'clock, but we have sitters with them. No school after two."

"I haven't had any experience working with children."

Adam patted her on the shoulder. "Sonya, you're going to be great at this job. Stop fretting."

But when he led her into a room housing more than a dozen active three-year-olds, Sonya's courage deserted her completely. Only Adam's hand on her arm kept her from bolting out of the room. A woman held the hands of a pair of blond girls, who were evidently twins. They tugged to get free of her hold.

Behind the woman two little boys threw play dough at one another. When Adam and Sonya appeared, one black boy raced to Adam, shouting, "Here's the preacher. Catch me," he said as he jumped into Adam's arms.

The scene was pure bedlam, and Sonya thought maybe Bryon was right about having children. But the door behind them banged suddenly, a whistle blew, and the children dived toward their assigned seats at the table. In a few seconds hardly a sound could be heard.

Sonya turned to see who had wrought this miracle. A small, gray-haired woman walked toward Sonya with outstretched hand. "Is this my new helper?" she asked. The woman radiated energy and efficiency.

"Sonya, meet our dedicated nursery teacher, Eloise Dedham. This woman could make twice the salary in a public school as she does here. We're fortunate to have her."

"Now, Adam, you know it's a ministry for me. I'm delighted to have you, Sonya," Eloise said. "The children are always hyper on Monday morning, but once we start our activities, they settle down. Don't worry about learning everything at once. You can mostly observe today, and I'll gradually fit you into the schedule."

Sonya was amazed at the many things the toddlers could do. They sang several action songs, listened to a Bible story, exercised, finger painted, and played with educational toys. Before lunch, they watched a video on proper table manners, and Sonya supervised three children during lunch to encourage them to observe the examples they'd watched on the VCR. The children had individual blankets for nap time, and they spread out on the nursery floor and rested for half an hour. Eloise assigned the other helper to monitor the children, and she took Sonya into her office.

"Our main purpose here is to achieve security, love and discipline for the children. We have fifteen little ones enrolled. Some of them are from broken homes, and they bring their troubles with them. Others have health problems, but some are normal, well-adjusted children. We try to meet all of their needs. Just follow my lead, and in a few days you'll know the ropes."

"I want to do a good job, and I'll do my best."

"It's an exacting position, but you'll do fine, and it will be good for you to be dog-tired when you go home."

"Reverend Benson has told you my situation?"

Eloise's blue eyes gleamed with compassion. "Yes, and we hope to extend help and healing to you."

In the hour left in the afternoon, the teacher guided the students in word pronunciation and numerical usage. When Eloise indicated the children should prepare to go home, Sonya looked at her watch in surprise. Where had the day gone? When most of the children left, Adam and Marie came into the room.

"What are your reactions, Sonya?" Marie asked. "Do you think you'll like this work?"

"Oh, yes. I've enjoyed today, and the time passed so quickly. I'm eager to start."

"Then we'll look for you at seven tomorrow morning. In the meantime, do you need anything? Are you settled into the apartment?"

Upon receiving Sonya's assurance that she needed nothing, Adam suggested, "You might find the adult program of the church of interest to you. Besides our Sunday and Wednesday services, we have an active singles group, which would be of help to you at this point. Every Wednesday evening we provide a fellowship dinner open to the entire congregation. You should join us. You'll meet people."

Time passed quickly for Sonya. She spent each day at the school, then went back to her apartment in a state of exhaustion. She read from her Bible each evening, and that kept her from despairing, but she wasn't sleeping well, and although morning sickness was slowly fading, she had no appetite. She ate at noon with the children, but when she was alone, she wanted nothing.

On Wednesday night she dressed in one of her most becoming dresses, noting with dismay that it was too tight around the waist, and set out for the fellowship dinner. She picked up a tray with meat, two vegetables, a salad, dessert and a roll, which cost only two dollars, delighted at the chance for a good meal at so reasonable a price. But the room was crowded with people chatting companionably, and she felt sadly out of place.

While looking around for a seat, Sonya came face to face with the lawyer, Daniel Massie. Her face flamed, and her new courage failed her. Even here, she couldn't escape her problems.

"Hello, Mrs. Dixon. How great to see you. Come and eat with my mother and me." He took her tray and carried it to a table that still had a few empty chairs.

"Mother," Daniel said to a gray-haired woman seated at one end of the long table. "Meet Sonya Dixon. This is her first time at our dinner. Let's make her welcome."

"By all means," Mrs. Massie said with a friendly smile that thawed a spot in Sonya's aching heart. "Sit down right here next to me."

Mrs. Massie had the same sparkling gray eyes as her son, and she was almost as tall as he, but she was a lanky woman, whereas Daniel was a big man, broad shouldered though slender of hip. Mrs. Massie extended a hand toward Sonya, and two large diamonds graced the long tapering fingers. Her voice exhibited the same tone of tenderness that Sonya had observed in the lawyer as Mrs. Massie introduced her to the others seated at the table, all of whom greeted her with warmth.

"I'll bring your beverage," Daniel said. "Coffee or tea?"

"Iced tea, please." Daniel soon deposited the desired beverage at her plate.

"Now may I bring you anything else?" he asked, and at Sonya's refusal, he seated himself beside her. It was a rarity for someone to wait on her and see to her needs, and Sonya enjoyed it.

Sonya had never considered herself talkative, although she could usually carry on an adequate conversation, but tonight she seemed tongue-tied. She pulled at her garments, wondering if her pregnancy was obvious, hoping that no one except Daniel Massie could tell she was pregnant.

Her companions continued a conversation started before she

arrived, and Sonya was grateful when Daniel chose to chat with her. "I'm glad to see you again, Mrs. Dixon." He lowered his voice. "I haven't been able to get you out of my mind. How are you getting along?"

"Then you don't know that I did contact Adam Benson?"

"I knew that you had telephoned him, but I've had no further report. Was he able to help you?"

"More than I can tell you right now. When I was at my lowest ebb, he and Marie came to me. They gave me a job in the nursery school and helped me find a place to live in the Washburn Complex across the street. Perhaps more than anything else, they led me to renew my faith in God and to trust Him for daily inspiration and guidance. I didn't know how low I'd fallen spiritually until I started reading the Bible."

"You couldn't be in better hands," Daniel said, and a look of relief replaced the concern previously on his face. "Working with the Bensons is the perfect place for you. They will be able to help in ways that I can't. It relieves my mind considerably to know that you're overcoming your problems."

Sonya glanced at him timidly. "Do you take such an interest in all of your clients?"

"Not all of them, although Mother does tell me that I go beyond the call of duty by becoming involved in my clients' lives."

Daniel looked up when a young man stopped by the table.

"I want to thank you, Mr. Massie, for providing the money for Johnny's camp fee," he said. "He wanted to go with the other fifth-graders, but we've been pressed for extras since my spouse has been laid off."

"Sending boys to church camp is a good investment, so it was my pleasure to do it, and incidentally, if I can help otherwise, don't hesitate to call me."

As Daniel talked to the younger man, Sonya observed him closely. She felt more uplifted than she had for months. He had left no doubt that he was sincerely interested in her personal problems as he was in the plight of this man's family. She had never encountered anyone quite like him. Bryon had never shown much interest in others' problems, and although her father had been considerate and helpful to his neighbors, on the farm he hadn't had many opportunities to meet needs.

When the young man walked away, Daniel said, "We have five minutes before the service starts. Let's clear the table, and I'll show you the way to the sanctuary."

"I don't intend to go." She looked down at her garment, which looked as if she'd been poured into it, and compared it to the neat, flowered polyester dress worn by Mrs. Massie. "I'm not dressed very well, and I don't know these people."

He made light of her excuses. "You're a beautiful woman, Mrs. Dixon. I can't imagine that you'd ever need to apologize for your appearance. Besides, you know Mother and me, and the Bensons, and since you know God, you're a member of this church family." He looked at her intently. "It would mean a lot to me to have you go, and it will be helpful to you, too. Adam is a heartening speaker."

"I've always been backward about making new friends," she admitted, "but I will go with you. I've been spending too many evenings alone the past few weeks." She picked up several of the used plates and cups and deposited them in a waste receptacle, while Daniel carried the silverware to the kitchen service window.

The sound of piano music drifted from the second floor and Sonya walked between Daniel and Mrs. Massie in that direction. When a man stopped Daniel on the stairway, Mrs. Massie said softly, "We won't wait for Daniel. He's been advising that man about a tax problem, and he may be delayed."

They found a seat near the front of the sanctuary, and Mrs. Massie informed her that the large room had a seating capacity of five hundred, and more than half of the seats were filled. The modern stain-glassed windows lent a worshipful air to the otherwise plain interior decorated in variegated blue tones.

The song service had been in process for about ten minutes

before Daniel came down the aisle and sat beside her. "Sorry," he whispered, "I didn't mean to desert you."

"I'm doing fine. Your mother introduced me to several people."

What was there about this man that caused her to feel secure and strong when he was beside her? When she had entered the church tonight, she felt unworthy and as low as a toadstool. Now she actually felt like singing, and when Daniel opened a book and extended it toward her, she sang with a fervor she hadn't known since childhood.

What a fellowship, what a joy divine
Leaning on the everlasting arms.

It was amazing that all Daniel Massie had to do was smile in her direction and her self-respect felt suddenly renewed. *Where did the man get the strength that he transmitted to others?*

When Adam called upon Daniel to pray, Sonya had the answer. She had never heard anyone pray with the earnestness Daniel exhibited. First he praised God for His mighty works in the universe and the transformation He had made in his personal life. He prayed for the needs of those who were hurting in physical and emotional ways, and Sonya knew he was thinking of her, for he reached out and took her hand. Surely some of the power he received in prayer must have been passed to her, for when he said, "Amen," she felt more spiritually aware than she ever had before.

At the close of the service, dozens of people spoke to Sonya and urged her to return again.

"Mother," Daniel said, "if you'll wait here, I'll walk Mrs. Dixon to her apartment."

"Oh, that isn't necessary," Sonya said hastily. "The street is well-lighted."

"It will only take a few minutes." He touched her arm lightly and steered her toward the side of the building that faced the Washburn Complex.

She didn't want him to accompany her, but she couldn't

make a scene, so she walked silently by his side as they crossed the street. Sonya absolutely refused to allow him to escort her upstairs. The apartment was so untidy she didn't want anyone to see it, and also, though she trusted Daniel, she rebelled at any sign of intimacy from a man.

In parting, he took her hand, and the warmth of his fingers was comforting. "If there is anything at all I can do for you, Mrs. Dixon, let me know. I'm not speaking as your attorney now, but as a member of your church family. Perhaps you will need someone to take you for doctor's appointments. My time is my own. I can easily help you. Will you telephone if you need me?" When she hesitated, he squeezed her hand. "Promise me."

"I hope I won't need your help, but I will call."

He left her with a cheery, "Good night," as well as a question. Even considering the depth of his Christian faith, how could Daniel have developed such an interest in her after their short acquaintance?

Saturday morning Sonya slept late. It had been a strenuous week, but she was pleased to know she'd survived. That was the important thing—she had made it. She'd proven she could make a life for herself without Bryon if she had to, and dealing with a roomful of wiggling tots kept her mind off her troubles, but she still dreaded nighttime. When she finally went to sleep, each night she dreamed that Bryon had come back to her, only to awaken sobbing to the reality of his absence. With each heartache, she prayed, "God, if he won't love me back, why can't I forget my love for him?"

Wonderingly, Sonya rubbed her abdomen where the baby moved vigorously. Hardly a day passed now that the baby didn't prod or kick her lightly, and each time, she mourned that she wasn't sharing the experience with Bryon. She was tempted to stay in bed, but she had to buy groceries. The few items she had brought from the apartment were almost gone. Dr. Hammer had been specific about the right diet for a healthy baby, and she intended to follow his advice.

She eyed the littered apartment with distaste. Bryon had always insisted on a spotless environment, and this place didn't look like her home. She had left dirty clothing lying on the chairs, dishes were unwashed in the sink, and because it was more trouble than it was worth, she hadn't folded up the bed each day.

Bryon wasn't here now to see it, so she left the room as it was, except to pick up her dirty clothes. She took them down to the basement where the manager had told her she would find washers and dryers. After she finished the laundry, she carried the basket upstairs. The bed looked inviting, so she lay down again.

The buzzer sounded, indicating that someone wanted to enter her apartment, and she went to the speaker.

"Sonya, this is your mother. Open the door, we want to come in."

"We?" Sonya said stupidly.

"Your father and I."

Sonya pushed the button to release the lock on the lobby door and looked wildly around the littered apartment. She quickly smoothed the sheets on the couch and folded it before her parents knocked on the door.

She didn't want her parents to know the depth of her unhappiness, but when they stepped into the room, she started sobbing and threw herself on her father's husky, squarely built chest. He patted her back, whispering as he had when she was a child. "Now, don't cry, baby. You'll be all right."

"This is worse than I even suspected," her mother said, sizing up the room in horror. "Why didn't you contact us before you moved in here?"

Sonya removed herself from her father's arms, closed the door and motioned them to sit on the couch. She drew a kitchen chair close to them, took a deep breath and wiped her eyes.

"I felt it was my problem—no use to involve you."

"It's our problem, too," her father said. "We've come to take you home."

"No, I'm not leaving. I have a job, and I intend to make it on my own."

"We'll see about that," her mother said. "Start at the beginning and tell us everything."

Efficient and determined Marilyn Sizemore always had the effect of making Sonya seem like a child again, and she found it difficult to reveal the complete facts about Bryon's infidelity. By the steely look in her father's eyes, Sonya knew he had no trouble reading between the lines.

"Do you think there's any chance of reconciliation?" her mother asked when Sonya finished.

"It doesn't seem so, but I'm not giving him up without a fight. I still love him, no matter what he's done to me."

"I can't understand why you didn't come to us immediately," her father said. "We're your parents. You should have known we would take you in."

"But you told me when I married Bryon that if I got burned I'd have to suffer alone with the blister."

Her father's face colored, and he swung his arm angrily. "It's true I didn't want you to marry him, but you should have known we would help you if you had a need."

"What's done is done," her mother said. "Let's pack your things, and we'll start home in the morning. We brought the pickup, and we can take most everything you have here."

For a moment Sonya was tempted. It would be comforting to be in her old home again, to awaken to the sounds of the farm—the lowing of cattle as they came to the barn for milking, the hum of the tractor as her father went to the fields. Her parents would shoulder the expense of the birth and support her and the baby without complaint. She would be loved and cosseted as long as she wanted to stay with them. But was that fair? Her parents had sacrificed to educate their four children, and since her marriage, they had accumulated some money and free time.

After one of their sons-in-law had become a partner on the farm, the Sizemores had been able to spend part of the past two winters away from the farm in Florida. If she went home, the money they should spend on their retirement would go to take care of her, and they would miss the small luxuries they deserved. She wanted to go home, but she wouldn't.

Sonya took them both by the hand. "I love you, and I appreciate having you come to help, but I won't push my responsibility on you. I'm going to handle this myself. I'm working now, and I'll manage."

Across the hall a door banged, and a husband shouted angry insults at his wife as he bolted down the hall. Mrs. Sizemore covered her ears.

"But surely, daughter, you aren't happy living in such a small place," her father protested.

"No, I'm not happy. I'm miserable, but I can't see any other recourse now."

"If you won't come with us, at least go to that lawyer and make Bryon give you some support."

"Mother, would you want to live on money from a man who didn't want to provide it? After being rejected the way I have, I don't have much pride left, but I do have some, and I refuse to beg from him."

Marilyn Sizemore threw up her hands in defeat. "Let's clean this place. I've never known you to litter a room like this. Don't you feel like cleaning?"

"I've lost any desire to have a clean house. There was no one to see it, and I didn't care."

With both of them working, it took only a couple of hours to clean the apartment, wash the dishes and do the necessary ironing. While they cleaned, her father checked the plumbing and electrical fixtures and took a general survey of the apartment.

"We must check into a motel," he said, "and then we'll take you out for dinner. I also intend to stock up these grocery shelves for you."

"Now, Daddy, I won't have it. I can manage on my own."

"I'll not have a daughter of mine go without food. Don't

you have a birthday coming up? Count it as your birthday gift, if that will make you feel better."

"Under those circumstances, I'll accept."

"And I'm going to have a telephone installed here and pay for it until you're able to do so. I'm not doing that for you, but for your mother and me. Don't you realize how we'll worry if we can't even contact you? Forget your pride and allow us that privilege."

"I don't have any choice, I suppose, but as soon as I possibly can, I'm going to assume all my expenses. And I don't want you to send me any money, either. I'll simply send it back. Besides, I have some money—I told you I've sold the furniture. I'm not destitute by a long way."

"But if you go through a divorce, you'll need plenty of money," he said.

"Remember one of Grandma's adages, 'I'll cross that bridge when I come to it.'"

"A lot of trouble can be avoided in this life if we attempt to build the bridge before we need it," her father said. "I'll remind you of this one time, and I'll never refer to it again. If you had finished college like we wanted, you wouldn't be in this mess now. In the first place Bryon would have married someone else, and even if he had waited, you would now have a profession to provide you with a good living. As it is, you're working for wages that a high school student would scorn. And frankly, I don't believe you can possibly make a living at that school job."

Sonya knew the wisdom of her father's speech, and she didn't defend herself. She alone was responsible for her present circumstances and would have to find a solution by herself.

Chapter Five

Having a telephone gave Sonya a stronger feeling of security. She kept the numbers of We Care on the table beside her bed, and a few nights she telephoned the agency. Mostly, however, she slept long fitful hours marked by horrible dreams, awakening each morning feeling as if she hadn't slept at all. She dreamed of a reconciliation with Bryon, but in the midst of their joyous reunion, Gail Lantz would appear, and Bryon would leave her arms and go with Gail. Other times she would see accusing fingers leveled at her from the darkness, and voices echoing back and forth, saying, "Forget him. You're foolish! Stupid! Imbecile!" Another time, she was sitting on a riverbank with a fishing pole in her hands. When she landed a fish, it turned out to be Bryon, and again the accusing voices called, "Throw him back. He's not worth keeping. He's been unfaithful. Why would you want to keep him? Let him go."

To avoid going to bed early, Sonya talked often on the phone with Leta. She called Bryon's parents to let them know she had a telephone, but she sensed a reserve in her mother-in-law's manner, as if she preferred not to talk to Sonya. No doubt they had been in touch with Bryon and had his version of their problem, so she didn't contact the Dixons again.

One night she telephoned the Shraders.

"Hello, Lola," Sonya said. "How are things with you?"

"I'm glad to hear from you, Sonya. Riley and I think of you

often. When I couldn't reach you at the Sandhill Apartments, I didn't know what had happened to you.''

''I couldn't afford to live there, so I have a much smaller apartment in west Omaha. I didn't have a telephone at first, but I do now, and I wanted to let you know how to reach me.''

''That's great. How about lunch someday?''

''I would love that, but it will have to be on Saturday, as I have a job now.'' She explained about her work at the nursery school.

''That sounds like a good place for you—you'll receive first-hand experience to help in raising your own child. How are you feeling?''

''All right, I think. Having never been through this before, I hardly know what to expect. I seldom have morning sickness now.''

''Good. Could we meet at Pierre's Saturday at twelve? Riley will be home then to care for the children. Let's make a day of it—we can shop afterward.''

Sonya hesitated momentarily. Could she afford Pierre's on her salary? But she didn't want to take a chance of losing Lola's friendship, so she agreed, ''I'll be there. Telephone if you can't make it.''

Sonya thought about the luncheon engagement all week. She had acquired new friends at the school, but she still missed the friendships she had made through Bryon. Thinking about seeing Lola brought back the enjoyable times spent in Bryon's company. The longer he stayed away, the more she tended to forget how he'd treated her the past four months, remembering only the love they had shared.

Saturday morning she was downstairs before seven o'clock to do her laundry, and she made short work of cleaning the apartment. She'd stopped cluttering, so it didn't take long to shape up the place. Her messiness had been intended to aggravate Bryon, but he wasn't there to see it, so why make her own life miserable?

Now that she could no longer afford a hairdresser, Sonya

styled her own hair, but she wasn't pleased with the results this morning. Since Bryon's absence, she'd allowed her short hairstyle to grow out again. She had no extra money for beauty salon appointments. She knew her hair would look mighty plain compared to Lola's modish hairdo. But she chose a dress that was full enough to disguise her expanding waistline and finally approved of the image she saw in the mirror.

Already Sonya had learned the truth of Leta's words about her clothes—there was hardly anything she could wear. She had gained five pounds, which the doctor said was normal now that she was four months into her pregnancy, but she had only a few dresses that were comfortable.

The gas gauge registered empty, and she grudgingly stopped at the service station for five dollars worth of fuel. She had received a paycheck yesterday, and although it was meager, she was thankful to have even that much. She guarded tenaciously what Leta had paid for the furniture to secure her hospital confinement, though she had drawn on that account to pay a month's advance on the apartment.

Lola waited in the lobby at Pierre's, and she embraced Sonya.

"I'm pleased to see you looking so well. I know this separation has been a blow to you, and I feared that you might have a complete breakdown."

As they were shown to a table for two, Sonya admitted, "I'm having lots of rough times, but working each day has helped me retain my sanity. I try not to think about the future, nor the past."

"I want the special," Lola said to the waiter. Sonya noted that the special cost fifteen dollars, and she knew she couldn't pay that price.

"Bring me a chef's salad and hot tea," she ordered, and to Lola she said, "My appetite still isn't good, and often I throw away food. I'd rather not order more than I can eat, especially at these prices."

Lola refused to meet Sonya's gaze. "I'll be happy to buy your lunch."

Sonya flushed and stammered, "It isn't that. I have money, just not much appetite." She forced a smile. "I may have some dessert later if I'm still hungry."

Perhaps sensing Sonya's embarrassment, Lola hurriedly changed the subject to chat about her children.

"Does Riley ever mention Bryon?" Sonya interrupted to ask.

"Not much," Lola said shortly. "He knows I've lost all patience with your husband, but he did say that Gail Lantz had been transferred to San Francisco. So you know what that means. I always thought she was on the make, ready to pick up the first man she could find dangling."

That information dulled Sonya's appetite, and she pushed the salad aside.

"What could I have done to keep him?" she whispered weakly.

"I think your question should be, 'Why would I want to keep him?' He's acting despicably. If he didn't want any children, he could have done something about it and not thrown all the responsibility on you."

"I know what you say is true," Sonya agreed quietly, "but I still want him."

Softening, Lola said, "I shouldn't be so bitter, I suppose, and no doubt I would feel differently if it were Riley."

"Do you think Bryon will ever come back to me?"

"No, I don't, and I think you should make up your mind to that fact."

Lowering her head into her hands, Sonya answered, "I can't give him up yet." Although, more and more, Sonya was wondering if her relationship with Bryon had been as perfect as she had considered it, she couldn't admit that to anyone else.

Lola patted Sonya on the shoulder. "If you want him that badly, keep hoping. He won't be the first man who's strayed and then returned home." Picking up her purse, Lola continued, "But enough of this gloomy talk. Let's go shopping. We can look at baby things, and you'll probably need some maternity clothes. I would let you borrow mine, but I'm so much shorter than you, they wouldn't fit.''

"Maybe just one new dress. Most of my clothing is too tight now.'' Sonya knew she couldn't afford any new clothes, but she didn't want to admit her poverty.

Lola led the way to the exclusive shops where they'd always made their purchases.

"You shouldn't tempt me this way, Lola. You know pretty dresses are my weakness, and I haven't bought a new one for weeks.''

"High time you did then.'' Waving the salesperson aside, Lola shifted the garments on the rack. "How about this pink one? You always look stunning in pink. And here's a jumper dress—just right for your coloring. Try both of them.''

"I really shouldn't, Lola. I have to conserve my money now.''

"But you'll need some maternity clothes! Buy one of them at least.''

The dress featured a striking earth-tone print jumper over a seven-button rust-colored Henley T-shirt. Although it was a comfortable one-piece with an elastic waist and straight skirt with back vent, it looked like a two-piece outfit. When Sonya took off her tight garment and eased into the jumper dress, she felt as if she'd been let out of jail. The price was almost a hundred dollars, a bargain price at that shop.

She modeled the dresses for Lola. "The jumper dress is definitely *you*, Sonya. And the way it's made, you can wear it throughout your pregnancy.''

Normally, Sonya wouldn't have thought twice about buying the dress, as Bryon always insisted that she be stylish, but she had only fifty dollars in her purse, and that had to last for the next two weeks until she was paid again. She had used most of the groceries her father had provided.

Sonya replaced the two garments on hangers and carried them from the dressing rooms. She handed them to the salesperson. "They're very nice, but I don't have enough money with me to buy them."

"You have an account here, Mrs. Dixon. I'll be glad to charge them."

"I'd forgotten about that."

"You can surely afford this one," Lola insisted as she held the jumper dress for Sonya to take another look. Not wanting her friend to know the depth of her poverty, Sonya said, "Oh, I guess I can at that. I'll take it."

Sonya drove home with a warm glow in her heart. The afternoon had been good for her—she loved to shop, she loved to buy new clothes, and it was great to have Lola treat her as she always had. Sonya hustled upstairs to her apartment and tried on the dress again. The dress would be serviceable all through her pregnancy, for the bloused waist would facilitate any weight she gained. Humming one of the songs the children sang at nursery school, Sonya made out a grocery list and went down to the car again. It was only five blocks to the shopping center, but that was farther than she wanted to carry groceries. After two blocks, the car lurched sideways.

"What happened?" Sonya wondered aloud as she braked to a halt.

She hurried around to the right rear of the car. The side had blown out of one of her tires.

"Oh, no!" she muttered. She was parked in front of a service station, and Sonya motioned to the attendant.

"Trouble, ma'am?" he said as he approached. Sonya pointed at the tire. "Guess you do have trouble. Take a new tire to fix that."

"I have a spare in the trunk." She lifted the lid, and the man punched the tire. "Tread is worn thin on the spare—it would do for a few miles in an emergency, but you'll be asking for trouble to drive far on it. Fact is, you need a whole set of new tires."

Sonya recognized the wisdom of his words when he pointed out the worn places.

"I don't have the money for a new set of tires."

"Take my advice and buy some before winter, or else leave the car parked when the streets are snow covered."

"How much will it cost to replace the damaged one? That's all I can afford today."

"I've got a good retread here that I could sell you for $40."

Which will leave me exactly ten dollars for two weeks' of groceries.

Sonya returned to the apartment as soon as the man replaced the tire. She draped the new dress over her shoulders and smoothed down the twill challis fabric. Glancing at the clock, she knew she must hurry. She reached the dress shop just a few minutes before it closed.

"I've decided to return the dress," she said to the salesperson.

"But I thought you liked it."

"I do...but I can't afford to buy it." Sonya felt her face grow warm as she forced herself to admit the truth.

"Perhaps I could lay it away for you, and you could pick it up later."

"No, thank you, and I want you to close my account. Anything I buy from now on, I'll pay cash."

Tears blinded her eyes as she stumbled out of the shop.

Sonya stopped at the grocery store and searched the shelves for inexpensive items. She passed by the produce and meat counters, although these should be part of her diet, and bought several cans of soup, some crackers, bread and milk. The total came to more than ten dollars, and, embarrassed, she asked the clerk to deduct one can of soup. The woman in front of her at the checkout counter had a cart piled high with groceries, and she paid her bill with food stamps. Would she come to that? If the choice lay between welfare and starving, she would have little choice.

Sonya warmed one of the cans of soup for her supper, wishing she had the chef's salad she hadn't finished at the restaurant. As she washed the dishes, she thought how long it had been since morning. She'd started out so happy, but the day had gotten steadily worse.

The doorbell rang, and Sonya moved toward it with lagging feet. She kept the chain on the door all the time for she didn't trust some of the neighbors in the apartment complex. So she opened the door just a crack. It was Adam and Marie Benson, who had been visiting an elderly woman on the first floor.

"Come in. May I offer you some refreshment?" Sonya asked, wondering what she would do if they said yes.

"No, nothing, thanks," Adam said. "We wanted to see how you're doing."

"We can stay for a few moments, though," Marie said as she took a seat on the couch. "The apartment looks nice now that you've brought your own possessions here."

"It's small, but about all I can take care of with my schedule at the school. And I do thank you for giving me that job. It's been a lifesaver."

"Our director is satisfied with your work. I wanted you to know that," Adam said.

Sonya flushed with pleasure. "I needed that compliment after today."

"What went wrong today?" Marie asked, peering keenly at Sonya.

"Nothing in particular," Sonya answered, loath to burden the Bensons with her problems, "just a Saturday."

"Are you still having financial problems?" Adam asked. "We don't want you to be pressured beyond your means."

"No, I'm doing fine," Sonya insisted. She couldn't let the Bensons know that she was out of money; they had done enough already. "My parents came to visit, and when I wouldn't go back to Ohio with them, Dad paid for the installation of a phone, and he'll pick up the tab until I'm doing better. They would provide more, but I won't accept it."

"Do you know that we have a clothing and food bank at the church?" Marie asked thoughtfully.

"No."

"We're going to stop at the church this evening so Adam can pick up some notes for his morning sermon. If you would like to go with us, you might want to look at the clothing—we received several nice maternity garments last week, and I think they would be your size."

Sonya shook her head stubbornly.

"Have you ever given to the United Way or other benevolent funds?"

"Yes, Bryon was always generous with charities."

"Then you shouldn't hesitate to receive when you're in need. You can't possibly make enough at our nursery school to provide a full living. Look at it this way—you're doing us a service by working at the school for less than you could get in many other jobs. Take some of the clothing and groceries and count it as part of your pay," Marie persuaded.

Sonya sobbed, and Marie gathered her close as Sonya divulged the events of her shattering day.

"Pride may be your worst problem, Sonya," Adam said.

"But it's also hard to become humble when you've had as much as she's had," Marie said severely, and Adam lapsed into silence.

When she could control her voice, Sonya told them, "I'll take the clothes and some food with thanks," she said. "Again God has sent you to me when I had a great need. I'm not sure I would have been able to make it through the night."

"Come along then. Let's see what we can find."

While Adam went to his office, Marie took Sonya downstairs to the clothing room.

"Why, this is almost like a store," Sonya said in amazement when she saw the numerous items available.

"Some of the clothing is unfashionable, but there aren't many changes possible in maternity garments," Marie said. "Look at these. I thought when they came in that you should have them."

She lifted several dresses from the rack, and while none of them were as pretty as the one she'd wanted at the shop, still they were adequate and looked almost new. Sonya chose two similar long-sleeved dresses with high waists and six-button front plackets. One dress was fashioned from royal blue wool, and the other in a multicolored polyester fabric.

"I imagine these belonged to a woman who only wore them through one pregnancy. And here are some large blouses that you can wear with those maternity slacks. You may need to lower the hem in the slacks though."

"I shouldn't take all of these," Sonya objected.

"No reason not to," Marie said. "After your baby is born, you can bring them back if you like." She motioned Sonya to another part of the room and opened several metal cabinets.

"Please choose enough food items to see you through the next two weeks."

Sonya covered her face with her hands. "I feel so cheap doing this."

"Sonya, will it help you to know that when Adam was in seminary, and we had two children and another on the way, there was never a month that we didn't have to take food from the church supplies?" Sonya looked at her with wondering eyes. "You see, I know how you feel."

"I'm ashamed for being so ungrateful. Of course I'll take some food."

She chose several cans of beef stew, tuna and macaroni and cheese mixes. She took a large box of cereal and some dried milk. Adding several cans of fruit, she decided she had enough.

"I'll help you across to the apartment house with these items," Marie said.

After Marie left, Sonya put away the foodstuffs and tried on the clothes with a spirit almost as light as it had been when she'd started out this morning. Another obstacle had been surmounted.

Chapter Six

Sonya went to early worship service the next morning and, upon Marie's invitation, attended the coffee hour between worship and Sunday School. Sonya already knew several of the parents who brought their children to nursery school, but Marie introduced her to many others. She received invitations to the singles group that met each month, but she didn't feel "single" yet, so she didn't intend to go.

When she left the church, the sunshine and breezy conditions made her think of summertime. She couldn't bear the thought of spending the afternoon inside, and she watched enviously as the families gathered into cars and started home. Even Daniel Massie, who was unmarried, drove off with his mother, both of them waving in friendly fashion.

She moped upstairs to the apartment, barely acknowledging the greetings of the other apartment dwellers. She hadn't made any effort to meet any of her neighbors, and she didn't intend to do so. She telephoned Lola, but didn't receive an answer. What could she do for the afternoon that wouldn't cost any money? She checked her stock of groceries and telephoned Leta.

"Say, Leta, how about coming over for lunch? Then we can drive to Fontenelle Forest and hike this afternoon."

"Are you sure you're up to it?"

"I'm fine, and I can't stay inside on this beautiful day."

"I'll be over soon. Don't fix dessert—I'll buy a strawberry pie."

Sonya had enough celery to make a bowl of tuna salad. She made grilled cheese sandwiches, and warmed some soup. She was mixing a pitcher of iced tea when Leta rang the bell.

"I've missed seeing you, Sonya. I returned from my mother's yesterday, but I was too late to telephone you." She looked Sonya over closely. "You're picking up some weight, aren't you?"

"Five pounds."

"You seem a little happier."

"I'm making friends at the church, and I keep busy at the nursery school, so that doesn't give me much time to brood. I'm forcing myself to accept the fact that Bryon may not come back, and if he won't, I have to go on living."

"Heard anything from Bryon?"

"Nothing since I moved out of your apartment."

"He probably doesn't know where you are."

"I telephoned his mother and told her, and I imagine she's relayed my whereabouts."

Sonya enjoyed her meal much more with someone to talk to, and she listened to Leta's chatter with satisfaction. The lives of her tenants were discussed at length.

"I've not rented your apartment yet. I want to be especially particular about the tenant who lives across the hall from me, and with your expensive furniture, I want someone who's responsible."

"If Bryon comes back to me, we might be able to move back in."

Leta gave her a look mixed with disgust and sympathy. "I suppose you'll take him back on his own terms if he shows up."

"I married him for 'better or for worse.' I've had the better for two years, and I won't give him up when I experience the 'worse.'"

Leta swallowed her last bite of pie. "Some people like to be martyrs, though I didn't think you would be one of them. But enough of that. We need to start if we're going to do much walking. The daylight hours are getting shorter all the time. Let's take the rest of this tea in a thermos.''

Leta insisted on driving, and Sonya didn't argue much, for she didn't want to be out of town with her unreliable automobile. They headed south to Fontenelle Forest, the largest unbroken tract of forestland in Nebraska. The paths were crowded with many others who desired a last taste of summerlike weather before winter arrived. After two hours of hiking, both of them agreed they'd had enough. Leta suggested they drive north along the Missouri. By the time they started south again, darkness had descended.

"Shall we stop at a restaurant for a snack?" Leta suggested.

Sonya didn't want to admit she didn't have any money, so she said, "There's still some of that pie left. Why can't we eat that?"

"Good idea."

Sonya left the nursery school at noon to keep a doctor's appointment. At the apartment she changed into the blue hand-me-down maternity dress. As she appraised her appearance in the mirror, she noted that her daily walks had given her skin a healthy tinge. She'd always heard that pregnant women glowed with an inner beauty, and although during the first months of unhappiness, she couldn't see anything beautiful about her body, she looked much better now. The woolen dress, obviously an expensive one, raised her self-esteem.

As she drove several blocks to the doctor's office, she peered constantly at the gas gauge. She hesitated to change doctors now, but knowing she must reduce expenses, she thought she should seek an obstetrician closer to the apartment.

Since she was midterm in her pregnancy, she was scheduled for several tests, including a sonogram and an Alpha fetoprotein test. The doctor commented favorably about her low weight gain and said her general health was excellent. He assured her that she had nothing to worry about, but when she received the

statement for his services and the lab work, Sonya cringed—
almost five hundred dollars!

"I don't have that much money with me," Sonya muttered
to the receptionist. "I'll go to the bank, then come back and
pay you." She had deliberately refrained from starting a checking account so she wouldn't be tempted to overspend.

More gasoline wasted to drive to the bank, where she withdrew five hundred dollars from her savings account. If she had
any more expenses like this, she wouldn't have enough money
left to pay for the delivery of her baby. She returned to the
hospital and paid the bill, but when the receptionist started to
schedule her next month's appointment, Sonya said, "I'm
sorry, but I can't come for any more checkups. I can't afford
it."

"But Mrs. Dixon, Dr. Hammer insists on seeing his obstetric
patients regularly. Surely you can make arrangements to pay
for that."

"I have just enough money to pay for the delivery costs, and
I must save that for my confinement. If he doesn't want to
deliver without seeing me regularly, I'll have to find another
obstetrician," she said hotly, for the receptionist's loud voice
carried throughout the crowded waiting room.

"I didn't suggest he wouldn't deliver your baby. It's just an
unusual situation. I'll discuss it with Dr. Hammer." The receptionist gave her a pitying stare. "You poor thing," she said.

Sonya said nothing.

Hoping none of her acquaintances had heard the conversation, Sonya abruptly turned away and rushed out of the room.
Her pride couldn't stand much more.

She hurried into her apartment, for once glad to be enclosed
within its four walls. She didn't know if she would ever have
the nerve to stick her head outside again. What a humiliating
experience! It was bad enough to struggle to pay every bill
without having it broadcast over the city.

Suddenly Sonya felt hatred toward Bryon for what he had
done to her. Up to this point, she'd considered herself at fault

for the situation, but now she transferred her resentment to Bryon. She jerked off the secondhand maternity dress and flung it across the room, where it fell in a heap. She unfolded the bed and collapsed on the wrinkled sheets, wondering how she could ever find comfort for her breaking heart. Her greatest agony came from her suspicion that the unconditional love she had reserved for her husband had not been mutual. Had he *ever* loved her?

She lay there until the room was completely dark, hoping she could go to sleep. She roused when a knock sounded on the door, snapped on a light and took a robe from the closet. She considered not going to the door, for it had to be someone from the apartment building. Checking to be sure the security chain was in place, she opened the door slightly. The short, handsome man who'd often tried to converse with her stood in the hall.

She started to close the door, but he stuck his foot in the opening. "I thought you might be lonesome and want some company," he said.

"When I do, I'll choose my own company. Take your foot out of the door."

He stood indecisively a few moments, and Sonya panicked, wondering what she could do if he refused to leave? But he withdrew his foot. "Sorry, ma'am," he said. "Guess I made a mistake."

Shivering, Sonya shut the door and staggered back into the room. She slumped into one of the straight chairs and leaned her head on the table. *So this is the opinion they have of me.* Her pregnancy was obvious now, and she supposed her new neighbors had deduced that she was an unwed mother. Had it come to this? That she appeared to be fair game for any lecherous man who crossed her path? She felt the child move in her body and she shuddered again. How could she possibly make a decent life for it?

The outside buzzer sounded, and Sonya eagerly went to answer. Maybe it was the Bensons! They always seemed to know when she needed help.

"Yes," she said.

"Sonya, this is Bryon. I want to talk to you."

Suddenly Sonya had trouble breathing, and she grabbed at a chair for support.

"Did you hear me, Sonya?"

"Yes. I'll release the door. I'm in apartment 405."

She looked wildly around the room. She rushed to fold up the couch. She picked up her dress from the floor and threw it in the closet. She recoiled at her image in the mirror, but before she could do anything with her personal appearance, his knock sounded at the door. Her heart pounded wildly, and her legs trembled so much they hardly supported her as she opened the door. His virile, stimulating presence overwhelmed her, and she threw her arms around him.

Bryon pushed Sonya aside; he wasn't alone! Gail Lantz preceded him into the room—a Gail Lantz, sleek and tantalizing, in a woolen suit that probably cost more than the doctor's bill Sonya had paid today.

Sonya didn't ask them to sit down, and she waited for Bryon to speak. Her throat was too dry to utter a sound.

"Why did you move into a place like this?" Bryon demanded, as if her dwelling had insulted him.

"I didn't have any choice."

"Why didn't you go back to your parents? I thought that's what you would do—the reason I cut off your expenses. I wanted you to leave Omaha."

"I had my own reasons," Sonya said shortly. Why bother to defend herself to Bryon? Why had she allowed him to put her on the defensive? She should have attacked him first.

"What did you do with our furniture? This stuff is junk," he said as he glanced around the room.

"I sold the furniture to Leta and put the proceeds in a savings account to pay for my confinement. Maternity care is expensive."

"I wouldn't know," he said. He motioned Sonya toward the

couch and drew up one of the straight chairs for himself. Gail still hadn't said a word, and the other two ignored her.

Bryon smiled, and Sonya saw him as the person she'd loved so long. "Sonya, I want to be fair with you, but I don't want to be married to you anymore, nor do I intend to be saddled with alimony payments. Let's admit we made a mistake, agree on a onetime payment and call it quits."

"But, Bryon, don't you even intend to acknowledge that you have a child?"

"No, I don't." His smile disappeared, and his face hardened. "You're responsible for the child, since I depended on you to prevent one. I'll give you a settlement that will pay for your medical expenses and support you for six months, and after that I'm through."

Sonya caught his hand and, ignoring Gail's presence, she said, "Bryon, how can you forget so quickly the love we shared? Don't you love me at all?"

His face softened, and his gaze failed to meet hers. He hesitated and returned the pressure of her hand, but Gail laughed ironically.

"Maybe I'd better leave, and you two can take up where you left off."

Her comment broke the spell, and Bryon threw an angry glance in her direction, but he dropped Sonya's hand. "What about it, Sonya? Will you agree to a onetime settlement? I'll be generous with you. That way we can both start our lives over again."

Sonya felt tears stinging her eyelids, but she refused to cry with Gail in the room. She lifted a hand to still her trembling lips.

"You can't expect me to make this decision without giving it some thought. How long will you be in Omaha, Bryon?"

"Three days. I'm here to attend the annual board meeting of the firm."

"Telephone me in two days, and I'll give you an answer."

Bryon's manner with Gail was curt as he ushered her out of

the room, and Sonya had a feeling she hadn't cemented her relationship with Bryon by the comment she had made.

Sonya sat in a state of numbed shock after they left. Her mind rioted with unanswered questions. Why had Bryon brought Gail with him? Was he afraid to be alone with her? Afraid he would succumb to their former relationship? How should she react to his suggestion of a onetime settlement? She had to talk to someone. Should she telephone her parents? Lola and Riley? The Bensons?

After more than an hour, she telephoned Leta.

"Bryon has been here."

"What! Tell me all about it."

Eager to hear the story, Leta didn't interrupt while Sonya related Bryon's visit. "And I don't know what to do next," she concluded.

"Go to see Daniel Massie. You'll have to consult a lawyer, and I don't imagine he'll think much of this onetime settlement."

"But what about his fees? I don't make enough money to pay my current expenses."

"I told you that lawyers often add their fees to the divorce settlement. He'll get his money out of Bryon. If necessary, I'll loan you the money, or give it to you for that matter. It would be worth it to help some woman escape the clutches of a man like Bryon Dixon."

"But, Leta, for a few minutes tonight, he was like the old Bryon that I love. I believe if Gail hadn't been along, he might have agreed to come back to me. I wonder if that's why he brought her."

"Possibly. But let's not stray from the point. Are you going to contact Daniel Massie?"

"I guess I'll have to."

Sonya telephoned Daniel from the church office the next morning and set up an appointment for after work at the nursery school. To save a parking fee and gasoline, she took public transportation to Daniel's office. While she waited at the bus stop, a young woman, whom she recognized as a resident of the apartment complex, arrived at the stop with three small children in tow.

Because of Bryon's visit, Sonya had forgotten about the man who had tried to come into her apartment the night before. Perhaps it was time she made her marital circumstances known to her neighbors.

"Hello," she said to the young woman. "I'm Sonya Dixon, and I live in Washburn Complex. Haven't I seen you there, too?"

"Yes," the woman said stiffly. "I've spoken to you several times, but you didn't act like you wanted to be friendly."

"I'm sorry, but I haven't been fit company for anyone, not even myself. My husband walked off and left me three months ago, and I haven't been able to deal with it very well. When I moved into the apartment, I couldn't have told you that, but I'm finally accepting the fact."

"Are you divorced?"

"No, and I'm hoping we won't be. He came to see me last night, and I'm going to a lawyer this afternoon, but I'm pregnant, you see, and I'd like to keep our home together."

"We'd kinda wondered if you had a husband. Lots of young women in the complex don't have a man. My husband tells me not to have anything to do with them, but a body's got to have some adult company. I'd climb the walls if I didn't talk to anyone but these kids, day in, day out."

"Maybe we can meet for coffee someday. I'm sorry I haven't been friendly."

"Sure, I understand. My sister went through the same thing."

"Does your husband work away?"

"He's a migrant worker, so he's gone most of the time. He'll be home next week for the rest of the winter."

"There comes my bus. Is this the one you're taking?"

"No. By the way, my name is Loretta Slinde. I live in 212."

"My number is 405. Let's have coffee one day soon."

Sonya was early for her appointment with Daniel, and though

she wanted to shop for a few minutes, she pushed temptation aside and went on to his office. She had to wait for a half hour, but reading one of his magazines wasn't going to cost her any money; shopping might break down her self-control.

Because she'd seen Daniel quite often at the church, she wasn't ill at ease in his presence as she had been on her previous visit. She explained briefly about Bryon's proposal for a divorce settlement.

"I won't have any money to pay for your services unless he does make an allowance for me, so there won't be any hard feelings if you don't want to represent me. I wouldn't blame you at all."

"Then your salary at the nursery school isn't adequate?"

She shook her head. "It might be if I didn't have anything except general living expenses, but last week I had to replace a tire, and my doctor's bill was five hundred dollars. I make enough for rent and food, but not for one thing extra, although I hope to manage my finances better. I'd sell the car if I could, but Bryon's name is on the title. So I'm using it as little as I can, and I've canceled my doctor's appointments. When my baby comes, I'll just have to enter the hospital as an emergency patient and take whatever doctor is on duty."

"Not a very wise procedure, Mrs. Dixon." When they'd met in church, Daniel had been calling her "Sonya," but here in the office, they were on a professional footing, which made it much less embarrassing for her.

"I don't seem to have any other choice."

"Oh, you have several other options, but you didn't choose any of them. Don't worry about my fee. Your husband will eventually have to pay it, or I'm not worth much to you. About the settlement, I think you're unwise to do anything until after your child is born. If the baby should have health or emotional problems, medical bills could run into thousands of dollars. There's no way those problems could be anticipated in a predivorce settlement."

"Then you think I should tell him no," Sonya said, with a

lighter heart. The longer she could put off divorce, the more likely that Bryon would come back to her.

"He would only have to wait another three or four months, and he's unreasonable to refuse that."

"He won't like it, but I'll hold firm."

"Refer him to me if he becomes difficult."

Sonya dreaded Bryon's call, and it was almost a relief when he didn't contact her that night, but she fretted all the next day, knowing she couldn't put off the controversy any longer. She hoped that he would come to see her, but the phone rang soon after six o'clock.

"All right, Sonya, I need your decision," he said briskly.

"Bryon, is there no possibility that you'll change your mind? You know I don't want a divorce."

"Don't start that. I only have a short time—our meeting reconvenes soon. But since you bring it up, I don't want a divorce, either, but neither do I want a child. If you'll give the baby up for adoption as soon as it's born without even seeing it, and have an operation to prevent another pregnancy, I'll forget about the divorce and come back as soon as you're back to normal. I only want you if we live as we did before you got yourself in this mess."

In other words he wants my undivided attention, wants to put me up on a little pedestal and have me decorate his home.

"I don't believe that would work, even if I'd agree to such a horrible suggestion. I'll admit that I don't particularly want a child, either, and with all the trouble it's caused, I have trouble looking forward to it. But I'm going to overcome that, and even if I don't love the baby, I can't deny my responsibility to it. I've seen the problems of too many unwanted children at the nursery school."

"That's my only bargaining point, and apparently you're rejecting it."

"Bryon, why don't you like children?"

He was silent for a few minutes, and Sonya didn't interrupt

his thinking. She had wondered about this often and hoped for an answer.

"I really don't know. Actually, I don't dislike children in general. I just didn't want any of my own. As long as I had you, I didn't need anyone else in my life."

Sonya's heart lifted. "Then you still love me?"

Her heart seemed to stop beating while he hesitated, and she waited for him to speak.

"We're straying away from my reason for telephoning. When can we meet with our lawyers to agree upon a divorce date and settlement? It's all over, Sonya, and you might as well accept it."

Sonya was so disappointed that she replied angrily, "It isn't all over for me and won't be for some time. I went to a lawyer yesterday, and he advised me to refuse any settlement until after the baby is born. That won't be until another three months."

"I won't accept that. Who is your lawyer?"

She told him, adding, "But I won't agree to a divorce, so you're wasting your time to contact him."

"Then you needn't expect any support from me, no maternity benefits, nothing."

"I've been getting along for three months on my own. I'll make it, Bryon. If you can live with yourself by denying your responsibilities, I can live without any support from you. You and Gail will just have to wait for a while."

"Not that it's any of your business, but we aren't waiting."

With a curse, Bryon slammed down the receiver, terminating the conversation and confirming Sonya's suspicions. They were already living together!

Chapter Seven

The classroom seemed unusually quiet. The children had gone for the day, but Sonya had stayed to help Eloise take down the turkey and pumpkin display on the bulletin boards and to put up the Christmas decorations. Each day she lingered beyond her scheduled hours, because she hated going home to an empty apartment. If she worked until she was exhausted, she could fall into bed at an early hour. Most of the time sleep wiped out her trauma, except for those nights when she dreamed— dreamed of Bryon still loving her, dreamed of Bryon in Gail's arms, dreamed of Bryon gone forever.

Adam and Marie stopped by the nursery room when Eloise and Sonya had almost finished. Plastic snowflakes tumbled at random on the windows, and a nativity scene, with figures as large as the children, stood in one corner of the room. On a low table a Christmas tree blinked red and green, and brightly wrapped packages dangled from the ceiling on colorful tinsel ropes. Each child would receive one of those gifts on the last day before the Christmas break.

Sonya loitered until Eloise was ready to lock the door. As they left the room, Marie put her arm around Sonya.

"Sonya, don't overdo. You don't look well. We appreciate all the work you're doing here, but you must be careful."

"I was doing fairly well until Bryon came to see me. I'm developing a bitter attitude toward him. I resent the way he's treating me. And, too, I'm not looking forward to the Christmas season.''

"Are you going to your parents' for Christmas? The school will be closed for ten days—you would have ample time.''

"My mother is expecting me to come and insists on sending me a plane ticket, but I haven't decided yet.''

"If you don't go away, we want you to share Christmas dinner with us,'' Marie said. "And in the meantime, we're always as close as your phone.''

"Thanks. I'm still using the We Care numbers, but not as often as I did. And I'm finding much comfort in the Bible, but I fear my faith is still very weak.''

As she trudged across the street and up to her apartment, Sonya wrestled with her decision about Christmas. During the past two holiday seasons, she and Bryon had enjoyed a succession of dinners and parties that started with Thanksgiving and continued through the New Year. She had hoped that she would still be invited to some of those festivities, but she hadn't heard from anyone, not even the Shraders. Lola and Riley always had a brunch on Thanksgiving morning, but Lola hadn't called her for several weeks. Not since their lunch date. She realized that a single would be a "fifth wheel" at a couples party, like the brunch, but couldn't Lola still remain a friend, anyway?

She'd made it through Thanksgiving with Leta's help. Leta had spent Thanksgiving Eve with Sonya. They'd attended church together, and then Leta had come back to the apartment and stayed until midnight. The next morning she'd come for Sonya, and they'd gone to a restaurant featuring a large buffet. Since the weather was good, they'd driven east on the interstate to Des Moines, and by the time they'd gotten home, Sonya was tired enough to sleep.

But Leta would visit her mother in St. Louis for Christmas, and although it was kind of the Bensons to ask her for the holiday, she had no intention of intruding. Sonya was gradually becoming more self-reliant. She had learned that when she helped one of the children at school overcome a big problem it made her own situation more bearable. *It's time I search for others who are as lonely as I am and reach out to them. I must stop expecting people to do for me. Perhaps I can find healing by helping others.*

Sonya heard the phone ringing when she reached her apartment, and she hurriedly opened the door.

"Hello, Sonya. You're late tonight."

"Yes, Mother. We decorated the room for Christmas after the children left."

"I need to know what day you're coming, so I can arrange for your plane ticket. If I don't do it soon, you may not get a reservation."

"I've decided not to come to Ohio for Christmas."

Her mother cried, "Sonya, do you realize you haven't been home for Christmas since you were married?"

"I know, and I'm sorry to hurt you, but, Mother, I'm hurting, too. I want to be at home, but my pride won't let me come back alone, proving that I've failed at marriage. Perhaps when the baby comes, and I have something to show for three years of 'wedded bliss,' I may lose my hurt, but I can't face my friends and the extended family now. Thirty or forty relatives on Christmas Day is more than I can handle. Please try to understand."

"What are you going to do?"

"The Bensons have invited me to spend Christmas with them." Her mother needn't know that she wouldn't accept the invitation.

"What can we send you for Christmas then? What do you need?"

The ogre of the hospital bill loomed closer and closer and without thinking, Sonya said, "Why don't you send what you would spend for a plane ticket, and I can apply it to my medical expenses when the baby is born?"

"Why, Sonya, don't you have insurance? Isn't Bryon taking care of that?"

Too late Sonya realized what she had done. So far she'd carefully concealed Bryon's total parsimony from her parents. Was that pride, too? Not wanting to admit that the man she'd chosen could behave so shabbily.

"I'm finding out there are many expenses besides medical bills," she said, trying to repair the damage she'd done. "I had no idea what baby clothes cost! I wasn't begging—I'm getting along all right—but you will buy me a Christmas gift, anyway, so it might as well be what I need rather than something frivolous. Or if you would rather, you can buy some baby items. You've reared four children, so you know what I'll need better than I do."

"I might just do that—it's fun to buy for grandchildren. But you're sure you aren't in actual need?"

"Mother, I'm doing fine, and I have to salve my ego by proving to myself and Bryon that I can manage alone."

"You don't think he'll come back to you?"

"It doesn't seem likely, but I'm still hoping."

"I can't understand why you would want a man who deserted you, but it's your decision."

This thought had often filtered into Sonya's mind, but it annoyed her to have her mother express it so bluntly.

"Daddy never left you, did he?"

"Of course not!"

"Then don't judge my reactions, Mother. You can't know how I feel. I love you, but I have to work this out myself."

Physically drained after the phone conversation and the long hours at school, Sonya made short work of dinner preparations. She warmed a can of soup and washed an apple. With these and a few crackers on a tray, she sat on the couch to watch the news while she ate. The ringing phone awakened her, and she glanced at the tray. She'd eaten about half of the food before she had fallen asleep. As she answered the phone, she noted the time was nine o'clock.

"Sonya, this is Daniel Massie. Am I telephoning too late?"

"No, not at all."

"I have something to discuss with you. Could we have dinner together tomorrow night?"

"Uh," she hesitated. "Is it something about Bryon or the divorce?"

"No, I want to discuss a proposition that might solve your financial problems."

"And you can't tell me what it's about?"

"I'd rather talk to you in person."

"Then I suppose we could go to dinner."

"Fine. I'll pick you up at your apartment. Will six o'clock be all right?"

Sonya sat for a long while before she took the tray to the kitchen and dumped the cold food into the garbage. She pulled out the couch and made up her bed, although she wasn't sleepy. What did Daniel want? Why couldn't he have told her on the phone? Although she didn't suspect Daniel of any romantic ideas, still she didn't want to be in a man's company. The more she thought about going out with any man who might approach her romantically the more upset she became. Sonya spent most of the night tossing and turning, unable to sleep. She couldn't go through with it.

But with morning, her common sense took over. Even during the years with Bryon, she had lunched occasionally with some of their mutual male friends, and she knew that Daniel Massie was interested only in her spiritual and material welfare. He was friendly toward all the women at the church—married or unmarried—so why make such an issue about a simple dinner engagement? There was something special about Daniel, Sonya had to admit to herself. She always got a good feeling being around him. He was so warm and kind. He seemed so sure of himself; confident, but not in an arrogant way like some men. No, it was his strong faith, she decided that made him seem so calm and clear-sighted. So grounded. She envied him that. And thinking about Daniel, she was amazed at how light her spirits were during the day as she looked forward to the evening.

Although she usually dawdled after school, when her duties

ended for the day, she rushed out of the building, eager to get to her apartment and make preparations for the evening. She took the blue dress she had discarded, after that disastrous incident at the doctor's office, downstairs to the laundry, and after running it through the wash and dry cycles, she was pleased with its appearance.

After showering, she styled her hair in soft waves, and her blond hair flowed freely around her shoulders. With her makeup kit that she hadn't used for months, she applied colors that brought out the gold tints in her hair and, draping the blue dress over her shoulders, she saw that it emphasized her blue eyes, making them seem brighter, but just a bit on the mysterious side.

Her hands hovered indecisively over her jewelry box. Bryon had pressured her to dispose of all of the jewelry that she'd had before they were married, so all that she possessed had been gifts from him. Would it be proper for her to wear his jewelry when she was dining with another man? She thought longingly of the gold chains she'd been given by the boyfriend she'd been dating when she met Bryon. She remembered Bryon's tirade when she'd worn one of those chains on their honeymoon. Hoping to avoid future unpleasantness, she had readily agreed to give away her jewelry, and he'd bought her more expensive necklaces. Did it show a lack of character on her part that she'd gone along with all of Bryon's suggestions? Boy! She had been putty in his hands.

Recklessly Sonya reached inside the jewelry box and withdrew the diamond necklace and earrings. Adding those to her attire really made her look elegant, and when Daniel sounded the buzzer, she went to meet him with a self-confidence that she hadn't felt for months.

For the first time Sonya was aware of Daniel's masculinity that Leta was always raving about. At the office he wore dark suits, but tonight he was dressed in a casual tweed sport coat with a tan shirt opened at the collar. He complimented Sonya on her appearance, took her arm and ushered her into his car as graciously as if she were royalty.

Driving away from the apartment house, he said, "And where shall we eat? Do you like Chinese, Mexican or plain old American food?"

"Yes."

He looked at her inquiringly, and she laughed. "I mean I like all of them, so choose any restaurant you want. My grandmother used to admonish us, 'Eat what's put before you,' so we grew up with a taste for all food."

"Then let's go to a steak house. I know a good one a few blocks from here."

The restaurant he chose was one where she had gone often with Bryon, and she almost asked Daniel to drive on to another place, but if she was ever going to forget Bryon, she might as well start tonight. But her resolve suffered a setback when they encountered Lola and Riley Shrader dining with another couple from the brokerage firm.

Sonya tried to maintain her emotional equilibrium as she introduced Daniel to her former friends, but her mind rioted as she and Daniel continued to their table. *This will be all over town by tomorrow, and Bryon will be sure to find out. Why did something have to happen to remind her of Bryon tonight? Even in his absence, did he monopolize her life?*

Perhaps realizing the emotional jolt she had received, while they waited for their meal, Daniel asked about her childhood on the farm.

"We have a dairy farm, milking Holsteins and a few Jerseys. Dad owns two hundred acres of beautiful, fertile soil. My brother-in-law has been operating the farm since Dad retired two years ago, although he still does a lot of the work."

"Didn't you have a brother who was interested in working the farm?"

"No brother, although I have three sisters. Needless to say, being the youngest in the family, my siblings often accuse me of being spoiled, which isn't true because our parents showed no favoritism. Dad sacrificed to give all of us a college education, and then I had to disappoint him by marrying Bryon.''

"Without any brothers, did you girls have to help with the farm work?'' Daniel asked, deftly shifting the conversation away from a subject that disturbed Sonya.

"My two oldest sisters did, and they became very good with the farm machinery. Dad took me to the fields when I was sixteen, but after I plowed out two rows of his best corn, he decided that tractors weren't my forte.'' A smile flitted across Daniel's face. "After that I helped mother in the garden some of the time, but mostly the two younger daughters were expected to help with the housework.''

"Do you miss the farm?''

"I've been home only once since I married, for Bryon didn't want me to go alone, and he was always too busy to take me. I missed the family at first, but I've grown accustomed to being separated from them.''

"I've always been interested in farming,'' he said. "My grandparents owned a farm in central Nebraska, and I spent all of my childhood summers there. Grandpa thought that I'd become a farmer, but my life took another direction.''

"You're probably better off as an attorney. Farming is hard work.''

"Any profession is hard if you give it your best, and that's what I try to do.''

"What made you decide to become an attorney?''

"Several factors influenced my decision. I mentioned when you were in my office that my father abandoned my mother when I was a child. Of course, a five-year-old isn't very observant, but I still remember my mother crying late into the night when she thought my sister and I were asleep. My paternal grandfather helped us, or we would have gone hungry because mother had married young and didn't have any job skills, nor did she have anyone to care for us if she had worked.''

"I can see why you compared my situation to hers.''

He nodded. "And although I'm not proud of this, growing

up without a father was difficult for me, and I started running around with the wrong friends. I refused to go to church with mother, my grades were poor, and I failed the eighth grade. That summer I was accused of breaking into a store and stealing a television set. I hadn't done it, but my reputation was bad, and when the police took me for questioning, I was terrified. If it hadn't been for a family friend who was a lawyer, I would have been punished for that crime. He believed that I was innocent and represented me without compensation. I was so happy when I was proved innocent that I made up my mind to stop my rebellion, to study law, and become the kind of attorney who would be more concerned about justice for his clients than his own aggrandizement. I especially wanted to help boys who needed guidance.''

Daniel paused while the waitress replenished their beverages and took away their salad plates, and Sonya noted particularly how considerate Daniel was of this woman as he stacked dishes and handed them to her.

''I started studying, and during my high school years, I managed to be an honor student.'' Daniel continued. ''About the time I was ready for college, my grandfather died and left his entire estate to me, so it was easy to finance my education and embark on the goal I'd set for myself.''

''You have certainly fulfilled your goal. You've been such a comfort to me, and I'm extremely grateful to Leta for bringing me to you. It's obvious to me that you are a caring person.''

''I take little credit for that. I owe it to that attorney who set a good example for me, my grandfather, and to God. When, as a teenager, I was struggling to find some meaning to my life, wanting to make new friends and chart a different path, I read a promise in one of the Psalms that I claimed for my own. *I will instruct you and teach you in the way you should go; I will counsel you and watch over you.* There has seldom been a day since then that I haven't asked God to fulfill that promise in my life.''

''Perhaps I shouldn't ask, but if you're so interested in helping children, why haven't you married and had a family of your own?''

Sonya thought she saw a shadow flicker across Daniel's warm gaze, but when he spoke his voice betrayed little emotion.

''At first I was too busy getting an education, helping mother and seeing that my sister was educated, to consider marriage. Now that my sister is settled, and Mother is comfortably established, I intend to marry.''

''I thought the many broken marriages you encounter in your practice might have discouraged you from taking a wife.''

''Those experiences have taught me to be wary, but I do intend to marry, because I've observed enough happy couples, like Adam and Marie for instance, to know that it is possible to have a Christian home and family. That's the kind I expect to have.''

As Sonya listened to him, she was impressed by his eloquence and his rugged good looks. When she first met Daniel, she hadn't considered him handsome, so what had happened to change her mind? Perhaps it was his infectious smile resulting in a crinkle in his forehead that made her smile. She was happier in Daniel's presence than with anyone else, and that realization made her squirm uncomfortably in her chair, as she lifted a hand to her flushed face. She didn't want to become emotionally involved with another man, especially when she thought there was a chance to reconcile with Bryon, and although Daniel was a cut above most men she had ever known, he was a man, and once burned, she knew to stay away from the fire. If she could simply be his friend, she would like to be more closely associated with Daniel, but could she see him often without wanting more than friendship? Sonya knew that she yearned for love, but could she ever trust another man with her heart? *Why couldn't she have met a man like Daniel before she made her disastrous marriage?* There was no doubt in her mind that the woman who married Daniel would never feel unloved or unhappy.

By the time they'd finished their salads, T-bone steaks and

baked potatoes, Sonya had pushed the meeting with the Shraders into the background, and while they waited for dessert, Daniel said, "I suppose you're wondering what I wanted to talk with you about."

Sonya laughed. "Actually, I've been enjoying myself so much that I'd forgotten there was a purpose to our meeting."

Daniel looked at her appraisingly. "Sonya, do you realize that tonight is the first time I've ever heard you laugh."

She sobered immediately. "I really haven't had much to laugh about the past few months. I used to be a happy, carefree person, who laughed a lot." She rubbed her cheeks. "I suppose that's the reason my face feels stretched. I haven't used my laugh muscles for a long time. I used to be pleasant company. I suppose all of my new friends think I'm a sourpuss."

He reached out and touched her lightly on the hand. "Let me say that I prefer the laughing Sonya. Try to think about the future with a smile."

Sonya withdrew her hand, her skin burning at his touch, but Daniel didn't seem rebuffed.

"I wanted to talk to you about an idea that I've been rolling around in my head for a few weeks. You may need some time to think about the proposition I want to make, and you may not be interested in it, but at least hear me through."

Sonya nodded and relaxed in the chair.

"You've been open with me about your finances, so I know you're having quite a struggle. My suggestion might alleviate your financial worries, and at the same time you could be a help to someone else."

With a smile Sonya said, "That's strange. In the past few days I've concluded that I'd spent too much time brooding about my problems, and that it was time I started reaching out to those in need."

"I have an elderly client who needs someone to stay with her at night. She has a maid who takes care of the house cleaning and that type of thing during the daytime, but Mrs. York isn't too well and shouldn't live alone. However, she resists moving to a nursing home.

"My idea is that you could give up your apartment, move to her home, be there with her at night, and still work at the nursery school. Those arrangements would free your salary for the hospital confinement and other expenses. I can't guarantee that my client will look favorably on this suggestion, but I feel the arrangement could be beneficial to both of you."

"That might be all right temporarily, but in three months, I'll have a child. No elderly woman will want a baby in her home, and if I give up my apartment for three months, I might not find another."

"She might welcome having a small one in the house. Her last close relative, a granddaughter, passed away about a year ago, and the old lady is quite lonely."

"Where does she live?"

"In a large house in the northwest section of Omaha. At one time her family owned a ranch there, but progress has encroached on her, and she now has only five acres surrounding the house. There's one bad part of my suggestion—you couldn't walk to work, and there aren't good bus connections. You'd have to drive, and that will take some expense."

"When opportunity knocks, it seems as if I should investigate, but shouldn't you find out her reaction before we discuss it further?"

"Do you know Edith York?" He observed her closely with questioning eyes as if to determine what the name meant to her.

"No, I don't think so."

"I'll go to see Edith tomorrow morning, and if she's receptive to the idea, perhaps I could take you out to meet her in the afternoon. Or would you prefer to drive out by yourself?"

"It might be better for me to go with you. I don't know much about that part of Omaha."

Sonya didn't go to bed until the early hours of the morning, for she kept thinking of their dinner conversation. For her nightly reading, she opened the Bible to the book of Romans, turning to a Scripture that often puzzled her. *And we know that in all things God works for the good of those who love him, who have been called according to his purpose.* Her faith in God was more secure now than it had ever been, but she had not yet figured out how it could be good for her to suffer through Bryon's abandonment and the heartaches it had brought, and now when she had found a man who seemed to be all one could want in a husband, she was so disillusioned that she even hesitated to be Daniel's friend.

She had once read a poem, "The Weaver," that compared one's life to a weaving fashioned by the hand of God, who alone could see the overall pattern. She couldn't remember all of the words, but one line had read, "I in foolish pride forget He sees the upper, and I, the under side" of the weaving. The poet had further explained that in a weaving dark threads were as important as the bright colors, and that only the Weaver knew the final outcome. Could this mean that to experience life to its fullest required dark, as well as beautiful days?

Was there a purpose after all to these months of trouble she had endured? Although she could see only the present, was God cognizant of the full scope of her existence? Was life a chain of events all woven together? If she hadn't married Bryon, she would never have come to Omaha, and if Bryon hadn't deserted her, she would never have met Daniel and through his loving concern become aware that all men were not like Bryon, and most important of all, if she was still with Bryon, her relationship with God would have continued to deteriorate. It was difficult for her to comprehend that God would go to such lengths to order her life, but that must be true.

Sonya didn't know anything about weaving, but she thought of the large jigsaw puzzles she and her sisters had enjoyed fitting together when they were children. When they first dumped the jumbled pieces out on the table, it was incredible to think they could assemble them to match the picture on the box. Piece by piece, however, the finished product took shape. Perhaps her life was like that, and she would never know the reason for disappointments and failures until the picture was completed. *But if life was a puzzle, where did Daniel fit in?*

Daniel stopped by the nursery school the next morning and spoke to Sonya briefly. "Mrs. York is quite eager to discuss my idea with you. What time do you finish here?"

"I can leave anytime after two o'clock."

"My secretary and I have an appointment with another attorney in that area. We'll stop by the school and pick you up, introduce you to Mrs. York, give you an hour for visiting, then bring you back to your apartment. Will that be satisfactory?"

"Yes, thank you."

While the children had nap time, Sonya asked Eloise for permission to go to the apartment to change her clothing. Being an elderly person, Mrs. York probably wouldn't want to see a pregnant woman in slacks, so she chose the multicolored polyester hand-me-down dress and was back in the classroom when Daniel and his secretary arrived.

Daniel endorsed her clothing change with a smile. "Mrs. York comes from an old line of aristocrats, and she has strong ideas about proper apparel. She'll approve of your appearance."

A beautiful old cast-iron gate marked the entrance to the buff-colored brick residence. Though Daniel had said a *large* house, Sonya wasn't prepared for the opulence of the estate. The driveway curved up a small hill toward a three-storied house that faced a magnificent lawn. A brick wall marked the rear of the property, and an iron fence based in buff brick surrounded the front and sides of the estate.

When Daniel stopped in front of the house, Sonya sensed the isolation of the place. Numerous trees on the property concealed the dwellings around it. Although others lived within a mile of the property, it appeared as secluded as it had been when the house was built many years ago.

Before they knocked at the door, Daniel said, "Please don't give Mrs. York an answer until I talk with you again. You need to know some facts that she probably won't tell you, but I didn't want you to know them, thinking they might sway your opinion. After you meet Mrs. York, I'm sure they'll make no difference.''

Sonya nodded.

"And be candid with Mrs. York. She'll understand your situation.''

Sonya doubted that an elderly woman who lived in these surroundings could possibly understand problems of divorce and rejection so common in the current generation, but she hoped Daniel was right.

In spite of the cold wind blowing across the wide porch, she felt hot and nervous. An older woman with a kind face answered Daniel's knock. She was a housekeeper or maid, Sonya assumed.

"Good afternoon, Mr. Massie. Mrs. York is in her living room."

Bug-eyed, Sonya followed Daniel down the wide hallway. She'd entered another world. An intricately carved walnut grand stairway led from the entrance hall to the second floor. On the landing a grandfather clock announced the time at three o'clock. A huge wrought-iron chandelier, holding electric candles, hung from the second-floor ceiling. Sonya would have suspected that a house this old would have suffered neglect, but judging from her quick inspection, the house was intact and orderly.

Mrs. York was tiny, fragile and gray-haired. Her hair was dressed in an upsweep that had been done at a beauty shop. She wore a fashionable blue dress that matched vivid, sparkling eyes, and a pair of diamond earrings dangled from pierced ears.

Sonya's heart sank when she saw this woman whom Daniel Massie thought might prove her benefactor. This woman needed nothing—she wouldn't welcome a pregnant nobody, nor would she want a howling infant to destroy the quiet and peace of this house. Sonya almost turned on her heel and walked out the door, but she didn't want to let Daniel down after he'd been so kind to her.

Daniel made the introductions, then said, "I'll return for you in an hour, Sonya. That should give the two of you time to become acquainted."

"Lay aside your coat and sit down, Sonya," Mrs. York said when Daniel exited. "Stelle will bring us some refreshments. Do you prefer tea or coffee?"

"Tea, please."

"That's what I always have. She'll be along soon."

While waiting for Mrs. York to speak, Sonya looked around the room. It might have been a drawing room once, but now it served as a bed-living-room combination. One side of the room had been partitioned into a bathroom. Near the bathroom door was a single bed. The section of the room where Mrs. York sat contained a small sofa, several chairs, bookshelves and a television. A telephone stood on the table beside the chair.

Sonya considered the most outstanding piece of furniture to be an ornately carved chest at the foot of the bed, although it contrasted vividly with the many antique items in the room. Nursery rhyme characters decorated the polished maple chest. Little Red Riding Hood and the Three Bears were delicately carved and painted on the light wood. This child's toy box seemed out of place in the room of an octogenarian.

"When is your baby due, Sonya?"

That was the last place Sonya expected the conversation to start.

"Around the first of March."

"Are you having any trouble physically?"

"No, and the baby is all right, too. I had a series of tests at midterm, and the doctor assures me all is well. My problem is emotional, but I suppose Mr. Massie told you about my situation."

"Just a few basic facts. He seemed to think it better if you told me what you wanted me to know."

Stelle entered the room with a tray on her shoulder. She placed it on the low table in front of Mrs. York. The maid poured a cup and handed it to Sonya, then she carefully measured a small portion of milk and some sugar into a cup, filled the cup half-full of tea and the rest water. She pushed Mrs. York's chair closer to the table.

"Help yourself to the cookies," Stelle said. "I made them this morning, special."

"Mrs. York..." Sonya began haltingly as Stelle exited.

"Call me Edith. My friends all do."

"My husband left me three months ago when he found out I was pregnant. He hasn't given me any support since, and I've been too proud to force him to do so, nor would I allow my parents to support me. I've been trying to make it on my own, and frankly I've had a struggle. Mr. Massie seemed to think we might be of some mutual help to each other, but seeing the way you live, I can't think I would be any help to you. Since I have a long way to go before I'll be over this situation, my company may not be good for you."

"But I'm in need of healing, too, and I need a companion. If I can't have someone in the house at night, I'll have to go to a nursing home. I don't want that."

"I can understand why you wouldn't want to leave here."

"I was born in this house soon after the turn of the century, ten years after my father built it. We were out in the country in those days, but the city has surrounded us. My husband sold off everything except these five acres before he died."

"Has your husband been gone long?"

"Almost twenty-five years."

"I'd think you would be healed by this time."

"Oh, I'm not grieving for my husband. I need healing because of the death of my granddaughter, whom I lost a year ago. She was my only close relative, and she was soon to bear a child, too."

"Then won't my presence be an unpleasant reminder?"

"No, on the contrary, I think it would benefit me."

"If you should invite me to stay with you, would it be temporary? I can't believe you would want a child in the house. I suppose I could take the baby to the church nursery during the day, but at night I would have it with me.''

"This is a big house, my dear. I'm pretty much confined to this room and the dining room now. I have a bad heart, as well as an arthritic condition, which won't allow much stair climbing. Indeed, I have no desire to go upstairs, anyway, but my point is, your quarters wouldn't be on this floor, and I wouldn't hear the child.''

Sonya laughed slightly. ''I know it sounds as if I'm trying to wriggle out of this arrangement, but how could I be of any use to you with a child to care for and in another part of the house?''

"I have a buzzer system, which sounds throughout the house. I summon help that way. Actually, I'm ready to die, and wouldn't care if I just slipped away alone, but my doctor and lawyer are worrywarts, and they insist that I must have round-the-clock companionship.''

"Haven't you been able to find people to help?''

Edith hesitated with downcast eyes, and her hands moved nervously in her lap as she said evasively, ''I hardly need a nurse, and I don't feel inclined to pay for a companion when I don't need one, but in this case, when you need a home and I need a night sitter, it would probably work to our advantage. I wouldn't monopolize all of your time, but I would appreciate having you share dinner with me. You would need to prepare your own breakfast each morning, as I sleep late, and Stelle doesn't come until mid-morning. The food would be my expense. You would, of course, be responsible for the support of your child.''

Sonya was ready to agree to the situation. She couldn't see anything except benefit to her. Edith York was personable. The living quarters were great, although something about the house did give her an eerie feeling, and she wondered how she would like being isolated up on this knoll with only an old lady for company. But by living here, she could save almost all of her salary if the daily drive back and forth to work didn't prove too costly.

"This sounds like a good deal for me, but perhaps it would be better if we think it over for a few days."

"That's fine with me, but you should see your rooms before you go. I would like you to stay in my granddaughter's apartment. She had a living room, bedroom, bath and a small kitchenette on the third floor. I'm sure you would find it comfortable." She rang the buzzer, and Stelle came in and picked up the tray.

"Will you show Mrs. Dixon to the third-floor apartment? She may be coming here to live, and she needs to see the quarters."

Stelle turned quickly, stared at her employer, and the tray tipped in her hands. The sugar bowl slid on to the floor. It didn't break, but sugar spread over the carpet.

Sonya looked at the woman in amazement. She had sized up tall, angular Stelle as a well-coordinated, capable woman. What had startled her into dropping the sugar bowl?

"Mrs. Edith!"

"Stop gaping, Stelle, and do as I asked you. It will be all right."

"Yes, Mrs. Edith. I'll sweep up the sugar soon."

Stelle set the tray on a hall table and motioned Sonya to the left. "Quickest way is up the back stairs." When they reached the stairway, she stood aside to let Sonya precede her. "Don't stop at the first door. Go to the door at the head of the stairs."

"Aren't you going?"

"No ma'am. I need to clean up the mess I made."

When Sonya came to the first landing, she opened the door and glanced about. This was the second floor and looked much like the downstairs. Doors opened into four rooms. Before she closed the door and continued upstairs, she admired the large chandelier suspended from the ceiling.

Edith obviously intended to put her in the servants' quarters, and she'd almost decided she wouldn't consider coming here, wondering how she could climb these stairs when her pregnancy became more burdensome. And how about carrying a baby up here each day? But when she opened the door into the apartment, she knew Edith had offered the best she had.

A large picture window commanded a view of farmland to the north, completely overlooking the houses surrounding the estate. It reminded Sonya of the farm at home. She would like that view every day.

Dust sheets covered the furniture, and the rooms had a neglected look. Had anyone cleaned the room since the granddaughter had died? Sonya lifted a sheet to peek at the furniture, finding it more modern than the rest of the furniture in the house. The small bedroom was as pleasant as the living room, and Sonya could tell these rooms, once servants' quarters, had been remodeled in the past few years by Edith for the grandchild she had loved and lost. The low ceilings gave her a sense of protection and comfort. After that one-room apartment, this place looked like heaven.

She went downstairs and entered Edith's room. The woman watched her with anxious blue eyes. "I forgot to tell you, we do have an elevator to the second floor, so you would only have to walk the last set of stairs. Did you like the rooms?"

"I do. Your granddaughter must have been very happy there."

Edith's shoulders shook with sobs, and as Sonya knelt to comfort her, the doorbell rang. Edith patted Sonya's hands and gently pushed her away. "That will be Daniel. He must not see me crying. You run along now and telephone me soon about your decision. I'm willing to have you move in whenever you want to."

"I'll be in touch soon."

Stelle reached the front door at the same time that Sonya left the room. Daniel stepped inside, bringing a flash of snow and cold with him. "Ready?"

"Yes." He held her coat for her and walked by her side out to his car.

"My secretary and I didn't finish. As soon as I take you home, I'll go back and join her."

"I'm sorry to bother you. I could have waited until you finished."

"No bother. I was eager to know how it turned out."

"I'm ready to move in anytime, and she said she was willing to have me. I think it would be great to live in that beautiful house."

"But beautiful houses don't always mean happiness. Edith has had her share of sorrow."

"Yes, she told me about her granddaughter."

"Did she tell you how she died?"

"No, now that you mention it, she didn't."

"I didn't think she would, and I didn't want you to know until you'd met Edith and sized up the situation." He paused again, and Sonya stared at him curiously. "She committed suicide by hanging herself from the large hall chandelier."

Chapter Eight

Sonya switched on the light and sat up, drenched with perspiration and trembling. Three o'clock! This same dream had occurred all night long. She would dream; awaken in fright; go back to sleep; dream again. Same dream, but the victim changed each time.

Sometimes it was a faceless person, and finally she saw herself swinging back and forth over the York mansion's large central hall. Then the scene changed, and she stood on the ledge at Sandhill Apartments ready to jump to her death. What had prompted Edith's granddaughter to take her own life?

Sonya left the bed and went into the kitchen. She heated water and made a strong cup of tea—no more sleep for her tonight. Why hadn't Daniel told her about Edith's granddaughter before she had gone there? The reason was obvious—he was pretty sure she wouldn't go. "Nor will I go now," she muttered. Could she ever walk into that house without remembering the tragedy? No wonder Edith didn't want to go upstairs anymore, and that Stelle avoided the third-floor apartment.

By daylight, Sonya decided that she wouldn't go. She'd made it this far without extra help. There had to be another way. She would ask Daniel to tell Edith that she wouldn't come.

As Sonya sipped on the tea, she kept remembering Edith's words, "I need healing, too." And she thought of her conviction that it was time to reach out to others, rather than to expect all of the benevolence to flow one way. Sonya wished it weren't

Saturday, so she could be busy at school and forget the decision she had to make.

While she cleaned the apartment, laundered her clothes and showered, Sonya kept weighing the pros and cons of living with Edith York. Did the benefits outweigh the liabilities? She would have free room and board for herself and a home for her child, thus enabling her to save enough money to pay for her hospital confinement and to continue her regular appointments with Dr. Hammer. She would have a pleasant place to keep the child and nice wide lawns for his or her stroller. As she looked around the tiny apartment, she admitted how crowded it would be when she moved in the necessary items to raise a child.

And in daylight perspective, she considered her reason for refusing to go as ridiculous. How could the tragic death of Edith's granddaughter have any effect on her? She smiled when she realized that Daniel had used psychology—he knew life with Edith would be pleasant for her, and he wanted her to see that before she heard the debit side.

She telephoned Daniel at his home. When she told him her decision, he asked, "When do you want to move? I'm sure Edith will welcome you anytime."

"The December rent is due in two days, so I might as well give notice and move Monday. I'm sure Eloise will give me the day off to do that."

"Will you need a moving van?"

"I moved here in the car. Except for my clothes and kitchen items, there isn't much to move."

"I'll give you any help you need to settle in your new quarters. Count on me to help with the moving, and I'm sure Adam will help, too."

Sonya felt warmed by Daniel's concern and murmured her thanks. He seemed to go out of his way to help her at every opportunity and she felt grateful for his friendship. She went to the office and notified the manager that she would be moving and returned to start packing. She'd always felt uneasy in this apartment, and it would be a relief to leave. Before she accomplished much, the doorbell rang. At first she didn't recognize the frail, unassuming woman standing in the hall.

"I'm Loretta Slinde. We met on the bus. You told me to come for coffee sometime. Is it all right now? My husband's at home with the kids."

"Certainly. Come on in. As a matter of fact, I'm going to move Monday, so this is probably our last chance."

"You didn't stay long."

"I've been given a chance to move in with an elderly lady. I can stay with her at night for room and board and still work at the school in the daytime. I need some extra money, so this will be a help to me."

She ushered Loretta to the couch. "Let's sit here—it's cozier than the table. Do you want sugar and cream in your coffee?"

"Yeah, I do."

Sonya carried the snack items on a small tray and placed it near Loretta. She was glad she'd bought the cookies yesterday.

"Help yourself to the coffee and cookies. Sorry they aren't homemade."

"Where did you say you were moving?" Loretta asked as she popped half a cookie in her mouth.

"To the home of Edith York. She lives in a big house in north Omaha."

Loretta choked, and bits of cookie flew from her mouth. Her face flushed, and Sonya rose to help her. Loretta waved her away.

"I'm all right. You just surprised me, that's all."

"Would you like a glass of water?"

Loretta shook her head. Although she still struggled for breath, she blurted out, "You can't go there to live—that house is haunted."

Sonya laughed.

"No, I mean it. A young woman who lived there; the old lady's granddaughter I think, well, she killed herself because she was afraid of her gangster husband. That's the reason the old lady can't find anyone to stay with her."

Well, thanks a lot, Daniel Massie.

"I don't believe in that rubbish!"

"Well, I heard it's a scary place. No matter what you believe," Loretta concluded.

"I've already said I would go, and what you've told me only confirms my decision. Mrs. York needs somebody to help her, and that somebody may be me."

Sonya switched the subject, but when the woman left, Sonya telephoned Daniel again.

"What was the name of Edith's granddaughter?"

"Alice Simmons."

"And her husband was?"

"Wade Simmons, a notorious criminal. No doubt you've heard of him."

Sonya swallowed convulsively for she recognized the name as the one on the pamphlet the Bensons had loaned her. "Don't you think it's time for you to tell me *everything* about Edith York?"

"I've always heard that what you don't know won't hurt you," he said with a laugh.

"In this case, I'm not so sure," Sonya countered. "If the ghosts show up, I need to be prepared."

"So you've heard that. You surely don't believe in ghosts."

"Not yet," Sonya joked. Her faith would never permit such a superstitious belief and she was sure Daniel knew that.

He laughed again. "When Alice married Simmons, she didn't know he was a gangster. After she became pregnant, she went back to her grandmother, not wanting to rear a child around Simmons' friends. That's when Edith remodeled the third floor apartment for her. But Simmons wouldn't leave her alone. He wouldn't allow her to make a new life for herself. Alice finally notified the police, and they arrested him at Edith's house. I suppose the shame she'd brought on herself and her grandmother, as well as the fear of reprisal from Simmons if he should escape from prison, drove her to suicide."

"So it was suicide?"

"Evidently. Now, that's the whole story as I know it. I haven't telephoned Edith yet, so if you want to back out, you can. I feel that I have taken advantage of you, but on the other hand, I did it for your own good. It will be a good home for you as long as you like."

"Or as long as Edith lives."

"Yes, I'll admit it's a gamble, as her health isn't good."

"I still intend to go," she replied decidedly.

The more Sonya thought about Alice Simmons the more she felt struck by the shocking coincidence, that of all places, she had been led to the young woman's home. Alice's life was so much like her own, her burden so similar, Sonya felt God's hand in this matter and believed there was a purpose to His leading her to Edith York.

On Sunday afternoon Sonya went to the Sandhill Apartments and found Leta at home. Leta had heard vaguely of Edith York and Alice Simmons, but laughed at the tales about the place being haunted.

"Sounds like a dreary house," she said honestly. "But it might be a better place for you to live now."

As she left Leta's apartment, Sonya looked longingly at the closed doors of her honeymoon home across the hall. Now that had been a nice place to live—for a while. She shook her head, squared her shoulders and refused to dwell on the past. She couldn't control her dreams, but in daylight she refused to mourn. Bryon was gone, and she had to make a new life, and more and more she was considering that she might be better off without him.

Monday dawned sunny and warm for a December day, so Sonya felt no misgivings when she drove her heavily laden car away from the apartment complex. Daniel and Adam waited for her at the York house, and they carried her possessions to the third floor. Daniel's presence helped her feel more relaxed and settled about her decision to live there. She realized that she trusted him; he had only her best interest at heart and believed this situation would work out.

The dust covers had been removed and the apartment cleaned. Edith must have used high-powered persuasion to force Stelle into the rooms, but Sonya was pleased to have the clean apartment. Edith came up on the elevator, and Daniel helped her to the third floor. After the men left, Edith reached a hand to Sonya.

"You've made me very happy, Sonya. I hope you will have some happy days here. I thought this would be a sanctuary for my granddaughter, but it didn't work out that way."

"We need to discuss a few details. What do you expect of me?"

"Just be here at night. And I don't mean that you should never go out. You're too young to sit with an old lady all the time—if you want to go to church or to other social activities, that's fine. My doctor insists that I shouldn't stay all night by myself, although that's a lot of piffle." Sonya was amused at some of Edith's casual vocabulary, which seemed at variance with such a sophisticated lady.

"When my baby arrives, I'll not be going out much, so that shouldn't prove any problem. If I'm away all day, then I feel I owe the baby the rest of my time. I'm old-fashioned, I suppose, because I think a mother should stay home and care for her child, but I won't be able to do it. The Bensons have recommended a baby-sitter until I can take him to their nursery facilities."

"As I told you before, you can prepare your own breakfast, but Stelle will serve our dinner at six o'clock. She also prepares a light lunch, and if you're here at noontime, as on Saturdays, you may eat with me."

"I suppose I can prepare my breakfast in the apartment's kitchenette."

"Of course, but you may have the run of the house—go where you want to."

"Do you mind if I receive telephone calls here? My parents check on me from time to time."

Sonya's parents had been skeptical of the move, but her

mother considered the York house such an improvement over the apartment that she had protested very little.

"Of course. And if they should want to visit you, the whole second floor is available for visitors."

"Thank you. I have the feeling that this bargain is increasingly one-sided."

"You won't think so if I buzz you in the middle of the night for some help." Edith rose from the chair with difficulty.

"The buzzer is connected to this apartment?"

"Yes, Stelle and I checked it when she cleaned the rooms."

"She needn't clean them anymore. I'll take care of that."

Dinner was served in the large dining room, with china and silver and crystal. "I enjoy modern conveniences, but in some ways I'm still an anachronism. I don't mind having pizza for lunch, but in the evening I prefer to honor the traditions of my father," Edith explained.

Sonya was amazed that this elderly woman was so conversant with world affairs. She must definitely watch the news more often, or she would feel illiterate during their discussions. They spent more than an hour over the bountiful meal. Eating was much more pleasant when it was shared with another, and they appreciated the company since both of them had been without companionship. Edith invited Sonya into her room, but Sonya said, "I'll need to unpack my clothing tonight and become oriented in my quarters. I'll visit other evenings, though. Shall I check on you when I leave in the morning?"

"No, I'll be asleep. I'm able to help myself quite a lot. The cane is just insurance against a fall. Don't fret about me. If I need you, I'll be sure to give you a summons."

The strangeness of her surroundings kept Sonya alert, and long after she finished unpacking, she still hadn't gotten sleepy. Except for the hiss of the steam heat as it moved through the old-fashioned radiators, she could hear nothing. From the window, she could see the glow of streetlights above the tree line on the back of the property. It was good to know that civilization was near, since the house and lot were swathed in darkness. Before she went to sleep, Sonya read a few pages of her Bible. Every day seemed to bring new changes to her life, Sonya reflected. She was grateful for the strength and courage her faith brought her. At least something good had come from all her misery.

The days passed easily in Edith's company. One snowy afternoon, as Sonya came in from a walk, Edith called out to her and Sonya quickly went to Edith's room.

Sonya knelt beside her chair. "Is everything all right, Edith?"

Edith patted her hand. "I feel fine, dear. But you look chilled. Sit here with me for a while and warm up. I want to talk to you about Christmas. Are you going to your parents for the holidays?"

"No, they want me to come and will even pay my fare, but I've too much pride to go back home now when my life is in such shambles."

"Then would you share Christmas with me? Perhaps we could prepare the meal ourselves and give Stelle the day off."

"Certainly. My mother taught me to cook, and although I won't be able to turn out a banquet, I can prepare turkey with dressing and that type of meal. And why don't we plan to attend the Christmas Eve service at the church? Do you feel up to that?"

"I seldom go out at night, but I probably can go if you'll do the driving. I have an automobile, but I haven't driven for a few years. Stelle takes me shopping and to the beauty parlor. The Christmas Eve service is a good idea," she agreed.

With the matter of Christmas Eve and dinner taken care of, Sonya entered into the holiday activities at church and school with a lighter heart. She felt needed at Edith's and knew that she hadn't been asked just as a charitable act. Edith wanted companionship, too, so they would be helping each other.

A careful check of her bank balance proved that she had enough for her hospital stay and for regular visits to Dr. Hammer until her due date. That gave her a feeling of security she hadn't possessed since Bryon left. Since it just didn't seem right not to do some Christmas shopping, she decided to buy token gifts for the family. She also wanted to buy something for Leta, the Bensons and Edith. Christmas cards would have to suffice for others.

The next evening, before she went to Edith's, she drove to a mall and found a few shops with good prices on the items she wanted. Since her family in Ohio would gather together during the holidays, she could mail all of the presents to her parents and ask her mother to distribute them in order to save on postage.

Though she tried to drive memories of last Christmas from her mind, thoughts of Bryon often intruded. They had spent Christmas Day with his parents, and then they'd flown to Colorado for a three-day skiing trip. Several people from the office had gone with them, including Gail Lantz. Thinking back, she tried to remember if Bryon had paid any particular attention to the woman then. She was reasonably sure that he hadn't.

During her shopping, several times she saw items that she would have bought for Bryon, and she longed to buy for him again, but on her meager budget, she couldn't have purchased anything that he would accept. Later, when she prepared her Christmas cards, on a sudden impulse, she addressed a card to him. She kept it on the table in her living room for several days, but she finally mailed it. Although she had the address of his residence, she sent it to the office. Perhaps Gail wouldn't know he'd received it. Within a week she had the card back stamped "Return to Sender." It hadn't been opened. Had Gail intercepted the card, or had Bryon been the one to return it? Last year Bryon had bought her a diamond necklace. This year he wouldn't even accept her card. How could he have changed that much?

The incident ruined Sonya's Christmas plans, but she tried to put up a front. She was loud and frivolous at school, while at Edith's, she laughed at every opportunity. Then, disgusted at herself for such foolishness, she lapsed into silence and spoke only when it was absolutely necessary. All she wanted to do was to crawl into a hole somewhere and lick her wounds. She dreaded going to school each morning, but on the other hand, she didn't know what she would do for the ten days the school was closed. Why had she tried to contact Bryon? She always came off second-best in any encounter with him.

One evening, however, a week before Christmas, when she stopped by to see Edith after she arrived home from school, Edith smiled at her.

"You look as if you're on your last legs."

Easing down into a chair, Sonya said, "That's the way I feel. My thoughts are burdensome, and certainly my body is the same way." She patted her bulky stomach.

"You need a change of pace, and I believe I have the answer. We've been invited out on a date."

"Oh, you mean we're going to double-date. I can't imagine anyone who would want to date me."

"There's only one handsome gentleman, but he wants to take both of us out on the town, and his mother as well."

Sonya smiled. "Apparently Daniel has telephoned."

"He has tickets to the university choir's musical tomorrow night, and he wants to take us out for dinner ahead of time. What about it?"

"It sounds like a great idea to me, but are you able to go?"

"Why not? I told him that if you agreed, we would meet him in town. I have some business at the bank tomorrow, and it's also the day for my hair appointment, so I'll have Stelle drive me into town, and after I'm finished, I'll meet you at the church. The performance is at seven o'clock, so Daniel said we should eat at five."

"Sounds great to me. I've attended the choir's Christmas musicals before. They're always excellent."

Feeling less burdensome than she had when she'd arrived home, Sonya heaved her body out of the chair. "I'll have to see if I have anything I can possibly wear. There may be something in my evening garments, but I haven't had them out of the boxes since I came here."

Most of her evening dresses were formfitting, so had to be rejected, but she did have one floor-length black velvet gathered skirt with an elasticized waist. She removed the elastic, tried the skirt on, and it fit very well. With it she decided that she could wear a sequined, belted satin blouse that fit over the bulge in her abdomen, and although it was obvious that she was pregnant, she didn't look too bad. A mink waist-length jacket would complete her outfit.

Walking downstairs more jauntily than she had earlier, Sonya presented herself in Edith's room.

"How do I look?"

"Stunning," Edith said, surprised. "I didn't know you had such beautiful clothes."

"Bryon was very generous with my clothing allowance. He always wanted me to look better than any of the other women in our group. I used to think it was because he loved me so much, but as I look back on it now, perhaps my impeccable dressing was important to him because it indicated his prosperity."

Her eyes clouded, and Edith was quick to change the subject.

"Where will you dress tomorrow evening?"

"I'll take my clothing along and dress at the church after the children leave."

"Well, I'll have to make an effort to look as well put together as you do. Of course, Jane Massie will be dressed to the nines. She always is."

When Daniel called for them at the church basement the next afternoon, he handed both Edith and Sonya a corsage box. The orchid put the finishing touches on Sonya's garments, and as she took a quick look in the mirror of the church's rest room, she agreed with Edith. She did look stunning!

Mrs. Massie and Edith were old friends, and during dinner they chatted amicably. Daniel devoted most of his attention to Sonya. She enjoyed the way his gray eyes lit with laughter before the rest of his face expressed amusement. He had no difficulty introducing subjects that she found interesting. With Daniel, she was alive.

The musical performance combined portions of Handel's *Messiah,* as well as secular Christmas music and the beloved church carols. Much of the music brought tears to Sonya's eyes, but new hope dawned when the choir sang:

"And ye, beneath life's crushing load,
Whose forms are bending low,
Who toil along the climbing way
With painful steps and slow,
Look now! for glad and golden hours
Come swiftly on the wing:
O rest beside the weary road
And hear the angels sing."

Had God sent her this particular message? Sonya believed that He had, because life's load had nearly crushed her, but for the first time since Bryon's defection, she began to believe that glad and golden hours would come for her again. In the closing moments of the concert, she prayed silently, *Thank you, God, for sending me the message of Christmas—hope for a brighter tomorrow.*

When Daniel delivered them to her car at the church's parking lot, she said quietly, "I can't express how much this evening has meant for me, but it has given me new hope. I owe much of this to you, Daniel. Thank you for a lovely evening."

Edith was already in the car, leaning back with her eyes closed, and Daniel bent over Sonya. His eyes sparkled mysteriously in the dim light, and he said huskily, "Oh, Sonya, you don't know how much this evening has meant to *me.* You've captivated my thoughts, and I'm constantly inventing ways to be around you."

Sonya was amazed at his words and his ardor. He spoke like a man in love, but surely that couldn't be. He wouldn't talk romantically to a pregnant married woman, but she found it hard to breathe, and Daniel's eyes held hers captive. He lowered his face to hers. "Sonya, I..." The moment was shattered when an automobile with its radio blaring, whizzed through the parking lot. Daniel stepped back and shook his head, as if he had just emerged from a thick fog. A stiff breeze buffeted them, leaving Sonya's hair in disarray. Smiling wryly, Daniel brushed the hair from her forehead and gave her a brotherly hug. Sonya knew that he had intended to kiss her, and although she reminded herself that she was married to another man, she couldn't deny that she would have welcomed his caress.

Opening the car door, Daniel said, "We must get together before Christmas. I'll give you a call."

The last day before the nursery school closed for the holidays, when they were distributing gifts to the toddlers, Sonya was summoned to the phone. The staff didn't usually take calls during working hours, but because so many parents were present, Eloise told Sonya to answer the phone.

"Sonya, this is Mother Dixon."

Sonya eased down into the chair by the telephone.

"Oh, hello," she answered weakly.

"I tried to call your apartment and learned the phone had been disconnected."

"Yes, I moved right after Thanksgiving. I'm living at the home of Edith York. Do you know her?"

"I know who she is, but I'm not acquainted with her. Why would you live there?"

"She isn't well, and a mutual friend recommended me to her. I can continue my work at the nursery school and not have to pay apartment rent. It's working out quite well. You can telephone me there anytime you want to."

"I called to invite you to have Christmas dinner with us." Sonya's mind worked overtime. Why, after ignoring her for three months, would they ask her to dinner?

To Mrs. Dixon she said, "That's nice of you, but I've already made plans for both Christmas Eve and Christmas Day."

"Are you going to Ohio?"

"No."

"We don't want you to spend the holidays alone."

Why was she probing? Did she think Sonya had a date?

"I'm spending the time with Edith. She's lonely, and I'm lonely, so it will be beneficial to both of us. I do appreciate your thinking of me, however."

"How's your health?"

"I feel fine physically—emotionally I'm not so well, as you might suspect. This is a difficult season for me."

Mrs. Dixon ignored that remark. "When is your child due?"

"The first of March," Sonya said shortly. Bryon had made it plain that this was her child, and she didn't appreciate Mrs. Dixon's questioning.

"If you can't come for Christmas, how about New Year's Day?"

"Will Bryon be there? I'm sure he wouldn't want to encounter me."

Mrs. Dixon laughed lightly. "Bryon is going to Hawaii for the holidays, so he won't be coming home. I'm not attempting to bring you back together if that's what you think. You and Bryon will have to work out your own problems, but I can't see why that should interfere with our relationship. We've always been on good terms."

"That's true, and I see no reason I can't spend New Year's Day with you. I'll telephone after Christmas to confirm the date."

Sonya replaced the receiver slowly. So Bryon was spending Christmas in Hawaii! That was to have been their next big vacation. He'd gone without her, and had no doubt taken Gail. Why did she continue to love a man who treated her this way? Here she was pinching pennies to save enough money to pay for the delivery of his child, living on the charity of others for her food, clothing and lodging, and he flew off to Hawaii with his paramour. Why couldn't she see that she was better off without him?

But when she thought of Bryon, she never pictured him as a wayward husband, but rather she remembered the handsome Bryon, the catch of the campus who had pursued her until he'd won her heart.

Chapter Nine

The organ was playing when Edith and Sonya entered the candlelit church sanctuary on Christmas Eve. The room was crowded already, but an usher approached them, saying, "Jane Massie told me to bring you to her pew. Come this way." Sonya welcomed this consideration since Edith was breathing heavily, and she didn't want to keep her standing while they looked for a seat.

Daniel smiled and placed Edith at his mother's side and made room for Sonya beside him. Daniel's sister and her family had come for the holidays and they sat beyond Mrs. Massie. Sonya was surprised at her personal serenity tonight. She almost believed that the Angel's message was for her alone.

Fear not: for, behold, I bring you good tidings of great joy,
which shall be to all people. For unto you is born this day
in the city of David, a Saviour, which is Christ the Lord.

She should be lonely spending Christmas Eve away from her family with people she hadn't known a year ago, but these three people had wrapped her in a love that couldn't be compared to familial devotion. Sonya missed a lot of the service because her thoughts had turned inward on her difficulties, recalling how the people in this church had united to help her.

At the close of the service, Daniel introduced Sonya to his sister's family, and under cover of Edith's conversation with them, he said softly, "I'm concerned about the two of you being alone on Christmas Day. Won't you and Edith spend the day with my family? Please say you'll come; it would make me very happy."

Sonya was touched by his heartfelt invitation but she had to refuse.

"Oh, we couldn't intrude, and besides, I don't believe Edith is up to it. Look at her—she's had trouble breathing all day, and I don't like her color."

"You're right," he said, obviously disappointed. "I'll give you a call sometime tomorrow."

He gently squeezed her hand and said goodbye.

Both Sonya and Edith were serene and content when they started home from the Christmas Eve service. The choir had presented a cantata, followed by communion, and Edith hadn't even seemed tired as they drove out of the church parking lot. As they approached a minimall, Edith said, "There's one thing we forgot that I always like for Christmas dinner. Let's stop here and see if we can buy a plum pudding. My mother always made them, but I have bought them since then. The deli at that grocery store may have some left."

The parking lot contained only a few automobiles, and Sonya went into the store to buy the plum pudding. A few shoppers like herself, who had come in for a few last-minute purchases, hustled up to the checkout counter.

Exiting with the plum pudding, she had almost reached the car when she noticed a woman running across the parking lot with a man in pursuit. She headed toward Sonya crying, "Help me. Help me."

Sonya stood like one turned to stone, and Edith rolled down the window. "Hurry, Sonya, get in the car. We can't be involved in this."

The distraught woman had reached Sonya by that time, and she grabbed her arm, begging, "Take me with you. I must get away from him." A quick glance showed Sonya that the woman's face was distressed and her clothing in disarray. She dodged behind Sonya when the man reached them, but he shoved Sonya aside, and she lost her footing and fell on the concrete.

"My baby!" she screamed, grabbing at her abdomen.

By the time she struggled to her feet, the man had dragged the woman across the lot and shoved her into a car. Tires squealed as he rushed down the street, and Sonya strained her eyes to see the license number.

Sonya leaned against the car, panting. Edith held on to the vehicle and maneuvered to her side. "Sonya, are you hurt? Do you feel all right?"

"My heart is racing so fast I can hardly breathe, but I'm not hurt."

"Such a fall could have caused a miscarriage."

"That's what scared me, but I don't have any pain of any kind."

"Let's hurry home, then."

They drove for several blocks in silence. "Poor woman," Edith whispered. "We should have helped her."

"I know. I'll never forget the look on her face. I didn't know what to do."

"You didn't have time to do anything. We're advised to stay out of domestic quarrels—even the police seldom interfere— but I feel sorry for abused women. My granddaughter was one."

"I'm still shaking. I wanted to help her, but right now all I want is to feel the safety of our own four walls."

Sonya helped a trembling Edith into the house and settled her on the couch.

"I know you think we shouldn't be involved," Sonya said, "but don't you think we should at least report the incident? I did get the license number."

Edith sighed wearily. "By all means, do what you think is best. I'd like to help that poor woman in some way, if we could."

Sonya dialed 911, and when the dispatcher answered, she

said. "I want to report an incident that happened at the Farmer's Mart parking lot on West Dodge street. A woman was running away from a man who forced her into a blue Plymouth Voyager. I believe the license plate was 1-679A, and the left front fender of the van was of a different color, maybe a light brown."

"Lady," the dispatcher said, "if we investigated every fight between husbands and wives tonight, we wouldn't have time to deal with real emergencies. You've done your duty, so just forget it."

Sonya angrily replaced the phone receiver. "So that's all the thanks we get for trying to help someone."

"Go on to bed, Sonya," Edith said, "and sleep late in the morning. We won't concern ourselves with a big dinner."

"I'm going to put the turkey in the oven before I go to bed, and I can prepare the rest of the food when I get up. We won't have to eat until mid-afternoon."

Sonya did stay in bed later than usual, not because she was asleep, but because she didn't want to disturb Edith. The incident of the night before continued to haunt her. She couldn't forget the terror displayed by that woman. She knew Bryon's treatment of her was a form of abuse, but at least he hadn't done her any physical harm. This Christmas Day would necessarily have been bleak, without the added trauma of seeing a woman mistreated.

Stelle had prepared a cranberry salad and rolls the day before, so all Sonya had to do was cook green beans and mash the potatoes. She set the table with Edith's bone china service and sterling silver, lit the candles and was pleased with the festive table when she summoned Edith for dinner. The woman trembled with fatigue, but they both ate a hearty meal.

Sonya filled the dishwasher and joined Edith, who was looking toward the small Christmas tree in the corner that Stelle and Sonya had decorated. "Do you realize we haven't opened our gifts? Are you too tired to look at them now?"

Edith watched with interest as Sonya unwrapped the gifts

from Ohio. Several boxes contained baby clothes as she'd requested, and a large one held a lovely maternity dress. The elegant two-piece red linen dress featured a jewel neckline and quarter-length sleeves with navy trim. Navy also marked the deep patch pockets, and the sharp knife-pleated skirt was accented by a navy band at the hem. Sonya could hardly wait to model the dress, but that would have to wait until tomorrow.

Leta's package contained two ballet-length nursing nightgowns delicately edged in lace trim. Scooped necklines and ruffled cap sleeves modified the versatility of the garments, which concealed nursing vents under center pleats. Just what she needed for her hospital stay.

Most of Edith's gifts had been received a few days before—a poinsettia from her nephew in California, and several fruit baskets sent by her elderly friends in the city. But she opened with pleasure the colorful scarf Sonya had chosen for her and a pair of house slippers, a gift from Stelle. While Sonya was disposing of the wrapping paper and ribbons, the doorbell rang, and she looked questioningly at Edith.

"Were you expecting guests?"

"No," Edith replied. She looked puzzled. Then a mischievous sparkle lit her eyes. "Unless..." Her voice trailed off and she smiled at Sonya. "Better answer it, dear. I think it's a caller for you."

Sonya reached the front door when the bell sounded again.

"Who is it?" she called loudly, through the thick wooden door.

"Ho! Ho! Ho!"

"Who is it?" she repeated.

"Santa Claus. Didn't you hear the sound of his sleigh and reindeer?"

Laughing, Sonya opened the door to a gift-laden Daniel. His broad shoulders filled the doorway and his smile warmed her. She held the gifts while he took off his coat and hung it in the hall closet.

"Sorry not to be here sooner, but it took a long time to open our gifts and eat a big dinner."

"Thanks for coming," Sonya said sincerely. "Edith will be glad to see you."

Daniel took the gifts from her. "And aren't you glad to see me?"

"Of course. It's cold in this hallway; let's find the comfort of Edith's room."

Edith opened her gift first—a high-intensity reading lamp. Then Daniel handed Sonya three gifts.

"Why three gifts?"

"Read the cards."

The small box bore her name, but two of the parcels were labeled "For Baby-to-Be."

"After hearing what I'd bought for your baby, my sister, who's the mother of three, said she wouldn't want me shopping for her children, but I believe in buying practical gifts."

Sonya's hands trembled as she opened her gift—a bottle of expensive perfume. It was her favorite and she wondered how Daniel knew. Then she recalled he'd complimented her once on the scent and she'd told him the name. But that was so long ago. His thoughtfulness and efforts to please her were touching, despite her resolve to remain just friends. Then she took the ribbon from the baby's gift and finding a football, dropped her head to the box and sobbed.

Daniel was on his knees beside her immediately. "Why, Sonya, what's wrong? I didn't intend to make you unhappy!"

She reached a hand to him, and he held it securely while she continued to sob. At last she lifted her head and wiped a tearful face.

"You didn't make me unhappy. You see, I've been concerned because no one really wants this baby. His father has disowned him, his paternal grandparents have practically ignored his coming, and my own parents would have preferred that I not have a child under these circumstances. And dare I admit that most of the time I haven't wanted the baby, either?

I've done all I can to ensure its health and a safe delivery, but I've looked on the birth as an ordeal that I want to put behind me."

Daniel still held her hand. "I imagine those are normal reactions under the circumstances."

"But when you bought this football, you were thinking of my baby as a person. He was real to you. I thank you for the perfume, Daniel, but the greatest gift you've given me is the realization that this child is going to be an important part of my life."

"We're all looking forward to his birth. Mother is planning to grandmother him. She doesn't want Edith to have all of the fun."

"Well, enough of the tears," Edith said, "I want to know what's in the other package."

Smiling now, Sonya tore away the wrappings.

"A computer!" she shouted.

Shamefacedly, Daniel said, "I didn't think it was too soon to start the hi-tech stuff, but my sister disagreed with me, saying I didn't know anything about shopping for newborns."

The box indicated that the toy computer was designed for ages one year and up. Daniel took it from the box, inserted the necessary batteries that he took from his pocket and demonstrated the utility of his gift.

"The man at the store showed me how to do this. There are several program disks available in the packet. This one, for instance, is designed to teach the child the alphabet. He can hit the *A* key, and a large capital *A* and cursive *A* appear on the screen. At the same time, a voice says, '*A.*' These programs will help a child learn the colors, plants, animals and all kinds of useful information."

Daniel spent the next half hour demonstrating the versatility of the computer, still convinced of the usefulness of his gift. His running commentary kept Sonya laughing and smiling as usual.

"I don't know whether my baby will learn from it," Sonya said, "but it's certainly entertaining for adults."

When Edith went to sleep, Daniel hurriedly took his departure. Sonya went down the hallway with him.

"She seems very weary tonight," Daniel said.

"And with some reason, too." Sonya told him about the incident they'd observed the night before.

Daniel shook his head. "There are always numerous incidents of spouse and child abuse during the holidays. Unfortunately the authorities can't investigate them all. Let's hope no harm came to the woman you saw."

Sonya agreed. Then she added, "Thanks again, Daniel. Between you and Edith, you've made this a Christmas to be remembered fondly, not a dreaded one as I had expected."

She reached out her hand, and Daniel took it, but then he leaned forward, tenderly brushed her hair aside with his hand and softly kissed her cheek. It was a gentle caress, but one that kindled a flicker of emotion in the region of Sonya's heart that she had never expected to feel again.

"Merry Christmas, Sonya, and I pray that your New Year will be a happy one."

As Sonya went back down the hall, she pressed a hand to her trembling lips, realizing that this had been the most satisfying Christmas she had experienced since her marriage.

The next morning when Edith was too weak to leave her bed, Sonya insisted on telephoning the doctor.

"I don't suppose he'll make a house call, so perhaps I should take you to the hospital."

"When I die, I'm going to die in my own bed. But he'll make a call here—his father was our doctor for years, and his son took over the practice two years ago."

Sonya didn't stay in the room when the doctor examined Edith, waiting instead in the hallway until he prepared to leave.

"Her heart doesn't seem to be any worse, but she should stay in bed. I've told her to have bed rest for a week, but if you can keep her in bed for three days, I'll be satisfied."

But Edith didn't even leave her bed in three days, for the evening's paper brought another shock. Sonya spent most of the day in the laundry room washing the linens they had used for the Christmas meal, as well as her own garments. When she went to check on Edith after Stelle left for the night, Edith sat with the paper across her legs, shielding her face with her hands.

"Look!" she said, handing the newspaper to Sonya.

"'Husband held for wife's murder,'" Sonya read the headline aloud. "Do you think it's the woman we saw?"

"There isn't any doubt. The murder occurred in the area where the grocery store is located, and that picture looks like the man. We could have saved that woman's life. I'll never forgive myself."

"You shouldn't reproach yourself, Edith. We didn't have time to do anything. He pushed me aside and grabbed the woman before I hardly knew what was going on. By the time I picked myself up from the ground, they were gone. Besides, it says here that an anonymous phone call led the police to her assailant. That had to be the call we made."

"The call *you* made," she said. "I didn't do anything but rush away from the scene, although I thought it best at the time. Well, I can't help her now, but if another opportunity like that comes along, I'm going to be ready."

Because Edith hadn't regained her strength, Sonya considered canceling the New Year's dinner date at the Dixons. She didn't want to hurt their feelings, but she considered she had a responsibility to Edith. However, when she told Edith that she wouldn't go, the older woman said, "You'll do nothing of the kind. I can get up if I want to, but I feel better lying in bed. Besides, you'll be going back to school the day after New Year's, and I'll be by myself then until Stelle arrives."

Still, Sonya was uneasy about leaving Edith alone, so she arranged for Stelle to take off the New Year's Eve day and then come to be with Edith on New Year's Day. "That'll suit me fine," the woman agreed. "My old man likes to party on New

Year's Eve, and we start out early." She laughed. "I may be pretty sleepy come the first of the year, but I'll be here, in case Mrs. Edith wants anything."

Sonya put on the new dress her mother had sent, thankful she had a really nice garment to wear to the Dixons' dinner. Her pride would have rebelled at wearing the hand-me-down clothes. She had gained about fifteen pounds, but the chic dress camouflaged her pregnancy. Her face and neck were too thin, but she added plenty of mousse when she shampooed her hair to give it body, and after she fluffed it around her face, she looked almost as pretty as she had a year ago. She put on eye shadow and lightened the dark circles under her eyes, then surveyed her image with satisfaction. As a final touch, she sprayed some of Daniel's perfume on her wrists and inhaled the pleasant fragrance.

As she approached the Dixon home, she drove more and more slowly. Mrs. Dixon had said twelve o'clock, and she didn't want to be late, but the thought of entering the house without Bryon frightened her. She had never visited his parents alone. It was no wonder she was having trouble adjusting to Bryon's absence. Except for the times he was at work, they had seldom been separated. Bryon hadn't gone anywhere that he couldn't take her.

She pulled her old car into the driveway, and her hands trembled as she unfastened the seat belt. Like a specter, Bryon stood between her and the house. Had his parents told him they'd invited her? Mr. Dixon came down the walk to meet her, and he took her arm.

"Happy New Year, Sonya," he said.

Mother Dixon greeted her at the door with a kiss on the cheek. "We're so glad you could come, dear. This would have been a lonely day for us without you. Here, Tom, hang up her coat. Come into the living room. We won't be eating for about an hour."

Just like old times, Sonya thought ironically, but if the Dixons were willing to befriend her in spite of Bryon's action, what did she have to lose? So she pushed thoughts of Bryon into the background and made up her mind she would be pleasant. She might enjoy the day if she tried.

Tom Dixon brought Sonya a cola, and she sipped on it slowly. She asked about other members of their family, who usually shared their Christmas dinner. Almost as if she were hoping for a middle ground of discussion, Mrs. Dixon launched into a commentary on the aunts, uncles and cousins, until it was time for dinner.

Sonya helped Mrs. Dixon clear away the dinner things and fill the dishwasher as she always had, and in spite of Bryon's defection, she felt a warm glow to be with "family."

Before they settled into the living room chairs again, Sonya pulled back the sheers on the picture window to check the weather. "Do you mind if we keep these open?" she asked. "If it starts snowing, I'll need to leave."

"You're welcome to stay here," Tom said, "if there's a storm."

"Thank you, but I need to go back to Edith. She's been ill this week, and the maid leaves at four o'clock."

"Do you like it there?" Mrs. Dixon asked.

"Very much. Edith York is a lovely person."

"You're looking well, Sonya," Mrs. Dixon said. "Have you had a sonogram to find out the sex of your child?"

Why should she resent the Dixons asking questions about the baby? she thought. Just because Bryon didn't want the child was no reason his parents wouldn't be interested.

"It's a boy."

"Are you pleased about that?"

Sonya shrugged her shoulders. "Doesn't matter much either way. Frankly, I've had trouble becoming interested in the child because of the difficulty Bryon and I've had."

"What do you intend to do with the baby?"

Sonya stared at her mother-in-law. "Keep it, of course. Bryon wanted me to abort the fetus or give it up for adoption, but I wouldn't consider such a thing. Tell me, Mother Dixon, why doesn't Bryon like children?"

"I don't know. As a matter of fact, I had no idea he didn't like children." Sonya saw her glance nervously at her husband. "We assumed that the two of you would have a family."

"There must be some reason. I feel very bitter toward him for the way he's treated me. It might make it easier if I knew the reason for his behavior."

Mrs. Dixon's face flushed, and Sonya knew she stifled an angry retort. *Of course, Bryon wasn't at fault!*

"You might as well tell her, Anna," Tom said.

"We've questioned Bryon's attitude as much as you have, and we've come to one conclusion. I suppose you know that Bryon isn't our only child?"

"Why I didn't know that!"

"We had another son born when Bryon was five years old. He was a Down's syndrome baby."

Sonya gasped and cradled her unborn child. He gave a vicious little kick as if to assure her he was alive and well.

"He lived only six years," Mrs. Dixon continued. "We were kept so busy with him that we probably neglected Bryon, although at the time we didn't realize it. Perhaps he resented those six years and grew to hate children in general," Mrs. Dixon explained.

"And don't forget your period of depression after our boy died, Anna. For two years," he explained to Sonya, "we had to send Bryon to his grandparents. She couldn't cope with an eleven-year-old in her condition."

"He did tell me that he had to live with his grandparents for a long time, but he seldom mentioned his childhood. Perhaps he felt rejected."

"It's possible that Bryon didn't want children because he feared you might have a handicapped child," Mr. Dixon continued. "What we went through with our son wouldn't be something anyone would choose voluntarily. You shouldn't have gotten pregnant, Sonya."

Sonya felt her face flushing, and she sputtered, "Don't blame me. I hadn't changed birth control methods since we were married. If he'd just leveled with me, discussed his hang-ups, there were many ways we could have prevented a pregnancy. I loved him so much, I would have chosen him over a child anyday."

"Tom wasn't being critical of you, Sonya, but since we couldn't find out much from Bryon, we thought you might enlighten us. We were very disappointed to learn you were having trouble. Is it all over between you?"

"Not as far as I'm concerned, but Bryon has asked for a divorce. My lawyer has advised me to do nothing until after the child is born. Now that I've learned about your handicapped child, perhaps that was a wise move, although I had an amniocentesis test that indicated that my baby is all right."

"How much longer do you intend to work?"

"Until they haul me off to the hospital, I suppose. I can't afford to lose my job."

"You shouldn't be working now," Anna insisted. "If you can't get along on what Bryon's providing, we'll be glad to help you."

So they didn't know that Bryon had cast her aside penniless. She wanted to shout the news at them, but they'd always idolized their son, and she wasn't mean enough to tell them about his conduct. She knew how she had felt when Bryon toppled from the pedestal where she'd placed him. The Dixons had always been good to her, so why should she repay their kindness by demeaning their son?

Sonya started talking about her work at school to avoid any further discussion of her husband, and the rest of the afternoon passed pleasantly enough. By four o'clock snow flurries danced around the windows, and Sonya took leave of her in-laws.

"We must get together again," Mr. Dixon said as he helped her down the steps and to the car. "Be careful and don't fall. This walk could be slick."

As she drove homeward, Sonya experienced a warm glow of thankfulness that she had spent some time with Bryon's family, who'd been a part of her life for two years. But her forehead creased with worry. What if she had a handicapped child? Was that the reason for Bryon's actions? And although the Dixons hadn't admitted it, Sonya could read between the lines. Bryon had apparently been neglected during the sickness of his brother and the time of grief following the child's death. Was that the reason he wanted to control her completely? Had he been determined that Sonya would be only his, afraid that a child would wean her affection away from him? But even that couldn't excuse his actions toward her, she reasoned.

With all of these things to worry her, Sonya didn't anticipate the advent of a new year.

Chapter Ten

Within a week Edith had recovered and seemed to be as well as usual, though she tired more easily. To escape the memory of her frustrating visit with the Dixons, Sonya enjoyed returning to the regimented school schedule, but the extra weight of the child slowed her down considerably.

The Christmas season had drained her emotionally, and she was pleased to have it behind her, but now, she had only two months until her child was born. The nearer the time came, Sonya, with dismay, realized that she dreaded having the baby—not the physical birth, but simply the thoughts of having a child around all the time. This distressed her because she didn't want the child to feel unwanted, and she'd read that the emotions of a mother before the baby was born could determine the personality of that unborn babe. Since Daniel's gift at Christmas, she was considering the birth of her son with some anticipation, but at times she blamed him for causing her to lose Bryon. She definitely had to get over that feeling, and she decided to have some counseling with Adam Benson, which would help her put motherhood in its proper perspective.

To offset her lack of enthusiasm for the child, she made an effort to be sure he was healthy. She walked around the York lawn several times each day and watched her diet religiously. Stelle, who had become a close friend, was as protective of Sonya as she was of Edith and prepared food suitable for a pregnant woman.

Daniel, too, continued to bolster her spirits as he had during the Christmas holidays. He often called at the house, and while Sonya saw him only in Edith's presence, he had a knack of knowing what to do to encourage her. He occasionally brought her chocolates, but more often, while Edith dozed, he encouraged her to talk about the activities at the nursery school. His ready laughter when she reported an amusing incident, or his compassion when she spoke of a needy child, not only filled the lonely hours of waiting for her baby, but gave her additional insight to the worth of this man. She actually enjoyed her work more, storing up incidents to share with Daniel.

One night when she met him at the door, she was chuckling. "Wait until I tell you what happened today."

He shook the snow from his hat and coat before he entered the house, and as they walked down the hallway to Edith's room, she continued, "We took the children on a tour of a church—a different denomination from ours. The children are well acquainted with our large baptistry and have seen people immersed in it. On the tour, the church's pastor pointed to their baptismal font.

'This is where people are baptized,' he said, and one boy went forward, peered into it, and scoffingly said, 'Baptized in that *little* old thing!'"

Both of them were laughing when they joined Edith. "Wait until your son gets here," Daniel said. "He'll be saying the same kind of cute things."

Daniel referred to her pregnancy often, and one evening, he said, "Sonya, I want you to telephone me when you need to go to the hospital for the baby's birth. It doesn't matter what time of day or night, I'll be ready."

"That's good of you, but Leta has already volunteered. She also plans to assist me in the delivery room." Daniel appeared disappointed, but Sonya felt uncomfortable imagining a man other than her husband helping at such a time—even Daniel.

When Sonya considered that the child would be born in eight or nine weeks, she knew she had to make plans for it. She needed clothing and a bed or bassinet. And where could she stay when she came from the hospital? She wouldn't be very active for a week or so, and she couldn't ask Edith to share that burden. What could she do?

Eloise lightened her load somewhat by suggesting one day, "If you don't have all the baby things you want, a friend of mine is having a garage sale tomorrow. She has some beautiful items. Her house is located along your way into work. Why don't you stop there in the morning?"

Sonya took her advice and bought a bassinet and a boxful of clothing for only twenty-five dollars. That evening after supper she spread out her purchases for Edith to see.

"I've wanted to ask you what you needed for the child, but until Christmas, you seemed so reluctant to talk about your pregnancy that I hesitated. However, I have several things you're welcome to use."

Leaning on her cane, Edith went to the chest at the foot of her bed, and she motioned for Sonya to follow her. When she unlocked the chest, Sonya saw layers of baby clothes, some still wrapped in their plastic coverings.

"I bought these for my granddaughter before her untimely death. I haven't felt right about giving them away, but I would be happy to see your child wear them. I've become quite fond of you."

Sonya lifted a small sweater and booties and held them to her face while she tried to stifle her tears.

"I'll be proud to use these, but when the child comes, shouldn't I go someplace else? It's an imposition on you to bring a baby here."

"Why, I thought that was the plan," Edith said, dismayed. "I'm looking forward to having a baby in the house. It will remind me of the time when my own son was toddling around this room."

"Then you'll *have* a baby in the house, but if the situation becomes a burden to you, please let me know."

"A burden? Nonsense, my dear," Edith said, "I'm looking

forward to the baby so much that I've come up with a plan that might keep both of you here all of the time.''

Edith shuffled back to her chair, and Sonya sat on a footstool at her feet.

''I want to stay here. You know how grateful I am to you for taking me in, but I'll have to work to support myself and the baby, and I must make some provisions to have the child cared for while I work. I'm not sure my salary will take care of a baby-sitter and the extra supplies I'll need for it. If not, I'll have to find another job. I'm so worried about all of this, and that's one of the reasons I dread having the baby.''

''Don't you expect your husband to pay child support?''

''I'm sure he won't if he can get out of it, and I don't intend to force him into it.''

''Would you rather stay with your child than have a baby-sitter?''

''Yes, of course. That's the way I was taught.''

''Then you may be interested in my plan. I've not been able to put that young woman we failed to help on Christmas Eve out of my mind, and I've prayed for some way to make restitution.''

She took a newspaper clipping from the table drawer. ''Did you see this?''

The article, headed, ''Help for abused women and children,'' reported on incidents of child and wife abuse in the city of Omaha. Sonya was stunned at the astronomical number of cases, and until this point, she hadn't really considered herself an abused wife, but the article stressed that verbal and emotional abuse brought on by desertion was just as devastating as physical abuse. The article concluded with an appeal for homes to shelter abused wives, stating that grants were available for those with suitable facilities. A telephone number was given if one desired additional information.

''After I thought about it for a few days, I telephoned that number. Seems this is a crisis-intervention agency supported by several church denominations. They check out the situations to be sure that the applicants really need help, then they send them to abuse centers. The grants also provide a small salary for a director. I've been wondering why we couldn't turn this house into an abuse center where you could be the paid director. You would have a job and can stay here and look after your baby at the same time.''

"That sounds like a solution to *my* problem, but it wouldn't work for you. You're used to privacy, and I don't believe you would like having your home turned into a public shelter.''

"I've considered that, but I've been pretty much confined to two rooms for a long time. As you know, I seldom go upstairs. We could put a partition in the middle of the hall, lock the door, and as thick as these walls are, I would probably not know anyone was in the house. Besides, I may not live long, anyway, and I'll die happier if I know this big house is being put to some use.''

"On Sunday Adam Benson said in his sermon that when God closes one door, He often opens another one, and he urged us to be aware of the open door of opportunity. It's strange, but if I hadn't gotten married, I intended to prepare for social work, but since I didn't get a degree, I doubt that I have the expertise to serve as the director. What would I have to do?''

"We must check out those details. I didn't want to proceed further until I had your opinion. I'm sure that the salary is meager, but probably as much as you receive at the school. If you're interested, I'll telephone Daniel Massie and ask him to have dinner with us tomorrow night. We'll see what he thinks.''

"I think you two women have all the trouble you need" was Daniel's instant opinion. "You would have all kinds of women and children coming here.''

"The agency screens the women," Edith said.

"I'm an abused wife, and you sent me to Edith," Sonya added.

"That's another matter entirely." Daniel's gaze met hers, his eyes glittering with unspoken emotion. "I will look into it for you. Our church contributes to the agency, so I know it's a reputable group.''

Daniel had his findings within a week, and he came one evening to discuss them.

''You would have to request enough money to do some remodeling on the house. Fire escapes must be added, another bathroom and probably one of the front rooms turned into a dining area, if you intend to keep the one across the hall for your own personal use.''

''What does being a director involve?'' Sonya asked.

''A crash training course to be qualified, but that shouldn't be difficult for you, since you told me that you were interested in social work. Then, too, you would need more help than Stelle. She's busy enough now with Edith, so plan another person to help with the cleaning and night monitoring. Don't say you can handle it all, because with a baby you wouldn't have the time. I'll consider those things in the grant application.''

''For how long will we be committing ourselves?'' Edith asked.

''Two years, when you would be evaluated before you could ask for more funding.''

''Would the grant proposal include food, medical attention and other special needs?'' Sonya questioned.

''Yes. There are several drugstores and hospitals in the area that cooperate with the agency. If this facility is approved, you would be covered with insurance—most of the funds come from the city and state governments.''

''I'm rather excited about it,'' Sonya admitted. ''It sounds as if it might solve my problem.''

''I don't think you should do this, partly because of Edith's health, and the fact that this project will take you away from your child quite a lot, but you may be assured that I'll be supportive in all that you do. Call upon me for any help you need.''

When Sonya walked to the door with Daniel, he said, ''Have you heard anything more from your husband?''

"No, except he returned a Christmas card I sent him, and his parents invited me to eat New Year's dinner with them."

"I had a rather nasty letter from him stating that we needn't think we could rob him, and insisting that I initiate divorce proceedings. I replied amicably that I would contact him sometime in March with our proposal."

"I'm eager now to remove him from my life, and perhaps I can start over again. Right now everything is in limbo until the baby is born."

"Yes, that's true," Daniel agreed. Sonya sensed that he was thinking about their relationship as well. Did Daniel hope to be more than a friend to her someday? The thought of any man's romantic interest had seemed repellent to her not so long ago, but Daniel had become such an important part of her life. Sometimes she believed God had sent Daniel into her life for a purpose, not only to watch over her and help her survive Bryon's abandonment, but to show her that, unlike Bryon, some men could be relied upon and trusted.

"How much longer are you going to work?" he asked.

"I've requested a leave of absence for six weeks starting in mid-February."

"And perhaps by that time, if the grant application is funded, you may not have to go back to the school at all."

"I hope so. I like the work, but I think my own child should be my first priority. Growing up without a father will be a big enough detriment, and if his mother is gone most of the time, the child will feel neglected right from the first."

"You will make a good mother, Sonya." He took her hand in his.

She flushed with pleasure. "I'm beginning to feel more like a mother now, so I hope you're right."

"And don't forget I'm taking first dibs on being a substitute uncle. I'm great with kids. And I know I'll love yours." His smile warmed Sonya's heart. Yes, Daniel was a good man and a blessing in her life.

The day Sonya left school for her leave of absence, the staff surprised her with a baby shower. The love and good will the women displayed meant as much as the needed items. With their generous gifts and what she'd collected, and with Edith's contributions, her child was going to be well clothed. Thinking back to the time of Bryon's desertion, when the future had looked hopeless, Sonya realized that time and God had a way of changing everything. Considering how Edith, Eloise and others had cared for her, she looked forward to managing the abuse center so she could pass along to others the good will she'd received. She thought often of Jesus's parable of the sheep and the goats. "Inasmuch as ye have done it unto one of the least of these my brethren, ye have done it unto me." Was this a way she could show her gratitude for how God had supplied her needs?

Leta agreed to be Sonya's support person during the delivery, and she attended the prenatal classes with her. During these sessions, Sonya lost what little fear she had experienced and learned many exercises to strengthen her muscles and help with the delivery. As the burden of the baby increased, and she could hardly find any comfortable position to sit or lie, she longed to have the birth behind her. She had a suitcase packed with the necessities for her and the baby, since Dr. Hammer had indicated during his last examination that she might deliver sooner than he had expected.

Daniel had also volunteered to take her to the hospital when labor began, and she told him, "If I can't locate Leta when the time comes, I may have to call on you. Besides, my mother is coming, so I won't be alone."

"You know you can always count on me, Sonya," he assured her. "Now more than ever."

Edith had insisted that Sonya's mother should stay with them, and Sonya had readied a room on the second floor. Dr. Hammer had set the date for March 2, and Sonya's mother was scheduled to fly in the day before.

Just a few days before her due date, Daniel reported that the grant application had been approved with funds to be available for renovation within a month.

"So that means you will be able to stay here and care for your child," Edith said, "which makes me very happy. I will look forward to hearing the sounds of a child in this house."

"If the abused women bring their offspring, you may have more sounds of children than you want," Sonya said. "But I'm happy, too, Edith, and I appreciate the help you've given me. Having this good home has meant the difference between hope and despair. I'm beginning to heal. There are days now when I never think of Bryon, and I often sleep through the whole night without any bad dreams."

"But you've helped me, too. Without you in the house, I would probably have given up and gone to a nursing home."

"Better get ready for a quick trip out of here, Sonya," Stelle said one morning near the end of February. Because of Sonya's cumbersome body, Stelle had delivered Sonya's breakfast each morning.

"What makes you think that?"

"There's a full moon tomorrow night, so you're apt to deliver anytime, and you may have to leave without much warning if we have a bad storm. We've gone all winter without a blizzard, and we're due one. My bunion says snow, the newscaster says snow, and when we both agree it's a sure thing."

Sonya laughed. "I don't have any insight about the weather, but I'm sure that I won't hold on until March 2. I had lots of pain all night long. Should I telephone the doctor?"

"Might be a good idea," Stelle agreed as she glanced over Sonya's body. "Looks to me like you're gonna drop that child any minute."

By noon Sonya's pains came regularly, fifteen minutes apart. She paced the floor of the apartment all morning, eyeing the lowering clouds, which promised that the predicted blizzard was a distinct possibility. When she contacted Dr. Hammer, he concluded that he should see her. So Sonya called Leta, but there was no answer. She thought of calling Daniel, as he'd offered, but then felt self-conscious about bothering him during a workday. She was preparing to drive to the hospital herself when Daniel stopped by with some papers for Edith to sign.

"Why didn't you call me, Sonya? How could you even consider driving yourself to the hospital," he said sternly, taking the suitcase from her hand. "The roads are slick, and the wind gusts are strong enough to sway a car. Stelle," he called as he started down the steps, holding Sonya's arm, "give those papers to Edith and tell her I'll pick them up tomorrow."

When the pains became more severe, Sonya was thankful that Daniel had offered to chauffeur her. He's doing what Bryon should be doing, she thought. It was a miserable trip; Sonya shook convulsively when the labor pains struck periodically, and she gasped for breath.

"Does it hurt very much?" he asked quietly. Sonya just nodded. "Don't worry. We're more than halfway there. I'm sorry I don't know what to do for you," Daniel added, a mixture of concern and affection in his expression. "I've never driven an expectant mother to the hospital before."

Sonya gritted her teeth and stifled a scream. Daniel laid his hand on her shoulder. "Don't fight your pain. Scream if you want to. It won't scare me." He patted her back. "I'll have you there as soon as possible." Daniel insisted on waiting out in the reception area while she saw the obstetrician. After the doctor had examined her he said, "You're definitely in the early stages of labor. Although with a first baby it may take a long time, I can't risk sending you back to that house with this blizzard blowing, and no one but an old lady to look after you. I'm going to admit you."

"I'll tell Mr. Massie not to wait for me, and then I'll need to make some telephone calls."

On trembling legs, Sonya waddled back to the waiting room. Daniel helped her into a seat beside him. His face showed his concern.

"He's going to admit me." Her lips quivered. "I've managed to be nonchalant about the delivery up until this point, but now I find that I'm afraid, terribly afraid."

Daniel tenderly folded her hand in both of his. "We're always afraid of the unknown. But you'll get through this, Sonya. I know you will. And afterward you'll have a beautiful baby. I telephoned Mother to tell her where I was, and she sent you a Scripture verse for comfort. After all the years, she says she remembers that childbirth was a frightening experience. When the discomfort seemed almost unbearable, she quoted over and over, 'Weeping may endure for a night, but joy cometh in the morning.' Those words helped her over the rough places. She wanted you to remember them."

"I learned those words the night Adam Benson visited me when I needed him so desperately. I would have committed suicide if he hadn't telephoned me that night. So that's another thing I have to thank you for."

She started to rise, then groaned and grabbed her stomach. Daniel instantly came to his feet and reached out to support her. With his strong arms wrapped around her, Sonya pressed her cheek to his chest. She felt a featherlight touch of his hand on her hair. "Dear Sonya," he whispered. "Don't be afraid." She felt his embrace tighten ever so slightly for a moment, then he stepped back and lifted her chin with his fingertips. Gazing down into her eyes he said, "Sonya, at this moment you feel very alone, but let me assure you that God will be with you through this experience. I'll be praying all night for your physical needs, as well as your spiritual assurance, and when this is over, you'll realize that never for a moment were you separated from His everlasting arms."

She nodded and walked away from him, but before she turned the corner into Dr. Hammer's office, she looked back. She waved her hand to Daniel, who stood where she had left him. She yearned to know the meaning behind the pensive expression on his face.

Sonya made her first call to Stelle, and the woman said, "Don't you worry about things here. I'll stay with Mrs. Edith.

We'll be praying for you and your little one.''

When Sonya telephoned her parents, her mother said, "I'll get a plane tonight. I can be there in the morning.''

"There's a blizzard here. You may have trouble landing.''

"The airport in Columbus should know whether or not I can land. Don't worry. I'll be there.''

She made a call to the Bensons, who promised to be in constant prayer for her, and to Leta. To Leta she said, "Dr. Hammer says it won't be for several hours, so if you're here early in the morning, it will be soon enough.''

But around midnight Sonya was brought awake by sharp pains, and she rang for a nurse. The intense pain, which built to a peak and then receded long enough for Sonya to catch her breath, kept her from counting her contractions, but the nurse monitored her every fifteen minutes. After a couple of hours, she said, "Mrs. Dixon, your contractions are about four minutes apart, and you're going to deliver soon. I'll put in an alert to Dr. Hammer, and then we'll take you to the delivery room and prepare you.''

Sonya gripped the side of the bed until another wave of pain receded and said hoarsely, "Should I ring my friend Leta? She's supposed to be my support person.''

The nurse pulled back a curtain and peered into the night. Snow swirled against the windows, and Sonya couldn't see the streetlights. Shrieking wind along the side of the building signaled that a full-fledged blizzard was pelting the city. She couldn't ask Leta to come—she would take it alone.

Because of the trying situation with Bryon, and the fact that at times she'd dreaded having a child, Sonya hadn't dwelt much on the pain of childbirth. She had often heard women talk about their difficulty during the long hours of labor. Throughout the months when she had carried the child, it seldom seemed real to her, almost as if someone else was bearing it, but now she was scared, and tears slipped from her eyes. Over and over, she kept repeating the words she had first heard from We Care:

"Weeping may endure for a night, but joy cometh in the morning." She sensed the prayers of Daniel and the Bensons, and their loving concern and petitions blanketed Sonya with the assurance of God's love.

When they took her to the delivery room and prepared her for the birth, she was aware of what was going on, but it was almost as if she witnessed what was happening to someone else. But the pain was real enough, and though the nurses made her as comfortable as possible and coached her with breathing and relaxation techniques during contractions, loneliness overwhelmed her.

"Oh, Bryon, come and help me," she screamed once, and then clamped her jaws tightly to prevent another outburst. Bryon wouldn't come, her mother and Leta couldn't, only God could help her tonight, and she reached out a hand to Him.

During the struggle to force the child into the world, two strong emotions manifested themselves and fought for control of her heart. As the pain intensified the child became real to her. He was hers, and she loved him, and strange as it might seem, as her love for the child surfaced, the indifference she'd felt for the baby was transferred to Bryon. The hold Bryon had held on her emotions disappeared, and she no longer cared about him. It was such a strange feeling—for two years Bryon had been the center of her universe, and tears stung her eyelids when she realized that now she felt nothing for him. She hoped she would simply remain indifferent to him, for she didn't want to hate him, although he had given her ample reason to do so.

"Oh, thank you," she breathed when the nurse finally gave her a shot to ease her labor pains and drowsiness calmed her, but she endured until she experienced an excruciating pain and heard Dr. Hammer say, "That's it—we've got a fine boy."

She awakened in the recovery room when Doctor Hammer came in with a nurse carrying a blue-wrapped bundle.

"You have an eight-pound boy, Mrs. Dixon, and he's healthy and alert. How do you feel?"

"Tired."

"You've a right to be," he said with a laugh, "and you probably won't believe this, but you had a much easier time than most women do. Physically, you're well built for bearing children."

"Rather wasted on me, isn't it, when I'm married to a man who doesn't want a family?" Sonya said bitterly. "And, Doctor, I will have to give my husband an answer now about the divorce, so I hope you'll examine the baby carefully to be sure he's physically fit."

"That's part of our routine here. We're required by law to test newborns for certain rare, inherited diseases. You can be assured that your baby will be screened before he leaves the hospital."

Sonya cuddled the baby and scrutinized his features. His little face was red, his eyes squeezed shut, and a bit of brown fuzz covered his small head. She'd seen baby calves on the farm with more beauty than that, but she smiled at the mite she held and whispered, "Doesn't matter if you're not a great beauty now, you'll change soon." She wasn't worried about the child's appearance, since both she and Bryon had more than their share of good looks. Up until this moment she hadn't decided on a name for her boy. If conditions had been normal, she would have named him after Bryon, but knowing he wouldn't want that, Sonya said, "Would you like to be called Paul?"

The baby didn't make any response, but at least he hadn't cried over the prospect, so Sonya kissed him and said, "Paul. I like the name, and I love you."

At daylight, her mother telephoned. "Sonya, we've finally arrived at the airport, but it will be a while before land transportation can bring me into town. How are you doing?"

"Fine, Mother, and you have an eight-pound grandson."

"You mean I'm too late," she said, and Sonya sensed the disappointment in her voice.

"The baby was born three hours ago. I was in labor about twelve hours. All is well."

"I'll still come to the hospital as soon as I can make it."

When the phone rang again, Daniel was on the line. "I checked at the front desk and learned that you had already delivered. How are you, Sonya?"

"Tired, but I understand that's a normal reaction. And, Daniel, I want you to know that my faith in God's providence remained strong."

"You're a courageous person, Sonya. I never once thought that you wouldn't come through it all with flying colors. And how's your son?"

"The most perfect baby ever born."

He laughed. "They always are."

They spoke about the baby for a few more minutes and Daniel told her he'd be coming in a few hours to see this perfect baby for himself.

Right after she hung up the phone, a nurse came in with a large bouquet of roses. "How beautiful!" Sonya exclaimed. She eagerly tore open the card, expecting to see Edith's or even Leta's name. But the flowers were from Daniel with a simple but touching note: "Wishing you and your new baby great joy this morning and every morning—Daniel."

Glowing with Daniel's good wishes and confidence in her, Sonya telephoned Leta and the Bensons, then she settled down to rest and contemplate the night's experience, destined to be a turning point for her. Becoming a mother had put her life into a new perspective. She savored a closeness to her own mother that she'd never known before and formed a deeper appreciation for what her parents had done for her. She experienced a peace that she hadn't known since Bryon had left her, but this was an incident they should have shared, and she sorrowed that Bryon had missed forever the wonder and beauty of the birth of his first child.

Mostly Sonya rejoiced in the miracle that she wanted the child, for her greatest fear had been that once the baby was born, she wouldn't feel any emotion toward him. Her apprehension that rearing the child would be a duty rather than a labor of love had disappeared forever when she first held and touched Paul. He was simply amazing to her. She had a son and she loved him! Perhaps that was the greatest miracle of all.

Chapter Eleven

With her mother on hand to help with the baby and to look out for Edith, too, Sonya didn't mind going back to the York home for her convalescent period. Her mother intended to stay for two weeks, and after that Sonya would be able to continue as Edith's companion. Edith gave Paul a heartwarming reception.

"I've longed for the sound of a baby's cry in this house, and I hope you won't think he's bothering me. Bring him to see me every day. I'll even watch him for you when your mother goes away, because you're going to be busy. Daniel telephoned yesterday that the inspectors will arrive in a few days to look over the house and see what changes have to be made to turn it into a refuge for battered women."

Sonya had telephoned Lola Shrader the news about the child, and while she was still in the hospital, Lola came to visit her bringing several sleeper outfits. Sonya had been resentful toward the Shraders that they'd ignored her during the Christmas holidays, but it was probably better that way for all of them. A single, pregnant woman didn't fit into the company Riley and Lola entertained.

Apparently Riley had reported about the child at the office, and Bryon must have heard. When Paul was ten days old, he telephoned.

"Are you ready to proceed with the divorce now?" he inquired bluntly, with no question about the baby, no comment upon Sonya's health. Wouldn't one think he would want to know his child's name, or if it were a boy or a girl? Perhaps his informant had supplied the information. Whatever the situation, his attitude annoyed Sonya, and she said angrily, "Yes, I'm ready for a divorce. I want you out of my life as quickly as possible, Bryon. I'll have my lawyer contact you."

She slammed down the phone without giving him an opportunity to answer. She punched in the digits of Daniel office.

"Daniel, my husband just telephoned about the divorce, and I'm ready to have you continue with it. When will it be convenient for me to see you?"

"I'll stop by the house this afternoon. I have to be in north Omaha, and that will save you a trip downtown."

Sonya had hesitated to contact Bryon's parents about the birth of her son, but since Bryon already knew, they probably had heard, too. The last time she'd phoned them they'd been preparing to go to California for several weeks, so she doubted that they had returned. For some reason when they didn't answer their phone, she was relieved, but she didn't feel it was right to restrain them from seeing Paul, especially since his face mirrored the distinctive features of their son. Even Sonya's mother, against her will, admitted that she could see nothing of her daughter in the child. "But let's hope he'll have your personality," she muttered.

A few months ago this fact would have frustrated Sonya, but now she could look at this little image of Bryon with unconcern. She loved Paul, but his visage didn't give her any longing for Bryon. She tried to convey something of her feelings to Daniel when he arrived for the appointment.

"I don't want Bryon anymore, so you take what measures are necessary."

Today, Daniel was her attorney instead of her friend, and he approached the matter of her divorce in an unemotional manner, but never again in his presence would Sonya be able to blot out the comfort he'd given her on the day that Paul was born. She now looked upon their relationship from a new perspective.

"What kind of divorce settlement shall we ask for? It isn't out of line to demand that he pay all of your hospital expenses, as well as child support, and even some alimony for you until you marry again."

Sonya laughed shortly. "This experience has soured me on marriage. I don't want anything from Bryon except complete custody of the child and that he sign away all of his rights."

Daniel frowned. "As your attorney, Sonya, I must tell you that is very foolish. He should pay for the care of this child. You don't realize how much it will cost to raise a child."

"I made it through the past six months on my own. I had enough to pay for the hospital bill and even a bit of money left over. I figure if I could manage that, I'll make it alone."

"I'm advising against it."

"If Bryon is sending child support each month, I'll not have a chance to forget him. I want to put the past behind me, Daniel, and I think this is the only way to do it. I do want you to make him pay your fees and any court cost involved. I don't want him to give *me* anything, but I want you amply compensated, and I know I can't afford to pay you what you're entitled to have. Bryon is the one who wants a divorce, so he should at least pay for that. Perhaps I am being foolish, and I certainly am not suggesting this as a precedent for other women to follow, but my pride prevents me from taking anything from Bryon."

"Sonya, I have mixed feelings about this. As an attorney, I oppose your action. Your husband should pay to support your child, especially since you don't have an adequate income. Many of my divorced clients can't make a decent living for their family when they have a good job *and* receive child support. On the other hand, I look forward to having Bryon Dixon out of your life forever."

Daniel had helped Sonya and Edith choose a well-known contractor to do the renovation, and on Monday morning three workers arrived. They first blocked off Edith's quarters by building a wall with a locking door in it.

It saddened Sonya to see the changing appearance inside the old house. She loved it because the walls had reached out and sheltered her when she needed a sanctuary, and she thought the renovations desecrated it. She figured Edith had similar feelings, because the elderly woman spent most of that day lying on the bed, but by evening the partition was in.

By the end of the week all the necessary changes in the house had been made and Sonya looked forward to starting her training classes.

Paul was a month old when Bryon's mother telephoned and asked if they could see the child.

"We returned from California yesterday," Mrs. Dixon said. "We could come by whenever it's convenient for you."

"Edith is doing quite a lot of renovation right now, and the house is rather untidy. Why don't I drive out with him tomorrow afternoon?"

"That will be fine."

The Dixons were obviously delighted with their grandchild, and Mrs. Dixon compared him to some of Bryon's baby pictures, confirming how much Paul looked like his father.

"It's almost as if we have Bryon again," she said.

Sonya stayed a couple of hours, and Mrs. Dixon held the baby all the time she was there. She seemed quite reluctant to give him up when Sonya prepared to leave.

"You said that Mrs. York is renovating her house. Seems a strange thing for her to do at her age," Tom Dixon said.

"She's turning the house into a crisis center for abused wives and children. I'm attending classes so that I'll be qualified to be the director. Since I wanted to care for Paul myself and avoid a baby-sitter, this arrangement seemed like a good idea. After my own experience, I think I have some knowledge to help other women, so I'm looking forward to the work."

"That doesn't appear to be a desirable environment to rear a child," Mrs. Dixon said.

"Oh, we have a delightful apartment for Paul and me. There

will be an attendant to supervise the clients at night, so I'll be looking out for him then.''

"But you don't know what kind of people will be living there,'' her mother-in-law insisted.

"They'll be screened carefully, and I don't have any worries about it. Actually, I have a lot of sympathy for the women who'll need to come to our center. From what I've learned in my training, I'll be dealing with women caught in troubled circumstances who are finally taking the first steps to make their lives and their children's lives better. No doubt by the time Paul is older, I will use this experience to find another job probably in social work as well. But I don't want to leave him when he's a baby.''

"Would you consider coming here to live?'' Mr. Dixon asked.

Sonya stared at him, dumbfounded. "Wouldn't that be an awkward arrangement? If I lived here, I couldn't possibly avoid seeing Bryon, and it would be too painful for me if he should bring home another wife. In spite of how he has treated me, I can't forget that he once loved me. Besides, I don't believe Bryon would come home if I lived in your house.''

"But if your divorce goes through and you have custody of the baby, we might never see him,'' Anna said.

"A few months ago, I was so mad at Bryon that I didn't care whether I saw any of you Dixons again, but before I could become the sort of Christian I want to be, I had to learn to forgive. I've forgiven Bryon for what he has done, and I certainly won't be mean enough to prevent you seeing your only grandchild, but I believe Bryon will not want you to have a relationship with Paul. If he broke up our marriage because he didn't want a child, he won't want to share you with our son, especially when I'm the boy's guardian. You may have to make a choice—either your son or your grandson.''

"I'm sure he will change his mind now that the child is born,'' Anna said confidently, with a significant look at her husband.

Sonya was glad to leave the Dixon house, and she doubted if she'd ever go there again. She had never loved the Dixons, but she had respected them. Maybe the break with Bryon would have to include his parents, too.

Paul was three months old, the house was almost ready for patrons, and still no word from Bryon about the divorce. Although Daniel had contacted Bryon's attorney and filed the necessary papers, he had received no response.

When Daniel telephoned that he needed to see her, Sonya wasn't surprised. "Do you want me to come into the office?"

"No, I need to see Edith on business, too, so I'll come there this morning."

Daniel's face was unusually grave when Sonya opened the door to admit him.

"Shall we sit in Edith's room? I've just brought Paul down for his visit with her. She enjoys having him for an hour or so each day. I think she pretends that he's her own great-grandchild."

"She's become quite fond of you, Sonya."

Daniel lifted Paul from his carrier when they entered the room. "How's my boy?" he greeted the baby and kissed his cheek. Paul was a happy child, and he gurgled at Daniel in reply. "He's a cute one, Sonya. And he's getting bigger every day. Pretty soon, I'll have to teach him how to toss that little football I gave him," Daniel said, testing Paul's grip on his finger as he cradled the child to his chest.

Sonya laughed. "I think we have a way to go before he's playing football, Daniel." She reached for the baby and Daniel unwillingly handed him back.

"Whatever you say. You're his mom. Maybe we'll start with the zoo, first," he added hopefully.

"Sounds like a good idea," Sonya agreed.

Daniel sat down, and he looked at Sonya with compassion. "Sonya, you have to deal with a rather difficult situation."

"Bryon?"

"No, I haven't heard from his lawyer, but now I think I know why. I had a visit from Bryon's parents yesterday. They want to adopt Paul.''

"Why, the nerve!" Sonya said when she finally found her tongue.

"Apparently they believe that Bryon will not have another child, and they want an heir. If you retain sole custody of Paul, they would have no legal right to him at all.''

"But what legal grounds could they have?"

"They're contending that a crisis center isn't a suitable environment for a baby, and that financially they're able to care for him, and you're not.''

Sonya reached for Paul and clutched him tightly. "Can they take my baby away from me?''

"I don't think so, but they have a lot of money, and they're determined.''

"And I don't have any money,'' Sonya said bitterly.

"I'll do everything I can for you, without charge,'' Daniel assured her. "That should go without saying by now.''

"And you're welcome to use my money, Daniel,'' Edith said, and her lips trembled. "It's inconceivable that anyone would say *my* home isn't a fit place for a child.''

"I don't believe there's a judge who will give them custody of Paul when he knows the true facts. We can have plenty of character witnesses, perhaps your friend Leta, Edith, Adam and Marie Benson, and the people you've worked with at the nursery school. I thought I knew your answer before I came, but I had to inquire. Your answer is no?''

"Of course.''

"They said they will give you one hundred thousand dollars if you agree to their plan without a court fight.''

Sonya hadn't felt such a surge of anger since she'd learned that Bryon had deserted her. She remembered distinctly the mutilation of the two Chinese vases, so she hurriedly placed Paul back in his playpen. She didn't want him in her arms if she had an urge to throw something. She paced the room while Edith and Daniel watched her.

"I'm trying so hard to come through this divorce without hatred, but it grows worse every day. Just when I think I can live at peace with everyone, the Dixons take this awful action. Do they have such a low opinion of me that they think I would sell my child? That's what it amounts to."

"If that's what they think, I'll soon take them your negative answer and then let them proceed. Though I was sure of your answer, I couldn't speak for you."

"Thank you, Daniel," Sonya murmured.

He favored her with an inquiring glance.

"For believing that I wouldn't give up my child for money."

He flashed a warm smile. "Sonya, it makes me laugh to even hear you say such a thing. There was never any question in my mind about your answer had they offered you a million dollars. What puzzles me is why they didn't work through Bryon to gain custody of the child," Daniel added. "That would be the logical way—for Bryon to fight for him."

"Bryon doesn't always do what his parents want him to, so he may have refused."

Daniel stood and looked down at Paul, who had gone to sleep, unconcerned about the battle that was brewing over his small form. He reached down and gently touched the baby's hair with his fingertips.

"I can't understand why a man wouldn't want a baby as sweet as this one, but unfortunately, in my line of work, I see this form of rejection every day."

After Daniel left, Edith and Sonya sat in companionable silence. Sonya's thoughts were so troubled that she didn't want to talk, and Edith must have understood this for she waited until Sonya stirred and said, "I must get ready to go to my class. I'll never be able to concentrate on my studies after this jolt. Do you want me to leave Paul here, or should I take him to Stelle so you can rest?"

"Since he's happy here, leave him, and tell Stelle to look in on both of us occasionally."

Sonya knelt beside Paul and laid her hand tenderly on his

face. "I can't believe they would try to take my child. For one thing, they're both in their sixties and certainly that is no age to start rearing a baby."

"I'm sure you have nothing to worry about, Sonya. Since you have such a good record, I can't see any judge taking the child from you. If Bryon fights for him, that's a different story."

"This could drag on for years, couldn't it?"

"I don't know, but there is something I do know. Do you realize that Daniel Massie is in love with you?"

Sonya turned startled eyes on the older woman.

"I was sure you didn't suspect that," Edith said gently.

"He's given no indication. I've been very grateful for his supportive friendship as well as some spiritual guidance, but love...no, surely you're mistaken."

"As an attorney, he knows you have to preserve your integrity until after a divorce is finalized, so he wouldn't ask you to do anything that would jeopardize your standing in the court. But you need to face the possibility that when your divorce is finalized, he may speak."

"I certainly hope you're wrong, Edith. I owe so much to him that I'd hate to hurt him, but right now I feel as if I will never marry again."

"Perhaps I shouldn't have said anything, but if he does approach you, I didn't want it to be a surprise."

But Edith's words had disturbed her mind, and she thought of the many times Daniel had helped her during these months, and she was convinced he didn't take that much interest in all of his clients. She thought of the many quiet talks they'd had together. They'd grown even closer after Paul's birth. She thought of Daniel's warm looks, his kind words and encouragement and his tireless efforts to be there when she needed him. Was that love? She didn't know the answer. But whatever Daniel's feelings for her, she felt honored that a man with so much to offer any woman wanted to be such a large part of her life and Paul's.

And if he is in love with you, what do you think about it?
Sonya could find no answer to that question.

It was over a week before Daniel contacted Sonya again, and
when he telephoned, he said, "The Dixons are going through
with their demand, so I've arranged a meeting before a judge
on Monday. You're to appear and bring Paul with you. Wear
something sedate and conservative, but dress up. We want to
make a good impression."

"I'll wear one of the expensive outfits I used to buy. I'm
almost back to my original size. They may not be fashionable
now, but perhaps the judge won't know the difference. Or is it
a woman judge?"

"No, we've been assigned a male judge—he's in his late
fifties and a solid family man. We have a good chance with
him. Shall I pick you up?"

Sonya would have liked his comforting presence rather than
to arrive at the courthouse by herself, but she remembered
Edith's comments about Daniel's interest in her. If they were
true, she couldn't place herself under any more obligation to
Daniel than an attorney-client relationship warranted.

"No, thanks. That would be out of your way, and my old
car is still running well enough. If I need transportation, I'll let
you know."

"As you wish. The hearing is at ten o'clock."

Three days to wait! Sonya tried desperately to fill in the
hours. She studied for her final exams in the social work course,
willing her mind to concentrate on the book before her. The
exams were on Wednesday, and if the decision didn't go in her
favor, she wondered if she might fail the course.

The night before the hearing, Sonya went to her room soon
after dinner. Clutching Paul in her arms and wondering if this
time tomorrow night she would no longer have him was an
intolerable burden to bear. She knew Paul should be resting in
his crib, for she didn't want him to be fussy tomorrow, but she
was reluctant to put him down. Only once before could she
remember a more trying time—the night she would have taken

her life except for the timely arrival of Adam and Marie. She had thought losing Bryon was the worst thing that could ever happen to her, but his desertion was nothing compared to the possible loss of her son.

Although she was worried, she didn't have the feeling of desperation she had experienced that other terrible night, for she had a hope now that she didn't have before. Sitting on the couch with Paul in her left arm, she opened the Bible to Romans 8:28. That verse didn't baffle her as much as it had once. *And we know that in all things God works for the good of those who love him, who have been called according to his purpose.*

She couldn't see why it would be right for the Dixons to take Paul, but she had experienced sufficient evidence of God working in her life to believe that, in some way, He would make tomorrow's hearing turn out for the best. She did love God, she believed He had a purpose for her life, and she had no choice except to leave tomorrow, and all other tomorrows, in His hands.

Sonya kissed Paul, laid him tenderly in the crib, and changed into her nightgown. "Weeping may endure for the night, but joy cometh in the morning," she whispered and turned out the light.

Surveying herself in the mirror on Monday morning, Sonya was pleased with her appearance. She'd found a classically styled navy wool suit, with a shaped blazer and slim skirt that seemed perfect for court. Small gold earrings and a pearl necklace completed her outfit. Most of the weight she'd gained during her pregnancy was gone, and her figure looked slim and attractive once more. The honey-toned hair flowing over her shoulders was shiny and alive. Only in her large blue eyes could one detect the unhappiness that had been her constant companion for so many months.

She dressed Paul in a new set of clothes her mother had recently sent. He looked like a miniature farmer with his red plaid, flannel shirt and blue chambray overalls. Edith was still in bed eating the breakfast Stelle had brought when Sonya walked down the back stairs and paused in the doorway.

"How do we look?" she asked, holding Paul aloft for inspection.

"Adorable! Come for a kiss. Remember, right is going to win, and it's right for you to keep this boy."

After Sonya buckled Paul into the used car seat she had found at a yard sale, she reached into her purse for a tissue to wipe the perspiration from her hands and dropped her head on the steering wheel to ask for God's help. After a few minutes she turned the ignition key with shaky fingers and drove slowly down the street. She had ample time, so she needn't hurry.

Daniel waited for her on the steps of the courthouse flanked by the Bensons, Leta, Eloise Dedham and the manager of the Washburn Complex. "Doesn't hurt to have plenty of backup troops when we go into battle," he said with a smile. "We probably won't need them, but I'm ready."

Leta took Paul from Sonya and hugged him. "Doesn't he look cute in this outfit? The Dixons will get this child over my dead body," she said dramatically.

Leta carried Paul until they reached the courtroom. "Sonya should carry him now, Leta. When we enter the room, the five of you can sit on the seat behind us. My defense will depend on what the Dixons' lawyer proposes, so I don't know when, or if, I'll call you to testify."

Daniel led Sonya to a table close to the judge's bench, and her spirits soared when she sensed her friends seating themselves behind her. She deflated again when the elder Dixons entered the room with their lawyer, completely ignoring her presence. She hated to think that their friendliness toward her since Christmas had been nothing more than a ruse to snatch her baby.

Paul began to fuss, and Sonya whispered, "Please, baby, be good today." She reached into the diaper bag and brought out a bear he liked, which silenced him for the moment. She'd brought a battery of things to entertain him and to feed him.

Turning to Leta, she whispered, "If he needs to be changed, will you take care of him?"

Fortunately the judge came in at that moment, and the clerk asked everyone to rise. Sonya hoped they would have the proceedings finished before Paul became too fussy. The clerk called the courtroom to order and the judge sat behind his large desk. As Sonya reseated herself, she felt Daniel briefly squeeze her hand. "Don't worry, Sonya," he whispered. "With God's help, we'll win this. He knows we have to."

The judge scanned the papers before him and turned to the Dixons' attorney. "It's my understanding that Tom and Anna Dixon are suing for the custody and adoption of their grandson, Paul Dixon. I have in the record here that the mother of the child, Sonya Dixon, is opposed to that adoption. What is the position of the father? I assume he's still living."

"Yes, and he has no objection to this adoption. He doesn't want the child himself," the plaintiffs' lawyer said.

"The court will listen now to the arguments advanced by the grandparents as to why they want to adopt the boy."

The lawyer approached the bench. "I have here a financial statement of my clients. It's their contention that they can provide much more for the child than his mother can. She's the director of a crisis center for abused women, where she makes less than the minimum wage. She lives in that center, and my clients believe that isn't a proper environment for the rearing of a child."

"I assume that the father is paying some support for the boy. Is that considered in an estimate of her income?"

"No, Your Honor. A divorce is in process, but it hasn't become finalized, necessarily delayed for the outcome of this hearing."

The judge glanced momentarily toward Paul, who chortled gleefully in Sonya's arms.

"Am I to understand, then, that you bring no charges against the character of the mother?"

"No, Your Honor, we haven't investigated her life-style. We

simply believe this adoption would be in the best interests of the child.''

The judge nodded for the attorney to take his seat, and he turned to Daniel.

"Mr. Massie, we're ready to hear your case."

"Your Honor, I want my client, Sonya Dixon, to tell you the events of her life the past year." Sonya turned startled eyes upon him, and he smiled slightly. "As you can see, this comes as a surprise to Mrs. Dixon. I hadn't warned her ahead of time, since I wanted the narrative to be completely unrehearsed." He smiled encouragingly at Sonya. "I believe her story is the only defense we need."

"Will you stand, Mrs. Dixon?" the judge said.

Sonya handed Paul to Leta, and he left her arms reluctantly, howling immediately. Leta snatched up the diaper bag and hurried down the aisle with the unhappy boy.

"I was happily married to Bryon Dixon for two years, but when I became pregnant, he turned into a different man. When I refused to abort the fetus, he abandoned me."

She swallowed and resumed with difficulty. For over an hour she talked, occasionally sipping from the glass of water that Daniel had placed on the table. She told of Bryon's surprise move to San Francisco, Gail's entry into the apartment to take away his clothes, how he had closed the savings account, leaving her with scant money, how he'd had the utilities turned off. When her voice faltered, and she felt unable to go on, she glanced at Daniel and drew strength and comfort from his calm, steady gaze. Tears streamed from her face as she recalled the move from the Sandhill Apartments to the tiny quarters, how she was compelled to wear used clothing, depend upon the church for food. Gaining control of her emotions, she wiped her face with some tissues the court clerk handed her. When she mentioned her move to Edith's home, the judge took on a new look of interest.

"There were times when I hated my unborn child because of all the trouble he has caused, but during the night I labored to bring his small form into the world, I fell in love with him. I want only what's best for him, and if Your Honor believes his interests can best be served with his grandparents, then I won't contest the decision of the court.''

Daniel stood up and interrupted, ''Your Honor, the client hasn't discussed such a statement with me. Please don't hold her to that decision.''

''Be seated, Mr. Massie. You gave your client the privilege of speaking without coaching. You'll have to take the consequences. Continue, Mrs. Dixon.''

Daniel eased back into his seat, and, taking a deep breath, Sonya said, ''But, Your Honor, I want my baby. I love him with all my heart and would do anything in my power to keep him safe and happy. I've provided for myself for over a year. I changed my life-style to scrimp and save to pay my hospital bills. If I could do that when I was pregnant and with a newborn child, surely I can take care of him now without doing him any harm. You can tell that he's a happy baby and that he won't come to any harm through me.''

''Do you mean that you haven't had any support from your husband?''

''No, Your Honor, not from him, his parents, nor mine. Since December, I've been a companion to Edith York for free room and board, and until a few weeks before Paul was born, I worked at a nursery school and saved enough to pay my hospital confinement. I'll admit that compared to the Dixons, my financial statement is meager. I own a six-year-old car and have less than two hundred dollars in the bank. Those are my total assets, except for some expensive jewelry, compliments of my husband.''

''May I ask about the divorce proceedings and terms?''

Daniel rose. ''May I speak to that, Your Honor.''

The judge nodded and said, ''Be seated, Mrs. Dixon.''

''My client's husband asked for a divorce almost immediately after he deserted her, and he wanted to give her a onetime settlement to pay for the hospital confinement and her expenses until she could get a job. I advised that she refuse the divorce until the birth of the child. When he was born without any health problems, I contacted Mr. Dixon's attorney and gave him our terms. That has been over three months ago without response from them.''

"May I ask what your terms are?''

"Again, Your Honor, Mrs. Dixon refused my counsel. She wants nothing from her husband except his renouncement of all claim to the child and that she be given complete custody. She wants to assume full responsibility. I think it unwise, but she is adamant.''

"Mrs. Dixon, you may remain seated, but I want to ask why you're taking a stand that might not be in the best interests of your child?''

"Perhaps it's stubbornness, Your Honor.'' A light smile played around the judge's stern features. "Bryon has never inquired about the child, never asked his sex or his name, although I assume he knows this from his parents or from our mutual acquaintances. I feel it's degrading to Paul to demand support from a parent who won't even claim him.''

"Mrs. Dixon, I'm going to ask you a question which may be difficult for you to answer, but I want the truth. Does your husband have any reason to believe that this child is not his?''

"Your Honor!'' Sonya gasped.

Bryon's father cleared his throat. "Your Honor, may I speak?'' And when the judge nodded assent, Mr. Dixon said, "We have no reason to believe the child is not legitimate, else we wouldn't have asked to adopt him. To compare Bryon's baby picture with her child, one would find them as identical as twins.''

Sonya ventured a look at her in-laws. Mr. Dixon's face was red, and he breathed with difficulty. Mrs. Dixon sat with her face buried in her hands. Had they had any idea before just how shabbily Bryon had treated her? Sonya's face seemed drawn and tight. Tears threatened to overflow again. She glanced at

Daniel and the sympathy and affection in his expression soothed her.

"I apologize for asking that, Mrs. Dixon, but I had to be sure before I made any decision."

"Your Honor," Daniel said, "if there is any question about my client's character, I have with me several witnesses to assert that Mrs. Dixon has lived an exemplary life both before and after her husband's desertion."

"That isn't necessary at this point. Normally I would deliberate several days before making a decision of this sort, but surely even the plaintiffs and their lawyer can see that justice can only be served by refusing this request for adoption." Sonya dropped her head on the table and sobbed. She heard sniffing all around her, and the judge halted momentarily. Even his voice seemed strained with emotion when he continued, "Mrs. Dixon, I believe the attitude that weighed most heavily in your favor was when you agreed to relinquish your son if this court decided his interests would best be served with his grandparents.

"I remembered when a judge, much wiser than I, was faced with a similar decision. You will remember that two women came to King Solomon contesting the motherhood of a child. When the real mother agreed to give up her child to save his life, King Solomon ruled in her favor. Can I do any less than he? It may be that the grandparents will appeal my opinion, but it's my decision that their request for adoption be denied."

Mr. Dixon leaned forward and spoke to his attorney. "Your Honor," the attorney said, "the plaintiffs will not appeal."

The judge turned again to Sonya, who lifted her tear-streaked face.

"You understand, Mrs. Dixon, that my only ruling is with the case in hand. This is not to indicate that your husband may not demand custody of the child. And although it isn't my place to advise you, I would strongly suggest that you rethink the terms of the divorce. Even if you receive custody of the child, your husband has some obligation for your welfare and that of his son.''

''Thank you, Your Honor.''

The judge left the courtroom, and Marie Benson snatched Sonya into comforting arms. Over Marie's shoulder, she watched Bryon's parents make their way slowly down the aisle. She'd never before thought of them being old, but they walked with the tread of the aged. Bryon had ruined their lives as well as hers.

Chapter Twelve

Sonya fretted because the elder Dixons might still acquire Paul through Bryon. Even if he didn't want Paul, Bryon could demand full or equal custody and turn the child over to his parents. This specter haunted her, but she finished her social work course, passed it and waited for the first client at Blessed Hope, the name they'd given to the crisis center.

Since many people still gossiped about the tragedy that had occurred at the York house, Sonya had difficulty finding a helper, and it was imperative that they hire an extra night worker as she couldn't leave Paul by himself all night. When she couldn't hire a part-time person through the unemployment agencies, she went back to the Washburn Complex to talk to Loretta Slinde.

Although Loretta was still skeptical, she agreed to work. "My man ain't working right now, and we need some extra money."

"It will be part-time work. We can't pay you if we don't have a patron. I'll probably call you frequently in the middle of the night."

Representatives of the organization assembled at the house for a ribbon-cutting ceremony, and a newspaper reporter from the *Herald* spread the story prominently in the next Sunday's issue. They still hadn't received a client when Edith had a telephone call from her indignant nephew, the first time she'd heard from him since Christmas. Sonya sat nursing Paul in Edith's living room, and since the man spoke loudly, she heard most of the conversation.

"Aunt Edith," Albert York said, "I can hardly believe what I've just read in the *Herald*. Why would you turn your house into such a place? And who is this Sonya Dixon you've taken under your wing? What kind of influence is she exerting upon you?"

Edith's lips trembled as she slipped a nitroglycerin tablet under her tongue. "I believe the newspaper explained it all, Albert. It was *my* idea to convert the house into a shelter."

"Well, I don't like it. It's degrading to the York name for one thing. The scandal connected with Alice's death was bad enough, and people are just beginning to forget that, and you have to start a crisis center. I don't wonder that Uncle will turn over in his grave."

Still with an attempt at calmness, Edith said, "Your uncle lived with me for several years, and I doubt he would be much surprised at anything I do."

"Since you know my objections, I trust you'll close down the place immediately."

"That's out of the question. I've signed a contract with the organization for two years. And I might remind you, Albert, you don't own this property." She eased the receiver back in place.

"Albert is worried about his inheritance," she said angrily.

"I could hear. It's too bad he doesn't understand."

"Albert has a dollar sign where his heart should be. He resents it that I've lived so long to use money that he thinks should be his. He's my husband's nephew and believes he's the heir to the York fortune, but he hasn't seen that in writing."

The first call for help came at three o'clock that night. A new telephone hot line had been installed in Sonya's apartment to avoid disturbing Edith.

"Mrs. Dixon, we have a patron for you. The police will bring her by shortly. She may be suicidal, so you should watch her carefully.''

Sonya put in a call to Loretta Slinde and dressed hurriedly. Paul slept peacefully, but she left the door open so she could hear if he cried.

Walking down the broad stairway to wait by the front door, Sonya shuddered at the sight of the big chandelier. She had grown accustomed to the house, and it had been a long time since she'd thought of Alice Simmons and her tragic death on that spot.

The woman who staggered into the house ahead of the policemen reeked of alcohol, and Sonya turned inquiring eyes upon the officers.

''Both husband and wife are heavy drinkers, but tonight he became abusive, beat up the woman and kicked her out of the house. We've got him in jail. Try to sober her up.''

Sonya led the woman upstairs and into the bathroom, where she promptly vomited on the floor. Seating the woman on the side of the tub, Sonya bathed her face and applied bandages over the worst places. She tried to talk to the woman, who gave her name as Tracey, but couldn't carry on much of a conversation after that. Sonya tried her best to simply calm her and make her comfortable.

By the time she had the woman ready for bed, Loretta arrived, and she cleaned the bathroom. Sonya returned to bed, but she didn't sleep, wondering if she'd done all she could for Tracey.

After she fed Paul the next morning, Sonya checked with Loretta, who sat in the upstairs lounge watching the shoppers' club program. She had the volume turned low, and Sonya whispered, ''How did things go?''

''Haven't heard a word out of her. I've checked in the bedroom often. She's sleeping it off.''

''I'll report to the agency and see what we do next.''

Sonya didn't like the monitor's report. ''Her husband has

paid his fine, the police have released him, and he's coming to get his wife.''

Indignantly Sonya repeated the message to Loretta. ''We'll have to awaken her and let him take her, I suppose. Seems futile to me.''

Loretta flipped off the television, stretched and stood up. ''Doesn't surprise me. I've seen abuse often at the apartment. Man and woman go on a binge, get mad at each other and call the police. When they sober up, they're lovey-dovey until they liquor up again.''

''Do you think she'll want to go back with him?''

''Where else can she go? She can't stay here forever.''

Loretta was right, and when a burly, unshaven man appeared at the doorway demanding, ''Where is she?'' Tracey meekly followed him out to his car.

After they left, Sonya telephoned the agency. ''Wasn't there anything else I could have done for her? I feel as if I'm wasting my time if women like Tracey are just going to go back to the same situations. I thought we were here to help them.''

''We see all kinds of cases,'' the director said soothingly. ''When a woman doesn't want to return to her husband, you can keep her until we find a place for her to live. Each case is different. Sometimes we find foster homes for children until the mother can determine some means of support. You're going to deal with many different situations.''

The woman was right, for throughout the rest of spring and into summer, hardly a night passed that Sonya didn't have one or more patrons. A few women spent a week or more at the house and actually proved a help with other clients, who came in sick or hurt. Sonya was always moved and humbled when she witnessed women who were suffering themselves reaching out to those even less fortunate.

After four months of dealing with the problems of abused women, Sonya was ready to believe that Bryon had treated her decently. He'd never hit her, never publicly humiliated her, nor had he forced sexual relations upon her. She knew she hadn't deserved the treatment he'd given her, but at least she had come to the place where she could think of it with some detachment. Both she and Daniel had thought there would be an immediate response from Bryon's attorney after the adoption ploy had failed, but the months passed without any contact.

After Paul's birth Daniel became a frequent visitor at the York mansion. Sometimes he had business with Edith, but more often, he simply dropped by for an hour or so just to visit. Sonya would have been flattered to think he came solely to see her, but she had to admit that he gave most of his attention to Paul. He fussed over the boy like a mother hen with a chick. He absolutely insisted on going with her when she took the child to the pediatrician for regular exams, and he rejoiced as much as she did when the doctor praised the baby's growth. If he visited at feeding time, he heated the formula, tested it carefully and held the bottle for Paul to eat. A few times when Sonya was busy with the shelter's clients, he even changed Paul's diaper. Since Sonya had no previous experience with children, they were learning child care together.

Sonya did appreciate Daniel's interest in Paul, for she had read articles by psychologists saying that a child's personality formed at an early age, and she thought it was important for Paul to have a male influence. Daniel was being the father that Bryon should have been, and she was grateful to Daniel for filling that void. Sonya's maternal affection, and the love he received from the Massies, as well as Stelle, Leta and Edith had molded Paul into a happy, well-adjusted child, who cried very little and smiled at everyone.

Jane Massie, too, insisted on helping with Paul, and when Sonya needed to take Edith to the doctor or attend workshops to keep updated on state regulations for the Blessed Hope shelter, she often took Paul to the Massies'. If Daniel could rearrange his work schedule, he was always there to help.

When Paul was six months old, weighing in at fifteen

pounds, and displaying his first tooth, Daniel telephoned. "This calls for a celebration. Mother and I are coming to visit tonight, bringing cake and ice cream."

A warm glow spread throughout Sonya's body, and a smile crinkled her face. "You can bring refreshments, but no presents."

But when Daniel and Jane arrived, they brought several brightly-wrapped packages, which Paul liked more than the cake.

"Are you determined to spoil the child?" Sonya said in mock severity. "Daniel, it's time you married and had children of your own. Then, you can spoil them." Although Sonya laughed when she reprimanded him, she realized that the idea of Daniel being married was not amusing.

The house was quiet tonight with only one patron, and Sonya relaxed, for a change. This job was more taxing than she'd expected, and she seldom had a chance to sit down and think. She felt like a prisoner—she wasn't married, she wasn't divorced. She didn't know whether she could have Paul all the time, or if Bryon would contest that. If he wouldn't contact them, she intended to do something. Daniel might not approve, but she decided to write to Bryon.

Dear Bryon,
Why haven't you contacted my attorney? Although at first I opposed the divorce, I now believe it's the only way we can go. Too many things have happened between us to ever have them resolved. It's been almost a year of indecision, and I want to leave the past behind me and begin to plan a new life. Although you've never asked my forgiveness, indeed you may think you've done nothing to warrant it, I want you to know that I have forgiven both you and Gail, and I wish you the happiness that we had during our two years of marriage. And you should be happy, because if you agree to the divorce terms that I want, you won't have any extra financial burden. You give

up custody of our child, and that's all I want from you. And may God forgive you as I have.

Sonya

A few days later, Mrs. Massie telephoned and talked to Edith, inviting her and Sonya and Paul for dinner. Edith didn't give her an answer until she talked with Sonya.

"Are you sure you feel up to it?" Sonya asked, for Edith seldom went out anymore. Her hairdresser came to the house, and she relied on Sonya and Stelle to do the shopping. When Sonya questioned her about her health, she always said, "I'm fine, dear, only wearing out. Remember I'm an old woman."

When Sonya finally succeeded in taking her to the doctor, he had told Edith, "You're living on borrowed time. I've told you that for years, but you always make a liar out of me. Just take it easy and do what you feel like doing."

"Sonya takes care of me. She won't let me do anything."

"And rightly so," the doctor agreed.

But Edith seemed to want to go to the Massies. "Jane Massie is one of my best friends, and I was a friend of her mother. I prefer to go for Sunday dinner, rather than some evening, if that's convenient for you."

"I can't be gone at night unless I have someone here to man the phones, so Sunday noon sounds good to me."

Edith didn't go to church, but she was ready when Sonya and Paul returned, and they drove to the Massies' in Edith's old Lincoln. Sonya looked forward to the visit as a break from her routine and as something to take her mind off the pending divorce. Although she'd agreed to the divorce, her mind wasn't completely at ease about it. She kept remembering her vow "Until death do us part."

"This house was built at the turn of the century," Edith commented as they drove up the circular driveway, "by Daniel's grandfather. The Massies have always known how to make money and to keep it. I suppose Daniel could live in ease without working a day of his life, but the Massies are workers, too."

Daniel rushed down the steps to greet them and to help Edith into the house. "Leave the car here in front," he said to Sonya. "We don't expect anyone else. If you need help with Paul, I'll come back soon."

"No help needed," Sonya said. "By the time you have Edith settled, we'll be up the steps."

Daniel met her at the door and took Paul from her arms. "He's getting to be an armful. Aren't you, little guy?" he asked Paul. The baby grabbed Daniel's hair and Daniel laughed out loud.

Daniel was so good with Paul. Sonya felt a warm glow, watching their rapport. She knew Daniel would make a wonderful father if he ever had children of his own.

Upon entering the Massies' home, Sonya's thoughts quickly turned to Edith. Sonya noted the blue shade on Edith's face, and she watched anxiously as Edith slid a small tablet under her tongue. How much longer could Edith live, and then what would happen to Blessed Hope and Sonya herself? She tried not to think of such things, but moments like these made her realize how shaky her future was.

Edith rallied and seemed in better spirits than she'd been in for days. After dinner, Mrs. Massie took Edith into a small sitting room to look at some old family portraits. Sonya could hear their voices through the open door as she and Daniel went into the large room overlooking the garden. The watering system arced in a rainbow as it tossed water on the flowers. Paul had slept through dinner and still seemed content in his carrier.

"It's nice for us to meet occasionally on something other than an attorney-client basis," Daniel said.

"We do that each Sunday at church. We're all members of the same family there."

"Sonya, I want to be more than that to you. And as your attorney, I know I shouldn't speak until your divorce is final, but do you realize that I love you?"

"I hadn't even thought of such a thing, until Edith suggested that you had a personal interest in me."

Daniel took Sonya's hand and pulled her into his arms. Her

heartbeat quickened when she saw the yearning and desire in his eyes.

"I've tried to conceal my feelings from you, for I know you aren't ready for another relationship. I thought that love at first sight was a foolish notion, but from the first day you came to my office, I've known you were the only woman I could ever love. I tried to argue myself out of it, especially when you were still declaring your love for Bryon, but I couldn't do it." His voice was husky, taut with emotion, and when she glanced upward, she saw that his face was white and tense.

"Should we be talking about this now, Daniel? I'm still married," she protested with her lips, but her heart was hammering in her chest, and as closely as he held her, she wondered if he could feel her rapid heartbeat.

"Don't think I'm not aware of that," he groaned in dismay. "I tell myself dozens of times every day, 'She's married,' but my love is so overwhelming that I can't keep it to myself any longer. I wanted you to be free before I spoke, but I have no will power where you're concerned."

Daniel lowered his lips to hers in a brief, soft kiss that tenderly expressed his depth of emotion. Surprised at first, Sonya didn't respond, but she trembled in his embrace. Could she be excused for accepting this moment? She still didn't know the depth of her feeling for Daniel, but she did know that no embrace of Bryon's had given her the pleasure and joy she experienced in Daniel's arms.

With a sigh, Daniel lifted his head, and with a gentle hand, placed her head on his shoulder and his hand caressed her hair. "I love you for your beauty, both physical and spiritual. I respect you as one of the finest women I've ever known. You've triumphed over a situation that has devastated many women. And even if I didn't love you so deeply, I would still want to marry you. You're the woman I want to rear *my* children. I want to marry you, Sonya."

Her words were muffled on his shoulder, but she whispered,

"You deserve someone far better than me—a woman embittered by a former marriage and mother of another man's child."

"I don't agree. I believe you're the one God intended for me, although He had to take the long way around to bring us together. I've often wondered why He hadn't led me to the right person when I've prayed for a Christian mate. I knew why the first day I saw you. I've been waiting for you all of my life."

While they stood in close embrace, and he waited for her answer, Sonya thought of how she had felt when Bryon proposed to her. That day she felt giddy, excited and triumphant because she had won the man so many other girls wanted. Today, her feelings were different. Being asked to share Daniel's life had restored all the self-esteem she had lost when Bryon rejected her. She felt secure, wanted, cherished. She had learned long ago that Daniel's handsome features mirrored the beauty of his soul. She would be safe with Daniel Massie; she would be loved; she would be respected. What more could a woman want?

Realizing that the silence had lengthened, she reluctantly pulled away from his arms and picked up Paul who had awakened. "I wasn't ready for your declaration, Daniel, and I can't give you an answer yet. There's a part of me that wants to accept you now. I'm tired of carrying the load alone, and it would be a relief to dump all my problems on someone else. The fact that you want me has restored my self-respect. I haven't really felt like a 'woman,' since Bryon rejected me, but when you took me into your arms, I was all woman. You made me feel whole again."

He smiled winningly. "Can't you give me a little hope?"

"I'm afraid to. You see, even after my divorce is finalized, I might still feel married to Bryon. He's treated me shabbily, but he still hasn't given me enough reason to justify putting him out of my life if he should change his mind."

"I knew it was too soon to ask you, and I know we'll need time together—a real, old-fashioned courtship if you like, for as long as you want. I want the chance to take care of you, Sonya, you and Paul. I want to make you happy. I know I can.''

''I can't answer you now, Daniel,'' she said honestly. ''But whatever happens, I'll always treasure your friendship.''

''I'll treasure yours as well.''

Sonya heard Mrs. Massie and Edith returning, so she said quickly, ''Thank you.''

On their return home, Edith smiled. ''So he asked you?''

Sonya laughed and threw a puzzled glance in her direction. ''How did you know?''

''It was written all over both of you—looked as guilty as two kids caught in some mischief. What did you tell him?''

''Nothing. If there's one thing I've learned from this past year, it's not to make hasty decisions. I've been burned once. I don't want to repeat the experience.''

''Living singly isn't any pleasure, and I'm sure rearing a child alone is difficult.''

''I realize that, but I've learned from the clients we receive at Blessed Hope that there are worse things than being a single parent. And besides, at this point, I still have a husband.''

''You've not heard anything from him?''

''Nothing, and it makes me suspicious.''

Chapter Thirteen

When the telephone rang, Sonya thought it was another case for Blessed Hope, as she was expecting no other calls.

"Sonya, this is Bryon. How are you getting along?"

His voice no longer contained the harsh, cold quality, and he sounded like the Bryon she'd once loved. She eased down on the couch and gasped to catch her breath.

"All right," she said, relieved that her voice sounded natural, but how could it when she found it difficult to breathe?

"When can I talk to you?"

"If it's about the divorce, you'll need to telephone my lawyer."

"But that's the point—I've changed my mind. I don't want a divorce; I want to come back to you."

Sonya started laughing, and she couldn't control her voice when she tried to talk. The phone jiggled in her shaky hand, and she blurted out, "I can't believe this—that you'd actually suggest walking back into my life as quickly as you walked out, especially now that I've agreed to the divorce."

"I'm in Omaha for a few days, and I must talk to you, Sonya."

"If you had suggested a reconciliation a few months ago, you would have made me very happy, but it may be too late now. I question that we could possibly have a happy marriage with all the bitterness that has passed between us."

"Certainly we could. I still want you, Sonya."

"Will you go with me to a Christian family counselor where we can discuss our differences? If you accept Christ into your life as I have, we can make a success of our marriage."

He didn't answer. "Bryon, did you hear what I said?"

His laugh was scornful. "Yes, I heard what you said, I'm not deaf, but you did send me into shock. What's happened to you? You don't sound like the girl I loved and married."

"If you feel that way, I won't talk to you anymore unless my lawyer is present. I'll telephone Mr. Massie, and if he's available, we can meet at his office at eleven o'clock in the morning."

"What I have to say can't be said before a third party."

"It has to be that way. Do you think I can trust you now? Is this something you and your parents have hatched up to take control of Paul?"

"No, it is not. My parents don't even know I'm in town. I'm at the Holiday Inn. If you can't get an appointment with Massie, telephone me here."

Sonya's hands shook until she could barely punch the digits of Daniel's number, and he listened in silence as Sonya hurriedly related the strange conversation with Bryon.

"You did the right thing," he said immediately. "As a matter of fact, your husband should bring his attorney, but he probably wouldn't take kindly to the idea if you suggested it."

"Then you can meet us."

"Yes. I may have to reschedule some appointments, but I consider this an emergency. Remember, Sonya, I have a personal interest in the outcome of this meeting."

Sonya telephoned Leta next—who better than Leta to deal with the perfidy of men?

"Doesn't surprise me at all," Leta said promptly. "Men want their little spurts of freedom until their freedom turns into a prison."

"Do you think I should take him back?"

"Mercy, no!" Leta exploded. "You have him right where you want him. Let him understand how it feels to be rejected."

"That isn't a Christian attitude, Leta."

"Ha! If I'd taken a Christian attitude in my divorces, I'd be sitting out on the street."

"Maybe I shouldn't even talk to him."

"I don't know how you can avoid it. He can keep calling you on the phone. You may as well talk it out."

"I'm afraid this is another attempt by the Dixons to get Paul. If I take Bryon back, he's liable to turn the child over to them."

"You may be right, but I'm telling you, don't take him back. Hold his feet to the fire and get your divorce. You don't owe Bryon Dixon a thing. He's on the begging end now. And, another thing, take Paul with you in the morning. If he sees the way you've bloomed out now, looking like you did when you were a bride, he's going to be determined to have you. Seeing you as a matron with a child in your arms might cool his ardor. And good luck. Be sure and telephone me as soon as you can."

Edith was still in bed when Sonya went down the next morning, and after Sonya explained where she was going, she said, "But I'm not sure I should leave you." Holding Edith's hand, she noted her pulse was faltering and weak. "Perhaps I should call the doctor."

"No," Edith said weakly. "Your situation is more important than my health. I'm going to stay in bed. Just ask Stelle to bring me some tea and toast. I'll be all right."

Sonya wasn't convinced. She had never seen Edith so low before. Cautioning Stelle to keep a close eye on her mistress and to call the doctor if her condition worsened, Sonya put Edith's problems behind her. She had enough of her own this morning.

"Paul, we have a very important appointment this morning," she said, when she left the car in the garage and caught the elevator to Daniel's fourth-floor office. "You're going to meet your father."

Bryon was already in the waiting room when Sonya entered, and she halted her steps suddenly. She had expected to be here first and to compose herself before he entered.

Bryon rose at once and came to her, and in spite of herself, Sonya forgot all of the mean things he'd done in the past fourteen months. He was the old Bryon—the man with the charm and good looks who had won and married her.

Dear God, don't let my better judgment be swayed again!

He stooped to kiss her, but Sonya backed out of his way just as Daniel opened the door of his office.

"I'm ready to see you now, Mrs. Dixon," he said as impersonally as if she were a stranger.

"Have you met Bryon?"

"Only over the phone." Daniel shook hands with Bryon and motioned them into his office.

When they were seated, Paul reached out his arms to Daniel. The attorney took him and threw him into the air a few times. Paul chortled and laughed, puckering up when Daniel handed him back to Sonya. Bryon watched the episode with a speculative gleam in his eyes.

Bryon looked closely at his son. "I'd heard he looked like me. I can't see the resemblance, but he does favor my baby pictures." He reached out a hand and patted Paul's head. "Don't you recognize your daddy?" But Paul nestled closer into Sonya's arms and eyed Bryon with suspicion.

Perhaps sensing Sonya's discomfort, Daniel interrupted the scene by saying, "Mrs. Dixon tells me that you've changed your mind about a divorce. It's always wise to discuss any legal changes with an attorney present. I'd expected you to bring your own counsel."

Bryon waved his hand impatiently. "My lawyer doesn't own me. I can make my own decisions. And what I wanted to say to Sonya is for her ears alone. It was her idea to meet here, not mine. We can work this out between the two of us, I'm sure."

"Mrs. Dixon," Daniel said, "the choice is yours—do you want me to leave the room?"

Always overawed by Bryon's dominant personality, Sonya found it hard to deny him anything, but she now had reason to fear both Bryon and his parents. Could she trust him? Her arms tightened around Paul.

"No," she said decisively. "Go ahead, Bryon. Mr. Massie knows all about our problems. After all, he's been representing me for months."

"Yes, and I'm beginning to suspect his interest is biased."

Ignoring this remark, Daniel said, "Mr. Dixon, I'll be taping the conversation, in the event we should need it for future legal proceedings."

Bryon stood up angrily. "I'm not used to being treated like this. Sonya, what's this guy done to you?"

"Why should I trust you after the way you've acted the past year? Sit down and say what you want to."

Surprisingly, Bryon did as she commanded. He turned his chair so that his back was to Daniel, and he took Sonya's hand.

"I've rehearsed over and over what to say to you, but in simple words—I've been a fool, Sonya. I knew that soon after I left you, but I became involved with Gail, and once she had her clutches into me, she wasn't about to let go. I reached the place where I hated her, but hated myself more. I was on the verge of suicide, but I don't suppose you'd understand that."

With a grimace Sonya answered, "I understand it all too well."

"My work suffered, and my supervisor suggested I needed some help, so he recommended a counseling service. I've been going for weekly therapy the past few months, and they've suggested changes in my life as well as our relationship. My therapist insisted that I delay the divorce until I was sure of what I wanted. I'm not back to normal yet, but near enough to realize I don't want to lose you."

Sonya glanced down at Paul, sprawled out on her lap, sleeping peacefully.

"Bryon, all I'm hearing is that you want to come back to *me*. You must remember that there would be three of us now, and Paul was the cause of the problem in the first place."

Bryon nodded. "I can't help it if I don't like kids. I hated my brother from the day he was born until he died. Because of his illness, my parents necessarily had to give him a great deal of time and attention. I suppose I really wasn't neglected, but I had a fixation on that idea. Until he was born I'd had all of my parents' love and devotion—when he came along, he got more than his share, or so I thought. My inner self told me the same thing would happen when you became pregnant. Does that make sense to you?''

"Yes, I believe that's the key to your problem, but now that you're at the root of the situation, how is it going to affect your behavior?''

"Don't expect me to become an affectionate father if that's what you mean. I had thought I might change my mind when I saw the boy, but I feel absolutely nothing. Why don't you give him up for adoption?''

"Why, Bryon! I wouldn't give my child away to save my life.''

Daniel growled and shoved back his chair. "I can't stay and listen to this, Mrs. Dixon. I'm going into my law library.''

He closed the door behind him, but Sonya was comforted to know he was nearby if she needed him.

"I have trouble believing this isn't a plot with your parents— I come back to you, and they'll take Paul.''

"I haven't talked with my parents since they telephoned that they had been denied the right to adopt him, but that might not be a bad idea. He can live with them.''

"No.''

"Then he can live with us as long as you keep him out of my way. Hire a nanny to look after him when I'm at home. You can spend your time with him while I'm at work, but at night you're mine.''

"That won't be satisfactory. I want our son to be brought up in the security of a Christian home.''

"What goes with you and this Christianity business? Is this something new you've gotten mixed up in?''

"You know I'd always gone to church before we were married, but you discouraged it by keeping me busy doing something else on weekends. Since you've been gone, I've rediscovered the security of a Christian faith that I'd been floundering without for years."

"What do you mean by that?"

Perhaps he was feeling the tension in the room, for Paul started fidgeting in her arms and when he began to cry, Sonya carried him into the law library. Daniel was pacing the floor, his hands knotted into fists, his face white with anger.

"Take care of Paul for me," she pleaded.

"Get rid of the man, Sonya, before I throw him out of my office."

"Give me another minute. He's asked a very important question, and I want to answer it."

She sat down beside Bryon and took his hand, looking deep into his eyes, trying to find there an image of the man she had married. She chose her words carefully for she knew that their whole future as a family depended upon his understanding.

"You asked me to explain my faith in God. He sent his Son to die and redeem mankind from sin, and to live in a right relationship with God, we have to accept His free gift of salvation. I've done that. You've heard the Gospel before—you've gone with me to church on Easter."

"Everybody goes to church on Easter. And certainly I've heard crap like that, but I didn't suppose anybody believed it except down and outers. I wouldn't have expected anyone of your intelligence to fall for such rot."

Believing there was a chance that she might penetrate the shell around Bryon's heart, Sonya didn't want to antagonize him, so she concealed how abhorrent his words were to her.

"I may as well tell you that when you left me, I was so low that I very nearly committed suicide. If it hadn't been for God's providential care and my renewed faith in Christ, I couldn't have made it through the past year. I won't abandon that faith to stay with you, and I expect to bring Paul up to believe the same thing."

Bryon laughed, and the contempt in his laughter seared Sonya's heart. "Something has happened to you—there's no doubt of that, but once we're back together, you'll forget all of this foolishness."

"I wouldn't even listen to you if it weren't for Paul. He needs a father."

"If it will satisfy you, give him any kind of religious instruction you want, but don't expect any help from me. I've made myself clear on that. This is just between you and me, sweetheart—neither Paul nor God are involved."

After this conversation, Sonya couldn't see any way to redeem their marriage, but if it was God's will that she reconcile with Bryon, He could make them into a strong and loving family.

Daniel reentered the room, more calm than he had been, and handed the sleeping baby into Sonya's arms.

"I'll have to think about it. How long will you be in Omaha?"

"Two days. I'll be at the hotel in the evening and at the office during the day."

"I'll have Mr. Massie telephone you my decision, which I need to discuss with him now."

Before he left the room, Bryon leaned over Sonya and brushed his lips over hers. Seated as she was and holding Paul, she couldn't evade his gesture, and her face flamed. "While you're considering, don't forget I love you."

Without a word to Daniel, he walked out of the office with his old buoyancy, already sure of her decision.

Daniel and Sonya looked at each other for a long time. "As I've told you before, every time it seems I have my life on an even keel, the Dixons disrupt it. What am I going to do now?"

"Go on with the divorce. You can't trust him."

"It's such a difficult decision for me, because as I told you when I first came to this office, I don't believe in divorce. As long as Bryon was pressing the action, I had no choice, so my conscience didn't bother me. Now, he's pitched the ball to my court—it's going to be my decision, and I don't like being put in that position.''

''Of course, my interest goes beyond that of a client-attorney relationship, but even if I didn't have a personal feeling for you, I'd say the same thing. It's a long chance that you can ever mend your relationship.''

''But there is a chance?''

''I suppose so, but not one I'd want to gamble on.''

''And there's Paul. In these few months I've learned how difficult it is to be a single parent. I can give him love, but not much more. Is it fair to deny him the support of his father? I'm so confused. How I wish I'd never laid eyes on Bryon Dixon!''

''But you have, so you'll have to deal with him. However, I wouldn't do it now. You have two days, and you could take more time if you wanted to.'' Daniel paused; his expression grew serious. ''And if it's a decision about raising Paul without a father, you know I'm more than willing to act as a father to him. If we were ever to marry, as I hope, you know I'll adopt him. I love the boy already.''

The phone rang, and Sonya detected Stelle's shrill, excited voice when Daniel answered.

''We'll be there right away,'' he said and slammed down the phone.

''It's Edith.'' He reached for his coat and hat on the rack. ''She had a 'sinking spell,' according to Stelle, and Stelle telephoned the emergency squad. They're taking her to the hospital.''

''You go ahead. I'll take Paul to Leta and join you as soon as possible.''

Sonya telephoned Leta to see if she could keep Paul, and Leta said, ''Sure, I'll meet you down in the lobby to save time. Just park in front of the building.''

When she delivered Paul, Sonya took time to tell Leta about the conference with Bryon. Although she was in a hurry, she thought she owed Leta a quick explanation.

''Think hard and long about it. Don't let the scoundrel rush you into a decision. You don't owe Bryon Dixon a thing. And don't let Paul's future sway you—he's better off alone with you."

When she rushed into the hospital, Edith was in ICU, and Sonya and Daniel could do nothing but sit in the waiting room. After several hours, Daniel finally contacted Edith's doctor.

"She's on the verge of a massive heart attack, and I don't see how we can prevent it, but she's rallied somewhat, so perhaps she'll surprise me. You and Mrs. Dixon might as well go home. I'll leave word to telephone if her condition worsens."

"I don't like having you up there alone," Daniel said as they left the hospital.

"I may not be alone. Remember, I'm employed as a social worker, and there may be a client for us tonight. I need to be there. As soon as I go for Paul, I'll head that way."

But she didn't protest when Leta insisted on spending the night with her and Paul.

When she arrived at the mansion with Leta, Sonya put Paul to bed, then shared a cup of tea with her friend. Leta was always good company and Sonya found herself confiding her deepest fears about Edith's condition. Edith had come to mean so much to her in such a short time. Would she lose Edith now, so suddenly? How would she cope with such a blow?

Leta offered her comforting words, but Sonya knew that Edith's condition might not improve and tomorrow could bring unhappy news. Before she fell asleep Sonya prayed long and hard for Edith's recovery.

Chapter Fourteen

Sonya awoke to the sound of the telephone. She picked up the receiver, her heart clutched with cold fear. She heard Daniel's familiar voice.

"Sonya—did I wake you?"

"Have you heard from Edith?" Sonya quickly replied.

"Yes, I telephoned at seven o'clock. The nurses said she's responded to treatment and may be moved into a regular room today."

Sonya sighed with relief. "Thank goodness. I'll visit her this morning."

"I'm sure you'll give her spirits a lift," Daniel replied. "I'll probably go see her tonight." He paused. "Sonya, don't forget that you must give Bryon an answer tomorrow?"

"I remember," she assured him, though she didn't confide what her answer would be.

She chatted with Daniel for a few more minutes, then telephoned Adam Benson. "May I see you sometime today? I have an important decision to make, and I need some advice."

"Will ten o'clock be convenient?"

"Fine, I'll be there."

When Sonya telephoned the hospital, she learned that Edith had just been transferred to a room. She was eager to see her and quickly got dressed and took Paul downstairs to Stelle.

"Stelle, I have an appointment this morning, and, also, I

should like to see Edith. Will you mind looking after Paul? I'll try to return by noon."

"No bother, Sonya. Me and Paul—we're friends."

"He's everybody's friend," Sonya said with a laugh. "I don't know where he gets it—from neither of his parents, I'm sure."

"He's God's special little child, that's what he is," Stelle said and picked the boy up to give him a big hug.

Sonya put her arms around Stelle. "You're pretty special yourself. I don't know what I'd have done without you and a few of my other good friends during the past year. You've made my life bearable again."

Sonya never worried about Paul when either Stelle or Leta kept him, but she tried not to impose on her friends. She could have taken him with her to Adam's office, but not into the hospital, and she went to see Edith first.

Edith sat in her bed, nibbling on something from her breakfast tray. She gave Sonya a cheery smile.

"All of this fuss for nothing! I want to go home."

Sonya kissed her cheek. "What does the doctor say about it?"

As if on cue, the doctor entered the room and said, "The doctor says she can go home tomorrow. But it wasn't fuss for nothing—if Stelle hadn't gotten you here to hospital, you could have had a major attack. You have to remember you're not a girl anymore, and you must take it easy."

"I've outlived my quota of time, anyway, Doctor," Edith said pertly.

When the aides came to give Edith a bath, Sonya left, and when she passed the nurses' station, Edith's doctor called to her.

"I probably shouldn't release her, since her heart is mighty weak. I've considered a pacemaker, but at her age I'm not sure it's advisable. She'll be happier at home. Just protect her as much as possible."

Knowing that Edith would be returning home gave Sonya a

lighter spirit to face the appointment with Adam. She told him about Edith, and he said, "I'll go to visit her this afternoon. But you didn't come to talk about Edith. What's troubling you, Sonya?"

She settled back in the roomy chair and breathed deeply. "My husband wants to come back to me. He's decided he doesn't want a divorce, and I need to give him an answer tomorrow."

"Does that make you happy or sad?"

"Do I look happy or sound elated?"

He smiled. "Not that I can notice."

"A year ago this would have made me happy, but so much has happened since then. I've built my life without him. I've found that I can get along on my own."

"Then why are you having trouble with a decision?"

"I was brought up to believe that divorce is unacceptable. You marry someone, you stay married. As long as Bryon was pushing for divorce, I felt it wasn't my decision to wreck our marriage. Now it is."

"But is the marriage already wrecked? Can the breaches be repaired?" Adam's soft brown eyes clouded with concern.

"That's what bothers me. If I thought we could return to the good marriage we had for two years, I'd be willing to try for Paul's sake. Is it fair for me to deny him a father-son relationship? I've read about the problems of single parenting. Am I ready for that? What should I do?"

"I'll be the first to admit that I don't have any hard-and-fast rule to hand out to those whom I counsel. Basically I oppose divorces because they are tearing down the foundations of family relationships in our country. Strong homes are the backbone of our society. But on the other hand, I don't approve of spouse abuse, either. If some woman comes to me, bruised and beaten, such as the cases you receive at Blessed Hope, I can't tell that woman she should live with the man until death parts them. If he continues to abuse her, it won't be long until they're parted by her death."

"Of course, Bryon never laid a hand on me."

"But you were abused emotionally and mentally. Changes come in a marriage that are hard to cope with sometimes." Adam removed his brown-rimmed glasses and rubbed his forehead. Sonya glanced out the window at the Washburn building, thinking of the miserable nights she'd spent there. *I've come a long way since then!*

Adam startled her when he spoke. "As customs have changed through the ages, so have people's ideas about divorce. What had once been unacceptable, might be perfectly agreeable to today's society."

"But taking a vow of staying together for better or worse wouldn't change."

Adam laughed, and Sonya was glad someone could find humor in her situation; she couldn't. "This is a strange counseling session. It sounds as though I, the counselor, am giving you reasons for divorce and you're trying to prove I'm wrong."

Sonya flushed. "Does that mean I want to go back to Bryon?"

"Not necessarily, and I want you to know that whatever you decide, Marie and I will stand by you. But it must be your decision."

Adam discussed several Scripture passages relating to divorce among the Hebrews and in the early church, and he said, "I'm not always sure when the New Testament is discussing the practice of divorce or talking about the ideal marriage. There are passages that seem to be emphasizing monogamy in marriage rather than dealing with the subject of divorce. The practice of plural marriages was not uncommon in Hebrew history, but slowly the trend was toward one man for one woman. The gospel writers indicated that one shouldn't search for ways to squirm out of the marriage contract, but rather stressed how two people becoming one can have a beautiful relationship that precludes any possibility of divorce."

"Do you know of any such ideal marriages?"

With a smile, Adam assured her, "Many of them. Marie and I have that kind of marriage."

"Come to think of it, so do my parents. Then it is possible in this day and age?"

"Most assuredly."

"If one divorces, then what about remarriage?"

Adam leaned back in his chair and scrutinized her closely. "Are you considering remarriage?"

"Not very much, although Daniel has asked me."

"Yes, he told me. I've had a counseling session with him. He wants to marry you, but he, too, is concerned about what is morally right."

"It would be much easier if there were only a few spiritual and moral rules to follow, allowing us to pinpoint the right or wrong."

"Unfortunately, it isn't that easy. We have to make our own difficult decisions. If you do go back to your husband, it will be necessary to forgive him and forget the past, and I doubt you can do that unless he has changed his habits. Both of you would have to change."

"Bryon has made it plain that he won't change spiritually. In fact he was very sarcastic about my Christian faith. Perhaps my biggest concern is whether I can be married to him and still live a committed Christian life."

"It can be done, but it won't be easy."

"Bryon has made no effort to change and I question that I can trust him. You can't have a good marriage without trust. Should I ask him to give me more time about this decision? It took me completely by surprise."

"I wouldn't dally long with it for you're going to be in a state of emotional suspense until the matter is resolved. And, Sonya, although I won't give you a definite answer about divorce, I am going to advise you about remarriage. At this point, you are definitely not ready for another relationship. You're not completely healed emotionally, and I do hope you'll take my advice about that."

"But sometimes I'm so tired of all this trauma that I'd like to drop it on another's shoulders."

"The very worst reason for a marriage. Occasionally marriages of convenience are successful, but my advice is to never marry again unless you meet someone you can't live without."

Sonya picked up her purse from the floor. "I have to go. Stelle is baby-sitting, and I told her I'd return before noon, but I do thank you for talking with me. You and Marie have been so helpful through all of this."

"But have I helped you with your immediate decision?"

She smiled slightly. "I don't know. I need to think about what you've said. Right now, my mind is muddled."

In spite of her need to relieve Stelle of Paul's care, Sonya parked her car along Happy Hollow Boulevard and entered the wooded area bordering the University of Omaha. She walked with downcast eyes, paying no attention to the people she met. She left the path and wandered into the deeper woods and sat under a maple tree near a small creek. She leaned against the large trunk and looked up into the foliage that was beginning to show a tinge of yellow. She watched as two squirrels hauled nuts to their winter storage. More than a year had passed since Bryon had left her. A year that had brought some heartbreaking moments, but also a year that had proven she could manage without him. She had matured spiritually and emotionally, and she had also gained friends, the kind of friends who helped without question. And she had a son! Sonya smiled when she thought of Paul, his small hands, his bubbling personality.

Yes, there was no doubt that she could live without Bryon now, but should she? She had suffered and survived. She felt sorry that she no longer wanted him. How could she have changed so much in a year's time? Should she keep the vows she'd made, "Till death do us part"? But the vows had already been broken, and she hadn't been the one to do it. She had blundered once by choosing Bryon—should she repeat the mistake?

Sonya walked back to the path and wended her way toward

the car, no nearer a decision than before, until she noticed a decrepit vine growing in the graveled path. The vine had obviously tried to grow strong, only to be trampled underneath the feet of those who passed by. The vine was hardy and would continue to grow and put forth an occasional bloom, but its beauty and purpose in life would always be stunted. The vine had taken root in an unsuitable place—if it could only send its tendrils elsewhere, it would have a chance of normal growth.

That's the way it is with me, Sonya contemplated as she slowly drove away from the park. She would always be stunted as Bryon's wife. Actually, what had she accomplished in the years of their marriage? Endless parties, vacations, ski trips, collecting a big wardrobe and piles of jewelry but she had never really made her mark in the world. She had been content to dwell in Bryon's shadow. She didn't want to do that anymore. Bryon probably had changed very little, but Sonya knew that she had grown beyond him. If they could go back to what life had been three years ago, would she really want to?

The answer, of course, was no. She had found out what living meant—loving her child, caring for those who were down-and-out, denying herself for others. She would be selfish to go back to the old, narrow way of living.

Sonya had put off the most important issue until the last. She had to face reality. If she continued as Bryon's wife, her faith would suffer. Bryon's dominant personality would assert itself, he wouldn't let her rear Paul as she wanted to, and she would begin to doubt the hope of eternal life that she had now. The words of Jesus reminded her that anyone who started to follow Him and looked back wasn't fit for the kingdom of God; she couldn't forsake Him again. Considering these aspects of her relationship to Bryon, there was only one choice to make.

When she reached the York mansion, she parked the car and walked into the house with a light step and new determination as she picked up Paul from his playpen in the kitchen. She felt as if she had taken a new lease on life. She'd been fighting a war, and she had won it—maybe not all the battles, but enough of them to claim victory.

"God's in His heaven—all's right with the world," she quoted from *Pippa Passes* as she headed upstairs with Paul.

When Daniel answered the phone, she said, "I've come to a decision. I want to continue with the divorce as soon as possible."

"You sound happy about it."

"Not really happy about the divorce, but happy I've made a decision. I feel as if I'm a newborn calf frolicking around the pasture. I've been weighed down with bitterness and unhappiness for over a year. It's a relief to be free of it."

"Then I'll telephone your husband's attorney and say we want to proceed with the divorce on the terms outlined in our previous offer. I can't say much now, Sonya, but you know how happy your decision makes me."

Sonya hoped she wouldn't have to talk with Bryon again, but later that night, when the telephone rang, Bryon was on the line.

"I'm hurt by your decision, Sonya. I thought you didn't want a divorce."

"A year ago I didn't, but I've too many scars on my emotions to start over again."

"But you said you had forgiven me."

"That's true, but I can't trust you again. There's a difference."

"Are you in love with someone else? Is that why you don't want me now?"

Sonya wondered if this was the only reason Bryon wanted her. Did he still look upon her as his possession, and he couldn't bear to let someone else have her?

Daniel's smiling face and lovable personality flitted through her mind, and she wondered if she could give Bryon an honest answer to his question. Her high regard for Daniel complicated her decision about the divorce. She loved Daniel as a friend and had no doubt that romance would blossom if she gave it the opportunity. She couldn't fool herself that wanting to be in Daniel's presence was only because he was good to her and Paul. Why did her pulse accelerate when she heard his voice? Why did her heart sing when she caught his glance across a crowded room? Why did she think of him when she awakened in the morning and when she closed her eyes at night?

"You didn't give me an answer," Bryon prompted.

"When you abandoned me, you lost the right to ask that question, but I can tell you that I don't want an intimate relationship with anyone right now, including you. Except for my responsibility to Paul, I'm free, and I like it. Please, Bryon, if you have any consideration for me, go on with the divorce. If you don't, I'll sue for it myself."

"Then it's goodbye?"

"Yes," Sonya whispered, "and I'm sorry it turned out this way."

"So am I," Bryon said, and he hung up the receiver.

Although Sonya had been happy with her decision, she sat with her hand on the phone for a long time. Was there still time to salvage their marriage? She didn't even undress and go to bed for she knew it was useless. Apparently Bryon would cause her many more sleepless nights. If a spouse died, it was final because there was a corpse to bury, but how does one bury a divorce?

Two months had passed since Edith's hospital release, and she still hadn't regained her strength. It took quite a lot of Sonya's time to care for her, but the doctor had found a nurse who consented to work at night, which was a great help to Sonya.

"With this work of Blessed Hope, you have about all you can do, and you're not getting much rest sleeping on the couch in her room. As far as that's concerned, Edith isn't resting well, either, fretting for you," he had said.

"It's a vicious circle, isn't it?" Sonya said with a smile.

"Yes, and we can stop it with some extra help. Mrs. York can afford it."

Sonya was glad for the relief, since Paul demanded quite a lot of attention, too, and hardly a night passed that they didn't have at least one client on the second floor. Loretta could usually come to help, but Sonya still needed to supervise.

One morning during Thanksgiving week, Daniel telephoned, and he said excitedly, "May I come out for a minute? I have some good news for you."

"Have you straightened up all the details of the divorce?"

"No—that will be another week or so. Bryon's lawyer hasn't been very cooperative."

Daniel's excitement had piqued Sonya's curiosity, and she met him at the door. His face beamed as he thrust an envelope into her hands.

"Congratulations!"

Daniel took Paul from her arms as she pulled a check from the envelope in the amount of $10,000, payable to Sonya Dixon.

"Is this real? What does it mean?"

"Mr. Dixon visited me this morning and asked me to give you this check. They feel badly that Bryon hasn't supported you, and the check is also an apology for their attempt to take Paul. He asked my advice about giving it to you, and I told him you would accept it. That's the least they can do, so I hope you will take it. I feel sorry for Bryon's parents."

Sonya kissed the check. "Of course, I'll take it. I want to make amends with them. It would be wrong to shun their generosity."

"Let's go tell Edith. She'll be delighted," Daniel said.

Edith was sitting in a wheelchair looking out the window, and her features broke into a beautiful smile when she saw the check. "My word, what are you going to do with so much money?"

"I don't know. Right now, I feel like going on a spending spree and blowing every dime of it. I haven't bought any new clothes for almost two years, so, Daniel, you keep it for a few days until I calm down."

After Daniel left, Sonya pulled Paul's playpen into Edith's room and sat down to visit with her. Paul was too heavy and active for Edith to hold anymore, but she liked to watch the boy as he played. Sonya brought a basket of clothing that needed mending. The quiet scene caused Edith to doze occasionally, but once she asked, "Surely you have some idea of what you'd like to do with your money?"

"My mind has been working overtime since Daniel brought the check, and I've thought of dozens of things. I suppose the wise thing is to save it for an emergency—so I'll have Daniel invest it for me. There is one thing I'd like to do, but I may have to wait until Paul is a little older. I want to go back to school and major in subjects to train me more adequately for the kind of work I'm doing. If I'd finished college as my parents begged me to, then I wouldn't have fouled up by marrying too young. I'm sure Bryon wouldn't have waited three years for me."

"Don't let the mistakes of the past burden you any longer. Everyone is entitled to a few of them, but it's how you deal with mistakes that determine your destiny. The idea of going back to school is an excellent one. We have good universities close by, and I'm sure you can manage financially."

"Yes, I will manage somehow," Sonya agreed. "It's what I really want to do, and I guess I've learned that I can accomplish more than I'd ever dreamed possible if I'm determined enough, and pray for God's help."

The next morning Edith's room seemed empty when Sonya walked in, and she looked around quickly. Had Stelle taken Edith out? But a glance showed that Edith was in her bed. Somehow she didn't look right, and Sonya rushed to her. One touch told her that the room was empty. Edith had died.

She rushed into the kitchen. "Stelle, come quickly." Stelle stalked into the room behind her as Sonya rushed back to Edith's side. Noting Sonya's tears, Stelle said softly, "She's gone, is she? I've been expecting it most every day."

"But I thought she was better."

"Better in some ways, but getting weaker and weaker. What do we do now?"

"I suppose we'd better telephone Daniel. He handles her affairs. I don't even know what funeral director to call. She never discussed her death with me."

Sonya could hardly control her sobs when she telephoned Daniel, for she'd grown as fond of Edith as if she were family. While she waited for Daniel to come, Sonya went to her apartment to check on Paul and to telephone the agency. She told the dispatcher about Edith's death and asked if they could be relieved of clients for a week.

"Certainly. You telephone us when you're available again."

"I don't know what will happen now. There's a possibility we'll have to close the home."

Even though Edith had signed a contract for two years, her death might cancel that. She deeply grieved Edith's death, for she was fond of her, but underlying that was concern for her own future. Maybe this was her answer about going back to college, since it would have been hard to manage Blessed Hope, look after Edith and Paul and carry a full load of courses.

Edith had left specific instructions with Daniel about her funeral. Her body lay in state in the large parlor where her parents' funerals had been. Because Edith had outlived most of her generation, there were few mourners of her own age, but many of the members at Community Lighthouse came to pay their respects, and Adam's simple funeral message would have pleased Edith.

Daniel had notified Edith's nephew, and he came to the funeral, but he hadn't chosen to stay at the house, although Stelle and Sonya had made preparations for him. He approached Daniel after the closing ceremony at the mausoleum.

"I have to catch an early-morning flight. Could we take care of the legal matters tonight? I assume Aunt Edith had a will."

"Yes. I'll meet you at the house at eight o'clock."

"Could we meet at your office? I'm uncomfortable there, never knowing when some of those women might wander in."

"There won't be anyone tonight. The dispatcher knows about Mrs. York's death, and no one will be sent."

"Very well. I'll be there promptly."

Daniel drove Sonya and Stelle back to the house, and she asked, "I'm wondering what I should do about Blessed Hope. Even if Edith's nephew doesn't like it, we have a contract with the agency that goes on for more than a year. Can he make us close the shelter?"

"I'll take care of Mr. York this evening."

Several of the church people had sent in trays of food, so Stelle and Sonya ate their evening meal from that supply. Sonya helped Stelle put away the food, and she said, "You can let Daniel and Mr. York in, if you will, please. I'll take Paul upstairs. He's about asleep now. You can tell that Leta let him play all afternoon without a nap."

After Paul was bathed and put in bed, Sonya sat down and tried to contemplate what the future held for her. Her musings were interrupted when the house phone rang. Daniel was calling from downstairs. "Could you come down to Edith's room for a few minutes?"

"I've just gotten Paul to sleep, but I'll leave all the doors open, and I can hear if he awakens. Will I be needed long?"

"Probably not."

Mr. York, robust and florid, sat pompously in Edith's chair. Stelle stood by the door.

"Come in, both of you, and sit down. As you're mentioned in the will, it's necessary for you to be present."

He didn't have to tell Sonya to sit down as her legs wouldn't hold her. She listened in stunned silence as Daniel read. At first it was a lot of legal jargon about the payments of bills and being of sound mind, but ten minutes later, Sonya pretty much understood the gist of Edith's intention. Ten percent of her estate was to be given to Stelle, ten percent to the nephew and the balance of her holdings to Sonya.

"But that's preposterous," Mr. York shouted. "This woman is little more than a servant in the house. She's moved in here, ingratiated herself with my aunt. Who knows what she's done to persuade Aunt Edith to leave her all the money!''

"Be calm, Mr. York. Your aunt was certain you would feel this way, so she gave an explanation." And Daniel read an addendum to the will, written in Edith's own hand:

"I'm sure that my nephew will be unhappy about this decision, but I want to remind him that the estate is mine, and I personally think I'm being lenient toward him to give him ten percent. My husband paid for Albert's college expenses, and he gave him a generous sum to make the down payment on his home. In return for that he did very little to show affection toward us.

"Sonya has never asked me for anything, and except for giving her and the child a home, I've done nothing for her. On the other hand, she has given me love and companionship, which I needed desperately, and she allowed me the delight of having a child in my home. She's proven that she can triumph over difficulty."

Daniel carefully folded the document and placed it in his briefcase, and the nephew shouted, "I'll break the will. It's my uncle's money, and she has no right to give it away."

"I have a copy of the will for you," Daniel said. "Any reliable attorney will tell you that there's no way you can break this document."

"When did she make this will?''

"Two months ago. But you didn't receive any more in her previous will. Mrs. York considered you had gotten your share."

"I suppose you brought undue influence upon her. What are you getting out of it?''

"I had no idea what she had in mind, until she summoned me to this room in October," Daniel answered calmly. "And I didn't get anything out of it. In fact, I've lost a good friend and a client.''

"Crooks and thieves, all of you. You'll be hearing from my attorney," Albert shouted.

He started down the hallway, and Stelle followed to lock the door behind him. Daniel smiled at Sonya. "How does it feel to be rich?".

"I still don't believe I'll receive this. Mr. York is very angry."

"I told him he wasn't entitled to any more in the first will than he was in this one, and I intend to send his attorney a copy to prove it. Before you came here, she had willed most of her estate to charities. Don't worry, Sonya, the will is airtight," he assured her.

"How much is the estate worth?"

"Maybe $100,000, plus this house. It's hard to tell what you could get out of it on the market. Sometimes people pay well for the old houses. It's not so much, not a large estate."

"Not much! Maybe not for you, but for someone who has lived as I have for more than a year, wearing used clothes from the church clothing bank, subsisting on groceries from the food kitchen, I feel as if I'm a millionaire. I only wish I could properly thank Edith for what she's done for me."

"She evidently considered that she was in your debt." He reached into his briefcase. "She also left this letter for you."

With trembling hands Sonya opened the sealed envelope.

Dear Sonya,
When you read this I will be with my Lord, so please don't grieve for me. I've lived a long, happy and rewarding life, and I'm not sorry to be gone. Believe that and dry any tears you might have for me. Your presence in my home for almost a year, and the advent of Paul, have made the declining months of my life very happy. I took courage when I saw how you battled and won against your own disillusionment and unhappiness.
When I saw the depth of your character as you accepted the directorship of Blessed Hope, I decided that you would make better use of my estate than the charitable organi-

zations I had previously chosen to receive it. It's yours
with no strings attached. If you want to continue Blessed
Hope—fine. If you want to sell the house, that's all right,
too, because I realize it is too great an expense for a residence. Above all, I want you to have my estate to ensure
that you can control your future. In time you may want to
marry again, but you won't have to for financial security
if you invest my estate well. You can trust Daniel to advise
you. I have found him knowledgeable and trustworthy.

Your devoted friend, Edith York

In spite of Edith's admonition, tears stained the page before
Sonya finished reading it.

"Have you read this?" she asked Daniel.

When he shook his head, she handed him the letter. He
cleared his throat noisily when he finished, for he, too, had been
influenced by Edith's life.

"It's strange, but all of these months when I've had no
money, I constantly thought of things I'd like to have for Paul
and myself. But now that I'm in funds, I can't think of anything
I need, except that I want to do something for those who have
helped me. I want to take you and your mother, the Bensons,
Eloise, Leta and Stelle out to dinner. I'll check with Adam and
see when he's free, and arrange the dinner soon. Without the
seven of you, I wouldn't have made it. I want to show my
appreciation."

"That's a great idea."

The dinner was arranged for the following Sunday after worship service, and it was a time of rejoicing for all of them, but
an incident marred the day for Sonya. While they waited for
their food to be served, Sonya saw Bryon's parents leaving the
restaurant. If they had seen her party, they had ignored them.
Both of the Dixons looked older, and they walked dejectedly.
For some reason Sonya felt guilty, but what could she have
done? She couldn't give Paul to them.

Sonya continued her work with Blessed Hope, but in spite
of her busy schedule, the plight of Bryon's parents haunted her.

And the day Daniel telephoned that her divorce had become a reality and that Bryon had given her full custody of Paul, she said, "I've been thinking about asking Bryon's parents if they would like to visit with Paul sometimes. I wouldn't make any legal commitment, simply let them have the opportunity. What do you think?"

"You're great to even consider it after what they tried."

"I'm thinking of Paul, too. I'm afraid that if I keep him to myself, I'll become too possessive. And is it fair for him to be cut off completely from his father's family? I intend to be honest with him about his lineage, but as he grows older and lives in the same city with his grandparents, it seems cruel for them to be strangers."

"You realize that if Paul visits his grandparents, he's apt to see Bryon."

"I've thought of that, but now that I have full legal custody and the funds to care for the child, I feel more benevolent. He's mine, but I can't make a prisoner of him, and probably the best way for me to be sure he remains with me is to set him free."

"You're a wise woman, Sonya, so I don't know why you ask me for advice. I would suggest that you follow your heart on this matter as well as others. You know in what direction I want your heart to lead you. I won't pressure you for a while, but whenever you're ready, I'm waiting."

"Right now just be my friend, Daniel."

After Sonya discussed with Adam Benson her thought of allowing Bryon's parents visiting rights and he agreed that she would feel better about sharing her son with his grandparents, she wrote them a short note. She had written to thank them for their generous gift, but had not spoken to them since the custody hearing. Still, she addressed them respectfully, as she always had:

Dear Mother and Father Dixon,
I want to apologize for my part in the unpleasantness be-

tween us that has marked the past year. It's unfortunate that the problems between Bryon and me also affected your happiness.

After that beginning, Sonya pondered long over her next sentence. The Dixons shouldn't think that her change of heart meant she wanted any financial help from them, but rather that she was being considerate of their feelings.

Perhaps you know that Edith York left most of her estate to me. It came as a surprise, but a pleasant one, as the extent of her holdings has guaranteed a secure financial future for Paul and me. For the present, I intend to continue with the crisis center, for it is a worthwhile project, but next fall I hope to enter the university for a degree in social work.

All is well with Paul and me; however, I can't be completely satisfied to keep you isolated from your grandson. Would you like to visit with Paul occasionally? If so, feel free to contact me when you want to pick him up for a few hours, or I can bring him to your house. I believe you'll enjoy him. He is an adorable, happy boy.

                                   Sonya

Two days later Bryon's father telephoned. "Bless you, Sonya. Anna's health has plummeted this past year. She's lost interest in everything, but your letter has done wonders for her. May I come and pick up Paul tomorrow afternoon, or do you want to come with him? Will he be afraid of us?"

"No, he's happy with everyone, and you'll enjoy playing with him. If you will come for him around one o'clock, it will give me time to do some Christmas shopping, and I can come by to get him after that."

"God bless you, Sonya."

The next day as Sonya prepared Paul for a visit with his grandparents, she thought how different her circumstances were from a year ago. Then she was almost penniless and with more worries than she could contemplate. A year later she had money, she had friends and the freedom to do what she wanted. But was she happy? This was a question that plagued her daily. She had everything but love, and could she expect happiness without love? She liked and appreciated her friends, but she felt no deep emotions for anyone except Paul, and that didn't seem to be enough. Why couldn't she be satisfied with her life as it was now?

The doorbell rang and she looked at the clock. Too early for Mr. Dixon, but she soon heard steps approaching down the hall, and she turned as Bryon entered the room. Anger stirred at his intrusion into her well-ordered life, and she sank down on the couch beside Paul. She stared at him, speechless.

"Please don't order me out, Sonya," Bryon said in a quiet voice. "I arrived home this morning for a few days, and I persuaded Father to let me come after Paul. Do you trust me to have him?"

"I've decided that it's selfish for me to keep the boy to myself."

"A lot of things have happened between us in the past several months, Sonya, perhaps things that can never be forgiven or forgotten, but I've come to ask you once more. Will you take me back? I want to be a part of your life, and of Paul's. Surely I deserve a second chance."

For a moment Sonya's thoughts turned to that May morning when she had stood beside Bryon and had taken the vow, "I, Sonya, take thee, Bryon, to be my wedded husband, to have and to hold, from this day forward, for better, for worse, for richer, for poorer, in sickness and in health, to love and to cherish, till death do us part, and thereto I pledge thee my faith."

Emotion tightened Sonya's throat, and she desperately wanted to relive the past, but it was no use. The spark was gone, and there was no way she could rekindle it. Instead of seeing the handsome Bryon she had loved, all she could remember was the long months of heartbreak, his rejection of her and his attitude toward his son. For herself, she might have taken a chance on Bryon's change of heart, but she couldn't risk having Paul's childhood marred by a possessive father. Yet the boy needed a father, and, unbidden, the words of Daniel entered her mind, "I'm more than willing to adopt him. I love the boy already." This thought annoyed her, for she had to make her decision independent of Daniel.

"No, Bryon, I will not give you another chance. I begged you for months to return to me, but now it's too late. My love for you is dead, and I can't revive it."

He turned on his heel, without even taking Paul with him. Sonya didn't shed a tear as she watched him leave the house.

Later, when Mr. Dixon came for Paul, he said, "Bryon telephoned from the airport. He's leaving this afternoon for San Francisco. I'll come back with the boy in a couple of hours."

After Mr. Dixon left, she realized she was too disturbed to go shopping. Had she really put the past behind her? Was she ready to admit she had made a mistake and start again? She reached for the telephone, but replaced the receiver. She walked around the room several times before determinedly she dialed a number, and when her mother answered, Sonya said, "Do you have room for two more people during the Christmas holidays? I've decided to come home for a few days. I want Paul to meet all of his Ohio kin."

Her mother's elation confirmed that the decision was wise. Last year she couldn't face her family, but now she was ready.

An hour later, after long deliberation, Sonya made another phone call.

"Daniel, I've decided to go to Ohio for the holidays. When I return, maybe we could start that long, old-fashioned courtship you mentioned?"

She laughed at his reply.

Epilogue

The field was alive with color as the T-ball players gathered, resplendent in their red, green and yellow jerseys. This was the first game for most of the youthful athletes, and from her seat on the bleachers, Sonya watched with mixed emotions as five-year-old Paul ran to join his teammates. Tom and Anna Dixon sat beside her, eager to see their grandson participate in his first athletic event.

Daniel managed Paul's team, and a smile played around Sonya's lips and her heart gave a little somersault when she watched her husband on his knees in the midst of the excited boys. The players spread out over the field, and Paul was first at home plate. The umpire checked to be sure the defense was ready before he shouted, "Play ball." Paul took a mighty swing and missed the ball. Looking toward the bleachers, Daniel caught Sonya's eye and laughed.

The Dixons looked fondly at the child.

"Not a very good start," Sonya said, smiling.

"No, but he'll improve," Tom said. "He's going to be a fine athlete."

Tom and Anna exhibited the same pride in Paul that they had once showered on Bryon, but they didn't overindulge him as they had their son. Bryon's actions over the past few years had apparently taught them a lesson.

As the game progressed, and Paul's playing improved, in light of her own happiness, Sonya experienced a touch of remorse for Bryon that he had separated himself so irrevocably from his son. Since the divorce became final, Bryon had never seen Paul nor had he evinced any interest in him. When Sonya and Daniel had married three years ago, Bryon had readily signed the papers for Daniel to adopt Paul, and they changed his name to Massie. As soon as he was able to understand, they had told Paul about his true parentage, putting Bryon in as good a light as possible.

The game was almost finished, and the score tied, when Paul stumbled over one of the foul line cones and fell headlong. Sonya jumped from the bleachers and started toward her son, but Paul scrambled to his feet, yelled, "Daddy," and raced toward Daniel.

Sonya resumed her seat and smiled at the Dixons. "Obviously he isn't hurt if he can run that fast. Daniel will take care of him."

"We have never ceased to mourn Bryon's broken marriage," Anna Dixon said, "but we are happy that you've found Daniel. He's a good father, and we appreciate that. Both you and Paul are fortunate."

Sonya took Anna's hand and pressed it warmly. Bryon seldom visited his parents, but the one day each month they had Paul to themselves seemed to make up for it. Sonya had kept up an amicable relationship with her former in-laws, and Daniel was hospitable toward Paul's grandparents when they brought the child home after his day with them.

Tom and Anna had to leave before the game was finished, and while Sonya waited for Daniel and Paul, she reflected on the past four years. She had managed the Blessed Hope shelter until she was married, and then with Daniel's blessing, she had deeded the house and surroundings to a private corporation that owned and operated homeless shelters and abuse centers throughout the state. She had enrolled in the university on a part-time basis and two more semesters of work would complete her degree.

When Sonya and Daniel married, Mrs. Massie elected to

move into a two-room apartment in an exclusive retirement complex and left the large house for them. Sonya stirred from her reverie and watched with amusement as Paul tried to match his stride to Daniel's as they walked along hand-in-hand. Her heart was so full of love for both of them that she felt light-headed.

"Mom, did you see me hitting the ball?"

"I certainly did, and I was proud of you. Grandpa Dixon said that you're going to be a great athlete. Did you hurt yourself when you fell?"

"Oh, Daddy said it was just a little scratch," Paul said, but he invited Sonya to take a look at his bruised knee.

Daniel put his arm around Sonya's waist as Paul ran ahead of them to the parking lot.

"You had a mysterious look on your face when we approached," Daniel said. "What were you thinking?"

"Oh, just being thankful for my happy home. When I think about five years ago..."

Daniel bent over and stopped her words with his kiss.

"No more thinking about the past," he said softly. "Those days will never come again."

"I don't expect them to, but I have to remember the past to know how fortunate I am now. I'm not sure that I deserve you."

He pinched her playfully on the side. "You probably don't," he teased, "but I'm going to keep you anyway."

"We're going to stop for a hot dog and cola," Paul called over his shoulder. "Daddy said we could."

Looking up at Daniel, her eyes full of tender affection, Sonya said, "If Daddy says so, I suppose that settles it. But don't forget we have another child to pick up at your mother's. She may be tired of babysitting by now."

"I haven't heard her complaining."

Although Daniel had told her to forget the past, Sonya's mind turned backward once more. Two years ago, their daughter, Jessica, had been born, and how different that experience was from the night of Paul's birth. Daniel didn't leave her once during a difficult delivery, suffering with her through every contraction, pain and scream, and in the midst of her suffering, Sonya thanked God for Daniel's presence. During Paul's birth she had nothing to rely on except the Scripture verse she had first heard from We Care on the darkest night of her life. *Weeping may endure for a night, but joy cometh in the morning.* She had put God's promise to the test and found it to be true. She had endured two years of grief, but happiness had blossomed in her life through Daniel's love and the support of her church family.

On the morning she bore Daniel's daughter, her joy was dampened momentarily. The position of the child had kept the sex secret until it was born, but when the pain was over at last, Dr. Hammer said, "You have a pretty girl this time, Mrs. Massie," and tears crept into Sonya's weary eyes.

"I'm sorry I didn't give you a son, Daniel," she whispered.

He bent over the bed and squeezed her gently. "But I wanted a daughter; I already have a son."

She had never doubted Daniel's love for Paul, but his words made her joy complete. Her life had been so abundant that Sonya no longer puzzled over the meaning of Romans 8:28. During the ups and downs of her life, she had learned that in all things God *does* work for the good of those who love him, who have been called according to His purpose.

* * * * *

Dear Reader,

Childhood on a hillside farm in West Virginia was not conducive to a literary career, yet the lessons I learned there in responsibility, self-discipline and faith in God have influenced my writings. At the age of ten I was inspired to write my first novel. Not one to dally, I took a pencil and spiral notebook when I felt the urge to write, went up on the hillside, sat under a hickory tree and started my first book, although that inspiration was soon superseded by other childish interests. The desire to publish a book persisted, but it was not until 1977 that I began to think of myself as a "writer." I completed my first novel, though it was not published until 1990. In the meantime, I had published other books. However, success in writing didn't come easily for me. As an editor once told me, "You can write, but you have to work at it." How right he was!

Child of Her Heart is my fifteenth novel. I have no firsthand knowledge of the trauma that accompanies divorce, for I've been married to the same loving and supportive husband for forty-one years. However, the many friends I have whose marriages have ended in divorce prompted my interest in the subject, and I hope that my fictional treatment of broken wedding vows in this book will be a source of inspiration to my readers.

I have devoted most of my writing to inspirational subjects encouraging readers to overcome their problems and redirect their futures by accepting God as an integral part of their lives, and I hope they will desire, as I do, to find and accept God's will for daily living. No problem is too big, or small, for God to solve.

In His service,

Irene B. Brand

DESPERATELY SEEKING DAD

Marta Perry

In loving memory of my parents-in-law,
Harry and Greta Johnson.
And, as always, for Brian.

Chapter One

"I believe you're my baby's father." Anne Morden tried saying it aloud as she drove down the winding street of the small mountain town. The words sounded just as bad as she'd thought they would. There was absolutely no good way to announce a fact like that to a man she'd never met.

In her mind and heart, Emilie was already her child, even though the adoption wasn't yet final—even though the father hadn't yet relinquished his rights.

He would. Fear closed around her heart. He had to. Because if he didn't, she might lose the baby she loved as her own.

The soft sound of a rattle drew her gaze to the rearview mirror. Emilie, safe in her car seat, shook the pink plastic lamb with one chubby fist, then stuck it in her mouth. At eight months, Emilie put everything in her mouth.

"It'll be all right, sweetheart. I promise."

Emilie's round blue eyes got a little rounder, and her face crinkled into a smile at the sound of Anne's voice...the voice of the only mother the baby had ever known.

Fear prickled along her nerves. She had to protect Emilie, had to make sure the adoption went through as planned so the baby would truly be hers. And confronting the man she believed to be Emilie's biological father was the only way to do that. But where were the right words?

Anne spotted the faded red brick building ahead on the right, its black-and-white sign identifying it as the police station. Her heart clenched. She'd face Police Chief Mitch Donovan in a matter of minutes, and she still didn't know what she'd say.

Help me, Father. Please. For Emilie's sake, let me find a way to do this.

A parking spot waited for her in front of the station. She couldn't drive around for a few more minutes. Now, before she lost her nerve, she had to go inside, confront the man, and get his signature on a parental rights termination.

For Emilie. Emilie was her child, and nobody, including the unknown Mitch Donovan, was going to take her away.

Parking the car, getting the stroller out, buttoning Emilie's jacket against the cool, sunny March day—none of that took long enough. With another silent, incoherent prayer, Anne pulled open the door and pushed the stroller inside.

Bedford Creek didn't boast much in the way of a police station—just a row of chairs, a crowded bulletin board and one desk. A small town like this, tucked safely away in the Pennsylvania mountains, probably didn't need more. She'd driven only three hours from Philadelphia, but Bedford Creek seemed light-years from the city, trapped in its isolated valley.

"Help you?" The woman behind the desk had dangling earrings that jangled as she spun toward Anne. Her penciled eyebrows shot upward, as if she were expecting an emergency.

"I'd like to see Chief Donovan, please." Her voice didn't betray her nervousness, at least she didn't think so.

That was one of the first things she'd learned as an attorney—never let her apprehension show, not if she wanted to win. And this was far more important than any case she'd ever defended.

The woman studied her for a moment, then nodded. "Chief!" she shouted. "Somebody to see you!"

Apparently the police station didn't rely on such high-tech devices as phones. The door to the inner office started to move. Anne braced herself. In a moment she'd—

The street door flew open, hitting the wall. An elderly man surged in from outside, white hair standing on end as if he'd just run his fingers through it. He was breathing hard, and his face was an alarming shade of red. He propelled a dirty-faced boy into the room with a hand on the child's jacket collar.

The man emerging from the chief's office sent her a quick look, seemed to decide her business wasn't urgent, and focused on the pair who'd stormed in.

"Warren, what's going on?" His voice was a baritone rumble, filled with authority.

"This kid." The man shook the boy by his collar. "I caught him stealing from me again, Chief. Not one measly candy bar, no. He had a whole fist full of them."

Maybe she'd been wrong about the amount of crime in Bedford Creek. She was going to see Mitch Donovan in action before she even confronted him.

She looked at him, assessing the opposition as she would in a courtroom. Big, that was her first thought. The police uniform strained across broad shoulders. He had to be over six feet tall, with not an ounce of fat on him. If she'd expected the stereotypical small-town cop with his stomach hanging over his belt, she was wrong.

"So you decided to perform a citizen's arrest, did you, Warren?" The chief concentrated on the mismatched pair.

She couldn't tell whether or not amusement lurked in his dark-brown eyes. He had the kind of strong, impassive face that didn't give much away.

"Not so old, after all, am I?" The elderly man gave his captive another little shake. "I caught you, all right."

"Take it easy." Donovan pulled the boy away. "You'll rattle the kid's brains."

The boy glared at the cop defiantly, eyes dark as two pieces of anthracite in his thin face, black hair that needed a trim falling on his forehead. He couldn't be more than ten or eleven, and he didn't appear to be easily intimidated. She wasn't sure she could have mustered a look like that—not with more than six feet of muscle looming over her.

"Okay, Davey, what's the story? You steal from Mr. Van Dyke?" His tone said there wasn't much doubt in his mind.

"Not me. Must have been somebody else."

The boy would have been better off to curb his smart remarks, but she'd defended enough juveniles to know he probably wouldn't.

"Empty your pockets," Donovan barked.

Davey held the defiant pose for another moment. Then he shrugged, reached into his jacket pockets and pulled them inside out. Five candy bars tumbled to the floor.

"You know what that is, kid? That's evidence."

"It's just a couple lousy candy bars."

"And I've got a couple lousy cells in the back. You want to see inside one of them?"

The kid wilted. "I don't..."

"Excuse me." Little as she wanted to become involved in this, she couldn't let it pass without saying something. Her training wouldn't let her. "The child's a minor. You shouldn't even be talking to him without a parent or legal representation here."

His piercing gaze focused on her, and she had to stiffen her spine to keep from wilting herself.

"That right, Counselor?"

He was quicker than she might have expected, realizing from those few words that she was an attorney.

"That's right." She glared at him, but the look seemed to have as much impact as a flake of snow on a boulder.

"If she says—" Davey caught on fast.

"Forget it." Donovan planted his forefinger against the boy's chest. "You're dealing with me, and if I hear another complaint against you, you'll wish you'd never been born. Stay out of Mr. Van Dyke's store until he tells you otherwise." He gestured toward the door. "Now get out."

The boy blinked. His first two steps were a swagger. Then he broke and ran, the door slamming behind him as he pelted up the sidewalk.

Anne took a breath and tried to force taut muscles to relax. At least now she didn't have to deal with Donovan over his treatment of the boy. Her own business with him was difficult enough.

The elderly man gathered the candy bars from the floor, grumbling a little. "Kids. At least when you were his age, you only tried it once."

A muscle twitched in Donovan's jaw. Maybe he'd rather not have heard his juvenile crime mentioned, at least not with her standing there.

"You tripped me with a broom before I got to the door, as I recall. You slowing down, Warren?"

The old man shrugged. "Still give a kid a run for his money, I guess." He shoved the candy bars into his pockets. "I'm going to the café for a cup of coffee, now that I've done your work for you." He waved toward the dispatcher, then strolled out.

Donovan turned, studying her for a long, uncomfortable moment. Her cheeks warmed under his scrutiny. He gestured toward his office. "Come in, Counselor, and tell me what I can do for you."

This was it, then. She pushed the stroller through the door, heart thumping. This was it.

The swivel chair creaked as he sat down and waved her to the visitor's seat. Behind the battered oak desk, an American flag dwarfed the spare, small office. Some sort of military crest hung next to it. Donovan was ex-military, of course. Anne might have guessed it from his manner.

Maybe she should have remained standing. She always thought better on her feet, and she was going to need every edge she could get, dealing with this guy.

Anne leaned back, trying for a confidence she didn't feel, and resisted the urge to clench her hands. *Be calm, be poised. Check out the opposition, then act.*

Mitch Donovan had that look she always thought of as the "cop look"—wary, tough, alert. Probably even in repose his

422 Desperately Seeking Dad

stony face wouldn't relax. He could as easily be an Old West gunfighter, sitting with his back to the wall, ready to fly into action at the slightest provocation.

She took a deep breath. He was waiting for her to begin, but not the slightest movement of a muscle in his impassive face betrayed any hint of impatience. This was probably a man who'd buried his emotions so deep that a dynamite blast wouldn't make them surface.

"I realize I have no standing here, Chief Donovan, but you shouldn't have questioned the child without his parents." That wasn't what she'd intended to say, but it spilled out more easily than her real concern.

"I wasn't questioning, Counselor. I was intimidating." His lips quirked a little. "Who knows if it'll do any good."

"Intimidating." There were a lot of things she could say to that, including the fact that he certainly was. "Please don't call me 'Counselor.'"

His brows lifted a fraction. "But I don't know your name."

Intimidating, indeed. She was handling this worse than an Assistant District Attorney newly hatched from law school.

"Anne Morden. I used to be with the Public Defender's Office in Philadelphia." She could hardly avoid identifying herself, but some instinct made her want to keep him from knowing where to find her—to find Emilie.

He nodded, but his face gave no clue as to his thoughts. Strength showed in the straight planes and square chin. His hair, worn in an aggressively military cut, was as dark as those chocolate eyes. Even the blue police uniform looked military on him, all sharp creases and crisp lines.

"A Philadelphia lawyer. Around here they say if you want to win, you hire a Philadelphia lawyer." His gaze seemed to sharpen. "So whose battle are you here to win, Ms. Morden? Not Davey Flagler's."

"Davey? No." The boy had been only a preliminary skirmish; they both knew it. For an instant she was tempted to say she represented someone else, but knew that would never work. The plain truth was her only weapon.

"Well, Counselor?"

Her mouth tightened at the implied insult in his use of the title. But one hardly expected police to look kindly on defense attorneys—and most times the feeling was mutual.

"I'm not representing anyone but myself." She glanced down at Emilie, who banged her rattle on the stroller tray. "And my daughter. I'm here because—" The words stuck in her throat. How could she say this? But she had to.

With a sense that she'd passed the point of no return, she forced the words out. "Because I believe you are Emilie's biological father."

Impassive or not, there was no mistaking the expression that crossed his face as her words penetrated—sheer stupefaction.

Donovan stared at her, shifted the stare to the baby, then back to her. If his eyes had softened slightly when they assessed Emilie, that softness turned to granite when his gaze met hers.

"Lady, you're plain crazy. I've never seen you before in my life."

For an instant Anne was speechless. Then she felt her cheeks color. He thought she meant they...

"No! I mean, I know you haven't." She took a deep breath, willing herself to be calm. If she behaved this way in court, all her clients would be in prison.

His eyes narrowed, fine lines fanning out from them. "Then what do you mean?" The question shot across the desk, and his very stillness spoke of anger raging underneath iron control.

"Emilie..."

As if hearing her name, Emilie chose that moment to burst into wails. She stiffened, thrusting herself backward in the stroller.

Anne bent over her. "Hush, sweetheart." She lifted the baby, standing to hold her on one hip. "There, it's all right." She bounced her gently. "Don't cry."

The wail turned to a whimper, and Anne dropped a kiss on

Emilie's fine, silky hair. Maybe she shouldn't have brought the baby with her, but she couldn't bear the thought of being away from her in this crisis.

The whimpers eased, and Emilie thrust her fingers into her mouth. Anne looked at the man on the other side of the desk, searching vainly for any resemblance to her daughter.

"I didn't put that well." She cradled the baby against her. "I'm not Emilie's birth mother. I'm her foster mother. I'm trying to adopt her."

Donovan shot out of the chair, as if he couldn't be still any longer. He leaned forward, hands planted on the desk.

"Why did you come in here with an accusation like that? What proof do you have?"

"I have the birth mother's statement."

That had to rock him, yet his expression didn't change. "Where is she? Let her make her accusations to my face."

"She can't." Anne's arms tightened protectively around the baby, knowing this was the weakest link in her case, the point at which she was most vulnerable. And Donovan was definitely a man who'd zero in on any vulnerability. "She's dead."

Mitch stared at the woman for a long moment, anger simmering behind the impassive mask he kept in place by sheer force of will. What game was this woman playing? Was this some kind of setup?

"What do you want?"

The abrupt question seemed to throw her. She cradled the baby against her body as if she needed to protect it.

From him. The realization pierced his anger. Protecting was his job, had been since the moment he put on a shield. Assist, protect, defend—the military police code. Nobody needed protecting from him, not unless they'd broken the law.

"You admit it, then? That you're Emilie's father?"

He leaned toward her, resisting the urge to charge around the desk. It was better, much better, to keep the barricade between them.

"I'm not admitting a thing. I want to know what brought you here. Or who."

Something that might have been hope died in her deep-blue eyes. "I told you. The baby's mother said you were the father."

"You also told me she's dead. That makes it pretty convenient to come here with this trumped-up claim."

"Trumped up?" Anger crackled around her. "I certainly didn't make this up. Why would I?"

"You tell me." It was astonishing that his voice was so calm, given the way his mind darted this way and that, trying to make sense of this.

One thing he was sure of—the baby wasn't his. His jaw tightened until it felt about to break. He'd decided a long time ago he wasn't cut out for fatherhood, and he didn't take chances.

"That's ridiculous." Even her hair seemed to spark with anger, as if touching it might shock him. "I came here because I know you're Emilie's father."

His life practically flashed before his eyes as she repeated those words. Everything he'd worked for, the respect he'd enjoyed in the two years since his return—all of it would vanish when her accusation exploded. If the story got out, it wouldn't matter that it wasn't true. By the time it had spread up one side of Main Street and down the other, all the denials in the world wouldn't make it go away.

Those Donovans have always been trouble, that's what people would say. *The apple doesn't fall far from the tree.*

"You're wrong," he said flatly. "I don't know who that child's parents are, but you're not going to get anything out of claiming I'm her father except to cause me a lot of grief."

The idea startled her—he could see it in her eyes. "I didn't come here to create a scandal." She stroked the baby's back, her mouth suddenly vulnerable as she looked at the child.

"Good." He almost believed she meant it, and the thought cut through his anger to some rational part of his mind. He had to start thinking, not reacting. He went around the desk and leaned against it, trying for an ease he didn't feel. "Then why did you come?"

She thought he was capitulating, he could tell. A smile lit her face that almost took his breath away. A man would do a lot for a smile like that.

"All I want is your signature on a parental rights termination so the adoption can go through. Once I have that, Emilie and I will walk out of your life for good."

"That's all?"

She nodded. "You'll never see us again."

"And if I don't sign?"

Her arms tightened around the baby. "I've taken care of Emilie since the day she was born. Her mother wanted me to adopt her. Why would you want to stand in the way?"

They were right where they'd started, and she wouldn't like his answer.

"I don't." He leaned forward, bridged the gap between them and touched the baby's cheek. It earned him a smile. "She's a cute kid. But she's not mine."

She turned away abruptly, bending to slide the baby into the stroller. Emilie fussed for an instant, until Anne put a stuffed toy in front of her.

When she straightened, her eyes were chips of blue ice. "I'm not trying to trap you into anything."

"I'd like to believe that, but it doesn't change anything. I'm still not her father."

She gave an impatient shrug. "I've told you the mother named you."

"You haven't even told me who she is. Or how you fit into this story." He was finally starting to think like a cop. It was about time. "Look." He tried to find the words that would gain him some cooperation. "I believe I'm not this child's father. You believe I am. Seems to me, two reasonable adults can sit down and get everything out in the open. How do you expect me to react when an accusation like this comes out of no-where?"

He could see her assess his words from every angle.

"All right," she said finally. "You know what my interest is. I want to adopt Emilie."

There had to be a lot more to the story than that, but he'd settle for the bare bones at the moment. "And the mother? Who was she? What happened to her?"

He gripped the edge of the desk behind him. He probably shouldn't fire questions at her, but he couldn't help it.

She frowned. Maybe she was editing her words. "Her mother's name was Tina Mallory. Now do you remember her?"

The name landed unpleasantly between them. *Tina Mallory.* He wanted to be able to say he'd never heard of her, but he couldn't, because the name echoed with some faint familiarity. He'd heard it before, but where? And how much of his sense of recognition did Anne Morden guess?

"How am I supposed to have known her?"

"She lived here in Bedford Creek at one time."

In Bedford Creek. If she'd lived here, why didn't he remember her? "I'm afraid it still doesn't ring any bells."

That was only half-right. It rang a bell; he just didn't know why.

"Doesn't the police chief know everyone in a town this small?" Her eyebrows arched.

Before he could come up with an answer, the telephone rang, and seconds later Wanda Clay bellowed, "Chief! Call for you."

Anne's silky black hair brushed her shoulders as she glanced toward the door.

He reached for the phone. "Excuse me. I have to do the job the town pays me for."

He picked up the receiver, turned away from her. It was a much-needed respite. He let Mrs. Bennett's complaint about her neighbors drift through his mind. He didn't need to listen, often as he'd heard the same story. What he did need to do was think. He had to find some way to put off Anne Morden until he figured out who Tina Mallory was.

"We'll take care of it, Mrs. Bennett, I promise." A few more soothing phrases, and he hung up.

Anne looked as if she wanted to tap her foot with impatience. "Now can we discuss this?"

The phone rang again, giving him the perfect excuse. "Not without interruption, as you can see. Where are you staying?"

She stiffened. "I hadn't intended to be here that long. Why can't we finish this now?"

"Because I have a job to do." His mind twisted around obstacles. He'd also better run a check on Anne Morden before he did another thing. He at least had to make sure she was who she claimed to be. "How about getting together this evening?"

"This evening?" She made it sound like an eternity. "It's a three-hour drive back to Philadelphia, and Emilie's tired already."

He was tempted to say *Take it or leave it,* but now was not the time for ultimatums. It might come to that, but not if he could make her see she was wrong.

"Look, this is too important to rush. Why don't you plan to stay over?"

"I'd like to get home tonight."

Her tone had softened a little. At least she was considering his suggestion.

"Isn't this more important?" He pushed the advantage.

She looked at the baby, then back at him, and nodded slowly. "It's worth staying, if I can get this cleared up once and for all."

Mitch took a piece of notepaper from the desk and scribbled an address on it. "The Willows is a bed-and-breakfast. Kate Cavendish will take good care of you."

He considered it a minor triumph when she accepted the paper.

"All right." Maybe she'd anticipated all along that this wouldn't be settled in a hurry. "If that's what it takes, Emilie and I will stay over. When can I expect to see you?"

He glanced at his watch, reviewing all he'd need to accomplish. "Say between six and seven?"

She nodded hesitantly, as if wary of agreeing to anything he said. "I'll see you then."

He didn't breathe until she and the baby were gone. Then it felt as if he hadn't breathed the whole time she'd been there. Well, the news she'd brought would rattle anyone.

Just how much stock could he put in what Anne Morden said? He leaned back in his chair, considering.

It didn't take much effort to picture her sitting across from him. Cool composure—that was the first thing he'd noticed about her. She'd reminded him of every smart, savvy attorney he'd ever locked horns with, except that she was beautiful. Hair as silky and black as a ripple of satin, skin like creamy porcelain, eyes blue as a mountain lake.

Beautiful. Also way out of his class, with her designer clothes and superior air.

Well, beautiful or not, Ms. Anne Morden had to be checked out. He hoped he could find some ammunition with which to defend himself, before she blew his life apart.

He reached for the phone.

Chapter Two

Anne put a light blanket over Emilie, who slept soundly in the crib Mrs. Cavendish had installed in the bedroom of the suite. Nothing, it seemed, was too much trouble for a friend of Chief Donovan's. No one else was staying at the bed-and-breakfast now, and Mrs. Cavendish—Kate, she'd insisted Anne call her— had given them a bedroom with an adjoining sitting room on the second floor of the rambling Victorian house.

The rooms were country quaint, furnished with mismatched antiques that looked as if they'd always sat just where they did now. The quilt on the brass bed appeared to be handmade, and dried flowers filled the pottery basin on the oak washstand. A ghost of last summer's fragrance wafted from them.

She would have enjoyed the place in any other circumstances; it might have been a welcome retreat. But not when her baby's future was at stake.

She had to get herself under control before her next unsettling meeting with Mitch Donovan. This afternoon—well, this afternoon she could have done better, couldn't she?

Her stomach still clenched with tension when she pictured Donovan's frowning face. She still felt the power with which he'd rejected her words.

She shouldn't have been surprised. A man in his position had a lot to lose. The chief of police in a small town couldn't afford a scandal.

The sitting room window overlooked the street, which wound

its way uphill from the river in a series of jogs. Bedford Creek was dwarfed by the mountain ridges that hemmed it in. What did people in this village think of their police chief? And what would they think of him if they knew he'd had an affair with a young girl, leaving her pregnant?

They might close ranks against the stranger who brought such an accusation. A chill shivered down her spine.

If Mitch Donovan persisted in his denials, what option did she have? Making the whole business public would only hurt all three of them. But if she didn't get his signature on the document, she'd live in constant fear.

What was she going to do? Panic shot through her. She pressed her hands against the wide windowsill, trying to force the fear down.

Turn to the Lord, child. She could practically hear Helen's warm, rich voice say the words, and her fear ebbed a little at the thought of her friend.

Helen Wells had introduced her to the Lord, just as simply as if she were introducing one friend to another. Until Anne walked into the Faith House shelter Helen ran, looking for a client who'd missed a hearing, religion had been nothing but form. It had been a ritual her parents had insisted on twice a year—the times when everyone went to the appropriate church, wearing the appropriate clothing.

They'd have found nothing appropriate about Faith House or its director, Helen Wells—the tall, elegant woman's embracing warmth for everyone who crossed her threshold was outside their experience. But Anne had found a friend there, and a faith she'd never expected to encounter. Helen's wisdom had sustained her faith through the difficult season of her husband's death.

Not that she was under any illusion her faith was mature. *God's not finished with you yet,* Helen would say, wrapping Anne in the same warm embrace she extended to every lost soul and runaway kid who wandered into her shelter. *The good Lord has plenty for you to learn, girl. But you have to listen.*

God could help in this situation with Donovan. She had to believe that, somehow.

But maybe believing it would be easier if she had the kind of faith Helen did.

I'm trying, Lord. You know I'm trying.

A police car came slowly down the street and pulled to the curb in front of the bed-and-breakfast. She let the curtain fall behind her, her heart giving an awkward *thump*. Mitch Donovan was here.

In a moment she heard footsteps in the hall beneath, heard Kate greeting him—fondly, it seemed. Well, of course. Bedford Creek was his home. Anne was the stranger here, and she had to remember that.

By the time he knocked, Anne had donned her calm, professional manner. But after she opened the door, her coolness began to unravel. He still wore the uniform that seemed almost a part of him, and his dark gaze was intent and determined.

"Chief Donovan. Come in."

He nodded, moving through the doorway as assuredly as if he were walking into his office. The small room suddenly filled with his masculine presence.

It's the uniform, she told herself, fingers tightening on the brass knob as she closed the door. That official uniform would rattle anyone, especially combined with the sheer rock-solid nature of the man wearing it.

"Getting settled?" His firm mouth actually curved in a smile. "I see Kate gave you her best room."

Apparently he hoped to get this meeting off to a more pleasant start than the last one. Well, that was what she wanted, too. *You need his cooperation,* she reminded herself. *For Emilie's sake.*

"Any friend of Mitch's deserves the nicest one—I think that's what she said." Anne couldn't help it if her tone sounded a bit dry.

He walked to the window, glanced out at the street below,

then turned back to her. "Kate said you took a walk around town."

The small talk was probably as much an effort for him as for her. She longed to burst into the crucial questions, but held them back.

Cooperate, remember? That's how to get what you want.

"I stopped by the pharmacy to pick up some extra diapers for the baby. The pharmacist already knew I'd been to see you." That had astonished her. "Your dispatcher must work fast."

The source of the information had to be the dispatcher. Mitch Donovan certainly wouldn't advertise her presence.

He grimaced. "Wanda loves to spread news. And it is a small town, except during tourist season."

"Tourist season?"

He gestured out the window, and she moved a little reluctantly to stand next to him.

"Take a look at those mountains. Our only claim to fame."

The sun slipped behind a thickly forested ridge, painting the sky with red. The village seemed wedged into the narrow valley, as if forced to climb the slope from the river because it couldn't spread out. The river glinted at the valley floor, reflecting the last of the light.

"It is beautiful."

"Plenty of people are willing to pay for this view, and the Chamber of Commerce is happy to let them."

"I guess that explains the number of bed-and-breakfasts. And the shops." She had noticed the assortment of small stores that lined the main street—candles, pottery, stained glass. "Bedford Creek must have an artistic population."

"Don't let any of the old-timers hear you say that." The tiny lines at the corners of his eyes crinkled as his face relaxed in the first genuine smile she'd seen. "They leave such things to outsiders."

"Outsiders." That seemed to echo what she'd been thinking. "You mean people like me?"

He shook his head. "They make a distinction between outsiders and visitors. Outsiders are people like the candle-makers and potters who want to turn the place into an artists' colony. The old guard understands that, whether they approve or not. But visiting lawyers—visiting lawyers must be here for a reason."

"So that's why everyone I passed looked twice."

He shrugged. "In the off-season, strangers are always news. Especially a woman and baby who come to call on the bachelor police chief." His mouth twisted a little wryly on the words.

She'd clearly underestimated the power of the grapevine in a small town. But his apparent concern about rumors might work to her advantage.

"No one will know why I'm here from me. I promise."

She almost put her hand out, as if to shake on it, and then changed her mind. She didn't want friendship from the man, just cooperation. Just his signature, that was all.

"Thanks."

He took a step closer...close enough that she could feel his warmth and smell the faint, musky aroma of shaving lotion. Her pulse thumped, startling her, and she took an impulsive step back, trying to deny the warmth that swept over her.

She must be crazy. He was tough, arrogant, controlling—everything she most disliked in a man. Even if she had been remotely interested in a relationship—which she wasn't—it wouldn't be with someone like him.

But her breathing had quickened, and his dark eyes were intent on hers, as if seeing something he hadn't noticed before. She felt heat flood her cheeks.

Business, she reminded herself. She'd better get down to business. It was the only thing they had in common.

"Have you thought about signing the papers?" She knew in an instant she shouldn't have blurted it out, but her carefully prepared speech had deserted her. In her plans for this meeting, she hadn't considered that she might be rattled at being alone with him.

Whatever friendliness had been in his eyes vanished. "I'd like to talk about this." His uncompromising tone told her the situation wasn't going to turn suddenly easy. "About the woman, Tina."

"Do you remember her now?" She didn't mean the words to sound sarcastic, but they probably did. She bit her lip. There was just no good way to discuss this.

"No." Luckily he seemed to take the question at face value. "Do you know when she was here?"

"Emilie was born in June. Tina said she'd been here the previous summer and stayed through the fall." He could count the months as easily as she could.

He frowned. "Tourist season. They come right through the autumn colors. That means there are plenty of transient workers in town. People who show up in late spring, get jobs, then leave again the end of October." He shook his head. "Impossible to remember them all or keep track of them while they're here."

She'd left her bag on the pie-crust table. She flipped it open and took out the photograph she'd brought. A wave of sadness flooded her as she looked at the young face.

"This was Tina." She held it out to him.

He took the photo and stood frowning down at it, straight brows drawn over his eyes. She should be watching for a spark of recognition, she thought, instead of noticing how his uniform shirt fit his broad shoulders, not a wrinkle marring its perfection. The crease in his navy trousers looked sharp enough to cut paper, and his shoes shone as if they'd been polished moments before.

He looked up finally, his gaze finding hers without the antagonism she half expected. "How did you meet her?"

She bit back a sharp response. "Isn't it more pertinent to ask how *you* met her?"

His mouth hardened in an already hard face. "All right. I recognize her now that I've seen the picture. But I never knew her name. And I certainly didn't have an affair with her."

That was progress, of a sort. If she could manage not to

sound as if she judged him, maybe he'd move toward being honest with her.

She tried to keep her tone neutral. "How did you know her?"

"She worked at the café that summer." He frowned, as if remembering. "I eat a lot of meals there, so she waited on me. Chatted, the way waitresses do with regulars. But I didn't run into her anywhere else."

His dark gaze met hers, challenging her to argue. "Your turn. How did you get to know her?"

"She answered an ad I'd put on the bulletin board at the corner market. She wanted to rent a room in my house."

His eyebrows went up at that. "Sorry, Counselor, but you don't look as if you need to take in boarders."

"I didn't do it for the money." She clipped off the words. Her instincts warned her not to give too much away to this man, but if she wanted his cooperation she'd have to appear willing to answer his questions. "My husband had died a few months earlier, and I'd taken a leave from my job. I'd been rattling around in a place too big for one person. The roomer was just going to be temporary, until I found a buyer for the house."

"How long ago was that?" It was a cop's question, snapped at her as if she were a suspect.

"A little over a year." She tried not to let his manner rattle her. "I knew she was pregnant, of course, but I didn't know she had a heart condition. I'm not sure even she knew at first. The doctors said she never should have gotten pregnant."

"What about her family?"

"She said she didn't have anyone." Tina had seemed just as lonely as Anne had been. Maybe that was what had drawn them together. "We became friends. And then when she had to be hospitalized—well, I guess I felt responsible for her. She didn't have anyone else. When Emilie was born, Tina's condition worsened. I took charge of the baby. Tina never came home from the hospital."

His strong face was guarded. "Is that when she supposedly told you about me?"

She nodded. "She talked about the time she spent in Bedford Creek, about the man she loved, the man who fathered Emilie."

He was so perfectly still that he might have been a statue, except for the tiny muscle that pulsed at his temple. "And if I tell you it was a mistake—that she couldn't have meant me...?"

"Look, I'm not here to prosecute you." Why couldn't he see that? "I'm not judging you. I just want your signature on the papers. That's all."

"You didn't answer me." He took a step closer, and she could feel the intensity under his iron exterior. "What if I tell you it was a mistake?"

It was all slipping away, getting out of her control. "How could it be a mistake? Everything she said fits you, no one else."

He seized on that. "Fits me? I thought you said she named me."

She took a deep breath, trying to stay in control of the situation. "While she was ill, she talked a lot about...about the man she fell in love with. About the town. Then, when we knew she wasn't going to get better, we made plans for Emilie's adoption." She looked at him, willing him to understand. "I've been taking care of Emilie practically since the day she was born. I love her. Tina knew that. She knew I needed the father's permission, too, but she never said the name until the end."

She shivered a little, recalling the scene. Tina, slipping in and out of consciousness, finally saying the name *Mitch Donovan.* "Why would she lie?"

"I don't know." His mouth clamped firmly on the words. "I'm sorry, sorry about all of it. But I'm not the father of her baby."

She glared at him, wanting to shake the truth out of him. But it was no use. It would be about as effective as shaking a rock.

"You don't believe me." He made it a simple statement of fact.

"No." There seemed little point in saying anything else.

Mitch's jaw clamped painfully tight. This woman was so sure she was right that it would take a bulldozer to move her. Somehow he had to crack open that closed mind of hers enough for her to admit doubt.

"Isn't it possible you misunderstood?" He struggled, trying to come up with a theory to explain the unexplainable. "If she was as sick as you say, maybe her mind wandered."

For the first time some of the certainty faded in her eyes. She stared beyond him, as if focusing on something painful in the past.

"I don't think so." Her gaze met his, troubled, as if she were trying to be fair. "We'd been talking about the adoption. Certainly she knew what I was asking her."

"Look, I don't have an explanation for this." He spread his hands wide. "All I can say is what I've already told you. I knew the girl slightly, and she was here at the right time. I don't know how to prove a negative, but I never had an affair with her, and I did not father her child."

Something hardened inside him as he said the words. He didn't have casual affairs—not that it was any of Anne Morden's business. And he certainly wasn't cut out for fatherhood. If there was anything his relationship with his own father had taught him, it was that the Donovan men didn't make decent fathers. The whole town knew that.

"If you were to sign the parental rights termination..." she began.

He lifted an eyebrow. "Is that really what you want, Counselor? You want me to lie?"

Her soft mouth could look uncommonly stubborn. "Would it be a lie?"

"Yes." That much he knew. And he could only see one way to prove it in the face of Anne's persistence and the mother's dying statement. "I suggest we put it to the test. A blood test."

That must have occurred to her. It was the obvious solution. And her quick nod told him she'd thought of it.

"Fine. Is there a lab in town?"

"Not here." He didn't even need to consider that. "We can't have it done in Bedford Creek." He hoped he didn't sound as horrified at the thought as he felt.

"Why not?" The suspicion was back in her eyes.

"You've obviously never lived in a small town. If the three of us show up at the clinic for a paternity test, the town will know about it before the needle hits my skin."

"That bad?" She almost managed a smile.

"Believe me, it's that bad. Rebecca Forrester, the doctor's assistant, wouldn't say a word. But the receptionist talks as much as my dispatcher."

"The nearest town where they have the facilities—"

"I'd rather go to Philadelphia, if you don't mind." She shouldn't. After all, that was her home turf.

"That's fine with me, but isn't it a little out of the way for you?"

"Far enough that I won't be worried about running into anyone who'll carry the news back to Bedford Creek." It was a small world, all right, but surely not that small. "I have a friend who's on the staff of a city hospital. He can make sure we have it done quickly. And discreetly." Though what Brett would say to him at this request, he didn't want to imagine.

"This friend of yours—" she began.

"Brett's a good physician. He wouldn't jeopardize his career by tinkering with test results."

She seemed to look at it from every angle before she nodded. "All right. Tomorrow?"

"Tomorrow, it is."

He forced his muscles to relax. Tomorrow, if luck was with him, a simple screening would prove he couldn't possibly be the child's father. Anne Morden would take her baby and walk back out of his life as quickly as she'd walked in.

He should be feeling relief. He definitely shouldn't be feeling regret at the thought of never seeing her again.

Chapter Three

Anne made the turn from the Schulkyll Expressway toward center city and glanced across at her passenger. Mitch stared straight ahead, hands flexed on his knees. He wore khaki slacks and a button-down shirt today, his leather jacket thrown into the back seat, but even those clothes had a military aura.

Nothing in his posture indicated any uncertainty about her driving, but she was nevertheless sure that he'd rather be behind the wheel.

Well, that was too bad. Riding to Philadelphia together had been his idea, after all. He'd said his car was in the shop, and if she thought he wanted to drive the police car on an errand like this, she'd better think again. He'd ride down with her and get a rental car for the return.

The trip had been accomplished mostly in silence, except for the occasional chirps from Emilie in her car seat. Mitch probably had no desire to chat, anyway, and her thoughts had twisted all the way down the turnpike.

Was she doing the right thing? A blood test was the obvious solution, of course, and she'd recommended it often enough to clients. She just hadn't anticipated the need in this situation. She'd assumed a man in Mitch's position, faced with the results of a casual fling, would be only too happy to sign the papers and put his mistake behind him.

But it hadn't worked out that way, and his willingness to

undergo the blood test lent credence to his denials. She was almost tempted to believe him.

What was she thinking? He had to be Emilie's father, didn't he? Tina would certainly know, and Tina had said so.

They passed a sign directing them to the hospital, and her nerves tightened. Maybe she shouldn't have agreed to let Mitch make the arrangements, but it sounded sensible, the way he had put it. They could be assured speed and secrecy through his connection.

"I hope your friend is ready for us." She glanced at her watch. Dr. Brett Elliot had given them an afternoon appointment, and they should be right on time.

"He'll be there." Mitch's granite expression cracked in a reminiscent smile. "In high school Brett was always the one with the late assignment and the joke that made the teacher laugh so she didn't penalize him. But medical school reformed him. You'd hardly guess he was once the class clown."

Somehow the title didn't sound very reassuring. She glanced sideways at Mitch, registering again his size and strength. "Let me guess. You must have been the class's star athlete."

He shrugged. "Something like that, I guess."

The hospital parking garage loomed on her right. Anne pulled in, the sandwich she'd had for lunch turning into a lead ball in her stomach. In an hour or two, she might know for sure about Emilie's father.

Mitch's friend had said he'd be waiting at the lab desk. Actually, he seemed to be leaning on it. Unruly hair the color of antique gold tumbled into his eyes as he laughed down at the woman behind the desk. So this was the boy who'd charmed everyone—all grown up and still doing it, apparently.

"Mitch!" He crossed the room in a few long strides and pumped Mitch's hand. "Good to see you, guy. It's been too long."

Brett's face, open and smiling, contrasted with Mitch's closed, reserved look, but nothing could disguise the affection between them. Mitch clapped him on the shoulder before turning to Anne and introducing her.

Brett gave her the same warm grin he'd been giving the woman at the desk, but she thought she read wariness in his green eyes. Then he turned to Emilie, and all reservation vanished.

"Hey, there, pretty girl. What's your name?"

"This is Emilie."

"What a little sweetheart." He tickled Emilie's chin, and even the eight-month-old baby responded to him with a shy smile and a tilt of her head.

Brett gestured toward the orange vinyl chairs lining the empty waiting room. "Since we've got the place to ourselves, let's have a chat about what we're going to do."

The woman behind the desk muttered an excuse and disappeared into the adjoining room. Anne took a seat, Emilie on her lap, and vague misgivings floated through her mind. *These are Mitch's arrangements,* she cautioned herself. *This is Mitch's friend.*

Brett pulled his chair around to face them. "The first step is to do a preliminary screening of blood type and Rh factors. We'll be able to give you those results right away."

"They're not definitive in establishing paternity." She didn't mean to sound critical, but she'd handled enough cases to know it usually went farther than that.

"Not entirely." Brett didn't seem put off by her lawyer-like response. "But there are some combinations that can exclude the possibility of paternity, and that's what we look for first."

Another objection stirred in Anne's mind. "Don't you need the mother's blood type to do that?"

"Yes, well, actually I got the information from the hospital where Emilie was born."

He exchanged a quick glance with Mitch. Obviously they'd arranged that when they talked, too.

"My military records show my blood type." Mitch frowned. "We could have gotten them."

"This is faster than waiting for the military to send something," Brett said, before Anne could voice an objection. "And in a legal matter, we can't just rely on your word."

Mitch's mouth tightened, but he nodded.

"Okay, so if the screening rules Mitch out," the doctor continued, "we stop there. If it doesn't, that still means he's one of maybe a million people who could be the father. So we go to DNA testing at that point. It takes longer, but it'll establish paternity beyond any doubt."

Emilie stirred restlessly on Anne's lap, as if to remind her she'd had a long, upsetting couple of days. Anne stroked her head. "I understand."

"Let's get on with it." Mitch seemed ready for action, and she half expected him to push up his sleeve on the spot.

"Fine." Brett started toward the laboratory door.

Ready or not. Anne picked up Emilie and followed him, suddenly breathless. She'd know something, maybe soon.

Mitch's stony expression didn't change in the least when the technician plunged a needle into his hard-muscled arm. Emilie wasn't so stoic. She stiffened, head thumping hard against Anne's chest, and let out an anguished wail that tore into Anne's heart.

"Hey, little girl." Mitch's voice was astonishingly gentle. One large hand wrapped around the baby's flailing foot. "It'll be over in a second, honest."

When the needle was gone, Emilie's sobs subsided, but Anne didn't have any illusions. The baby was overtired and overstimulated, and she desperately needed to have her dinner and go to sleep. That wouldn't hurt her mother any, either.

"It's all right, darling." She stroked Emilie's fine blond hair. "We'll go home soon."

Brett nodded. "This won't take long. Make yourselves comfortable in the waiting room, and I'll bring you some coffee."

A few minutes later they were back in the same chairs they'd occupied earlier. Anne tried to balance a wiggling Emilie while digging for a bottle of juice in the diaper bag. The juice remained elusive.

"Here, let me hold her." Before she could object, Mitch took the baby from her. He bounced Emilie on his knees, rumpling the knife-sharp crease, his strong hands supporting the baby's back.

The ache between Anne's shoulder blades eased. She watched Mitch with the baby, realizing the ache had just shifted location to her heart. If Mitch was Emilie's father...

She bent over the diaper bag to hide the tears that clouded her eyes. Ridiculous to feel them. Nothing had changed. She blinked rapidly and fished the juice bottle out.

"I'll take her now." She flipped the cap off and dropped it in the bag.

Mitch shook his head and reached for the bottle. "Give yourself a break for a few minutes. I can manage this."

She leaned back, watching as he shifted Emilie's position and plopped the nipple into her mouth.

"You didn't learn that in...the Army, was it?"

He nodded. "Military Police. Matter of fact, I did. A couple of my buddies had families."

She thought she heard a note of censure in his voice. "You have something against that?"

His eyes met hers, startled, and then he shrugged. "Up to them. I just never figured family mixed very well with military police work."

Emilie snuggled against him, fingers curling and uncurling on the bottle, eyes beginning to droop.

"I see you hung around enough to learn how to give a bottle."

His face relaxed in a smile. The effect was startling, warming his whole countenance and demanding an answering smile she couldn't suppress.

"Not too difficult. Besides, I could always give the babies back if they got fussy."

"Of course."

Something hardened in her at the words. The three of them might look, to the casual observer, like a family. That observer couldn't begin to guess how skewed that impression was.

Emilie had fallen asleep in Mitch's arms by the time Brett pushed through the door, a clipboard in his hand. Anne inhaled sharply and saw Mitch's already erect posture stiffen even more.

"Well?" Mitch's voice rasped. "What's the verdict?"

Brett's green eyes were troubled. "Skipping all the technical details, the bottom line is the tests don't exclude you, Mitch. Your blood type means you could possibly be the father."

"Me and a million other guys," he snapped.

Anne's mouth tightened. He'd obviously been hoping against hope he hadn't been caught. Maybe now he'd give up this pose of innocence and sign the papers. But she had to show him she'd keep pressing.

"About the DNA test—" she pinned Brett with her gaze "—I'd like it sent to McKay Labs. I've dealt with them before. And I want a copy of the results sent directly to me."

Brett blinked. "That'll need Mitch's permission."

"You've got it." Mitch moved, and Emilie woke. Her whimper quickly turned into a full-fledged cry.

Brett looked ready to escape. "Expect the results in three to four weeks, then."

Anne nodded goodbye, trying to reach for the diaper bag and her crying child at the same time. "Let me have her."

Mitch handed over the baby.

"There, sweetheart, it's all right." She rocked the baby against her, but Emilie was beyond comforting. She reared back in Anne's arms, wails increasing.

Mitch picked up the diaper bag. "You can't drive home alone with her in that state." He took her arm. "Come on. I'll drive you and then call a cab."

She wanted to protest, but Emilie's sobs shattered her will. She nodded, letting him guide her from the room.

The baby's wails seemed to fry Mitch's brain as he followed Anne's directions through the city streets to a high-rise apartment building. He needed to think this whole thing through, but thought proved impossible at the moment. Who would imagine one small baby could make that much noise?

He took a deep breath as the cry reached a decibel level that had to be against the law inside a small car. Okay, he could handle this. It was no worse than artillery fire, was it?

Besides, it would soon be over. He'd deposit them at Anne's and call a cab. He'd be back in Bedford Creek in a few hours, and the only contact he'd have with Anne Morden and her baby would be when the DNA test came back, proving he hadn't fathered this child.

A padded, mirrored elevator whooshed them swiftly to the tenth floor. He took the baby, wincing at her cries, while Anne unlocked the door. He wanted only to hand her back and get out of there.

She scooped the baby into her arms as the door swung open, and her eyes met his. "This may not be the best time, but I think we should talk the situation over, if you don't mind waiting while I get the baby settled." She managed a half smile. "It won't take as long as you might think. She's so exhausted, she's going to crash as soon as she's been fed."

He pushed down the desire to flee, nodded, and followed her into the apartment. Anne disappeared into the back with the baby, and he sank onto the couch, wondering when the ringing in his ears would stop.

Anne had sold the house she'd talked about and moved here with the baby. He'd found that out in the quick background check he'd run. He glanced around. Expensively casual—that was the only way to describe her apartment. Chintz couches, a soft plush carpet, a wall of books on built-in shelves with what was probably a state-of-the-art entertainment center discreetly hidden behind closed doors—all said money. Assistant public defenders didn't make enough to support this life-style, but there was wealth in her family. This woman was really out of his league.

No question of that, anyway. All she wanted from him was his signature on the parental rights termination—not friendship, certainly nothing more.

Sometime in the last twenty-four hours he'd given up any thought that Anne was somehow attempting to frame him. No, all she wanted was to safeguard her child.

Unfortunately the one thing she wanted, he couldn't give her. Someone else had dated the unfortunate Tina; someone else had fathered her child. But who? And why on earth had the girl said his name? The answers, if they could be found at all, must lie in Bedford Creek.

The baby's cries from the back of the apartment ceased abruptly. Anne must have put some food in Emilie's mouth.

He got up, paced to the window, then paced back. What did Anne want to talk to him about? What was there left to say?

He sat back down on the couch, sinking into its comfortable depths, and reached automatically for the book on the lamp table. A Bible. It nestled into his hand, and he flipped it open to the dedication page. *To my new sister in Christ from Helen.* The date was only two years ago.

Anne came back into the room, her step light and quick. She glanced questioningly at the Bible in his hand, and he closed it and put it back where he'd found it.

"She settled down, did she?"

"Out like a light."

Anne sat in the chair across from him. Her dark hair curled around a face that was lightly flushed, probably from bending over the crib.

"You're probably as beat as she is by this time." She'd put in a couple of high-stress days, driving all the way with a baby, and on a mission like this.

"I could sleep a day or two. But Emilie won't let me."

She leaned forward and her hair brushed her shoulders, moving like a living thing. He had an insane desire to reach out, let it curl around his fingers, use it to draw her close to him.

Whoa, back off. Of all the inappropriate things he could be feeling right now, that was probably the worst.

"You wanted to talk."

"Yes." She nailed him with those deep blue eyes. "I hoped that you might be ready to sign the papers now."

He should have seen it coming. She still wanted what she'd wanted all along, and the inconclusive blood test results had just given her another bit of leverage. But it wasn't going to work.

"I know you don't believe this, but I never went out with Tina Mallory. I did not father her child." He took a breath, hoping he sounded calm.

She raised her chin stubbornly. "Then how do you explain Tina's words?"

"I can't. But there has to be an explanation somewhere. Someone in Bedford Creek must remember Tina, must know who she dated that summer. So while we're waiting for the DNA results, I'll do a little quiet investigating."

Her hands twisted involuntarily, as if she were pushing his words away. He couldn't blame her. She had what must seem to her to be incontrovertible proof of his guilt. All he could do was continue to protest his innocence.

"Bottom line is, I'm not going to sign anything that says I'm that child's parent. I can't, because it's not true. In three or four weeks, you'll know that as well as I do. Maybe by then I'll be able to point you in the right direction."

"I don't want my private business splashed all over Bedford Creek."

"Believe me, it's in my interest to keep it quiet even more than it is yours. I'll be discreet. But I'm going to start looking at this problem like a cop."

Her eyebrows went up at that. "Funny, I thought you always had."

He reminded himself that cops and defense attorneys went together like cats and dogs. "Look, Counselor, I am what I am." Her sarcasm had effectively doused that spurt of longing to hold her, which was just as well. He stood, picking up his jacket. "I'll be on my way now. I don't suppose we'll see each other again."

"I'm afraid you're wrong about that." She stood, too, her gaze locked on his.

He gave an exasperated sigh. "You're assuming that in three or four weeks you'll have proof I fathered Emilie. I know you're wrong."

"Actually, that isn't what I was thinking." She took an audible breath, as if building up to saying something she knew he wasn't going to like. "Emilie and I aren't staying here. We're going back to Bedford Creek until the results come in."

"What?" He could only stare at her. "Why? Why on earth would you want to do that?"

"You're right about one thing—the answers have to be in Bedford Creek. That's where Tina became pregnant. That's where the truth is. I can't just sit here and wonder for the next month. I need to find out, no matter what."

"After the results come—" he began.

She was already shaking her head. "I'm supposed to have a hearing on the adoption in a little over a month. Before then I have to resolve this, once and for all. And that means I'm coming to Bedford Creek."

He lifted an eyebrow skeptically. "Don't you mean you want to keep an eye on me?"

A faint flush warmed her smooth skin. "Let's say I have a high respect for the power of a police uniform. I don't want to see it used against me."

He fought down the urge to defend himself. If a man found it necessary to defend his honor, it must be in question. He took a careful step back.

"No point in my telling you not to worry about that, is there?"

She shook her head. "I won't interfere. You can pretend I'm not even there."

"Now that I can't do." He smiled grimly at her perplexed

look. "You're forgetting—people in Bedford Creek already know you and Emilie came to see me. They're probably speculating right this minute about where we are today. You can't come back and pretend we don't know each other, not in a small town."

"I'll say I'm there on vacation. You told me Bedford Creek is a tourist town. My presence doesn't have to have anything to do with you."

Obviously she hadn't thought this far ahead. "Nobody would believe that. If you come back, we'll have to keep up the illusion of friendship. And if we're both going to be looking into what happened when Tina lived there, we'd better figure out a way to cooperate on this, or at least not step on each other's toes."

He could see just how unpalatable she found that, and at some level it grated on his pride. He wasn't that hard to take, was he? It wasn't as if he were asking her to pretend a romantic interest in him.

Her eyes met his, and he could read the determination there. "I suppose you're right. You know a lot more about your town than I do. But I'm still coming. So that means we're in this together, for as long as it takes."

Chapter Four

"Now let me help you with that." Kate Cavendish took the bundle of diapers from Anne's arms before she could object. "Believe me, I remember how much you need to bring when you're traveling with a baby."

"I can manage…"

But Kate was already hustling up the front steps to The Willows, white curls glistening in the late winter sunshine. She propped the door open with an iron doorstop in the shape of a cat, then hurried inside. Anne lifted Emilie from the car seat.

It was silly, she supposed, to be made uncomfortable by so much open friendliness, but she just wasn't used to it. She could only hope Kate's enthusiastic welcome wasn't because the woman thought Anne was here to see Mitch.

That was ridiculous. It wasn't as if they'd returned together. She'd taken two days to organize this trip. Surely she could take a brief vacation in Bedford Creek without the whole town jumping to conclusions about why she was here.

Kate was probably just delighted to have paying guests at this time of the year. No matter how many tourists might show up in the summer, early March was clearly a quiet time in Bedford Creek. She glanced up at the mountain ridge that cut off the sky. It was sere and brown, its leafless trees defining its bones. She shivered a little.

"Here we go, sweetheart," she said to Emilie. "We'll just pop you in the crib while Mommy unloads the car, all right?"

Emilie wiggled, her arms flailing in the pink snowsuit. After three hours in the car, she was only too ready to practice her new crawling skills. She wouldn't be pleased at the crib, no matter how enticing Anne made it sound.

As they reached the center hall of the Victorian, Kate hurried down the winding staircase. The colors of the stained-glass window on the landing tinged her hair, and a smile lit her bright-blue eyes at the sight of the baby.

"Oh, let me take her, please. I'd just love to hold her." Kate held out her hands.

Emilie leaned her head against Anne's shoulder for a moment, considering, and then smiled, her chubby hands opening toward the woman. Emilie had apparently decided anyone who looked like Mrs. Santa Claus had to be a friend.

"You little sweetheart." Kate settled the baby on her hip with the ease of long practice. "We're going to be great friends while you're here, I can just tell."

"Thank you, Kate." Anne touched Emilie's cheek lightly. "I appreciate the help. It will just take me a few minutes to unload."

"Take your time." Kate carried the baby toward the wide archway into the front parlor. "We'll get acquainted. I'm surprised Mitch isn't here to get you settled. He's always so helpful to his friends."

Was that a question in Kate's voice? Maybe this was her chance to refute any rumors the woman had heard. Or started, for that matter. She moved to the archway.

"Mitch and I aren't that close. He probably didn't even know when we were arriving."

"Oh, I'm sure he did." Kate turned from the breakfront cabinet, where she was showing Emilie a collection of china birds. "He keeps track of things. And when his old Army friend's widow comes to visit...well, you can just be sure he'd keep track of that." Kate's round cheeks, like two red apples, plumped in a smile. "It's so nice that you could keep in touch."

"Old Army friend...how did you—" *Leap to that conclu-*

sion—that was what she was thinking, but it hardly seemed polite to say so. She'd mentioned that she was a widow when she'd checked in the first time. Kate seemed to have embroidered the rest.

"Wanda had all sorts of ideas about why you were here." Kate tickled Emilie's chin. "I told her, 'Count on it, that'll be why. Mitch's friends from the service have dropped by four or five times since he's been back in Bedford Creek. That's why Anne and her baby are here, too.'"

Mitch clearly knew his town a lot better than Anne did. She owed him an apology for thinking he was wrong about the stir her presence would create. As he'd said, she needed a reason to be here.

Anne opened her mouth and closed it again. What exactly could she say? Wanda, the dispatcher, had probably floated some much more colorful theories about Anne's visit. If Anne denied Kate's story, she'd just fuel the curiosity. She certainly wasn't going to lie about it, but maybe the safest thing was to say nothing and let them think what they wanted.

"I'm sure Mitch is busy." She settled on noncommittal. "I probably won't see much of him while we're here."

Kate swung around again, eyebrows going up in surprise. "Not see much of him? Well, of course you will. After all, his house is right across the street."

"Right—" She stopped. Anything she said now, she'd probably regret. Instead she headed back to the car for the next load, fuming.

So Mitch lived right across the street, did he? He might have mentioned that little fact about The Willows at some point in their discussion. He hadn't wanted her to come back to Bedford Creek at all; that had been clear. He certainly didn't want her to join in his investigation. But apparently he felt that if she did come, she should be under his eye.

Well, they'd get a few things straight as soon as possible. She was used to doing things on her own, and that wasn't about to change now—

It looked as if she'd have a chance to tell him so in the immediate future, because his police cruiser was pulling up directly across from The Willows.

Mitch got out. He closed the door, hesitated a moment, and then headed straight for her.

"Anne. I see you arrived safely. Any problems?"

"Not at all." She tried for a cool politeness. It would help, she thought, if she didn't experience that jolt of awareness every time she saw his tall figure. "We just got in a few minutes ago."

"I'll take that." He reached for the suitcase she'd begun to pull from the trunk, but she tightened her grip.

"I can handle it."

"I'm sure you can." His hand closed on the bag, his fingers brushing hers. "But why should you?"

"Because I don't need any help." Mitch Donovan had to be the only person in her life with the ability to make her sound like a petulant child.

They stood staring at each other, the bag trapped between them. Then his lips twitched slightly. "Something tells me that's your favorite saying."

"There's nothing wrong with being independent." She'd had to be, even when she was a child, even when she'd been married. She didn't know any other way to behave.

You can't do it all yourself, child. Helen's voice echoed in her mind. *Sometimes you have to let go and let God help.*

"You can be independent and still let me carry your bag upstairs."

She held on for another moment, then released the handle. With a half smile, he hoisted the bag, then grabbed a second one with his other hand.

Typical cop, she thought, following with an armload of her own. Give him an inch and he'd take a mile.

Unloading the car took only a few minutes with Mitch helping. She glanced around the same sitting room they'd had before, amazed as always at the amount of gear required by one small baby. Mitch set the stroller behind a bentwood coat rack.

"Looks like that's it."

She nodded. Maybe this was the chance she needed to set some ground rules for this visit. He had to understand that she wasn't going to be a passive bystander to any investigation he planned.

"We need to talk. Have you found out anything more about Tina's stay here?"

His eyebrows lifted. "It's only been a day."

"I don't have much time, if you'll recall. The hearing is in less than a month, and the results—"

The sentence came to an abrupt halt when Kate, holding the baby, stuck her head in the door. "Getting settled?"

Anne managed a nod, her heart thumping. In another instant she'd have said something about DNA testing, and Kate would have heard. She'd have to be more careful.

Mitch gestured toward the stroller. "Why don't we take Emilie out for a walk? I'm sure she's tired of being cooped up in the car."

Now that was exactly what she didn't want: to have the whole town see them together and speculate about them. "I don't think so. I need to put things away."

But Kate was already handing the baby to Mitch. "Good idea." She beamed. "This little one could use some fresh air, and the sunshine won't last that much longer. I'll help you put things away later, if you want."

Mitch bounced Emilie, who responded with a delighted squeal. She patted his face with her open palms. He looked at Anne, eyebrows raised, and she knew exactly what he was thinking. If she wanted to talk to him, they might have more privacy on a walk.

With a strong sense of having been outmaneuvered, Anne reached for the stroller.

When they reached the sidewalk in front of the house, Mitch bent to slide Emilie into her seat. His big hands cradled her, protecting her head as she wiggled. Anne's heart gave an un-expected lurch at the sight. His gentleness dissolved some of the irritation she'd been holding on to, and she tried to retrieve it.

"I understand you live right across the street." *And you should have mentioned that.*

Mitch straightened, nodding. "I bought the house a year ago." He shrugged. "Got tired of living in rented places. I wanted something of my own, where I could decide on the color of the walls and pound a nail in if I wanted to."

The cottage, with its peaked roof and shutters, pristine front door and neatly trimmed hedges, proclaimed its owner's pride.

"It's charming." The house was an unexpected insight into the man. She'd have expected him to live in a furnished apart-ment, something closer to spartan barracks. "Convenient to the station, too, I guess."

"Just a couple of blocks." He shrugged. "But nothing in Bedford Creek is very far away, as long as you don't mind walking uphill." He smiled. "Or down."

He held the gate open as Anne pushed the stroller through it to the street.

"You might have mentioned this was your neighborhood when you suggested The Willows."

He paused, looking down at her with a quizzical expression. "Does that make a difference?"

"It certainly adds to the impression I'm here to see you." She felt herself blush.

"Believe me, nothing I did or didn't do would change that idea." His hand closed over hers on the stroller handle. "Why don't you let me push?"

She'd put mittens on Emilie, and maybe she should have done the same for herself. If she had, she wouldn't have to feel the warmth and strength of his hand over hers. And Anne wouldn't be struggling with the ripple of that warmth traveling right to her heart.

"Fine." She snatched her hand away. "As long as you push

it by the café where Tina worked. I want to see the place for myself.''

His answer would tell her whether he was ready to accept her role in finding out the truth about Tina, whatever it was. This would certainly be easier if she didn't have to fight him every step of the way.

But unfortunately, even that wouldn't eliminate the problem that became clearer each time she was with Mitch Donovan. She was ridiculously—and unsuitably—attracted to the man who might be Emilie's father, and who might have the power to take Emilie away.

So Anne wasn't giving up on her determination to play detective, Mitch thought. It would have been too much to hope she might, but somehow he had to convince her. Because if he had a civilian meddling in this situation, he could forget any hope of keeping things quiet while he found out the truth about Tina Mallory and her baby.

''I'll take you to the café.'' He tried to keep reluctance from showing in his voice. ''I'll even buy you a cup of coffee there, if you want.''

She glanced up at him as they walked along the street. ''Do I sense a 'but' coming?''

He shrugged. ''But Cassie Worth, the owner, isn't the most forthcoming person in the world, especially with strangers. I haven't had a chance to sound her out yet. Maybe you'd better let me see what I can find out first.''

''Give me a little credit. I didn't intend to cross-examine her.''

''Like birds don't intend to fly?''

Her lips twitched in a smile he suspected was involuntary. ''Meaning I can't help being an attorney any more than you can help being a cop?''

''Something like that.'' He eased the stroller over a patch of ice on the sidewalk. He frowned, glancing up at the storefront of Clinton's Candles. Clinton would have to be reminded to keep his walk clear.

"How will I find out anything if I don't ask?"

"If you start asking a lot of questions, it'll get around. Make people curious—more curious than they already are."

They walked in silence for a few minutes, as she apparently considered that.

"I'll be discreet," she said finally. "That's the best I can do."

He glanced at her. Silky hair brushed the collar of her black leather jacket as she moved. There was nothing remotely discreet about the presence of such a beautiful stranger in Bedford Creek, especially one accompanied by a baby. It probably wouldn't do any good to tell her that, but he had to try. Maybe a blunt reminder would get through.

"I have a lot to lose if you're not."

She looked up at him. He seemed to feel her intense blue gaze penetrate the barriers he kept around him.

"I don't see..." She shook her head. "They're your people. Seems to me they'd take your word over a stranger's, if it came to that."

The apple doesn't fall far from the tree. The refrain he'd heard too often in his childhood echoed in his mind, but he wasn't about to share it with Anne. Would anyone, other than Brett and Alex, his closest friends, take his side? He didn't care to put it to the test.

"I thought we agreed neither of us wanted this to become public knowledge."

She glanced at the baby, and her mouth softened. "I don't relish publicity any more than you do. But I have to find out about Tina." She looked back up at him, and he could read the fear in her eyes. "If you're telling me the truth, then I don't have much time."

"I know."

He felt the clock ticking, too. It must be much worse for Anne, with three to four weeks to get back the DNA test results he knew would prove him innocent. And about the same time until her hearing. No wonder she wanted to launch into an investigation.

His steps slowed. "We'll find out. I don't expect you to trust me on this, but I'm telling you the truth. We'll find out."

She nodded, and he thought he saw a sheen of tears in her eyes. "Yes." She cleared her throat. "The café…is it near here?"

"Right across the street." He gestured toward the Bluebird Café. "Let me buy you that cup of coffee."

The baby seemed to enjoy bouncing down over the curb and across the street. She pounded on the stroller tray with both tiny fists.

The Bluebird Café, its façade painted a bright blue to match its name, was one of a series of shops that staggered down either side of Main Street. They were like so many dominoes, looking ready to tumble to the valley floor, but they'd stood where they were for a hundred years or so.

A bit different from Anne's usual setting, he knew, a vision of that luxury high-rise flitting through his mind. What did she think of Bedford Creek in comparison? Of him?

Whoa, back up and erase that. It didn't matter what Anne thought of him. Not as long as, in the end, she accepted the fact that he wasn't Emilie's father.

Anne held open the frosted glass door, its placard advertising Cassie's chicken-and-dumpling soup. He lifted the stroller up the two steps from the street and pushed it inside, not wasting time looking up for either admiration or approval in those sapphire eyes.

"Not especially crowded," Anne observed, unzipping Emilie's snowsuit.

"Empty, as a matter of fact. It's too late for lunch and too early for supper." He gestured. "So you have your choice of seating."

She picked a booth halfway back, and by the time they were settled, Cassie had appeared from the kitchen.

"Afternoon, Chief." She twitched her bluebird-trimmed

apron and shot Anne a suspicious glance. "What can I get you?"

"Coffee?" He raised his eyebrows at Anne, and she nodded. "Two coffees."

"That's it?" Cassie made it sound like a personal affront that they didn't order anything else.

Again he looked at Anne, and she shook her head. "I had lunch on the way." She gave Cassie a hundred-watt smile. "Another time I'll try your chicken-and-dumpling soup."

That smile would have had him picking himself up off the floor, Mitch thought. Cassie just jerked her head in a nod, but her usual grim expression seemed to soften slightly as she plodded back toward the kitchen.

"Does she give all her customers such a warm welcome?"

He leaned against the blue padded seat. "I told you she wouldn't be very forthcoming."

"A clam is more forthcoming." She took an animal cracker from her bag and handed it to Emilie. The baby pounded it once on the stroller tray and then stuffed it into her mouth. "Why did she open a restaurant, of all things, if she didn't want to be around people?"

He shrugged. "Not that many ways to make a living in Bedford Creek. You either work at the furniture factory or you make money off tourists. And Cassie is a good cook. You'd better come back for that chicken-and-dumpling soup."

"I guess I may as well sample the local cuisine while I'm here."

"And chat with her about Tina while you're at it?" That was obviously in her mind. "Maybe you should let me bring the subject up."

She pierced him with an intent look. "Would you, if I didn't push? Or would you ignore it?"

"I said I'd work on it, and I will." He couldn't keep the irritation from his voice. Persistence was a good quality, but he didn't appreciate having it turned on him. "I've already started a couple of lines of inquiry."

She looked as if she'd like to believe him. "What did you find out?"

The *clink* of coffee mugs announced Cassie's return, and Mitch shot Anne a warning glance. Cassie might not be the yakker Wanda was, but he still didn't want her knowing his business.

Cassie slapped down the mugs, more bluebirds fluttering on the white china. She took a step back, then looked at Anne.

"Fresh apple dumplings tomorrow. Get here early if you want it."

He suspected laughter hovered on Anne's lips, but she didn't let it out. "Thanks, I'll remember."

When Cassie was safely back in the kitchen, he shook his head in mock amazement. "Apple dumplings. Believe it or not, you've made an impression. Cassie doesn't offer her apple dumplings to just anyone."

Amusement lit Anne's eyes. "Dumpling soup and apple dumplings? I'd look like a dumpling if I ate like that."

He let his glance take in her slim figure, sleek in dark slacks and a sapphire sweater that matched her eyes. "You don't look as if you need to worry."

She couldn't meet his eyes. "I didn't know investigating was so calorie-intensive."

"Maybe you ought to leave it to the pros. I can tackle the apple dumplings for you."

She shook her head, smiling but stubborn. "What were you going to tell me before Cassie came back out?"

Right. The message was clear: he'd better keep his mind on business.

"I did some preliminary checking on Tina Mallory. She lived in town for six months, worked for Cassie from June to October. Once the tourist season ended, Cassie let her go. Far as I can tell, she left sometime the following month."

"Why Philadelphia, I wonder? She never told me that."

So, he could tell her something she didn't know about her friend. "Turns out she lived awhile in Philadelphia. I'd guess when she realized she was pregnant, she wanted to go somewhere familiar.''

"Familiar? Do you mean she still had friends or family there?''

Fear probably put the sharp edge in Anne's voice. Maybe it hadn't occurred to her that Tina might have family. Family that could possibly have a claim to Emilie. He shook his head quickly.

"Not that I can tell. Apparently it was always just her and her mother—no father in evidence. And her mother died about four years ago.'' He curled his fingers around the warm mug. "She'd apparently lost touch with any friends she once had. But there certainly had to be more job opportunities in Philadelphia than anywhere around here.''

"That makes sense. I just wonder why she never told me she'd lived there. In fact, I'm sure she said she was from Los Angeles.''

"Sounds as if Tina was a little careless with the truth at times.''

She gave him a level look, one that said she knew just what he meant. "She was young,'' she said finally. "She tried to make herself interesting. But that doesn't mean I should discount everything she said.''

He'd better not let himself enjoy the way Anne's eyes lit up when she smiled, he thought. Or try to figure out a way to prolong moments when they laughed together across the table as if they were friends.

They weren't friends, and Anne obviously intended that they never would be.

Chapter Five

By the next morning, Anne had nearly succeeded in convincing herself she'd imagined that unsuitable attraction to Mitch. It must be a product of emotional stress. She'd ignore the feelings—she'd always been good at that, thanks to her parents' example.

She maneuvered Emilie's stroller over the curb. One thing she knew about parenting without a doubt: Emilie wouldn't grow up in the kind of emotional desert she had. If she and Terry had had children... But she'd finally realized her husband had no desire for a family. In marrying him, she'd just put herself in another emotionally barren situation.

No, not for Emilie. She bent to tuck the snowsuit hood more closely around the baby's ears, since the weather had turned cooler. Emilie would have love overflowing from her mother. If...

The Bluebird Café, she hoped, might provide some answers. At least today she wouldn't have Mitch sitting across from her when she dropped Tina's name into the conversation. If Cassie did know whom Tina had dated, and if that person was Mitch, she might not want to say anything in front of him.

The hardware store carried a display of window boxes and planting tools. Anne hurried past. Not even the most rabid gardener would be buying window boxes today, she thought. But it was easy to imagine the narrow wooden houses, tucked along the steep hillside, decked out with flowers in every window. Bedford Creek would look like a village in the Swiss Alps.

She pulled the café door open, to be greeted by a wave of warm air scented with apples and cinnamon, and accented with chatter. It wasn't noon yet, but the Bluebird was crowded already. It was obviously the place to be when Cassie made her famous apple dumplings.

She glanced around, aware of the flurry of curious looks sent her way. The only empty table, a small one set for two, was in the front window. She maneuvered the stroller to it. Bringing up Tina's name in a casual way wouldn't be easy with the number of people in the café. She would have to linger over her lunch, hoping to outlast most of them.

"Hi. Can I help you?" The waitress was younger than Cassie, with a name tag showing her name: Heather.

Anne felt a spurt of optimism. This girl, close in age to Tina, might remember more about Tina than Cassie did, assuming she'd worked at the café then.

"I'll have the chicken-and-dumpling soup." She put down the plastic-coated menu and smiled at the girl, whose spiky hair and multiple mismatched earrings had to be a fashion statement in a small town. "I've heard it's your specialty."

"You bet." Heather's hazel eyes ticked off every detail of Anne's slacks, cashmere sweater and gold jewelry. "Cassie's famous for it. Anything for the baby?"

"No, that's it."

She'd wait until the girl came back with her food to build on the conversation. Maybe by then she'd have lost the feeling everyone in the place was listening to her.

She bent to pull a jar of baby peaches from the diaper bag. As she straightened, the door swung open again and Mitch walked in.

Her cheeks were warm because she'd been bending over, that was all. She concentrated on Emilie, aware of Mitch's voice as he exchanged greetings with what sounded like everyone in the place. With any luck, he'd be joining one of them for lunch.

Apparently luck didn't have anything to do with it. Mitch made his way, unhurriedly, to her table. The chair scraped, and he sat down across from her as if they'd had a lunch date.

"Somehow I thought I'd find you here." He bent to greet Emilie, who responded with a crow of delight when he tickled her.

"Probably because I mentioned yesterday I wanted to come back for the chicken-dumpling soup." *And a private conversation with Cassie.*

His smile told her he knew exactly what she was thinking. "Good day for it." He waved across the room to Heather. "Another bowl of the chicken soup here, Heather."

The girl nodded. "You bet, Chief."

"You guessed—" At his warning glance she lowered her voice. "You guessed I wanted to talk with Cassie myself. I'd rather do it in private."

"You mean without me around." His face kept its relaxed expression, probably for the benefit of anyone who might be watching, but his eyes turned to stone. "I have an interest in this, remember?"

"I remember." She could so easily see his side of it. If he was innocent, naturally he'd want to protect himself by knowing anything she found out. Unfortunately, if he was guilty, the same thing applied.

"Then you can understand why I'm here." His square jaw seemed carved from granite.

"All right." She didn't have much choice. She needed his cooperation, whether she liked it or not. "Let me bring it up."

"Go ahead. But don't be surprised if she can't tell you much. If you haven't been here during tourist season, you can't imagine how crazy it is."

The soup arrived in huge, steaming pottery bowls. Heather put down a basket of freshly baked rolls nestled in a blue-checked napkin. She looked from Anne to Mitch.

"Anything else I can get you? Chief, don't you want a sandwich with that? Cassie made pulled pork barbecue."

"I'm saving room for a dumpling. You've got one back there with my name on it, haven't you?"

"Sure thing." Heather smiled, touching one earring with a plum-colored nail.

Anne could so easily imagine Mitch having this conversation with Tina. Could imagine this sort of encounter, day after day, leading to an invitation, then to an involvement he might later regret.

"Sounds as if you've been waiting on the chief for a long time." That probably wasn't the most tactful way into what she wanted to ask, but she couldn't think of a better one.

Heather shrugged. "Almost a year I've been working here. You get to know the regulars, believe me." The girl frowned at the sound of a persistent bell from the kitchen, then spun away, bluebird-trimmed apron rustling.

"I could have told you Heather didn't work here when Tina did."

"I'd rather find out for myself."

He shrugged. "I figured." He dipped the spoon into his soup.

"Attorneys prefer to ask the questions." She took a spoonful, and rich chicken flavor exploded in her mouth, chasing away the chill. "It's in my blood, I'm afraid."

"A whole family of lawyers?" He sounded as if that were the worst fate he could imagine.

"Just my father. He has a corporate practice in Hartford."

"Your mother's not a lawyer, too?"

She tried to imagine her mother doing anything so mundane, and failed. "My mother's social life keeps her occupied. And I don't have any brothers or sisters." The last thing she wanted to discuss right now was her parents. Their reaction to Emilie had been predictable, but it had still hurt. "What about you? Big family?"

She'd thought the expression in his eyes chilly before; now it had frozen. "One brother. My mother died when I was in high school. My father was long gone by then."

"I'm sorry." She suspected pain moved behind the mask he

wore, but he'd never show it, not to her, probably not to anyone. "That must have made you and your brother very close."

He shrugged. "Link works heavy construction, mostly out west. He hasn't been back to Bedford Creek in a couple of years."

Anne's heart constricted. Loneliness. She recognized the symptoms. He probably wouldn't believe her if she said she knew how he felt. He probably wouldn't believe having wealthy parents who'd stayed married to each other didn't guarantee a happy family life. Didn't guarantee you wouldn't marry someone just like them. She felt the familiar regret that her marriage hadn't been...more, somehow. Deeper.

By the time their apple dumplings arrived, most of the crowd had filtered out of the café. Anne took one look at the immense dumpling, served in its own small iron skillet, and swallowed hard.

Her face must have given her away, because Mitch chuckled. "Somebody should have warned you, I guess. But you have to make a stab at it, because Cassie will be out to see how you like it."

"That's more dessert than I eat in a month."

Mitch plunged his fork into flaky pastry, and apple syrup spurted out, mixing with the mound of whipped cream. "Live dangerously. It's worth it."

The first taste melted in her mouth. By the time Cassie appeared, ready to accept applause, Anne had made a respectable dent in the dumpling.

"Wonderful, absolutely wonderful." She leaned back in her chair. "I couldn't eat another bite."

Cassie's thin lips creased in what might have been a smile. "I'll wrap it up for you. You can finish it later."

There was nothing to do but smile and nod. "I'll do that. It was just as good as I'd heard it was."

Cassie smoothed her apron. "You hear that from Mitch?"

"It might have been Mitch who told me. Or it might have

been a friend of mine who used to work here. Maybe you remember her. Tina Mallory?''

Cassie frowned. "Little bit of a thing? Big blue eyes?''

"Yes, that's Tina.'' She held her breath. Was she about to find out something?

"Let's see...it wasn't this past season. One before, I guess. Good waitress. What's she up to now?''

"I'm afraid she passed away a few months ago.''

"A kid like that?'' Cassie shook her head. "You just never know, do you? I'm sorry to hear it.''

"I'd hoped to meet her friends while I'm here in Bedford Creek. Do you know of anyone she was especially close to...a boyfriend, maybe?''

The woman sniffed. "Got enough to do without keeping track of the summer help's boyfriends, believe me. Can't recall anybody offhand. She came in, did her job, got along with the customers. None of my business who she hung out with after work.''

Anne's hope shriveled with each word. It looked as if this would be a dead end, like so much about Tina. "If you think of anyone, would you let me know?''

"If I do.''

Cassie's tone said she doubted it. Apparently Tina had passed through Cassie's life without leaving a trace.

She picked up the dumpling pans. "I'll put this in a box for you.''

When she'd gone, Anne met Mitch's gaze. His look was unexpectedly sympathetic.

"Sorry. I know you hoped she'd remember something.''

"It's a small town. I thought everyone knew everything in a small town.''

"They do, believe me.'' There was an edge to Mitch's words. "But that's only regarding the other locals. When the town is flooded with tourists and summer help, you might not notice your best friend on the street.''

She still found that hard to picture, but apparently it was true.

If so, the chances of finding anyone who remembered anything about Tina had diminished.

"You think I ought to give up." That was what he had in mind; she was sure of it.

He shrugged. "I think you ought to leave it to me. But I suspect you're not going to."

"If you—" She stopped, realizing Cassie had emerged from the kitchen with the leftover dumpling.

"There you go." Cassie deposited the package in front of her, patting it as if it were a pet. "And I thought of something. About that friend of yours."

Anne struggled to keep the eagerness from her voice. "Did you remember someone who knew her?"

"In a manner of speaking. Seems to me she roomed with another one of the summer waitresses—girl named Marcy Brown."

"Is she here?"

Cassie shook her head almost before the words were out of her mouth. "Summer help, that's all she was. Went off at the end of the season. None of those girls stick around once the season's over. No jobs for them."

Anne tried to swallow her disappointment. "Do you know where she went from here?"

"Seems to me she was headed someplace warm for the winter. Key West, I think it was." Cassie's expression showed disapproval. "Those kids...they just flit from place to place. I might have an address for her, if I had to send her last check, but she's probably long gone by now."

"I'd like to have it just the same, if you can find it."

The woman nodded. "See what I can do, when I have the time." She frowned. "There was one other thing."

"What's that?"

"Seems to me both those girls got into that singles group Pastor Richie had at Grace Church. Maybe someone there kept up with her."

"Thank you." She was past worrying about what Cassie thought of her interest. "I appreciate it."

It was something. Not much, but a little something that just might lead somewhere.

And as for the frown in Mitch's brown eyes...well, it wasn't unexpected, was it. She'd just have to live with his disapproval, because it probably wouldn't change.

So, it looked as if he'd been wrong about how helpful Cassie might be. But then, Mitch had been wrong about a lot of things since the moment Anne walked into his life.

Those blue eyes of hers were intent on her prize. This lead to Tina's friend would encourage her. If he didn't get control of her search, she'd be chasing it all over Bedford Creek. And sooner or later someone would find out why.

"I suppose you want to rush off to Pastor Richie right now."

"Maybe not this precise moment. But it is a lead to Tina's roommate."

"That was eighteen months ago. The chance that Pastor Richie knows where to find this Marcy Brown isn't very great."

"I have to try."

A stubborn look firmed her mouth, and he suppressed the urge to smooth it away with his finger. That would really be counterproductive.

"Look, I know Simon Richie. Why don't you let me talk to him?"

"How do you know him?"

She'd probably think this coincidence suspicious, but it couldn't be helped. "Because I go to Grace Church."

Her eyebrows lifted. "Did you also belong to the singles group?"

"No." People went to that, for the most part, because they wanted a social life. He didn't, so he didn't attend. "But I know Simon Richie pretty well. The questions would come better from me."

"I'd rather ask him myself."

Somehow this sounded familiar. If Anne Morden ever depended on anybody but herself, he had yet to see it.

"Look, if you go walking into Simon's office asking about this girl, it's going to make people wonder."

"I don't see why. I'll just say I'm a friend of a friend."

She clearly still didn't see the rampant curiosity with which people in town surveyed her every move.

"Let me find a less obvious way of going about it."

She seemed to be weighing that, and for a moment he thought she'd agree.

"Grace Church...isn't that where Kate belongs?"

He nodded.

"Kate's invited me to go to a church potluck supper with her tonight. I'm sure I'll have a chance to meet your Pastor Richie. I can bring up the subject casually."

He pictured her mentioning it in front of several of the most notorious gossips in town. She was determined, so there was only one thing he could do.

"Fine." He smiled. "I'll pick you up at ten to six, then."

Her eyes narrowed. "What do you mean?"

"Didn't Kate tell you? We often go to the church suppers together." *Sometimes, anyway.*

He was doing what he had to. If he expected to stay in control of this situation, he needed to keep tabs on Anne.

Unfortunately, he had a strong suspicion he had another motivation.

"Well, don't you look nice." Kate turned from the kitchen stove to assess Anne and Emilie. "Both of you."

Anne brushed one hand down the soft wool of her emerald skirt. It matched the green of Emilie's jumper, so she'd decided to wear it. "Is it too dressy?"

Kate shook her head. "You look as pretty as a picture. I'm sure Mitch will say the same."

Oh, dear. There it was again: Kate's insistence on pairing the two of them up like bookends.

When she'd returned to the house earlier and told Kate they

were going to the potluck, the elderly woman had been delighted. Anne had tried to dissuade Kate's all-too-obvious matchmaking, to no avail.

Well, what should she say? That Mitch wouldn't care how she looked? That the only reason he'd decided to take them to the potluck was to keep her from blurting out something indiscreet to Pastor Richie? It was only too obvious that that was behind his sudden desire to go with them.

There wasn't a thing she could do about Kate's misapprehension, so she might just as well change the subject. "Are you sure I can't fix something? Or stop at the bakery and buy a cake?"

"Goodness, no. There'll be more food than we can eat in a week, as it is. Everyone brings way too much stuff to these suppers."

Anne had to smile. Kate's righteous assertion was undercut by the fact that she'd prepared an enormous chicken-and-broccoli casserole, and even now was putting a pumpkin pie into her picnic basket.

"You don't think you're taking quite a bit yourself?"

"This little thing? Why, Mitch will probably eat half my casserole himself. That boy does love home cooking...probably because his mother never had time to cook much for them." Kate's eyes were filled with sympathy. "You do know about Mitch's family, don't you?"

"I know his mother died when he was in high school." She held Emilie a little closer.

"Well, his father had left before that. Poor woman worked to take care of those two boys. I'm sure no one could blame her if she wasn't there to cook supper every night. Or if she went out now and then, just to cheer herself up." Kate yanked open a drawer, muttering to herself about potholders.

Reading between the lines, it sounded as if Mitch had pretty much raised himself. Probably that, along with the military, had made him the person he was.

And what kind of person was that? Anne stared out the window above the sink, where dusk had begun to close in on Kate's terraced hillside garden. A man who'd buried his emotions—that's what she'd thought the first time she'd seen him, and nothing had changed her mind about that. A man who had to be in control, whatever the situation.

That might make him a good cop. But it wasn't a quality, given her strong independent streak, that she'd ever found appealing in a man. Besides, she wasn't interested. In future, her family would consist of Emilie and her, that was all.

She'd told herself she could ignore the attraction she felt for Mitch. Unfortunately, it didn't seem to be working. That attraction kept popping to the surface every time they were together.

Well, if she couldn't ignore it, she could at least control it. She'd remind herself twenty times a day, if she had to, that he wasn't the kind of man for her, even without the complication of Emilie's parentage.

The doorbell rang. Kate, her hands full of casserole, nodded toward the front hallway. "Would you mind getting that, dear? It'll be Mitch, I'm sure."

"Of course." Carrying Emilie, she walked down the hall. This was a good chance to test her resolution. She swung open the door.

"Come in, please. Kate's almost ready."

Mitch stepped into the hallway, seeming to fill it. "Hey, there, Miss Emilie, are you ready to go to church?"

Emilie bounced and held out her arms to him.

"Let me take her."

Anne started to turn away just as he reached for the baby, and his hands clasped her arms instead. For a moment they stood touching, the baby between them.

Mitch's large hands tightened, their warmth penetrating the soft wool of her sweater. They were so close that she could see the network of lines at the corners of his eyes, the sweep of his dark lashes, a tiny scar at the corner of his mouth. Those chocolate eyes fixed on hers, and she could hear his breathing quicken. She had to fight the urge to step forward, right into his arms.

She took a deep breath, released Emilie to him, and stepped back. "I'll just get our coats." Astonishing, that her voice could sound so calm.

Obviously reminding herself twenty times a day wasn't going to be enough.

Chapter Six

It was a good thing Anne had pulled away when she did, Mitch decided as he drove them to the church. A very good thing. Because if she hadn't, he just might have kissed her.

Disaster—that's what it would have been, plain and simple. The woman already suspected him of seducing a young girl and leaving her pregnant. What would she think of him if he tried to kiss her?

He pulled into the church parking lot and found a space. He'd better get his head on straight where Anne was concerned. The best way to deal with his inappropriate feelings was to solve Anne's problem for her so she could leave, as soon as possible. And the next step in doing that was to get the information from Pastor Richie himself, and do it without arousing anyone's suspicions.

"Looks like a good turnout." He held open the door to the church's fellowship hall.

"Goodness, half the town must be here." Kate bustled in, depositing her picnic basket on the nearest table. "Now, Mitch, why don't you get one of the high chairs for Emilie before they're all gone. I'll find us a nice place and introduce Anne around."

A warning bell went off in his brain as he went reluctantly in search of a high chair. Who did Kate have in mind for Anne to meet? He could think of at least a half-dozen gossips of both sexes he'd just as soon she avoided.

He'd have to keep an eye on her while looking for a chance to talk to Simon Richie before she did. Right at this moment, he could use a little help.

And there it was. With a sense of relief, he spotted Alex Caine's tall, lean figure. Alex, like Brett, was a friend he could count on. He'd help keep Anne out of trouble.

He deposited the high chair, muttered an excuse to Anne, who seemed to be avoiding his eyes, and worked his way through the crowd to Alex.

"Alex. I'm glad to see you."

His friend, leaning on the stick he sometimes used since surviving a plane crash a year ago, gave him a sardonic look. "Don't you mean you're surprised to see me?"

He grinned. "That, too." Another legacy of the accident seemed to be that Alex didn't socialize much.

"I decided this was my best chance to see your Ms. Morden. And baby."

"Not my Ms. Morden." *And not my baby.* But he didn't need to say that to Alex. He'd said it once, and it was a measure of their friendship that Alex accepted his denial without question.

Alex's gaze rested on Anne. "Kate seems to have adopted her already. Are you sure it was a good idea to bring her and the baby here?"

"Kate invited them. And once Anne found out Simon Richie might have some information on the girl's roommate, there was no stopping her from coming."

Alex took a step or two toward the wall, so they were safely out of the flow of traffic and of earshot. "Have you remembered anything else about the girl—Tina, was it?"

"Tina." He gave a frustrated shake of his head. "What's to remember? I barely knew her. She was a nice kid who poured my morning coffee, that's it. I can't figure why she'd lie about something like this."

"I'd hate to believe you're never going to know the reason."

He could see Alex's mind ticking over possibilities. Even

back in high school, Alex had always been the one with the analytical approach to everything. Where Brett had relied on charm and Mitch on strength, Alex had been the thinker of the team.

"The roommate's the best bet, I suppose," Alex said. "If anyone knows who the girl dated, she would."

Mitch frowned, watching Anne settle Emilie in the high chair. "It just keeps eating at me. Why me? Why did she give my name?"

Alex was silent for a long moment, so long that Mitch turned to look at him. He encountered a searching gaze. "Have you thought about Link?"

Mitch's stomach twisted at the name. *Link*. His brother. "Yes." He bit off the word. "Of course I have. I know what you're thinking. Using my name would be just the sort of sick joke he'd find funny. But you're forgetting, the girl knew me. Besides, he wasn't in Bedford Creek then."

"You sure?"

"I'm sure." Link had a tendency to show up on Mitch's doorstep whenever he was broke or in trouble. "We had a fight the last time he was here, that previous spring. A bad one. I told him I was done bailing him out. He hasn't been back since." He managed a half smile. "I'd like to believe that means he's gotten his act together, but I doubt it."

"People change."

"Not Link." *Not our father.*

Alex shrugged. "I'll take your word for it. Look, they're starting to get the food ready. You need my help with something before I round up my son for dinner?"

"Just keep an eye on Anne. I want to see Simon alone before she has a chance to collar him. But I don't want her getting the third degree from any of our local busybodies."

"And you expect me to prevent that?" Alex lifted an eyebrow. "You're underestimating them."

"But I'm not overestimating you." Mitch grinned. "You

know they're intimidated by the Caine name. And you can flatten anybody with that superior look of yours. Just use it.''

Simon Richie charged into the hall then, filled with an energy that never ceased to amaze Mitch. Simon had to be close to sixty, but nothing slowed him down when it came to taking care of his flock. If either Tina or her roommate had left an address, Simon would find it.

''I'm going to try and catch him after he says the blessing,'' Mitch said. ''Remember, keep your eye on Anne.''

Alex sketched him a mock salute. ''Will do.''

He bowed his head and tried to concentrate on the words of the prayer. Simon had an informal way of addressing God that made Him sound like a personal friend Simon was inviting to share their meal. It always made him vaguely uncomfortable. Mitch believed, of course. But Simon seemed to have found a closeness that had always eluded Mitch.

The prayer over, a wave of people swept toward the long serving table. Anne still stood at her chair, eyes closed in prayer for another moment. The sight seemed to clutch his heart. What prayer kept her so still, so focused?

Anne gripped the plate Kate had given her and edged closer to the serving table. Kate had insisted on watching Emilie so she could go first, since Mitch seemed to have disappeared. She'd noticed him talking to a man Kate said was Alex Caine, owner of Bedford Creek's only industry. The next time she looked, he was gone.

Not that she cared. The memory of that moment in Kate's front hall made her uncomfortable. She hadn't come to this dinner to be with Mitch.

''I don't think we've met.'' The woman in front of her smiled a welcome. ''Let me introduce you to some of these hungry people.''

By the time she'd reached the end of the buffet table, half-a-dozen names buzzed in her mind and way too much food had found its way onto her plate. She'd begun to feel that all she'd done since arriving in Bedford Creek was eat.

"I'm finished." She deposited her plate across from Kate, next to the high chair Mitch had put at the end of the table. "You go on now, Kate."

Kate rose and looked around the crowded room with a frown. "I don't know where Mitch is. He'd better get back here before the food's gone."

"I don't think there's any danger of that." And she'd probably have a more placid meal if he weren't sitting next to her, drawing her awareness with every breath.

She'd just given Emilie a biscuit to chew on when she became conscious of someone standing across from her. She looked up to meet an intent stare.

The older woman's narrow face formed a brief smile. "You'll be Kate's new guest."

Anne nodded. "Anne Morden. This is Emilie."

"I'm Enid Lawrence." The woman's gaze swerved, sharply curious, to the baby and back again. "Tell me, what brings you to Bedford Creek?"

Anne should have been better prepared for a direct question, she thought. As she groped for an answer, someone intervened.

"Excuse me, Enid." It was the man she'd seen Mitch talking with earlier. "I think your daughter is trying to get your attention." He diverted the woman smoothly away from the table, taking the chair she'd been blocking. "I'll keep Anne company until Kate gets back."

Enid Lawrence frowned. For a moment Anne thought she'd argue, but then she nodded, giving Anne a frosted look. "We'll talk later." It almost sounded like a threat.

She moved away, and Anne assessed Mitch's friend, Alex Caine. He was tall, nearly as tall as Mitch, but not as broadly built. His lean, aristocratic face was handsome, but marred by a scar that ran along one cheek. He had the inward look Anne had seen before in people who lived with pain.

"Alex Caine." He held out his hand. "Sorry if I interrupted, but Enid can be overwhelming at times. 'Curiosity' is her middle name."

She lifted her eyebrows. "Did Mitch suggest I needed protecting?"

She caught a flash of surprise mixed with amusement in his dark eyes. "You caught us, I'm afraid. Mitch thought you might prefer not to explain why you're here too many times tonight."

Now it was her turn to be surprised. "Mitch told you?" She'd have expected him to guard that information more carefully.

"Mitch and I go back a long way. He doesn't keep many secrets from me. Or from Brett."

"I see."

He frowned. "I'm not sure you do. I know Mitch as well as I know anyone. He tells me he didn't—" He stopped, probably reminded of the number of people in the room. "Let's just say I'd trust him with my life." Some emotion she couldn't identify flickered in his eyes. "In fact, I already have."

A dozen questions bubbled to her tongue, but she didn't have a chance to ask any of them. Kate came back, and in the flurry as she settled, Alex excused himself. The next instant, someone slid into the chair next to her. She didn't need to look to know it was Mitch. That aura of solid strength touched her senses.

He brushed her sleeve. She looked, startled, to find he was handing her a slip of paper.

"What's this?" She started to unfold it, but his hand closed over hers.

"It's that information you wanted—"

His fingers tightened a little, and her skin seemed to tingle from their pressure.

"—the latest address and phone number Pastor Richie could find. I had him jot it down for you."

She looked at the address, somewhere in Florida, written in an unfamiliar hand on church stationery. She folded the paper and slipped it in her bag.

"I didn't expect you to do that. Thank you."

"My pleasure." A smile tugged at his mouth. "No ulterior

motives, I promise you. I just thought it would cause less comment if I asked. I hope you find her.''

Perhaps he didn't expect her to believe that, but it sounded genuine. He'd given the information to her, rather than following up on it himself. Almost as if they could trust each other.

Careful, her lawyer's mind cautioned. *Look at all the evidence, then make a decision.*

She'd like, just this once, to rely on her instinct, the instinct that said he was telling the truth. That he could be trusted.

Unfortunately she couldn't. Not with Emilie's future at stake.

Anne rolled the stroller through the police station doorway, the memory of the last time she'd done that flickering through her mind. Only a few days ago, but it seemed like a lifetime. Odd, that she'd begun to feel at home in Bedford Creek so quickly, almost as if it had been waiting for her.

"Ms. Morden!" Wanda exclaimed. "Look who's here, Chief.''

Mitch stood in the doorway to his office, ushering someone inside. He swung around at Wanda's words. Anne wasn't mistaking the warmth in his eyes at the sight of her, was she?

"Anne. I hoped I'd see you today.'' He sent a glance toward his office. "Trouble is, I have someone here right now. Can you wait?''

Aware of Wanda's sharp eyes dissecting every gesture, Anne nodded. "Actually, I have a couple of errands to run. Why don't I come back in, say, half an hour.''

"Sounds good.'' He reached past her to hold the door for the stroller, and his hand brushed her shoulder. "I'll see you then.''

She pushed the stroller up the sidewalk, still feeling that casual touch. When the number Pastor Richie had passed on proved no longer valid, directory assistance and even the pastor had been unable to help her further. She had no choice but to ask Mitch for his help in tracking down Marcy Brown. But now she wondered if she'd made the right decision in bringing this to him. Everything Mitch had done was consistent with his being an honorable man who was telling her the truth. But could she rely on him to trace Tina's roommate?

The street staggered its way up the hill, and by the time she reached the pharmacy she was winded. She purchased shampoo and a teething ring, then glanced at her watch as she went out the door. Another fifteen minutes before Mitch expected her.

Someone had placed a bright yellow bench outside the pharmacy, probably for the convenience of all those tourists everyone assured her showed up in the summer. She sat down, positioning the stroller so the baby was out of the wind. The weak sunshine touched her cheeks, a promise of summer to come. A fat robin, back from his trip south, perched on the edge of a sidewalk planter and cocked his head.

A shadow fell across her. "Ms. Morden."

She looked up at the woman who'd introduced herself at the church supper the night before—the woman Alex had seemed determined to help her avoid. Her mind scrambled briefly, then came up with a name.

"Mrs. Lawrence. It's nice to see you again." Or was it? Alex had steered the woman off, implying she was a gossip, and that avid look in her eyes seemed to confirm it.

"I hoped I'd run into you." The woman perched on the bench next to her, tucking her brown wool coat around her legs. "We didn't have a chance to get acquainted last night. I'm Enid."

"I met so many people last night. Your congregation is so friendly to a stranger. It made me feel at home."

"You're from Philadelphia." The woman made it a statement, as if docketing facts. "Kate told me that. But she didn't say why you're here."

Anne edged an inch farther from that blatant curiosity. "Didn't she?"

Enid Lawrence shook her head with an affronted look, as if she had a right to every morsel of knowledge she could collect. "She didn't. It's not to see Chief Donovan, I hope?"

Anne weighed the probable results of outright rudeness in

deterring the woman and decided even that wouldn't work. "Not exactly," she evaded. "Bedford Creek is so charming. I understand you have quite a lot of visitors."

"Tourists." She sniffed. "But I'm glad you're not here to see that Mitch Donovan."

The venom in the woman's voice startled her. Everyone she'd met thus far seemed devoted to Mitch. Enid Lawrence seemed to be the exception.

Enid apparently took silence for interest. "He's not really one of us, you know."

"One of us?" She'd certainly had the impression Mitch had grown up in Bedford Creek. What was the woman driving at?

"He's a Donovan." Enid sniffed again. "Everyone in town knows what the Donovans are like. Worthless, the lot of them. The father would steal anything that wasn't nailed down, and those boys were just as bad. Carousing, getting into one scrape after another. Troublemakers, both of them. As for the mother and her drinking..."

The venom had spilled out so quickly that Anne hadn't had time to react. Suddenly revulsion ripped through her with an almost physical shudder. She got up quickly. "I'm afraid I have to go."

Enid frowned. "I'm just telling you because you're a newcomer. I wouldn't want you to be taken in."

"I don't care to discuss Chief Donovan with you." Her anger surprised her. Shouldn't she be taking the opportunity to find out anything she could about Mitch? Instead, she felt the need to defend him.

The woman rose, bringing her eyes to a level with Anne's. "Fine, if that's all the thanks I get for taking an interest. Mitch Donovan wouldn't even be here if Alex Caine didn't owe him something."

Anne managed to get the stroller out from beside the bench, her hands shaking a little. "Excuse me, please."

She swung the stroller around and set off downhill, heels clicking in her rush to get away from the woman. No wonder

Alex Caine had intervened last night. The woman was absolutely poisonous.

Her words trickled through Anne's mind. Mitch was not trustworthy—that was the gist of it. The woman was convinced Mitch was no good, apparently because of his father's reputation.

Unfair, her instincts shouted. That was unfair. The woman had no right blackening Mitch's reputation because of what his father had done.

But she'd also talked about trouble Mitch and his brother had gotten into, had implied that made him not trustworthy. Trusting him was what she was about to do. And it was something she didn't do easily.

Her impetuous charge down the hill had already brought her to the police station. If she saw Mitch while Enid Lawrence's bitter words echoed in her ears... Fair or not, she just couldn't do it. She'd have to go back to the house and think this over.

"Anne." Mitch opened the door and held it for her. "I've been watching for you. Come in."

She could feel herself flushing. "It was nothing important. I don't need to bother you now."

His brown eyes seemed to frost over. He stepped onto the walk and closed the door. "Don't you mean you've just had an interesting discussion with Enid Lawrence?"

She felt as guilty as if she'd sought out the woman. "How did you know she was talking to me?"

He jerked his head toward the bench outside the pharmacy. "I was watching for you to come back. I saw your little chat."

"I certainly didn't instigate it."

"You didn't avoid it, either." His jaw looked tight.

Her faint feelings of guilt changed to anger. "I walked away from her, in case you didn't notice. I'm not interested in gossip, even if—"

"Even if it supports the things you'd like to believe about me?"

His expression froze as a passerby eyed them. She seized a chance to gain control.

"I didn't go looking for the woman." She lowered her voice. "I'm not soliciting gossip about you, if that's what you think."

That probably was exactly how it looked, and there wasn't a thing she could do about it.

Or maybe there was.

The words pressed on her lips, wanted to be said. She could take the woman seriously or not. If she didn't, there was an easy way to prove it, by asking for his help.

She took a deep breath. "Now can we forget Enid Lawrence?" She wasn't sure she could, but she wanted to try. "I need your help. I want you to help me find Marcy Brown."

A few minutes later they walked back toward the house together, in tacit agreement that the subject was better discussed away from the station.

Anne looked carefully at her feelings. Could she forget Enid's poisoned words?

"Worried about it?"

She glanced up at Mitch, startled and guilty, then realized he was talking about the roommate, not about what Enid had said.

"No, not worried, exactly." She could hardly tell him she was trying to sort out her opinion of him. "Concerned about the time element, I suppose. How will you try to find Marcy?"

"Plenty of ways to track people down." He frowned. "The trouble is, this isn't a police case. It limits what I can do."

That hadn't occurred to her. "What *can* you do?" She hoped her question didn't sound as sharp to him as it did to her. If he couldn't or wouldn't use police resources, what good had it done to ask him?

"Believe me, if people knew how easy it is to get information on them, they'd be shocked. I can follow up on her social security number and credit reports, for a start."

"That should lead somewhere, surely. It's not as if the woman is trying to hide from us. She doesn't know we're looking for her."

"We'll find her." He slowed while she eased the stroller over a bump in the walk. "I just hope she knows something useful."

"Girlfriends do talk to each other."

He nodded. "That's about what Alex said. He thinks Tina had to have confided in someone, and who better than her roommate."

"I hope we're both right." She stuffed her hands in her jacket pockets. "He surprised me last night. When I realized you'd told him, I mean."

"We don't keep many secrets from each other."

It was much the same thing Alex had said. "He told me he'd trusted you with his life." She hadn't intended to say that, and knew it sounded like prying.

"Ancient history."

Enid had implied Alex's friendship was somehow owed to Mitch, and the thought left an acrid taste in her mouth. She didn't want to think that about either of them. She wanted to believe they were who they seemed to be.

"Is it something you can talk about?"

His gaze rested on her face for a long moment, then he shrugged. "If you want to hear it. It's not a big secret. Just some trouble we got into when—"

He stopped abruptly, then swung away from her. "Just a second."

Before she could say a word, he'd vaulted over the picket fence in front of the house they were passing. He plunged into the shrubbery by the porch and emerged a second later with a wriggling captive. Davey Flagler.

Apparently Mitch's police instincts never shut off. That was something important to remember as she tried to understand him. He was always a cop.

Chapter Seven

Great. As if things weren't already bad enough, now Davey had to act up again. Mitch tightened his grip on the boy, who wiggled like a fish on a hook.

He couldn't kid himself. Anne's opinion of him had probably taken a nosedive after her little chat with Enid Lawrence, and no wonder. He could just imagine what Enid had to say about him and his family.

Davey was going to make matters worse. Anne would go into her defense attorney mode; she wouldn't be able to stop herself. And they'd be adversaries again, armed with their own visions of what was right.

Well, it couldn't be helped. He had a job to do, and he was going to do it, regardless of what Anne thought of him.

"Trespassing, Davey?" He eyed the culprit. "You wouldn't have been thinking about that package on Mrs. Jefferson's porch, now would you?"

"I don't know what you're talking about." Sullen black eyes stared up at him. "You're crazy."

Over the boy's head he caught the flicker of surprise that crossed Anne's face. She hadn't noticed the package, any more than she'd noticed the kid. Being a cop had heightened his ability to register what other people didn't.

"Crazy?" He glared at Davey. "I'd be crazy to take your word for anything. Go ahead, tell me what you were doing in Mrs. Jefferson's yard."

"I wasn't after any package." Davey nearly spat the words at him. "I thought I heard a cat."

He could almost see the wheels turning in Davey's brain as he tried to come up with a plausible story. At least the kid wasn't an accomplished liar—yet.

"It looked like it was hurt." Davey put on a righteous expression that wouldn't have convinced the most gullible person in the world. "I was just trying to help. You always think I'm doing something wrong."

"That's because you usually are." Anger surged, and he shoved it down. A cop had no right to feel anger. That wasn't part of his job. Mitch didn't know why Davey set off a firestorm within him every time he dealt with the kid, but he had to stay detached.

"The boy didn't actually take anything, as far as I can tell." Anne's intervention didn't do a thing to douse his anger. "Only because I grabbed him first," he said, tightening his grip as Davey wiggled again. "Guess I'll have to speak to the delivery man about leaving things on porches. Looks like that's just too much temptation."

"You're declaring him guilty without any evidence at all." Anne's eyes shot angry sparks. "You don't know what was in his mind."

"Just stay out of it, Counselor. I don't need advice on how to do my job."

"Maybe you do. You can't accuse someone of something that hasn't been done yet."

"Look, this isn't the big city." Anne would never understand what things were like in a small town. Or why.

"Believe me, I'm only too aware of that. You wouldn't get away with this there—not without someone filing a complaint, anyway."

He counted to ten. It didn't help. "A cop in a small town is different. People expect us to anticipate trouble, and most times we can. And they expect us to prevent it, not wait around until it happens."

He had a sudden mental image of himself explaining, talking too much in front of the kid, and knew it was because he wanted Anne to think well of him. And that was probably an impossible goal.

"You can't—" she began.

"Yes, I can."

He turned to the still squirming boy. He had to concentrate on his job, not on what Anne thought of him.

"I want to see you and your father at the station tomorrow, right after school."

"But my dad might have to work. Or maybe—"

"No excuses, just be there. Because if you're not, I'll come after you. Got it?"

Davey's mouth set, and he nodded.

Mitch released his grip. Davey didn't bother trying to act macho. He just ran.

Mitch watched him go, then turned back to Anne, knowing he'd see condemnation in her eyes.

"I suppose you're proud of yourself, bullying a boy like that."

"What do you know about 'a boy like that'?" His anger flared again, startling him.

"I know anyone would respond better to kindness than to threats."

"Kindness!" She didn't understand. She never would. "Let me tell you what it's going to take for Davey Flagler to turn into a decent citizen instead of winding up in big trouble. He's going to have to work harder, perform better, be smarter than anyone else, because he's starting a lot of steps behind. And he won't do that if people make excuses for him."

Anne looked at him for a long moment, blue eyes blazing in a white face. "Are you talking about Davey Flagler? Or are you talking about yourself?"

She didn't wait for an answer. She walked away quickly, head high, pushing the stroller toward Kate's place and leaving Mitch fuming.

Hours later Anne slowed as she approached the front porch of Mitch's house. She stopped just beyond the pool of light from the street lamp. When she'd told Kate she needed to talk to Mitch, Kate had been only too eager to watch Emilie for her.

The windows of his small house glowed with a warm yellow light. She shivered, huddling a little deeper into her jacket. The temperature had dropped like a stone the moment the sun went down, and the stars were crystalline in a black sky.

She couldn't stand out here in the dark and the cold. She might as well march right up to the door and get this over with.

Her cheeks went hot in spite of the cold air. She couldn't believe she'd spoken to Mitch the way she had. Even if she had been right, they didn't have the kind of relationship that allowed her to say something so personal.

Lord, I'm sorry. I let my temper get the better of me again. I acted as if I knew what was right for everyone.

Confessing her mistake was one step in the right direction. Now she had to tell Mitch. She bit her lip. She had to tell him, because that was the right thing to do. It was also the only way to get things back on an even keel between them. That was all she wanted.

She went quickly up the steps and rang the bell.

Mitch opened the door, a dark bulk against the light behind him in the hallway. She couldn't make out his expression, which might be just as well.

"Anne. I'm surprised to see you."

He said the words in such a neutral tone that she didn't know what to make of his mood. "I came over to apologize." It was better just to blurt it out. "I said things I shouldn't have this afternoon, and I wouldn't want you to..."

The sentence died out. The problem was that she really did think she knew why he reacted to Davey as he did. She just didn't have the right to say so.

"Forget it." He stepped back, opening the door wider. "Come in. You don't have to stand out there in the cold."

"I shouldn't. I left Emilie with Kate, and I wouldn't want to impose." And going into his house felt like stepping too far into his life.

He moved under the light. "I'll bet Kate is having the time of her life. If you come back too soon, she'll be disappointed."

He gestured. "Come in, please. We can't talk with you hovering on the doorstep."

He was probably right about Kate. She stepped into the tiny hallway, and he closed the door behind her.

"In here." He ushered her through an archway on the right. "Make yourself comfortable. I have coffee brewing."

Before she could protest, he'd vanished through the door at the back of the hall. She shrugged, turned to the archway, and stopped in surprise. Whatever she'd expected of Mitch's house, it wasn't this.

Pale yellow walls and warm wooden wainscoting set off a living room that might have appeared in a country living magazine. The room was brightened with chintz; braided rugs accented the wide-paneled wooden floors. A fire burned cheerfully in the brick fireplace. It certainly didn't look like any bachelor's apartment she'd ever imagined.

She crossed slowly to the fireplace. It took a moment to realize what was missing. There were no family pictures. Mitch had a family-oriented room without any hint of family. In fact, only one photo graced the mantel. She moved closer, holding out her hands to the blaze, and looked at it.

Mitch, Brett and Alex. She should have expected that. They couldn't have been much more than high school age in the picture, but she recognized each of them at first glance. The photo had been taken outdoors, with the three of them lined up on a log.

"Looking at the three monkeys?" China mugs rattled on a tray as Mitch came in with the coffee. He put the tray on the coffee table and came to stand next to her.

Too close, that was all she could think. He stood too close for her peace of mind. He was dressed as casually as she'd ever seen him, in jeans and a cream sweater that made his skin glow. She couldn't breathe without inhaling the faint musky scent of his after-shave lotion.

She forced herself to concentrate on his words. "Why three monkeys? You mean like 'hear no evil'?"

"Something like that. It's what Brett always calls that picture."

Something almost sad touched his eyes as he looked at it, and she found herself wanting to know why. "You were pretty young there, weren't you?"

"Teenagers." He shrugged. "Thought we had the world by the tail, like most kids that age."

He gestured toward the couch, and she sat, then wished she'd taken the chair instead. He left a foot between them when he sat beside her, but it was still too close.

Businesslike, she reminded herself. *You want to get things back on a nice, businesslike basis.*

Then he smiled at her over his coffee mug, and her heart thumped out of rhythm. They were alone together. Maybe she should have brought the baby, as a sort of buffer between her and Mitch.

"I really am sorry." She hurried into speech, because it seemed safer than sitting in silence.

"Forget it."

"Have you?"

"No," he replied.

She met his gaze, startled, and he gave her a rueful smile.

"I decided I'd better not forget it, because I think you're right."

That smile was doing such odd things to her that she wasn't sure she could say anything intelligible. Luckily, he didn't seem to expect anything.

"I've been sitting here going over it. Trying to be angry." He frowned into the flames. "Instead, I kept seeing Davey's face, thinking about his family. Wondering if you're right about me." He shrugged. "It would account for a lot."

"Your family..." She stopped, remembering the unpleasant things Enid had said about his family. About him.

His face seemed to freeze. "I could never count on my family for anything."

"I'm sorry." It seemed to be all she could say.

He reached forward, picking up a poker to shove a log into place. The flames leaped, casting flickering shadows on the strong planes of his face.

"When I look at Davey, I guess I see the kid I was. Running

the streets with no one who cared enough to make me behave myself.''

Maybe it was safer to keep the focus on Davey, instead of on Mitch. "Does Davey have anyone?" she asked.

"Just his father." His expression eased slightly. He'd probably much rather talk about Davey than himself. He leaned elbows on his knees, letting the poker dangle. "Ed Flagler doesn't mistreat the boy, as far as we can tell. He just doesn't pay attention to him. Davey's headed for trouble if something doesn't change."

Obviously she'd been wrong. He did care what happened to the boy.

"You're planning to talk to the father. Do you think you can get through to him? Make him see the damage he's doing to his son?"

"It's worth a try." His mouth tightened into a grim, painful line. "At least he's still there. That counts for something."

Pain gripped her heart suddenly, but it wasn't for Davey. It was for Mitch. He betrayed so clearly the lonely boy he'd been. Maybe he still hadn't admitted to himself how much his father's leaving had hurt him.

This house—she glanced at the room with new eyes. Mitch hadn't just bought a place because he was tired of renting. He'd created a home here—the home he'd never had before.

She cleared her throat, trying to suppress the tears that choked her. "If talking to the father doesn't do any good, what will you do about Davey?"

"Guess I can't just throw him in a cell." He sent a sideways glance at her. "Some smart lawyer would probably get after me if I did that."

"Probably," she agreed.

"So I'm going to put him to work."

"Work? Isn't he kind of young for that?"

He shrugged. "Never too early to learn the value of work, especially for a kid like Davey. I figure I'll offer to pay him for doing some odd jobs around the station, maybe even around here. That might make him see he doesn't have to steal if he wants something."

He understood the child better than she'd thought. He was going to a lot of trouble for Davey.

"Better watch out. He might start looking up to you."

His mouth quirked. "That'll be the day. Far as he's concerned, I'm the enemy."

"It's pretty obvious the boy needs a role model. Maybe he's found one."

Some emotion she couldn't identify shadowed his eyes. "I'm not setting myself up to be a substitute father. With the example my father set for me, I don't know how."

There wasn't anything she could say to that, was there? But it was pretty clear that her goal of getting things back to a businesslike basis between them was doomed to failure.

The pain in her heart for the lonely boy who lurked inside him told her she'd already started to care too much.

What was the matter with him? He was saying things he'd never said to a living soul. Not even to Alex, though Alex probably guessed most of it. Somehow in a few short days, Anne Morden had managed to touch a part of him he'd closed off a long time ago.

She looked as if she didn't know what to say. *Change the subject,* that was what he had to do. Get off the painful topic that touched too close to his heart.

He nodded toward the mantel photo of himself with Brett and Alex. "That picture was actually taken on the trip I started to tell you about today."

"Trip? Oh, you mean the incident Alex mentioned."

"Our adventure." He felt his voice get lighter as he steered away from the painful subject of fatherhood.

"I'm almost afraid to ask what kind of adventure, especially since Alex seems to think you saved his life."

He shook his head. "Alex exaggerated. If anything, he saved my life. Or maybe we all saved each other's lives."

Anne picked up her coffee mug and leaned back. The plain gold band she wore on her right hand winked in the firelight. "That sounds like a story."

Probably she was as glad as he was to get off painful subjects. "Our senior camping trip. The three of us were assigned to work together. We were orienteering—you know, finding our way in the woods with just a map and a compass."

"I know. Believe it or not, I went to summer camp once upon a time. I can even build a campfire."

"You get the idea, then. We were supposed to find our way to a meeting point. Trouble was, nobody'd counted on Brett losing the map. Or on a torrential rainstorm. The three of us ended up trapped in a quarry with the water rising." Amazing that he could smile about it now. "It was like every bad disaster movie you ever saw."

"It doesn't sound like much fun to me. How can you joke about it?"

"You know what teenage boys are like. We thought we were indestructible. Right up until the moment we realized we might not get out."

He'd been making light of it, but all of a sudden the memory got a little too real. He felt the cold rain pelting his face, felt the wind threatening to rip his slicker from his back. Felt his hands slipping from cold wet rock.

"What did you do?"

"First we blamed each other. Then we fought about how we were going to get out."

"That sounds predictable."

"That almost got Alex killed."

In an instant he was back in the quarry, grasping Alex's hand as the water pulled at him. His hand slipping, muscles screaming...

"What happened?"

"Brett and I managed to get him onto a rock." They'd huddled, drenched, clinging to each other, sensing death was only a misstep away. "That got us smart in a hurry. We prayed. And we realized working together was the only way we'd ever get out."

He'd never forget the next few hours. They'd struggled up the rock face, helping each other, goading each other on. They'd finally reached the top, exhausted but alive.

"No wonder you've stayed close all this time. It changed your lives."

She was too perceptive. She saw right through him, saw the things he didn't say.

"I guess it did." His voice had gone husky, and he cleared his throat. "Before that, I figured people were right about me, so what was the use of trying? Afterward...well, it seemed that if God bothered to pull me out of that quarry, He expected something from me."

"That's when you went into the military?"

He nodded. "Nobody needed me here." She probably knew he was thinking of his family, disintegrated completely by that time, thanks to his father.

She reached toward him, as if to offer comfort. But when her hand touched his, something far more vivid than comfort flashed between them.

Firelight reflected in the eyes that met his—wide, aware.

He shouldn't. But he couldn't help it. He leaned forward until his lips met hers.

The kiss was tentative at first, and then he felt her breath catch. Her lips softened against his. He drew her closer, inhaling the warm sweet scent of her. He didn't want this to end.

Her hands pushed against his chest, and he released her instantly.

She drew back, cheeks flushing, eyes not quite meeting his. "I think I'd better go." She shot off the couch.

Choking down his disappointment, he nodded.

He could try to pretend it hadn't happened, but that wouldn't work. He'd blown it. This time he'd really blown it. He'd given in to the need to hold her, and now she'd never want him near her again.

Chapter Eight

Mitch shoved his desk chair away from the computer hard enough to hit the wall. Why wasn't he finding anything on the elusive Marcy Brown? It was as if the woman had vanished off the face of the earth.

Wanda would probably do this search better than he could, but he wasn't about to involve her in it. No, he'd just have to struggle on and hope he didn't drive himself crazy before he came up with something.

He couldn't kid himself that his current state of frustration had much to do with his lack of success. The problem gnawing his gut and tangling his nerves was a lot more personal than that: Anne, and last night's kiss.

How had he let himself do that? In fact, how had he let the entire situation happen? He'd told Anne things about himself that he'd never told anyone else, and what he hadn't told her she'd guessed. And then he'd capped his indiscretion by kissing the one woman in the world he should have had sense enough to keep his hands off.

The trouble was, he'd let himself become attracted to Anne. He frowned at the chair where she'd sat that first day, when she'd dropped her bombshell into his life. She'd been an unwelcome intrusion, maybe even a threat. Now…

Now she'd become important to him. But even if it hadn't been for the complication of Emilie's parentage, she was out of his league. And even if none of that existed, there would still be an impenetrable barrier between them. All she wanted was a family, and that was the one thing he'd decided a long time ago that he'd never have.

His fists clenched on the arms of the chair. *The apple doesn't fall far from the tree. Those Donovans are all alike.* You hear that often enough when you are a kid, you get the message. He wouldn't risk being the kind of father his had been.

He reached toward the keyboard. *Find Marcy Brown.* That was the only useful thing he could do.

The telephone rang. He frowned, snatching it up. Hadn't he told Wanda not to disturb him?

"Mitch, Wanda said you were busy, so don't you go blaming her." Kate sounded more flustered than usual. "I just had to talk to you, and I've got to leave in a few minutes."

"Leave? Where are you going?" Kate never left the bed-and-breakfast when she had a guest. It was unheard of.

"My sister's had a bad fall, maybe broken her hip." Kate's voice trembled on the verge of tears. "I just don't know, at her age, what we'll do if it's broken." She took an audible breath. "I've got to go, right now."

"Of course you do," he soothed. "I'm sure Anne won't mind moving to another bed-and-breakfast, under the circumstances."

"Well, we've got that taken care of. Anne says she'd rather stay here, since she's got the baby settled and all. There's plenty of food in the kitchen, and she says they'll be just fine."

"Then you don't have to worry, do you? You just get on to your sister's and call if there's anything you need."

"That's just it. I need your help."

"You've got it." Kate surely knew by now that she could count on him.

"I want you to look in on Anne and the baby. Promise me, now."

"I'm sure Anne..."

Doesn't want me looking in on her. That's what he wanted to say, but he couldn't.

"Please." Worry laced Kate's voice. "Anne didn't feel well

when she came in last night, I could tell. I want you to check on them.''

If Anne hadn't felt well, it was probably because of what had happened between them, but he could hardly say that to Kate.

"All right. I promise I'll look in on Anne and the baby."

And somehow or other I'll keep my hands off her and my feelings in check.

"Are you sure you're going to be all right?" Kate hovered at the door, car keys in hand, a worried expression on her face.

"We'll be fine," Anne said for what seemed the tenth time. Kate's worries about her sister were undoubtedly spilling over onto everyone else. She balanced Emilie on one hip and gave Kate a reassuring smile. "We're used to being by ourselves, don't forget."

"You've been looking a little pale since last night." Kate frowned. "Are you sure..."

"I'm fine." *Except for a monster of a headache and the feeling I've made a complete fool of myself.* "You go on. And if there's anything else you want me to do here, just call and let me know."

Kate nodded, finally edging her way out the door. "Mitch will be by to see if you need anything. He promised."

She felt the smile stiffen on her face. "He doesn't have to do that."

"I'll feel better if he does." Kate turned, waved bye-bye to Emilie, and started down the steps. Apparently the thought that Mitch was in charge gave her enough confidence to leave.

Anne closed the door and leaned against it. The last thing she needed or wanted was to have Mitch checking up on her. After last night's fiasco, she didn't know how she'd manage to look him in the eye.

What had gotten into her? She'd practically invited him to kiss her. And when he had, she'd bolted like a scared rabbit.

She hadn't been prepared for the devastating effect of his lips on hers—that was the truth of the matter. She'd been in-volved in the closeness of the moment, responding to his openness with her. She'd told herself they were becoming friends. The next moment they'd touched, and she'd known this was something much more powerful than simple friendship.

She rubbed her temples wearily. Maybe if she could get rid of this headache, she could think about the whole subject rationally. Her cheeks felt hot, and her ability to reason seemed to have vanished. Emilie's teething had given her a restless night and too much wakeful time remembering that moment in Mitch's arms.

"How about a nap?" She stroked the baby's cheek. "Okay? Emilie will take a nap and Mommy will, too. Then we'll both feel better."

And then maybe she could get her composure back in place before she saw Mitch again.

It was nearly suppertime, and none of those things had happened. Emilie fussed, chewing restlessly on a teething biscuit, then throwing it on the floor. The fourth time Anne picked it up, she decided her head would probably explode if she bent over one more time.

You couldn't get sick if you were a single parent. She'd come to that realization at some point in the last few months. You just couldn't, not unless you had a reliable baby-sitter on tap. At home in Philadelphia there were a half-a-dozen people she could call.

But she wasn't at home, and the only person she knew well enough to call in Bedford Creek was the one person she definitely would not call.

She bounced the wailing baby on her hip and started down the stairs. She'd better get the teething ring she'd put in the refrigerator to chill. Maybe that would soothe Emilie.

A wave of dizziness hit her halfway down. She sat abruptly, clutching Emilie, and leaned her head against the rail.

"It's all right." She patted Emilie, wishing someone would say that to her. "It's going to be all right. We're fine."

The knock on the door sounded far away, too far away for her to do anything about it. Maybe whoever it was would just go away.

Thirty seconds later the door clicked open. Mitch appeared in the hallway. "Anne?" He looked, then took the steps two at a time and knelt beside her. "What is it? What's wrong?"

"Nothing." She made a valiant effort to straighten up. "I'm fine."

"Funny, you don't look fine. Your cheeks are beet red, and your eyes are glazed."

"Thanks," she muttered. She should have been offended, but it took too much effort.

He put his hand on her forehead. His palm felt so cool. She just wanted him to leave it there until the throbbing in her temples went away.

"You're running a fever." He touched Emilie's cheek. "What about the baby? Is she sick, too?"

She struggled to concentrate. Okay, she was sick. No wonder she felt so bad. "Just teething, I think."

"Come here, little girl." He lifted Emilie from her arms. "Are you feeling cranky? Let's give Mommy a rest."

To her astonishment, Emilie's wails ceased. The silence was welcoming.

"Thank you." She forced herself to focus. "If you could just bring me her teething ring and a bottle, maybe I can get her settled."

"Settled? You don't look capable of picking up a marshmallow, let alone a baby." His arm went around her. "Come on. I'll help you to bed."

She couldn't resist leaning against that strong arm, even though she knew she shouldn't. "I'm fine, really I am."

"I know." He sounded amused. "You can do it yourself. But this time you can't, literally."

He stood, taking her with him, apparently not having a problem carrying the baby and lugging her, too. She forced herself to put one foot in front of the other, aware Mitch was almost carrying her.

When they reached the suite, he plopped Emilie in her playpen, to which she immediately objected. Anne winced at her cries and reached for her.

"No, you don't." Mitch steered her toward the bedroom.

"The last thing that baby needs is to get whatever bug you have. Do you want me to call a doctor for you?"

She shook her head, the movement making her wince again. "It's probably just the twenty-four-hour virus Kate says has been going around. I'll be fine, honestly."

"After you get some rest." He half carried her to the bed and sat her down. "Don't worry. I'll take care of Emilie."

She wanted to object, but the bed felt so good after a mostly sleepless night. She slid down bonelessly, her head coming to rest on the cool, smooth pillow.

"Just a little nap," she murmured. "Then I'll be fine."

"I'll bring you some water." Mitch pulled up the quilt and tucked it around her gently. Her eyes closed. She thought she felt his fingers touch her cheek, and then she heard him move away.

Just a short nap, that was all she needed. She slid rapidly toward sleep. Just a short nap.

The baby was still crying. Well, one thing at a time. Mitch crossed to the playpen and picked up Emilie. This time no magic happened—she continued to wail, although the volume decreased.

"Okay, little girl, it's okay." He bounced her on his hip the way he'd seen Anne do when she fussed.

"Everything's going to be all right. Mitch will take care of you."

Yeah, right. It was one thing to give a baby a bottle and then hand it back when it cried. Taking complete care of one was something else entirely.

Emilie seemed a little calmer when he talked, so he did his thinking out loud. "I guess I could call somebody else to help. Wanda, maybe."

It seemed to be working. The baby's sobs quieted to whimpers, and she looked up into his face.

"But do I really want to do that? Open us up to her curiosity? No, I don't think so."

Besides, he'd told Anne he'd take care of them.

"So I guess you're stuck with me." He smiled at Emilie.

She smiled back, and he felt as if he'd struck gold. "Let's get some water for your mommy, and we'll look for that teething ring she mentioned."

He tickled Emilie, getting a belly laugh that startled and amused him, then headed for the kitchen.

It was harder than it looked to manipulate a glass of ice water, a bottle of aspirin and a baby. He didn't want to put her down, because she might start crying again. He had an uneasy suspicion that if she did, he wouldn't find it so easy to stop her.

"Okay." He stuffed the aspirin bottle in his back pocket and set the water pitcher back in the refrigerator with his free hand. "Let's get this up to Mommy. Maybe I'll have to ask her where the teething thing is."

He started to close the door, then realized that pink, gel-filled donut looked out of place in Kate's refrigerator. "Hey, is this yours?" He held it out to Emilie, who grabbed it and stuffed it in her mouth. "I guess so."

He picked up the glass. "One more time up the stairs, okay?"

Emilie seemed content to be put in her playpen now that she had the teething ring to chew on, so he deposited her and tip-toed into the bedroom.

Anne lay on her side, one hand under the pillow. Her black hair tumbled about her face, curling damply on her neck. He brushed it back, resisting the urge to let his fingers linger against her soft cheek.

"Anne." He hated to disturb her, but she probably should take something for the fever.

She stirred, and her eyes opened, focusing on him.

"I brought you some aspirin and a glass of water."

She nodded, propping herself on one elbow long enough to down the tablets with a thirsty gulp of water. "Emilie..."

"Emilie's fine. I found the teething ring, but you'd better tell me what to feed her and when."

"I'll get up." She started to push the quilt aside, and he tucked it back over her firmly.

"No, you're not getting up. I can feed Emilie. Just tell me what I need to know."

She sank back on the pillow, apparently realizing she wasn't going anywhere very soon. "The baby food's down on the kitchen counter. Give her—" she frowned, as if trying to concentrate "—give her something with meat and a fruit. That'll be fine for now."

Her eyes drifted closed.

Which fruit? he wanted to ask. *What about a bottle?*

But already she'd slid into sleep, her breath soft and even, her lashes dark against pale skin. She looked vulnerable, and he had a ridiculous urge to protect her. He shook his head. In such a short time she'd touched some tender place in his soul, and he wasn't sure how he was going to get her back out again.

Mitch went quietly back out to the living room of the suite and looked down at Emilie, who was gnawing on the teething ring. "Well, I guess it's just you and me, kid. Tell you what, you cooperate, and we'll get along just fine."

Supper, he decided. Feed her, and then she'd go to sleep, right? He carried her down to the kitchen.

Luckily, Kate had already set up a high chair. Unluckily, Emilie didn't seem to want to go into it. She stiffened her legs, lunging backward in his arms.

"Come on, sweetheart. A little cooperation here."

Emilie didn't agree. Trying to put her in the high chair was like trying to fold an iron bar.

He'd seen Anne put some small crackers on the tray when they'd been in the café. Maybe that would work. He gazed around the kitchen, looking for inspiration. He found a small box of crackers stacked with the jars of baby food. Quickly he shook a few onto the tray.

"Look, Emilie. You like these."

She stopped in mid-cry at the sight.

Holding his breath, he slid her into the high chair. She snatched one of the crackers and stuffed it in her mouth.

"Okay, one problem solved." He fastened the strap around her waist, then turned to the array of baby food on the counter. "Let's see what looks good."

Actually, as far as he was concerned, none of it looked good.

He reminded himself that he wasn't eight months old. Maybe to Emilie this stuff looked like filet mignon.

He heated up the chicken-and-rice mixture.

"Here we go, Emilie." He shoveled a spoonful of chicken into her mouth.

She smiled, and most of the chicken spilled right back out of her mouth, landing down the front of her ruffled pink outfit.

Half an hour later Emilie was liberally sprinkled with chicken, rice and pears, to say nothing of the cracker crumbs. Also well adorned were Mitch's shirt, the high chair and the floor. The way things had gone, it wouldn't surprise him if some of the chicken had found its way into the house next door.

"Maybe we're done." He lifted her cautiously from the chair, holding her at arm's length, a new admiration for Anne filling him. She did this every day, and she didn't have anyone to spell her.

"Okay, let's get you cleaned up." He glanced at his shirt. "Me, too."

He carried her upstairs and eased open the door to the bedroom. Anne slept, still curled on her side. He tiptoed to the bed and touched her forehead. Her skin seemed a little cooler than it had earlier, unless he was imagining things.

Okay, he could do this. He carried Emilie into the bathroom. He looked at the tub, then shook his head. No way. Emilie would do with a sponge bath tonight.

By the time they were finished, Emilie was clean and he was wet. He bundled her into a sleeper and carried her out to the playpen. She settled without a murmur.

He stretched out on the couch, wedging one of the small pillows under his head. He closed his eyes. Peace, heavenly peace...

Sometime later a piercing wail split the air. He catapulted off the couch, heart pounding. Emilie. He reached her in a second, bent to scoop her up.

"Hey, it's okay. Don't cry."

The wail went up in volume and in pitch. Anne would never be able to sleep through this, would she?

But apparently she could.

"Shh, Emilie, it's all right. Don't cry, okay?" He felt like crying himself. If there was a more helpless sensation in the world than this, he didn't know what it was.

"It's all right. Honest." He bounced her, walking across to the windows, then back.

Strangely enough, that seemed to soothe her. The wails decreased. He settled her against his chest and turned to walk the length of the room again. Maybe he could walk her back to sleep, then get some rest himself.

That was only half right. Emilie dozed against his chest, her head nestled into the curve of his neck. But the instant he tried to put her down, her eyes popped open and the wail started again.

Okay, that wouldn't work. Looked like he'd have to keep walking.

This wasn't so bad, was it? He circled the room for the twentieth time or so. He'd walked guard duty longer than this and been more tired. He could do it. It might not be the way he'd pick to spend this evening, but he could do it.

His father's face flickered briefly in his mind, and he banished it instantly. He didn't think about Ken Donovan, not anymore.

But his father wouldn't have put in a night like this—not in a million years.

Chapter Nine

Anne came awake slowly, pushing herself upward from fathoms-deep sleep. Something was wrong, and for a moment she couldn't think what it was. Then she realized it was the first morning in months Emilie hadn't wakened her.

She shot upright in the bed, then grabbed her head. The headache had disappeared, replaced by the sensation that her head was about to drift off into space. Slowly, cautiously, she swung her feet over the side of the bed.

Mitch had been here, hadn't he? Or had she dreamed it? No, of course she hadn't. Mitch hurrying in the door, helping her up to bed, saying he'd take care of Emilie.

The crib was empty. Where was Emilie?

She forced herself to her feet and stumbled to the door, yanked it open. Emilie—

Mitch lay on the floor, sleeping. He cradled Emilie between his arms. She slept, too, her head pillowed on Mitch's chest. His strong hands held her firmly even in sleep.

She could fall in love with this man.

The realization hit her like a kick to the heart, followed immediately by a wave of panic. What was she thinking? She didn't intend to fall in love with anyone, certainly not with Mitch.

She tiptoed across the rug and reached for Emilie. Her touch was so gentle that the baby didn't wake, but Mitch's arms tightened instantly. His eyes flickered open, warming when he saw her. He smiled.

Her breath seemed to stop. She wanted to reach out to him, to touch the firm lines of his face, to wipe away all the reserve that hid his feelings. She wanted...

She took a step back. This was dangerous. She couldn't let herself feel this way.

"Good morning. Feeling better?" Mitch shifted position, and Emilie woke. She cooed, patting Mitch with both small hands.

"I'm fine. Really." Anne reached for the baby. "Let me take her. Goodness, I never expected you to stay all night. You should have wakened me."

He grinned. "That would have taken an earthquake. Besides, we got along fine." He stood, still holding the baby. "I'm not sure you should be up yet. You look a little dizzy."

"I just need a shower to clear my head. Then I'll be okay. Really, you don't have to do anything else. I'm sure it's time for you to get ready for work." And the sooner he was out of here, the sooner her breathing would return to normal.

He glanced at his watch. "It's early yet. Suppose I take Emilie downstairs and start some breakfast while you get that shower. Then we'll see how you feel."

Anne would have argued, but he was already out the door with Emilie. Short of chasing him down the stairs, there wasn't much she could do. And a shower might clear her head and help her get rid of thoughts about Mitch that didn't go anywhere.

Standing under the hot spray helped her body, but it didn't seem to be doing much for the rest of her. Her heart and mind still felt jumbled with confused feelings. She couldn't—shouldn't—feel anything for Mitch under these difficult circumstances.

She tilted her head back, letting the water run down her face. After Terry's death, she'd made a deliberate decision that she'd never marry again. Maybe she wasn't cut out for marriage; maybe she just didn't have the capacity for closeness that it required.

It might be different with someone like Mitch. The thought slipped into her mind and refused to be dislodged.

By the time she dried her hair and pulled on a sweater and slacks the light-headedness had eased. She certainly wouldn't be running any marathons today, but she could take care of Emilie. Mitch was probably itching to get out of here.

The picture that met her eyes when she entered the kitchen didn't suggest any desire on Mitch's part to run out the door. He was spooning cereal into Emilie's mouth, sipping at a mug of coffee between bites. Both of them seemed perfectly content. Mitch looked too casually attractive with a slight stubble of beard darkening his face.

"You didn't need to do that. I can feed her."

"Hey, I'm just getting good at this." He caught a bubble of cereal that spilled out of Emilie's mouth when she smiled. "And this time I remembered the bib."

The coffee's aroma lured her to the counter, where she poured a steaming mug. "You tried to feed her without a bib? That must have been messy." She should have told him that when she'd explained about the food, but her mind had been so foggy, it was a wonder she'd said anything coherent at all.

"Messy isn't the word for it. We both needed a complete washup afterward, to say nothing of the kitchen."

Guilt flooded her. Emilie was her responsibility, not his. "You should have wakened me."

"Really?" He lifted an eyebrow, and amusement flickered in those chocolate-brown eyes. "If Emilie's screaming didn't wake you up, I don't think I could have."

"I'm so sorry." Embarrassment heated her cheeks. "I never should have…"

"What? Gotten sick? Give yourself a break, Anne. You're not some kind of superwoman."

"I know, but I still feel guilty leaving Emilie to you when she's teething and miserable."

He paused, spoon half in Emilie's mouth, looking at the baby intently. "If that clink I just heard means anything, the teething problem might be solved for the moment."

"Really?" She hurried around the table and bent over Emilie. "Let Mommy see, sweetheart." She rubbed Emilie's gum, feeling the sharp edge of a tooth. "Look at that! Emilie got a new tooth."

Mitch's smile took in both of them. "Good going, Emilie."

The baby cooed. The image of the three of them, smiling at each other, seemed to solidify in Anne's mind. It might almost be the picture of…a family.

She blinked rapidly. She shouldn't think things like that. "I can finish feeding her."

"No, you can sit down and eat something, so you won't almost pass out on me again. How about some cereal? An egg?"

Actually, she did feel a bit hollow inside. "Maybe a piece of toast."

Mitch reached out to put two slices of bread in the toaster. "Will you please sit down? You're making me nervous."

"I didn't really pass out." Her memory of those moments on the stairs was a little fuzzy, but she was sure of that. She sank into the chair he pushed out for her. "I'm grateful you came in just then. I'm not sure what we'd have done without your help."

"Kate made me promise to check on you two. I guess she knew what she was doing." He scooped the last spoonful of cereal from the bowl and offered it to Emilie, but she turned her head away.

"Better stop there," Anne advised, grinning. "Her next move will be to swat the spoon, and you'll be coping with flying cereal."

"You're the mommy. I guess you know best." He set the bowl on the table. "Anything else I should give her?"

"Let her work on that bottle of juice." He'd turned her thanks away so easily that she felt compelled to say something more. "I want you to know how much I appreciate your help. Getting sick is a big problem when you're a single parent. You don't have anyone to spell you."

He nodded. "Believe me, sometime in the wee hours I got the picture. Parents should come in sets, if possible." His smile turned into a searching look. "I guess you and your husband must really have wanted a family."

It was a natural assumption. She was tempted to let it stand, but that seemed wrong.

"I don't think having a family was ever part of Terry's idea of marriage. He saw us as the classic yuppie couple—two jobs, no kids." Her mouth twisted a little. "He never seemed to want more than that. Two busy professionals with no time for kids and not much time for each other."

She hadn't intended to say that much, and surprise at her candor mingled with embarrassment.

His hand covered hers for a brief moment, sending a flood of warmth along her skin. "I guess that's why you feel the way you do about Emilie."

"She means everything to me." She blinked back the tears that suddenly filled her eyes.

Emilie, apparently feeling she'd been out of the conversation long enough, pounded her bottle on the tray. "Ma, ma, ma, ma, ma!"

"The experts say that's babbling, but I think it's 'Mama.'" Anne covered her ears in mock dismay at the onslaught of noise. "Oh, Emilie, stop."

Mitch caught the flailing bottle, closing his large hand around Emilie's small one. "Hey, little one, enough."

Emilie fastened her wide blue gaze on him. "Da, da, da, da, da!" she shouted.

Anne didn't know which of them was the more embarrassed. Mitch's cheeks reddened beneath his tanned skin and hers felt as if they were on fire.

"It's just nonsense syllables," she said quickly. "She doesn't know what they mean." Embarrassment made her rush to fill the silence with words. "Not that you wouldn't—I mean, I'm sure you'd make a great father." The words slipped out before she had time to think that they might not be wise.

His face tightened until it resembled the mask he'd put on against her that first afternoon in his office.

"I guess that's something I'll never know. I decided a long time ago I wasn't cut out for fatherhood."

She must have murmured something, but she wasn't sure what. She was glad she hadn't believed in that image she'd had of the three of them as a family. For a lot of reasons, it was clearly impossible.

Mitch's office was his refuge. Trouble was, it didn't seem to keep out thoughts of Anne.

Her vulnerability. Her strength. Her determination to take care of the child she saw as hers.

He'd tried to tell himself that last night was nothing—or at least, the sort of thing he'd do for anyone. But he couldn't. It was just too tempting. He'd been part of their lives last night, hers and Emilie's. He'd been important to them in a personal way—not as a cop, but as a husband, a father, would be.

One night. He shoved his chair away from the desk. It had only been a few short hours. Maybe he'd held up to that, but in the long run, there were no guarantees he wouldn't turn out to be just like his father. He wouldn't wish that on any kid.

The sound of raised voices in the outer office interrupted the uncomfortable thoughts. He opened the door to find Wanda and Davey glaring at each other, toe to toe.

Wanda turned the glare on Mitch. "You were the one who hired this twerp. Are you going to let him get away with this?"

He suppressed a sigh. "Maybe I could tell you, if I knew what he'd done."

Wanda flung out her hand toward the big front window. "I told him to wash the window. Did he do it? No! He messed around and let the cleaner dry on the window, and now it looks worse than it did before. He ought to be paying me if I have to clean up after him."

"You're not going to clean up after him."

"Go ahead, take her side. I figured you would." Davey threw down the roll of paper towels. "I'm getting out of here."

Mitch grabbed the kid. The look in the boy's eyes was familiar. He knew what that feeling was, because he'd been there himself. It was wanting someone to care whether he'd done something right or not, and being afraid of that wanting.

"Davey's going to do it again, and this time he'll get it right. That's what I'm paying him for."

"What if I don't want your stupid old job?"

This was familiar, too. He knew what it was like to want to bite someone for taking an interest.

"You don't have a choice, remember? Your father and I agreed you'd work for me, and I'd forget the little incident with the package." Anne would probably call it blackmail, but if it worked, it was worth it.

"All right, all right!" Davey snatched up the roll of towels. "I'll do your stupid windows, but then I gotta get home for supper."

"If he's going to do that window, you can stay right here and watch him." Wanda planted her hands on her hips. "Baby-sitting isn't in my job description."

"Baby-sitting! Who you calling a baby?"

Mitch gestured Wanda toward her desk and turned Davey to the window. He wasn't going to give up on the kid, not this easily.

But what had happened to the quiet life he'd had before Anne walked into it?

The late afternoon sun warmed the air enough to flirt with spring as Anne pushed the stroller up Main Street. Getting out for a while was a good idea. She'd hung around the house until she'd begun to drive herself crazy.

Thinking about Mitch too much, remembering those moments in the kitchen this morning—she couldn't dwell on it. There wasn't anything between them and there never would be, because he was determined to avoid the very thing that had become the most important in the world to her.

So she wasn't going to think about it anymore. She and Emilie would enjoy the sunshine, she'd pick up a few things at the grocery store, and they'd have a cozy supper, just the two of them. They didn't need anyone else.

"Ms. Morden! How nice to see you out and about. I heard you were sick."

Pastor Richie hurried down the sidewalk, beaming at her.

"I'm fine now, thank you." And how on earth had he heard about it so quickly? "Just one of those twenty-four-hour viruses, I guess."

He shook his head. "Nasty things going around." He bent to pat Emilie's cheek. "This beautiful little one didn't get anything, I hope."

"Nothing but a brand-new tooth." She couldn't help sounding like a proud mama some of the time.

"Well, isn't that nice." His round, cherubic face grew a bit serious. "Have you had any luck with your efforts to find that young lady you were looking for?"

"No, not yet. Mitch is checking out some leads."

"I looked back over the roster of the singles group for that time, and it jogged my memory. Ellie Wayne was a member then, and I believe those girls hit it off. She might have stayed in touch."

Anne's pulse jumped a notch at the possibility. "Is this Ellie Wayne still in town?"

"Goodness, yes. She runs the gift shop just the other side of the police station. Would you like me to ask her about the girl?"

"Thanks, but I'll do it." She couldn't help the size of her smile, which probably betrayed the fact that her interest was far from casual. "That's so nice of you. Thank you."

"My pleasure." He beamed at them both impartially. "Will I see you in church this Sunday?"

"Yes, of course. We're looking forward to worshiping with you. I hope the baby's not a problem."

He patted Emilie's cheek again. "How could she possibly be a problem? We have a nursery, but if you feel more comfortable keeping her with you, that's fine."

How much was she giving away to his wise eyes? He seemed to guess or to know more than she'd said.

"Thank you. We'll see you Sunday, then."

A lead, at last, she thought, pushing the stroller forward with renewed energy. And it was one she could follow up herself. She didn't need to involve Mitch at all, which was probably for the best.

She walked on down the street. Many of the shops were closed, probably until spring. She looked up at the mountain ridge. The faintest greenish haze seemed to cover it—not spring, but maybe a hint of it.

The bell over the gift shop door tinkled as she lifted the stroller up the step from the street. The mingled aroma of herbs, dried flowers and candles swept over her.

"Help you?" The woman behind the counter wore her thick dark hair in twin braids that swung almost to her waist. She had a strong, intelligent face, innocent of makeup, and a welcoming smile.

"Just looking."

Anne lifted the baby into her arms. Trying to push the stroller along the narrow, crowded aisles would be a recipe for disaster.

"Are you interested in something special?"

She glanced around. It would probably be diplomatic to buy something. "I'd like a dried-flower arrangement. Something with mauve and blue in it."

"This way." The woman came out from behind the counter. "You're Chief Donovan's friend, aren't you? Staying at The Willows?"

She couldn't get away from the mention of him, not in this town. She nodded. "Anne Morden."

"Ellie Wayne." She touched Emilie's hand. "What a beautiful baby."

"I think Pastor Richie mentioned your name to me. We were talking about a…well, a friend of a friend who used to be in the singles group with you. Marcy Brown. Do you remember her?"

Ellie nodded, her eyes assessing Anne.

"I just wondered if you happened to have her current address."

"Why do you want it?" Ellie's question was blunt.

"We had a mutual friend who passed away a few months ago. I wanted to let her know." And ask her some questions, too.

"I'm sorry." Ellie's eyes darkened with sympathy. "I have an address from a Christmas card, if that'll do you any good.

I think she was moving, but her mail might still be forwarded. So I guess a letter could reach her.''

''I'd really appreciate it.'' A few-months'-old address was better than nothing.

''I'll get it for you.''

As the woman moved away, the bell on the door jingled.

Anne turned. Mitch stood in the doorway, and her heart was suddenly thumping loud enough for her to hear.

Chapter Ten

What exactly is Anne up to now? Mitch had glimpsed her from the window where he was supervising Davey's reluctant cleaning. He'd expected her to turn into the station and had been ridiculously disappointed when she'd gone past. And somewhat surprised when she'd walked into the gift shop.

Her slightly guilty expression told him she was doing something she thought he'd disapprove of—some sleuthing, in other words. If she had some reason to believe Ellie knew something, he wanted in on it.

"I'm helping a customer. I'll be with you in a moment." Ellie gave him a wary look. He didn't think she disliked him; the uniform raised that response in people sometimes. Ellie was generous with others, cautious with him.

"I know." He responded with a bland smile. He turned to Anne. "I'm surprised to see you out already. You must be feeling better."

"Yes, I'm fine." That faint flush in her cheeks probably wasn't from the fever. She was embarrassed at being caught.

"Excuse me, Chief." Ellie brushed past him to lift down a dried-flower wreath, which she held out to Anne. "What about this one?"

Anne touched it gently. "It's beautiful. Did you make all these yourself?"

Ellie smiled at the praise. "And the baskets. Some of the pieces are on consignment from local artists."

Anne had managed to get more out of Ellie in two minutes than Mitch had in two years, he thought. But he didn't think she had come in here just because she liked Ellie's crafts.

"I'll take this one. And I'd love to have that address, if you don't mind writing it down for me."

Ellie glanced from her to Mitch, then nodded. "It'll be in my files in the office. I'll get it."

When she'd disappeared, he lifted an eyebrow at Anne. "Address?"

"It seems she received a Christmas card from Marcy Brown."

"She just happened to volunteer that information?"

"No, of course not. I asked her."

He suppressed a flicker of irritation. "I thought we agreed you wouldn't go around town asking questions of everyone you meet."

"I didn't do any such thing." Her eyes snapped. "I happened to run into Pastor Richie, and he suggested I talk with Ellie. Apparently she and Marcy struck up a friendship in the singles group, and he thought they might have been in touch."

Mitch winced. Looked as if he owed her an apology. Again. "Guess I shouldn't have jumped to conclusions."

"No, you shouldn't have." She sounded as if she wanted to hold on to her annoyance a bit longer. "And how did you know I was here?"

He gestured toward the station next door. "I was standing at the window, supervising."

"Supervising what?"

"Davey's window washing."

He liked the way her face softened at the boy's name. It would be nice to imagine that it did so at the mention of his name, but he doubted it.

"He's been testing the limits to our arrangement, and Wanda refuses to have anything to do with this project."

She actually smiled. Apparently he was forgiven. "You'll do a better job of it, anyway."

"I doubt it, but it's nice of you to say so."

They were standing close together, so close that he could

smell the faint, flowery scent she wore. He had to fight the urge to step even closer.

She looked up at him, and her blue eyes seemed to darken. "I'm sure—"

Ellie bustled in from the storeroom or wherever she'd been, her gaze darting from one to the other of them. "Found it." She waved a slip of paper at Anne.

Anne turned to her with what Mitch suspected was relief. "Thank you. I really appreciate this."

The woman shrugged. "No problem. I'll box up the wreath for you."

Ellie busied herself at the far end of the counter, and an uneasy silence grew between him and Anne. What was she thinking? Was she remembering the moment when they'd kissed? Or was she wishing he'd leave her alone?

Anne glanced up at him. "I wouldn't want to keep you from your work."

That seemed to answer the question. He shrugged. "Yeah, I'd better get back to the station. I'll see you tomorrow."

"You will?" She looked startled and not entirely pleased at the thought.

Well, she'd just have to lump it. "I promised Kate a while ago I'd paint the sunroom for her. Davey and I are going to work on it tomorrow, since it's Saturday."

"I see." She managed a smile, but it didn't look particularly genuine. "I'll see you tomorrow, then."

"One more bite, sweetie." Anne spooned cereal into Emilie's mouth as morning sunlight streamed through the kitchen windows. "We need to get you dressed, because Mitch is coming."

Emilie smiled, cereal dribbling onto her chin, just as if she remembered who Mitch was and looked forward to seeing him.

"There. All done." She wiped away the cereal and put the bowl in the sink. Whether or not either of them wanted to see Mitch was beside the point, anyway. He was coming, and she couldn't do anything about it but try and handle his presence better than she had the day before.

That encounter in Ellie's store had been a miserable display. She'd let her confused feelings for Mitch make her uncomfortable and awkward in his presence.

She had to cope with the attraction she felt for him, and she had to do it now. She couldn't go on this way.

Emilie banged on the high chair tray with both fists, as if in emphasis, and Anne lifted her out. She smoothed the fine, silky hair off the baby's forehead.

Maybe the most important question to ask was whether she still believed him to be Emilie's father. She tried to look at it as an attorney, instead of seeing it personally, but she couldn't separate the two.

Anne had grown to know him too well during her time in Bedford Creek. She'd seen the man behind the uniform and the shield, and she liked what she saw.

Integrity. That was the word for it. Every moment she spent with him made her more convinced he was a man of integrity. Every moment lessened her conviction that he was Emilie's father.

She put her cheek against Emilie's soft one. If her father wasn't Mitch, who was it? Time was ticking away, and she didn't seem to be getting anywhere. Was she letting her tangled feelings for Mitch distract her from what was really important here?

Well, if so, that was coming to an end. Regardless of what she might feel for him, the truth was that there would never be anything between them. Everything else aside, Mitch's attitude toward having children made it impossible.

Being Emilie's mother was a full-time job, and giving Emilie the warm, close family relationship Anne had never had herself would fill the empty spaces in her heart. She didn't need or want anything more.

A clatter on the front porch told her the workmen had arrived. Ignoring the way her heart lurched, she went to open the door with Emilie in her arms.

"Good morning." She caught Emilie as the baby made a lunge for Mitch. "I see you're ready to work." She was going to be pleasant, she told herself. She would act as if none of the events of the last few days had happened.

Mitch had a stepladder balanced on one broad shoulder, and he carried two cans of paint in the other hand. His faded jeans had definitely seen better days, as had the T-shirt that stretched across his chest, showing every muscle.

"We'll have the sunroom looking brand-new before you know it." A smile warmed his face, erasing the remnant of annoyance over their last meeting.

A tingle ran along her nerve endings. Her heart didn't seem to have listened to the lecture she'd just given.

She focused on Davey with a welcoming smile. The boy carried a bucket filled with painting gear and wore a disgusted expression. Obviously, this wasn't his idea of the way to spend a Saturday.

She waved toward the sunroom that adjoined Kate's kitchen. "I'll leave you to it. I'll be upstairs getting Emilie dressed if you need anything."

He nodded. "Come on, Davey. This way."

The boy trudged after him down the hall as if headed to his own execution. Suppressing a smile, Anne started up the stairs. Mitch had his work cut out for him in more than painting.

Half an hour later, Anne admitted the truth. She was delaying returning downstairs, delaying seeing Mitch again; she didn't want to put her resolution to the test. But it was time for that to stop. She picked up Emilie and headed downstairs.

"Goodness, you two are fast." They'd already stacked the furniture in the middle of the room and covered it with a drop cloth.

Mitch looked up from opening a can of paint. "I'm paying this guy by the hour, so I've got to get my money's worth."

"Looks as if you're doing that."

Anne realized Davey's gaze was directed at the baby with a mix of curiosity and trepidation. She smiled at him. "This is Emilie."

He jerked a nod in response, then came closer. "She's pretty little, isn't she?"

"She's almost nine months old." She bounced the baby. "This is Davey, sweetheart."

He took another step closer. "Can she say my name?"

"Probably not. She doesn't say much yet." She tried not to think about the moment when Emilie had looked at Mitch and said "Da-da."

"I never been this close to a baby before." Tentatively, Davey held out one rather dirty hand toward Emilie.

With a happy gurgle, Emilie lunged forward and latched her fist around his finger, smiling.

"Looks as if she likes you," Anne said.

Davey looked at the tiny hand, then up at Anne. "She does, doesn't she."

A smile spread across his face, changing him from the sullen, angry delinquent into a little boy who liked being liked.

That smile... Her heart warmed at the sight. Somehow seeing a smile like that from the boy made Mitch's efforts seem worthwhile.

"I'm sure she does." She glanced at Mitch. Had he seen what she had?

His gaze met hers and he nodded slightly, as if they shared a secret. The intimacy of his look closed around her heart.

She cleared her throat. "I'll put Emilie in the playpen here in the kitchen. That way she can watch you paint without smelling the fumes. They wouldn't be good for her."

Davey nodded gravely, as if storing that information for possible future use. He detached his finger carefully.

"You watch," he said. "You're going to see some good painting."

He returned to the sunroom with determination. Whether it would last or not she couldn't guess, but it was nice to see.

She plopped Emilie into the playpen, sliding it over so the baby had a view of the sunroom. Emilie seemed to enjoy the unusual activity. She clutched the playpen's mesh and watched every movement with wide blue eyes.

Mitch paused, roller in hand. "Have you heard anything from Kate yet?"

She'd nearly forgotten. "She called last night. It looks as if her sister didn't break her hip, after all. She's badly bruised, so Kate plans to stay and take care of her a bit longer, but she sounded very relieved.''

"I'll bet. Kate loves her independence, and I gather the sister can be pretty bossy at times. Kate will be glad when she can get home again.''

"She asked about you." Actually, Kate had asked if Mitch was taking good care of her. "I told her you'd be coming to paint today. She kept saying you didn't need to do it and she could manage herself.''

He grinned. "That's Kate. She's always doing kind things for other people, then is surprised when they want to do something for her.''

Was that behind Mitch's friendship with his elderly neighbor? Maybe Kate had been kind to him at a time when he needed kindness.

"She's a good friend," Anne said.

He nodded, smoothing the roller along the wall in a swath of pale yellow. "The first year I came back, she invited me to spend Christmas with her. Alex and his son had gone away, and I didn't have anyone else. She made it sound as if I did her the favor.''

Anne leaned against the door frame. "I'm sure she enjoyed it as much as you did.''

"She didn't eat as much." He paused, a reminiscent look in his eyes. "She kept saying she loved to see people eat what she'd prepared, so I made her happy.''

"Turkey and all the trimmings?''

"What else would you have for Christmas?''

"Hamburger and fries." The words were out before she knew it.

Mitch stared. "Why on earth would your folks serve that?''

It was clearly not the mental image he had of her family life. She shrugged. "They didn't. They'd gone away for the holidays…Gstaad for skiing, I think. The housekeeper didn't want to fix a big dinner just for the two of us, so we hit the burger hut instead.''

"Sounds like some of the Christmases I remember as a kid.

I always figured other people got the magazine-picture type of Christmas dinner, with the whole family around the table and the father carving a turkey.'' His voice betrayed the longing he'd probably felt as a child for that kind of Christmas.

Her heart clenched. She knew something about lonely holidays. "My ideal of Christmas was always the one in *Little Women,* where they all sacrificed to give to others and didn't need anything but each other to be happy.'' She'd reread that story every year at Christmastime.

"I remember it.'' His eyes met hers. "I'm sorry.''

She knew he wasn't talking about Louisa May Alcott.

She bent over the playpen to hand Emilie a toy. "Actually my happiest Christmases have been the last few, once I figured out what it was we were celebrating.''

"I wanted a bike for Christmas.'' Davey's voice startled her. She'd nearly forgotten the boy was there. "I asked for one last year, but my dad didn't have the money for it.'' He sat back on his heels. "It wasn't his fault, you know.''

"I'm sure it wasn't,'' she said gently. Her heart hurt for him. "Maybe you'll be able to make enough money to buy a bike yourself.''

Davey shot a glance at Mitch, then stared at the paintbrush in his hand. "Maybe.'' He didn't sound very optimistic.

Mitch reached over and touched the boy's shoulder lightly. Davey let the hand stay there for a moment, then pulled back.

Mitch looked at Anne, his smile a little crooked, and she knew he was as touched by the boy as she was. The sudden rapport, the sense of knowing what he was thinking—where had that come from? And what was she going to do about it?

"I'll start some lunch.'' She escaped to the other end of the kitchen, pulling open the refrigerator door to cool her face.

She'd never intended to let her guard down, never intended to see so deeply into someone's heart. She leaned her head against the edge of the refrigerator door. She and Mitch had begun to open up to each other in a way she hadn't expected. Now that he'd come so far into her life, how was she ever going to get him out again?

* * *

Anne pulled the mail from the box and checked it quickly. All for Kate. There was nothing that could be a response to the letter she'd sent to Marcy Brown's last known address.

Shivering a little in the cold wind, she closed the mailbox and hurried back inside. Emilie was napping, and the house was too quiet. She stacked the mail on Kate's hall table. Something to do, she thought. She desperately needed something constructive to do.

Maybe Mitch's inquiries had gotten somewhere. But then, he'd have been in touch immediately.

She'd avoided him for the last few days. Maybe he'd been avoiding her, too, and for pretty much the same reason. After all, they both knew there couldn't be anything between them. The kind of closeness they'd experienced on Saturday could only be bittersweet in light of that. It was safer not to see much of each other, safer not to take the chance of wanting something she couldn't have.

She glanced at the phone. She'd called Helen in Philadelphia yesterday. Helen was the only one of her friends who knew the whole story, and so the only one she could talk to about it.

But Helen had been involved in dealing with a runaway in crisis, and Anne hadn't wanted to tie her up with her worries. So she'd just asked Helen to keep on praying about the situation.

"Always, child." Helen's voice was as warm as her heart. "You know I'm always praying for you and that dear baby God has given you. Trust Him."

Anne was trying so hard to trust.

If only she could think of something useful she could do. She'd tried Cassie again, but the woman hadn't remembered anything more. Then Anne had gotten a list from the pastor of everyone in the singles group. But no one seemed able to help. It was as if poor Tina hadn't made any impression at all in Bedford Creek. And Marcy Brown had disappeared, leaving no trace but a single Christmas card.

She walked restlessly back through the house to the kitchen and picked up the teakettle—

She stood still, kettle in hand, staring out the back window. Why was the shed door standing ajar?

She blinked, leaning a little closer to the window. Mitch had put the stepladder away in there on Saturday; she'd watched him do it. She'd seen him close and latch the door. Now it stood partially open.

Her heart began to thump. She should call the police, she should—

Now, wait a minute. The rational side of her brain kicked in. It was the middle of the afternoon. She was in Bedford Creek, not the big city. Why was she letting her imagination run away with her?

She grabbed her jacket from the hall closet and slipped out the back door. It would only take a moment to check. Probably the wind had blown the door open. Or maybe the latch had broken.

She crossed the wet grass, caught the door and pulled it wide, letting light flood the interior. It showed her the ladder, the lawn mower, the folding chair, an old croquet set.

And Davey Flagler, curled up under a wicker table, sound asleep.

"Davey?"

He woke instantly at the sound of her voice, and sat up so fast that his head brushed the table.

"Are you all right? What are you doing here?"

He slid out from under the table, face sullen. "Just sleeping, okay with you?"

"Seems like a cold place to sleep." Carefully, she thought. She had to handle him carefully. Whatever was wrong, she wouldn't get it by pushing. "Why don't you come in the house where it's warm?"

"Nah." He grabbed a small backpack he'd been using as a pillow. "Guess I'll get going now."

Anne didn't move from the doorway when he approached, and he glared up at her. "You going to let me out, or what?"

"Tell me what's going on, Davey." She gave him a level look. "You obviously should be in class, and here you are sleeping in Kate's shed. Is something wrong at school?"

He stared another moment, then his gaze slid away. His thin shoulders shrugged. ''School's okay.''

''Something wrong at home, then?'' The little she knew about his family situation flashed through her mind.

''Look, I don't have to tell you anything. You're not my boss.''

''No, but I'd like to be your friend. Come on, Davey. Tell me what's wrong. I won't tell anyone else, unless you say it's okay.''

''Promise?'' His tone was skeptical.

''I promise.''

He stared down at the ground, his face troubled as he tried to put on a brave front. ''We got evicted, that's what. Guess my dad was late with the rent again. Landlord threw us out.''

His father must have been very late, if the landlord had gotten far enough in the legal process to evict them. She longed to touch the boy, but he was like a porcupine with all its quills standing on end.

''Is your dad out looking for another place?''

He shook his head.

''Then where is he?''

Davey didn't say anything, and a suspicion grew in her mind.

''Davey, you can trust me. Where's your father?''

He hesitated a moment longer. Then he looked up, and she thought she read fear behind the defiance in his eyes.

''He's gone, all right? He's gone, but he'll be back. I know he'll come back for me.''

Oh, Lord, tell me what to do. My heart is breaking for this poor child, and I don't know how to help him.

Slowly, very slowly, she reached out to touch his shoulder. ''Davey, I think you need some help with this one. You can't hide out in Kate's shed forever, you know.''

''I don't want help!'' He jerked away, fear leaping in his eyes. ''You tell anyone, they'll maybe put me away.''

''Nobody's going to put you away. I'm a lawyer, remember? I won't let them, okay?''

He studied her face for a moment, as if assessing the chance she was telling him the truth. Finally he nodded.

"Okay."

She let out the breath she'd been holding. "Maybe we ought to go down to the police station and—"

He went back a step, shaking his head. "No! I don't want to go there."

"What if Mitch comes here to talk to you? That's all—just talk."

His mouth set, and he stared down at his shoes. "All right," he said finally. "Long as all he wants to do is talk. He starts thinking about anything else, I'm outta here."

Luckily, Emilie was awake when they got into the house. Davey, fascinated, played with her, while Anne called Mitch and explained quickly.

He didn't bother asking for details or second-guessing her actions. "I'll be right there."

By the time Mitch arrived, they were all in the kitchen having a snack. Emilie gnawed on a biscuit while Davey wolfed down one sandwich after another.

"Hey, Davey." Mitch moved into the room easily, his voice low. He seemed to know without asking how skittish the boy was.

Davey eyed him suspiciously over the top of his grilled-cheese sandwich. "You can't put me away. Anne already told me, and she's a lawyer. You can't put me away."

Mitch sank into a chair, reaching out to filch a quarter of a sandwich from Davey's plate. "Who said anything about putting you away?"

"Well, I'm just telling you." Some of the tension seemed to go out of him.

"You do need a place to stay, Davey," she pointed out. "You can't live in the shed."

"I can take care of myself. I'm almost eleven. I don't need anybody."

"You're not going to be put away, and you're not going to live in the shed." Mitch's voice was firm. "Way I see it, you just need a place to stay until your dad comes back. So, I figure the best thing is for you to move in with me."

Chapter Eleven

For an instant after the words were out of his mouth, Mitch couldn't believe he'd said them. What did he know about taking care of a kid, especially one with Davey's problems?

"Do you mean that?" Anne's gaze held his, warning him, maybe, that it was a bad thing to say if he didn't.

"I mean it." It felt right to him. The problem would probably be convincing the kid that it was right.

He glanced at Davey, who was looking at him with a startled, disbelieving expression. Was there a little hope in that look? He wasn't sure.

But he was sure of one thing. He'd begun to take some pride in the way the boy was shaping up, and he didn't intend to give up on him now.

Anne rested her hand lightly on Davey's shoulder. "Seems like a really good idea to me."

It was nice to see the approval in her eyes, but he wasn't doing it for that. He just couldn't let the kid slip through the cracks the way he almost had.

"What do you say, Davey? You willing to stay with me for a while?"

Davey stared at the tabletop, as if fascinated by it. "You don't need to. I'll be okay."

"Davey..." Carefully, now. He didn't want to scare the kid. "I know you're used to being pretty independent. But the law says you can't live on your own yet. So you've got to stay with someone. You have any relatives you'd rather be with?''

The boy shrugged. ''Just my dad.''

It had a familiar, lonely sound that reverberated in Mitch's heart. He didn't want to have to call Child Services on the kid. He wanted to work this out, somehow.

''Well, then, what do you say? I'm not that hard to get along with.''

Davey stared at his hands. ''Okay. I guess so.'' He looked up. ''Just 'til my dad gets back. He'll come back for me.''

''Sure he will.'' Mitch wouldn't dream of challenging the defiant note in the kid's voice. He'd have a look for Davey's father himself, but from what he'd seen, maybe the kid would be better off without him.

He wasn't about to sign on for the long haul, but he could do this much.

He could practically hear Anne's sigh of relief.

''You'll need to get approval as an emergency foster home from Child Services,'' she said. She was thinking like an attorney again. ''I've been through that with Emilie, so I can help you out.''

''Sounds good. I know the caseworkers. I don't think they'll raise any objections to Davey staying with me for the time being.''

He'd always believed God had pulled him out of that quarry all those years ago for a reason. Maybe this was it.

Anne stood at the front window the next morning, watching as Davey, schoolbooks in hand, trudged down the street toward the school. She'd found it surprising how quickly and smoothly the question of Davey's custody had been settled. Maybe it was because Bedford Creek was a small town, or maybe because Mitch was the police chief. Nobody made waves about the situation.

He was now waiting in the doorway, maybe to be sure Davey headed in the right direction. Then Mitch went back inside, and the door closed. Apparently, he wasn't headed to work yet.

Anne stared thoughtfully at the house. If Mitch weren't at

the office, he wouldn't see her heading into Ellie's gift shop. She bit her lip, torn by conflicting arguments.

So far she had nothing, absolutely nothing, to present at the adoption hearing about Emilie's father. Mitch's search had come up empty; everything Anne tried was a dead end.

But Ellie—Ellie might have had more to say if Mitch hadn't walked in on them. Anne could go back to see her. She could even bring up Tina's name and see if the woman remembered anything about her that might be a lead.

Ellie was too bright to interpret a second visit as something casual. She'd know this was important to Anne. She'd be curious; she might talk about it.

But the clock was ticking. Maybe the time had passed for the caution she'd agreed to when she'd come to Bedford Creek. If there was the faintest possibility Ellie had answers, Anne had to go after them.

Kate, who'd returned the previous evening, leaped at the chance to watch Emilie when Anne said she wanted to go out. Anne hurried to the car. It would be faster to drive, with less chance of running into Mitch coming or going and forcing her to explain why she was talking to Ellie again.

A parking space in front of the shop, no other customers... She couldn't imagine why Ellie bothered to open until tourist season, but she was grateful for it.

Ellie raised her eyebrows when she walked up to the counter. "Are you interested in another wreath?"

"Not exactly." How much did Ellie guess of her motives? "We didn't really have a chance to finish our conversation the other day."

Ellie shrugged, dark eyes wary. "We were interrupted, remember?"

"Yes, well, I thought we might talk about it a little more." The woman was so cautious, it was difficult to read her.

Ellie stared at her for a long moment, then leaned against the counter. "Did you have any luck with the address I gave you?"

"Marcy had moved, and there wasn't a phone listing for her. I sent a letter, hoping it would be forwarded, but I haven't heard anything yet." And maybe she never would.

"What else do you want? I don't know any other way to find Marcy. She's not good about keeping in touch, and we weren't best friends or anything."

"I wondered..." This was the tricky part, and there didn't seem to be any casual way to bring it up. "I wondered if you remembered another friend of hers—Tina Mallory."

Ellie stared at her, eyes unreadable. Then she shrugged again. "I remember her. I never knew her very well, though. Are you trying to find her, too?"

Obviously she found Anne's interest suspicious, to say the least. "No. Tina was the mutual friend I mentioned. The one who died a few months ago."

"That young girl?" Ellie's reaction was much the same as Cassie's had been. "That's hard to believe. What happened to her?"

"She had a heart problem that had never been diagnosed." Anne felt as if she were using Tina's death to gain the woman's cooperation. "I know she and Marcy were good friends, and I thought Marcy ought to be told, but I haven't been able to locate her."

Ellie shook her head. "Wish I could help, but I don't know any other way to find her."

"Maybe you remember other friends Tina made when she lived here." Surely she remembered something helpful. "I'd like to get in touch with them, too."

"I can't think of any." Ellie frowned. "She was a dreamy kid, kept pretty much to herself. I never got to know her very well."

"What about boyfriends?" The opportunity was slipping through her fingers, dissolving away into mist like every other lead to Emilie's father.

"Boyfriends?" Ellie looked at her with an expression Anne couldn't interpret.

"Yes, boyfriends." Maybe she didn't sound as pushy as she feared she did. "She was a young girl. She must have gone out with someone while she was here."

"Funny you should ask me about that." Ellie picked up one

of the dried-flower arrangements on the counter, tweaking it as if to keep her hands busy.

"What's funny about it?"

"Funny because you're such good friends with Mitch Donovan."

"What do you mean?" A heavy weight seemed to press down on her, as if she knew the answer before the woman spoke.

Ellie twisted a flower into place, then looked at her. "I thought he was the man Tina dated."

Pain ricocheted through her. It carried a clear message. She'd gotten far too involved with Mitch Donovan—been far too willing to believe him.

She cleared her throat, trying not to let her voice or her face express any emotion at all. "What makes you think that?"

Ellie frowned, dark braids flapping as she shook her head. "Not sure, really."

Anne had to have more than this. "Did you see them together?"

"No...no, I don't believe I ever did. Unless maybe it was at the café. Tina worked there, you know."

"Yes, I know. But you must have some reason for thinking they went out besides seeing Tina wait on him."

Or did she? Anne wondered. Sometimes body language between two people told you all you needed to know about their relationship. Her stomach knotted at the thought.

"Maybe it was something Tina said. Or Marcy said." Her face brightened. "Yes, that's it. It was something Marcy said."

Anne's heart pounded loudly enough for her to hear, but she'd keep her voice level in spite of it. "What did Marcy say?"

"Well, I don't remember exactly."

She gripped the counter, holding back the need to shake the truth out of the woman. "What *do* you remember?"

"Seems to me..." She paused, head cocked as if listening to voices in the past. "I know what it was. Marcy said Tina was crazy about the chief. 'Head over heels in love with him'— that's what she said."

* * *

Head over heels in love. Anne wanted to grapple with Ellie's revelation, to assess it the way she would any piece of evidence in a case, but she couldn't seem to make her mind work that way. Ellie's words had blown a gigantic hole through her heart.

This is crazy. How could her instincts possibly be so far off the mark? She thought she knew Mitch. How could the person who helped her when she was sick, who took in young Davey, possibly have been lying to her all along?

She couldn't reconcile the two images of Mitch. They just didn't fit.

She'd begun to trust him. That was what drove the hurt deep into her heart. She didn't rely on people easily, thanks to her parents' example, but she'd begun to count on Mitch. How could she possibly be so wrong?

There was only one thing to do, one way to cope with this. She'd have to confront Mitch and find out the truth, Anne decided as she left Ellie's shop and got into her car.

But her courage left her when she reached Mitch's house. What was she going to say? How could she believe him?

She had to confront him with it, that was all. Nothing would be more unfair than to condemn him on the basis of a rumor. No matter how difficult, she had to face him. She rang the bell.

She had rung it a second time before she heard answering footsteps in the hall beyond.

"All right, all right." The masculine grumble sounded annoyed. "I'm coming." The door swung open.

"Anne." A quick smile lit his eyes. "Come in." He gestured with the hand that didn't hold the overflowing laundry basket. "I'm getting caught up on a few things before I go to the station."

She followed him into the hallway.

"We picked up Davey's clothes last night. Poor kid doesn't have much, and what he does have needed to be washed." He set the basket down. "I thought I'd…"

He stopped suddenly, his dark brown eyes focusing on her face. He went still, his gaze probing as if he could see into her heart.

"What is it? What's wrong?"

"I... " She opened her mouth, then closed it again. This was so difficult. The home he'd created surrounded her, warm and welcoming. It didn't seem the right place for the accusation she had to make. And she couldn't fool herself, any more than she could fool him. It *was* an accusation.

"Tell me." He reached toward her, but stopped before his fingers touched her arm.

Maybe she was putting out warning signals, she thought.

"What's going on?" he pressed.

"I talked to Ellie this morning." *Just get it out, any way you can.* "I asked her about Tina. She remembered something."

His face stiffened. "It can't have been anything good."

"Why do you say that?"

"Because you look ready for a fight, Counselor."

If he wanted the facts, he was going to get them. "Ellie remembered Marcy talking about Tina. And you."

"There was no Tina and me." He narrowed his eyes. "No matter what Ellie says."

"Ellie wasn't making any accusations." Her voice grew stronger as the woman's words rang in her mind. "She was just repeating what Marcy said."

"And that was...?"

"That Tina was crazy about you. 'Head over heels in love'— that's what she said."

He looked...astonished. That was the only word for it. "Ellie said that? I knew she didn't like me, but I didn't think she'd make up something about me."

"She wasn't. At least, I don't think she was doing anything other than repeating what Marcy had said to her."

"Hearsay, Counselor?"

She stiffened. "We're not in a court of law. I'm trying to find the truth. The two things don't always go together."

"No, I guess not." He took a step toward her. "But I thought we were beginning to trust each other."

She winced at the pain in his voice. That had to be genuine, didn't it?

"I just...I just don't know."

"We're back at the same old impasse then, aren't we." His mouth hardened. "All I can say is that I barely knew the girl. If she had feelings for me, I wasn't aware of it. I certainly never dated her."

"Then why?" Her voice threatened to break. "Why would she say those things?"

She flung out her hands, and the question seemed to vibrate in the air between them.

"I don't know." His voice was heavy, final. "I guess there's nothing else to say."

She swallowed hard. "I guess there isn't. When the DNA results come—"

"When the DNA results come, you'll know I'm telling the truth. I wish you could trust me until then, but it's pretty clear you can't."

Everything in her cried out to believe him. But she couldn't. She could only shake her head and walk away.

Mitch tried to ignore the emotions that surged through him. It didn't work. They pounded at him. Anger, pain, disappointment. He'd thought... *What* had he thought? That she'd begun to care for him? That she returned the caring he'd tried so hard not to admit?

He couldn't deny it now. He looked bleakly at it. He cared for her. And she didn't trust him. That was it, bottom line. She didn't trust him.

Just like his father. Nobody'd trusted Ken Donovan, with good reason. He'd betrayed everyone who'd made that mistake—every friend, every employer. Everyone who'd given him a chance to make something of himself.

And then he'd betrayed his family. To Mitch, looking at that was like looking into a black hole. Worse, it was a hole that threatened to suck him in.

The doorbell rang. Anne? Impossible.

But he crossed the hall in a few long strides, grabbed the knob and flung the door open. And looked into the face of his brother.

"Link."

"Hey, big brother." Link slouched through the door without waiting for an invitation. He dropped an overloaded duffel bag on the floor and turned to Mitch. "Don't look so glad to see me."

In spite of everything that experience had taught him to expect from Link, he couldn't help a surge of affection. Link, looking at him with that boyish grin, hair falling in his eyes, was for a moment the little brother he'd tried to teach and protect.

He held out his hand. "It's been a long time."

Link gripped his hand briefly. "Can't say it looks like much has changed in Bedford Creek while I've been gone."

"Don't suppose it has." Be careful. He couldn't let Link in on the biggest change in Bedford Creek. The one in the house right across the street. Link wouldn't be any support. In fact, he'd probably enjoy seeing Mitch embarrassed.

"Small town attitudes, small town minds." The familiar mocking note came into Link's voice. "How do you stand it?"

"I'm happy here. Some people wouldn't be." He snapped the words.

"Happy? How can you be happy knowing everyone in this town is looking down at you?"

"Nobody looks down at me." His temper flared. That was Link, pushing the familiar buttons. "Not anymore."

"Yeah, right." Contempt saturated the words. "You're the police chief now. That just means they'll use you to clean up their messes. But don't make the mistake of thinking they have any respect for you."

"You'd know a lot about that, wouldn't you? You don't have any respect for anyone or anything."

They were back to the old arguments, the ones they never seemed to get past.

Link shrugged. "I just look at the world a little differently from the way you do. Realistically. Nobody's going to give you a break, so don't expect it, and you won't be disappointed."

Like Anne, who didn't trust him, Mitch thought. He stared bleakly at his brother, wondering how, in a few short moments, Link had managed to zero in on his pain.

Chapter Twelve

Anne looked out the front window the next morning for what must have been the twentieth time. The police car still sat in the driveway, so Mitch hadn't left yet. Also for the twentieth time, she longed to run across the street, to tell him she believed in him. DNA results or not, she believed in him.

But she couldn't do it. Each time she thought she was ready to take that step, something held her back.

When she thought of the pain in Mitch's eyes the day before, she wanted to do whatever it would take to wipe it away.

Then the doubts crept in, poisoning her thoughts. What if she was wrong? What if Ellie's presumption was true? What if Mitch really had been the man in Tina's life?

Why can't I know, Lord? Why can't I know the truth, and then I could trust him?

No calmness came to still the tumult inside her. No answer presented itself, fully formed, in her mind. She didn't know, she just didn't know.

She heard the steps creak outside and turned back to the window in time to see the mail carrier going down. Kate was busy in the back of the house; Emilie safely napping upstairs. She might as well bring the mail in.

Anne carried a fat bundle inside and began to sort it on the hall table. Most of it was for Kate, of course, but—

She stared at the envelope with McKay Laboratories on the return address, and her heart started to hammer uncomfortably.

It was here. The DNA report was here, a week earlier than she'd hoped. When she'd called the lab to give them her address in Bedford Creek, she'd been told they were backed up with tests.

"Anne? Is something wrong?"

She'd been so preoccupied that she hadn't heard Kate come in from the kitchen. The elderly woman was drying her hands on a tea towel, looking curiously at her.

"No, no, nothing." Her face must betray that as a lie. "I'm fine. Excuse me."

Clutching the envelope, she hurried up the stairs. Kate would think her rude, but she just couldn't help it. She had to get away from the woman's curious eyes while she held Emilie's fate in her hands.

She slipped into the sitting room quietly and sank into the nearest chair. It was here, and now that it was, she could hardly bear to open it. She wanted to know; she was afraid to know.

Help me, Lord. Please help me. I'm afraid.

Suddenly the conviction she'd been seeking filled her, taking her breath away. The certainty pooled inside her, deep and sure. It wasn't Mitch. Whoever it was, it wasn't Mitch.

She opened the envelope and pulled out the results. They confirmed what she already knew. Mitch Donovan hadn't fathered Tina's child.

Thank you, Lord. Thank you.

She had to tell him. She folded the envelope and stuck it in her pocket. She had to tell him, now.

Kate stood in the hallway, glancing through a catalog. She looked up as Anne came down the stairs.

"I don't know why they keep sending me these things. I never order anything from them." Her gaze was keen on Anne's face, but clearly she wouldn't intrude.

Anne swallowed hard. She'd like to confide in Kate, but she couldn't. "I need to speak to Mitch for a moment, and Emilie's napping. Would you mind…?"

"Of course not." Kate's response was immediate. "You go on. Take as long as you want."

She'd reached Mitch's door before the thought occurred to

her that he might be angry. He might well say, "I told you so."

Well, he deserved to be able to say it, and she had to give him that chance. She knocked at the door.

Mitch pulled it open, his gaze both surprised and wary when he saw her. "Anne."

"May I come in?"

"Of course." He stepped back, his expression giving nothing away.

She walked in, trying to find the right words. Funny, she'd felt just that way the first time she'd seen him. Apprehensive, tense, struggling to find the right words. Maybe there weren't any.

She swung toward him and held out the envelope. He took it automatically, staring from it to her with a frowning intensity.

"It came." She took a breath. "I want you to know this. I don't see any reason why you should believe it, but it's true. Before I opened the envelope, I knew what it would say. I knew it wasn't you."

He flicked at the opened envelope flap with his finger. "I see you still had to look."

All right, she deserved that. "Yes, I guess I did."

He nodded, his face expressionless. Then he handed the envelope back.

"Aren't you going to look at it?"

He lifted an eyebrow. "Why? I know what it says."

She turned away from that searching gaze. "I wish..." Her cheeks grew warm. "I wish things could have been different. I'm sorry I put you through this. Maybe I never should have come to Bedford Creek."

He took a step closer, not touching her, but close enough that she could feel the heat of his body. "If you'd never come, I'd never have met you."

She tried to smile. "I would think you'd consider that an advantage."

He shook his head. "I'll trade the suspicion for the chance to know you any day of the week."

For a moment her eyes met his. The barriers he usually put

up were gone, and she seemed able to see right into his soul. To see the integrity. He wasn't a man who hid his weaknesses behind a façade. The only thing hiding behind his mask was strength.

He reached out to touch her cheek. His palm was warm and strong against her skin. The feel of him seemed to spread out from his fingers, coursing along her nerve endings, warming her all the way through.

"Mitch." She barely breathed his name.

He slid his hand down her neck, leaving longing in its wake. He grasped her shoulder and drew her toward him.

It was all right now. He hadn't been involved with Tina; he wasn't lying to her. She could trust him. She could let herself care about him. She leaned toward him, expecting to feel his lips on hers.

Instead he held her close, his cheek against hers.

"Will you tell me something?" His voice was soft, a whisper in her ear.

"Tell you what?" How she could think clearly enough to tell him anything, she couldn't imagine. Her mind seemed totally involved in the feel of his cheek was against hers, how strong his muscles were under her hand, how the two of them fit together perfectly.

"Tell me why it's so hard for you to trust."

The words brought her back…back to a world where explanations had to be made, where people had a right to know things, no matter how painful.

She met his eyes. "Are you sure you want to know?"

Mitch watched the play of emotion on her face. She'd come so far into his life in such a short time and now he couldn't imagine doing without her.

"I think I already know some of this. It has to do with your parents, doesn't it?"

He could feel the resistance in her. She didn't want to tell him this. The muscles in her neck worked, as if she had swallowed something unpalatable.

"Poor little rich girl." Her voice mocked herself. "That's what it sounds like, so I don't talk about it."

"You can talk about it to me." He led her to the sofa, sat down next to her. "I want to understand." He managed a smile. "After all, you know the worst about me, don't you?"

She stared down at her hands, still resisting, still holding back. Then she looked up at him, her eyes defiant. "My parents never hit me. They never mistreated me. I had everything I needed."

He rested his hand on the nape of her neck, feeling the tension there. "You couldn't have had everything you needed, or you wouldn't feel the way you do."

Anne stiffened. "There's nothing wrong with the way I feel. I just..."

"You just can't rely on anyone."

"Well, maybe I can't. Maybe people aren't very reliable."

"Some aren't." He met her look steadily. "But some are."

"I guess I have trouble telling the difference. After all, I was married to someone who recreated the same pattern. That wasn't smart, was it?"

Her anger was still there, but he recognized it for the defense it was. If they were ever going to get past this, he had to get her to level with him.

"I think I can almost fill in the blanks." It could be that throwing it right at her was the only way. "Your parents provided you with every material thing you needed. They just neglected the little things—love, attention, support."

"They probably thought they were doing the right things for me. I should have been stronger. I should have been able..."

"What? To tell them how to be parents?" Anger licked along his veins, at two selfish people he'd never known. "They had a beautiful child, and they never bothered to let her know just how precious she was."

"You don't know that."

She tried to smile, but it was a pitiful effort that wrung his heart. He could feel the pride that had kept her silent slipping away.

"I used to think maybe I wasn't pretty enough, or special

enough, or what they wanted." She shook her head. "I used to think if only I'd been a boy, it would have been different. My father always wanted a son."

He slid his hand comfortingly down the long sweet curve of her back. "Used to think?"

She glanced at him, and he saw the tears that sparkled on the verge of spilling over. "Then I met my friend, Helen. And through Helen, I found out I had another Friend. One who considered me precious, even if my parents hadn't."

He nodded. "I thought it was something like that. When I saw the dedication in your Bible."

Her blinding smile broke through the tears that had gathered. "First it was Helen, introducing me to the Lord. And then God brought me Emilie. Once I had a child, I realized how wrong they'd been. Emilie opened me up to a whole new dimension in my life. I could never ignore her the way they ignored me."

The smile hurt his heart. He wanted her to smile that way for him. To light up because he was part of her life, too.

"She means everything to you."

"She means—" Her voice choked a little. "If I have Emilie to love, none of the rest of it matters. If I don't..."

She stopped, and he saw the pain that filled her eyes. Pain and fear.

"What if I lose her? What if I go into that hearing with nothing, and the court decides to put her into a foster home? It could happen. I've seen it happen."

"It's not going to happen. Not to you and Emilie."

He wanted to wipe the fear away, banish it for good. Why couldn't he do that one thing for her? *Assist, protect, defend.* He wasn't doing a very good job of any of those for Anne.

"You don't know that." Her hands clenched. "No one knows."

"Don't." He drew her close against him, wanting only to comfort her. "Don't torture yourself like this."

"I can't help it." She turned her face into his chest, and he felt her ragged breath on his skin through the thin cotton of his shirt.

"It's going to be all right." He cradled her face between his palms so he could see her eyes, will her to believe him. "You've got to hold on to that."

Her gaze locked with his, and as her eyes darkened, all the breath seemed to go out of him. Her lips were a scant inch from his, and he longed to close the gap, to taste her mouth, wrap his arms around her and not let go. But how could he? What she needed from him was comfort now.

Then she lifted her mouth to his, and all his rational thought exploded into fragments. He drew her closer, the blood pounding through his veins. Her mouth was warm and sweet, and the two of them fit together as if they'd been made for each other.

This was right. It had to be.

"Well, well—"

The voice was like a splash of icy water in Mitch's face.

"—looks like my big brother has company."

Mitch let her go so suddenly that for an instant Anne was totally disoriented. She had to force herself out of a world that had included no one but her and Mitch. Someone else had come in. What was a stranger doing in Mitch's house?

Except that it wasn't a stranger. Mitch had said his name. *Link.* This had to be the brother—the one Mitch didn't want to talk about.

"Mitch, aren't you going to introduce me to your friend?" He crossed toward them from the hall, his walk an easy slouch as different as possible from Mitch's military bearing.

Mitch didn't speak, and his silence made her nervous. She held out her hand.

"I'm Anne Morden." She bit back any further explanation. To say anything more would show her embarrassment, would imply she had some reason to feel embarrassed.

Link took her hand, holding it a bit longer than was necessary. "Link Donovan. Mitch's little brother."

He was slighter than Mitch, not quite as tall or as broad. But the same dark-brown hair fell on his forehead, longer and more unruly than Mitch's military cut, and the same chocolate-brown eyes assessed her.

"Link is here for a visit. A brief one." Mitch seemed to make an effort to rouse himself from his silence.

"He works out west."

"Sometimes." Link eyed him. "Sometimes my travels bring me back to Pennsylvania, and good old Bedford Creek. My big brother would rather I stayed out west."

"I didn't say that." Mitch grated the words.

Anne looked at him. Mitch had the closed, barricaded look he'd worn the first time she met him. She thought she sensed anger seething underneath, but he obviously didn't intend to let it out.

"Close enough." Link shrugged. "But here I am back again, like the proverbial bad penny. And Mitch still wishes I'd go away."

That was clearly an appropriate time for Mitch to protest that he didn't want to be rid of his brother, Anne thought. But he didn't. He just gave Link that daunting stare.

She, at least, would have found it daunting. But Link seemed unaffected.

He shrugged. "Well, guess I'll let you get back to…whatever it was you were doing."

He sauntered back out again, and in a moment she heard the front door slam.

She'd opened her mouth to say some conventional words, but Link had gotten out the door before she could muster them.

Mitch shot off the couch. He strode to the window and looked out, as if assuring himself that Link was gone. "Sorry. Link just showed up yesterday. He does that."

"Not very often, it seems." She tread warily, not sure of his feelings.

"It's been two years," Mitch said. "I could see your mind working when you looked at him. You were wondering if he could be Emilie's father."

"I suppose I was." That should hardly surprise him, under the circumstances. "I wonder that about every man I meet in Bedford Creek."

"You don't need to wonder about Link." His voice was harsh. "I know exactly when he was here last. Two years ago next month, right at Easter. Wanting me to bail him out of trouble again, like he always does.''

His anger seemed all out of proportion, and she felt her way, unsure what was driving it. Or what she could do to defuse it.

"And did you help him?"

Mitch's frown darkened. "I lent him money again. Although I don't think *lend* is the right word, since he's never repaid a cent. And then I told him it was the last time. That he'd better find someone else to get him out of trouble, because I wouldn't do it again.''

Thoughts tumbled through her mind, most of which were probably better not expressed. "I see." But she didn't.

"I never figured I'd say that about my own brother. When we were kids, I used to think we'd always be best friends."

He went silent, and she tried to find the words that would get him talking again.

"I always dreamed of having a brother or sister," she began. "I imagined it would be the best thing, to have someone to share things with."

"There wasn't much to share at our house." His mouth became a thin line. "Except maybe a slap or two when our father had had too much to drink."

"You tried to protect your brother." She knew that much without asking. It was in his nature.

"I tried. But Link figured out early how to talk his way out of trouble. And he did it even if that meant he blamed me."

Anne could sense the pain he'd felt at his brother's betrayal. "Mitch, you can't still hold him responsible for that. Any kid would—"

He swung toward her. "I don't blame him for that." The words shot toward her, loud in the quiet room. "I blame him because he's turned out just like our father. I can't understand that, and I don't think I ever will."

The pain came through in his words so clearly that it pierced her heart. She suddenly saw a younger Mitch, trying to protect his brother and having that protection thrown back in his face.

"No." She said it softly. "I guess I wouldn't, either."

For a moment he didn't respond. Then his head jerked in the briefest of nods.

Let me in. Please don't shut me out. "Have you been in touch with him at all since that last time?"

"No. I didn't expect to hear from him. He'd stay away until he thought I had time to get over it. Until he thought he could hit me up for money again."

"Maybe he's changed. Maybe he's done some growing up since then."

He shook his head. "Look, there's no point in rehashing this. Link is the way he is, and I don't figure I'm ever going to change him. I'm just sorry he came in when he did."

"Because we were kissing?" She smiled, inviting him to see the humor in it. "That's not so bad, is it?"

"You don't understand." His face refused to relax. "Link would like nothing better than to embarrass me."

She raised her eyebrows. "Why is it embarrassing to be caught kissing someone? You're not hiding a wife in the closet, are you?"

He shook his head stubbornly. "It's not funny. You don't know what he's like."

"I know what you're like." She closed the space between them, putting her hand on his arm. It was like a bar of iron. "Link doesn't matter to me, except for the way he affects you."

"I shouldn't have kissed you, knowing he could walk in at any minute. I should have had more sense."

Her patience abruptly ran out. She was trying to be reasonable, trying to be on his side, and he just wouldn't let her. "If that's the way you feel about it, maybe you shouldn't have kissed me at all." She snatched her jacket from the chair. "I think I'd better go."

He didn't try to stop her.

Chapter Thirteen

"Finish up that homework before you watch television." Mitch leaned over the history book and notebook Davey had spread out on the kitchen table. "Mrs. Prentice said you're behind in your assignments."

Davey gave him a rebellious look. He picked up the yellow pencil with an elaborate sigh.

At least there was one person in his life who wasn't arguing with him. Mitch picked up the dish towel and started drying the silverware from dinner. Davey might be unhappy about having someone keep an eye on him while he did homework, but maybe at some level he understood Mitch was doing it because he cared. Mitch hoped so, anyway.

Understanding didn't extend to other people in his life. Anne didn't understand why he felt the way he did about his brother. As for Link... Who knew what Link understood? How to get his own way—that was all that had ever mattered to him. He didn't care about anything else.

He tossed a handful of spoons into the drawer. Link's return had upset too much. He should be with Anne right now, helping her, mapping out a plan for the adoption hearing. Instead she was so angry she'd probably slam the door in his face if he went over there.

He couldn't blame her for that. He hadn't intended it, but to her it had probably sounded as if he were ashamed of kissing her. Of caring about her.

I didn't mean it. He tried saying the words in his mind, tried imagining what her response would be.

Nothing encouraging appeared. Instead, he could only see her face the way it had looked earlier—angry, hurt, disappointed.

"You two look busy." Link's tone made it clear he didn't mean that as a compliment.

Mitch turned toward the doorway. Link's hair was wet from the shower, his shirt and pants freshly pressed.

"Going somewhere?"

"You're not wishing me gone, are you, big brother?"

Aware of Davey's dark eyes watching them, Mitch shook his head. "I already said you were welcome." *As long as you don't cause trouble.* "I just wondered where you were off to."

Link swung a leather jacket around his shoulders. "Going to meet up with some of the guys. It'll be just like old times."

"Not too much like old times, I hope." Link had run with a rough crowd in high school, and Mitch had no desire to have to arrest his own brother.

"You never did think much of my friends." A defensive note crept into Link's voice.

Mitch gave him a level look. "I think of them as little as possible. You'd be better off if you did the same."

"Hey, you've got your friends, and I've got mine. Can't say I ever cared for yours, but maybe your taste is improving. Your Anne's a cut above most of the local talent. You seeing her tonight?"

He should be. "No."

"Too bad." Link didn't sound sorry. "Maybe you scared her off. Maybe she'd like to try out a different Donovan brother."

The plate he was holding clattered into the dish drainer, and Mitch took a step toward his brother. "You leave her out of this, you hear?"

Link lifted a mocking eyebrow. "Little bit of a sore spot there? Hey, don't worry. She's not my type, anyway." He turned away. "Expect me when you see me."

Mitch counted to ten, then made it twenty. Nobody could make him madder than Link could. Maybe that was because nobody knew his trigger spots quite so well. Or enjoyed pushing them quite as much.

He turned back to the table, to discover Davey was gone. The history book still lay there, and the notebook was pristine. If any homework had been done, there was no sign of it.

Fuming, he went in search of the boy. He found him in the living room, parked in front of the television. Mitch snapped off the set in the middle of a car chase, earning a glare from Davey.

"Hey! I was watching that."

"How about your homework?"

"Done." Davey's tone was airy. "All done."

Mitch held out the text and notebook. "Show me. You were supposed to write the answers to ten questions. Show me."

"Listen, I know all that stuff. I don't need to write it down."

"If you knew all that stuff, you wouldn't be getting a *D* in history."

"It's dumb, anyway." Davey glared at him. "I'll bet you never did your homework. I'll bet your brother never did. So why do I have to?"

"Because I said so!" There were a lot better reasons than that, but at the moment his fuse was so short that he couldn't think of any. He tossed the book at Davey. "Get up to your room, and don't come out until the work is finished. And don't count on watching TV again any time soon."

"You're not my boss!" Davey let the book fall to the floor. "I don't have to do what you say. When my father comes back—"

"If your father comes back, you can argue with him. Until then, you'll live by my rules." He scooped the book off the floor and shoved it into Davey's hands. "Now go upstairs and get started."

Davey glared at him for another moment. Then he turned and stamped up the stairs, each footstep making its own protest. The door to his bedroom slammed shut.

Mitch held on to the conviction that he was right for about another minute-and-a-half. Then his anger cooled and the truth seeped in. He'd just blown up at Davey because he was angry with Link. To say nothing of being angry with himself.

Oh, he was right: the kid had to do his homework. But Mitch was the grown-up in the equation. He shouldn't have lost his temper. He certainly shouldn't have said anything about Davey's father.

He glanced uncertainly toward the stairs. Should he go up and apologize? Or say something about the boy's father? But the man seemed to have done an excellent job of disappearing.

He could have stood some impartial advice. If he hadn't made Anne thoroughly disgusted with him, he could have asked her. She and Davey seemed to have connected. But that door was closed until he managed to make amends.

Maybe the best thing was to leave the kid alone for a bit. He glanced at his watch. He'd give Davey an hour, then see how he was getting along. If he hadn't done the questions by then, maybe he could use some help. Then they could have a snack and watch something on television together, the way he'd always imagined families did.

Mitch sat down with the newspaper and tried to concentrate on the printed words. Unfortunately, too many things kept intruding. Was he doing the right thing for Davey? What was he going to do about Link? And most of all, how could he make things right with Anne?

Her face seemed to form against the black-and-white page, angry and hurt. The two of them had been closer than they'd ever been this afternoon. They'd reached a new level of understanding and trust, quite apart from the kiss that had shaken him as he'd never been shaken in his life.

And then it had all fallen apart.

Finally he put the paper down and looked at his watch: forty-five minutes. Good enough. He'd go fix things with Davey. It would be practice for trying to fix things with Anne.

He went up the steps quickly, forming the words in his mind. No indication that he was backing down on the homework issue, just a friendly offer to help—that was the right tone to take.

He tapped lightly on the door, then opened it. "Davey?"

He was talking to an empty room. The history book lay on the crumpled bed, and the window stood open to the cold night air. Davey was gone.

Anne put a light blanket over Emilie, tucking it around the sleeping baby. Emilie sprawled on her back, rosy face turned slightly to the side, hands outstretched. The pose spoke of perfect trust, perfect confidence. In Emilie's view of the world, everything was secure.

A lump formed in Anne's throat. Emilie didn't know it, but things weren't as secure as all that. Anne was the only person standing between her and an uncertain future. She'd never before felt so alone.

For a few brief moments that afternoon she'd begun to think life didn't have to be this way. She'd started to believe she really could have the kind of relationship she'd always thought was a mirage—one based on trust and openness. Something very good had begun between her and Mitch.

And then Mitch let his feelings about his brother spoil everything. Why couldn't he talk to her about it? He'd been so determined to hold everything inside, so irrationally angry. She didn't understand, and she probably never would.

The doorbell rang, suddenly and persistently, breaking the stillness in the old house. Startled, she closed the door to the bedroom gently, then went out into the hallway. She leaned over the stairs. What on earth was going on?

She saw Kate hurry toward the door. If something was wrong, she shouldn't let Kate face it alone. She started down the steps as the older woman unlocked the door and pulled it open.

Mitch erupted into the hallway. "Have you seen Davey?"

"No, not today." Kate ushered Mitch in and closed the door. "Why?"

Heart pounding, Anne hurried down the rest of the stairs. Mitch wouldn't look like that unless something had happened.

"Mitch?"

He looked over Kate's head toward Anne. "It's Davey. He's run away."

She barely registered Kate's exclamations of dismay. She was too occupied with the message Mitch's dark eyes were sending her.

Help. For the first time in their relationship, he wanted—needed—her help.

"What can we do?" Knowing why the boy had run could wait. Finding him—that was the important thing.

"I thought maybe he'd come over here." He glanced at Kate.

"We haven't seen hide nor hair of him." Kate clasped her hands in front of her. "Poor child. It's getting cold out, too. He shouldn't be out there in the cold and the dark. If he goes into the woods—"

"What do you want us to do?" she asked again. Mitch needed their help, not Kate's woeful predictions.

He shook his head. "Not much you can do if he hasn't come here. I'll get some people together and start a search."

"Maybe he'll come back on his own. Once he cools off, I mean."

"I did that a time or two." A muscle twitched in Mitch's jaw. "But I was a teenager then, not a ten-year-old. And it's supposed to drop below freezing tonight. I don't think it's safe to wait."

"No." She shivered, thinking of the lonely mountainous woods that surrounded Bedford Creek. "Let me get a coat. I'll help look."

"You don't know the area well enough." His rejection seemed automatic, but she wasn't going to be left behind to worry.

"I'm another pair of eyes. I can go with someone who does know." *Like you.*

Mitch gave a curt nod, obviously too intent on the search to argue.

"I'll watch the baby." Kate seemed glad to have something constructive to do. "I'll put the outside lights on, so he'll know someone's home if he wants to come here. And I'll start the prayer chain, if that's all right with you."

Mitch nodded. He looked at Anne. "Ready?"

"Right away." She grabbed her jacket from the coat tree.

"Let's get down to the station. I'll call the search team out from there."

She hurried after him down the steps, his anxiety palpable, pulling her along. *Hurry, hurry.* The cold wind, whistling down the mountain, made her thrust her hands into her pockets.

"He'll be all right." She said it to Mitch's back. "We'll find him."

He yanked open the cruiser door, and she slid into the passenger seat. When he got in beside her, his face was taut in the glare that spilled from the dome light.

"I hope so. Looks like I was the wrong choice for the boy."

She shook her head. "If you made a mistake, you can fix it. The important thing now is to find him."

For a moment longer he stared at her. Then he nodded, and his usual stoic mask seemed to fall into place.

"Right." He clasped her hand for an instant. "Thanks."

He started the police car, and it lurched forward.

She peered out the side window as the car spun around the corner. Dark, too dark to see much. She leaned her forehead against the window, hoping against hope that Davey would spring suddenly into view, safe and sound.

But he didn't.

Please, Lord. She stared out into the darkness. *Please, Lord. Be with us and guide our search. And be with that poor lost child.*

She hugged herself, shaking a little. A lost child. At the moment it seemed they were all lost children, in one way or another.

"Shall we have a moment of prayer before we start?" Pastor Richie stepped to the front of the group of searchers who'd gathered at the station.

Anne could sense the urgency seething in Mitch, but he nodded. She clasped her hands in prayer. They needed all the help they could get. Twenty searchers, armed with powerful flashlights, looked like a lot, especially when coupled with those who were already cruising the streets in cars. But it probably wasn't enough—not when they were looking for one small boy in the dark.

Pastor Richie lifted his hands. "Loving Father, we come to You in desperate need. One of Your children is lost. Guide our search, that we may restore him to safety. We know You're watching each of us as a loving father tends his children. We put our search in Your strong hands. In Christ's name we pray, Amen."

Please, Lord.

She saw Mitch's hands flex, as if he were trying to relieve the tension. Again she felt the urgency that drove him.

"Okay," he said. "You have your assignments. Everybody know what to do?"

She nodded with the rest. It had already been decided she'd go with Mitch, giving him another pair of eyes to search the blocks around his house.

"All right. Let's go find him."

The crowd scattered quickly.

Mitch slid into the car and turned the key in the ignition before she even got the door closed. "I don't think he'll have gone far."

The streetlights they passed first illuminated his face, then cast it in shadow.

She clasped her hands. "What if he has some destination in mind?"

He sent her a sharp glance. "What do you mean? What destination?"

She didn't want to say this, but she had to. "Maybe he wants to find his father."

"He's said he doesn't know where he is. Anyway..." His voice trailed off.

She thought she could fill in the blanks. Mitch wouldn't have gone after his own father, or at least that's what he told himself now. So he didn't want to believe it of Davey, either.

Help him, Lord, please. This is really hurting him. It reminds him too much of his own past.

Mitch pulled to the curb at the end of the block and grabbed a flashlight. "Look, we've got to make some assumptions to go on. I don't think he's on a wild-goose chase after his dad, but if he is, the team checking the road out of town should spot him. Meanwhile, we've got to get on with the search.''

"I know." She slid out, grabbing her own flashlight and zipping her jacket against the cold. "I wasn't trying to second-guess you.''

He nodded. "Second-guess away, if you want. I know you care about him.''

"Yes." *And about you.* But that was something she'd probably never have a chance to say.

Mitch swept his light in a wide circle, illuminating shrubs, trees, barren flower beds. "Let's start with the front. Check under every hedge.''

She nodded and followed him into the yard, whispering a silent prayer.

They worked their way through one yard, then a second. Mitch was an organized, meticulous searcher, leaving nothing to chance. For the most part they worked in silence, occasionally consulting in low voices.

Three houses later she paused after checking under a lilac bush and watched Mitch swing a beam of light through low-hanging branches. "You act as if you've done this a lot. Conducted a search, I mean.''

He bent to direct his light under a porch. "Often enough. We have a pretty well-organized search-and-rescue routine. It's a lot more difficult when someone's lost in the woods.''

He straightened, looking up, and she followed the direction of his gaze. The bulk of the mountain was black against a paler black sky, looming over the town in an almost menacing way.

She shivered a little. Maybe people who lived here all the time got used to the mountain's presence. She hadn't, yet. Often it seemed protective, but tonight she was aware of its dangers.

"Davey wouldn't go up there. Would he?''

The beam of the flashlight showed her the tight line of his mouth. "I don't think so. I hope not.''

"Please, Father." The prayer came out almost involuntarily. "Please be with that child.''

"You sound like Simon Richie. I'm sure he's praying and searching at the same time."

The strained note in his voice caught her by surprise. "Aren't you?"

He shrugged. "I guess I figure God wants me to get on with my job, not go running to Him every time things get tough."

She checked a row of trash cans. Nothing. "Don't you think the Father wants to hear from His children when they're in trouble?"

Mitch swung his light toward her, maybe in surprise. For a moment he didn't say anything. Then, his voice harsh, he said, "I don't know. I don't have much experience with a good father."

The undertone of bitterness in his voice startled her. She kept forgetting, God forgive her. She kept forgetting how complicated his feelings were toward his own father. If that had spilled over into his relationship with his Heavenly Father, it wasn't surprising.

Be careful, she warned herself. *Don't make things worse.*

"I know what you mean." She tried to keep it light. "If I believed God was a father like mine, I'd never be able to pray at all."

He stopped, the flashlight motionless in his hand. Had she gone too far?

Then he nodded. "Maybe you've got something there." His hand closed over hers warmly. "Let's search and pray."

An hour later they'd completed their grid as best they could. Looked like he'd been wrong about where the kid was likely to be found, Mitch thought. Where *was* he?

He slid into the cruiser next to Anne. She was shivering a little, and he started the heater before flipping the radio switch.

"Wanda. Got anything?"

"Nothing, Chief, sorry. Most teams have finished their first grid and gone on to their second." Wanda sounded briskly efficient. "You have anything?"

"Nada." His jaw clenched. Where was the kid? "I'll check in again in an hour."

Anne stirred beside him, leaning forward to look down the empty street. "Every house has its porch light on."

He nodded. "Word's spread. People want Davey to know he could walk up to any door in town right now."

"I didn't—" Anne's voice sounded choked. "I hope he sees. And understands."

"Yeah. Me, too."

Davey, where are you? Where did you run to?

Where would he run? Mitch tried to look at it rationally. If he were the kid, where might he go?

Home? But Davey didn't have a home, not anymore. Flagler had never bothered to provide his son with even minimum security.

Some people thought they didn't have homeless people in Bedford Creek. He knew better. Maybe they didn't have people sleeping on the streets, but there were those who didn't have a safe place to live.

Home. The word kept coming to him, refusing to go away. *Home.*

Are you trying to tell me something, Lord?

He glanced at Anne. That was the kind of conversation she probably had with God all the time. He hadn't realized, until tonight, that it was lacking in his own life. Or why.

He started the engine, and Anne looked at him.

"Where do we go next?"

He shrugged. "Maybe I'm wrong, but I've got a feeling. Let's go down to River Street and have a look at the place where Davey used to live."

A few minutes later they pulled up in front of a dilapidated house. It was dark and appeared empty. Still, something inside Mitch kept driving him. He had to check it out.

He approached the front door and tried it, sensing Anne coming up behind him and looking over his shoulder. A brand-new padlock glinted in the light from his flash. Looked like the landlord hadn't been taking any chances. But there might be another way in, a way a kid would know.

"I'll check the back. Why don't you stay here?"

She nodded, rubbing her arms against the chill, and he stepped off the creaky porch.

He prowled around the house, checking windows. The side door, too, bore a shiny new padlock. No sign anyone could have gotten in, not even a skinny kid.

He stopped at the back of the house, shining his light along the black windows. Nothing. This had turned into been a wild-goose chase. He'd better get back to his assigned grid and stop following hunches. One of the other searchers would cruise this neighborhood, anyway.

As he turned, his light flickered across the dirt-bare space stretching between the house and the river. He stopped. The light touched a decrepit building sagging into itself at the edge of the river.

Check it. The voice in his mind was insistent. *Check it.*

He stalked toward the building—little more than a shed, really. There were plenty of other places that would be warmer and drier for a kid out in the night.

Still, something drove Mitch. He had to look. He grabbed the sagging door. It stuck tight, and for a moment he thought it was locked.

He rattled it, putting his shoulder into it. The door popped open.

He took a step forward, flashing the beam of light around the interior. Nothing. Some battered boxes, a stack of lumber on one side, broken glass littering the floor.

"Davey!" His voice echoed in the cold darkness. Futile. The kid wasn't here.

He turned away, stepping through the open doorway. Then just as he started to shut the door, something creaked behind him. He froze.

His hand tightened on the door frame, and he swung the light toward the lumber pile. There might be—could be—just enough room behind it for one small body.

"Davey?" He reached the stack, moved to the side of it and peered along the wall. "Davey? You there?"

"Go away!" The boy's voice was shrill. "Go away! I hate you!"

Chapter Fourteen

"Davey, listen to me."

Behind him, Mitch could hear Anne's running feet. She must have heard. He held out a warning hand. No use spooking the boy by having too many people around. From the corner of his eye he saw her stop.

"No!" A scrabbling noise accented Davey's answer. The kid was trying to get around him to the door.

"Come on, Davey, I just want to talk."

This time Davey didn't bother with a verbal answer. He just spurted past.

Mitch grabbed, caught the sleeve of a windbreaker, and pulled the boy toward him. He wrapped both arms around the kid, trying to still his frantic struggles.

"Let me go! I don't wanna be with you. Let me go!"

"Davey—" Mitch clamped his arms tighter "—you have to let me talk to you. To tell you I'm sorry."

The slightest pause in the boy's flailing encouraged him to continue. "Listen, I was wrong. I was mad about something else, and I snapped at you instead." *Just like my father used to do.* The lump in his throat threatened to choke him. "I was wrong."

"Yeah, you were." Davey sounded angry, but he stopped struggling. "That stupid history—"

"Hey, I wasn't wrong about that. You still have to do your homework." He eased the pressure of his grip. He could sense

Anne moving closer, but kept his focus on Davey. "That's part of the bargain. But I should have helped you, not yelled at you."

"Yeah." The boy's voice was muffled. "I thought maybe you…"

He put his hand gently on the kid's head. "What did you think?"

"I figured you were going to tell me to get out." The words came out defiantly, but Mitch could hear the fear underneath. "So I just figured I'd go before you got around to it."

Pain was an icy hand around his heart. *Lord, give me the right words. Please.* It was the kind of prayer he'd never felt comfortable with, but it came out so naturally now, warming him.

"Hey, we have a deal, remember? I don't go back on a deal." He held the boy a little away from him, so he could see his face in the dim light. "You're going to stay with me until your dad comes back. Right?"

Davey nodded, then looked down at his toes. "What if I do something you don't like?"

"Then I might yell. But I wouldn't tell you to go. No way." That was what he'd always wanted, but never had—the assurance that someone was there, whatever he did, no matter what. Just always there. "You've got my word on it."

Holding his breath, he released the boy. "We okay now?"

Davey peered up at him. Apparently whatever he saw satisfied him. He nodded.

Some of the tension slipped away. "All right. Let's get you home."

"Okay."

Davey took a step away. Then he stopped, waiting while Mitch shut the rickety door. He fell into step beside him as they walked to the patrol car.

Anne's gaze met Mitch's as she joined them. Her eyes were bright with tears. She touched Davey lightly on the shoulder. "Hi, Davey. I'm glad you're okay."

Davey nodded. Then he slid into the cruiser. Anne brushed a tear away with the back of her hand and followed him.

Thank you, Lord. He got in and picked up the mike to let Wanda know to end the search. *Thank you.*

Davey fidgeted.

"Mitch?"

"Yeah?" He glanced at the boy.

"People were looking for me?"

"You bet people were looking for you. What'd you think, we'd just let you go?" Mitch gestured down the street, where every porch light was on. "See those lights? They're for you. Because people heard you were out there and wanted you to know it was okay to come to them."

He could see the muscles in Davey's throat work. "You sure?" The kid's voice wavered.

"I'm sure."

With a little sigh, Davey leaned back against the seat, hands relaxing.

Mitch saw Anne surreptitiously wipe away another tear.

Davey would still be a handful; he was sure of that. But if this night had convinced the kid that people cared what happened to him, they'd come a long way.

Anne climbed a little stiffly from the car when they pulled up in front of Mitch's. They'd stopped at the burger hut for sandwiches, and Davey had wolfed down two. Now he looked so tired he could hardly hold his eyes open, and she was in about the same shape.

"I'll say good night now."

Mitch caught her arm. "Come in for a minute." His smile flickered.

She wanted to stay. She wanted to go. Finally she nodded.

As soon as they got inside and he'd disappeared up the stairs with Davey, she had second thoughts. What was the point of this? They'd said everything there was to say that afternoon, and still Mitch had shut her out. He had been ashamed or embarrassed about kissing her. Could she believe any of that had changed, just because they'd come together over Davey's crisis?

She picked up her jacket, then tossed it over the back of the chair. She wouldn't be a coward about this. If Mitch wanted to talk, they'd talk.

She was sitting in the living room, leafing through a copy of a police magazine, when he came back downstairs. He'd shed his jacket, and the sleeves of his flannel shirt were rolled back, as if he'd been helping Davey get washed up. He glanced at the magazine in her hands.

"Getting up to date on the latest weapon regs?"

She shook her head, let the magazine drop onto the end table. "How is he?"

"Okay." Mitch sank to the couch next to her and leaned back, closing his eyes. The lines of strain were obvious on his face. It had been a difficult night for all of them—Mitch, Davey, the searchers who'd looked and prayed.

"Thank heaven you thought of looking there."

Mitch sat up. "Thank heaven is right. Something led us straight to him."

Yes. Something… Someone…had. "A lot of people were praying."

"I know." His face relaxed a little. "Thanks for your help tonight. That's what I wanted to say." His hand closed over hers. "Thank you. For everything."

"You're welcome. You and Davey both."

"I don't want to let him down."

Was that what was eating at him? Doubts over his ability to care for Davey? "You won't."

He shrugged. "Donovans don't have a very good record." His tone was light, but she knew him well enough to hear the pain under the words. "My dad left. My mother escaped into a bottle. Link turns tail at the sight of responsibility."

Her heart hurt for him. He was so sure, so in control on the outside. But inside he measured himself by his family. That was obviously behind his determination not to have a family of his own. The fear he'd turn out just like his own father.

"Maybe…" She went slowly, trying to find the right words. "Maybe you inherited everyone's share of responsibility. Assist, protect, defend. Like that crest in your office."

His smile flickered. "Military Police. I adopted that motto

when I went in. They're good rules. They let you know what's expected of you.''

She could see so clearly the boy he must have been, trying to make up for a bad start by finding something solid to hang on to. ''We all need that.''

''I need something else, too.'' His eyes darkened. ''I need to say how sorry I am. About today.''

The quarrel seemed to have taken place an eternity ago. ''It's all right.''

''No, it's not.'' He smiled wryly. ''You got to see the worst aspect of having a brother. He knows me better than anyone, so he can push all my buttons. I was wrong to let that come between us.''

His fingers moved softly against her wrist, tracing circles on the delicate skin. Each touch seemed to go right to her heart.

''Yes.'' Her breath caught on the word. ''You were wrong.''

His dark brown gaze was intent on her face. ''Will you let me make up for it?''

Some faint warning voice told her she was getting in too deep, in danger of being swept away, like that story he'd told her.

She could retreat to safer ground. Go back to being the person who'd decided against having a man in her life. It would be safer, but it wouldn't be better.

She touched his cheek, feeling warm skin, the faint prickle of beard. He put his hand over hers, pressing her palm against his skin.

Her heart was so full that it stole the words. But she knew she loved him. She'd seen it coming, tried to avoid it, but nothing had done any good. She loved him.

Mitch drew her into his arms. She could feel the steady beat of his heart as she wrapped her arms around him. Her own heart threatened to overflow. She held him tightly. They had both come home at last.

Mitch lingered at the kitchen table over a second cup of coffee the next morning. Davey had gone off to school a little heavy-eyed, grumbling a bit, but he'd gone. At least he'd seemed confident Mitch would be there when he came home.

He lifted the cup to his lips, smiling. Funny thing, how he'd found himself smiling at odd moments ever since last night. Ever since he'd held Anne in his arms and dared to think about having a family.

Given the way Anne felt about Emilie, given the family wars she'd been through herself, she wouldn't trust a new relationship easily. But she'd taken the first painful steps from behind her safety barricades, and so had he.

Noise in the hallway wiped the smile from his face. It was stupid of him to tense at the very sound of his brother's footsteps.

If just knowing Anne could bring him this far from the person he'd been, he ought to be able to get through one breakfast conversation with his brother without snapping. He could try, anyway.

Link wandered through the doorway, spotted the coffeepot and made straight for it. He didn't glance at Mitch until he'd taken several long gulps from his mug.

Maybe it was up to Mitch to get the conversational ball rolling. "How did your reunion go?" At least he hadn't heard any damage reports, so it couldn't have been too wild a time.

An expression of disgust crossed Link's face. "You wouldn't believe it. The old gang is going domestic. Getting married, buying houses, having kids…I thought I was in an old television rerun."

Mitch grinned. "Wedding bells are breaking up the old gang, huh?"

"That might be okay for them." Link responded with an answering grin that reminded Mitch of the little brother who'd once looked up to him. "But it's definitely not in my plans."

"What are your plans?"

Link shrugged. "The company wanted to send me to Anchorage on a project, but I turned it down." He shook his head. "Not for me. A two-year commitment, responsibility of crew chief…definitely not for me."

That was Link all over: running from any hint of something

settled. "A little responsibility isn't a bad thing," Mitch said. He tried to keep the words light, but he could tell from the tightening of Link's expression that he didn't succeed.

"This town is getting to you, big brother. Be responsible, settle down, act just like everybody else and maybe they'll like you. Maybe they'll forget what you came from."

His hand tightened on the coffee cup. "That's not what's important to me."

"Sure it is." Link slammed his mug down on the table. "You think I don't know? I watched you at that fall festival when the mayor called you up on stage, said what a great job you'd done. You were eating it up. You'd have licked his boots for that praise."

Link's words moved slowly through his mind. The foliage festival Link meant wasn't the most recent one. It was the one before.

His heart turned to lead. It was the one that was held when Tina Mallory was in town, when Link wasn't supposed to have been anywhere near Bedford Creek.

He looked at his brother. "That was the festival before last. I thought you weren't here then."

He could see the wheels turning in Link's mind, see him backpedaling. See him deciding it didn't matter.

"Yeah, so? That was after you'd told me never to darken your door again. I didn't bother to tell you I was in town. Place was so crowded with tourists, you'd never have noticed unless I'd walked right up to you. I wanted to see my buddies."

"And who else did you see?" The words tasted like ashes in his mouth.

"What do you mean?"

"I mean Tina Mallory." He could see it, rolling inexorably toward him. Link and Tina Mallory. Emilie. He almost didn't need to ask. He knew the truth, bone deep, and it was crushing him.

"Tina?" Link shrugged, turning away, not meeting his eyes. "Don't know her."

"You did." Mitch stood, feeling as if he forced his way upward against a huge weight. He pressed his fists against the table. "You knew her. You went out with her. You left her pregnant."

"Pregnant?" Link's face lost its color. "What are you talking about?"

"Tina Mallory. Cute little kid who worked at the café. A little kid you got pregnant." He hammered the words at his brother. "She's dead now, if you care."

"No!"

He could see Link's mind working feverishly, trying to find an excuse, an evasion. He felt suddenly very tired, as if the past had rolled over him and flattened him, and he'd never be right again.

"Don't bother to deny it. I can see the truth in your face."

A hunted look flickered in Link's eyes. "All right, I dated her a couple times. We got close. But I didn't know anything about a baby. I went back to the job. Tried to call her maybe a couple months later, but she'd left town. I never heard from her again. She never told me anything about any baby."

Given Link's history, the words rang true, but it didn't seem to make much difference whether his brother had known about the baby or not. He could only think it was the end of everything.

"It wasn't my fault!" Link slammed his fist down on the table. "I know what you're thinking, but it wasn't just me. It was her, too."

"She was a kid."

"She was old enough to know what she was doing. And if you think you're going to tangle me up in this, you're wrong." He thrust away from the table and reached the back door almost before he finished speaking.

"Wait a minute." Mitch reached toward him. "We have to talk about this. For once in your life you have to face your responsibility."

"*You* talk about it, big brother. I'm getting out of here." He flung open the door before Mitch could get around the table, then looked back over his shoulder. "And think about this, while you're at it. The only reason she even went out with me was because I was your brother."

That stopped Mitch in his tracks. "What are you talking about?"

"That's right." The old mocking, defiant Link was back. "She went out with me because she had a crush on you, and you never gave her the time of day."

He slammed out.

Mitch stared at the door, pain wrapping around his heart. It looked as if he and Link, between them, had just proved that everything people had ever said about the Donovans was true.

That was what Anne would think. *Anne.* A fresh spasm of pain hit him.

He had to tell her, even though it might mean the end of everything between them.

There was only one thing he could do before he faced Anne with the truth. He'd catch up with Link and make him agree to sign the papers before he disappeared again. At least he could spare Anne that much pain.

She'd take the baby... *His niece.* An even stronger pain slammed his heart, shattering it. She'd take Emilie and the papers, and leave. He'd never see them again.

He wasn't sure how he'd go about living with that.

Chapter Fifteen

"There we go, sweetheart." Anne snapped Emilie's romper. "All clean and dry and happy."

Emilie waved both arms, seeming ready to launch herself into space from her diaper change. Anne lifted her, planting a kiss on the soft round cheek.

"That's my girl. We'll just go downstairs and maybe..."

Maybe they'd look out the window and see Mitch? That was what she was thinking; she couldn't deny it.

Happiness seemed to bubble up inside her. Last night had been frightening, but it had been good, too. Thanks to Davey, she and Mitch had found their way past some of the barriers between them.

Arms snug around Emilie, she started down the steps. For the last eight months, she'd believed having Emilie in her life was all she'd ever need to be happy. Now...now she was looking beyond just herself and Emilie, to the possibility of a real family.

Even a month ago she wouldn't have thought it possible. But she'd already trusted Mitch more than she'd ever trusted anyone in her life. Maybe she really could take that next step, a step toward the kind of emotional intimacy she'd never imagined having. If she and Mitch could reach that, they'd share the kind of love she'd never believed would be hers.

The telephone rang in the hall below, and Kate rushed in

from the kitchen to snatch it up, smiling at Anne and Emilie as they came down the stairs.

"Good afternoon. The Willows."

She listened for a moment, then held the receiver out to Anne.

"It's for you. Let me take that sweet child while you're talking."

Anne exchanged Emilie for the telephone. Kate, cooing to the baby, walked back toward the kitchen.

Anne lifted the receiver. Mitch? There was no reason to think he'd call this afternoon, but even so her heart beat a little faster. "Hello?"

"This is Marcy Brown." The girl's voice was hesitant. "You wrote me about Tina?"

Her stomach turned over, and she gripped the receiver. Marcy Brown, at last. "I'm so glad you called. And sorry I had to break such bad news to you. The thing is, Marcy, I need to find the baby's birth father in order to finalize the adoption. I'm hoping you can tell me something about him."

Silence seemed to press along the connection.

"I—I don't...well, didn't Tina tell you who it was?"

Careful, careful. "Tina mentioned one name. Mitch Donovan. But I know he's not the father, and I can't begin to guess why Tina would lie about it."

Marcy's sigh came over the line clearly. "She said that, did she? I told her not to, but she wouldn't listen."

"You know, then." The blood seemed to be pounding in her ears. "You know who Emilie's father is. You know why she named Mitch."

"Yeah, well, that part's nuts, but Tina went off the deep end sometimes. Thing was, she really liked the chief, always talked about how nice he was to her and what a great guy he was. I think maybe when she realized the other guy was gone and wasn't coming back, she sort of pretended. You know, pretended that Mitch Donovan was the one, so everything would be all right. She didn't mean any harm by it... At any rate, it was Link Donovan. You know who I mean? The chief's brother."

The hallway did a slow spin around her, and she sank down abruptly on the bench. "How... But how can that be? I thought he wasn't even in Bedford Creek when Tina was here." That was what Mitch had said. He wouldn't lie to her.

"He was there—"

Anne could almost hear the shrug.

"—just for a couple weeks in the fall. It seems to me I did hear him say he didn't want his brother to know he was in town. Like they'd had some big fight or something."

The certainty settled on her like a weight. Mitch had mentioned the quarrel. Probably he'd never suspected Link was back in Bedford Creek at the crucial time.

"You're sure?"

"Oh, yeah. He was the only guy she went out with, and I think she just went with him because he sort of reminded her of the chief."

"I understand." She did. Tina, reaching out for love, had snatched at whatever was offered. But it hadn't been love.

A few more exchanges, a promise to send a photo of Emilie, and Anne put down the receiver. She knew now. She had the information she'd come to Bedford Creek to find.

And after asking Kate to watch Emilie, she headed out to find Mitch.

Ten minutes later, she stopped on the sidewalk outside the police station, stomach knotting. This would be difficult, so much more difficult than that first day, and she'd thought nothing could be worse than that.

Help me, Lord. Help me find the words. This news is going to hurt Mitch so much. I don't want to cause him pain, but he has to know.

She took a deep breath and opened the door.

Wanda looked up at her entrance, smiled, and waved her toward the inner office door.

Anne tapped, then opened the door. Mitch stood at the desk, head bent, just hanging up the phone. Her heart gave a little jump at the sight of him. For an instant thoughts of her reason for being there slipped away, and she was back in his arms again the night before, knowing she loved him.

No. She couldn't let herself think about that, not now. Not when she had to tell him something that would hurt him so badly.

"Anne."

She half expected him to round the desk toward her, but he didn't. "I have some news," she said, then stopped. This was so difficult, but she had to do it. She'd tried handling everything on her own, and it hadn't worked. Surely she and Mitch had come far enough to deal with this together.

"What is it?" He did come around the desk then, reaching toward her as if expecting the worst.

"Marcy Brown called." There wasn't any way to say this but to get it out. "She knew about Tina's pregnancy. Knew who the father was." She swallowed hard. "She even knew why Tina named you."

He didn't say anything, just stared at her from under lowered brows, his face expressionless. The mask was back in full force, as if he needed its protection.

"She said..." She took a steadying breath. "She said it was Link."

There, it was out. Mitch would be shocked, denying it, but...

But he wasn't. He just stood there, looking at her, and she read the knowledge in his face.

"You already knew." The words were out before she thought about them. He *knew*.

Pain gripped her. All this time she'd been desperate to find the truth, all this time...

"How could you do this?" The blood pounded in her head. Later she'd need to weep, but not now. Now she had to react to this betrayal.

"Anne, it's not what you think."

"You knew how important this is. How could you lie to me?" Maybe she wouldn't be able to hold back the tears until later. They stung her eyes, salty and bitter.

"I didn't!"

Her heart turned to stone. "You knew. You didn't tell me. What is that but a lie?"

He reached out to her, as if to touch her, and she recoiled. He let his hand drop, eyes darkening.

"I didn't know, not until today. You can't believe I've been lying to you all along—"

"When today?" It was like being back in a courtroom, but she'd never tried a case that held so much personal anguish for her.

He stiffened. "This morning. Link told me the truth this morning."

"And you kept it from me." Her head throbbed. "How long were you going to keep it from me, Mitch? Until after he was gone again? Until he wasn't here in Bedford Creek to embarrass you?"

"No! That's not why I didn't tell you. Anne, you have to believe me. I only wanted—"

She shook her head. "You're wrong. I don't have to believe you." She could barely breathe against the heartache. "I was wrong ever to trust you. It's a mistake I won't make again."

Mitch stared at the door that had closed behind Anne—that closed on any chance he might have to make things right.

He could go after her, but what would he say? *I was wrong?* She knew that already, and nothing he could say would make it any different.

He'd ruined everything with his black stubbornness. If he'd gone to her with the truth right away, maybe there would have been some small chance to make things right. Now there was none.

He'd told himself he was trying to spare her, to delay telling her until he could find Link and try to repair the damage. But maybe she was right. Maybe he was really trying to spare himself.

He hadn't fixed anything. He'd lost his brother and he'd lost Anne, and this was one thing he couldn't blame on his father. This one was all his fault.

One way or another, he had to find Link. Getting Link to cooperate wouldn't change things between himself and Anne.

How could it? But at least it would make things right for her and Emilie. That was all he could expect.

Getting Link's signature was the only thing left Mitch could do for Anne, and he wasn't going to fail.

But two hours later the possibility of failure loomed a lot larger. He drove down River Street one more time. He'd tried every friend of Link's he could remember, tried every place his brother might be staying. He met nothing but blank looks. No one had seen his brother since the day before.

He seemed to be out of options. His stomach twisted. He'd have to see Anne, let her know what he was trying to do. She wouldn't want to see him, but he had to tell her he wouldn't give up until he had Link ready to sign.

He stopped in front of Kate's place, took the steps two at a time. He rapped on the door.

Kate swung it open and looked at him, her gaze a little startled. "Mitch. Is something wrong?"

"I need to see Anne. Will you let her know I'm here?"

But Kate was shaking her head. "I can't do that."

"What do you mean?" He could sense bad news coming, see it in the way her gaze slid away from his.

"Anne's gone." Kate gave a helpless little gesture. "I couldn't talk her out of it. She took the baby and went back to Philadelphia."

The road snaked ahead of Anne, glistening a little in the gray afternoon light. The cold, light rain slicked the pavement, and she slowed as she started up the steep hill. Maybe if she kept her mind on the road conditions, she could keep the pain at bay a little longer.

It didn't seem to be working. Her breath caught on a little sob.

Mitch, how could you do this? How could you betray me this way?

Emilie wiggled in her car seat, just beginning to fuss. She hadn't been happy to be packed up so abruptly. And Kate... Kate hadn't understood at all, but Anne hadn't been able to explain her sudden need to leave.

She still couldn't, not even to herself. She'd just known she had to get away from Bedford Creek, away from Mitch.

"Hush, Emilie. It'll be all right. We'll be home soon."

That was what she needed to hear someone say to her. *It will be all right.* But there was no one to do that.

Why, Lord? she prayed bleakly. *Why did You let me begin to trust, begin to care, only to face betrayal?*

She could have handled the fact that Link was Emilie's father. She could even understand Tina's convoluted reasoning in naming Mitch as the father.

Tina had thought Mitch was everything Link wasn't—solid, responsible, trustworthy. She'd probably thought she could count on Mitch to do the right thing.

Anger pulsed through her; she tightened her grip on the wheel. She'd thought that, too. And they'd both been wrong. He'd chosen to protect his brother instead of her and Emilie.

What would Link do? Her throat tightened. She should have stayed, tried to see him, tried to get his signature on the forms. That was why she'd come to Bedford Creek in the first place.

But she wasn't the person she'd been then. That Anne Morden would have put on her lawyer's armor and faced down both the Donovan brothers. Now she'd started to care too much, and she couldn't do it, not without letting Mitch see exactly how much he'd hurt her.

So she'd go home. She'd go back to Philadelphia, hire a private investigator, put the whole thing in professional hands.

Emilie's cry went up an octave, and Anne winced. She turned her head to take a look, and felt the car swerve. Her fingers tightened on the wheel. She must be more tired than she'd thought. She couldn't—

The car swerved again, sliding across the road, and she fought the steering wheel. It wasn't her—it was the rain. She touched the brake, barely tapping it. If she could just get onto the gravel berm, they'd be all right.

The car swung across the road, out of control. Her stomach turned over. She clenched the wheel, jerking it, but it was no good—she'd lost control entirely. They careened sideways, nothing between them and the steep drop-off but a narrow gravel stretch and a ditch.

She couldn't stop. Her mind flashed ahead to an image of her car sliding off the mountain, tumbling down the steep slope, plunging into the trees below.

Help us, Father! Help us!

Seconds became an eternity…spinning trees, whirling lights, frantic prayers. And then the car slid gently to rest against the opposite bank.

The sobs she heard were hers. Emilie's crying had stopped, maybe out of her amazement at the ride. Anne twisted in the seat, touching the baby with frantic hands.

"Are you all right? Emilie, are you okay?"

Emilie batted at her hands, then stretched, twisting irritably in the car seat.

She was all right. Anne leaned her forehead against the seat back. The baby was all right. They were both all right, no thanks to her.

"Thank you, Lord." She patted Emilie, then wiped away the hot tears that spilled down her cheeks. "Thank you."

I wasn't in control. But You were.

She turned, leaning back in the seat, relief flooding her. God had been in control. Even though she hadn't trusted, even though she'd been trying to do it all herself, God had been in control.

"I haven't been trusting You, have I?"

Helen would probably smile at the question. Wise Helen had seen what Anne needed. Believing wasn't enough. She had to trust, too.

She brushed her hair back from her forehead. "I'll try, Lord. I'll try."

She couldn't have a relationship with God unless she could trust. She couldn't have a relationship with another person unless she could trust.

She looked back over the last twenty-four hours. She'd told herself she loved Mitch, but she hadn't trusted him enough to give him a chance to explain. Maybe things could never be right between them; maybe there were too many barriers. But whatever happened, she couldn't run away. She had to give him a chance.

Something else was crystal clear in her mind. Unless Mitch could open up, unless he could find a way to deal with the family problems that haunted him, they didn't stand a chance.

Her heart turned to lead. Dealing with that pain might be more than Mitch was able to do. But she'd learned something in these difficult weeks. Having a relationship built on trust, based on openness, really was possible.

She'd never believed that before, but now she knew it. And she couldn't settle for less.

Slowly, carefully, she put the car in gear and started back toward Bedford Creek.

Chapter Sixteen

"Look, just stay by the phone for me, okay?" Mitch frowned at Wanda. "I've asked half the town to call me if they spot Link. Someone's bound to see him."

"All right, all right." Wanda dropped the purse she'd picked up, preparing to going home. "But you owe me for this one."

He owed a lot of people—Anne most of all. But she was gone. He looked bleakly down the years he would be missing her. Why couldn't she have given him a few minutes' grace? That was all he'd wanted. Now—

He heard the door, spun around, and his breath caught in his throat. Anne stood there, holding the baby. He'd never seen a sweeter sight in his life.

She was pale, and she clutched Emilie too tightly. The baby wiggled restlessly.

"What's wrong?" He took a step toward her, battling pain, grief, regret. Something was wrong besides the obvious, but whatever it was, she probably wouldn't accept help from him. The only thing he had left to offer her was Link's signature on that form.

She shook her head. "Nothing. We're all right. We just... I decided we needed to come back."

"I'm glad you did." Easy, don't push. "I'm trying to find Link, so I can—"

The telephone rang, and he nearly leaped across the desk.

Wanda said a few words, then hung up and turned to him. He could read the message on her face. Someone had spotted Link.

"Behind Grace Church. His truck's parked there."

Adrenaline pumped through his veins. Something positive to do, thank heaven. He turned to Anne.

"You wait here with Wanda. I'll find Link and bring him back."

But she was already shaking her head. "We'll go with you."

The last thing he wanted was Anne observing an ugly scene. "That's not a good idea. I'll do better with him alone."

"I'm going." Her mouth set stubbornly, she turned toward the door.

"Anne…"

Frustrated, he shook his head. He didn't want her there when he confronted his brother. But it didn't look as if he had a choice.

If he'd picked the worst place in the world to confront his brother, this would be it, Mitch thought as he pulled up to Grace Church Cemetery. His throat tightened. Link was on one knee in front of a double headstone, carefully clearing away the dried leaves that littered it. He looked very young, kneeling there in the brown grass in front of their parents' graves.

Mitch and Anne's footsteps grated on a patch of gravel. Link swung around, his face hardening when he saw them. "What are you doing here?"

"Looking for you." Mitch stared down at his parents' headstone. "Guess I should have thought sooner to look here."

"Why would you?" Link stood, fists clenching. "Not a place you spend much time, is it?"

"I guess not." He stared down at the epitaph. At his father's name. His father hadn't come back until it was too late to say the things that needed to be said between them. Maybe he could keep from making the same mistake with Link. "Look, we need to talk."

Link shrugged, his face cold. "I've got nothing to say."

"Fine, just listen, then." He couldn't let himself think about Anne, standing so silently beside him.

"Sorry, don't have time." Link spun, but Mitch grabbed his arm.

"Make time, Link. This is important."

"To you?" His expression made it clear that didn't weigh with him.

"To this baby girl." He jerked his head toward Emilie, his eyes never leaving Link's face. "She deserves a chance in life."

Link's gaze swiveled to Anne and the pink snowsuited bundle she carried. "Tina's baby." Link said it with certainty.

"That's right. How did you know?"

He shrugged. "Wasn't hard to figure out, once I knew part of it. Why else would Anne and the baby be in Bedford Creek?"

"Listen to me, Link." His throat was so tight that he had to force the words out. "When Tina knew she wasn't going to make it, she wanted Anne to adopt her baby. She wanted to give her a chance at a good future."

"Okay, I'm giving her that chance, too." Link's gaze slid away from the baby. "I'm getting out of here. That's the best thing I can do for her." He nodded toward the headstone. "After all, that's what he did for us. Like father, like son, right? He just should have done it sooner."

The bitterness in his brother's voice seeped into Mitch's heart. He was used to it in himself. He'd never guessed it ran so deeply in Link. He felt a sudden revulsion. It wasn't doing either one of them any good.

"Don't, Link. Don't think that about yourself."

"Why not? It's true, isn't it?"

Conviction pounded through his veins. He knew, now, what he had to do. What they both had to do, if only it wasn't too late.

"What he did doesn't matter anymore. At least, it only matters if we let it." He reached toward his brother. "Don't you see what we're doing? We're still letting him control our lives."

"Not you. Not Mr. Upright Citizen. Your life is as different as it can be from his."

"Don't you get it?" Mitch caught his brother's arm. He had to make him see. "I'm doing everything I can to be different from him. You're doing everything you can to be like him. That means we're both still letting him run our lives."

For a moment Link stared at him, dark eyes unreadable. "Yeah, well, there's not much we can do about that, is there?"

"We can stop." The conviction settled into his soul, so strong he didn't even mind the fact that Anne was hearing all of this. "We can forgive him."

He hadn't known it was true until he'd said it. A sense of release slid through him. All this time, trying to be the opposite of everything his father stood for, he'd still been holding on to his resentment. Letting it control his life.

Link jerked free of him. "I can't!" A shadow crossed his face. "And what difference would it make if I could? He's gone."

"It won't make a difference to him. Just to us."

He put his hand on Link's shoulder, feeling his brother tense at his touch. It drove a knife through his heart. He never should have let things get so bad between them. Link was the only family he had in the world, probably the only family he ever would have.

They stood side by side, looking down at their parents' graves. "Let it go, Link. Let them go."

"Not what you'd call a perfect set of parents, were they?" Bitterness still laced Link's words.

"No, I guess they weren't. But that doesn't mean we have to repeat their mistakes." His hand tightened on his brother's shoulder. "I haven't exactly been a perfect big brother, either. Maybe I can do better, if you give me a shot at it."

Mitch felt the tension begin to seep out of Link. "So…if I were trying to do better than they did…" He choked, but went on. "What would I do about this baby?"

That one Mitch knew the answer to. "Sign the papers so Anne can adopt." He looked at her, seeing the way she cradled the baby close, as if defying anyone to take her away. "Nobody could possibly be a better parent to that little girl than she will be."

Link looked at Anne and the baby, not speaking. Then he let out a long breath. "Okay. Let's do it."

Mitch's eyes stung with unshed tears. He nodded. "Follow us back to the office. We can take care of it there."

A few minutes later Link stood by the desk in Mitch's office. His hands clenched into two tight fists. "I'm ready."

Anne looked shell-shocked, as if she couldn't handle much more. "Are you sure?"

Link took a step forward and touched Emilie's soft curls. An emotion—sadness?—crossed his face. Then he nodded.

"I'm sure. She belongs with the mother who loves her." His voice roughened. "I guess Tina knew that. I won't interfere."

Mitch tried to swallow the lump in his throat. This had been a long time coming, but he finally was getting to see his little brother step up and do the right thing, instead of running away. Maybe there was hope for Link...hope for both of them.

Anne juggled the baby as she fumbled with the catch to her bag.

"Let me take her." Mitch reached out, and Emilie came eagerly into his arms.

For a moment he thought Anne would snatch the baby back, but then she nodded.

Give me a chance, Anne. Give us a chance. He wanted to say it, but he couldn't.

Anne unfolded the paper slowly, then held it out to Link.

He took it to Mitch's desk, leaned over to read it. A muscle worked in his jaw, the only outward sign of his feelings. He reached for a pen and scrawled his signature in a quick slash across the bottom of the page.

Anne's breath escaped in an audible sigh. She had to be thinking that it was over, that Emilie was safe at last.

Link handed the paper to her, and she folded it quickly.

"That's that, then." Link tried to smile, but it didn't quite work. "You don't need to worry I'll cause problems. I won't."

Mitch's heart hurt for Link. His little brother had finally started to grow up, but it was a painful process.

"What are you going to do?"

Link shrugged. "Think I'll take on that job in Alaska I told you about.'' He aimed a light punch at Mitch's arm. ''Who knows? Next time I come back, I might have turned into a responsible citizen. Like my big brother.''

''Stranger things have happened.''

Link glanced from him to Anne. ''Looks to me like you could stand to talk things out.''

Mitch, cradling Emilie in his arms, nodded. *If Anne will talk to me, that is.*

Link crossed to the door, then looked at them. ''You know, I'm not cut out to be a father.'' He paused. ''But I think I could be a darn good uncle, if the position opens up.''

He closed the door before either of them could respond.

Anne looked at her baby...hers now, for good. The three of them were alone here, just as they'd been that first day when she came to break the news to Mitch. Emilie was perfectly happy in Mitch's arms.

''We do need to talk.'' Mitch's voice was a low rumble.

She nodded. ''I guess that's why I came back. I couldn't...''

How could she say it? The words didn't seem to exist to explain the tangled emotions she felt at the sight of him.

Mitch looked at Emilie's face, as if trying to discern some resemblance to his brother. ''I really didn't think it could be Link. I was so sure he wasn't in town when Tina was here. Sure that was one thing I couldn't blame on him.''

''I know.'' She hesitated, feeling her way. They had to get this out between them. ''But I don't know why you didn't tell me when you found out.''

Because you couldn't trust me? Just like I couldn't trust you?

He shook his head. ''How can I make you understand? The truth just hit me like a sledgehammer. All I could think was that it proved the Donovans were just as bad as everyone always said.''

She saw the anguish in his face as he said the words, and it reached out and gripped her heart, too.

''I wouldn't have thought that. I don't think it now. Link was wrong, but at least he's starting to face up to it.''

''Maybe he'd have faced it sooner if I hadn't blown up at

him." He touched Emilie's hand, and she latched onto his finger. "Anne, you have to know I never intended to hurt you and Emilie. I just wanted a chance to find Link and clear things up with him before I told you. That's all. I would have told you today." He looked at her, dark eyes intense. "I wish you could believe that."

Her heart started to pound. He wanted to know she trusted him. Was that so much to ask?

"You...you and Link have made a start at working things out." That wasn't what she wanted to say. Why was it so hard to tell him what she felt?

He nodded. "The truth is, I let my feelings about my father color everything else in my life. My relationship with my brother, my career, even my relationship with you. I finally saw I had to forgive him, if I wanted any kind of a future." He looked at her, his dark eyes steady. "What about you, Anne? Are you ready to put the past to rest so we can move on?"

That was the question she'd started to face out on that road. She'd let her relationship with her parents govern her relationship with God, just as Mitch had. She hadn't even recognized she was doing it. It was time for both of them to stop.

She looked at Mitch holding her child, and her heart swelled. "I'd like to try."

The love in his eyes took her breath away. "We've got a few hurdles to get over. But God's not finished with us yet." He took a step toward her. "I love you, Anne. I want to try and make this work. Will you stay? Will you marry me?"

If she didn't take this chance, she knew she'd miss the best God had to offer her. She moved forward, letting Mitch's arms enfold both of them. "We'll stay."

Epilogue

"Da, da, da, da!" Emilie stood in the stroller and banged on the tray.

"All right, Sweetheart." Anne maneuvered the stroller through the summertime crowds on the sidewalk. "We'll go to the station and see Mitch."

The baby plopped back into her seat, apparently satisfied. Emilie hadn't mastered the sound of "Mitch" yet, but that didn't matter. After their wedding this fall, he really would be her daddy.

Anne dodged a tourist with a camera and pushed through the station door. Wanda gave her a welcoming smile.

"Chief!" she shouted. "Anne's here."

Davey dropped the broom he'd been wielding and rushed to Emilie. "Can I take her out of the stroller, please? I want to show Wanda how she can walk."

"Of course." Anne smiled. Emilie held her arms out to the person she considered a big brother, and he lifted her carefully from the stroller.

In the months Davey had been living with Mitch, he'd blossomed. That wary, sullen look was completely gone from his eyes. Neither his father nor any other relative had been located, but Davey's permanent placement with Mitch gave him the security he'd never had before. Perhaps, one day, she and Mitch would be able to adopt him legally, but that wouldn't make him any more their son than he already was.

Trust in the Lord with all your heart. She still had to remind herself of that each day. God would work out what was right for Davey, in His own time.

The office door opened, and Mitch came toward her quickly. ''Anne.'' Love shone in his eyes as he kissed her. The mask he'd once worn was gone now entirely, and his face no longer hid his emotions. His feelings were written plainly for her to read.

His arm still around her, Mitch reached for Davey and Emilie. The baby toddled toward them, clutching Davey's hand, beaming.

Mitch swept Emilie up in his arms, and Anne put her hand on Davey's shoulder, drawing him close.

Family. They were a family. She looked up at Mitch, her heart overflowing with love. She hadn't really known the meaning of the word before. Now, each day, she and Mitch discovered how deep, how blessed their love could be.

She'd come to Bedford Creek to find Emilie's father. God had seen to it that she found so much more.

*   *   *   *   *

Dear Reader,

What happens when a man is confronted with the claim that he fathered a child, a claim he knows isn't true? Mitch Donovan popped into my mind one day, complete with all the baggage of a difficult family background that had made him determined never to have children of his own. All I knew about the story was that he'd fall in love with a woman who came complete with baby, and that he wouldn't be able to have the love God intended for him until he learned to forgive.

Thank you for reading my book. I hope you enjoyed Mitch and Anne's story, and that you'll look forward to visiting Bedford Creek again.

I love to hear from readers, and I hope you'll write to me c/o Steeple Hill Books, 233 Broadway, Suite 1001, New York, NY 10279

Best wishes,

Marta Perry

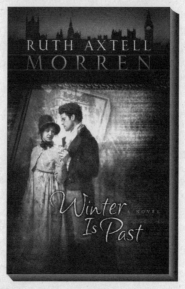

Hideaway

E.R. doctor Cheyenne Allison
seeks a break from her
stressful life, but instead finds
a dangerous vandal and terror.

Will trust in her charismatic
neighbor and faith in
Providence get her through
a harrowing ordeal?

HANNAH ALEXANDER

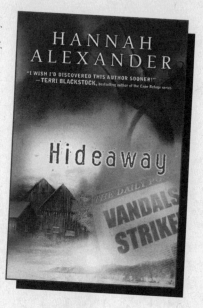

Available October 2003 wherever hardcovers are sold.